DYIN'S EASY

DYIN'S
EASY

A Novel

Gary Prisk

Published by
Hybrid Global Publishing
333 E 14th Street
#3C
New York, NY 10003

Manufactured in the United States of America, or in the United Kingdom when distributed elsewhere.

Prisk, Gary.
Dyin's Easy
   ISBN: 978-1-957013-51-0

Cover design by: Joe Potter
Copyediting by: Dea Gunning
Interior design by: William Groetzinger

Jackie —

Thanks for standing up

for America —

DYIN'S
EASY

A Novel

Gary Prisk

Gary Prisk

Published by
Hybrid Global Publishing
333 E 14th Street
#3C
New York, NY 10003

Manufactured in the United States of America, or in
the United Kingdom when distributed elsewhere.

Prisk, Gary.
Dyin's Easy
   ISBN: 978-1-957013-51-0

Cover design by: Joe Potter
Copyediting by: Dea Gunning
Interior design by: William Groetzinger

This book is a work of fiction. The settings are real.
Incidents, characters, timelines and names are either the
product of the author's imagination or used fictitiously.
Any resemblance to actual persons, living or dead,
events or locales is entirely coincidental.

My Thanks to

Captain Michael B. Edwards, US Navy
A lifelong friend
A legend
A member of the "Brown-Water Navy" During Vietnam's War

Southern Burma. 18 August 1939.

Delirious, searching for his weapon, Hardin spits through a choking spasm. The bitterness of the monsoon is harrying his vision, the jungle a mass of swirling vegetation. And yet, at times, the driving rain and pulsing wind is a tolerable distraction from the wound in my thigh. Suddenly clear-eyed, catching rainwater in his mouth, he massages his humping tackle. There is little else to comfort his survival in the jungle of southern Burma—in the jungle of northern Malaya nothing at all.

Disoriented, laughing, then screaming at a young girl, twice and then again. He is jumping from the Shackleton into a thick mist, into the night, fighting his parachute's torn risers. Tonkin mercenaries are firing from every turn… or are they Chinese?

"Who are the sods chasing me?" Captain Hardin's mouth is as dry as burlap, and his tongue is swollen. "Where are my bloody boots?"

Then instantly he is at ease. The narrow trackway, the wooden cart, laying amongst a pile of straw-filled sacks, his chest rocking with the rhythm of the water buffalo's step—he tries to swallow. He laughs a cough. "Where the bloody hell am I going?"

Nearly naked, a native girl runs past his cart speaking broken English. "Wake up. Wake up. Wake up."

Then again his team is ambushed. In Burma. Screams echoing in counterpoint with the gunfire's roar. Death's lingering smell wafting. The rot oozing from the jungle floor reeks with the bile of malaria and yellow jack fever.

Suddenly, silence snaps to. Captain Edward Hardin's chest twists into a knot, and his mind begins again—ratcheting through images—his lovely wife Katherine, his mother Mary, Willie Hockey, his special-ops teammates. He begs each to respond. Sir John Poston, Admiral Sinclair, and Uncle Dingo offer but muted echoes.

A picture of his grandfather spars gently with an echo of Katherine's laughter.

With the cadence of indifference, the sequence keeps on flashing on and off. Weapon, parachute, mercenaries, family, friends. Uncle Dingo and Katherine mostly.

Even Uncle, that Aussie swagman, seems happy.

As his mother Mary stands to, Hardin's world whirls into a black void.

*   *   *

Tucking Mill, Cornwall, England. April 1924.

At this time of year, the damp in Mary Hardin's two-room badger hole stained the small window next to her front door. Her only door. It kept raining. Spring had not come to Cornwall.

Even France had climate.

"I've a warm pasty for you, Edward." Mary set the pasty on her son's plate and poured him a glass of cold milk. "The last bit of beef and cabbage." Patting her twelve-year-old on the shoulder, she rubbed his back. Her son was getting too big for her small home.

"I'll let it cool a tic."

Mary wrapped a woolen scarf around her neck, put on her coat, and opened the door. "I'm off to clean the mine owner's home."

"I know, mum."

Sitting on the floor near the fireplace, Edward held a grainy photograph. "Is the soldier in this snap my grandfather?"

"Yes. He was twenty-four in that snap. Proud to be a faithful soldier. A foot in the Duke of Cornwall's Light Infantry. He died in 1902. In South Africa fighting the Boers."

Edward stood up and set the photo next to his cheek. "I'm going to be a soldier."

"Not today, you're not." Mary held the door open. "Practice your sums, Edward. If you know your sums, the mine owners will have a proper job for you."

"Go on mum. Off you go."

Mary Hardin longed for her earlier days in Portsmouth when she was a sprout. The clear air, the streets washed by channel rains, the blue hour between night and dawn. She missed her mother and her aunties most of all.

Mary's mother, a stout gentle soul, worked as a cutter in the Colour Loft of the Portsmouth Dockyard making flags, canvas overalls, and tool bags. Mary's father had worked as the porter for the dockyard, standing watch in the Porter's Lodge, marking the hours by ringing a bell four times per shift.

With hugs before bed, and stories of growing up in Chatham, and of her Aunt Ginny, Mary could still feel her mother's calloused hands, her fingertips. Aunt Ginny's as well.

Ginny hand-stitched ribbons for Mary's hair. Yellow mostly. Ginny worked in the Chatham Dockyard, spinning yarn in the quarter mile long

Double Rope-House since the end of World War One. Ginny spun the shake-rag Mary used to call Edward's father for supper.

Riding her bicycle to work now, Mary thought the slag waste from the mine gave her town a depressingly gray tone, coating mortar and stone with a pollen that would color her son's future with enduring shame.

The mine owners are a bloody merciless lot, she thought.

Men working in the mine eventually came to naught. Stooped shouldered, they shuffled in lockstep along worn paths, their faces charred black, their salt misspent, their shift-mates, one as the next, trapped in pitiless work. Yet somehow grateful.

Richard Hardin, Mary's husband, was a miner. He liked his drink, and his prideful boast—South Crofty Tin Mine; the deepest black-tin mine in the world. Almost all the men of Tucking Mill worked a shift, some nearly a mile underground. Working in a tin mine or a coal mine, living in a badger hole or a two-room hovel, a miner no longer able to work would be pensioned into the South Crofty Tin Mine's workhouse.

Will my Richard ever get hold of tomorrow? Or next week? Mary wondered as she left the mine owner's home and walked to her second job, working as a barmaid.

From drink to drink, and song to song, Web's Public House lay in the fog of another sodden dusk. Six nights a week, leaving Sunday for the Lord, Mary would put on one of the three dresses she owned and ride her bicycle to her second job as a barmaid at Webb's Public House on the east end of Tucking Mill—not for the money, but to temper her husband's roaring with timely gestures of delight or disgust.

Setting religion aside, Mary entered the pub to the miner's singing and raising their pints.

Several of the men waved, suggesting she join the chorus. Taking her station near the beer taps, she tied her apron strings, soaked several bar rags in hot water while measuring the condition of the customers she could see.

With her coat and scarf hung on a peg between barrels of grog, Mary set to her evening chores. She was frightened. That morning, while she was cleaning his home, the mine owner had tried to molest her in the parlor of his home. When she confided in the Reverend Gosden, the vicar dismissed her with a shrug.

"Tired-looking sods, don't you agree?" Mary alerted with a frown at the comment. These well-dressed buggers leaning on the bar must be engineers, she thought.

"Not much leeway. Mankind's virtues cost more than five bob a week. No footrest in the Isles of Scilly for these lads. A dutiful future it is, Cornwall's Light Infantry or the mines. That's the meat of it. The Boers gave chuff to these lads at Kimberly and Ladysmith—Mafeking as well. Not a history to be hedged about." The larger man shrugged and emphasized his point by eating the smaller man's last chip. "Gold and diamonds cost a good deal more than money."

"Ah, too true, I suppose—sacrificed to stern duty and all that." The smaller man toasted his stout to the rhythmic song the miners were singing. "The Welsh go on and on until they drop, like gun horses, they are. They're a down-market lot, that's certain." Mary pushed a wet cloth near the smaller man's jacket and squeezed water under his elbow.

"Fair enough, I suppose. One does one's best." The strangers finished their pints and pushed their way to the door of the pub as the chorus gained ground.

Mary's gaze centered on the strangers, their hacking jackets rubbing against her natural grace. Angry, she kept wiping the bar, watching the men leave, and summing their comments with a sigh. Suddenly... her sarcasm freshened with disgust, Mary screamed down the bar, countering Richard's foolish grin and his humbly offended tenor voice.

Richard Hardin thrived as Tucking Mill's tinker, an itinerant mender at the service of any widow wanting a bit of repair, all in good fun, mind you—tending the business of the households in the town. To support his family, Richard worked the early shift in South Crofty, hiding from the clock while banging an unsupervised shovel on the floor of the tailings bay, or dressing gangue from the minerals tin and wolfram.

His charm made shift with a continual chatter, fostered by those unexpected resources of indignation. Being comically arrogant, Richard tried to fashion the fuss and the prudery of Mary's Methodist minister—the reverend Gosden—into a song with his Welshman's tongue.

But the vicar wouldn't wear it.

A devout Methodist, Mary embraced Wesleyan teachings at a time when heresy was a remote favor. Mary and Edward spent their Sunday afternoons looking for God through a scattering of trees and reading the Bible at the Chynhale Wesleyan Sunday School.

At Mary's suggestion, to offset the devil's work, Richard became a loosely knit Freemason, attending meetings at the Freemasons Hall on Saint Nicholas Carriageway—a member of the 'One and All Lodge' No. 330. While his tinkering enjoyed a bit of respectability, he stuffed himself with certainty.

With his sponsoring lodge in Camborne, he wasn't regular enough to can much status. Proud to be a Third-Degree Mason, Richard presented his fidelity to anybody who would listen.

Nights found Richard at Webb's Public House, a fox cheering the hennery, his joy wrapped halfway around a pint. He played cards and sang with his mates, the lot toasting the doings of those salad days when young men could wrinkle a peach into a wagon rut.

After the cards were massed into a stack and the brown ale had its way, Richard would grab Mary's hand and dance her around the pub to the cheers of his mates.

Mary didn't mind the dance. She adored her stubby Welshman. She was a gentle soul, tall and lean, well set up, and titted-out, Mary's laugh could crumb a fresh biscuit. Laughing without warning, she spoke through a mischievous grin. Her pale-green eyes held a sparkle, and her plump cheeks held a glow whenever she wrapped her smile in one of the handwoven woolen scarves she cherished—the signature of Mary's dress and her profound belief in moderation.

She spent her house cleaning money ensuring Richard and Edward met each day with fresh, well-mended clothes. Tattered on all fours, her shake-rag's *wop* sounded at a low enough frequency to penetrate the tenor of Richard's tongue when she called him for dinner. His mates knew the sound and showed him the door at first *wop*.

Quite stout, he was a forcibly robust sort, prone to larceny and partial to cricket.

After Mary discovered Richard's gambling chits tucked under a candle base on the fireplace mantle, she wept. She and Edward were in for a scuddle. Richard gambled on cards or cricket, or any game at hand. He carried a copy of the *Wisden Cricketer* magazine in his lunch pail. He bet on the Penzance cricket club whenever they had a match.

By June 1924, after years of wagers, Richard's hire-purchase debt owed to South Crofty Mine, Ltd., had invested his family with disgrace.

Richard Hardin could not live long enough to feed his family and pay his debt to the mine owners. As the debt grew more burdensome, his dreams slipped away. Passing the workhouse, the hollow expression of an old miner screamed at his way.

With fear running duty to its limit, he bagged his insufferable pride and asked his shift-mates for a loan. Without a ha'penny amongst them, every man suggested Edward lend a hand.

Richard was ashamed. To indenture his son would be unforgivable—a Welshman's dowry. Edward, a fair-sized lad for his twelve years, had a quick eye for mischief and precious little time for books—not hard to imagine, given his mother's quick smile and his father's galloping tendencies. The mine was a trap.

In the fall of 1924, Richard Hardin, the gambler, with nowhere to turn, signed a contract indenturing his son to general duties in the tin mine. Young Edward Hardin had become chattel—his labor assigned to South Crofty Mine, Ltd., until his family's debt was satisfied.

Arrested by the local warden, taken from his school, wide-eyed and silent, Edward's classmates sat glued to their chairs.

Mary's broken heart toiled as the joy in her son's face faded to a frown. Edward became boy with old eyes. His posture, his shoulders, gradually fell forward under the weight of the water he hauled to the down-shaft miners. He rarely saw his father, and when he did, his father shunned him with an "Off you go."

"Richard, can't you help our son?"

"Now, Mary. Edward has a knack for sums. He's better for the work."

"The truth's too much, is it? Forgive me, Richard. Edward and I have three jobs. It's time you work a second shift."

In the winter of 1924, to escape the shame of Mary's demand and her modest dreams, Richard Hardin left work, stumped off to the Royal Army Regimental Barracks at Shire Hall, and within a matter of an hour enlisted in the 1ˢᵗ Duke of Cornwall's Light Infantry.

On January 27, 1925, the 1ˢᵗ Battalion of the regiment sailed from Gunwharf Quay next to the South Railway Jetty inside the wall of the Portsmouth Dockyard for Calcutta, India, to fight Indian insurgents.

Richard began in earnest, sending his pay home. But the money he sent home wasn't steady, and it wasn't enough. By June, after nine weeks of waiting for word, Mary assumed her Welshman was dead. Frightened, she began eating one meal a day at a small table in the storeroom of Web's Public House, wrapping the leftovers in her apron to help with Edward's dinner. She devoted the bulk of her wages to Edward, his meals and clothing.

Richard's mates lent a hand, bringing pasties to the mine for Edward.

Wiping the bar at Web's Public House, Mary set her teeth when a corporal from the Royal Army Regimental Barracks, looking a fraction of his age, entered the pub and presented her with a cable and stood at attention.

Realizing the corporal was the message, Richard's mates stopped talking and crowded near the bar. Mary read the words aloud.

> Richard R. Hardin, a Foot in the 1st Duke of Cornwall's Light Infantry Regiment, died in an ambush while on patrol with a contingent from the Ceylon Planter's Rifles, near a remote outpost in the West Bengal region of India on 19 July 1925.

With her best ceremonial expression, she wrinkled the death notice into a ball and dropped it on the bar. "Shoveled into an early grave, was he? With a bunch of bloody farmers." The corporal picked up the cable, smoothed the edges, and quietly read it.

"What about his pay? Do you have his pay-book?"

"No, ma'am. His kit and pay-book have been shipped to unit headquarters from the front, mum." The corporal handed Mary a script. "You have a 30-pound death benefit your husband's unit will send, and whatever his pay-book indicates he is due."

Crying, Mary took the death notice and tucked it in the pocket of her apron. "Why couldn't you wait until the morning?"

"Orders, ma'am."

With tears at the ready, Mary put a log in the fireplace, and looked at her son's black fingernails. "Eat your cabbage, Edward."

"I'm turning into a cabbage."

A horse nickered. An army lorry had stopped in the lane in front of Mary's home. She opened the door as a trunk was being pulled from the lorry's bed, splashing into the muddy lane. Mary and Edward hauled the trunk into the house and set it near the fireplace.

"Do you want me to break the lock?"

Mary didn't answer. Edward took his father's ballpeen hammer and broke the lock and hasp. The trunk contained a never-worn spare uniform, an envelope containing Richard's pay-book, and a sealed envelope.

"You know your sums, Edward. What does the paybook say we're due?"

Edward, surprised to find the paybook written in pencil, exclaimed, "43 pounds."

"Hide the paybook. We'll trick the blokes—say we didn't receive it."

"You'll have to present it to get paid."

"I'll wait until I get his death benefit. I can buy vegetables and meat on credit."

The news of Richard's death set its cap. Still in debt to the mine owners, Mary sat crying. With Edward carrying water in the mine and her husband's tenor voice howling with dust, his smile torn at its edge, her nightmare now complete. Her chest settled through a sigh as she opened the green envelope and read the dispatch—Richard's final words:

msg: p5a. Dateline Simla, 27 February: Subject=Cornwall's movement to India.

My Dearest Mary,

I will love you always. I am dreadfully sorry for the burdens I have left you and Edward, and if I've made you cry. The Wesleyans will help you.

My lodge will help you. Please forgive me, Mary. I could not face the workhouse the mine owners had waiting for me.

A hug for Edward. Give his hair a toss.

Good-bye, Mary.

Love Always, Richard.

With her heart holding sway, Mary's grief churned so. She became more frightened. Alone and impoverished, Mary read the dispatch again, realizing her stubby Welshman had abandoned his family—and Richard's note had been written shortly after he arrived in India.

For Mary, the next night meandered, dark and then darker.

By mid-afternoon, the word of Richard's death had run the whole of Tucking Mill, stirring a familiar wake of decaying leaves. Mary slapped Reverend Gosden when he tried to fondle her breast. He chastised himself with a smirk, derisively pestering her over the sins of alcohol and working in a public house.

Hours later, the majority owner of South Crofty Mine tried to massage Mary with a rush of old fondness, suggesting favors for the interest due.

Badgered and harassed by the sons of the mine owners, fighting became a passage for Edward as he walked to and from the mine. As summer became fall, Edward tired of the beatings the gang of young boys were giving him and turned to stalking his enemies—the lads his size first off. With mitts like single jacks and cat-quick feet, Edward nearly killed the first lad.

The bull ring, the hunt, and the complete destruction of his adversaries excited him. He thrashed them good.

Without remorse, the local ruffians turned on Mary, threatening to kill her if Edward didn't mend his ways. Mary was safe while working at Web's Public House. Richard's shift mates stood at hand. She was not safe while cleaning houses for the mine owners. At wits end, Mary posted Richard's ship dispatch to her cousin Karen, in Cardiff, Wales.

Days and weeks appeared without a word from Karen.

On the fourth Sunday Mary and Edward watched as Reverend Gosden argued with a stranger. The vicar looks frightened. The stranger was wearing a houndstooth hacking jacket, trousers fit for the rich, and highly polished leather boots. Repeatedly poking the reverend in the chest while pointing at Mary, the stranger was clearly angry.

Through the clouded glass of old sight, the craggy seams that framed the stranger's smile frightened Mary. He's an odd bit of work, that young man, she thought. Does he know who I am? Mary's chest ached. She held her breath, put her arm around Edward, and stepped into the churchyard.

He looks like the mason's carving at the entry to the nave—the vicar's green man. Standing near the entry to the churchyard, the stranger seemed to blend into the landscape. Stout, with a large nose, thick hands and hay-colored hair, his eyes sat watery-gray as though glazed stones on the bottom of a winter brook.

He's following me.

The stranger reached for Mary's elbow and drew her to a halt as she reached the gate to her front yard. "A minute of your time, Mary. I'm a traveler from Temple hamlet in the parish of Blisland, on Bodmin Moor, in Cornwall."

Stepping away, Mary stood erect. "What do you want?"

"I'm William Hockey, Willie if you like. I'm the Tyler of the Masonic lodge in Cardiff, Wales. I helped your cousin Karen with her difficulties some months back. She asked me to help you. I read Richard's final dispatch. Did it come in a green envelope?"

"And how would you be knowing that?"

"A guess. A green envelope means the dispatch wasn't censored by his unit." Not wanting to push a claim, Hockey smiled as he took a deep breath. "If you don't mind, Mary. I'd like to look in his kit that came from India."

Mary let her guard down as she ushered her son and the stranger into her home. Reluctantly she closed the door. Adding dry leaves to the coals in the fireplace followed by a handful of kindling, Edward looked over his shoulder with pride as the fire took hold.

Mary's heart shook with a quickening as the stranger's eyes iced over. Warming herself near the fire, she kneeled and reluctantly opened Richard's trunk. Her house grew suddenly cold as though the man had found satisfaction in her fear.

"Nothing wrong with the Welsh." Hockey talked as he rummaged through Richard's kit. "Make damned fine soldiers under white officers. That's the lot then, is it, Mary?" He turned a quick smile into an inquiry.

"Yes, that's the whole of Richard's life." Timid, standing amid scraps of firewood, Mary checked a tear with her apron, and answered Hockey's challenge.

"What's that about the Welsh?"

Hockey drew the trunk near the fire. For a long while he knelt on a rush mat near the hearth, examining the stitching of the trunk's lining. With the hiss of sap for a chorus, he extended his hand. "No offense, Mary. Welshmen are Taffy buggers to the lads in London. Barely fit for fodder. Thought London might have used his kit to send a bit of gold back."

"There's gold in the tailings at South Crofty," Edward blurted. His dark brown eyes widened as if shocked by his voice. Mary squeezed his shoulder.

Hockey stepped to the fire and extended his hands. The window near the door reflected his image, and the oddments near the fireplace. He shrugged through a smile, seemingly dismissing the young man's announcement. He touched Mary's shoulder lightly. As though offering friendship, he gave Edward's hair a possessive toss.

Alarmed, Mary bunched her apron tie in her hand, trying to hide her fright. This well-dressed stranger had acknowledged Richard's request. His eyes seemed to search her being. The gift—he's a Druid—he has the powers of divination. If so, he knows me better than I like.

Edward drew erect, smiled, and took hold of Hockey's hand.

"I'll drop 'round, Mary. Cobwebs want removing."

Censoring herself, not sure she wanted this man with his chilly, tranquil demeanor and gritty eyes in her home again, Mary mustered a smile.

"What are you going on about, then?"

"I need to get on. There's a reverend needs putting right. Good-bye, Mary."

One month later, on the first Sunday in November 1925, William Hockey visited Tucking Mill with a group of well-dressed men. Less than an hour later, after reading Richard's dispatch, the men bade their good-byes. Hockey stopped in the doorway and stared at the fire. With a vacant pause, his eyes seemed hollow as he surveyed the room, landing on Richard's trunk.

"Cobwebs want removing, Mary."

The following day, the Masonic lodge in Cardiff, Wales, paid Mary's debt owed to South Crofty Mine, Ltd. Reminding the mine owners that South Crofty, the deepest mine in the world, produced black tin, wolfram, and minor amounts of arsenic. Wanting to arouse their fear, Hockey spoke to each mine owner of a conflict of loyalty and warned that one of the owner group would die in the mine if Mary Hardin was abused or mistreated by anyone.

The principal owner chose a measured personal apology as his response. Additionally, South Crofty would deliver a packet of food to Mary's home once a week.

The next day the Reverend Gosden walked into the garden of the cloister on the southern flank of the church and offered Mary a scuppered expression of nicely judged indifference.

"Look at you, Mary. Dolled up like a sore finger. I judge your work at Webb's Public House is preferable to being on the gate."

Reverend Gosden had received a donation from the lodge along with a warning to leave Mary and her son alone.

One of the ruffians who had berated Mary in front of young Edward fell off the windlass in the main shaft of South Crofty mine. His chest had been branded with an eight-pointed cross. Taking a full measure, the ghosts of religious retribution had rattled their chains. The mysterious death put Tucking Mill and the whole of Cornwall on edge.

Young Edward decided to bide his time before he settled with the second ruffian, Alfred Gosden, the vicar's son. When I'm grown, I'll beat him every Friday.

In the shadows of confinement, the attrition of despair weighed on Mary's soul. The pretend people, Mary's friends, and neighbors began greeting Mary and Edward with a whisper of fear and respect. From garrets and cellars the intonation was clear—being Mary Hardin's friend had become a necessity.

Days passed and weeks as well. An ominous silence grew into an array of gestures replacing the obligation of friendship with practiced avoidance. The isolation grew calmly, without hatred.

For the next three years, on the first Sunday in November, William Hockey came to visit Mary to pay his respects and refresh her neighbors' memories. In time Mary found Hockey friendly but unsettling.

In the spring of 1929, an English gentleman came to Tucking Mill with Hockey.

"My, my, Willie, look what you brought to Tucking Mill?" Mary wiped her hands hurriedly and examined the detail of the Hockey's elegant friend.

"Mary Hardin allow me to introduce Sir John Poston. Sir John's a member of the Masonic Lodge in Cardiff, and a lifelong friend."

Mary's cheeks flushed as she clasped her hands in front of her. Sir John stood tall, and stately, sporting thick gray hair that sat atop an expression that seemed to expect surprise. As though moved by Mary's modesty, he scanned the meager trappings around the room.

With expansive black eyes, he seemed to welcome Hockey's comment while evaluating its author and calculating its worth.

With a smile for Edward, Sir John warmed his backside by the fire. Issuing a long, relaxed sigh, as though setting his wealth aside, he laid his Harris-tweed jacket over the back of a chair, looked at his pocket watch, and took out his pipe.

Sir John engaged Edward with predictions for the Penzance cricket club's season. After lighting his pipe with an ember from the fireplace, he complimented Mary on the comfort of her home and suggested he needed a cook on staff in London who practiced the Welsh custom of cooking with saffron.

Mary was embarrassed. Her modest home and her son's coarse appearance were faults she could not mend. Ashamed, as if the tatters at the edge of her tablecloth were her own, Mary pressed her apron against her thighs with her palms.

Cornish pies sat ranked, cooling on the hob. A pitcher of cold milk stood nearby. "We've pasty for our supper."

"Your home smells wonderful, Mary." Sir John sat to the table.

"The smells have nowhere to go," Edward happily declared.

After dinner Sir John offered Edward a working apprenticeship with Poston and Sons, Ltd., not in London but in a leased warehouse on the docks of New York City. Tired of the mines, Edward accepted the offer with a dance around the table. Realizing his mother would be alone he stopped rejoicing, lowered his eyes, and cocked his head.

"I can't leave. I've my mum to look after."

Mary nodded ruefully but didn't speak. With tears streaming down her cheeks she gave her son a hug. At last—Edward would be free of the mines. "It's time you left your father's life behind, Edward." She gave his black, curly hair a toss.

Sir John moved to the fireplace and began to fill his pipe. "Will you come to Saint Albans, Mary? To help on staff?"

She drew up in hardened reproof and nearly hollered. "Why would I? Tucking Mill is better now. It's the home I know. I grew old here." Angry that Hockey didn't come to her defense, she raised her chin. "Willie has the gift. He knows you scare me. You've no reason to come to such a poor village, waving your pipe about." Mary's chin quivered as she wiped the tears on her cheeks with her apron. A part of her wished this London swell had never come. He knocked his pipe on the inner wall of the fireplace.

"Why did you come?" she asked, sweeping pipe tobacco into the fire.

Shrugging into his jacket, Sir John seemed contrite. "Willie's been boasting about Edward for quite some time. I had to see for myself. And my company has been shipping black tin from the South Crofty mine for decades. Wolfram as well." He extended his hands toward the fire, then he stood more erect. "I've been paying the Crown's seven percent coinage dues on South Crofty's smelted tin for a good many years."

"I see. So, you know these mine owners." Taking a deep breath, Mary pressed a fist against the tabletop. "You paid our debt?" Sir John nodded. She moved a pot from the fireplace. "I've been grateful these many years, but we would have managed." Her hands shook as she cleared a dish from the table.

Mary caught Hockey's arm as he passed through the door and whispered, "Willie, please watch over my son—his father sold him like he was a jar of stout."

There had been a time, three or four years ago, when Edward had given up. He tried to look out sharp for his mother, but it seemed the town enjoyed her despair—her dependence on William Hockey. Suggesting reasons why he came around at odd hours.

At age seventeen, standing at six foot plus one, with shoulders as wide as an ax handle, and fists wider than mallet heads, Edward bid good-bye to his mother with a warm, tender embrace. He promised to write and send for her by year's end. A tear blessed his eye.

Afoot, he set out for London looking for Poston and Sons, Ltd., a midsized international shipping company situated amid the Surrey Commercial Docks on the east end of London, near Rotherhithe, on the south side of the River Thames.

All wool and a yard wide, mad keen to astonish, packing an indefinably foolish expression, Edward mounted the stair to Poston and Sons, Ltd. Taken for a pretend person by the secretary, he was directed to a wooden chair in the foyer, and told to wait until Sir John returned from an appointment. A fan massaged the hot air. Trying to stifle a yawn, Edward was barely up to scratch when Sir John entered the foyer.

An hour later, holding a finger to the light, his voice rising, Sir John shook Edward's hand. "You must not break faith with those who die, Edward. Your father did his best."

In return for his conditional support, Sir John made demands of his young charge: become a devout Freemason and send money home on a regular schedule.

After a thorough hashing of the dangers of the world, including the pitfalls of New York's streets and prostitution, Sir John gave Edward a fitting of new clothes, a Union Steamship Company second-class ticket to New York, and a bundle with three packets—each containing five hundred American dollars.

Edward thought, this money will dry the dampness of Tucking Mill. Yet his father's betrayal lay amid the odors of the mine, clinging to his trust. "I'll not sell my son as property," he whispered to himself.

With a sense of pride, Edward ran his hand across the top of a cigar box perched in the spill of Sir John's desk lamp. The oaken box braced an inlay, a ruby-red, eight-pointed cross. Nodding his recognition, something breaking from the past, he tucked the money packets into the hidden waist pockets of his trousers.

Willie Hockey has a cross tattooed on his forearm, he thought. Same color. The thug who fell off the windlass in South Crofty was branded with a cross.

Standing now by the door, Sir John put a hand lightly on Edward's shoulder. "You will be required to join the Longshoreman's Union, in New York, Edward. I suggest you learn how to button that lip of yours. That or become a pugilist."

Edward admired the young women of London. The gamers admired his shock of curly black hair, laughing as they teased his mischievous smile. Being free of the cast of down-shaft mining, his day was happily his own.

On August 4, 1929, with their agreement signed in contract form, Edward set sail for America on the British ocean liner *Aquitania*, with twenty-one dollars.

Amid the excitement and confusion common on the docks of New York City, Edward found loyalty led to argument and nationality led to trust. Tough and stubborn, he stood the morning shape-up for his union with primary-school zeal. He made shift on the dock next to the livery at 17 Battery Place, saving money and searching for a wife.

Late one afternoon a cable from Hockey arrived that left Edward unstrung. His mother had been assaulted by two men in the keg locker of Webb's Public House. One of the men was the vicar's son, Alfred Gosden. After a few minutes, an hour at most, he read the first part of the cable again with a mounting sense of rage.

His words seemed to melt together. "I've money enough. I should have sent for mum months ago." Edward wiped the tear coursing his right cheek.

Drawn damp in the mire, William Hockey's not-so-discreet inquiries into the assault revealed the dead man found in South Crofty mine was one of Mary's assailants. Did Willie carve a cross in the man's chest? Edward wondered. My mum might think so.

As though an insistent question, Edward whispered, "Willie's cable doesn't seem urgent. He's escorted mum from Tucking Mill. She has her treasures, her woolen scarves and her shake rag, and he promised to look after her to help the family of a fellow mason."

Edward had matured into a robust, byproduct of pasty pies, horse barns, and stern religious discipline, with a flair for boxing—his hands as leaden as the head of a double-jack. His corner man's ringside chant didn't need a drum: "Can the bluster, Eddie, and start the dance." His minister agreed. The vicar coached boxing at the local YMCA.

Being the first of the Hardin clan to graduate from any school, Edward became a steward in the local longshoreman's union. In 1931, on his nineteenth birthday, one year after graduating from PS 33, he received a cable from Sir John Poston.

> Edward
>
> I have arranged a working scholarship for you to pay for your attendance at the Royal Military College, Woolwich, in southeast London.
>
> The college is called The Shop, because the first building at the college is a converted workshop of the old Woolwich Arsenal. It's England's foremost military college. The college was established to train artillery and engineer officers."
>
> I suggest you become an engineer.
>
> John Poston

Shunned by his upper-crust classmates at the Royal Military College, Woolwich, Edward joined a local gun club that offered archery lessons. Shooting targets mounted on hay bales with a bow seemed to temper his frustration.

In June 1935, Lieutenant Edward Hardin graduated from Woolwich as a Royal Army engineer officer, his English sufferable, mixed with an occasional American syntax.

Passing out without honors earned him an adverse posting—the central vehicle-storage facility, part of the Royal Army Ordinance Center near Ashchurch, England.

*   *   *

Royal Army Ordinance Center. Ashchurch, England. 8 October 1935. 0830 Hours, GMT.

Convinced the ordinance-center posting adversely marked his career, Lieutenant Hardin decided to match the mark by devoting himself to becoming a damned poor military excuse.

Bolstered by Sir John's recommendation to the Masonic lodge, he met with Masonic guides for three months of study. Testing with zeal, he received acceptance as a First-Degree Mason. Study and further testing followed by oath taking—vowing to protect the women and families of other Masons—he was elevated to a Third-Degree Mason.

Fellow Masons sprang from hiding, the butcher on the town square, a solicitor, the ordinance-center commander, and the lead engineer for the Cornish Main Line of the Bodmin and Wenford Railway.

Corporal Akens, his newly assigned signals sergeant, handed Edward the phone. "It's a Sir John Poston on the line." Hardin frowned a little.

"Hello, Sir."

"Congratulations, Edward. Your father was a Third-Degree Mason. I'm sending your father's trunk to you. It contains the remnants of his service in India."

"Sir, my father didn't care about being a Mason. He was a tinker and a gambler. The debt he shoveled onto his family—my mum and me, brought years of hardship. My mum's still being shoveled about, insulted. Never to be free of the shame."

"Hockey will ensure Mary is safe."

Edward had heard enough. "He's either her signpost, or her problem. But is he both?" It could only have been an instant later that he heard Sir Poston ring off.

Activities in and around Ashchurch rubbed along at a lumbering pace, unchallenged by the prospects of war in Europe. As the center's junior training officer, Hardin challenged his boredom by engaging all gears simultaneously, promoting confusion while watching the base commander measure the folly a vehicle-storage depot could sustain.

Nothing challenged Edward's quick wit. Deciding almost all British officers were tea-minded and serious in their need for decorum and discipline; he began misinforming them at every tick of the clock. These officers, in Edward's opinion, needed more black coffee.

He spiced drills in crating and uncrating an artillery piece and loading and unloading a railcar with regulations designed to frustrate any off-wheel who happened by, while, at the same time, stimulating all worn bearings to maintain a spirited gait. Hardin scheduled inspections for the hour after tea to ensure dimness could set its cap.

Bored with the pace of British army life, he decided to resign his commission after he served his hitch and return to New York.

The letters he received from William Hockey, the Tyler of the Masonic Lodge in Cardiff, Wales, although welcome, increasingly packed an impatient tone.

Lieutenant Edward Hardin,

I am distressed by reports of you putting about like a young disappointment. If you intend to represent Free Masonry in any capacity, anywhere in the world, or prosper with the help of myself or Sir John Poston, I suggest you stop acting like the captain's bit and have a go at perfection.

It's the Tarpeian Rock from where all failures are thrown to their doom.

Caveo Dominus,
William Hockey

Stretching, and yawning a second time, Hardin dumped his coffee in a slit trench. "The captain's bit. Caveo Dominus—beware the master. I should have stayed in New York." Nearly spitting the words, his face creased into a brace, and he tossed Hockey's letter in the waste bin.

"That iron-gray old bastard couldn't melt enough wax to touch up the youngest peach in Piccadilly." Hardin grabbed Hockey's letter and tore it to pieces.

"Pardon me, sir?" Corporal Akens asked.

Surprised to find the man standing next to him, Hardin smiled. "Nothing, Corporal." Then he grabbed his gym kit and left the hangar for a morning jog.

The narrow roads around Ashchurch wove over the low-rolling countryside through canyons of hay and stonework, each turn giving way to the next. His favorite route crossed the Tirle Brook, circled Dowty's Engineering Works, and crossed the Tirle Bridge near the town square. Abreast of Cowfield Mill, he realized his pace had reached its highest mark.

Alert to any challenge, as he tried to gain ground on a bicycle, his shoes met the roadway with a scuffing *thump*. Pushing his stride, he came to a stop to catch his breath. Suddenly the bicycle he was chasing swerved to avoid an oncoming motorcycle, careened off the road, and smashed headlong into a ditch. A girl flew over the bicycle's handlebar, over the ditch, and landed in a stack of hay.

Hardin sprinted to the scene and vaulted over the ditch—instantly helpless. The girl had recovered nicely and stood smiling, her sweater holding sway and her hair strewn with straw. Looking every bit a member of the Fraser Clan, she radiated the soft beauty of the West Highlands. Bunching and fluffing her ginger-red hair to shake out the straw, she flashed her apple-green eyes and stole a glance, and playfully returned his gaze. Her smile and the geometry of her equipment started Edward's tackle to whirling.

Struck dumb, Edward's mind rattled with his nerves.

"Try to stop fidgeting, sergeant, and lend me your hand." She tilted her head, seemingly amused by the lack of composure of her boyish admirer, her eyes showing a trace of delight.

"Lieutenant Edward Hardin at the charge, my lady. Sword in hand." Embarrassed by his impish chat-up line, he extended a hand to the young woman, his thoughts nudging his smile.

This doll's a beauty. All decked out in her straw-covered togs.

"Do stop staring at me like a startled cow." Her smile filled with mischief, she watched him lift her bicycle from the ditch, pointing a finger as she went on. "Is gawking a temporary affliction for you Yanks, or do you regularly loll about, lusting in silence?"

The girl's forward nature had Edward off his game. Racking his inventory for any line he could use, even the words he thought of kept fumbling about. There had been girls and adventures of sorts. None of these torn pages more than half helped him know what to say.

Taking deep breaths, the joy of the encounter began warming a deeply felt emotion.

A truck motored by, and a whistle played the air. Edward matched the whistle note for note. With enthusiasm tacking under a full sail, his cleverness dismayed, he admired the first thing that caught his eye, the girl's natural beauty, her natural endowments.

With a half-amused way of talking, his grin tried to slur his words. Wanting to buzz on, he blurted, "I'm glad you landed on your keister. Look at the mess you made of that haystack."

Blushing, her eyes quick to laughter, she raised her chin. "Ah, wheel, it's a grand, soft day." Not waiting for a response, she burst on. "My name is Katherine Burnside. I teach at the primary school in Ashchurch. If you wish to visit, come by the school next Tuesday afternoon. Good-bye, Lieutenant Hardin."

Decked for the Christmas season, they married in the Church of Saint Nicholas and settled into Katherine's flat overlooking the Tirle Brook, near the Ashchurch town square. Bored with jogging, Edward started boxing as an undercard in the Saturday night smokers on the base. Durable, punching above his weight, he took a pounding.

He enjoyed fighting.

Making love with Katherine fired his enthusiasm, rushing home to lose himself in her beauty. As the weather turned cold, they would meet in the pub below their flat for a glass of wine, before mounting the stairs and laughing as they made love again and again.

Life is good, he thought, watching Katherine sleep, listening to her laughter. We'll have lots of children and live in the country. I'll muster out of the army and work as an engineer. Katherine can teach school if she likes or concentrate on being England's best mum.

"Akens, tell me about your signals school at Catterick Camp, in North Yorkshire."

"The basic course is nine weeks. Mostly classroom stuff. Last winter."

"Is there an advance course?"

"Yes. For special service blokes."

Corporal Akens had a wool scarf wrapped twice around his neck, winter flight gloves to prevent having to type, and boots corralling a kerosene heater under the front lip of his chair.

"Today's mighty cold, Lieutenant."

Hardin raised his cup. "You're right, Sparky. Battalion operations declared February '36 the coldest on record in England."

"Sir, let's close shop and be off to the pub."

"We're off for the day."

In early March, sitting in their flat overlooking the town square, Katherine handed Edward a cable from Sir John Poston. The union steward who had befriended Edward, had been killed in a crane accident on the New York docks. Several crates of machine parts from Poston and Sons, Ltd.'s, Bayonne warehouse had burst open spewing packets of opium onto the quay.

The shipment was the third cargo the company had transported for Bosch America, a large German subsidiary financed by Enskilda Bank, in Stockholm. If any of the financial giants associated with Bosch decided Poston and Sons, Ltd. was smuggling drugs, bankruptcy would be Sir John's end.

Sir John accepted the news with anger touched with suspicion. Measuring the weight of varying probabilities, and the mounting criminal activity in Bayonne, France and on the New York docks, he sent Hockey to New York to investigate and informed Lloyd's of London.

For Hockey, only time and place were accidents. The union steward's death was not an outlier. The steward was a target. Willie found himself convinced by the obvious: the Corsican stamps stenciled on the broken crates.

Sir John,
   The crane operator who mishandled the crates was found dead, floating in New York's East River. Dockers claim he was paid to drop the cargo. Be alert. Dockers think contraband is being shipped regularly in your cargoes.
   I believe Poston and Sons is being set up to divert attention from a smuggling operation in southern France. Run out of Lyon or Marseille.
   Caveo Dominus,
   Willie

For Edward, the news of the union steward's death lay sequestered, distant in time, obscure. The cause seemed plausible: a crane accident—thick ice and an overloaded boom. That opium was found in Sir John's cargo was puzzling.

Setting the cable aside, he searched the confines of his father's trunk, inch by inch. He drew his hand over the emblem of the 1ˢᵗ Duke of Cornwall's Light Infantry Regiment. With a welling sense of self, he started reading Willie's files—Tucking Mill; South Crofty mine owners; Reverend Gosden; Alfred Gosden; Mary Hardin; Richard Hardin; Gordon Dewar.

What am I looking for?

Opening his father's Masonic bible, he found a sheet of yellowed paper. On it, a drawing of an eight-pointed cross. The left arm of the cross bore the name Alfred Gosden. The right arm bore the words *The Lady of Wisdom.* Who was the artist?

Why is Willie looking for Alfred Gosden? What else has the vicar's boy done? Edward extended his hands toward the fire. Someday I'll find the sin-shifter's son. God won't help him.

Katherine rubbed Edward's shoulders to ease his mood, to draw him from the past, to draw him to her breast. He accepted her gesture, his expression the true reflection of her own. They decided to focus on her teaching post and his job offer from Dowty's Engineering Works.

That and sleep themselves happy.

*   *   *

Ashchurch, England. Royal Army Ordinance Center. Central Vehicle Storage Headquarters, 12 March 1939. 1645 Hours, Greenwich Mean Time, GMT.

Hardin laughed at the orders promoting him to captain. Hockey wrote a letter fobbing the honor as "gating a layabout in Ashchurch," rather than sodding a better man with the post. Edward dismissed the old man's sarcasm and threw the letter in the waste bin.

A week of gales had filled the slit trenches near the gun storage hangar to the brim. Gusts of wind blew water onto Hardin's desk. Chilled to his core, sporting a naturally shriveled bag, he wiped the desk with a towel before posting the weekly training schedule. Word-for-word—he used the schedule twice for the Artillery Gun Assembly Point.

Glancing across the tarmac, he spotted, Akens, the signals corporal, sprinting toward the hangar. Water splashed from the corporal's boots as he leaped through the open bay.

"Captain Hardin!" The corporal's face was bound in unctuous gravity. Shifting his feet, his eyes moistened. "Sir!" A rain-sodden overcoat pulled at his slight frame. He turned away as he handed his captain an envelope stamped "Most Immediate."

"What is it, Corporal?" Hardin hesitated for an instant before opening the note. The notification had been written hurriedly.

"No officer would use the blower, sir." Rain brought a long stroke of cloud, a soaking drawn across the air strip. "And the red caps aren't worth a shilling. Those self-righteous scuffers, claimed they weren't couriers."

Captain Hardin,   1620 Hours.
    Your wife has gone missing.

She was riding her bicycle near Aldershot. An auto fled the scene and was found some miles away, smashed into a stone fence. The driver was shot through the head.

A foot from the 1st/5th Infantry Brigade, the Queen's Own Cameroon Highlanders witnessed the obduction. He's given a statement.

So far, your wife hasn't been admitted to the local hospital. She was taken from the scene in an army ambulance. Royal Army red caps and the local constables are searching for the ambulance.

We collected her belongings from her room at the Spread Eagle Hotel in Liphook and left them with her landlord.
    Sergeant C.

"You're dismissed, Corporal." Hardin, the large, strapping, thick-chested Welshman, sat into the remnants of a tragic circumstance, looking, unseeing. God's a frightful bastard, he thought. My West Highland lass. I'll keep looking for her smile.

Standing in the mouth of the empty maintenance bay, Hardin stared across the vehicle park. At first glance, he found the acres of close-knit grass seemed to ease into a turbulent, cloudy horizon.

"I'm sorry, Katherine. I hope we can find you and make you better."

Crying, a gust of rain hit his face. "What in hell do I do now?" He kept walking, heading for the bakery on the Ashchurch town square for coffee and a pastry. It was a special time of day—the time to meet Katherine at the bakery on the town square.

Angry. He was nearly running. Screaming into the wind. "Is there a reason for all this shit? I've come from the tin mines. My family comes from the fens of Wales. We escaped the workhouse, and my mother can't find peace."

And now his Katherine was missing—abducted outside of Bordon Camp near Aldershot.

Tragedy must have a limit, he thought. Water that's run by and all. Mixing British and American axioms of rage and retribution, he was reluctant to respond to inquiries. With a heart full of hell, he reached for the blower and rang the ordinance-center switchboard for a patch-through to Sir John Poston's London home.

After tapping the phone rest several times, badgering one operator after another, and finally the switchboard supervisor, Hardin heard the phone line ring clear. "Poston residence." The butler's voice packed a frosty sort of gravel.

"May I speak with Sir John Poston, please?"

"One moment, sir."

"My God, Edward! I've been expecting your call. I am worried about Katherine. Hockey rang me, muttering quiet warnings about circumstance."

With a clipped, refined insolence in his voice, Hardin asked, "Sir John, is her disappearance tied to the tin mines of Cornwall?"

The brittle spike of his voice brought silence. "I'm sorry, Edward. What did you say?" Sir John's tone cast a hint of disbelief.

Slightly the worse for drink, Hardin asked, "Was Katherine murdered?"

Again, the line was silent. "I shouldn't think so, Edward. Katherine's a schoolteacher. Hockey will put the shingles in place. If we're fetched up against old bones, we'll know soon enough." Sir John's tone drew a legible note of caution.

"Katherine was pregnant."

"One of God's ruddy little games I suppose.," Sir John exhaled a deep, exaggerated breath. "Do carry on, will you, Edward?"

"Ruddy little games? Damn Poston. Is that all you can say?"

As if there was much more, Sir John cleared his throat. "Willie's looking for Katherine through a storm of deceit, mixed with odd doings." Catching his wind, he went on. "I lost a son many years ago, now. I do apologize if I seem callous."

Exasperated, wiping away the tears, his throat full, Edward could barely speak. "My billet here at Ashbrook ends next month. We were looking forward to my transfer to the RAF base at Mildenhall. If Katherine's not found soon, I won't be able to assist the authorities."

"Might be best all 'round. You'll have to eat what's on your plate eventually."

Hearing that, Edward hesitated, considering the problems before him. "I think I'm going to chuck." His staccato marking how drawn his face had become.

"Back-chat aside, that might help."

"Any luck locating my mum?"

"She's living in a village near Newcastle. Willie's gone there, and all. We've let Mary have her way, Edward." Sir John seemed to stifle a cough. "Fear runs in circles tossing bits to the side. Your mother's finally returning my calls. We talked yesterday. I'll stay in touch with her."

"Forgive me, sir. I've been limping along expecting to see Katherine. The way things have gone, if she's not found soon, I'll have to leave Ashchurch." Edward's frustration had put on weight. "Can you arrange a posting overseas, to New South Wales or Malaya? Singapore? Anywhere out of England."

At first there was no reply. Then the rustle of paper. "Those postings tend to be in the back of nowhere, Edward." And after a series of coughs, "I'll make some inquiries. But you're far from qualified for special operations."

"I've heard units are siding up for bush-ranging in Burma and Southeast Asia."

"I believe that's Force 136, Group *A* and *B*—elite provisional units as yet unsanctioned—all hush-hush, mind you. The Interservice Research Bureau is proposing a Group *A* and *B* as part of a provisional executive, the Special Operations Executive, SOE. Yes, that's it."

"If it's unsanctioned, what kind of squaddie are they looking for?"

"Fugitives, I suppose. Irreverence might be required. Admiral Sinclair, the head of Special Intelligence Service, SIS, may be of assistance. Perhaps Sir Nigel Stuart as well—I know both men. Cheeky buggers."

"Thank you, sir. I'll look forward to your call."

"A warning. Sir Nigel Stuart is an enigma. Complicated. Desperately loyal to the crown. He grinds his enemies to dust. If he sponsors you, you'll be on a tight wire."

"Fair enough."

"I judge Force 136 is a rough posting, Edward. You'll have to do a stint at the RAF Central Landing School at Ringway, near Manchester, first off, followed by a stint in the colonies at Fort Benning, Georgia. Panama as well. If you pass muster, you'll be off to New South Wales."

Hesitantly, Edward came plain. "I need to leave Ashchurch. The coppers often scoff at my grief." He knew the time had come to move on. His Katherine was missing and many in the constabulary believed she was dead. Even the cobles in the Ashchurch town square brought memories of his Highland Lassie.

"Mind you, Captain Hardin. This provisional executive, the SOE, has been boiling in the bowels—the 'Hole' below Whitehall for months—a merger between the War Office and the Ministry of Economic Warfare. The PM's not amused."

Wondering what Sir John was trying to tell him this time, with a huff, Edward put in: "Chamberlain's a flowering nitwit. The bugger doesn't give a jot about squaddies like me. While SIS is addling on about the idea of war, an expedited posting should get their bags off."

Sir John knew this too. "Attentive idiocy can blossom in the brightest wards. Sick-making. Well beyond accountability. Today, however, these habits will help your cause."

Edward paused, considering his plan for getting out of Ashchurch. "Yes, I know. One is keeping my mouth shut. The other, keep my head down."

"Quite right!"

Looking across the air strip the evening light shone like watered whiskey. "Sir John, give my regards to Hockey. Let him know I'm no longer the captain's bit."

"Yes, of course. I'll tell him just that. Willie's filled with the souls of Celts come and gone. Indifferent to the values of this world, he's not of our time, Edward. He has the power of prophecy. He always seems to be watching from the side."

"Well, that should settle it, I suppose."

"Willie's on to Newcastle. I asked him to visit your mother to bring her this news and see to her needs."

"Check on her, sir—just check."

"Mary's fine, Edward. Your mother resolutely refuses my invitations to come to London. She's a sentimental woman. She will be well cared for.

Willie will see to that." A door knocker sounded, followed by a commotion in the background on Poston's end of the phone.

"Excuse the fuss, Edward. The ice delivery came to the wrong entrance."

"Give my regards to your sons."

"Yes, I will. They're nearly thirty years old and well on their way. We've been following your progress. Look after yourself, Edward. Do carry on, will you?"

"I didn't get to say goodbye."

Sir John Poston rang off. Edward held the receiver waiting for more words. Retracing the years, the months, the days, he thought of their moments of joy; of Katherine's mischievous grin and their first straw-strewn encounter—the happiness she found each morning, the Ashchurch town square, the bakery.

The image of her smile swept through the hangar, raced along the duckboards, and dwindled to a flutter, playing out the door into the rain.

Gale-force winds and rain pounded the French coast. Alone on an isolated quay in Bayonne, France, Sir John set a torch under his arm, and started as he had before—inspecting a shipment of machine parts bound for Rotterdam. The instant the clipboard holding his papers shattered, and the corner of the packing crate near his face blew into pieces, he heard the shots.

Sir John dove for cover as the sniper fired three more quick shots. The first round tugged at the shoulder of his overcoat and a second round burned his right side. Out of the line of fire, he scrambled along the front apron and into the adjoining go-down.

"Damn, it is a rough enough time I've had of it."

When the dawning came upon him Sir John woke with a start. A docker was shaking his foot. Fighting leery optics, he eased out of the tunnel of truck tires where he had spent the night.

The right side of his shirt was caked with dried blood. As he arched his back, a shivering pain shot through his chest. I must have a cracked rib, he thought. After following the docker to a wharf shack near the end of the pier, accepting a cup of coffee, he eased onto a wooden stool.

"Shall I call the *gendarmes, monsieur*?" the docker asked, offering Poston a pastry from his lunch pail.

Accepting the pasty, Poston set his feet. "No, monsieur. There's not much a gendarme can do. A pry-bar to open the rest of my crates would be helpful."

Poston left the comfort of the warm shack, pry-bar in hand. Examining the damaged crate, he found packets of opium salted throughout the machine parts. Putting a packet in a canvass sack, he opened the rest of the crates.

Every crate contained opium. The packets had common Asian markings. The Corsican syndicate headquartered in Corsica and Marseille controlled the smuggling in southern France.

Certain the sniper had meant to kill him; he warned his family with a phone call—alter your daily routines. Within the week, he received a telegram from Willie:

> Sir John,
>   The foot from the Queen's Own Cameroon Highlanders who witnessed Katherine's obduction has gone missing. If their weaving ropes from the sand of Givenor Cove, they've gone Bodman.
>   *Caveo Dominus,*
>   Willie

With a war brewing in Europe, in order to put the world right, we may have to stop shipping through Bayonne, Poston thought. The Nazis and the Japanese are driving up the cost of shipping throughout the world. Raw silk and pot ash are at a premium.

And Edward has lost his lovely wife. It's no wonder he's gone bush-ranging—if nothing else but to test his chances.

*   *   *

Candle Creek, New South Wales. Two Months Ago. 15 June 1939.

The enlisted men's bar at the upper reaches of Candle Creek lay in shambles thanks to the commandos selected for the Special Operations Executive, Provisional, Force 136 Group B, Team 7. The roustabouts had just completed sixteen weeks of training, bush ranging for hundreds of miles, living on short rations, honing their movement and communication skills for Operation Snow White, a deep-penetration rescue mission into northern Tonkin near the Chinese border.

Captain Edward Hardin stood at a brace before the camp commander, waiting to hear the disciplinary charges against his team members. Stating their case, he put in, "Sir, these month-long training cycles, parachute, and bush ranging, have convinced the lads they're bullet proof. Combined with their twenty-odd year old cocks made almost all of their abilities a retched mess, including their penchant for drink and whores."

"What do you suggest, Captain Hardin?"

"Put the tent back up. Dock my paybook. Dying will be easy for the lads where Team 7's off to. On the back side of Burma."

Laying in the shade of a coolabah tree, near the verge of a dirt airstrip, on a plateau above Cattage Point at the mouth of Cowan and Candle Creek, drinking a last round of gunfire, tea mixed with rum, the commandos laughed and joked as they waited for an extraction aircraft.

Cocksure lads they were, plucked from the ranks of the 1ˢᵗ Duke of Cornwall's Light Infantry—one of Mother's finest fighting units. Trained in the school for bloody mayhem, in the jungles of Panama and the outback and waters of New South Wales—considered the best guerrilla fighters in the world. The lads who volunteered to scour the jungles of hell.

There is an instinct born of training, of understanding. But, to trust this instinct, a squaddie must have a gift that goes beyond learning. To a man, members of Team 7 had the gift.

Captain Edward Hardin, code-sign "Doc," was their team leader. Sporting a hangover that made his hair hurt, he gathered his team around a small fire. "Snow White's definitely a long-range mission. If all goes well, we should be in and out in five weeks. We run through Laos and Thailand down into southern Burma and onto the Malay Peninsula."

"Snow White's a halfpenny whore," Linc Jensen shouted. None of the commandos liked the operational code-signs MI6 had selected—strictly bollocks was Sleepy's charge.

"A bit like you then, eh Jensen?" Hardin pointed at his signals sergeant.

"Ah, but it's grand tits she has." Only Sleepy seemed to relax much, but everything came easy for him.

Hardin laughed. "The drop has been changed to 2200 hours, a night jump into northern Tonkin. Mission change: we no longer secure a weapons drop for the communist guerillas. We snatch Burma's Catholic Bishop being held near the Chinese border. This could get sticky. These guerrillas are being supplied by countries around the world to fight the Japanese in Southeast Asia. Including the Yanks."

"We'll drop like bloody sandbags," Wingrove chirped.

"Cods and sods, that's us." Hardin lit a fag.

"Bloody hell," Jensen chopped in. "A night jump on the tail of the monsoon. We're going to be hanging in the bloody trees, with manky bastards shooting at us."

"Good chance 'a that." Hardin agreed. "Spicy, that's Snow White—a tart. One of Mother's creations." With the wind freshening, Hardin kicked Bashful's boot to wake him.

"Within a mile of our objective the Viet Minh have an emergency landing strip. Six hundred meters of knee-high grass southeast of the prison compound.

"West is the bishop's name. He's a Yank. According to Dewar, he works the Vatican's black-market in Indo-China—trading rubber, tin, and opium on behalf of the Vatican's Prefecture of Extraordinary Affairs. West was recruited in '37 by MI6, Section D, to trade for the Household—the Windsors. As double blind.

"The Queen Mother's crowd, MI6 and the lot, want this priest alive and back in England."

Sleepy came awake with his spaniel eyes afire and a robust chest rattle. "Only one reason Mother would want that papist alive. The bugger's got his hands on some intel MI6 wants to slide under the rose. Incriminating bits that can tickle the Queen's buttons."

"In full cry, who cares?" Hardin searched the confines of his shadow. Why was a priest in northern Tonkin? "Let's hope he's on church parade and ripe to be plucked."

"The priest will stay alive if he can keep our pace." Jensen, code-sign Grumpy, minced in, he alone prompting a wicked parting. "What gets on my tit is we've gone from living on the dragon's lip, hunting Japs, gathering intel, to being browned off by a bunch of staff weans."

"Boredom takes courage." Acknowledging Jensen without lending him credit, Hardin shred his cigarette. "Phase Two: we escort the bishop to Haiphong's British passport office."

Pacing, Jensen stood-to and kicked his rucksack. "How fat is this bastard?"

"I don't know. He'll have to fry his own lard."

"Odds are, this one'll be skinny by the time we reach Burma," Wingrove chimed while scratching his arse.

"Raised in a giggle house, eh, Wingrove. You're bloody Dopey, that's flat." Jensen laughed, finishing his gunfire. "It's the Welsh fiddle, that itch you're scratching?"

Ignoring Wingrove, Hardin offered Jensen another shot of rum. "Phase Three: we infiltrate through Laos and Thailand into southern Burma gathering information on Japanese activity in the region.

"Last phase: we rendezvous with Captain Baxter Corcoran's steamer near Ross Island in the Mergui Archipelago for extraction. Uncle Dingo has been about everywhere in the Bay of Bengal and the Andaman Sea where his boat could go. He'll make the rally.

"Grumpy will set the pace." Hardin picked a small twig out of the fire and lit the corner of his mission briefing notes. "If I don't survive this show, Jensen's in charge."

"If the priest slows us down, I say we shoot the derby bastard and rattle his beads," Jensen declared. "The silk crowd won't know."

"They won't care, either." Hardin shook his head. "Fat or thin, we're not shooting a Yank." Certain and hard are these bushrangers of SOE Team 7. Keeping Jensen or any of the others in harness will be like keeping a badger at bay.

"My eye's at the back site, Doc." Linc Jensen, code-sign Grumpy, gave his balls a boost, soliciting the approval of the rest of his mates.

Robin Wingrove held a bewildered expression, as if pondering Jensen's last remark. He was code-sign Dopey. He spent most of his day with his face bound in secret, parsing words for their hidden meaning. Tall and lanky, with crystal blue eyes and a pointed jaw, he carried a spoon and fork in this breast pocket of his battle dress, as if a ration was closer than the next second.

Living on the verge of boredom, Wingrove's eyes had a crisp bounce. From man to man, or tree to tree. Truck to truck, or plane to plane. With 10/15 vision in each eye, he could find the details common to game trails. Any trail. Robin was Snow White's point man.

Dudley Sutton was eight-months married, couldn't stop smiling, and talked to a tattered picture of his bride—my saucy girl. Over chipmunk pouches in his cheeks the play of the muscles in his face showed a gleeful mind. Frame by frame. He was code-sign Happy. Sutton, a harry prat, was an inch short of six feet with a square jaw, and a neck that was part of his shoulders.

Without his glasses his eyes became confused, as if they enjoyed their competition. Dudley Sutton had toiled slowly into his duties as the team's medic, giving a series of shots to each man, along with Atabrine antimalarial tablets. He knew Atabrine was poisonous. That it caused night tremors, insomnia, and sweating fits. But the drug was better than malaria, so he couldn't tell his team mates why they were getting skittish.

Nathan Everett was code-sign Bashful because he didn't know the meaning of the word. Remote and detached, he was dribbling to be at the Japs. Bashful was constantly fingering the locking ring on his bayonet.

That and his ball sack. Barely over five foot and six, he liked to stand somewhat removed from the team. Bashful had a presence, a knowing. He seemed to feel his surroundings, its trees and vines, its topography, its creatures. And he was dangerous. Sporting square, powerful hands, Everett would fight at the drop of a hat. Often for reasons no one else could fathom.

Rory Campbell, code-sign Sneezy, had a log for a mustache. A man badgered by hay fever and loud nasal exchanges, Sneezy packed rag to extract the bush oysters from his log, and a muffler to deaden the noise. Antsy, Campbell could not stand still, his shadow so often confused, he ate lunch when it disappeared. Hyper-alert, muffler in hand, his parting words for a mate, "Look out sharp for yourself." Linc Jensen's response, "Bugger off, fuck-stick."

The medics at Candle Creek assured him the muffler was useless. The training center phycologists praised adrenaline as the human body's natural antihistamine, confident that Campbell would not sneeze under stress. Rory was the team's boobytrap expert.

At twenty-six years of age, obviously too old to muster an oak-hard stiffy, Harlin Rogers was code-sign Pops. With hair that ringed his head like a wreath, and cheeks that nearly covered his eyes, he packed an indefinably foolish expression. And, being hung like a battery mule, Rogers liked to show off his cock when he took a pee. He'd laugh while enjoying a good shake, claiming, "A good looking head doesn't come with hair on it."

At five feet plus ten Rogers was rake-handle skinny. He needed a rucksack to cast a shadow, and his chin stuck out like a traffic arrow. His mother was from Nepal, and he liked the picture of her holding a bolo next to his father's neck. "I come from a long line of Gurkhas."

Rogers was the team's demolition expert.

Emrick Blaney was code-sign Sleepy. Physiologically scuppered, he only slept in short intervals—any commando unit's asset. His favorite phrase, "Up ya get." He could pull night outpost duty without impacting his ability to function during daylight hours. Looking a fraction of his nineteen years, he was in first rate condition and eager to let chaos have its way.

With his large dark eyes cloudy and his rusty colored hair in knots, the booze bogies Blaney experienced after the team trashed the bar at Candle Creek, kept traipsing through his large chest and shivering his bowels. Emrick was the team's sniper.

Linc Jensen was Grumpy. An all-England football legend who never smiled, with thighs bigger than Sleepy's chest, he could run for days without rest. Jensen was born ornery. He liked to argue with his superiors. Any subject would do. As Team 7's wireless-radio operator he prompted uncertainty, saying anything to anyone over the radio net.

His most valued radio procedure; he had mastered the art of "listening out", and never transmitting a response.

For Captain Edward Hardin, Jensen was the perfect signals sergeant. He sensed Hardin's changing moods, Hardin's frustration with boot-polishers, and was eager to tell them to bugger off. Or piss off. Or any number of declarations designed to end a radio transmission.

With every sense alert, Captain Hardin knew Sergeant Linc Jensen was not fully invested in the mission. Grumpy had withdrawn into the hard-eyed shadows of clipped speech, where casual moments seemed a crap shoot.

Hardin was the Doctor—Doc. Team 7's team leader.

"Sutton's not going to get laid for months," Rogers chimed. "He's packing a pair of her nickers so he can sniff her trail."

"He's not like you, Rogers. Too old and slow to get it up." Jensen laughed as he opened his rucksack. "Hell, Rogers, your hand has even worn out its blisters."

"You're definitely a grumpy bugger, Jensen." Everett prompted a facetious glare.

"Doc. Where's our airplane?" Wingrove asked.

"Well Dopey, you'll know where it is when it lands." Hardin finished his gunfire and looked at each face. "Your identity discs only have your code-signs. Code-signs only after we exit the aircraft over Tonkin."

Edward Hardin, a large, square-built Welshman, had a hard, sure way about him. He moved like a woodsman; with an assurance few could muster. Months of brutal training and the jungle had carved away thoughts of empathy and left hard thoughts of vengeance, leaving a warrior's spirit even a jungle could not defeat.

The men of Team 7 were bush-rangers, cast by the casual way they wore their day—laughing and jaw-jacking as if it weren't raining. Taking the odds, many, if not all of the team would die during Operation Snow White.

In the summer of 1939, in Southeast Asia, a long-range penetration mission might last a lifetime and be shorter than a rainy day.

They had been in the air for hours when Hardin nudged Jensen's arm. Hardin set his jaw. To hell with it, he thought. "Jensen, what the hell are you on about?"

"I've a grim feeling, Doc. A bit packed up. Early graves and all. MI6 has us dancing on a tightrope while they marinate rose petals for the Queen Mother." The rasping intensity of Jensen's voice set sail. "We didn't bring any shovels."

"Bloody hell, Grumpy. Get a grip. Grave digging, is that what you're on about?"

Jumping into a thick mist at night was like jumping into a well. Team 7 exited the aircraft in less than ten seconds. With Hardin's right boot flashing a small green light at five second intervals, the other seven team members, slipped their chutes into an eighty-meter cluster.

The drop zone turned out to be a plateau covered with knee-high grass. The Viet Minh landing strip was empty. No structures, no broken grass, no sign that anyone or anything had crossed the plateau for weeks. Moving through a heavy ground mist before first light, with the whisper of wet knee-high grass across their canvas boots, the team went to ground.

A man screamed. Then came a short burst of an automatic weapon.

"Doc, Sneezy hasn't made a sound since he hit the ground," Jensen said.

"Adrenaline. He's scared. From here each step is a crap shoot—waiting for an echo."

The gray light of dawn cast the prison compound in silhouette. Sleepy set the sight of his Springfield sniper rifle on the communist guerilla who was pointing his instructions.

"I got the blighter wagging his tongue in my scope hairs, Doc." Sleepy began taking slow deep breaths, waiting for orders.

"He'll be a memory soon enough."

"Doc. I don't see any perimeter wire. The wankers are just scratching about. They don't know we're here."

"I don't hear any birds." Hardin kept scanning the compound. "No automatic fire, lads."

Team 7 crawled through the tall grass until Doc and Sleepy lay sixty meters of the first hut. Waiting while Sleepy acquired his target again, Hardin moved the balance of the team into an arc. Whispering, "Find a target," he got the nod from Grumpy, gave Sleepy a nod and the plateau turned into a roar. Team 7 hit eleven guerrillas in the first volley and killed eight more guerrillas as they ran through the compound.

Standing in the confusion of twisted shapes, Hardin set fire to a cigarette. "Look for anything we can use. We're in a rush. There's bound to be more guerillas nearby." The guerilla commander, the man Sleepy shot first, had a hole right between his running lights.

"Cocksure you are, Sleepy. Nice shooting."

"Bit of a lark, really. Got one more on the hop. Blew up his pump."

"Scan the jungle beyond that last hut."

As the team swept the compound, removing the bolts from the enemy's weapons, they found the bishop's head inside a hut, mounted on a bamboo spike, dripping fluids.

"Ruthless, bloody bastards." Bashful set to his kit, crossing himself. Raising his chin, he caught Hardin. "There's a young tosser watching the village. Just inside that tree line, right side, sixty meters north."

"Keep a sight on him."

To increase the rush, Hardin barked, "Spread out and set up a perimeter. Sleepy, Dopey, see if you can find ammunition we can use. And water."

Moments later Happy found the remains of the bishop's body. A brace of shakes crimped his strained voice. "Holy hell. God's pissy with his favors." The bishop had been dragged some thirty meters from a hut, split shoulder to crotch and thrown on a mammoth bed of fire ants, rosary, and all. "The bugger was sawn off before losing his head."

Jensen moved to Happy's side, annoyed by the man's embalmed face. "On the razzle, are you, Happy? Fondle your bloody beads. Four Hale Marys, and whatever else you piffle-shits drag around. Shift your arse and keep away from me."

Alone, picking the bishop's rosary out of the ant heap, Jensen spotted a leather pouch tucked under a pile of shattered bamboo. On guard, he washed blood off the pouch with the water in his canteen and examined the wax-covered brass seal.

Bingo, this is the pouch Sir Lewis Poston ordered me to find—at all cost.

To a man, the commandos wanted answers. Why did this bishop have a pouch bearing the seal of England's royal family? Was he England's own or our enemy?

With no answer and an old French map, the short result of the firefight left the team in the back of nowhere, checked by close country, with limited ammunition, and a need to clear northern Tonkin as fast as possible.

Grateful he didn't need to bury a team member, Hardin began walking. "Dopey, you and Bashful look to our flanks. We're running southwest. Sneezy, you're the trailer. Set a booby trap across our backtrail, one hundred meters out."

Hardin half closed his eyes. "Why are we here?" The team had been lucky. "Catholics are well hated. Represent all that's evil in this patch of woods."

Dopey scoffed. "Any woods, I'd say."

Withdrawing across a grass covered knoll, the team stopped in a saddle one hundred meters southeast of the prison compound. Standing in a seam of thick vegetation Hardin searched the charred compound, hut by hut. Tendrils of smoke drifted through the canopy, muted by a cornflower-blue sky.

Laying belly down in a thirty-meter perimeter, the team fell into a scripted silence. Hardin studied the team's backtrail leading from the compound. The vegetation near his head hung still in the hot, lifeless air. With a long glass he brought the compound into focus. The dead guerrillas lay like heavy stones. Fire ants. The rats and wild dogs would come by midday.

"Grumpy. Give me an all-good. Weapons, ammo, water, leeches."

After tying off the bottom of his pant legs, Hardin drank the last of his water. The roar of their small arms still echoed. But a medley of doubt was swelling in volume.

"We're all-good, Doc." Jensen gave Hardin a thumbs-up.

Not a man one could easily ignore, Jensen had not engaged the enemy during the raid on the compound. Linc did not fire a shot. Hardin knew men who were slow to muster and others who found fear debilitating. Hardin had no such fearful inhibitions. Casting a questioning eye to the jungle bordering the drop zone, Hardin pushed a finger and thumb on his left hand against his eyes. Jensen's actions were out of character.

What are the odds that Jensen is a bin-pusher for the admiral?

The next day, with a sunrise like a straight rainbow, Hardin measured the tree shadows, ensuring they lanced the grass to his hard right. Satisfied he was facing south, he set the team's initial pace running out of northern Tonkin.

Near midday, Jensen grabbed Hardin's arm. "Some jackass wants to talk, Doc."

Fumbling with the radio handset, Hardin took the radio and walked twenty meters into the jungle. After hearing the authentication code, *tightrope,* Team 7 was directed to proceed to Haiphong and rendezvous with three MI6 operatives.

Jensen watched suspiciously, peering into the jungle. His eyes carried a rimy cast. Jensen fell in beside Hardin, away from the team. "Doc, we've got damn little time to get to Burma and rally out of this shit. If that transmission was relayed by the Yanks, they may be trying to delay our trek overland and cut us off."

"Why would the Yanks do that? We've nothing they want. They're all one to me."

Jensen jerked Hardin's arm and spun him face to face. "Bollocks, Captain. Think about where we are. That priest was a Yank. He's in three pieces. Those MI6'ers in Haiphong are gunslingers, not staff infants."

Indignant, Hardin marshaled a scrap of corrosive laughter. "Stand easy Sergeant Jensen. Grumpy needs to amount to himself. He's the Team's second." Blinking as he changed focus, Hardin checked the breech of his Mark MK1 submachinegun.

Adding a gram of garlic, Hardin took off his bush hat. "Backchat or gospel, Jensen, no Yank's going to soak our powder."

Hardin handed Jensen the radio handset. "When we reach the resupply grid, do a recon on our backtrail before you contact that radio relay and sort out their last transmission."

"Where will you be?"

"I'm going to limit the doings of these three MI6 contractors. If they are the wild cards you claim, the team needs to know."

Hardin returned to the perimeter to brief his mates. "Our current status puts us on mission. We're short of ammunition and rations. To get extracted on schedule we'll need to run through Thailand and beyond.

"Even you, Sleepy."

The commandos laughed—except Grumpy. He looked tense. When Hardin spoke again, Grumpy stiffened. "We run as a team to our resupply location. After our traps are packed, half the team will run to Haiphong with me to meet up with three MI6 mercenaries working for our Special Intelligence Service."

"Do any of these mercenaries have a name?" Bashful asked.

"Our old friend Lucien is team leader."

Grumpy stood with his hands on his hips. "Butchery aside, Captain. If that Frenchman's involved, you better meet him alone. Without the team. Mercenaries working in this region, smuggle drugs and work both sides of the wire."

"Fair dinkum. You have the team until I get back." With a nod from Jensen, Hardin drove on. "Mark this grid coordinate for the resupply cashe on your maps. We have a three-day window to put on flesh and get refit."

The sky was turning gray in the east as the team approached the first clatter of huts on the outskirts of Haiphong. Hardin set the team in a dense patch of vegetation and left his rucksack. An old woman led Grumpy to one of the huts and then ambled away.

Hardin found Mother's MI6 mercenaries drinking Three Feathers Whiskey to a chorus of sarcasm at a sidewalk stall in Haiphong, laughing through a cloud of beaten French tobacco. Lucien, a self-proclaimed parachute master, insisted Hardin meet them again after dark at the Red Mill, a restaurant in Saigon.

Leenstra, a Dutchman with a somewhat craggy countenance, rose and slapped him on the shoulder. Recognizing Hardin's Hart MK1 submachine gun, he opened his rucksack and handed Hardin a 32-round ammo box loaded with 9x19mm parabellum cartridges.

Hardin, with his eyes centering on Lucien, took a chair from an adjoining table and sat apart from the three strangers. "Thanks for the ammunition."

Leenstra adjusted his bush hat. "That ammo box is the short result of a contact with Jap prickers in northern Tonkin. Running from our drop zone in the back of nowhere."

Noting their weapons, Hardin remembered the French army had purchased several hundred Thompsons from Birmingham Small Arms, a company headquartered in Small Heath, England. Then decided not to buy the gun for general issue and had shipped the weapons to Annan, in Indo China to arm the Vietnamese supporting French rule.

Lucien, Leenstra, and a German named Steiner, were wearing weathered French jungle fatigues, driving a British Bedford K-series lorry, and carrying a ten-dollar BSA 1926-9mm French Thompson tethered to loosely arranged combat webbing.

Smoking expensive cigars, drinking expensive whiskey, they must have plenty of money. They're back-shooters. Never at odds with their kills.

When Team 7 had received mission briefings at Camp Z, in Broken Bay, New South Wales, Lucien had been the subject of a situational brief-up, typifying the for-hire slags fighting for Ho Chi Minh. Leenstra's picture also on display.

Piecing bits of their conversation together over a beer, Hardin learned the three had recently jumped into southern China with thousands of weapons and tons of ammunition to help the communists fight the Japanese, their mission paid for by the Americans.

Hardin studied their expressions, their humor—their stories bouncing from pussy to killing with equal enthusiasm. Although they looked comically different, a cryptic fire flickered in their eyes, as if they loved the adventure, and something else. The killing.

"Let's drink to our next mission: bush ranging from here to Burma," Lucien announced.

"That's a long haul. Are you running over ground?" Hardin asked.

"Not initially," Steiner declared, his English somewhat metallic.

"Night jumps can be tricky." Hardin cocked his head.

"In the dark all cats are gray, *mon ami.*" Lucien's counsel came with a nod from Steiner. Lucien probably didn't know his picture was posted on the ready board at the SOE Training Base in Broken Bay, New South Wales—next to Leenstra's. Branded as players in Southeast Asia's drug trade, transporting drugs through Malaya's Neck for more than a decade.

"If you're one of the cats, your mission must be a secret." Hardin set his eyes to a crease.

"You're our mission, mon ami." Lucien nudged Hardin's foot and flashed a joking grin. Then he pointed at Leenstra and Steiner. "My friends are the best trackers in the world."

"I'll bet they couldn't find their ass if they had a rope tied to it." When Leenstra burst out of his chair, Hardin held up a hand and laughed. Then asked, "Why has Steiner memorized the tread-pattern on the bottom of my boot?"

Lucien invited Leenstra to sit, then said, "Uncivilized Krauts have nasty habits. We're being paid to find Jap prickers along the coast of Burma and northern Malaya."

After ordering another round of beer, Steiner invited Hardin to join their table, all the while measuring the heft of Hardin's weapon. Stupid Kraut's an anxious bastard, Hardin thought. He's looking for a reason to kill me—a clue, the heft of my rucksack. Hardin set his feet outside his chair legs, and laid his weapon across his knees, pointed at Lucien's crotch. This meeting was an MI6 ambush. Lucien's handlers were expecting the whole of Team 7.

Deciding to shoot Lucien first, then Steiner, Hardin set his right foot near the back of his chair. "Nazis do have nasty habits."

Toasting his beer, Leenstra laughed a nervous cough, then spoke with boyish pride of Tonkin's Vietnamese communists, of playing hide-and-seek with Jap patrols, and of leveraging one employer against another.

Lucien abruptly asked about the condition of Team 7. Hardin's jaw tightened as he set his finger through the trigger guard.. "Why do you want to know?"

"You'll never reach Malaya, mon ami."

"Is that where I'm off to?"

At the man's challenge, Hardin felt his rage surging, wanting to lay a horizontal butt stroke on the bastard's jaw. "Frenchman, I'm not your bloody friend."

The game's plain enough now, he thought. He poured his beer on a potted palm and set the glass on the table. How do they know Team 7's heading for Malaya?

Shaking hands with the three mercenaries while they were still sober enough to trail him, Hardin left Haiphong on foot running northwest for three hundred meters before turning west southwest. Choosing a route through a series of small villages, he checked his back trail at odd intervals. Deciding he wasn't being followed, he rallied with the team.

Why did Mother order me to meet with Lucien? Is he working for MI6? Why are they hunting my team? Do they know the location of our extraction point?

Team 7 left their resupply location long after dark of the second day, heading southwest. On the third day out, Linc Jensen disclosed his separate intel mission and gave Hardin the sealed pouch—with a warning. "There's a spy in MI6, London."

"A spy. Is that what they call you, Grumpy?"

"I'm just part of the main, really."

With a sideward glance and a thin, cryptic smile, Linc Jensen leaned his head to the right. "Captain! Doc! You and I volunteered for this long-range mission. And we've ended up in a gum tree. On paper we're left to run the whole of Southeast Asia looking for Jap prickers."

"Then what's with the pouch?" Jensen looked away. "You've no bloody idea, do you?"

Linc Jensen's eyes came to a sudden judgement. "I'm your signals sergeant, Captain. The rest you don't need to know."

There are no beginnings like the dawns that come to a jungle teaming with life, nor are there colors anywhere to match the vibrant greens and browns of a distant hill. The mist and the smell of the expectant rain, the vegetation yawning as it dries out—and still, it holds death so close, always ready, waiting.

For the next eight days, Hardin pushed the team south and east, spotting and killing a six-man Japanese patrol. Then came nine quiet days to the coast of Burma, turning south onto the Malay Peninsula. There had been the usual stops, to barter for food from the locals to dry socks and massage feet, to clean weapons and repair uniforms.

A grass-covered hill bulked before them now, and by midday lay behind them. At point, descending its western slope, Hardin slowly went to ground. With the team dispersed in a small perimeter, Hardin and Jensen searched the matted grass near the wood line.

"Doc, I found the remains of a shredded fag. The bits of paper were dry."

"How many men?"

"Over twenty. Enough to make a weasel think twice."

"A platoon of Jap prickers?"

"Not likely, that. We're in the middle of nowhere."

"Move the team into that wood line. Set up a laager. No fires. No cooking."

Of the five escape routes, out of Southeast Asia, Ratline 4-Charlie ran through forgiving terrain—the caches well stocked, the bridges well-tended. These too were anomalies. The cashes were too well stocked. The guides spoke French.

The commandos had been warned—the smugglers spoke French.

4-Charlie's regularity had drawn the team into a trance, into a loping, rhythmic pace. Burma's section of the ratline followed a track worn bare by animals that used the terrain for ease of movement to hunt their prey. Men new to the jungle found no track.

For Team 7, the track may as well have been paved with stones.

Three days later, hampered by the rains and winds of a tailing monsoon, Hardin skipped a step when he saw a broken vine. Dismissing the anomaly, he kept his pace. After running for nearly thirty hours without a break, fatigue had set in. The team was bunching up. Not keeping proper intervals. He stopped the team and signaled for them to separate.

Hardin's eyes ranged to the end of the trail, where the trail seemed to turn left. He sank into a squat, watching heat waves rise from the jungle floor. For hours now, something had not felt right. Wetting his lips, Hardin studied Jensen's face. Deciding something but saying nothing.

Hardin studied Jensen more carefully. "I don't hear any birds."

"Aye. And the temperature has hit bottom." His voice sounding a damp beckoning, Jensen stood and nudged Hardin's shoulder. "Pick up your rucksack, Doc. We've a boat to catch."

With that, the team's pace quickened and became uncommonly decisive.

Suddenly Grumpy, the second in line, the slack man, shouldered Hardin forward off the trail. Falling through a tangle of vines, Hardin heard the team open fire with their Bren guns, screaming as they were shot to pieces in the kill zone of the ambush.

Wounded, unnerved, unable to defend himself, he surveyed the slaughter. Sweating, he tried to slow his heart rate. His heart kept pounding. Heavy beats drumming pain through his thigh.

As team leader, Hardin always ran at point. Team 7 had moved with a tactual, ranging cadence, each man assuming a contrived solitude, the lot ignoring nagging bits of recognition—a broken vine, a frayed large leaf.

Slammed from behind by Jensen, as a bullet tore a trough across the front of Hardin's right thigh, and three solids cut through his rucksack, momentum and a thumping slice of luck sent him rolling off the trail into a dense hollow, out of notice. He crept to the edge of the trail, to a vantage where he could cover the kill-zone and held himself still.

Hardin counted the mercenaries—twenty-six—all harvesting the slaughter, emptying rucksacks. If I fire, I might hit three of the bastards, Hardin thought. Need to save one round for myself. If they bunch together, I could kill a few more.

These bastards are well trained. Odds are Lucien supplied their weapons.

Bashful's boots were blown off with his feet still in his boots. The high keen of his scream had been lost in the roaring drum of weapons tearing apart his mates. He cried for his mum and his God until he bled out—the echoes made wage with the remnants of chance.

Happy was propped against a rock and his midsection beaten with bamboo rods until his stomach sack spewed from his mouth. A moaning roar rumbled in his chest. He frantically pushed at his stomach sack and clawed at his throat.

Grumpy was strapped forward against a tree and sodomized with the barrel of a rifle until his entrails hung down into the leech-infested mud.

Dopey was strapped backwards against a tree. Yelling as his throat was slit open; his yells became hollow as his tongue was pulled out through the front of his neck. Dopey was dead before the mercenaries cut off his cock and muzzled it into his mouth with an empty rice sock.

Sleepy and Sneezy were hit so many times, Hardin saw solids explode threw their bodies as they turned and fell. Solids dragging bits of flesh and uniform threads. Excited, the mercenaries started counting the holes as they secured the squaddie's weapons and rucksacks. And then laughed as they cut off their right thumbs.

Sweating, breathing through clinched teeth, Hardin's finger began vibrating against the trigger guard. Moving his eyes constantly to keep from staring at one target, he realized more and more of the mercenaries had filtered away from the kill-zone.

The bastards are lighting a bloody cooking fire. Stench and all, they're going to sit in this shit to eat and divvy the team's kits. Bully beef will give 'em the hab-dabs.

They're too big to be Burmese. Cambodian. Not Tonkin.

The muscular expression on the largest mercenary did not change as he walked through the carnage shouting orders. He stood for an instant just inches from Hardin's left arm looking up and down the trail. Suddenly he hollered a mouthful of vowels, pointed at Sneezy's bullet-riddled body, laughed, walked down the trail, and urinated in the commando's face.

Damn, that was close.

The mercenaries began shouldering their rucksacks.

Afraid to move, Hardin set his head on his hand and wiped the sweat from around his eyes. Slowly he placed his right hand over his leg wound to stem the bleeding. Not knowing the direction they would choose, Hardin slid down a short incline away from the trail.

With a confusion of retreating sounds, the mercenaries began ranging north.

Keeping to the darkness away from the trail, Hardin moved to where he could scan the kill zone through a slit in the foliage. Climbing out of the hollow was risky. He waited for several minutes, listening. As the silence gained ground, he grasped a vine, tested it, and carefully lifted himself onto the trail.

"Those rotten bastards," he whispered, his first utterance in over an hour. His canvas water carrier was shredded.

After drinking the remaining water, Hardin hobbled toward his dead mates, whispering a pledge, watching for movement. Holding to the weak-stemmed vines bordering the trail, with a Royal Welsh Fusilier's trench knife in his left hand, Hardin moved closer to the bodies.

The scene was a mud-laced bit of hell… dying the way of it.

Hardin took his time. His eyes strayed up the trail. Bits of flesh hung in the vines. A thin tendril of smoke flowed from the mercenary's cooking fire into the canopy. Catching his breath, he took off his bush hat and ran his fingers through his hair, then cupped his hand over his mouth, grappling with the smell.

It's down to me, then.

Alone in the glow of twilight, huddled under a shroud of shame, he inspected his mates—the slaughter was a message for his experience. Feverish, his breath came in spurts. Only now did Hardin realize his mates, these strangers, all looked alike.

This… This jungle carnage was the wicked swarming, a brutal testament. Memories of their laughing, of trashing the club at Candle Creek, of parachute training at Ringway, flicked in and out of his thoughts.

Determined to defend their honor, Hardin whispered his devotion through a crack in his mouth. Instantly the interlude fell away—self-hatred took its place. He was exhausted. The many weeks of endless watchfulness, of continual awareness had taken its toll. Under the compost Hardin found his prison, one of enduring loneliness.

Swarms of black flies gathered in pools of blood.

Sheltered from the mess by the rags of Happy's shirt, Hardin punctured Happy's stomach sack, spewing fluids into the man's screaming eyes. Hardin stumbled backward, catching his balance. An indifferent rain accentuated the reality of dying in the jungle.

All but Linc Jensen were dead. His pulse barely showed cause.

"You're in a bad way, Grumpy." Jensen's body stiffened when Hardin pinned him against the tree and cut him loose. His legs folded into a heap. Hardin cradled Jensen's chest and rummaged in his kit for a rubber-encased *L* pill.

"No worries, cobber." Jensen squeezed Hardin's hand.

"Dyin's easy, Doc."

"We were done up, Linc. Stitched. Betrayed." Jensen's eyes opened with a flutter. He looked from side to side as if his mind was photographing each image.

"Make the rally, Doc. For the lads." Jensen's hand fell to the ground.

"I owe 'em that." Holding the suicide pill to the light, wondering why he hadn't died with his mates, Hardin thought of Baxter Corcoran—how Uncle Dingo had fought to survive after being pulled from the waters of Refuse Bay.

"You saved my life, Grumpy."

Hanging a thread of saliva, cinching his brow, Jensen's eyes dilated to a distant focus. "Aye, that, Doc. You were in my way."

Shaking off an anxious grin, Hardin checked north down the trail. Adjusting Jensen's head, he stuck the *L* pill into Jensen's mouth. "Bite down, Grumpy. Give it up as a bad job." Hardin forced Jensen's teeth together. Mustering the remnants of a sigh, Linc Jensen died, his expression driven 'round the bend where his vitals lay piled.

Hardin's rage warped into vacant despair, and his guilt ran to carelessness. Linc Jensen, his mate, died in the stench of his bowels, while the roar of the ambush rang a vicious note and ended before its knell found an echo.

My mates have gone west.

Once stripped of their kits and weapons, each man's right thumb had been severed. The bloody bastards are counting thumbs. The ambush was planned. Somehow, a desk-mucker will find out one of the team escaped.

Examining the bodies of his mates, smothered by the stench of their bowels, he whispered, "So, this is what death will be."

Then, in a moment of twilight's calm, he began allaying sorrows and sorting consoles.

Hardin nodded in recognition; his throat full. He tried to remember the smell of fresh bread and burnt sugar wafting in the air near the bakery on the Ashchurch main square.

"Will I ever see my Katherine again?"

Lying in a hollow thirty meters from the kill zone, near the end of his tether, Hardin lost consciousness. A dark cast had enveloped the jungle by the time he woke.

Urgency kicked its way through his mind. He cut the identity disc from Jensen's waistband. Fumbling his trench knife, his smatchet, into the mud as he tried to hurry, he wiped the leaf-shaped blade on Jensen's pant, and then tied his identity disc inside the lace of Jensen's boot.

As darkness gathered around the bodies, a rain squall crabbed along the top of the canopy. With water dripping from his bush hat, Hardin presented his weapon to his mates at port arms.

With a voice stiff in his throat, firing on every other cylinder, he whispered. "Since you blokes aren't going to speak to me, I'm going to get cracking. I'll make the rally. You can fit that in. Me and Uncle Dingo. He's a good mate. Full on, if you lads muster those Muslim virgins that Swagman bragged about, leave a trail of breadcrumbs. Coming down from the end of that fable, the Abigail's are either in hell or in Piccadilly."

The confluence of fear and time pushed Hardin to move, to gain distance from the ambush site. Twilight had but minutes of life. Wild dogs would be on the hunt within the hour.

"I'll kill the bastard who betrayed us, Grumpy. Take good care, mate."

Hardin propped Jensen's boot in the mud. The vulcanized fiber identity disc was hidden below the knot in the boot lace. "Those Muslim virgins might be a good turn, Grumpy—might get a bloke like me interested in religion again."

Jensen was a mess.

Dark brown rats scurried from the trees, forming wads, racing around the east side of the kill zone. Hardin remembered the team's briefing in Candle Creek: Mountain Giant Sunda Rats.

Hardin winced as he pulled himself up, accepting a painful sense of resolve. He wanted to shoot the rats scavenging the area around the cooking fire. A well-fed rat sat sniffing the air, staring at him. Gradually the chorus of rats took up station. A perfect perimeter.

Hoping the remnants of the *L* pill would poison the rats, he muttered, "I'll look for you in Piccadilly, Grumpy." Reluctant to leave, Hardin wanted to bury the bodies. Standing cocked legged, without an entrenching tool, he spit instead. "Good-bye lads."

Sweating profusely, limping across the trail, his leg wouldn't support his weight. He stared at the pure, vicious green of an impenetrable jungle.

To move he needed to find a navigable route tracing the topography and favoring his wounded leg.

Packing three days of water—less with the water he needed to clean his wound—his rations would last five days.

His can of M&B 693 sulfa powder had been shot to pieces. Salvaging what he could, he filled the wound with the light tan powder and wrapped a battle dressing around his thigh. The round had torn a thin layer of the large muscle on the front of his thigh. Gradually letting his weight settle, he hobbled away.

His boots touched the ground with a whisper and a thump.

Blood quickly soaked the battle dressing, saturating his pant leg. Packing his rucksack on his left shoulder and carrying his weapon in his left hand, his right hand was free to carry a stave. Jumping the bags, the first steps were pure hell.

He needed to find water.

Hardin hobbled through a small grass clearing tap-dragging his right boot—his tracks rife with broken vegetation. The draw spilled out into a wide, flat table of knee-high grass bordered on three sides by thick, single canopy jungle. Before entering the clearing, he stopped and searched the tree line on the far side and each flank.

Listening for several minutes, he knew twilight would come with a rush, sucking the light off the jungle floor, leaving less than twenty minutes to find a badger hole with water and lay up.

A man's hard to track if he's not moving.

As he started again, a fine brush of rain swept through the grass. Ranging with hesitant steps, rescuing his stave from the damp soil, he moved with caution. On the far side of the clearing he climbed to the top of a small ridge and stopped to search his back trail.

Detecting movement, he froze. Brief, as though two shadows had changed places, he swore it was real. He swore it was a girl. Then nothing. Just the raw demands of fear.

Cool air flowed in a river up a narrow draw. The floor of the jungle was growing quite dark. Day's end would bring a chorus of ambient noise too loud for a man to detect the anomalies. Twilight was a time for predators, the wrong time for a man to be wounded, and casting off the smell of fear and blood.

Days ago, just after his team was ambushed, automatic weapons fire had lanced the canopy above his head. Wounded, he changed direction and hobbled until the pain ripped at his stride. Gasping, stumbling, he fell against a rock. Hardin lowered his head to shield his face, breathing with his mouth open. A tumult set to his mind with a clatter of blurred pictures.

Wind-whipped rain rattled off his head. He fell again, pulled off balance when his stave penetrated a bog. Covered with rot, he pushed himself to firm ground, then stood up.

"Bastards are hunting me."

At twilight Hardin crawled into a cavern behind a jumble of vine-covered boulders. A small, clear pool of water sat atop a gravel bottom. After drinking until his thirst was satisfied he closed his eyes. Mosquitoes pushed the foliage aside and swarmed down on his face to have a slap. It's always a bunch of pregnant females, he mused, their wingbeats in full stretch as the day wore out and he lost consciousness.

Lips swollen and coffin faced; Hardin woke with a jerk. For a moment his focus seemed to pinwheel. The glare of the tropical sun was parsing the canopy. Listening for movement, for vegetation being brushed aside, he set his shoulders against the base of a tree and waited. Feeling flimsy, he took a strip of his shirt and tied it around his upper thigh to help staunch the flow of fluid from his leg wound. His rucksack was a sodden mess.

His essentials were dry—cigarettes and matches.

Satisfied he was alone, he used his last bit of plastique explosive to heat a cup of tea, took his last salt tablet and lit a cigarette. During the next hour he barely stumbled on, pausing in the shelter of a tree from time to time to search his backtrail.

Later, after drinking from a stream, he picked his way at a faster pace. The game trail he found drew him into a corral of sorts. Tangled in a patch of interwoven vines he fell on his face. Try as he might, with his hands under his chest, he rocked backwards onto his knees, but he did not have the strength to stand. How long he lay in the compost he did not know.

Waking, he found that his shivering had settled his face into the mud.

After burning a leech off his neck with a cigarette, he started walking... falling... crawling... standing, a collusive cycle. Exhausted, he leaned against a tree. Struggling with the buttons on his pants, he hauled out his cock and stood shivering, finally able to pump ship without his left kidney howling with pain.

By half-twelve the jungle had fallen into a pulsing silence. Not an even pulse, more a conniving. No movement... no life. The odor of a mud flat mingled with the sea mist had lingered as the morning opened around him, and, in the intrigue particular to this silence, a wet, infectious, heavy smell.

Hardin closed his eyes to picture Ross Island, a jungled outcrop three hundred meters north of his rally point in the Mergui Archipelago.

Instead, the sea off Lizard Point, near his childhood home in Cornwall, crashed along a rocky shore.

Curlews and gulls were screaming.

Katherine's picture was cracked with lines and creases. She was smiling. Thank God I have this snap. Distant memories seemed close by, perched next to a bag of regrets.

Hesitant, uncertain, he realized no jungle birds were calling out the day, and no rustle rattled in the palm fronds. Only silence. The jungle lay vacant until a murmur rose throughout the canopy—a high, minuscule hum, nearly beyond reach of his ear.

Much of the overcast had broken. The mist made a sound as it spilled into the canopy—a soft hissing whisper. The air around him seemed to flow and billow with mist. Hardin knew if he listened long enough, its whisper would be gone.

He walked steadily with his usual, unusual step, keeping rhythm with his stave. Given a proper measure of luck, he might make it home.

Wild thoughts kept colliding. Of the outside world he was unaware. The betrayal of his team ran a disturbing gamut. Neither grief, nor fear, however, was a luxury he could afford. Exhausted, he wiped mud from the stock of his Hart MK1. The sub-machine gun had gained weight. Something had scared the birds.

At twilight Hardin stared out to sea. The draw spilled out into a wide expanse of sand just in from a palm covered beach. Dimly, at the end of the game trail, through a thin veil of mist, he glimpsed a flash of white, a schooner near the shore heading north, and then a faint outline of a transport framed against a far-off gathering sky. The sea was running north.

Warily, too clumsy to remain undetected, he hobbled across an open sweep of knee-high grass. An oily sweat, a pore-fungus, had joined with the mist, coating his face. Standing inside a tree line to listen, cussing his fortunes, he knew he should set booby-traps for the for-hire guerillas hunting him.

The wind dropped off as he started again.

Ginning up a moment of hope, Captain Edward Hardin reasoned that if number 10 Downing knew of Team 7's fate, one of the six radio relay stations in the Bay of Bengal area of operations must have sent signals detailing the team's status.

I wager it was the radio intercept station at Lion Rock on the island of Ceylon. Admiral Sinclair's a good bloke. Like old acid. He'll search for his commandos... dead or alive.

To hell with Mother, though. Her bloody pride—never checked or resigned. She mops the seas, from continent to continent, never at odds with

Greenwich Mean Time. She won't find the man I used to be. I've acquired a soiled mind.

In the tranquility of exhaustion Hardin's memories persisted. He thought of home many times, wishing to hear Katherine's voice, wishing she was safe, and they could share a pastry in the bakery on the Ashchurch town square.

Long before dawn he was moving again. The dense vegetation marked the emptiness of the jungle. Yet he knew it was crawling with death. Daylight came… one instant the sky was gray, and then his shadow was as wide as his feet. He walked on, reluctant to get away from the trail.

At odd times throughout the day, he thought of Captain Baxter Corcoran, the Swagman. The steam ship driver whom his mates and crew called Uncle Dingo. Will the Aussie make the rally near Ross Island on time?

Uncle ground the corn of his missions. Every detail and variable run to ground. Threats segmented by type, location, and probable timing. Mother's weans headquartered in China Bay, Ceylon, could tell Uncle what to do. They could only imagine what he was going to do.

"Have a piss," was the Swagman's way of saying, sod-off.

Hardin's mate was a raucous Aussie with unforgiving guile—a touchy-as-hell Jack who looked at life through dusty fly wire. With rum and a good cigar, Uncle could blind himself with sheer belief, donating half his pay to the sailors' home near Broken Bay, in New South Wales, a home managed by the Returned Sailors and Soldiers Imperial League of Australia.

Australia was a hard land, but he wished for no other. Nothing in his youth had been easy. He had worked with his father, protecting sheep herds, hunting dingoes and red fox mostly, and then when his father had been killed in a fall, he had tried to support his mother and his two younger brothers.

His mother died when he was fifteen, working to make ends meet. Baxter Corcoran left his two brothers at a neighbor's ranch and headed for the outback near Broken Bay.

My mate is bobbing about in the Bay of Bengal. The scruffy cobber is sitting in a warm cabin, drinking rum and smoking cigars with Molly. You can trust him for that.

By the next evening, stopping at the top of a rise, Hardin stood into a small recess between large leaf trees and lit a cigarette. A moment later, remembering the aroma of tobacco lingered in dense vegetation, he took a final draw and shredded the fag. On his mettle, he knew he was still being followed.

As he moved off the beach and back into the darkness of the jungle, a flat-bottom hollow lay before him. Weary, he cut to the south side of the hollow and picked up another animal trail.

The sun was sinking into the Bay of Bengal. Shadows had gathered at the base of the rainforest spires. The mist was cool and heavy. Mud pulled at his feet as he walked away from a stream, trailing his wounded leg. Struggling to keep moving instead of laying-up, he changed directions— east, south, west, south.

Stopping to listen, he shouldered his rucksack, checked the bolt housing on his weapon, and was watching a mosquito drill into the back of his right hand, when he caught the flash of a bamboo rod as it crashed into the side of his head, divvying his right ear.

Dark then light, he saw himself falling, his face drawn tight across his jaw. Then the mud, the slime and nothing at all.

*   *   *

Burma. 19 August 1939, 1438 Hours, Greenwich Mean Time, GMT + 6.5 Hours.

When Hardin came at last awake, he was four days beyond death. He scoffed a futile laugh. Reasoning was barely possible. He had not eaten in two days—or was it six days? A large- shouldered Welsh lad comes easy upon hunger.

An old chest wound throbbed with a distant ache that spiked whenever he coughed. The bullet wound across the front of his right thigh wept a sticky, yellowish fluid. When he tried to bend his knees, pain from his thigh shot through his balls and into his lower back. The sequence made him grunt and lift his chest to absorb a hacking cough.

Why do I always get bit by the same bloody dog?

Hardin in his prime had had a raven's presence. A jungle-worn squaddie, uncommonly decisive—wise with the wisdom of a young man who never had time to be a boy, fear was something strange to him. And, although he had known danger, it had passed him by.

Hardin was not a man given to talking. He spoke only after his mind was wound up. Once he took hold of an idea or circumstance; any contrary tosser was in for a gnawing. That was when he was a soldier—before he was clobbered with a bamboo rod, lost his weapons, was thrown into a rickety cart, and lapsed into the profane.

Wedged in a corner of the bullock cart was a freedom of its own. It wasn't much, just roofless planks cobbled above the mud. Gripping the top sideboard, Hardin pressed his cheek into his hand. Slime mold coated the cart's sideboards and its worn wooden deck.

Awareness returned slowly. The jungle looked as it had before except now Hardin knew he was dying. He glanced around. With a pang, Hardin's lips flattened against his teeth. I may as well be west of hell, he thought. My mates are dead. I've lost my Mark MK1 and my trench knife. I'm being carted by a bloody water buffalo and tracked by a native girl.

In the steaming heat, the clinging wet fingers of the jungle lay heavy on his face. In and out of the day, the minutes seemed like hours and the hours hard to follow. A tragedy it is. A special ops commando flogged, and hog tied, brought to ruin by a small girl while running from mercenaries and drug smugglers. Of course, MI6 well knows what Burma's outback is about. They fawn over scraps of the East's mystic intel.

The captain was a tall, hard-bitten man, with a shock of black curly hair, his gaunt, wide-jawed cheeks covered with a blue-black scruff of twisted hair. For weeks, he played Mother-May-I with a jungle more tuned to savaging his vitals than lending a hand—his body pitted by leeches boiling from the rot on the jungle floor, finding blood through the eyelets on his boots.

His humping tackle spared; his little-used piss tube arcing like a shriveled twig.

Of late he realized his left pant leg had more holes than a fisherman's net. The panels of his jungle blouse had been torn, front and back, and the buttons were gone. Better yet, someone had cut away the front of his right pant leg, exposing the wound he picked up during the team's ambush in Burma.

"I've no choice but to plug on." Hardin gave a hoarse snort, nearly chewing the words. "Without a weapon. I'm a festering, pathetic tart."

Flinching from pain, Hardin began whispering, rage edging his voice. "Do any of these soft-sods know where this cart's going?" Then it came to him. If they find out I'm a British officer, I'll be executed. Trying to open his right eye, he praised his luck. "Damn good thing they didn't hit me with a bloody cricket bat."

Since being shanghaied, there had been days and nights of misery, lying in a rickety ox cart cussing the water buffalo and mumbling to himself. No one spoke to the water buffalo driving the cart. The fat bastard must be heading home.

The beetroot colored knot on the right side of Hardin's head had swelled over his right eye, and the blood flowing from the wound had soaked into the tatters of his uniform blouse.

For weeks now the jungle during the day had not seemed dangerous—the sun streaming through the leaves. But with yellow jack fever, the jungle during the night had been an appalling mystery, a sensory overload—a hellish maze of insanity itself.

A wind stirred and grew stronger and struck along the track way. Frustrated, Hardin searched the foliage for symmetry, odd shapes, waiting for Lucien's man to kill him.

Come on you slimy bastard.

Hardin's options were few. Did he have any? Sure. Wait for death or fight to survive. Fight with what? His crippled hands? Instinct told him the secrets in the pouch Linc Jensen had stuffed into his rucksack were toxic, the bloody reason Team 7 was ambushed, and most likely, why he was being hunted.

Sergeant Linc Jensen died to save my life—for what? Surely not for this sodding pouch.

No one will see that man as I saw him, his belligerent, wry smile—his icily silent glare. A wily communicator, a trusted man, he must have been one of Mother's best.

Jensen did die. He lay rotting in the jungle, his caustic asides a thing of the past. Suddenly energetic, falsely so, Hardin braced through a fit of anger, then sorrow. He came alive, boasting; Uncle Dingo will sort out the silks who posted Team 7 to this hell.

"Heaven or hell, we'll meet again, Grumpy. Fondling echoes, I'll keep you close by."

The water buffalo ambled along. Hardin peered at it, wondering why the animal kept walking. Finding black humor in timing the cadence of the buffalo's ass, his laugh sounded like a choking grunt.

The beast must be heading home.

Hardin anchored himself against the roll of the bullock cart and stared at the rutty track way along his back trail, a long-used stock route. The trace wove through a rainforest of ancient canopy trees. Glistening colors from creamy gray to black and tan to ochre brown stained the massive spires. The trees gripped the moist soil with long, stout, gnarled buttress roots.

The jungle lost a drop of wind and began closing in. Dark and dank, an arched tunnel ran away from Hardin's view. Weak, with blood from his leg wound staining the cart's deck, instinct kept him searching the foliage for a trailer.

In the silence, there were always ambient sounds. The vegetation liked to hum, then pulse—its radiance black one moment and glowing the next. Wisps of cloud rushed along the ground, sparring with the oil palms, and fending the light sweeps of rain… torn rags battered the sky.

As twilight drew darkness around him, he thought of Ashchurch, England, of the bakery on the town square, sitting with his lovely bride—his Katherine. She liked to cup his cheeks in her hands before she kissed him, laughing with the charm of sensual sureness, her kisses a confusion of affection.

He needed help and a good bit of luck to make it out of Burma alive. Think, Eddie. What will Uncle do if I'm late for the rally? Will he have to leave to get fuel? Will his control let him cycle back through the rally point?

Slowly the hours drew on. Twilight brought a pounding rain, and movement throughout the canopy. The chill of the wind set to his chest, channeled by the track way.

Trying to sit up, he gasped for air, each movement a painful, deadening drag. Lucid and losing strength, he struggled to see. An odd opaque cast held his eyes, as if their quicksilver were tarnished. Losing control of his mind's eye for minutes at a time, the shock of his team's ambush had receded into bouts of guilt and rage, and the putrid smell of death.

In the diminished light his mate's faces seemed to change color, to a pale paste botched by puddles of blood and streaks of mud.

Mother Mary full of grace and that priest's bloody pouch can't be dismissed. Horse shite is what it is. I'd like to see the reason the team was ambushed. And why I'm being hunted.

A lifetime ago, Team 7 had run as one through the jungles of Thailand without a hint of fear, or Japanese prickers. Anxious to press on, heading for the boatyards of Portsmouth and Southampton, the commandos had a boat to catch; a tramp steamer driven by Captain Baxter Corcoran, Uncle Dingo.

Now, fighting the fever, Hardin kept muttering. Then Grumpy grabbed his arm. Fear leapt in the sergeant's jasper eyes, as a rush of static blared from the team's Paraset radio. "The priest has documents we need to secure," he whispered.

Lucid for a moment, Hardin slumped against the cart's sideboard and fell silent, listening to the metallic clatter of the buffalo's harness, the drum of the wooden lynchpin, the teeter of the yoke pole, and the drag of the worn leather traces hanging at the buffalo's side.

Reaching for the cart's gunwale, he saw himself stumble into a mindless scramble—again the night parachute drop, then rally points Ac and Beer, Haiphong, Lucien, the team's ambush. A relentless stream of images circled in a roily brine stirred by a headless bishop.

Wet with fever, Hardin's vision pinwheeled into a black void. Suddenly he was jumping from a plane. Pulling the parachute's O-ring, falling into the night, the T-4's canopy catching air and deploying, he was drifting in a cloud, soaking wet—the drone of the modified RAF Shackleton transport fading in the east.

Conscious, exhausted, Hardin could barely lift his chest.

Moaning through a surge of pain, he saw Corcoran's smile. His thick chested mate was a roughhewed, leather-skinned roustabout—mean as a pack of dingoes. Branded by his mates as Uncle Dingo, Corcoran was a raspy wild man. With curly black hair covering his weathered hide, except where Lucy, a buxom Mayfair Mama tattooed next to his gold bracelets, Corcoran would do anything to protect his crew.

Quick to muster, Uncle liked to lie even if the truth led to a better grade of rum.

Uncle Dingo liked to howl when he drank. If Clive Mauldin, his chief engineer was out of money, if Molly couldn't fix his jack, Uncle would boost his balls, then stuff a fiver in Molly's beer glass, and scream, "Have a piss, Molly."

Hardin licked his hand hoping for salt.

Struggling with the haunting rattles of betrayal, he rubbed his face and tried to sit up, alert but confused. A series of rhythmic footfalls sounded through the wind—a sloped shouldered man? Might be an animal. Looking for his knife, Hardin's thoughts ran wild, vast frustration mixed with quick calculation—a sense of being stalked.

Where's my bloody weapon? My Mark MK1? "Be careful who you talk to, Doc."

Hardin clutched his near-empty rucksack. A shoulder strap was wrapped around his left wrist. The thin leather straps of Jensen's pouch filled his right fist.

"Listen, dammit," he whispered, spitting air, "there's a hound nearby." A pant leg, or the shoulder of a cat pushing aside the vegetation.

Searching his back trail, the tunnel of vegetation began vibrating and warped through a spiral. Fighting to find a clear focus, vagrant bits of sunlight lanced the canopy only to be blurred and scattered by fluctuating shades of gray and green. Wind-blown shapes swooped into the tunnel, fractured, dancing as they disappeared.

"This fever's killing me."

The steady saunter of the water buffalo, the pause before the drag, one hoof muffled by the next, forced the ponderous rhythm of the bullock cart. Odd sounds interrupted the pattern—footsteps. Gusts of wind rustled the leaves and fronds.

The angle of the sun shafts meant the day had slipped away. Looking down his back trail, the mud ruts merged and then disappeared.

"Stay awake, Eddie."

Of course, there was, there had to be a reason he was being hunted. It's funny, in a way—laughing at death. My balls are swollen, my leg's rotting,

I'm being hauled to hell knows where, to a fire-ant heap, and there's a manky bastard stalking me.

A searing bolt of pain shot through his frame, sending his mouth racing through a medley of infectious slurs, giving rise to a coupling of recall and fear. Unable to concentrate, he shook the empty canteen. His body was running out of water. A black, resinous sap of the Rengas tree had blistered the skin on both forearms, leaving cavernous, rotting sores.

If they took my weapon, they mean to kill me.

A girl scurried past the cart and slipped into the jungle on the bullock cart's right flank. She seemed to float across the jungle floor, her bamboo hat gliding evenly through the gusts of rain, her course unaltered by the motion of the vegetation.

"Is she tracking me?" Talking to himself had become involuntary. Putting a sliver of wood in his mouth, he drew saliva into his throat. "I need salt."

The pouch Linc Jensen gave him was sturdy enough, scarred by jungle vegetation and the variants of pursuit. Entrusting him with England's survival, Jensen had warned, "Guard this pouch. Keep it under seal. Give it to my uncle, Sir Lewis Poston in Cairo. No one else."

As if saying goodbye, Jensen had brushed the pouch seal with his sleeve. With a glance over his left shoulder, he whispered. "Be careful who you talk to, Doc."

The contents of this pouch must have MI6 dancing on a penny.

Jarred alert by the cart's sudden stop, he lost focus. The jungle, the cart, the rain; all were an enveloping blur. He set an ear to the left side of the cart. A faint noise seemed near yet remote. A passing sound. The sequence accelerated. Hallucinating, he could not separate the sounds.

Distant lightning illuminated the periphery of the track way, and far-off thunder drummed with the rain beating on the canopy. Hardin watched his back trail. He cocked his head. "Who is she?" Mopping sweat from his face, he licked salt from his wrist.

Searching the funnel of vegetation behind the cart his vision showed two frames, one for each eye. In seconds, his vision cleared. As the visual frames rushed to join, a man leapt across the track thirty meters behind the cart. Hardin's pulse carried on with a sickening force.

Hardin's memory keyed on the man—something about him. His massive bulk reminded him of Linc Jensen. Code-sign Grumpy. But the stranger was slope shouldered. It was Leenstra, carrying a rifle. No, a machete. Hardin rubbed his eyes, struggling with the dim light.

"The bastard!" Not a man he could avoid, Hardin knew why he was being tracked. Leenstra means to kill me. He shivered, thinking. Reality does have a certain beauty.

Shocked by a surging sense of isolation, Hardin tried to roll onto his left side. His memory but a membrane of cottony twine, soiled with the bile of regret.

The jungle had grown cold and hazy, strapping his hope with an endless array of futile gestures. Leenstra ran across the track way. Hardin tried to sit up. No luck. Unease grew.

Who's driving this bloody cart?

Hardin's vision cleared. A flash of light swept across his face—light reflected off a rifle barrel, or machete. A young woman appeared near the cart.

Her black eyes darted, as if dissecting the track way. Suddenly the foliage near her bamboo hat came alive, jousting with gusts of wind and rain. Hardin fell sideways into a jarring rut, fighting to absorb the shock.

Where's my weapon? A sharp pain shot through his leg. Stifling a scream, he tried to locate the girl, the black-haired wisp.

At almost the same moment, without a sound, she ran past the cart whispering in English, "Wake up. Wake up." Instantly, the ambient noise died to a tick-over. With a sense of recognition, she slipped into the jungle, leaving the cart to navigate the mud-gullies.

"Good luck, Sweet Pea." A surge of adrenaline brought pain to his flanks, to his kidneys. His body was out of protein—eating itself.

The crack of a branch brought him erect. He strained to react. As his hands came off the cart's deck, the girl's machete sliced through the rain and split Leenstra's head—brains exploding into the air, an eye flying free. Leenstra collapsed as if thrown to the ground. His throat hit the gunwale, tossing brain matter onto Hardin's feet.

Hardin recognized the Dutchman's fiery eyes, narrowed by thick brows. He drank beer with the bastard in Haiphong with Lucien and the German.

Smiling, the girl ripped the machete from Leenstra's skull.

With a stoic grin, her peasant beauty seemed to wash its way into a compliant resolve—her expression mixed with contradiction. Hardin fell back exhausted. He wanted to clean his feet, to rid the cart of the smell, but he did not have the strength.

Reaching into the cart she jerked on the hemp rope tied around his ankles. She lifted his feet and slammed them onto the deck. At once, her eyes turned on Hardin, and he felt their impact. Death's beauty had come to call—the girl was an enigma—her eyes seemed hollow.

Hardin's concentration remained absolute as the girl rolled the heavy man into a muddy rut. Appearing serene, she set a silken face into the rain, sloshed through the mud, slid her machete into a wooden scabbard at the front of the cart, picked up a single-shot carbine, and nudged the buffalo forward.

"Steady yourself. The kraut will be next. Steiner." Hardin's bush hat overspread his view. For him, the rain had soaked his will into a sense of dread. Whispering through a pathetic chuckle, he summed his fate. "I'll be sold as a slave. That, or left in pieces."

The girl handed him a short section of bamboo filled with water. He held water in his mouth before slowly swallowing. An ease pushed its way through his body. Sip by sip he drank the water and presented the bamboo tube for a refill. She ignored him. He threw the tube at her as she ducked into the jungle.

Try as he might, Hardin didn't have the strength to remain erect. Shivering, he laid on his side and picked at the knots binding his feet. Trying to focus, a futile scrap crossed his mind. *I hope that girl didn't tie these bloody knots.*

"Do stop whining, Doc," Jensen's words. "There's always time for dying."

Replaying the ambush, he realized an operative with access to sensitive information in MI6, had betrayed his team. There was no other explanation for the sequence of events.

Gordon Dewar, an MI6 operative, had flown from England to New South Wales to brief the team. That the wanker wore a houndstooth jacket in Australia's outback should have been a clue.

If I make England in decent trim, I'll shoot him in the head. Even better, the lower belly, just above his ball sack.

The bullock cart kept rocking, slowly moving along the jungle track. Hardin rubbed his eyes to clear his head of the dwindling fog. The rain beat on the canopy with a steady drum. Soaking wet, he could not stop shivering. Listening for the fear that rode his shoulders, the echo of the rain on the canopy rang out.

This stinking jungle. Little can match it, or the bloody monsoon. Without a weapon, dying was the easiest thing a squaddie could do—a barely noticeable distraction. Linc Jensen had been fated to die—his tortured body wrapped in a torn khaki guise.

In the vague light Hardin spit at the rain. *I miss how my mates laughed at life's mud.*

The glassy brightness of recent fever shone in Hardin's eyes. Calm at times, he could not stop shivering. Time seemed to warp and wobble. Closing his eyes, he saw himself rush from a churchyard into the jungle in an instant. Gravestones warping into muzzle flashes.

Searching the clouds in silence, he wondered about the young native girl with black eyes—with a machete? A picture of Katherine flashed, and then flashed again. Her sudden smiles.

As the cart stopped, muffled voices sounded below the rain with the same sharp notes that followed the teams ambush—those maddening, singing vowels. Men began arguing. Four or five. Without warning, Hardin's body swung through the air, suspended among four men whose grip ignored the fluids flowing from his wound.

Why are they keeping me alive?

A thick hemp rope bound his chest. Suspended, he was lowered through a hole—into a cave. From bright sunlight to darkness, unable to discern definition, his feet touch a dirt floor covered with small stones. Trying to stand, he fell onto a bamboo mat, his chest hit the corner of a wooden crate as the rope he was hanging from collapsed around his head.

"Bloody hell, that hurts. Where am I?"

A small fire burned near the entrance to the cave. A man was arguing with the girl. Large sacks filled with prickly durian fruits lay near Hardin's side.

His vision ran in and out of focus.

Delirious, Hardin saw himself talking on a primitive, tactical field wireless. His shoulders felt like wire knots as he fumbled the handset into the dirt, trying to secure the talk-box. He lost the image. Brutal days of running warped into defeated days of dying, his ears fending the roar of small arms fire, his hands and forearms pocked with jungle rot.

Registering a low chime, he realized he was naked.

How many days have I lost? Have I covered enough ground to make the rally on time? The lagoon just there means I'm facing south. The right direction for catching a ride on Uncle's tramp steamer.

The details of his new surrounding brought a welcome calm: the bamboo mat; the hut frame dancing in an oil lamp's flame; the damp smell of attap thatch; the palm fronds, and the azure shades of a lagoon. His tattered shirt had been washed and hung to dry.

The remnants of his kit lay scattered on the floor; pants, socks, a sealed container of M&B 693 sulfa powder; Salvarsan cream for abrasions; his empty tin for Mepacrine malaria tablets; and his last Wilkut razor blade.

No shit. A battle dressing, a can of sulfa powder, and well-worn khaki pants.

A kindly, liverish looking old woman with a frail, worn face, sat on a stool near Hardin's feet. She plastered pulverized Daun Kentut leaves over the rotting sores on his forearms, wrapped the leaves with a thin animal skin, and tied the dressing off with strips of intestine.

I'm being sold into slavery. There's no love for Brits in Malaya. An officer's worth a good deal of money. Any Brit, really.

Instantly the echo of Lucien's counsel— "You'll never reach Malaya, mon ami." Knowing Leenstra was a right bastard, with chaos raging in his top paddock, Hardin was beginning to believe Lucien was right.

Admiral Sinclair's intelligence memo marking Lucien had been clear: This clandestine operative makes money acting as America's point man in Southeast Asia. Lucien's a French American mercenary hired to parachute into northern Tonkin with weapons and ammunition for the Vietnamese communists fighting the Japanese. Lucien has the easy manner of a sleeping snake. He speaks Mandarin, Vietnamese, German, French, and English fluently. He's dangerous and will kill anyone. There's a jagged scar under his left eye and a notch in his left ear lobe.

Lucien's picture, along with a picture of Leenstra, the man the girl killed, were posted on the Candle Creek's ready board in New South Wales—side by side—accused of hiring well-trained mercenaries for years to protect their drug smuggling operation.

Exhausted, wet, and shivering, Hardin dismissed Lucien with a flick of his fingers and lit a cigarette. "It's been near-as-dammit since the parachute drop, Grumpy—so much for siding up."

*   *   *

The Bay of Bengal. Uncle's Steamer. 21 August 1939. 1035 Hours. GMT + 5.5 Hours

The met mechanics, those masters of cumulus thought, had misjudged the storm's intensity, leaving the tramp to wallow under smoking clouds. Green water washed the boat deck wing to wing and shot out opposing scuppers.

Captain Baxter Corcoran was tired of fighting to keep his flush-deck steamer above water level. Sheer waters boiled around the pilothouse door. But the squall pounding the pilothouse was not nearly as annoying as Mother's intelligence dicks camped in the steamer's chart room.

Mother's agents had fallen to Corcoran's care in Singapore, smelling of cloves. Their assignment cloaked in the deepest obscurity—debriefing long-range penetration teams. Their cover—intelligence sergeants assigned to the 2nd Argyll & Sutherland Highlanders, headquartered near Finlayson Green.

"If you know your duty, Captain, you'll cooperate with our enquiry."

"Have a piss." Bare chested, hairy as an ape, Corcoran shouldered the tallest agent out of his way, opened a locker and picked up his spare pistol.

"You twats are on my boat. I'm the bloody captain. You'll do what I tell you to do, or you'll be in for a swim."

"You best watch your mouth, Captain."

Laughing, putting on a dry shirt, Uncle lit a cigarette and pushed the ashtray away from his left hand. "The tar-pots in my crew want you posh lollies off their patch. All they know how to avoid are spoiled whores, and bad booze." Opening a small compartment below the radio mount to check his primary weapon, he pointed a pistol at his guests.

"The lads like to throw six-bob-a-day tourists like you dunny rats over the aft rail."

"You'll give us the status of Snow White's Team 7."

"Why would I tell you dwarfs anything?" With nudged-up raillery, Uncle set to the clutter on his desk, loosening those shingles of guile London's pugs liked to fashion into a frenetic stew.

"You'll give us situation-updates on that team at the bottom of each hour. If you refuse, we'll have the Royal Navy out of China Bay board your ship and put you in chains."

Uncle slammed his fist on the radio mount and declared, "You empty-baggers are stupid, that's flat, testing your cocks to distraction. Your words ring like farts in a jam jar. Full due, you swiggers could fiddle with Abigail's arse and only get whispering steam."

"Do button it up, Captain."

"Piss off."

The agents pumped their fins with an air of urgency. Uncle drew his eyes to a measured frown. These ruddy buggers—Stuffy Dimness and Censorious Admiration don't seem to realize they're sparring with one of maritime's fairer elements of farce—Me. Captain Uncle Dingo Corcoran. I'm a double-jack aspiring to be Mother's favorite sailor—in the provisional Special Boat Service (SBS).

After gulping his rum, Corcoran looked into the empty mug. Tapping his mug on the radio mount, he couldn't resist a smug grin.

Evaluating the frayed end of his kola-root toothbrush, he dropped it in his mug. If those look-sticks piss off Molly, their hides will be jumbled trying to evade the big man's fists.

Uncle, a swagman of rural sarcasm, thought the shorter agent was dimmer than kangaroo piss, and constipated beyond relief. He decided to give the stubby clocker a new handle—Mutt-the-Dwarf. And since the taller agent looked to be fresh from tidying the sand of The Ladies Mile in Hyde Park, his lips pursed by chided matrimony, Uncle decided to call him Pucker.

Mutt and Pucker.

Moving about the cabin, pausing to grin, as if admiring what appeared in the reflections he discovered, Pucker became inquisitive, searching British Admiralty Chart #829 for the Bay of Bengal, North, dissecting the sheen of the chart table with a small torch.

Did the wanker ask the Queen Mother if he could read her charts? Uncle mused. The twit doesn't know a fathom from an exit buoy, or a meter from a cable.

Pointing at the taller agent, Uncle cocked a grin. "On this steamer every man gets a handle. Your stubby mate here is Mutt because he's short and fat. You're Pucker because you look like you've been sucking on a lemon. Mutt and Pucker."

"I'll have my associates teach you some manners after we dock, Captain."

Poking Pucker in the chest, Uncle laughed. "If you're still on board."

A man with a thick-set regard for British royalty, Uncle found simple delight in peeling away the layers of time Mother's twats required to construct their illusions. In his view, Mother's intelligence service was rife with inertia, laden with artifacts, confused when deceived, and forever perched on the cusp of being offended—tastefully offended, of course.

If his expression ginned up an artful dodge, few could help grinning. Larcenous to the core, Corcoran was devoted to the art of the some-what-straight answer—have a piss, his favorite retort. Uncle was a large man, covered with hair—thick and black. The frosty rime of his cheeks set his laugh afire. Knowing dying was the way of it, luck came with be-ing elusive.

His outsized forearms, his pump handles, were his signatures of fact. He liked to lean into a stranger's insistent conversation using his ham hocks as props, and let his eyes begin to vibrate and fill with menace.

Uncle was a plank-splitter from Australia's dusty red-plain outback.

His head was sheltered by blue-black hair that curled without regard to form. These curls sat atop whiskers that had been aggravated to mask his intent. These hallmarks held form until his crystal-blue eyes and sun-bright teeth were brought to bear.

If he didn't like a man, he would wave his chew-stick, his kola root, then brush his teeth with it while the man talked and lean forward to ensure his forearms took center stage, all the while cultivating a tacit confession of his adversary's weakness.

His clothes were an even sharper message. Light tan denim, his shirt, and pants were one weave short of being canvas, worn to a soft, wrinkle-free texture. Clean but frayed, his shirts were open to his diaphragm, with the sleeves rolled above the elbows. The man was a beast.

Baxter Corcoran was a Jack, a man with a flexible tongue, a man with more wrinkles on his horns than an Adeni whore, his life shaped by hard music without a thimble of waste.

The air in the chart room reeked of stale sweat and cigar smoke. Stiff, fostering a cloying insistence, Uncle set to measuring the ball-weight of the agents. "You wizards have been banging your bags, bullying Snow White's progress. Intel operatives from the Sutherland Highlanders my ass. I'll bet you're MI9'ers: escape-and-evasion twits straight out of The Beano. Comics sniffing Mother's nickers."

"Just so. I'm The Beano's Dead-Eyed Dick."

"You're a dick, that's flat."

"Try to remember who employs this lot, would you, Captain?" Mutt put in.

"Employ is it now? Have a piss, Mutt! Snow White's gone off the rail, and you bastards, are posting a bloody ledger." Uncle rolled his head around his collar, exhausted by London's sawn-off instincts.

"Your extraction schedules are too thick for this sailor."

"Quite right, Captain, circs are a bit pinched."

Throbbing, as though suddenly braced, the agents left the cabin. The blighters even make latching a cabin door a bloody event, Uncle thought. Nib-sniffing bastards.

Uncle was fed with worry, realizing his mate Edward Hardin was in trouble and may damn well be dead. A hard man, the well setup Welshman had saved the Aussie's life during a training exercise at Camp Z in Refuse Bay, an offshoot of Broken Bay, in New South Wales. Hardin had pulled Uncle ashore on the beach of Lion Island, near the mouth of the Hawkesbury River.

A licensed ship's captain and a man prone to cracking the shits, during a break in their survival training, Uncle had matched 1.25-liter Darwin stubbies with Hardin until dawn. When a square pusher tried to brace them, they went absolutely jungle and destroyed the officer's bar at Candle Creek.

By noon the next day both Captain Corcoran and Major Hardin had their officer commissions scrubbed and graded as General List Commissions: emergency use only.

Within hours Major Hardin was hosted by No. 40 Squadron RAF aboard a Bristol Blenheim ferrying construction supplies to Alor Star, a Royal Air Force Base in the Kendah region of northern Malaya, twenty miles up the western coast from Penang. Headquarters of the Kendah Volunteer Force.

Uncle found himself traveling the next day, assigned to the Special Boat Service (SBS), a provisional unit yet to be set to paper, whose sponsors claimed to be SBS Detachment 4, stationed near Colombo, Ceylon. The unit did not exist. Uncle had become a ghost.

One month after being reassigned, Corcoran received orders from Admiral Hugh Sinclair, the head of SIS, directing him to take command of the Portuguese-flagged steamer, SS Iron Knight, anchored in Port Kembla, Australia, and sail to the Royal Naval Base at Trincomalee, Ceylon, and await further orders.

His orders: pick-up and extract SOE Force 136 Group B's, four long-range penetration teams, including Hardin's Team 7.

As a cover, the tramp steamer had taken on bulk cargo at No. 4 jetty in Port Kembla—a modest load of pig iron slated for delivery to the Port Talbot Steel Works in South Wales. A representative from Port Kembla's Waterfront Workers Federation WWF had inspected the ship's log to ensure the scrap iron was not bound for Japan.

'No Scrap for the Jap' signs stood on the port's front apron. Port Kembla's Breakwater Battery's six-inch guns stood along the jetty. The guns had a range of sixteen kilometers.

The British Admiralty had ordered the light cruiser HMAS *Adelaide* to sail from Port Kembla west into the Indian Ocean to conduct antisubmarine patrols. With the sloop HMAS *Swan* entering the Persian Gulf.

"There's a reason our deck's ridin' low, Captain." Molly fired his Model 1897 trench gun at a passing seagull, blowing feathers into a bloom.

"Olive Oil smokes when she gets her way," Uncle said, setting fire to a cigar.

"We're in the gun, Captain." Molly threw the empty shell casing into the sea. "Mother's lads don't want us to run for home."

Driving a ten-knot steamer about the only craft they could outrun was a sampan. And that on a clear day. Running from the Japs or the Bosche was impossible—a recipe for lifeboats and saltpeter. That, and if they couldn't tackle the winds, the tramp would flounder, roll their scuppers under, and start shipping seas.

Uncle stood at the starboard rail and drank the cold, dark ale. He shook out a fresh fag as HMAS *Adelaide* cleared the port's exit buoy. With a tone of regret he whispered, "Latest goss: War has come to Australia Station and New South Wales."

For weeks after leaving Port Kembla the tramp sailed laboriously around the Bay of Bengal, running a course from Colombo, Ceylon, to Singapore, and north to Rangoon, Burma, the sailings a ruse to disguise his mission:

conduct coastal patrols looking for Japanese surface ships, submarines, and amphibian aircraft; and extract four commando teams.

Up to a point, excluding the weather, Uncle had planned each move. The risks of Hardin's rally point would be the extreme. Both of his missions contained a do-not-engage unless fired upon order. So, he loaded the twin 40MM guns mounted on the stern of the ship and covered the guns with a canvas dodger.

Uncle had lost radio contact with Team 3 with small arms fire echoing in the background and the team's signals specialist screaming into the wireless for his mother and for his God. Each time the tramp sailed through Team 3's rally point, Uncle tried to raise them with no luck.

Team 4 and Team 6 had rallied as planned and were delivered to the Royal Naval Station at Trincomalee, on the northwest coast of Ceylon, an elephant's walk north of the Royal Air Force base at China Bay.

Restless, Uncle slapped at the ship's intercom. "Scratch the tart's ass, Molly. Set your foreskin at one-third ahead. Steady on." He waited with a grin for the engineer's response, knowing Clive Mauldin would be shaking up a mouthful of broken biscuits.

"Right-oh. She fancies the short strokes." Molly spoke to a pause. "Did you send these two bomb-pots down here?" He charged, scoffing at Uncle's authority. "Wet bags of brown wind by the looks of 'em."

"Show 'em your trench gun, Molly. Show 'em Olive Oil's twelve gauge bore." Even as he laughed, the best part of his mind was sorting problems that lay ahead.

"The cog-wheels got their balls in a five-0 clutter."

Uncle encouraged Clive Mauldin's forty-grit way, knowing his chief engineer relished a proper measure of mistrust, mixed with Olive Oil's heavy shot. Molly enjoyed kicking at the crust of a world he could not alter.

"They're in sensitive health, Molly—fresh from the Ice Works—trying to patch a leaky bellows." Uncle spiced his coffee with a bit of rum,

"Be cheerful, Molly."

Uncle wanted to brief Clive Mauldin on the details of Operation Snow White, but such a brief-up would have hampered Molly's liberty ashore. Given the mission, he could barely foster a proper sense of caution. Besides, Uncle did not believe the mission's briefing details. Carving eddies in the Bay of Bengal, hauling pig-iron from Australia to England, it will be weak tea and Burmese medals for this crew.

After twenty minutes in the head spent trying to outfox his disturbed bowels and dancing with a tuneful sea, he keyed the wireless handset to reach Hardin's team.

"Doc, this is the Princess. Doc, this is the Princess. Come in, Doc." He let deviltry twist into a gallop when a rush of static snapped into a series of partial syllables.

Annoyed by the reentry of the MI9 agents, Uncle keyed the handset again on the Hallicrafter, HT-4, 350W, maritime transceiver. "Doc, this is the Princess, over."

Nothing—no one spoke. The cabin seemed purposely empty.

With a canned tone Mutt put in, "It's bad luck ploshing about in this soup."

"Fair to shit, I'd say." Uncle turned the chair to face the agents. "Doc's a crafty lad, true to his salt. Team 7 will make the rally." Not waiting for the usual bumf, he blew smoke over his shoulder and burrowed closer to the transceiver.

"Doc, this is the Princess here." Uncle lowered the volume as static burst into a crisp bounce. The light over the radio mount dimmed.

"Grumpy here, Princess." Uncle flinched inwardly. The rush of static had cut the air as a dullard rips the soil. With the wireless signal fair to good, nearly a strength six, Team 7 had to be near the coast. Cussing the tenacious pause, with Grumpy holding the frequency open so no one else could transmit, Uncle chewed on his kola root, recognizing the voice, realizing Hardin had changed his code-sign and was indeed alive.

"Grumpy here: heaps of bad apples, Princess. A bit like yesterday, really. There's a mistral on the way, over." The echo of his mate's voice picked at Uncle then raced him for cover. The code word *mistral* brought Uncle to his feet—only one commando from Team 7 was alive.

The MI9 agents focused on the transceiver's speaker, as though analyzing scenarios. Uncle reset the fold in his shirtsleeves as Mutt, with his quick evil eyes, clumped around the cabin, his brow cinched into a doubtful crown.

"That's the spirit, Grumpy. No worries." Uncle emphasized the code-sign. "Leave your location status, Grumpy. We'll hang the gong on a post—a VC for good measure."

"I'm in for a penny, Princess. A pint of the best will do."

"Good on you, cobber. No worries. See you in King's Cross, Grumpy."

The wireless snapped and went quiet. Catching the snap with a brace, Whitehall's lads picked up the usual wrinkles. Had they seen it all? Done it all? Uncle sighed as he scrubbed his beard with the side of his fist, wanting to move the tide of the conversation along.

Raising a hand in a toasting gesture, acknowledging the agents, Uncle announced, "Luck is trooping her colors. We'll sail north to a staging near Rangoon." Not wanting a reaction, he made a chore of turning off the wireless. "Team 7's churning mud, that's flat."

Pucker, the tall weasel-sharp bastard, sighed through a series of clipped tones, and shrugged as if finished with his mission. "We could gas on for days, I suppose. Team 7's the last of the lot. Not many of those lads will make the dole."

With a calculating nod, Uncle offered the agents a shot of rum, wanting to tease the lords into believing what their minds were inventing. The agents exchanged cynical grins as if they had accomplished their mission.

The bastards are looking to do Team 7. Dead and missing.

Corcoran reset the fold in his shirtsleeves as Mutt clumped around the cabin. Giving Mutt the finger, Uncle started brushing his teeth with his chew stick. Brazen-lunged, slurring words, Uncle stood. "Mutt and Pucker. The Bing Boys. Is there something Molly can help you cane toads with? Something Mother has detailed? Something in the wind, perhaps?"

Returning his finger, the agents turned as one and left the cabin. Washing his mouth with rum, Uncle decided to throw lines in Rangoon and ditch Mother's clowns.

*   *   *

London. The Athenaeum Court Hotel. 22 August 1939. 1340 Hours, GMT.

The luxury of the hotel's furnishings and the elegance of its wood carvings elevated a traveler's behavior no matter his origin. Such refined beauty, combined with three tots of brandy, could spawn solutions to complexities yet to be contrived.

Gordon Dewar preened his lapels, the signatures of a fading homosexual. Well pastured by any standard, his cheeks filled with helium, ballooning from his dimples to his ears, from his lower eyelid to his jowls. When he smiled, his mouth became an exaggerated oval, capped with a nose pitted with large pores and striped with capillaries.

His shoulders were narrower than his hips.

A man who made immobility appear responsive; Dewar admired himself in a mirror—a well-connected dandy. He came from money. His eyes could smile even if he hated the words or who he spoke to. One of three station chiefs in Mother's MI6 Section D, on paper he was John Poston, Jr.'s boss.

Dewar found August 1939 to be unseasonably warm and cold as England prepared for war. A dangerous time for an unconnected spy to be prancing about. A lucrative time for those with intelligence information for sale, especially with financial trading cycles gaining velocity and intensity. And Dewar had such information.

"Please, Johnny." Dewar filled Poston's glass, then his. "The French are God's doing, and wholly consonant with his gifts. Absent the French, and their library of metaphors, even Churchill would be speechless."

"The French, as a group, are uniquely stupid." John Poston raised his glass, trying to curtail Dewar's tripe.

"The row festering in Europe is consuming a good many Jews." Dewar was devotedly antisemitic. "Even the Americans refuse the Jews—907 Jews on the steamer *Saint Louis* were denied entry to the US last June. They landed in the alleyways of Marseille."

Amused by Dewar's expression of bewildered haste, Poston put a hard word on. "Some mighty powerful Yanks have been supporting Hitler. Henry Ford. Joseph Kennedy. And, the British White Paper denying entry to Palestine, will leave the Jews of Europe with few options."

John Poston, Jr. managed an obscure desk in MI6, responsible for tracking the doings of crime syndicates throughout the world. His current focus centered on the unprecedented concentrations of cash being traded by German industrial companies—arbitrage plays that had spread into Asian markets sending centuries-old players scrambling for a share of the profits.

Pressed and styled as if requested at court, boasting an internal mental consistency at odds with his conditional sense of inference, Poston's linguistic skills were agile and acute. Having studied mathematics under Szolem Mendelbrot in Paris for three years, he was recruited to give guest lectures introducing Chaos Theory to postgraduate students at Oxford and Cambridge.

John Poston could rinse outcomes from limited data as if sorting a child's crossword, his mind an abundance of brilliant and insane ideas.

Lewis, John's older brother, on the other hand, was the plodder. He was a quiet man of sturdy build, broad in the shoulders, slim in the waist, with an elegant, sun-brown face and coal-black eyes.

Evidence to Lewis was something tangible. That, and he was cursed with a taste for honesty. As an operative assigned to headquarters of the Security Intelligence-Middle East (SIME) he was directed to establish an office in, Cairo. His "A" Force would run deception operations in the Mediterranean area of operations.

The placard on his office claimed he was the head of the Inter-Services Liaison Department (ISLD), a guise for MI6 in the Med.

Last week Lewis fell to speculation while speaking to Johnny.

"Admiral Sinclair's gravely ill. Owing to his failing health he may soon resign his functions to a successor. In the near run, the new chief of SIS will rely on Dewar's judgment. If this occurs Johnny, you should resign to prevent being assigned abroad. A lieutenant colonel from the Horse Guards is thought to be the next in line as SIS chief."

The Poston brothers knew after twenty-seven years in the MI6, Dewar had a good many clandestine friends—too many.

For a moment, Dewar's face relaxed enough for Johnny to see a worried man. "Is that what Mother pays you for, Gordon? Making declarations about obvious outcomes?"

Dewar took his watch from his waistcoat pocket, and gave Poston a sidelong look, filled with suspicion. "Really, Johnny, Mother only fights for the shadows she can leave—the Bay of Bengal, Bombay, Yemen, Malta." He swirled his Old Sporan Malt Whiskey.

Adding a dose of self-lacerating cynicism, Dewar put up his hands in a placatory gesture. "For years now, Buck House has had me flame-dodging in Mother's draft, poorly paid, topping up bits of data, and sorting pots of gruel."

"Come now, Gordon. We all oscillate between grass and hay. Being bound in servitude comes by degree." Johnny spoke whimsically, knowing any meeting with Dewar would be lighted, here and there by a touch of comedy. "Are your actions without stain?"

"It's not the oscillation that's bothersome. It's realizing I've become socially ornamental." Envying the cold demands of money, Dewar had become aware of a shadow in the Poston family's transactions, and in that shadow, a Jewish lender who required darkness.

Poston shook his head and donned a lecherous grin, recounting Dewar's idiosyncrasies, likes and dislikes—habits. "Still and all, we can thank God for marble floors and hard leather heels. That bird in the black dress could oscillate your data."

Dewar swung his chair around and became well invented. But Poston's boss preferred the short pipes of the bird's bodyguards—a gentleman's slant on life.

"And just so, Johnny." Dewar adjusted his grin as the woman's bodyguards passed by. "Here's a gram that confounds. A bit of an Oliver, really. The National Gallery is moving its paintings to Wales. Why would anyone trust the Welsh with such valuable works of art?"

"You know I'm Welsh, I assume."

"I do."

"And so, Gordon. Your membership query to the Army and Navy Club in Pall Mall was turned back. It seems the members of the Rag are not impressed with your other-rank particulars. Perhaps you could attend to one of the members—ease into the morning room for coffee via the garage off Cleveland Place."

At first Dewar did not acknowledge the comment. After scanning the dining room, he smiled. "Cumbered once again—Admiral Sinclair's doing, I'm sure. Giving me the meal."

"The Admiral must have declared your diminished station, your enlisted rank, a function of some sort of guilt."

"Akin to the War Guilt Clause in the Treaty of Versailles, I suppose."

Unperturbed, Dewar sipped his whiskey, closing his eyes as the drink bit his throat. His hatred of consular types like Admiral Sinclair and John Poston Jr. had deep roots. That the Admiral sponsored young Poston's membership in Boodle's, the exquisite gentlemen's club on St. James's Street, promoted social schisms Dewar reduced to honorable inference.

Having more than an ample share of low cunning, the aspects of life for Dewar, often governed by the circular nature of circumstance, had brought his dealings with the swells of the Poston family full round. His dealings beginning in the fall of 1921, first with Sir John Poston, now centered on the lord's two sons.

Dewar winced, then anchored his tumbler with a sharp crack on the wooden tabletop. "You realize, Johnny, after the last lot, Mother, and her allies, established a Reparations Commission to collect one billion pounds sterling in war reparations from Germany. An impossible sum without surrendering capital assets."

Poston countered as he raised his glass. "American and British investors, as a ruse, claimed the market was cracked beyond repair. They knew the German State was substantially uninjured. With their help, Settlements Bank in Basel has become a wash tub, converting Reichsmarks into foreign currency."

Dewar evaluated his charge. This young mucker plods on with a deepening will, knowing the workings of Settlements Bank as a blind man knows his cock.

Having a bit more, Johnny put in. "These indemnities were designed to be burdensome. Foreign investors expected Germany's default. Germany's bankers have been speculating on currency fluctuations, anticipating Hitler's next move.

"That's why the chaps pulling the strings at Settlements Bank met with Hitler in January 1933, to restructure Germany's foreign debt, and thus guarantee Fritz the funds required to pay the indemnities. Plus, the funds required to continue rebuilding the German economy, including its military."

After a moment, Dewar tapped the tabletop with his tumbler. "American investors have spurred the transition of Settlements Bank from a debt collector to a currency floor for the Nazi state. And the Americans continue to issue high interest loans."

"Probable derivatives for our former colony," Poston chimed. "Kennedy's to blame. He and his friends have been funneling investment capital to the Germans from the moment the Treaty of Versailles was signed, knowing the Germans could be pressed to pay the indemnities. Kennedy knew the reparations demanded by the victors exceeded the cost of stabilizing the German economy, and that the German State would reconstitute its military."

Poston continued. "American diplomacy is reacting to an ever-changing mood. Roosevelt's quite canny. He runs a course between calculation and deceit knowing the two are twins. And so, he controls the spot price of gold. The old boy's far too bright for our lot."

Dewar tossed off his drink. "It's a big circle, Johnny—one of those wondrous theories of the even minded." Looking as if he were weaned on a pickle, the old punter scanned the room again, his gaze centered on his subordinate.

There's that facetious nod Poston prompts so well.

"Not to put too fine a point on it, it's Rome's game, Johnny. The Vatican has long-standing contracts with the Assassini, and the Javanese, through Royal..." The conversation stopped in mid-sentence. Licking the edge of his glass, Dewar set it down and signaled the waiter for a top-up. "Royal Dutch Shell has agreed to reserve seventy percent of its Java crude oil production for the Japanese."

"Well below the cost of production, according to the admiral."

Dewar stood, adjusted the waistband of his trousers, and sat with a grimace, then sighed as if he were about to lecture a room filled with dolts. "The Vatican has been financing French East India Company's investments since the late 1600's through its Institute for Religious Works. At this moment the Vatican's Secretariat of State and their Prefecture for Extraordinary Affairs direct their Asian financial matters.

"Tonkin's bishop must have run out of gold."

Through decades of intelligence work, Gordon Vivian Dewar had become a disciple of Leon Blum, a Jewish Freemason, and former head of France's Popular Front government. As with Leon Blum, Dewar remained clinically devoted to hauling the Vatican into courts of condemnation.

"No bishop runs out of gold. It's the oil of angels." Poston didn't wait for a reply. "Yank dollars, maybe. Although by now, there should be enough of those out of service to finance illicit franchises from Hong Kong to Marseille. Even the Vatican's."

Dewar sniffed at the remnants of his whiskey, absorbing the soft rustle of its aroma. "The Japs and the Corsicans will control the whole of Southeast Asia for the next ten years. Opium's getting expensive, as are the resins of Indian hemp. Even worse, the Singing Houses of Southeast Asia are being soiled to their core."

"Of course. Those starlings of a lighter virtue," Poston chimed. "Did you notice that there's always a new silence when the starlings are gone?"

For a moment Dewar looked annoyed, his hand playing a nameless melody on the table. Then he rose. "Piccadilly still has a full round."

"What's your view of Poland, Gordon?"

"Of course, there's Poland." Dewar waited for Poston to look his way. "There are virtually no negotiations between Poland and Germany. Mutual recrimination over the persecution of minorities is growing in volume, and Danzig is seething with rumors and excitement."

"That's where the row will start," Poston declared. "The Nazis are on a clock. Last week they informed Polish customs officials on the Danzig-East Prussian border that they would no longer be permitted to carry out their duties."

"That scrap of intel missed my queue."

"Came in August 4th."

"That's why the German press is savaging the Poles. A classic misdirection."

Dewar's chant matched his tired-looking smirk. Because the old boy had been brown shagging in secret for many years, his arse suffered from trigger itch, and his hair had jumped into a twist, trailing an expanding bull's-eye.

"With a bit of spin…" Poston stopped talking and adjusted his chair.

"With a slight of hand, Hitler will land in France after he carves up the Polish cavalry. Fritz has been conducting tank maneuvers in the Black Forest for months. The Bosche plan to pour through the Ardennes. Petain will usher them in—with ribbons and bouquets. It's a mess, really—Yanks training our conscripts, Indian troops guarding the Suez, Italy wishing for earlier times, our expeditionary force forming up to head for France to secure the Belgian frontier, and the bankers in Zurich lending money to the lot."

"It's as linear as a circle can be, I suppose." Dewar raised a finger, ordering a top-up. "Be careful how you run 'round it, Johnny. Stupidity's in bloom, I'm afraid."

"You and Hitler have much the same approach to life, Gordon. Excessive aspirations mixed with long-minded calculation and arrogant impulse provoked by resentment."

"I do say, that's a bit ripe."

On cue, luggage tumbled from both sides of a porter's cart—three suitcases and a storeroom worth of hat boxes. Disturbed, Dewar stood as a stunning woman entered the hotel. Her black, tailored suit was cut to accentuate a buxom figure.

Dewar was mesmerized.

Grinning in silence, as though reverence and sex had joined, the tall sylph with elegant legs glided to the reception desk, dismissing her escorts on the way. The woman's vulpine beauty, though breathtaking, showed signs of cruelty.

Her long black tresses ebbed and flowed as she drew the attention of the guests in the hotel lobby, men, and women. With an expression of cunning intensity, a nod fixed her escorts in place, and an impassive stare challenged Dewar's gaze.

Never at odds, Dewar practiced his airs for good-looking women. He enjoyed his deceitful madness—his homosexual desires, and interludes. "MI6 has a file on that beauty. Petra Laube-Heintz. She's a German bank-er tied to Schroeder Bank and Stein Bank. Banks that manage Hitler's personal accounts."

"What's she doing in London?"

"Ah." Dewar began calculating odds. "The Bank of England might be washing gold for the German state. Her minders, perhaps."

"Her elegance is definitely an asset. A situational distraction."

Noting Poston's grin, Dewar spoke quietly, as if to beckon the lady's needs. "Hitler and the Vatican are partners, Johnny. Postulates in hand, with their predilection for group intrigues, they'll destroy her Jewish banker. Even von Schroeder's emissary. Fritz will get his empire, and Rome will get gobs of washed gold."

"If you know, does the woman have contacts in London?"

Loath to accept Poston's implication, he set his glass upon the table and tipped it onto its side. "Fritz and the Pope are in harmonic balance—concordant drones. They have webs and spies everywhere. Their charity is hand-in-glove. It's only money—nothing to die for."

"On balance, gold's more than money." Adjusting their chairs, they smiled as the woman took the stairs.

"You've a gram there, Johnny." Dewar accepted the drink with a toast to the waiter. "Settlements Bank gave the gold they were holding in London for Czechoslovakia to the Reichbank. Lord knows why—barter between sovereigns, I suppose—*valuta*."

"A pound says Miss Heintz came to London to manage that gold transfer."

"That Czech transaction is well by the board. I've been correlating gold-related intel decrypts for weeks. The Bank of London has been washing gold for Germany weekly—flooring commercial transactions with German banking interests."

"Where will Mother hide her gold, Gordon?"

"Lord knows—Canada perhaps. Or wherever the starlings are hiding. Did you notice that Mother's janissary of parapet and flue have vanished from London? No. I don't guess you would miss those East End songbirds."

"Have you been brought up to scratch on operation Snow White?"

"Bits and pieces have come my way."

Sir John's youngest son had created Operation Snow White to jar the minds of British intelligence specialists, to force MI6 and MI9 to devote resources to deal with the Japanese invasion of China, and to consider how a Japanese invasion of Singapore might occur. Often absent at odd times, the Home Office dismissed his ideas as obvious fantasies.

Cast as a wet spot by Admiral Sinclair as a ruse: John Poston's current assignment—fish for a spy. To date he had chronicled the cobs of Dewar's past, gathering cabinets of dun-colored files and no useful information. The prominent facts—Dewar traveled to Lyon and Marseille in southern France regularly. And the island of Malta occasionally.

Considering the three cities Dewar visited, the admiral gave Poston an additional task. "Find out if Dewar's tied to the Corsican Syndicate."

Guiding Dewar, Poston led on. "The Admiral's relieved. Snow White's commando team flew out of Malaya on the dot, and their parachute drop into Tonkin went off without a hitch."

"I say, now there's a turn up—when the Queen Mother farts." Dewar guffawed. "You're talking turds." Ambling to the reception desk, Dewar exchanged words with the concierge and scribbled the woman's room number in his diary.

As if the provocation was a trifle over the score, Poston replied, "Turds, is it?"

"Under the circumstances, it's turds indeed." Dewar lit a cigarette. "A night parachute jump into the jungles of northern Tonkin, on the backside of a monsoon—I'd wager their brollies were scattered like billiard pills." Dewar pointed toward the billiard table in a sunken arena, where the woman's escorts had gathered.

"You're right, of course, Gordon. We'll have to let the rain have its way."

Dewar knew how to be careful. "With a good many of the lads assigned to Force 136 Group B off the net… presumed dead"—he looked about, admiring the waiter—"there's no reason to believe Snow White's lads are better off."

Dewar had been facing east since his sojourn to the 1936 Olympic Games. Nothing was right with his job. Nothing was right with England. Maintaining five separate government accounts, he made a game of laundering money, spending far more per month than his salary. His end game was scheduled for January 1940—an escape to Argentina.

After being expelled from Woolwich, the Royal Military College, for misconduct, he dedicated himself to the art of crude flatteries—that and keeping a tight measure on the admiral's cancer treatments. Like Dewar, the admiral's chief physician was as queer as a nine-bob note. Dewar's wounded treble barely kept up with the doctor's sturdy baritone.

Tracking the tail of the desk clerk's stride, Dewar drew slowly on his cigarette. His fingers drummed at Poston with a resonant tone. "My God, that female banker might agree to help you amount to yourself, Johnny."

"Do you enjoy the effects of a woman's allure, Gordon?"

"No. No I don't actually." Dewar narrowed his eyes and cocked his head slightly. After drawing deeply on his cigarette, he exhaled as he said, "You and Lewis are shackled to that rack. A bit of flannel I suppose. You're both prone to being played by a passing fancy."

"Gordon. I'm surprised you noted the woman in your ledger. I wager her legs go right to the top." Poston rose to leave. "I've a gram of disgust for your quiver. A bit of wisdom from my father, Sir John—trench wisdom. 'If you stand women on their heads, they all look like sisters.'"

"That's sparkling. Sends the sausage up like a railway signal, eh, Johnny?"

"Let's meet at the Savoy tomorrow," Poston suggested. "I want to fill you in on the current details of Snow White. And I've a meeting nearby to amend the first casualty listing."

*   *   *

London's Savoy Hotel. The Grill Room. 23 August 1939. 1930 Hours, GMT.

Famous for its many first, for its four-hundred-and-twenty-foot-deep artesian well supplying the sweetest drinking water in London, for its steam generators supplying enough surplus electricity to light its neighbors along the Strand, the Savoy Hotel had drawn Winston Churchill and his cabinet to its table by roasting its own Savoy Coffee in the basement.

Cabinet lunches were topped with a half-pound of dark roast for each guest.

To aid the War Department, the Savoy had constructed the finest air raid shelter in London in their basement next to their coffee grinders. And to set an example, the hotel's kitchen set their maximum price of a war-time meal at five schillings.

The Household's account at the Savoy Hotel, one of London's dearest bowers to transgress, promoted benefits Gordon Dewar abused with regularity. Young and now old past belief, he imagined these luxuries. Expecting accolades with each of his twenty-seven years of service to the Crown, he had reached a position of sufficiency, a position well beyond his dream—assigned as aide to Admiral Hugh Sinclair, Chief of the Secret Intelligence Service, SIS, MI6.

Insiders called the admiral *C*. His nickname was Quex. Dewar called him sir.

Dewar's desk governed the doings of Room 39, in "The Zoo," a labyrinth located beneath the First Lord of the Admiralty. Advertising his good fortune to any handsome beauty, more concerned to preach than to listen, he enjoyed playing the role of a kindly old stick.

A back-sliding Catholic, he worked out his angst railing the debauchery of papists at Center Court and Whitehall. Dewar framed his pride of station with whiskied discussions burrow-shagging John Poston Jr., his senior charge.

The Zoo, or "Broadway," as it was known outside the organization, had become the high-strung, much-acclaimed audit chamber of British Intelligence: a placket hole with battered desks and drab walls.

To draw attention away from his opium smuggling operation, before a trip to France or Malta, Dewar would monkey-wrench the Zoo's intricate cogs, scoffing at the particulars who quivered, encouraging the center shaft to vibrate madly, and cast the main bearings asunder.

Wrapped in the pied bark of municipal splendor mixed with social deceit, the tumblers of Gordon Dewar's mind had a peculiar tolerance of the royal family, half contemptuous, half pitying—more the pity since the abdication. But for Dewar, subservience was always bad form.

Dewar had no regard for Poston, suspecting he was Admiral Sinclair's plant. He was   certain after he had discovered Poston received mail at Post Office 850, a classified and treasured post box for Britain's intelligence elite—those men who worked secretly for the admiral. *C*'s announcement memo was clear: Poston has been selected to compass our flanks because of his acute attention to deceit and mindfulness amidst operational chaos. His mind for detail is extraordinary—logical inference being conditional.

John Poston, Jr., the Benjamin of his family, played his part nobly.

Being the younger son of the late Sir John Poston, a lifelong friend of Admiral Sinclair's, did not help Poston remain obscure. That this familiarity brought supervision from every quarter, including London's legal center, the Temple Bar, was another story no less interesting.

Johnny was a tall, shy analytic with an exquisite taste in women and an excellent tailor. With his wardrobe augmented weekly, he changed clothes at 1400 hours each day to ensure his appearance bolstered the day's underlying message.

Poston held his posture and manner to complement his dress. His older brother, Lewis, liked to suggest he relax—that or learn how to bob-and-curtsy. For John's taste, Lewis was too casual, and far too comfortable during social and business encounters.

Johnny's conclusions derived from bits of data. A statistical wizard, he understood the value of simply being clever and the dominance of detail. He deduced his father had been attacked by an opium cartel with connections to Marseille.

Parsing the words of colleagues for clues or missteps, he decided a spy lay within British Intelligence, with a controlled enemy agent, in the aversion of an off eye.

Rummaging through a pile of discarded documents, Poston had found an MI6 decrypt titled Drug Imports Specific. The decrypt referred to shipments of machine parts. Sir John was shot at by a sniper while inspecting a crate of machine parts. A crate salted with packets of opium. Johnny's calculus had been tedious. Streaming nine strands of data, his deductions flowed from a critical path centered on the timing of Gordon Dewar's trips to France.

"Listen, Johnny..." Dewar scratched his head and settled into an expression of sneering pride. "There's a fuss doing with Snow White. The Admiral and Electra House are bypassing my door on this one." Dewar's voice banged at the flagpole with a quizzical tone.

"Conditions drive probabilities, Gordon. Can you be more precise?"

Poston had been misleading Dewar for months, feeding him oblique information to obstruct his view. Poston was receiving classified data from Electra House, even the communiques for Dewar's eyes only, and channeling his conclusions to Sinclair.

Of late Dewar realized he had become overly anxious, fishing about to bid up tactical data, stalking the Southeast Asian deployments scripted exclusively for the provisional doings of the SOE, the Special Operations Executive.

"I've been preaching for cooperation among departments for years, Johnny. After months of redoubtable defense, MI6, Section D, has agreed to information-sharing procedures with MIR, the prime minister's guerrilla research group. These two decrypt henneries have officially proclaimed their allegiance to each other and to the prime minister's Propaganda Department EH, at Electra House."

Poston seemingly decided to throttle Dewar as the man's expression continued to be crisp and insistent, fostering a worthy's image, as though his existence depended on a clever notion.

"You're on form as usual, Gordon—your dishonored genius. Full square, Gordon; semaphores and tocsins, even warnings well received, test loyalty to its destruction." Having declared victory, Poston set his glass to the center of a coaster.

"Order breeds habit, actually. It's part of our existence," Poston declared. "Are these carpings your fond of something from your early period, Gordon—from your age-old romance with knocking shops and the horse cavalry?"

Poston arched his back to relieve an amused stomach. A burst announced itself. Dewar paused as though surprised. As Poston extended a hand to apologize, Dewar jumped in with a quick barb. "You qualify, Johnny. Your lineage allows for spilling wind; I suppose—giving birth to a Welsh polly. The best part of that ceremonial expression reminds me of Chamberlain."

As if bored after annoying Dewar for hours and minutes, Poston decided to pass along Admiral Sinclair's appraisal of the twit. "You and Chamberlain have the lineage of wet lamps, Gordon—sputtering glimmers waiting for gas to make a comeback."

"Just so, Johnny." Dewar bunched his napkin, and leaned into the table. "If First Grenadier Jensen escapes Burma and reaches Alexandria with those documents, we'll be able to keep the Windsors out of the frame and assign the whole affair to the Vatican."

Poston peered without giving way to a changing expression as he assumed the hush of a stuffed chair. Poston set his glass aside, sorting Dewar's words.

Dewar's miscue was the first classified reference to Operation Snow White uttered outside of the "Hole" and completely unexpected. How does Dewar know about the protected documents? Does he fear the documents detail the Windsors' dealings in Southeast Asia, or other damaging information about the Household?

The strain wrinkling Dewar's forehead set in motion, jumping from one watch-fire to the next as if looking for an outpost—looking for a regime to suggest to memory.

Of record, only two members of SIS and MI6 were privy to the parachute manifest listing the names of the men assigned to Snow White's long-range-penetration Team 7—Admiral Hugh Sinclair and John Poston.

Four men are in the photograph Admiral Sinclair handed me, Poston thought—Rudolf Hess, the duke of Hamilton, Albert Hartl, and Gordon Dewar. The old boy's either fronting for Hess or the Vatican.

Fabricating surprise, Poston asked, "Do you know this first grenadier, Gordon?"

"Linc Jensen. Isn't he one of the lads kicking up a wake of leaves in Burma? That's where Snow White's Team 7's operating."

Augmenting his surprise, this time offering an open palm, Poston pulled a notebook from his jacket pocket and made a quick entry. "I don't have the foggiest. That team manifest was off the boil—more than secret—from the outset."

"What the devil. I must be getting cloth headed. I need to recruit my nerve and demand convalescent leave. In the earlies no one remained on staff long enough to get this demented."

Dewar stood as if to finish his defense.

"Did you lie to Team 7, Gordon?"

"Sinclair wrote the briefing notes."

Why is Dewar still messing about in Snow White? "Cloth headed is it? You briefed that team near Candle Creek in New South Wales before they parachuted into Northern Tonkin. By now you must have their manifest listing memorized."

"Just measuring your depth, Johnny."

"Given that other SOE teams have been extracted from the Bay of Bengal area of operation, there's no reason to believe Team 7 won't make their rally in decent trim."

Not ten hours past, Poston had tied Dewar to powerful Nazis, confirming Admiral Sinclair's suspicions. The warp and weave of Snow White's trousseau, combined with the long-fibered texture of Dewar's turning east, had given Sinclair enough grist to have Dewar coiled up and shot. Dewar had met secretly with Rudolf Hess and Max Ilgner.

Max Ilgner was a ruthless, powerful man—I. G. Farben, International's intelligence chief. By extension, he controlled the world-wide distribution of I. G. Farben's synthetic oil production, brokering private sales for gold. While tracking synthetic oil sales, Poston connected Ilgner to an opium smuggling operation—six intel flimsies had led to a *Most Immediate* decrypt—a meeting between Dewar and Ilgner in Lower Fort Saint Elmo, on the island of Malta.

Enjoying a sigh to alleviate the tension, Poston decided groveling with the self-righteous clot might shift Dewar's focus and give the old boy an opportunity to create an alternative cover.

"Well, sir, from what I've gleaned, at least one man from that long-range team is left standing. His code-sign has been confirmed as Grumpy. How have you hashed Jensen from that?" He let his voice soften, guiding Dewar's attention to the women being seated to his rear.

"Yes, of course." Dewar acknowledged the women with a smile, and Poston with a nod. Seizing the lead, he leaned over the table. "The intel decrypt listed the code-sign Grumpy as the lad transmitting. What do you make of it?" His voice packed a dry bite, as if he suspected his charge of hesitant portions of deceit. "If you knew, you would tell me, Johnny."

Resenting the threat, Poston iced his expression. "You're off the peg on this one, Gordon. According to the admiral, that data came from a wireless intercept, not an intel decrypt." Poston moved a potted plant and adjusted his chair. Always before he had been positive that he could control Dewar, yet he began to recall that such had never been the case.

"You see, Gordon, the Baker Street Boys are holding the ribbons on that operation. They run Mother's intel group. This proposed Special Operations Executive is Baker Street's bird—close hold between the prime minister and Admiral Sinclair, a special operation executive yet to be sanctioned—with secrets so lewd, they are banned by the Catholic index."

"Right you are, Johnny. Papists want to ban smoking, drinking, and— you know the rest. The confessional is sport for them." Something spoken had Dewar scurrying, his expression mixing anticipation with opportunity. "Yes, of course. Where's your brother, Johnny?" He waved a hand, seemingly answering his question with implied understanding.

Noting Dewar's agitation, Poston was quiet for a time. "Lewis is running in circles like the rest of the lot I suppose."

Johnny's brother Lewis, the chairman of British Petroleum Acquisitions and Exploration, spent his day negotiating oil contracts from a luxurious complex in a drab, stench-laden backwater—Alexandria, Egypt. A spy, Lewis Poston was an eighteen-year operative of MI6. Clandestinely assigned to quietly help the Special Operations Executive plan future operations for SOE Force 133 in the Mediterranean region, his office was swept daily for listening devices.

"You seem a bit brittle, Gordon." Adjusting his chair, Poston stood to redress his trousers, then turned to admire the ladies.

"Nothing brittle about those bouncers, eh, Johnny?"

"A postulate held to be obvious—such chaos breeds life, Gordon. Opposing sine waves actually. Unanchored breasts and secret codes get on well together, chasing passing trolleys—just part of the show, really."

At this stage of his investigation regarding Dewar's activities, Poston had assembled three intercepts related to the documents in the wayward leather pouch. Even with such scant data, he informed Admiral Sinclair the documents in the pouch should have a priority of: *Most Immediate*—the Windsors might be at risk.

"Tell me, Gordon, you dropped this business card near your desk: William E. Calver & Co., Ltd., Casablanca. Do we have an operation in that region I should know about?"

"Mother does not have an operation in Morocco. Calver is a fellow I met in the Caxton Bar at Saint Ermins Hotel, here in London." Dewar glanced at the women behind him and changed the subject.

"Lucien's dropped off the grid."

Poston plucked a flower from a vase to search the thin membrane of its petal. "Lucien's a poor excuse, even for a Frenchman. One of your early hires, wasn't he? Years ago, by now."

"Eight years ago. Lucien's a Yank of French extraction. A cunning synthesis. A breed with prevailing disorders, I'm afraid. After an age, even patriotic Frenchmen need mending."

Dewar gave ground with a brusque nod. His breathing had become labored.

"I'll put you in the picture, Johnny. Before the snows fall, the French will be of two minds. The weak will choose the Nazis, the rest will choose a resistance league—Paris or Marseille. Although cloaked in an aromatic kinship, Frenchy's hatred of his brother is called patriotism."

Poston shrugged. "The Nazis or the resistance? There's money in smuggling contraband and the Lyon-to-Marseille smuggling route is one of the best in the world. Weapon sales will be at a premium. Ammunition as well."

Dewar spoke through a huff. "Of course, the resistance groups will have Marseille." Poston caught a glimpse of anger in his eye. Or was the clit sorting options? "But the Nazis and Paris will have I.G. Farben and synthetic-oil."

Poston knew Max Ilgner, I. G. Farben's intelligence chief, played solitaire, using shills to front and camouflage Farben's activities. If Ilgner communicated with Dewar, at least three message dead drops were in play. That this Nazi had penetrated British Intelligence left Admiral Sinclair's replacement in the frame for further scrutiny.

After correlating variables and estimating probable derivatives, Johnny had decided the Vatican was dealing with false intel concerning the documents in the pouch. False intel to confuse or cover a tangential operational trail. And, if Dewar supplied the Vatican with the bogus intel, he used Rudolf Hess, Hitler's secretary, or Albert Hartl, Germany's Vatican specialist as the conduit.

Additionally, he knew Ilgner had co-opted the fears of European banking houses, using their soiled hands as a tool, intending to run them to ground if they sought leverage over I. G. Farben's intelligence network, NW 7.

I. G. Farben had been raiding competitors since 1927, and the company's synthetic-oil production was disturbing currency markets throughout the world. NW 7 had been trading currencies in the world's arbitrage market for a decade and the volume of their currency plays had increased dramatically.

Fantasy perhaps, Poston mused. The day before, he set nineteen intelligence flimsies in an array on a drafting table. Sorting words, drawing implications here and salutations there, he deduced Max Ilgner planned to boost Farben's financial stature by raiding specific German industrial giants.

Correlating the dates on the flimsies, Johnny had celebrated Ilgner's sense of irony. The date chosen for the hostile raids would be well received in the Muslim world. Ilgner planned to set his strategy in motion on September 11, 1939—the day Allen Dulles, I. G. Farben's principal attorney, had negotiated for Saudi Arabia and Iraq to publicly sever ties with Nazi Germany.

For John Poston, Jr., one recursive computation remained to be sorted. Given the intelligence data relating to Dewar, the timing and location of his travels, the German industrialist he's meeting, and the Nazis he's in bed with, is Gordon Dewar swimming in money?

If so, where is he hiding his money?

*   *   *

Burma. Small Coastal Village. 23 August 1939. 1720 Hours, GMT + 6.5 Hours.

Major Edward Hardin had lost his Christian name. Doc even lost his operational code-sign. As Grumpy he had paid toll on Charon's ferry so often; accepting his bondage, he did not care where he was heading or where he got off.

Mired in the throes of self-loathing, as Doc ran at point he missed the signs of the ambush. His mates died because he was not worthy. He ignored the scuff marks on the trail and missed the manicured firing lanes covering the kill zone.

In the summer of '38 Edward Hardin was teed up and in splendid trim. In the fall of '39, packing the slops of war, he walked with a stave, and needed help to stand.

His eyes were a hollow for the attrition of hope—specked with misery's numbness.

The day broke humid and hot. Awakened with a start, frowning at the foul taste in his mouth, brief gusts of pain coursed through his thigh and into his lower back. His chest vibrated from breath to breath. Dehydrated from losing blood, he drank until the water bowl was empty.

Alert but tired, he studied the jungle near his hut—plants, soil, lagoon, birds. The hut sat away from the shore amid water palms and clusters of bamboo.

Weary, he knew the jungle's simplicity could be deceiving.

The natives: where are the bloody natives? The village is too quiet. The smells. Wet thatch and sulfa powder. They cleaned my wound, dried my socks, and took my boots. Why?

A used battle dressing lay against the far wall. An old woman peered over the edge of the veranda and scurried up the beach when Hardin looked at her. His throat was so raw he could hardly swallow. Out of gas, he curled into a ball drawing his knees into his chest.

I'm being sold into slavery.

Needing sleep, he wanted to fade into another time, another place. The silk-clad, black-haired girl took center stage, slipping through a crack in the foliage, bounding into the track way, cycling moves as if timing her stride.

Had the girl spotted the Dutchman? Had she waited for Leenstra's attack? Was she that well trained? Of course. She's killed before. Leenstra was reaching for Hardin's rucksack when he fell to her machete—dead before he could scream—dead before he hit the ground. Hardin tried to get up, but the fever claimed him, and he lost the image of the girl.

A torrent of rain burst from the near cloudless sky—hollering and suddenly dying.

Rapidly warming air steamed the wet thatch of the hut. Striated shafts of sunlight streaked through the palms, gaining leverage on the beach, setting the azure water of the lagoon in sharp contrast to the creamy-white shells and pale-brown sand.

Hardin cleared his ears. The sound of small-arms fire rang in the distance—north. East. He couldn't be sure. Jap prickers must be gaining ground.

As lightning strikes through the heart of a black horizon, scenes of the team's ambush flashed and accelerated—the muted roar sounding a muffled thrum, as if a drum's skin-tray were being dampened by a Proto-Celt's hand.

Hardin struggled to draw air into his lungs. He could not set his despair aside.

The smell and the agony of the kill zone had grown with time. Wherever he stood, he found himself on the leeward of these memories. With eyes regarding something beyond their focus, pictures played at variable speeds, at times cast in single frames.

We have a specific for men who break faith with those who die—Admiral Sinclair's signature words for ending formal mission briefings—words of farewell.

Breathing as though desperate for air, his rib cage hide-bound, straining to expand, Hardin held his right foot above the floor. Half-clad, he pulled himself along the wall to the doorway and onto the veranda facing the beach. The hut was aged. Built many years ago, the structure held the look of seasoned strength.

The hut stood forty meters from the palm trees crowding the water's edge.

Designed to withstand violent onshore winds, the hut's bamboo frame had been reinforced with heavy hemp line. Propped above an isolated expanse of gray, sandy soil, bordered by clumps of bamboo, scattered palms, and a stiff wedge of grass, the floor system was lashed to eight bamboo poles, three feet above the ground.

Searching for a sentry, Hardin categorized the vegetation and terrain again. The hemp rails of a bamboo footbridge swayed with an onshore breeze to the north—sixty meters north. Escape had to be instinctual. Day or night, he could not hesitate. A Raleigh all-steel bicycle would be the ticket, he thought. That cart's too slow. A whiskey or a cup of coffee would be good. Rather a shot of gunfire—tea spiced with rum.

Hardin set his chin into a freshening breeze. Palm fronds rustled a soft, crackling summons—a sunny day near Port Washington, running through the corn stalks. "I need my boots and a walking stick."

Crouched on his left knee inside the doorway to avoid detection, Hardin shaded his eyes against the glare and searched the area to the north, near the beach. A small group of armed natives had gathered near a fishing boat, arguing. One man kept pointing toward Hardin's hut.

I'm running out of time. The villagers know I'm worth a good deal of money. I'll die slowly if I'm sold into slavery.

The rest of the village was empty of life. A scattering of huts stood to the south through a funnel of open ground. A thin belt of palm trees and dense foliage screened these huts from the beach. A wall of bamboo interlaced with vines fenced a portion of the northern sector.

Giving his tackle a boost to ensure he hadn't become a gelding, he leaned against the door frame. No longer agile, to move swiftly was impossible.

To escape he needed his gear. A fevered chill ran through his chest. Escaping Burma was so near, and he desperately wanted to make the rally with Uncle Dingo—to get back to England and his Katherine.

And at the end of this unfettered chaff, Hardin found a man standing near him with a chiding finger. The black-haired girl peered over the lip of the veranda. Hardin stood between utter exhaustion and subtle defiance.

"This is my daughter, Tu."

Catching the strident tone of the old man's voice, Hardin said, "She's her father's child."

Hardin blinked as he changed focus. The rush of his thoughts began drumming a brand of mongrel chit. On your game, Captain—this lovely lass stalks the jungle like a cat. Hankered, the fever ignited his urges. Without her machete, she's a slice of grand beauty.

Her eyes shone as black as Newcastle's coal—she stood firm and erect. After being isolated for weeks, Hardin waited for the old man's next comment.

"We have cleaned your wound." The set to the old man's expression was deep and cold. "You cannot use the wireless again. Javanese pirates have been looking for our radio for months. We spotted five of them in the mountains to the north yesterday, near the shoreline."

Flagged under the heat, Hardin clutched the door frame and fixed his gaze intently upon Tu's father. The old man's black eyes were dark with intent as they looked into those of Hardin's. He was a powerfully built man with a dark, native, deeply weathered face. He was larger than Uncle Dingo.

Hardin's right shoulder ached as he raked his fingers through his bushy hair, donning a faintly astonished look. The other men he had seen in the village were barely tall.

"I'm afraid my mind's a mess. When did I use a wireless?"

"Yesterday, in our cave up the beach."

Hardin raised an eyebrow, and asked, "I don't remember. Am I a prisoner?"

"Not of ours—we are fishermen. You must leave our village."

"Where's my equipment—my rifle and kit—my boots?"

The old man hesitated. "We'll give you your equipment when you leave—we will keep the French language books." As though selective in his favors, the old man drew a deep breath and his expression grooved to a rigid mask.

A grain of wind brushed the old man's hair. Hardin stared at him. He's like most guerilla fighters. His mind's made up and there's no arguing with him. If that's truth in his eyes, I might live long enough to run south.

Hardin steadied himself against the door frame. "I want my boots." Breathing through a resonant shudder, doubts pestered his tone. The calm of the old man's brow had an edge—a voice smoothed by age—his nature that of the jungle.

Sensing uncertainty, Hardin changed tack.

"Your English is good."

"The Catholics are determined teachers." The old man projected a thin, icy understanding as he peered across the lagoon.

"Do you speak French?" Hardin asked.

"Of course. You are not the first to pass this way." The dense substrate beneath the old man's frown flared crimson, too abrupt to ignore—dogged, synchronized, and eagerly ruthless. The old man set his teeth. "I speak many Italian dialects as well."

A distinction and a warning—the old man must work for an offshoot of East India Company, Hardin thought. If he's looking for intel, he'll have trackers follow me.

"How did you find me?" Hardin asked, trying to stand still.

The old man hesitated—either undecided or formulating a response—watching Hardin. Tu's eyes turned to her father. He flicked his hand outward. Tu ran away.

"We have trail watchers throughout southern Burma."

"Did your friends ambush my team?"

The old man's face leveled into a propitious stare. When the distant drone of a plane filtered through the canopy, he looked across the lagoon, as if evaluating the sound. "So far you have been lucky Englander. British coastal patrol flights are only looking for Japanese ships."

Tu appeared without a sound and set a bowl of rice near Hardin's feet.

"And, Englander, if my friends ambushed your team, you would be dead."

Hardin grabbed the door frame to keep from falling. Sweating profusely, his vision faded from clear to fog, then to clear. His body was still fending a low-grade fever.

The old man moved to the edge of the veranda and cocked his head as if setting his ear to a sound. "Do not leave. Many are searching for you. Tu will bring chicken eggs." With a nod from her father, she ran off, bouncing from one dry patch of ground to the next.

"We have been paid well for your safe passage, Englander."

"Who paid you?"

"A large man with gray-green eyes."

The old man's speech had gained a precise pattern of enunciation, causing Hardin to alert. "Give me a pot of coffee, five days' rations, and my equipment. I'll leave today."

The old man's eyes glinted with sudden anger. Taking a step toward Hardin, he closed the gap, and cocked his head. "You will not leave without Tu. She remains your guide."

The confrontation ended as it began, without satisfaction.

It had been raining off and on for six weeks. The jungle dripped with misery. Rotten leaf bogs governed the low patches of ground. Hardin couldn't stay near the coast. He needed to find a game trail heading south.

Knowing he must keep a steady pace to make the rally south of Ross Island on time, he started memorizing the location of the channeling vegetation—trees, ground cover, bamboo, wedge grass. Instinct would govern his escape. Each step required a sense of touch—his leg wound forced him to accept a lurching gait.

Amid a stirring of unrest, the black cicadas had started their rasping, throbbing chorus.

For hours Hardin sat on the veranda sipping hot tea, rum, and citrus. A potion mixed by the old woman, thought to combat malaria.

Relaxed, yet vigilant, searching the night he found a sky spangled with stars. None of their glow reached the jungle floor.

Sparring with fever, Hardin's body needed time to heal.

*   *   *

Garmish, Germany. 24 August 1939. 1930 Hours, GMT + 1 Hour.

The storm had consumed the Alps from north to south, through Bavaria and Italy.

"I can see why Hitler comes to Bavaria," Eaton whispered as he looked at a brochure featuring the 1936 Winter Olympics.

Garmish, a mountain retreat with a vibrant hostelry, lay in a lush, narrow valley framed by massive granite tors that defined the beginning of the Bavarian Alps. Populated by wood carvers and farmers, butchers, and grocers, Garmish was famous for hiking in the summer and skiing in the winter. "The clanking of pails and the lowing of cows. What could be a more deceitful backdrop for Hitler than a mountain valley filled with farms."

Eaton knew the railway station lay three hundred meters from an Olympic venue built to form the landing arena for a now-famous ski jump. I'd like to see that ski jump.

A cold sleet matched wits with the station lights. Steam blasted from the engine's undercarriage, fogging the cobblestones as the black train eased to a stop, blowing white clouds into the signal gantries and the wrought iron eves of the stationhouse. Guards with Nazi armbands stood at the platform's only exit.

A shrill whistle echoed into the night. Steam shot from the train's undercarriage and continued to flow through the iron skirting of the station's roof. A porter set a step stool and opened the carriage door. Eaton stepped onto the metal platform at the rear of the carriage. Instinct brought a sense of recognition and of foreboding. A cold, crisp wind touched his face.

It's time to sort the pieces of this German puzzle. Samuel Eaton, arbitrage specialist for J. P. Morgan banking house, pushed at his legs to iron out the kinks.

An elegant woman appeared near the station exit in the penumbra of a hooded light—the same woman he admired during his layover in Frankfurt. As if inventorying the passengers leaving the train, she turned her head ever so slightly and spoke over her shoulder to the man behind her.

That lady's beauty is ungovernable, Eaton thought, embracing delusions of adequacy. Alive to indecent suggestion, he admired her radiant hair. With a humorous expression of attentive indifference, her eyes seemed to gather his thoughts, and reckon each one.

A black Mercedes sedan idled nearby, adding a confident expectancy to her presence. Ice crystals trimmed the sedan's windows.

"Samuel Eaton!" Her voice sent soft, thunderous explosions through Eaton's chest as he stepped onto the granite platform. Excitement wheeled him away from caution, instantly challenging his composure. The cold glow in her face belied the easy motion of her hips.

His trip had been planned for weeks—a meeting with an unknown representative of the Five Arrows Fund. The subject of the meeting was the accelerating opportunity to capture the profits from wartime currency fluctuations caused by real-time tactical decisions and derivative gold-price fluctuations—currency arbitrage.

As an incentive, his boss, the chief operations officer for J. P. Morgan, had awarded him a luxurious follow-on vacation in Paris. Eaton had made over $128 million dollars for J. P. Morgan through international currency arbitrage in past years, accurately predicting the storms and calms of Nazi Germany's takeover of Austria and Czechoslovakia.

My god the woman is gorgeous, he thought, trying to gather his wits. "Yes, I'm Samuel Eaton." She took hold of his elbow, guiding his step toward the sedan. Bypassing the pleasantries, she signaled her escorts. A man wearing a long, black leather coat ushered Eaton and his escort into the sedan and closed the doors. Another man slid behind the wheel.

"The meeting has started." The woman's tone was stiffening.

"Why are you following me?"

"I am your escort, Mr. Eaton." She was tall, her eyes light blue with specks of black, her dark hair drawn tight to the back of her neck.

There was something more than breeding in her face, more the hint of steel being honed to a cutting edge.

"Do you represent the Five Arrows Fund?"

"No. I represent a consortium of German bankers"

Aware of a dimming of the station lights, Eaton scanned the platform as the sedan moved forward. Concerned yet composed, he started dissecting information. The woman's English had a smooth Bavarian flow in sharp contrast to her efficient clothing and symmetric figure.

"We missed you in Frankfurt, Mr. Eaton."

"Are you going to tell me your name?"

"Petra Laube-Heintz."

Restive, Eaton caught the profile of a Luger under the arm of one of her escorts. The sedan's cruciform began consuming his senses as if he were in a museum. Odors of lost time set him in search of logic. Calculating, anticipating, he sank into the deeper hallows of the sedan's comfort, waiting for more definition.

"Protocols must be respected, Mr. Eaton." What in hell's she talking about?

"If you're inferring that I'm late, the train arrived on time. And German railways are more reliable than any of the others in Europe." The woman's a blooming Nazi.

Eaton sighed audibly, instantly regretting his lack of guile. "Whose protocols?" he asked.

Somehow Samuel Eaton, New York banker and graduate of the London School of Economics, had plunged headlong into a netherworld of mutually exclusive commitments. Could he back away and remain productive?

As was often the case, Eaton felt trapped by financial dwarfs. Fighting a sudden rush of anger, squinting to hide the tiny facial spasms that played around his eyes. Eaton drew air into his lungs to steady his breathing. The woman's words contained a questioning, but why?

Anticipation shook his frame as the woman exchanged words with the driver, then acknowledged the driver's smattering of laughter. His escort told the driver, he, Eaton, would not live out the week. As a queer chill traced his shoulders, Eaton turned toward the fogged window. His throat knotted with a quickening. His fluency in German and his greed were colliding, exposing the integral that had drawn him to Garmish—the continuity of financial variables.

I've been shanghaied. When these Nazis finish with me, I'll be executed and dumped in the woods. Why am I here?

Even though the patterns of international currency arbitrage were purposely disconnected, a thread of gold tied Singapore and Bombay to

Marseille and London—massive amounts of gold were flowing into England. And Mother was moving her liquid assets to Canada.

The sedan turned into a narrow gravel drive lined with low granite walls. The windows of a small chateau were alive with light. The drive wrapped around a dry, circular fountain. Petra Laube-Heintz walked him up the front steps, past a pair of sentries, and turned him over to a concierge with pale skin, a knife-like nose, deep set eyes, and thin lips.

What in hell am I into? They're all packing heat.

*   *   *

Diamond Harbor, India. Headquarters Annex, East India Company. 24 August 1939, 1140 Hours, GMT + 5.5 Hours—Indian Standard Time.

The monsoon rains set loose a tide of lost souls as mud-clogged spirits jostled with the rot of daily obligations. Bodies of the misplaced and fragments of rural cocoons washed to the sea, scattering missives of predictable grief.

In the growing prosperity of Diamond Harbor lurked an ample measure of intrigue. The Headquarters Annex of the East India Company and the adjoining go-downs stood on piles above a matting of sewage and flotsam containing millions upon millions of refugees—rats, dogs, monkeys, snakes, fire ants, and bloated human remains.

The east was not only an enigma; it was a weariness.

Four disused go-downs sat apart from the primary docking aprons along Diamond Harbor's waterfront. The most secluded go-down housed the armory of Alex von Cleve, a Templar assassin. His latest acquisition, eight crates of Mauser, MG42 machine guns from a Nazi arms dealer in Khartoum, held for resale to Muslim insurgents in northern India.

A second go-down held von Cleve's food exports—grains and jute primarily. The South African's trading company sold weapons and grains in every port or hidden bay from Shanghai to Durban.

The sun was just past half-eleven and the temperature was well over one hundred degrees. A platoon of jet-black Schipperkes foraged the gated compound. Frenzied by the rats assaulting the docks, these small dogs, with their barrel chests, large shoulders, big heads, and boundless energy, struck without warning and without sound, racing in and out of the go-downs.

The air in the grain storage go-down was laden with a faint colloid and reeked of jute. Von Cleve had soaked his massive hands in walnut juice and was locking his private weapons storage bin, when a monk and two large men were escorted into the go-down by archers patrolling the compound.

"Sikh, sit at the table and keep quiet," von Cleve whispered. The monk's escorts must have concealed weapons. While the monk sat across from the Sikh, von Cleve alerted his archers.

"Iced tea will cool you, Monk."

The monk ignored von Cleve's gesture and declared himself a financial emissary from Malta—one devoted to faithful transactions—the eight-pointed cross tattoo warned those he met of his Templar devotions.

Von Cleve had his own cross, and he did not like surprises. For a time, they did not talk, each busy with his own thoughts. The monk stared hard at von Cleve, but the eyes that stared back into his showed only contempt.

When the monk claimed he represented Compensation Brokers Ltd., von Cleve alerted without expression causing his archers to close the exits of the go-down. Compensation Brokers Ltd. was one of the million- pound contracts he had negotiated for retrieving sensitive financial documents.

"Monk. Why are you in Diamond Harbor?"

"Retribution!"

"Retribution!" Von Cleve was incredulous. He raised his hand, and an arrow sank into a wooden spar near the monk's head. "Did Compensation Brokers Ltd. dispatch you from Malta to offend me?"

With one hand on the arrow's shaft, the monk stood, leaned over the table, insistent. "As you are aware, von Cleve, we represent many of the world's most powerful bankers. Their clients remain hidden from the world. Your Sikh killed one of our clients." Measuring the six-foot seven-inch Sikh, the monk seemed fearless. When the Sikh stood the monk's bodyguards alerted, eased away from the table, set their right hand to their weapon, and spread out several meters.

Von Cleve grabbed the monk and pushed him into his chair. "Monk. No man comes to my headquarters and threatens my associates." As von Cleve drew away from the table he peered at the Sikh. At six foot plus seven, the man's beard, made larger by his bright red turban, billowed over his mammoth shoulders. But it is the Punjabi's eyes that should warn this monk, von Cleve mused. They matched the Schipperke's, black orbs that lack dimension.

That, and each time the monk opens his mouth, the Sikh drops his hands and rests them against the front of his thighs. This Punjabi is no mere Jaat. He is a dangerous man. The Sikh and von Cleve sat down when a small Asian woman brought three classes, a pitcher of iced tea and a small bowl of sliced lemons. The Sikh moved the pitcher away from his hands.

Incensed, on the cusp of a killing rage, von Cleve drew a knife from his ankle scabbard and held it behind his right hip, cutting edge up. This Punjabi bastard works for the Thule Society as an enforcer throughout India. I have to be careful. The monk and the Sikh represent two of my three contracts. That he was paid in advance, in gold, to retrieve the documents in Hardin's pouch, by three clients, must never become known.

If these competing contracts come to light, Ion Crilley will have me killed.

"Whom do you represent, Sikh?" The monk hollered.

Instantly enraged, the light-skinned giant swept the tabletop with his left hand, strewing glass, and iced tea across the floor. Lurching across the table, his right hand holding his kirpan followed in an opposing arc. Yelling, he slit the monk's throat.

Fountains of blood spewed into the air. The monk let out a gurgling clamor as his body bounced off the tabletop and slumped to the floor.

In the vacuum that followed, the monk's bodyguards sank into a crouch. Bow strings drawn, as the bodyguards brought their weapons level with their hip, arrows lanced their chests, with one protruding from each man's mouth.

A cold, mystic tremor swept through the go-down.

The Sikh hesitated, threw the table aside and wiped the kirpan's blade on the monk's robe. Turning, he stared at von Cleve. "The Thule paid you in gold, Dutchman. My employer wants the delivery date for the documents."

In this world of money, von Cleve was an outlier. He wanted to be a gentleman. He became an assassin instead. Dispassionate, on his nod, his archers had killed two men of God. Blood ran into a pool near his sandals.

"I thought Punjabi Sikhs were men of God." With a nod, von Cleve posted his archers throughout the go-down. "Killing this monk complicates matters."

"Your monk knew the game." The Sikh scanned the go-down. A frown gathered between his eyes. "His client was a thief."

"My monk, is it?"

Eleven archers had notched their bows and stood separated by forty feet in an arch around the Sikh. "The Thule Society has many ornate precepts." The Sikh spoke, punctuating words. "Many are dedicated to the occult. If the documents we want are made public, and London untangles the web, I will kill you first, Dutchman."

Iced with rage, von Cleve pointed at the Sikh. "You have now negated my obligations to the Thule. I will keep their gold. And you, Sikh, will worship whatever God they require."

Killing this giant will take less time than blinking an eye.

Von Cleve took note of the Sikh's posture as the man slid his kirpin behind the sash at his waist. Watching as the big man spread his feet, when the Sikh jumped and turned in the air swinging his kirpin in an arc toward von Cleve's face, six archers let fly their shafts.

Only a moment, a matter of an instant, six arrows drove deep into the Sikh's chest, soaking his Sulthan with seeps of blood.

* * *

The Andaman Sea, East of Port Blair. SS Iron Knight. 24 August 1939. 1240 Hours, GMT + 6 Hours.

My coffee's hot and the sea's flat, Uncle mused, rubbing his rum-soaked eyeballs, trying to put the lips of a tattooed pussy together while he depressed the wireless transmission key. "Grumpy, this is Princess, over." Grumpy was First Grenadier Linc Jensen's code-sign. That Hardin had assumed the code-sign meant the grenadier was dead.

Baxter Corcoran, maritime operative, ship's captain and tuft-hunter extraordinaire, aimed the transmission signal northeast, across Tavoy Point, hoping his mate had reached the vicinity of the rally point in decent trim. He pledged his pledge with a swig of rum—to rescue the man who saved his life in 1938 during a Z-Special training exercise in Refuse Bay, New South Wales.

That Hardin was his mate, he knew. That Hardin could fight, or sing and drink the night until dawn, he knew. That his mate liked to keep his own counsel, he knew. Slow to anger, Edward Hardin could explode. He did not like to be touched. Uncle found that out the hard way—when he nudged the squaddie's shoulder to cap off a joke, Hardin decked him.

Drumming his fingers across British Admiralty Chart #825 for the Andaman Sea, he laughed at the essentials of life, preferring the mutual benefits of booze and pussy. The echoes were all the same to him—all but the death of his son.

Picturing the dusty red soil plain near his childhood home, this Australian had been hewed by his family's struggle to survive. His jaw always set; he was more at home in the bars along a harbor's strand than braced upon the bridge of his ten-knot steamer.

"The SS Iron Knight. What shining numb-nut names these tubs?"

Drinking rum, he rolled his fingers in and out, watching the tendons in his forearm push Lucy's hips up and down. Lucy could quick-up any man's blood, he decided. Hardin had bayed with delight after Uncle sobered down, clumping on about Lucy, the big-titted Mayfair tart Uncle found tattooed next to his watch.

"Grumpy, this is Princess, over." Nothing. "Come on, Grumpy, pick up." He wanted to talk to Hardin without Mother's lads eavesdropping or caning him with monotonous chatter.

But here the MI9 agents came, amusingly odd and comically different. For the better part of a day the dicks had been requesting the jump manifest listing the team members—not the name of the man transmitting, but the original manifest. Their pestering being at odds with their official charge as facilitators, he decided the twats must have been thoroughly briefed on the operation, except for each commando's code-sign.

Why do they give a toss about Team 7 or the remaining lads?

After twenty-plus hours of oral mechanics, jousting with the agents, Uncle retreated to his cabin to fashion a new jump manifest. Hardin didn't make the jump.

In the morning he presented the modified manifest. "Here's Mother's jump manifest. Five cobbers, that's the lot." Allowing an expression of exuberant fatigue, he dropped the manifest on the chart table.

"All hale and well met." Pucker didn't appear to believe Corcoran.

Mutt's expression sharpened, casting lines of stern duty to stalk about the cabin. Then his face creased into a vengeful grin. "That team had septuple. Seven dwarfs, plus one."

London's pugs appeared to conspire in an instant, spot-painting Corcoran as their latest problem. Pucker seemed keen to muster Corcoran's goolies as he pointed a long, bony finger at the captain's face. "That was written in stone—Lucien confirmed that an eight-man team made the night jump into Tonkin. Lucien showed us a copy of the team's manifest, including code-signs. I believe Grumpy is First Grenadier Jensen's code-sign."

"Lucien's a rousting, hard-shelled bastard." Now Uncle turned from the chart table, about to continue, he was distracted by a lost thought. After hesitating for the merest second, he shouted, "Lucien gutters like a whore's streetlamp—aiming off his targets. He's a liar."

As the agents reached the cabin door, Uncle burst from his chair, tossing papers into the air. "That team's been bush-ranging for weeks. At least one lad's unemployed. You're holding a copy of the jump manifest, and all you soft sods can do is prose on about bloody dwarfs."

Uncle alerted as the mission briefing data he remembered from Candle Creek marched about the cabin, and his mouth outran his reason. "Seven seas, seven dwarfs, seven deadly sins..."

He stopped shouting to light a cigarette and draw his Webley pistol from under the radio mount. "Hold on. What's that again? When did you nob-heads talk to Lucien?"

Needles of doubt fostered empty words as the agents assumed a guarded stance, as if concentrating on the immediate—Corcoran's weapon. Their bullshit was clear: a wireless signal made from Tonkin through multiple radio relays, could take days to reach the Andaman Sea, and Uncle's signals mate had been monitoring the three mission frequencies twenty-four hours a day and had received no transmissions from Tonkin.

Dismissing the observation, Uncle eased his silenced Welrod pistol from a holster mount under a recess in the transceiver's console. Fingering the odd-looking trigger, he sat and laid the weapon on his thigh aimed at Pucker's balls. Obviously recognizing the silenced weapon, known throughout British Intelligence as a Special Intelligence Service priority issue, Pucker became as civil as fresh nickers.

Uncle smiled. "This Welrod has a silencer. Seventy-three decibels. Not much louder than a docker's fart. Sanitized. Fluorescent paint on its sight. With a round that will blow your cock out through your arsehole. My cousin's an SIS engineer named Major Reeves. He designed the weapon at Station IX, north of London in the town of Welwyn Garden City in Hertfordshire. It's blokes like me who fancy a good toy."

Uncle adjusted his weight to confront the twits, allowing them to gauge their predicament. Clearing his throat with a hacking grunt, he laid his Webley MK4 revolver on the radio mount near his left hand.

With a pistol at the ready for each hand, he jabbed the agents. "Talk now or have a piss."

Mutt turned crimson. Pucker shook his head. "We met Lucien some weeks back—in Hong Kong, before being dispatched to Singapore."

"You lying, sodding rat bag..." Uncle took hold of the Webley, tipped the barrel up and pulled the hammer back. Then he slowly pushed smoke out the corner of his mouth. "You're cutouts! Blinds for some mahogany shit-pile festering in Mother's crotch."

Uncle had done business on Hong Kong's waterfront for many years, exchanging intelligence information with the local triad. Lucien had stolen money from a Chinese triad in Macau. Lucien's death was a certainty if the triad caught him anywhere near Hong Kong. Uncle chose a bar-keep's patience to buy time and slid the Welrod into its holster.

"At the end of the day, Grumpy's exposed. In full fig. Rather like a turd served cold on fine china. Grumpy could be one of five lads. But if it spots your ball, he can be one of seven or eight lads—makes no odds to me."

The agents looked askance, a bubble off plumb. Given the circumstance, they had to agree. They counted fifteen salty men in the steam ship's crew— sailors savoring a variety of retributions. Men shackled to buggering the Crown, or any of Mother's pimps.

Captain Baxter Corcoran was a fan of Linc Jensen. He had won a good deal of money betting on the young man's football team. The strapping, curly haired lad from Wolverhampton, the All-England football player, could run for days without rest. During the South Coast Derby—the FA Championship match held at Wembley Stadium last April—Jensen scored the only goal in the Wolverhampton Wanderers' 4-1 loss to the Portsmouth Pompey Football Club.

Soon after the '39 South Coast Derby, Parliament suspended football for the duration of the war. Linc and his brother Dirk joined the army the next day, requesting service with Special-Service Troop, drawn by the challenge of long-range penetration work.

Uncle did not know that if any member of Hardin's SOE team reached the tramp steamer, the MI9 agents had orders to neutralize the commandos, then double-out and deliver the pouch to 13 Rue du Four, Paris VI—post haste.

"You. You tall, boney dingo. Before you rack off, we're going to play a game of Two Up with these gold coins. If you lose, I shoot your twat friend here, and use his guts for gaiters."

The cabin fell into a crudely fashioned dance as the agents separated. Uncle waved the Webley about the cabin. "No worries, Abigail—Lucien cocks gallopers like you sods. That Frog's a clever bastard. Practices his knacks religiously. Why don't you two stop playing pussy and tell me what your mission is? Six, seven, eight lads, it's an odd question don't you think?"

Reading their eyes for signs of resignation, he continued. "If even one brave heart's left standing, that lad's buckled to a bee's ass." Uncle didn't want the agents to respond, so he leveled his Webley at Mutt's chest and picked up the radio's handset to transmit.

"Sit down, you bloody shit pile."

"Grumpy, this is Princess, over." Nothing…

"Grumpy, this is Princess, talk to me, cobber." Nothing…

Uncle stood into a brace, pointing at the farthest corner of the cabin with his weapon. "Set your hereditary arse on that locker and leave your paws out front." The agents strained through a palsied come-uppance; their expression ripe for a good flogging.

After the agents settled, Uncle finished his coffee and keyed the ship's intercom. "Molly, bring Olive Oil up here—and a bit of lashing for Mutt and Pucker."

Laughter roared through the ship's intercom touching Uncle's reason as Clive Mauldin, a WWI veteran of Flanders Field, hollered, "The brown wind had chips, did it?"

"Right away Molly. We're taking on a harbor pilot. Pretend we're busy."

Burma's tropical rain came in blistering sheets, rending the bunkering docks of Rangoon Harbor a nasty piece of work, soaking dockers in the gases of deliverance, offering harm to young manhood and slanging the rest. Men died without notice in Burma in 1939. Unmistakably Asian, the temper generated by the tail of the monsoon had ripened in the lassitude of the acrid, delta air.

Contract killings were routine this time of year. Anytime really.

Uncle filled his pipe, watching his chief engineer prod the agents with shortsighted views of the barrel of Molly's prize Model 1897 shotgun, fondly known as Olive Oil.

"Give the clock a tic, Molly. Then put these bush crickets down the gang." Uncle put on a dry shirt and stretched to work the kinks from his aging frame.

"Without their kits, Molly."

Clive Mauldin held his wind as he settled into Uncle's chair, sizing himself into a smug posture, then farting to register his station. Pleased with the report, Molly threw a key on the floor at Mutt's feet. As ankle chains formed a pile, Molly and Olive Oil found their sync. Working together for decades, Olive, with her 5-round tubular magazine, never one to whore on Pug Street, could aim and discharge herself.

I knew a woman like that once, he thought.

Molly extended the barrel of his friend into Pucker's face. "No worries, Captain. It'll take these branding-paddock bastards a lifetime to sort their cowberries."

"They don't know a ranker from a wog, Molly. Don't give 'em an inch."

Uncle had been beyond sanction long enough to know that the escape-and-evasion morons working for MI9 were his adversary—Hardin's enemy. Either Mother remained clip-cocked over the commando team, or she had become the team's sheepdog—the answer being subject to a notional prime minister.

And whose whore does Lucien fancy?

Certain his wireless was being monitored; Uncle suspected MI9 had planted a transceiver on the steamer. That pegged at least one crew member as a spy. Reluctant to use a land line or the wireless to contact Sir Nigel Stuart, his MI6 control for Snow White, he dispatched a runner, with five pair of nylons for trading stock, to find the old veteran.

Three hours later the runner returned with a case of whiskey, minus one bottle for the customs agent, and a negative report. Uncle sensed operation Snow White had too many alpha dogs. Uncle was smoking two cigarettes as he ran down the gang. Flipping his right-hand fag into the harbor, he moved swiftly along the front apron, dodging a sea of wharfies, pushcarts, and dock bulls, and registering the images cast on the oil-stained water.

Remaining on the quay, standing pressed against a go-down's wall to stay out of the traffic, he studied a lascar's blunt face, thinking, Stuart's late. Nigel's never late. Grinding his teeth, he searched the quay entry from the harbor strand. With dock bulls clogging the wharf, a man could be stabbed and sent into the harbor without care.

An hour, what's another hour when you're beached?

Suddenly men shouted. Uncle froze, then merged with a gang of laborers and wharfies, trying to isolate the threat and sort the din. Mutt and Pucker ran by.

Where are those bastards off to?

"G'day, Baxter." Uncle's cigarette slid from his lips. Only one man called him Baxter. "Nasty sort of carry-on for old sweats, I'd say." Stuart nudged his shoulder. "Snow White's picked up a bit of a wrinkle, I'm afraid—nothing to lose your wool over."

"Indeed, and Bob's your uncle. For Christ's sake, Nigel. Where have you been? I mean fair play. This operation's a bloody chunder. You better stop chasing that bloody slave trade and give this mission its due. Mother has her snouts squarely in my queue. One's a dwarf wallaby, and the other's a burrowing cockroach."

As Uncle talked, he was watching the agents scurry into a forest of bad plumbing along Rangoon's waterfront. If the bastards are off to a singing house, I can ditch them here in Rangoon. He grinned through a patched-up nicotine stain, blowing bluish rings of smoke into Stuart's face. Sorting, and mincing facts, Uncle continued to weigh Stuart's shifting sand, to weigh Stuart's loyalty. First off, did Stuart place a snout on board my steamer?

After a hard draw on his cigarette, Stuart flipped a fag into the harbor. "Have you lost any of your crew, Baxter?"

"Baxter, my ass. Those snouts are your bloody mates. I'd put a two-penny stamp on it."

Stuart looked askance and scanned the dock, then turned a hard hawk into Corcoran. This time he was not grinning. "Not much of a wager, Captain. Typical intel niners, I'd say. Right out of the Corinthia Hotel, London. Fledglings, really, dry-nursing old times."

How does Merlin here know Mother's agents work for MI9?

"Your intel niners met with Lucien. A mate of yours. They're stirring Team 7's soup, and so are you." Uncle's comment seemed to nudge his old mate.

Sir Nigel Stuart, Clive Mauldin's platoon leader in the spring of 1917 on Flanders Field, stopped talking when a dock bull crushed a wooden crate.

His expression turned to listening, tunneling. As if chiding himself, he offered Corcoran a small scrap of brown paper. "Here's the latest radio message, Captain. Burn it. Give my regards to Molly?"

Uncle put the message in his pocket without reading it. His anger raced into its natural refuge—a need for rum and a raucous brawl. "Snow White's down the pan. It's been a near-facer since the lads jumped off. Rough as bags, and Team 7's still bobbing about."

"Get hold of yourself, Captain. The operation's a piece of cake, really."

"I know at least one lad's left to muster. No matter how you add your sums, Nigel… I'm betting there's three more." All was quiet for a few seconds as Uncle glanced at his watch. "The sum I figure says this operation's a cock-up—a bloody cock-up."

"There's more than one man you say?"

"Go on, Nigel. Rack off and add your own sums."

Stuart registered Corcoran's disrespect. "I could do with a pint." As was his custom, he dismissed Corcoran with a hard-eyed nod, and stepped into a mural of dockhands and slipped past the broken crate.

Bending his head into the rain, weaving his way through the activity on the quay, Uncle mounted the steamer's gang on the run. He now knew Stuart was Hardin's enemy. He decided to throw lines and ditch Mother's weens.

"Keep a tight fit, Molly." Uncle locked the cabin door, sat on the corner of the chart table and surveyed his private cobbles. Flanked by the muted hum of generators, settling into the stale air and the cast of a dim red light, he opened the packet.

He set fire to a cigarette and to the corner of the short message: "Pay attention. Don't look in the mirror." Nigel and his snouts can have a piss, he thought. The message matched the signal sent by the Far East Combined Bureau from Singapore three days before. First the boys at FECB and now Stuart—ordering him to scuttle Hardin's team. The "mirror" was the rally point for Team 7, open water south of Ross Island in the Mergui Archipelago.

Mother will be on her knees tugging me off before I'll scuttle Hardin's team. If Stuart's the blighter directing Far East's end of this operation, why did he come to Rangoon to shovel a load of old cod. Answer. He's tying up loose ends. MI6 operatives. If it's an outlier like Lucien, the bastards mean to kill Hardin as well.

Pissed, Uncle slammed open the overhead locker and grabbed a bottle of rum. A seaman, a spy on his crew—a rat bag in need of a swim in the bow-wash and a bottle of new bubbles. The MI9 agents on board had received the same message Stuart passed to him on the quay.

Nodding, he smiled. The discovery was good oil.

Captain Baxter Corcoran and his crew were on their own. The Aussie decided to live up to his reputation as Uncle Dingo and deceive Sir Nigel Stuart at every turn.

That Stuart and the MI9 agents were working in concert literally left Uncle without a port. Reclining in his chair with his feet on the chart table, he lit a cigar, and drank his rum. He decided to chart a course for China Bay in Ceylon, and once clear of Rangoon's exit buoy, turn south and sail to Singapore.

* * *

Burma: Vicinity of Tavoy Point. 24 August 1939. 0540 Hours, GMT + 6.5 Hours.

Dawn broke hot and calm. Hardin watched the clouds lift above the palms. Quiet—the presence of old women made the village seem empty.

Hours of rain left the huts stained a sodden tan. Sunlight cooked steam from the jungle floor. Listening to the ambient sounds he could hear thatch drying with a subtle flutter. Life can be simple, I guess. Rather like unground corn. Welcoming the fit of clean socks and the remnants of his stiff, dry boots, he dropped his pants and sat at the edge of the veranda to let the sun warm his balls and dry the skin around his leg wound.

The trough-shape crease across his thigh had grown a thin protective hide from the inside out. Tender and easily ruptured, this membrane had to be covered with a dressing for it to thicken. Examining the pulpy flesh bordering the wound, Hardin doused the trough with sulfa powder and waited for the sun to have its way. The swelling had not gone down. If he had to run, the inner hide of his wound would split open, and blood would flow.

For days now, an older woman with wrinkled hands had cleaned his wounds morning and night, covering them with a poultice that looked and smelled like rotten eggs.

His uniform pants had a two-ply, pale gray-blue silken patch stitched across the front of the right thigh. The map pocket on the left leg had been used to mend holes in the buttocks. The new-old pants the old man had given him didn't fit.

His uniform shirt had been torn into strips and placed on top of his bunk. A thin, muslin smock with long sleeves lay next to these rags.

Are they helping me? Or setting me up? Hardin knew the warm morning air, mixed with the surety of food, were deceptive friends.

The pouch sat on a stool near the front wall of the hut. Hardin ambled from the veranda and picked it up. "Seal or no seal, I should chuck this thing. Mother wouldn't know. Grumpy found it—he had his orders. I watched him cram it in my rucksack—insisting the pouch was filled with secrets critical to fighting the Japs."

Arguing with himself didn't help.

The quiet came again. After a moment, he opened his eyes. The things he thought about, lying in that cart with his feet bound, came to mind. Stories of the fens of Wales and the South Crofty tin mines of Cornwall. His mother darning by candlelight, her jelly-bag dripping its best.

Hardin yearned for his Katherine. He stitched her name into his heart at twilight, next to the prayer his mother recited with him at bedtime.

The memories were enduring. Katherine was in the bakery in Ashchurch with her blouse hanging open as she leaned over to cut his pastry. I want to be there again—to be in bed with her, turning up from down—is she safe? If she's alive she'll be hoping for her squaddie.

A cracking noise brought him searching the foliage that screened the village. Through an alley of scrub vegetation, a man with a carbine ducked into the bamboo north of his hut. For part of a moment, he waited for the man to reappear.

Tired of wondering about the game, he yelled. "All you right bastards do is muck about." Nine men with carbines sat in a circle up the beach—near a fishing boat. The nearest man pointed his weapon at Hardin and laughed. The others filtered into the jungle.

How many rounds do they carry with their carbines?

He squinted as sand spirals cast images of the team's ambush amongst the reeds. Dead men peered through the monsoon's charm in search of an unfulfilled promise. Hardin had enemies to kill and deaths to avenge. Life could be short and get even shorter if he delayed his escape.

Wind-worried and battered, he should have been tired. He hardly had time to lay about and no time for grief. With high tide gathering, he watched as a man with a carbine slung across his back appeared behind his hut.

Carefully maneuvering, he steadied himself on the veranda. In the sprawling scatter that cluttered his mind, he found one disconcerting scrap. The black-haired girl with her machete
was walking toward the hut.

Native girls in this region must have a brief blooming.

The girl placed a burned, wrapped leaf on the bamboo mat near his feet. Smiling through a complex mosaic, speaking through gestures of deliberate scrutiny, her offering brought relief and disgust. Eggs had been scrambled, mixed with a rice and cockroach paste, spiced with the fires of hell, and presented as a Javanese delicacy designed to load the body with protein. Akin to a rotting carcass, the smell made Hardin retch.

While he forced himself to eat, he measured the vagrant portions of the young girl's body. When she stopped moving and accepted his gaze, her face creased into a cautious calm. As if pleased with the stranger's recognition, her eyes flashed with a certain spark. She bounded off the veranda, around the corner of the hut, her athletic frame the picture of ease.

She's a mystery.

With the white caps outside the lagoon fighting for space, he ate with his left hand and examined the Hart MK1 submachine gun with the other. The Hart MK1 SMG was England's special-issue weapon for paratroopers. Still in the testing stage, the weapon was designed by Harold Turpin at the Philips Radio Works in Perivale, Middlesex.

"The old man and Lucien. All this rum lot are packing French Thompsons." The Hart's 32-round ammunition boxes and 9x19mm cartridges had been cleaned and oiled. "At this go, it makes no odds. My MK1's meant for short-range, heavy fighting. Same as the Thompson."

Hardin's kit lay in a sprawl on the floor of the hut. As promised, the old man had kept the French currency and the French language books. Hardin inventoried his equipment, three quarter-pound, reddish brown packets of Nobel's Explosive No. 808, six blasting caps, a battery, ten meters of trip wire, four grenades, eight new rations, Salvarsan ointment, and a small tin box containing three Monoject ampoule syringes of morphine.

"No *L* pill."

How am I going to haul this shit on a bum leg?

Tacking this close to the wind, the mere thought of running for days brought dread. The answer was obvious; he needed to find a place to hide after he escaped and lay up. Curious, he picked up a small tin that had been added to his gear. It contained a fresh packet of British made M&B 693 sulfa powder.

Why would this remote village have sulfa powder? He scanned the empty doorway of an adjacent hut. And where are the chickens? Ignoring the silence, Hardin turned his attention to the leather pouch.

Branded with a seal known in diplomatic circles the world over, a five-petal rose incised in lead and coated with red wax, the leather pouch sat perched on a bamboo stool leaning against three quarter-pound tubes of Nobel's Explosive No. 808.

Are the secrets in this pouch reason enough to be killing special-service troops?

With what's left of my uniform, nobody will know I'm an officer? If I become a prisoner, my kit and this pouch will be sold to the highest bidder.

The members of SOE Force 136, Group B, Team 7 had been drawn from various British military units, and assembled for the first-time near Camp Z, in New South Wales. None of their wives, friends, or relatives knew where they had gone.

The only record of the team that Hardin had seen was their parachute manifest, and that listing had the code-signs of eight commandos. No proper names or ranks.

Who the bloody hell is Gordon Dewar? All of Sinclair's intel group know the Special Operations Executive is not included on Whitehall's War Establishment listing. For me and my mates, for Team 7, SOE doesn't exist. We're expendable. They can erase our paper trail.

Hardin assembled his gear, shouldered his rucksack, and walked across the interior of the hut. Escape would not be easy. Worried, he picked up his weapon and ammunition and walked to his bunk. Dropping his gear on the floor he picked up the pouch.

MI6 must have an operational file. The admiral wouldn't bugger us. If the admiral knows we're here, others besides Dewar know we're here. There might be a spy in London who means to eliminate Admiral Sinclair.

Hardin replayed his meeting with Lucien in Haiphong. The Frenchman had described huge profits from the rubber and drug franchises operating from Hong Kong, Malaya, and Singapore, on to Malta and Marseille. Put off by such doings being run out of a basement in Whitehall, Lucien had claimed that a spy in Mother's house was getting rich.

Lucien had scoffed at Hardin's loyalty, saying, "Loyalty's not on—it's the Windsors' game. There's a new Round Table: solicitors and bankers. You're nothing but dry paint, mon ami."

Lucien's sarcasm could linger in any weather.

As Hardin doused the cockroach spice with rainwater, the black-haired girl appeared on the veranda from the brush of an onshore mist wearing a silk sarong. Hesitantly, Tu slipped inside the hut, glistening, erect with a mounting intensity.

Hardin dismissed her father's image, scratching at the layers of time, awakening his sense. Feeling his pulse skip into a polka, his weathered eye recorded the marvelous detail. A timid gust tightened her skin into a beautiful glow as orphaned drops of water rolled across her chest.

Her expectant sigh gave rise to complete supplication as Hardin moved to his right, allowing the light from the oil lamp to pass through her sarong, accenting her body. Her figure under the thin garment was lithe and eager.

It was months ago when Katherine went missing. Was she alive? No one seemed to know. With uncertainty came the guilt of her memory. He had not kept her from harm. And now, barely able to walk, he knew he may never see her again.

With an awkward, forgotten motion, he slid an arm around Tu's waist. The muscles in her neck and shoulders stiffened, then warmed into a tossing anticipation. She moved her hands frantically, her lust reverberating. Her body was in full bloom as she worked him into a frenzy.

Forcing him to respond, she lowered herself onto the bamboo mat. Drawn by her simple delight, his body exploded to the rhythm of an ancient art, to the applause of ancient pleasures.

Young and chasing, she held him tightly. Her breathing was audible, clamoring with an anxious pulsing. Her fingers were relentless: bursts of energy laying him aside. The coupling ached with a steaming sweetness, wet with the salts of consuming passion, devouring the smells, erupting again, lost to the realities beyond their demands.

She caressed Hardin as if leaving for the last time, lingering through a cascade of long black hair, the sheen of her body dancing with the sweats of sexual satisfaction. Her sarong hung at her shoulders. Water dripped from the hem. She stood with the sun backlighting her frame, a black cutout—naturally beautiful, easy with her passion, and dangerous.

You've played hob now. What would Katherine say?

*   *   *

Garmish, Germany. 24 August 1939. 1130 Hours, GMT + 1 Hour.

Samuel Eaton noticed the umbrellas dripping in the brass boot—a boot blazoned on its sides with the Nazi crest. A rank of men flanked the corridor leading to a set of double doors. Their greetings for Petra Laube-Heintz always clipped with veiled demands, dispensed with a mocked, scripted dialog—tangents spoken to burden the discernible with implied urgency.

A cold-looking man gripped Eaton's elbow as if measuring his worth. "You are here, Mister Eaton, because you are considered by my superiors to be one of the world's foremost arbitrage specialists. You should pray that this is true."

Immediately furious, Eaton forced the man out of his path. Then confronted Petra. "Is there a loyalty oath to be signed? Morality aside, are there religious precepts you Nazis fancy?"

"Your insults will be cataloged."

Petra became distant as she ushered Eaton into a darkened room, and to an isolated cubicle. Eaton leaned forward against a table and set a forefinger and thumb to the corners of his mouth. Pinching his lips, he felt his brow arch involuntarily. Worried, he shifted his weight to lessen the tension as the arena grew more confidential.

Emphatic whispers came with a muddle of arrivals.

A faint hue highlighted a series of partitions arranged in a staggered V. Eaton sat at the apex of the V, facing a black void that consumed the stage. A podium was flanked by large Swiss and Swedish flags. *Neutral countries.*

Nothing like New York boardrooms? This is handsome fantasy, he thought. A scuffle to his right was followed by a body hitting the floor. A body was being dragged from the room. As Eaton tracked the sound his escort placed a hand on his shoulder as if to caution his response.

During the balance of the day an Austrian outlined the purpose of the conference and the structure of a currency arbitrage play much larger than Eaton thought possible.

As he listened, he became nervous. He knew international money traders working in concert could generate tens of billions in profits. If these profits are concentrated, investment capital will race into markets that would otherwise be ignored. Or the expectation of profit will be used to create false markets anywhere in the world.

One banking house from five countries—America, Sweden, Switzerland, England, and Canada—and two from Germany were represented at the meeting, each by one man, each bank pledging funds in amounts unparalleled in history. Each banking house was expected to function as a hub for the other six banks, redirecting differential increments of currency and gold through algorithms at such intervals, and in such amounts, as to drive the effective interest rate on billions of dollars of industrial loans for the target companies to zero.

The plan is certainly extreme. Eaton thought. Banks being used to draw companies into a routine of exuberant borrowing until they are statistically overleveraged. Then Harrison, at the Federal Reserve Bank in New York, will raise the discount rate dramatically without warning when a moderate decline is expected. Once done, the banks will call notes, thus driving company stock prices down.

When stock prices fall to target levels, the bankers will raid the companies—buy fifty-one percent of a company's stock on the exchange and buy the balance of the stock with the company's own money.

There's nothing crueler than justified Christians... Jews.

Stunned, Eaton imagined being caught. Insider trading. He was knee-deep in a dangerous scam—currency arbitrage designed to take over the industrial giants of the Nazi state. Another hour passed with strangers describing the mechanics of the scheme.

Clever. Too clever. Too many paper trails. This bullshit will get people killed. Will any trader live to see the end of this deal? Hitler is cunning. He'll catch on. When he does, every one of the conspirators will be hunted down and executed.

Bankers and Industrialists.

As he watched, the room grew heavy, as though burdened by centuries of intrigue, as if the cormorant's lust for money had ruptured into a loathing of lesser men—a brutally final solution. Anticipation in the room gradually turned from shock to a cautious murmur.

A sudden clamor in the cubicle to his right brought Eaton to his feet. A man's breathing had stopped, and accelerated into a heaving, followed by the shuffling of hard-soled shoes and the sound of another body hitting the floor. Except for an open-door allowing light to play across the ceiling, the room remained dark. Again, Eaton's escort gripped his shoulder.

For Eaton, reality always came late in the day. Cinching his right hand, he tried to work out a cramp. As he did so, Eaton's pulse rose to a fibrous beat.

This must be a bad dream, he thought. Ensuring his expression registered blank, he waited for a light to come on. Not knowing what his options were, Eaton decided to call New York and ask for guidance. The facts of life—sex and the compounding cost of capital. To stay within an ace, time will cost money—it always costs money.

Before the Grand Duchy of Hessen-Kessel financed the Second Boer War or joined in formalizing the accelerating principles of compound interest, a man could hardly "spend time" or "waste time." But in this meeting, in this room, in this small Bavarian village, the transactions scheduled would circulate currency at velocities and margins unrecorded in history.

If the proposed currency transfers were well synchronized, the bankers servicing the industrial giants of the Third Reich, Keppler's circle of friends, would amass such large concentrations of cash as to guarantee their viability well beyond Hitler's dream.

The meeting fell into a cold silence. Eaton's throat tightened. The traders intended to leverage the wealth of Europe, collect the principal on industrial loans with confiscated company stocks, while the Hesse/Fugger banking empire processed the payments, manipulating the base price of gold in such a way as to generate their own fees.

Eaton nodded reluctantly. The arbitrage specialists summoned to Garmish, using new trading algorithms, were charged with generating sufficient margins at accelerating intervals to fund the stock raids plus their own brokerage fees.

Cyclical symmetry—free money.

Seven of the largest international banking houses, targeting Germany's industrial giants, planned to gain control of the wealth of Europe using the cultists of the Thule and the Aryan of the New German Order as scheduling tools.

The president of the United States had been announcing the daily spot-price of gold. Roosevelt's pattern of price adjustment had been analyzed and factored into the currency-trading algorithm by its author.

Samuel Eaton squinted, shouldering the weight of isolation. Enlisted by compulsion, fear pummeled his system. He stepped away from his chair. Breathing carefully to temper his asthma, his heart rate soared. A door at the front of the room opened bringing an ocean of light. Nazi soldiers stood at the four exits.

A silhouette appeared on a fabric screen, then turned facing Eaton, tunneling at his memory. This was not a man he could forget. Eaton's throat filled with a silent scream. Damn! I thought he was dead. What in hell am I doing here? Did the jackass next to me just die. The man who crashed to the floor. Might be stage-play. A ruse calculated to intimidate the rest of us.

Eaton wanted to run. Only once had he been this frightened. He was ten when a neighborhood shop keeper was shot in front of him. This arbitrage scheme, the opportunity of what could be a short lifetime, would force him to find a way to hide his fees.

His escort began massaging his shoulders, her hands hard and firm. Sighing with a whispered comment, "Relax, Mr. Eaton, and listen." Balanced, as if coated with the ease of being a lifelong friend, her voice had softened. A door behind him closed.

Cloaked in obscurity, the silhouette on the fabric screen cleared his throat. "You will establish control accounts, one for each of the other six banking houses." Eaton remembered the man's voice, even muted by the fantasy. Austrian—one of Europe's well-connected money men. A gaunt man, pre-middle age. Allen Dulles had claimed the man was killed in an automobile accident near Frankfurt.

Dead men and gold, Eaton thought. This is a dangerous game.

There was no morality in this deal. Eaton's membership in this club, in life, would expire if he betrayed anyone in this room, including his Nazi escort.

He met the Austrian in passing while negotiating a series of debentures last spring near Essen, in Germany.

I'll bet that's why I was drafted for this scam.

The Austrian continued. "You will establish subordinate accounts within each control account: one for each of seven companies—forty-two accounts."

You've screwed yourself this time, Sam. Trapped. Eaton knew he was trapped.

"Your brokerage fees will be paid in gold with weekly deposits made in Geneva at Credit Suisse. You can expect fees in excess of eight million pounds."

"Or die running," Eaton whispered. "That's more likely."

Impatient shuffling sounds at the front of the room led to the unlatching of a heavy door and a rush of cool air. Again, light poured into the room. Realizing the meeting had ended, Eaton rubbed his brow and surveyed the room.

As the cool air swept the room, dust motes rose in swirls above the desk lamps.

The seven arbitrage specialists had been sequestered in a cubicle, with a female attendant. Guards in greatcoats stood at the rear exit. Eaton listened for a familiar voice, for an accomplice, for anyone to share his fear. The woman's touch was electric, frightening. Her hands were beautiful—the creamy white of Bavarian and southern Germanic women.

With no apparent emotion, Eaton's escort took his arm. "Here's your account number at Credit Suisse. Memorize it. I will show you to your quarters." Pausing, looking at her watch, she slipped her hand behind his arm. "In three minutes and twenty-one seconds." The allure of her voice drew Eaton to his toes. Her touch sent his traps into an expectant rush as he scanned the outline of her body.

Why the exact time?

Eaton glanced at the calendar in his valise. He was scheduled on a flight out of Frankfurt the next day. "I need to be on the first train out of Garmish in the morning, and a lift to the station."

"You will adhere to our schedule, Mr. Eaton." Petra Laube-Heintz led Eaton to a small suite overlooking the parking arena. "Do not leave this room, Mr. Eaton. I will come for you."

She smiled, just a little.

Faint sensual tremors stirred his mind. Chasing skirt was a year-round New York City sport. Could he absorb a dalliance with this gorgeous kraut? As he was shown to a room, he embraced the yearning, the infantile delight. I'm always wanting something.

The night had come with snow when she left, when the door to his suite latched, and Eaton measured his predicament. *What are my options? I can't hot-wire an automobile, there are Nazis everywhere. And it's snowing. Apart from this filly spending the night in my room, helping me show the flag for God and country, I'm on my own.*

Financial edicts, the staple of his moral sense, could not supplant the sexual mania Eaton had fancied through the years. The ensuing hours would bring the vagaries that usually stole in upon his mind, chinks hewed out of his honor.

*   *   *

London. Simpson's-on-the-Strand, 100 The Strand. 24 August 1939. 2020 Hours, GMT.

Wind and rain with a predictable chill, what else could there be? At least London's fog has cleared off. Even the smells of Alexandria will be a welcome change. That's until the heat steams the olio into my linen.

Lewis Poston, Sir John's oldest son, an account executive for British Petroleum, preferred the sirloins of beef to the saddles of mutton offered by the 'God of the Fatted Plenty' at Simpson's on the Strand. Stepping from the hansom cab, he smiled at the familiar entry.

The white marble arch, topped with a chessboard and its opposing pieces, welcomed him into a dining room like none other he could remember—dark oak wall paneling with white coffered ceiling sectionals dressed in shades of gold velvet.

Even though Johnny's frazzling was often tiresome, Lewis welcomed the opportunity to dine with his younger brother. Blessed with a trace of wealth's gilding and a crop of richly colored hair, Lewis projected a quiet air of proficiency devoid of arrogance.

A roughly handsome, muscular, soft-spoken sort of man, he viewed circumstance to be as broad as it was long. This religious indifference left his daily routine in an incessant scrum, spiced with an occasional bit of luck. He classified good fortune as imaginary.

He judged jealousy the trademark of a corrupt mindset.

Months before, Lewis and his brother had been clandestinely rescued from financial disaster by one of their father's school chums working at the Bank of England. Investment capital for the rescue had been routed through Durban, South Africa, and Antwerp, Belgium. The resulting arrangement bore the trappings of a friendly foreclosure, leaving Poston and Sons, Ltd., tethered to an investor with stodgy, mysterious, parchment-like qualities.

Before he was murdered, Sir John Poston had assembled shipping assets, transporting goods between Durbin and Rotterdam—these and the eight hundred pound note he planned to pay off by selling his Durbin properties. The company owned dozens of go-downs and lighters spread from Antwerp, to Rotterdam, to London. Sir John was an old horse. A hard-edged rasher, he could read the rhythm of war's economies of scale.

With millions of pounds to be made or stolen and buncoing opportunities for ghillies to game, Sir John had given his sons cautionary advice: "Let the war find its way, then ring as many bells as you are able."

Sir John, stabbed in January 1939, died in a dense fog on a London wharf while inspecting a load of machine parts stenciled for shipment to Bayonne, France. Functionaries in British Intelligence ignored the queries from the family, not caring to foster baggage that could sniff on for years. Sir John's death, charged to the devil-we-know, found a home in the misconduct of a time rife with passport discrepancies.

For months after his father's death, Lewis had searched for a name plate to aim his disgust and loathing. Gradually he embraced the passions of revenge, hoping he could sort out his target, hoping his traitorous hatreds were soluble in time.

Lewis sighed, savoring the roasted beef and horseradish, thinking, *something is amiss.* Curious, he settled his shoulders near his brother. "You've a face like a sea boot, Johnny. That mortal slouch of yours needs a lift."

With frankness that was deliberate and premeditated, Johnny declared, "Dewar's a spy!"

"More of your feverish sweat, I suppose." Carefully measuring a piece of roast and scooping enough horseradish sauce to clear his sinuses for a week, Lewis used his napkin to dry his eyes.

"I'm spot on with this one, Lewis—C agrees with me."

"Parliament has been recalled, army reservists have been activated, civil defense forces have been put on alert, and you're dicing a bloody spy."

Lewis let his thoughts riffle through the record of Dewar's past. Considering that Admiral Hugh Sinclair, the chief of the Special Intelligence Service, agreed with Johnny troubled the sensibilities.

Johnny continued. "The SIS is Churchill's earpiece designed for highly irregular operations, all sanctioned by Whitehall."

After several bites of roast, not wanting to inspire any sparkling conversation, Lewis led his conclusion by pointing with the back of his fork. "You've gone daft, Johnny. Sinclair purchased Bletchley Park with his own money in the spring of '38 to be an intelligence station. Away from Whitehall. The admiral doesn't trust the first lord."

"I'm on the mark this time. I've found a self-similar system of time—a purposeful chaos generated by Dewar's movements. I'm certain he's been facing eastward for years."

Lewis warned his younger brother with an extended look of exasperation and again with the back of his fork. "You've a flat battery. Dewar's war record is better than all of the other intel ratings from the last lot."

"When you stop sharpening that mockery, Lewis, you might have a go at listening."

Johnny's posture got shirty. Lewis erupted. "Don't pick at his strings, Johnny. Dewar has always been a nasty bastard."

"Sequence governs his treachery, Lewis. He leaves London for France on calendar days, five, eight, thirteen, or twenty-one of any given month. Each trip lasts three days."

"Dammit. That's torn it. That jellied old bugger hasn't the salt for close country. Sir John soaked his powder in the summer of '38 when he refused a posting to the Suez."

"Let me resurrect the last episode of the life of Sir John Poston. Our father lost his life in January of '39—murdered, I believe—on the night of 21 January. Dewar was in France."

As though confused, Lewis sat brooding. Wanting to prompt a flaw in Johnny's logic, he dismissed his brother with a slight nod. That historic forces had the capacity to corrupt was absolute. Did Dewar murder their father because of something Sir John had discovered?

"Damnit Lewis. Periodic five-fold symmetry does not occur in nature. It must be constructed—constructed for a reason—to create opportunity from the chaos."

Dismissing Johnny's logic, he ginned up a flicker of humor, charting a woman's passage out the door. "Keep your resolves, Johnny."

Lewis's brow arched into a cautious expression, faking the appearance of concern. In time, he echoed a familiar response. "You do have a natural appetite, Johnny. I had hoped this meal would stem iteration's tide for one afternoon."

Lewis came erect, embracing a genuinely inspiring vision. He motioned his brother to look at a splendid pair of bouncers marching hard heel down the line, playing "loose buttons on parade." His portside stoppings throbbed with delight.

"In spite of what the clerisy may say, in every way that matters, with that woman, even if a friend put me up to it, I'd be joyously smothered." Lewis remained standing for a lasting look.

The brothers sat without speaking, absently examining the guests milling about the foyer.

Lewis leaned into his brother's ear and spoke softly, measuring the mood of the neighboring table. "Unlicensed blighters are sailing our steamers on routes we have no logs for." Silent, Johnny seemed to distill the news into a sharp round. "I've confirmed that our steamers have been fitted with the latest classified wireless transceivers—the Hallicrafter-HT series. The response to my inquiries has laid the expense to the war."

Silent for several minutes, for Johnny the answer was obvious. Dewar was a spy. Shaking out a derivative, he said, "Cloaked in the deepest obscurity, there's a kernel to every scheme."

Lewis unfolded a letter and sent the waiter for a whiskey. Then he presented Johnny with Poston and Sons, Ltd.'s eight hundred-thousand-pound note drawn on the Bank of England by their father, stamped paid in full.

Pointing at the document, Lewis put in, "And, tomorrow is a summer bank holiday."

"Not for Scotland." Johnny spoke with an air of astonishment. "This could be the kernel. It will be if we don't deal with whomever holds the note on Poston and Sons?" The brothers' eyes met briefly, blooming—a collusive gesture cascading into mutual apprehension.

"We've lost the shield of our father's school chums."

"On top the payoff seems proper enough. A syndicate headquartered in Colombo, Ceylon invested on the advice of a chap named Schiff, operating through a solicitor in Geneva and an export-import bank in Singapore."

Johnny put in: "Schiff. A well-known German Jew. Old and honest bankers. As a group, they are a calculating lot. We might have to learn how to be an ugly child and wait for the scheme's second iteration."

"Right, let's look at what we've got. We're nose deep in profits, odd cargoes, expensive old men, and few answers. We're coupled to the upside of a money pump."

"We've been through all that."

Johnny's expression mirrored a mental process of frazzling data, isolating anomalies, forcing countless combinations through probable scenarios until patterns emerged from the backcloth, and common elements became obvious.

Johnny stalks at a diligent pace when he's dampening the chaos, Lewis thought. Even if the variation in an expectation is because of chance alone, the outcome may be far from random, far from normal, and far from probable.

"Dewar arranged the note purchase to add a bit of old-world quaintness," Johnny declared.

"Bollocks. You don't know what you're banging on about." Lewis sat back, folded his arms, and set his eye to a distant focus. His father's office came to life: bustling and energetic. The warmth of this memory receded into resignation.

Johnny put in first: "And so, brother mine. Do we gin up money in a rush? Sell a property and buy the note?"

*　　*　　*

Diamond Harbor, India. 25 August 1939. 1050 Hours, GMT + 5.5 Hours.

Morning found von Cleve angry, reading a piece in the colonies section of the *Illustrated London News.* It read like a novel. The Dutchman's head had been split; his entrails cast over his right shoulder—an odd ritual for Burma. Leenstra, von Cleve's cousin, lay rotting in a monsoon weary jungle.

Leenstra was family.

Warders and sentries, with eyes keen and shoulders firm, stalked the quay's apron, in and out of the go-downs, relentlessly guarding their charge. Black and silent, they worked in a Dutch enclave, for a dangerous man.

Alex von Cleve stood inches over six feet, with ebony hair and a square jaw that topped shoulders wide enough to fill the door of a loading bay. A broker, he traveled the world constantly: weapons, food, hemp, opium, gold—any transaction that paid a fee. Only the substantial qualified—the Bank of England, the Institute for Religious Works, M. M. Warburg Co., J. H. Stein Bank, Royal Dutch Shell, Sun Alliance Assurance Co., et al.

Ruthlessly cunning, von Cleve brokered death. The upper chambers of the banking houses of Europe and Asia knew he was treacherous, complicated, and illogical; contracts with this artifact were replete with skillful deceit, cultivated chaos... and were final.

Only when situational risks fell beyond the bounds of humanity would this noisome artifact of death's ancient trade be approached. A contract with this disciple of the Lady of Wisdom meant the banking house, corporation, or individual who initiated the agreement became inured to the constitutions of the least scrupulous and closed society on earth.

Any communication with von Cleve brought fear. Contracts negotiated with this assassin contained an unwritten warrant—your death is my choice. If you lied to Alex von Cleve, you died. This principle formed the core of his being. All else, including any unexplained lapse of time, relied on the vagaries of chaos, tied to an eight-pointed cross, to the apex of a pagan, to an asocial sense of assurance.

Born in the depths of malice, his contempt for men of lesser strength or timid will, fevered a killing rage. Skilled in intrigue and without scruples, he was wildly ambitious.

Aside from his current contracts, he was busy brokering the sale of privately held sums of Nazi gold for the Bank of England.

The Sikh, who killed a monk in von Cleve's go-down, had been a disciple of the Thule—a stupid, short-seeing man. Archers hobbled the Sikh, then suspended his carcass upside down on a wall at the far end of an abandoned go-down. As one, archers screamed a perfect scream when von Cleve threw the giant's turban into the harbor and then emptied his torso to retrieve their arrows. All while calmly explaining the fellowship of brotherhood.

This Sikh killed a simple man who came in peace. Von Cleve had not been sure, and still was not sure if the monk's killing had been expected.

Out in the harbor a ship sounded its departure.

Now, savoring a rich Brazilian coffee and a morning without rain, frowning curiously, he watched two pear-shaped men be surrounded by his archers outside the go-down. Ignoring them as they edged around a mountain of jute bales, a needling apprehension caused von Cleve to get to his feet. Too fat for their suit jackets, breathing with difficulty, and awkwardly changing direction to avoid the jute bales, they balanced their way through the maze.

Announced as solicitors representing the Vatican., escorted to a cubicle near the far wall of the go-down, a situate fewer than twenty meters from von Cleve's armory, a thin smile traced the assassin's face.

The blade of a black-handled sickle showed purples and reds, its tip driven into a spar above a table made from well-worn shipping crates. Von Cleve stood near the spar waiting for the men to select their seat. He looked at his gold and rather rare watch, and then demanded additional fees, his custom anytime a client questioned his work.

Setting their valises at the side of their chair, reaching as one for their chair, they leaped as one, stumbling into bales of jute, pointing their horror, suddenly realizing the tabletop was awash in the sweetness of fresh blood.

Silent, stoic, von Cleve mused at his visitor's newfound reality.

Just as they came free of the jute bales, the strangers seemed, for a time, to be frozen in space. When the moment lapsed, von Cleve's eyes held on the fattest man as he extended a hand, insisting his guest sit down.

The man was sweating profusely.

Rolling conduits of heat swept through the go-down. Abruptly, without waiting for the fat man to sit, von Cleve counted his sentinels. Why is one of my nine archers missing?

The heat mixed with an olio of smells. The residue from old cargoes of copra, tea, sago, and nutmeg made breathing an audible delight. Placing a crystal vase of orange-yellow flowers from the chompaco tree into the sea of blood, he drew at the aroma and laughed.

Now finally, he could go to work. Von Cleve's humor came alive whenever he made institutional gallopers nervous. Solicitors have such weak egos. They're wired to an oak-paneled certitude, gazing through centuries of solicitous law—never at odds with a transaction.

His visitors represented the Vatican. They carried British passports. He examined their letter of introduction, signed by the Deputy Consul of the British Legation in Stockholm, confirming they worked for British Petroleum, listing their headquarters as Ankara, Turkey.

Von Cleve held three contracts—three separate requests for the same assignment, each with a tailored outcome. The first request had come from Stockholm, channeled through the Thule Society and Rudolf Hess. The second request had come from Paris, channeled through Compensation Brokers, Ltd., and Max Warburg. The third request had come from Rome, channeled through the Vatican's Secretariat of State, the Prefecture for Extraordinary Affairs, through an East India Company and a bishop with no name.

Linking the three groups were ladders of clandestine functionaries detailed to bridge the communication gaps. Simple contracts: eliminate an SOE team operating in Burma and retrieve a sealed pouch. All three employers had deposited the required fee—one million pounds in gold at Enskilda Bank in Stockholm.

Von Cleve had traveled to Bangkok, Thailand, and hired Cambodian mercenaries from the Cao Dai Society, an ancient crime syndicate operating throughout Southeast Asia. As a backup, he hired a freelance ensemble of old comrades—French, German, and Dutch mercenaries operating out of Bayonne in southern France, led by a French American—Lucien. Leenstra, the Dutchman, was von Cleve's cousin. Steiner, the German, was Lucien's counterweight.

Sizing up his guests, focusing on the fat man with the nasty scar, von Cleve spoke with a rapid, harsh rhythm. "The Vatican is my employer. You are their agents." He searched the go-down as he poured iced tea. The hair on the back of his neck prickled.

"We expect positive returns from our investments." The fat solicitor had spittle at the upturned corner of his mouth.

Von Cleve parsed the words. He hated fat people. They were unnecessary. Curious, he tried to correlate the message from his control in Calcutta, its timing, and the need to meet these men. He surveyed the rice storage activity in the warehouse as was his habit and realized a fifth archer was missing.

"I know people like you can be useful in certain situations. And I suppose it's remotely feasible you would be willing to help. But agents like you don't make investments. You don't have any money. If you want to leave here alive, you will give me your word that you will deposit my additional fee tomorrow."

Who arranged this meeting?

The solicitors had been briefed by Max Warburg—if you lie to this man, you will never leave India. "We want assurance—collateral." Both men sat marinating in a predictable quandary. Von Cleve's words lugged an uncertain tone. Obviously frightened, sweat beads covered their faces. An ebbing silence gripped the go-down.

Von Cleve sipped the iced tea, watching their expressions grow more apprehensive. After they spent a few minutes, he smiled and brought a Beretta level with the tabletop. Raising his voice, he declared, "I will assure your death—now if you refuse, next week if you lie."

Iced tea is such a civil drink, von Cleve thought.

"We will pay the additional fee."

"One million pounds worth of gold."

"Yes, of course. Why are we being followed?"

Von Cleve seized his knife as robed attackers rushed through the loading bay carrying BSA Thompson submachine guns. He bolted forward, sending the table over the fat man's head. Warburg's agents jerked about, suspended in a fanciful pose, breaching, and then collapsing as the solids marked their black suit jackets with a jarring pattern of dust spurts.

Running and crawling, von Cleve propelled himself along the base of the wall as fragments of decking tore at his face. Automatic weapons fire burned his neck and tore at his clothing. Scrambling along a plank wall, he somersaulted over a row of bagged rice as a hammer hit his skull. Wounded, he fell to his knees. Who's the target?

Losing focus, exchanging words with images, von Cleve sank into a doorway. He wasn't angry. He resented being betrayed. His memory kept coming back to Ion Crilley. Von Cleve was sure Crilley wanted him sanctioned. Off the scent. Off the chase for the pouch. But why?

And yet it wasn't Crilley. The coppery skinned mercenaries reeked the distinctive rural smell of for-hire thugs from northern India.

Are they stealing my weapons?

Blurry figures rummaged in and out of von Cleve's armory. Again, a hard voice trailed off. Strange hands moved in a tatter, alerting, unsettling, tearing at the front of von Cleve's shirt. The soggy tang of the wharf was replaced by an antiseptic whirl as a rag passed over his face. With a sharp jab in his arm, the voices began to fade.

The euphoria was nearly as wonderful as opium.

"He'll live. Keep him quiet."

*   *   *

Innsbruck, Austria. 24 August 1939. 1450 Hours, GMT + 1 Hour.

Max Ilgner was far less benign than his studied manner allowed, his velvet tones modulated to emanate a pliable disposition, his words tailored to mask a calculus of hate. For Rudolf Hess, the meeting with Ilgner, was tarnished, here and there, with undercurrents of fear—the more so for being shocked. Yesterday he discovered a one-page document listing nineteen names of prominent Nazis, all scheduled for assassination.

Rudolf Hess was number eight on the list. A line had been drawn through his last name. Was there another Rudolf?

Having been invited to spend the weekend at the mountain retreat of Max Ilgner, head of NW 7, the espionage arm of I. G. Farben, International, for Hess anxiety came with the arrival of Max Warburg. The Jew had foreclosed on his father's property in Essen. Needing some air, Hess made his way to the terrace. After the train ride from Berlin his suit was soiled.

He sat listening to a clandestine briefing organized by Walter Schellenberg, head of the Council of Twelve, a group of industrialists who supported the ascendancy of Heinrich Himmler and the establishment of a New German Order. The statistics being presented, although worrisome, were known to the attendees.

As of August 1939, the operations of German-American I. G. Farben supplied ninety percent of the foreign exchange to Nazi Germany, ninety-five percent of the imports to Nazi Germany, and eighty-five percent of the military and commercial goods for Herman Goering's four-year plan to put Germany's military on a self-sufficient war footing by 1940.

Hess worshiped these international merchants and their bankers. He saw himself as a fellow conspirator and supported their end-game—the ascendancy of Himmler as the new German monarch. For this to happen, Germany needed an increasing influx of foreign capital to overthrow Hitler.

He studied the guest list, estimating the worth of each. Shaking his head, he shrugged with a heavy sigh. Ilgner's assassination document featured two of the individuals. Winthrop Aldrich of Chase Bank and Edsel Ford of Ford Motor Company.

The rest; Sosthenes Behn of Swedish Enskilda Bank; Gerhardt Westrick of ITT; Walter Teagle of Standard Oil; Charles Mitchell of National City Bank; Lewis Weis of Sterling Products; Axel Wenner-Gren of US Electrolux; Sven Wingquist of SKF, International; Kurt Baron von Schroder, director of J. H. Stein Bank; and Max Warburg of the Warburg Institute.

"I'll volunteer to shoot Max Warburg," he whispered.

Sven Wingquist of SKF International proposed a toast to Sosthenes Behn. He acknowledged the head of Sweden's Enskilda Bank. Raising his glass, he said, "Without the financial floor provided by Enskilda Bank, Balfors' munitions production, and SKF's ball- bearing production could not keep pace with Germany's military expansion."

Max Warburg, the head of German intelligence during World War I, proposed a toast.

"Hitler's removal of Dr. Hjalmar Schacht as president of the Reichsbank last January is a clear signal the corporal is unstable. Without the twelve billion marks Dr. Schacht created through a four percent instrument he called a ME-FO bill, none of the progress we enjoy today would have materialized."

Warburg followed the toast with a note of caution. "The Fuehrer was surprised by this new money and is not capable of using this prosperity for the general welfare of a greater Germany," Warburg continued. "Bank accounts have been established to ensure the ascendancy of Heinrich Himmler as chancellor of a new German monarchy. The first is a personal S account at J. H. Stein Bank in Cologne with a personal contribution of five million dollars from Princess Stefanie Hohenlohe. The second is the R account at Dresdnerbank in Berlin for sustaining Himmler's private army, the Gestapo.

"We expect contributions from George Jones at Standard Oil, Irene du Pont's Black Legion, Lammont du Pont's American Liberty League, Errol Flynn, the Duke of Windsor, the Duke of Hamilton, Lord Montagu Norman, J. P. Morgan, Hugo von Rosen, James Forestall, and many, many other notables around the world."

Hess didn't believe Warburg because the Jew had pulled his assets out of Germany and moved them in total to England.

Charles Mitchell, of National City Bank of New York, offered a boast. "We control the Federal Reserve Banks of America, all of them. We therefore control the discount rate, and by extension, we can factor Roosevelt's pattern of setting the spot price of gold into any future trades we consider.

"Having the Federal Reserve discount rate in our folio will ensure the timing set forth in the currency arbitrage algorithm will maximize our returns and keep us on track to raid the stock holdings of the target companies."

The industrial members of the Council of Twelve recognized the Warburgs and the Rothschilds as powerful banking groups, along with Schroder Bank—and the banking and investment decisions in Europe in the summer of 1939 were directly or indirectly tied to I. G. Farben, International; to Baron Eugene Rothschild, the French commercial attaché to Sweden; or to Enskilda Bank of Stockholm.

This could get complicated, Hess thought. Thanks to Warburg we have industrialists and bankers on a fence, tossing money to both sides of Himmler's ascendency. The bankers, especially Warburg, had better choose their poison. Ilgner will not tolerate duplicity. Any banker or industrialist who interferes with I. G. Farben will be hung in their own home—Ilgner would do it himself.

Hess left the meeting focusing on a tangent, a minor, more speculative opportunity. He wanted to explore using Ceylonese transport to import, silk, tin, rubber, and drugs from Indochina; pearls from Bangkok; and rubies and sapphires from Rangoon and Bombay, into Europe through Marseille.

* * *

Garmish, Germany. 24-25 August 1939. 1900 Hours, GMT + 1 Hour.

Eaton stood at the window of his room, looking into the courtyard. Heavy black Mercedes sedans sat idling, mixing exhaust clouds with flurries of snow. Men in greatcoats hesitated near the stone driveway arch, then proceeded carefully, carrying what looked like the body of a man.

Feet spread on the icy surface of the car park, they stopped behind the open boot of the lead Mercedes, nodded in agreement, and tossed the body into the boot.

The driver of the hearse waved a luger in the face of the pallbearers. Monitoring their dismissal, as if announcing himself, he fired two solids into the body and closed the boot. After a cursory scan of the courtyard, he bid the other drivers *adieu* touching the brim of his hat, sat behind the wheel and drove into the night.

With the gunshots came the stark realization; these Nazis will kill me someday. Worried, Eaton tried to put his escort out of his mind. Her eyes told a story, a soldier's story.

The night and the snow had consumed the village of Garmish. The wind howled, rushing, harassing shutters and trees. Chauffeurs as well. The pallor of the storm charged the valley boasting coils of lashing, pitiless sleet, and chinks of lighting.

Thunder crashed, rattling the windowpanes of the chateau. A window near Eaton burst from its latch. Wet to his waist, he took off his shirt. I could climb out of the window but where would I go? At least one Kraut likes shooting dead people. The lights throughout the grounds went out, then, one by one began to glow, regaining life.

Watching the courtyard, he found the Austrian—Nicholas, stepping into a sedan. His distinct profile—Austrian aristocracy, flashed briefly, noting the lightning, creating in Eaton a surge of recall, promoting renderings of meetings past.

Exasperation drew a wry grin as he started a three-way dialogue with his conscience and his memory. Earlier, during the arbitrage briefing, he recognized the man's voice. By reputation the man was a financial anomaly, moving money in amounts that made sovereigns cringe.

Petra Laube-Heintz, Eaton's escort, received an unexpected message from her handlers at Stein Bank. A secretary of Eaton's was scheduled to be terminated—in the morning—in New York. She unlocked Eaton's room. "Take off your clothes, Mr. Eaton. Your garments will be cleaned and pressed for your travels." In the spill of his athletic frame, she accepted his clothing, looking toward the window as if distracted.

"Do you require the services of a young woman or a young man, Mr. Eaton?" She seemed prepared for either answer.

Standing naked in the dimly lit room, remembering those nights in New York City, he spoke his lust. "Will you stay?" He was playing an impulse.

He felt her looking at him with new interest.

Taking her time, she remained silent, leaving the invitation in the weave of a manner-less void. As though weighing her decision, she traced a path from the window to the door. Eaton sensed a contradiction. First obscure, then elusive, her movements portrayed a history of well-rehearsed encounters.

She took her time getting to the door. Stopping in the doorway, she seemed resigned.

"I will send a young woman directly." The latch on the door echoed in the hallway.

Immediately Eaton switched off the headboard lamp and stepped behind the curtain at the left side of the window. Snow packed the cobblestones lining the courtyard. Men in black leather greatcoats and jackboots stood-to just beyond the vegetation, Schutzstaffel, their appearance made larger by the light passing through the snow-laden branches.

For Eaton, the driving snow disguised the haste of the special security force, their voices, but not their meaning. The sedan containing the Austrian crept toward the stone exit. If Eaton could identify the man as the author of the arbitrage plan, he could leverage his own arbitrage bets and stay alive to enjoy his commissions.

Minutes before 3:00AM Petra opened the door carrying Eaton's clean clothes. She reminded him of a large cat on the prowl. There was a sense of expectancy about her, as if she was waiting for a vibration, a gesture. In the darkness, Sam's profile shone on the lace curtains. *A dalliance with this Nazi can be reconciled after I return to New York.*

*   *   *

Rangoon Harbor, Burma. 26 August 1939. 1010 Hours, GMT + 6.5 Hours.

Rangoon's air was heavy with the heavy odors of another day. In all the war-time prosperity there lurked a sense of fatigue.

War had come to Burma. Jap prickers had penetrated its eastern provinces. Rangoon's salt storage go-downs had been confiscated, set aside—under guard, patrolled by the Royal Army's Rangoon Battalion at the request of the Chinese Nationalist Government. Desperate for transport facilities, the Chinese Nationalists had requisitioned the go-downs to store war material and ammunition. The first shipment from America was stacked on the wharf's front apron.

Tempers were short. Ship traffic had increased beyond the harbor's ability to control the inspection of imports or exports. Harbor pilots were in short supply. Docking procedures were routinely abbreviated. Sailing schedules were fluid. Manifests, passports, and liberty documents were all but ignored.

With this chaos came rumors of Japanese patrols in upper Burma.

Rangoon's harbormaster was an Irish drummer—a ruddy, truculent sod. A man with new boots, ideas, and ignorance. He was fiercely fond of his post. Robert 'Darkie' McPhee, the harbormaster, had the nasal tone of a hungry sow. As often as sobriety led to a reflective signpost, he presented the Catholic question to any Englishman he could give a flogging. With a temper up to ninety, and a paddock of lemony-red hair, at six-foot minus one, his protruding jaw and tin-money eyes had received more than an equal measure of abuse.

'Darkie' wasn't slow of thought. He bragged his notions. Looking in the mirror just never occurred to him. And so, when somewhat puzzled, he liked skipping over well-trod ground. A wiry, rugged figure in waterfront clothes, McPhee was by looks and habit, Shanty-Irish—a bay with a rough-grained sailor's face that wrinkled like dry leather.

Raised in the Irish quarter of London's Seven Dials district, he was never short of breath. Steeped in the convenience of vagrancy, 'Darkie' McPhee was weaned on lowly air in the slum leading to Buckingham Palace. One sundial short of a proper design, he was constantly changing his mind. A freebooter answering any challenge with a profane, tenor groan.

Initially McPhee had dismissed Captain Baxter Corcoran's request to throw lines eleven hours ahead of his scheduled sailing. But a sailing for an Indian steamer had been delayed, and McPhee wanted the gold coins the captain had spread out on his chart table. He needed the gold to pay a gambling chit held by Rangoon's master in chancery, a fat, vengeful buffoon careering away in Rangoon—the capital of British Lower Burma—Burma's celebrated muck-smeared sewer.

Of late, the master in chancery's fondness for games of chance had found solace in either the misconduct of gambling, or skewering McPhee's goolies.

McPhee opened a packet of black-market Egyptian cigarettes, manufactured by the Aden Tobacco Company. Fondling the gold coins, he glanced out his office window and doubled his take. Permitting himself a short burst of laughter, he shook a cigarette to his lips and hurriedly stashed the coins in a pouch under his shirt.

Spitting bits of tobacco, he whispered, "Tastes like bloody camel dung."

The chief magistrate—Rangoon's docket for the head copper, came plowing along the quay's apron, leaning into the wind. The old duffer looked perturbed to be hauling two stern-looking weans at his heel, pulling at his load with wine-flown fits of weaseled nonsense, signally encouraging their step.

Basking in the light of sobered reason, the chief magistrate burst into the cabin and started rummaging among McPhee's papers. "Robby, my boy, you've sharped these lads, letting that Portuguese flag off the quay ahead of schedule."

"Never have done. I'm a Cat-lic."

"Let's have the strait of it, Robby."

"Fetching bread for cog-wheels, are we now, Chief Magistrate?" McPhee peered a toss-off Irish peer. "There's little enough for a mick to do, I suppose."

"Now, now, Robby—let's have it straight. What do you have to say for yourself?"

The weans blossomed into full reach, as if winding their minds into a scram—slipping past the magistrate's words, their expressions anticipating a link between McPhee and Captain Corcoran. Chopped ends of words bounced between the two strangers.

Taking his time, McPhee groaned through a hack, squinting under his cap. He had a name for these agents. Annoyed, he replied evenly, "A natural occasion, I'd say—sailing ahead of a short sea." McPhee turned a shoulder into the chief magistrate and flipped through the day's log.

"Is it linen we're rolling, Inspector?"

Pucker, the taller agent, tightened into a muster. "British Intelligence Escape and Evasion, MI9. Where's that Portuguese flag heading?"

"Aye right. Never heard o'such."

McPhee leaned into the man's plum-colored face and furled a concerned brow. "Always been Singapore—City of the Lion and all that." McPhee lit another cigarette and drew a deep breath. "Now that 'The Wet' is over, Chief Magistrate, it's a feeling I have. Wondering why Mother's look-sticks are flogging the doings of a tramp steamer?"

McPhee, having made his point, nearly burst into a shout when the agents moved to opposite sides of the cabin, braced while blocking the exit doors, as though the word *always* had implied a familiarity beyond a brief encounter.

"Has Corcoran thrown lines in Rangoon before?" Mutt, the shorter agent, squawked.

Keeping an off eye on the chief magistrate, McPhee pointed at a passing barge. "Now who might Corcoran be?" he asked, his smile thick and mocked with guile.

"Leave it out, you rumpy dotard. You're already nose deep." The way some men are prone to skipping about, Mutt burst into a series of short steps, nodding as if a conclusion had his mind at half-speed and frowning because his foul sensibilities had his bowels rumbling.

'Darkie' McPhee threw the sailing schedule across the cabin. "Nose deep in Mother's end-o'quay bullshit. And it was a grand time it was we had."

The cabin air seasoned to a sarcastic soup, while McPhee carped his best curl. "It's a time of vigor it is. The rainy season's over. Is it a ceremony your blisters are starved for? That ship's never thrown a line in Rangoon. I gave the loopy bastard wide currency. The ship's captain set a bearing for China Bay, Ceylon."

Abruptly, ignoring the others, the chief magistrate bellowed. "Good show, Robby. Keep us posted." As though relieved, the pompous git threw open the cabin door, pushing at the agents with an expression of solemn haste. He knew 'Darkie' McPhee had practiced his implied slights for years and could torment the Pope with his tuneful grovel.

"I'll want the groundage port charge, Robby. Tonight."

'Darkie' danced, needing a rum ration. Turning suddenly, he bumped Pucker as the agent stepped toward the door, knocking him into a slop locker. Watching the three men muck down the stairs, McPhee grabbed the envelope that had fallen from the agent's pocket and found its way into a scupper at the base of the cabin wall.

A 1,000 pound 5%, one year note drawn on The Central Bank of India, LTD, Rangoon. And would Pucker be paying the Chief Magistrate a fee?

A ten-pound, Malayan Postal Order—A069056. On its back, a handwritten address—W.I. 13 Rue du Four, Paris. And would this be the post for Pucker's doss house?

* * *

Burma. 26 August 1939. 0730 Hours, GMT + 6.5 Hours.

There is never a gentle season in the jungle.

A hollow blue sky plunged into the sea, grappling with puffs of white cloud near the edge of the horizon. Tavoy Point, an eyebrow propped above the lash of a two-foot sea, was a continuum of dense, wet vegetation along the shore. Vines hung to the sand, fishing for critters. Warm, variable winds swept the sand, sending tiny dry shells scurrying. A gust brushed the trees.

Captain Edward Hardin accepted a weary smile, listening to the sago palm fronds fight for space. Yet, how often he thought of his love for Katherine. In the space he had cleared for her, in the course of a long search, he assumed she was not alive.

Or was he ashamed of his dalliance with Tu?

Circling back, he would stop, compose himself for Katherine's sake, and put the mockers on this patch of grief. Hardin glanced seaward again, tempted by the windy green chop, knowing the Bay of Bengal was more than a place. For Doc, team leader for Operation Snow White, the sea was an endless obstacle, now an integral part of his being.

Grabbing his kit and starting to slip into the bamboo, even as he shouldered his rucksack, four men with carbines appeared in front of his hut. He was in a spot and knew it. Knowing these natives were a notional lot, that they might shoot him if he tried to leave, he dropped his ruck.

Getting home will have to wait.

The leaves, large and small, inhaled, absorbing the morning heat. The tail of the monsoon had brought a rolling coda of violent gusts, brief downpours, and general chaos.

Today the sky's clear. The old man has been gone for days. With or without his daughter, I'm leaving tonight.

Dismissing his clogged spirits with a vigorous cock massage, rehearsing a fantasy about Tu, peering through clumps of bamboo, he searched the beach north of the village. Suddenly the women and children were running into the jungle. The men guarding his hut had vanished. Grabbing his Browning and kit, Hardin jumped from the veranda and nearly fell into the foliage.

The wound on the front of his leg burst open. Running, he crashed into the bamboo. Stumbling, he collapsed, catching his weight with the butt of his weapon, and rolling to his right. Pulling the Browning from the mud, he hobbled into a recess formed by adjoining clumps of bamboo. Sitting with his leg lying flat on the ground, he applied pressure to his leg wound to stop the bleeding.

The refuge was a danger, an island of bamboo with no escape route.

Hidden behind a fence of sedge grass he slid the barrel of his weapon through the vegetation forming a crease he could look through. Bandits began shouting and firing their carbines in the air. Separating the heavy grass blades with their stiff, yellow spines, Hardin braced. Sucking air through the corner of his mouth, he huddled farther into the grass.

Tu was running. She didn't have her machete.

She vaulted onto the veranda and scurried into the hut. Seconds later, she leaped from the veranda and pushed Hardin's used battle dressing into the mud with her foot. Slowly backing up, she came to a stop in the middle of the clearing, as if measuring her fate.

Cambodian bandits appeared through the breaks in foliage—eighteen all told. Hardin searched their faces. His eyes narrowed. "By God, those are the bastards who ambushed Team 7. That killed Grumpy and pissed in Sneezy's face."

With Tu surrounded, the bandits hollered and ripped off her sarong. Waving for the rest to hold her still, they screamed their vile intent, their breed's choice. Five men sacked Hardin's hut with a swelling sense of excitement.

They aren't looking for me. Where are the villagers?

Hardin spotted Tu's father at the edge of the far tree line near the beach. With his hands tied to the trunk of a palm tree, the old man has nothing to offer the bastards. So they'll just rape his daughter. Celebrating, the guerillas took their pleasure, beating and raping Tu, dragging her father around the tree, and forcing him to watch.

The Cambodes were extolling their cruelty.

Tu lay silent—her body limp and lifeless. Is dyin' that easy? Studying the situation frame by frame, Hardin set the front sight of his weapon on the center of mass of the man raping the girl, his finger vibrating on the trigger as he took up the slack.

They're too spread out. For seconds and minutes Hardin remained still. His face felt heavy. I can kill a couple before they take me out. But they'll just kill Tu and the rest.

Finished, the Cambodes joyously fired their weapons into the air, stomping Tu's sarong into the mud. Finished, they tossed their prize onto the veranda and left her sprawling—her body battered, her eyes opaque, consoling herself with pleas, crying a soft, cry.

Weeping, Tu watched as they beat her father. Three of the guerillas rode south on bicycles, the others ran along holding a vine tied around the old man's neck, nearly dragging him. When he fell, they threw the vine aside and left him belly down in the mud.

Grinding his teeth, Hardin waited. He wanted to make sure the bastards had left the area. Picking his way through the clumps of bamboo, he moved to Tu's side. Her father stood and started stumbling toward his daughter—his lips bloody and his eyes but swollen seams.

When the old man reached Tu's side, she lay crying. She extended a muddy hand to his cheek, and he began to moan. Watching the villagers filter back, Hardin went to a knee, set his ammunition next to his knee, and began scanning the outskirts of the village.

He turned his weapon toward the back of a hut, toward the sound of splashing feet in the mud. The Cambode who had ripped Tu's sarong off burst into the clearing. Smiling. Hardin fired one round from twenty meters and blew his head apart.

Bloody dumb shite!

Hardin rolled the nearly headless body over and dumped the man's rucksack on the ground. In a small leather sack, he found seven thumbs. "Well, Grumpy and our mates will be glad to know this bastard's been done and dusted."

The cadence of small arms fire erupted in the south. Down the beach. Sounds like two or three kinds of weapons, Hardin thought. A hundred meters away—ten, twelve minutes.

Eight locals with carbines filtered into the village from the north and were directed by the old man to firing positions on the south side of the village.

Assuming the Cambodes might backtrack, Hardin stepped into a clearing. Seeing Tu up close, he handed his weapon to the old man with a nod. He could not afford to be emotional, yet the girl had been the grip he needed to survive. She had saved his life, over and over—thrice, and now again, burying the used battle dressing.

She should have given me up—run into the jungle with the rest of the villagers.

"My God," he whispered, his attachment gaining depth. Tu's body lay bruised and swollen. With the new bandage on his leg wound soaked with blood, Hardin lifted her gently and turned toward the lagoon. Her father followed.

"I'll get you washed off."

Clearly in a bad way, Tu didn't respond.

Mindful of her wounds, Hardin coaxed her head to his shoulder. Lurching from step to step, seeking concealment, winding through a maze of knife-like leaves, he waded into the lagoon and found a pool tucked in the recess of two rock outcroppings. Tu seemed to welcome the water's cooling salts, sighing as pockets of warm, then cool water caressed her skin. Finding no open wounds on her extremities, Hardin washed her mud-filled abrasions.

As he carried her to the hut his chest grew tight. Shame filled his heart. Could he match her resolve? With the taste of hate in his mouth, he would find someone to kill.

Bits of candlelight marked the walls, brief glisters marking the time between wind and calm. Hardin laid Tu on a mat. An old woman urged him out of the hut as she covered Tu with a silk blanket. Hardin eased himself off the veranda and hobbled into the bamboo to secure his kit.

With his rucksack for a pillow, he fell asleep in seconds.

The old man kicked Hardin's boot and then gave him his weapon. "We wait to fight the Japanese. We have no ammunition to spare. With better weapons, we could kill these bandits."

Hardin opened the small leather sack and showed the old man the seven thumbs. "The Cambodes who raped Tu, are the bastards who slaughtered my mates. They count thumbs so they can get paid for the men they kill."

Several women attended Tu at intervals throughout the day. The afternoon heat steamed the mud, and time made mention of a soft twilight breeze. Mosquitoes swarmed through the canopy, badgered by an onshore breeze.

Composing himself, Hardin returned to the hut as the twilight mist turned to rain. Tu lay tucked in a ball, calmed by opium a peasant resolve. Except for a soughing vibration in her chest and her swollen cheeks, she appeared unbroken by the day's events—a better soldier than him.

Growing fond of his vengeful plans, the raping of Tu ate at Hardin worse than the slaughter of his mates and worse than Grumpy's tortured dying, his final sigh. Remembering her muffled screams, remembering the blade of her machete, wondering how she would butcher the next wog she caught alone, he decided to shoot anyone who tried to harm this young girl.

I'd rather be dead than bear witness again.

A hostile silence ran through the village. Anxious children mingled in doorways, staring, pushing their elders with insistent whispers. The few natives preparing food made the village seem more vacant than before. If the Cambodes were looking for him, they might layup outside the village and watch it after dark.

Hardin decided to leave at twilight when ground visibility in the jungle was limited. Favoring his thigh, he pulled Tu's sarong from the mud and rinsed it in the lagoon. A group of villagers with single-shot carbines stood north up the beach below the face of a rock escarpment. Another eight men with carbines had moved into a perimeter south of the village.

I'll bet Uncle has weapons he would give these people.

As he checked the jungle to the east, Hardin spotted a man with a carbine behind his hut. Am I worth guarding—worth money?

Captain Edward Hardin, code-name Doc, with a pouch in each hand, shook the dust-colored bag containing his mate's thumbs—his sanctuary for reflection. Everything is for sale.

* * *

Rangoon Harbor, Burma. 26 August 1939, 2340 Hours, GMT + 6.5 Hours.

What time was it? Was it the right time and the wrong place? Or was it the wrong time and the wrong place? Too drunk to sense the question, Rangoon's harbormaster, Robert 'Darkie' McPhee, could not keep pace with his own spraddle-legged stride.

Finally, it became so for McPhee. The premonitions were impatient, unruly at times, conjuring those sentinels posted by a legion of odd lights. He was an hour getting to the waterfront from his whoring. Menace possessed him again and again. For an instant he lay on his back staring upward. From time to time he stood up and moved a bit.

Rangoon's waterfront reeked with the charm of alarming insinuation, the hum of insects whispering as 'Darkie' weaved past the front of the Silver

Grill and stumbled into a burst of speed, dancing sideways through the tar-painted bollards quartering the quay.

Rain or shine, the insects liked to hum when 'Darkie' was steamin' drunk—mainly in his left ear, his cauliflower ear, the ear he liked to lean toward.

Colored diesel sheens, those strange moving shapes, ran spurting ahead of his feet. His thighs were heavy—gelatin-wobbling. Rum-soaked, his figure was athwart, stunted by opportunity's folly. Wet and careless, a dormitory corporal at his best, McPhee could give out and play a persistent melody of sloshing unrest.

The wind sang in and out of tune, playing the loose tiles along the quay.

The rain squalled. Banging the side of the go-down, the drops slapping his head caused 'Darkie' to stand erect and then fall into a scuttle of quick steps.

Sauntering now, in spurts, weaving the width of the apron, banking off a fender pile, a bitt and then a petrol drum, he settled into a wobbly gait—a victorious imitation of his boyhood parade. Full of whiskey and a good bit of rum, he was soaked with folly.

His prophecy—the world was as cunning as he imagined.

With the cast of the harbormaster's office perched in silhouette, he skipped his step and nearly fell. A battalion of boots were pounding on the quay, racing toward him. Focused for a second, chatting with an imaginary friend, he was the first to make up his mind. "Hide, Robby."

Blinking his eyes like a rooster to shield the rain, to clear the cobwebs, muttering in lugs, he swore blind. "Muster your bag, Robby."

The boot falls grew nearer. Alarmed and barely able to reason, he swung around a splintered fender pile and slid below the deck of the quay. Nearly falling into the harbor, he curled into a tight ball. Drunkenly he peered around the pile just above the quay's deck. Within the splashing sounds the British agents ran past, inches from his hands, drawing out with long strides.

Bloody bent coppers.

Sobering, waiting for the noise of their boots to wane, he crawled onto the apron. Kneeling on the slimy deck, he strained to see, to listen. Cold and wet, with fear at a gallop, his hands glistened with the sting of piling oils.

Seating himself against a fender pile, he waited. Nothing moved. The rain had hidden its squall. He stood and began to trudge. You'd best be on the trot, Robby, and nothing else at all.

McPhee spread his legs for balance, his wiry frame virtually immobile and his reason bobbing about in a back eddy. Gasping, coddling his balls, he blessed himself, skipping the words, and started for his office. Those spendable fuckers. The sods sacked my castle.

Bellowing at the night, hurling his words at the sky, chanting a dirge for man's fate, his stoke-hole erupted, spewing rum, fish, chips, and pubic hair into a fan. Frowning at the foul taste, he wiped his sleeve across his mouth. He stumbled and began choking and spitting chunks.

He could barely see the apron.

With his bowels rollicking from loose knit to knotting cramps, and his vision bound by a pair of palsied eyeballs, he started to scramble down the apron. As his vision fumbled with booze boogies, he stumbled, fighting a sleeting squall.

The concussion threw McPhee against the side of the go-down, blowing him to buggery, dumping his arse into a stack of empty crates and petrol drums. The explosion blew the sides of his office laterally in an eerie display. Pieces of the harbormaster's office fell in scripted arcs, joining the rain and then the squalor of Rangoon harbor.

Wood and glass shards rattled against the side of the go-down.

McPhee's mind, a frightful warehouse of textual misery, foraged for a sober thought. The concussion had hit his chest, lifted him into the air, and gushed over his carcass as if he were wind-driven seagull shit. Satisfied, the blast echoed down the canyon formed by the adjoining go-downs and shoved its way into the whorehouses along the waterfront, dressing the whole affair in high comedy.

Pontoons of debris swirled and lapped against the jagged pedestal that once supported the harbormaster's domain.

And so, after the explosion's echo, 'Darkie' McPhee laughed with fright, amused by the residual authority of his station. This bullshit has a certain beauty, it does. Dun-colored scraps of manifests, cargoes, and schedules are scattered across the water, swimming in all possible directions, controlling Rangoon's ship traffic.

With his perceptions floating light boned, stumbling on to matters of the Crown had put him in the frame—assuming the worst, the chief magistrate owned the flat where he lived.

Buggery shit. It's your legacy, 'Darkie'. Come here till I tell you it's a fine thing you've done. McPhee searched at his waist for his money belt and then counted Captain Corcoran's gold coins. Calculating the odds, he whispered, "It's tomorrow night I have to be out of Rangoon. Out of Burma."

By the next afternoon, after first crawl, he was so hung over his hair hurt. Dressed as if he had come down in the last shower, his mind so wobbly his eyes were blind stabbing single frames, looking in the mirror his face looked like it had been scrubbed with the rough end of a pineapple. His hands would not stop shaking. Mounting the stairs to enter the plane, he vomited over the handrail onto the tarmac, wiped his sleeve across his mouth, ginned up a bewildered expression, and tried to become a different person.

It could be worse. It's the scutters I could be having.

Flying out of Rangoon, sitting in one of Germany's newest aircraft, he tried to play with the gadgets—the cloth window sash and the levers on the fold-down typewriter mounted on the forward cabin wall were far too clever.

With an expression that begged McPhee's attention, an elderly woman seated across the aisle handed him a small green and gold tin cylinder—Tums for the Tummy, an advertisement for Horace Heidt radio. "Thank you."

To his mother, he made sure to say thank you. Watching clouds slipping past the window he ginned up a bit of self-control.

A sudden pang in his ears set him to tilting his head from side to side. Opening and closing his mouth, he tried to clear his ears—to equalize the pressure. The wind drag from the three 410 Kw 550hp Pratt & Whitney Hornet engines on the Junkers 52/3mce and the groan of the propellers had turned the passenger cabin into a throbbing, echoing tube.

Both his ears cleared with a painful squeal.

Now, sparring with his subconscious, he scribbled in his diary. After chronicling the destruction of his shop, he maintained that the chief magistrate owed him three hundred quid.

There was but one regret to flush down the pan. He missed Rosy, his live-in maid.

Eurasia Flight 93 to Singapore flew smack into remnants of the monsoon and diverted to the airport at Port Blair, on South Andaman Island. Rather than catching a flight to Singapore, McPhee shared a cab to the nearest pub and the nearest phone box.

"Hawkes, you blistering sod, McPhee here."

Recognizing the raspy voice Hawkes laughed. "Gum tree 'Darkie' McPhee—you drizzling, down-market, spot of shit. Have those brown birds been barking at your nib again?"

"Just so, Hawker. I've touched down in Port Blair—hurled into the bloody soup. Would you be pulling tits again?"

"Let's not dance about. What is it this time?" Hawkes liked McPhee because Paddy was the good, stupid kind he liked marching next to him. Always gummin for a pint, 'Darkie's criminal weakness is always good for a laugh.

"You'll not find jam on this egg, Hawker. Is your wireless up to scratch?"

"Dead as mutton, I'm afraid." Hawkes did not want to be seen with this Irish skiver. "Robby, you're the ropey turd. You're either in shackles at Hopetown, or you've fallen foul of the coppers, and they won't let you off the quay."

"Bugger off, Hawkes," McPhee shouted, recounting his acquittal. "The chief magistrate in Hopetown had me hands in darbies and me feet in chains until I agreed to arrange his whistle-bait whenever the gossamer turd found his foreskin inverted."

"Robby, you're about as thick as a ditch. If you don't want me to ring off, let go of your stem and give me a damn good reason. Start by giving me your post."

"There's gold afloat, bound for Singapore. I've popped into Ritchie's Pub. I'm into Mother's nickers, barney-mugging the old twat, and she isn't happy."

"Ritchie's, is it? Have a go at another pint, Robby. I'll only be a tic."

Hawkes rang off. On his desk, the usual work awaited; schedules to be memorized, cargoes primed for pilfering, smugglers to be paid. And now McPhee's excessive chatter.

With a Browning HP pistol in his pocket, he listened to the petrol flow from the can into the wagon. A lonely black beauty, well-known on South Andaman Island and overpowered for its existence, the lumbering, Canadian-built Ford station wagon could easily outrun the short wheel-based, 1938 Hillman saloons' the police drove.

The wagon, a pot-bellied oil burner, idled in a blue haze with a low, syncopated rumble. Like its owner, one cylinder refused to function on time. The muffler had given its guts to the salt air and Hawkes had just soldered the seams of the radiator.

Flying Officer Jeffrey Hawkes was a third, his title a burden he avoided. His father, Lord Jeffrey, had made millions in the jute and lumber markets around the Bay of Bengal from an opulent office in downtown Singapore. Studying to be a concert pianist, young Jeffrey was quite gifted, performing in concert at the age of twelve at the Royal Albert Hall in London.

There he met young Phillipa, the daughter of another lord, who fancied Jeffery's pedal work and his winsome smile. Christened in the joys of the Hallelujah chorus, his flat and diminished chords turned sharp, and he lost interest in the rigors.

Lord Jeffery purchased a membership for his son in the Singapore Flying Club. With the memories of Phillipa in hand, women, whiskey, and flying became the hallmarks of Hawkes's military career. His problems surfaced with certainty whenever he mixed the hallmarks.

Routinely he fell to inexpensive booze and overdone tarts.

Hawkes sipped his drink and leaned against the bar, chatting up a local lass. Surveying the pub, he spotted McPhee sitting hump-shouldered, facing the slop-sink the barmaids were using in the far corner.

"By the look of your gear it's been the slops of the livery for you, eh, Robby?"

"Go on outta that, Hawker," McPhee said, running a flea rake through his hair.

"For Micks like you, 'Darkie', the Household's remedies can be many and various."

"'Darkie' is it now?" McPhee lowered his chin. Rubbing the base of his neck as though trying to relax and keep his foul disposition from creating a scene, he said, "Burma's in for a rooting, and I'm left to rabbit on."

Jeffrey Hawkes set his face to a disgusted cast. "You're a smelly mess, Robby. A mixture of rum, coal dust, and diesel fuel. Or remnants of your Burmese tart."

"Two o'Mother's look-sticks jumped the rails—MI-Niners." McPhee looked out the rain-streaked windows through a glow of stale smoke, then touched his lips with his tongue. "They tried to kill me last night." A thin shadow of doubt fell on 'Darkie' McPhee. "Bugger all. If the latch on my bog hadn't gone off with a gust, I'd be a restless bit of seaweed."

"Intelligence blokes are free of shame, Robby." Assuming McPhee had nothing to lose, Hawkes hesitated. "The bastards work under Mother's rose."

"It's the Household, sure enough. Fogging about like a fishwife's fart. After the sods blew my ditty-box out, the wanks kept bobbing about, looking for me."

Listening and not listening, Hawkes pegged two strangers across the room for their niggling ways. "When you're fumbling about under the rose, you're kicking at old bones, Robby. Some of Mother's finest hours have been fashioned in the Bay of Bengal." Hawkes peered into the public bar where a tall, thin stranger seemed to be checking faces. The stranger then huddled into a booth in the far corner, with a shorter man.

"Full on, the twats think I'm in league with that steamer I'm tracking." McPhee's tone was soaked with intrigue. "I had to leg it."

"What sort of shit have you stepped in, Robby?" Hawkes studied the strangers more carefully. They had ordered pints and were bartering over the charge.

"Not the foggiest. Bit of cackle-shite really. I scheduled an early sailing for a rather hefty ballast-bag and a handful of gold. Yesterday, Rangoon's chief magistrate gave my shop a toss and Mother's look-sticks pissed a dot in each corner."

Spicing his words with annoying amusement, McPhee seemed anxious to end the discussion and get on with his story. "Last night they booby trapped my shop. A gray day, an early tide, and I hook the only herring in a basket of squid. I'm doubled-out by the looks of it."

"If the Household wants to ring your bell over a tramp's schedule, that tramp must be packing a nasty cargo."

"It's bad plumbing, that's for sure. It's my way to do. If I had the doing of it again, I'd do it different. I need a leg up, Hawker."

"Mucking with Mother isn't tits duty, Robby. MI-niners have odd doings." Hawkes's shoulders shivered at the weight of his damp sweater. He knew what the stake if he threw in with 'Darkie' McPhee. "I gather you're recruiting."

Jeffery Hawkes had been an exceptional pilot, enjoying the latest crusades from Kota Bharu, an unfederated Malay State in northern Malaya near the Gulf of Siam. Standing in the dock, in shackles, as a guest of the Federated Malaya States Volunteer Force, Hawkes's judgment found *TM Magazine*'s front cover above the fold:

> Flying Officer Jeffrey Hawkes has been discharged without pension for flying his Lockheed Hudson Bomber into Kuala Lumpur, doing a smashing cart-up landing, interrupting a football match on the pitch in front of the Federal Secretariat Building.
>
> With the crowd cheering, Flying Officer Hawkes waved his arms and celebrated his amazing feat. Drunk to the point of being shot to ribbons, he stumbled from the cockpit, threw a yellow jacket onto the pitch, inflated the dingy, sat in the dingy, raised his flask, and declared to the cheers of the crowd that he just "hit-for-six."

Arrested before his cheering fans, Hawkes landed on civvy street the next day. Jeffery Hawkes, the drunk, a notable member of Kuala Lumpur's premier social club known as The Spotted Dog, was accustomed to boozing with the staffs of anyone capable of guiding his imagination. General Chennault wanted him shot for protracted misconduct, had ordered him shot. But pilots were hard to find.

Now, drunk, or sober, officially he could not fly.

After being cashiered from the Royal Airforce, Hawkes offered his services to commodity brokers operating in the Andaman Islands—brokers buying and selling rubber, coconut, sugarcane. Anything really.

The best hires were the rounders, the lumber brokers—scupper teak, rosewood, marblewood, and padauk. They preferred their whiskey large, their whores frisky, and poker high stakes. Lumber brokers chartered aircraft for him to fly and paid hundreds of dollars in undocumented commissions.

"Well, here's a slice of Big Edna's ass." Hawkes circled an entry on the docking schedule. "There's a Portuguese flagged steamer, the SS Iron Knight, due in Port Blair on the late tide."

Gradually the mood of the old friends joined the warmth of the rum. Discounting McPhee's judgment, Hawkes turned his thoughts to the tidy-looking strangers huddled in a snug in the opposite corner. They were West Brits, imports, and neither man had touched his pint. The tall, thin man was negotiating, emphasizing a point with the end of a banger. These hucksters hung like cheap, twatlike bastards, niggling over peanuts.

Pressing on, Hawkes decided. "Let's shift ourselves to the airstrip." He finished his whiskey and lit a cigarette. "Make sure none of Neville's boys stopped off for petrol. If the air's clear, we can shift to the Coral Bar at Sinclair's Hotel and cabbage a crumpet to chew on. And 'Darkie', you're buying."

*   *   *

London. The Round Table, 175 Piccadilly Road. 26 August 1939. 1300 Hours, GMT.

"**M**ax, why did your nephew set our financial plan to paper?" Max Warburg had long thought Victor Rothschild was a complicated, museum of natural sociality, a brilliant man who understood the import of forgiven sin.

Having posed this dilemma to Lord Norman weeks before, the legal representatives from three American investment firms—Kuhn Loeb, Cromwell and Sullivan, and Samuel and Samuel –now sat quietly, waiting for Warburg's response.

Lord Montagu Norman spoke again. "Max, your nephew Frederick has left us adrift on a restless sea. I've been praying for God's help." Frederick Warburg, whose father, Felix was Max Warburg's brother, had been the director of the Prussian Life Assurance Company of Berlin, and had, in a fit of youthful spasm, crafted a financial circuit diagram of the arbitrage scheme, detailing the raid on Germany's industrial giants that left even the witless in shock.

"Well, my Lord, I think God should just be allowed to watch."

Rothschild stood silently looking into the face of a sunny afternoon. He rarely contributed to consensual speculation, preferring to listen, to allow solutions to evolve to his needs.

Lord Norman continued. "As we know, the funds we guaranteed the New German Order in January '33 have been augmented with massive industrial levies routed through the Schroder Banking House. And now the principal goal of our endeavor, the control of Europe's industrial base, is in jeopardy. I cannot accept Frederick's canine appetite for written records."

Max Warburg was livid. His voice sounded as he rose from his chair. "And yet, Lord Norman, you and Dr. Schacht instigated the transfer of twenty-three tons of Czech gold held for the Bank of International Settlements in London to the Reichbank. Please explain why Settlements Bank is financing Adolf Hitler."

"Max, please. We can discuss this privately."

"Gold, Lord Norman, twenty-three tons of gold." Warburg's expression showed manic frustration. "You must be aware that approximately twenty-eight percent of the Reichbank's own notes are partially secured by 'dead loans' issued by Special Loan Banks Dr. Schacht calls *Darlehnkassens*! These dead loans will never be repaid."

"A telling reason to transfer gold to the Reichbank." Lord Norman was defensive. Standing and finishing his sherry he continued, "We want these companies to borrow aggressively and continue this trend until they are statistically beyond recovering. This gold transfer helps create the environment for such exuberance."

Warburg scoffed. "Walter Funk is the head of the Reichbank and a director at Settlements Bank. He's a homosexual and an alcoholic—easily bribed. Surely, he and you, Lord Norman, are aware that much of the Reichbank's deposits consist of gold stolen from conquered territories—including taken from the Jews."

Lord Norman seemed overly eager to speak as he stepped across the room. "Funk assures me that all the Reichbank's gold deposits are safe and carefully graded. What's the term he used? Ah, yes. *'In good delivery.'*"

John Schiff of Kuhn Loeb spoke softly. "Our efforts to absorb and control Keppler's creation, the companies represented by his circle of friends, must not become obvious. It's the only way we will stop Hitler and put Himmler in as chancellor."

Schiff accepted another sherry from the sommelier as he used a pen to check the name of the men he invited to London. Young James Warburg worked for Roosevelt's Office of Budget. His membership in the Round Table and support of the takeover scheme as a means of eliminating Hitler was a closely held secret. Schiff did not want Roosevelt to find out because Roosevelt might alter his pattern of setting the spot-price of gold and disrupt the scheme's trading algorithm.

Schiff addressed Lord Norman. "Herman Abs of Deutsche Bank works closely with your protégé, Charles Gunston, at Settlements Bank. Abs and Gunston are the ones who tried to give Frederick's document to the Americans. You alone, Lord Norman, are responsible for our current problems."

Drawing young Warburg from Washington D.C. was risky—a risk Schiff was willing to take to keep the Round Table functioning and the takeover scheme viable. Schiff scanned the names again, recounting their political and financial pedigree.

James Paul Warburg:	His father, Paul Warburg, authored the Federal Reserve Act for the United States. Former Director of Management and Budget for the United States. Director of M. M. Warburg & Co.
Max Warburg:	Head of German intelligence during World War I. Director for the Schroder Banking House Director of M. M. Warburg & Co.
Frederick Warburg:	Director of the Prussian Life Insurance Company, Berlin. Director of M. M. Warburg & Co.
John M. Schiff:	Partner, Kuhn, Loeb and Company.
Victor Rothschild:	Director, The Five Arrows Fund. British Intelligence, MI5.
Lord Montagu Norman:	British Intelligence, MI6. Governor of the Bank of England.
Sir Lewis Wiseman:	Head of British Intelligence during World War I.
John Foster Dulles:	Attorney and associate partner, Cromwell and Sullivan.
Allen Dulles:	Attorney and associate partner, Cromwell and Sullivan.

Sir Lewis Wiseman, Max Warburg's clandestine cohort since 1915, laid an open palm toward the Dulles brothers. "I'm told you met with Hitler in January 1933. Did he give you any indication of the scope of this final solution?"

"No!" Allen Dulles had been asked this question many times. "Propaganda created the illusion Jews were to emigrate. After the British White Paper effectively closed Palestine, doors have been closing throughout the world. Seven hundred and fifty Jews a month can emigrate to Palestine through the port of Haifa. That many Jews are being displaced from the towns and villages of Europe by the hour."

"What's your opinion concerning the United States?" Wiseman asked. "Will this displacement of Jews be enough to drag the colonists into the war?"

"Time has no meaning for the United States." Dulles set his cigarette down and picked up a newspaper. "I've a copy of the *Palestine Post* for you to read. The lead article is titled 'Getting US to Pull Out the Chestnuts.' The Jews of Palestine are asking the same question. Currently there's no interest in the United States for fighting this war."

"Will Hitler stop with Czechoslovakia?" Max Warburg asked.

Allen Dulles seemed to search for an answer as he paused and glanced around the room.

"I don't think so. Not if the Russians invade Finland."

Max Warburg stood abruptly, ready to explode. "Will Hitler insist on occupying the Danzig Corridor? Will the Nazis invade Poland?"

"The intelligence reports I have seen are clear," John Dulles offered. "The Nazis have been conducting tank maneuvers in the Black Forest region for over a year. For what it's worth, I believe they intend to invade Poland and the low-countries."

The sommelier came through the room refreshing each glass of sherry. Silence followed as the man left the room.

Wiseman burst from his shell. "As far as we know, Frederick's document is still under seal. The financial circuits detailed are explosive. Losing control of the document is disastrous—and Alex von Cleve knows this. Compensation Brokers Limited, hired von Cleve, knowing his propensities. He has already received millions from us.

"We must continue our dialogue with the Hong in Bangkok. We may need them to deal with von Cleve and his associates. So far, our dealings with the Hong are restricted to importing tin and rubber from the Malay States."

Max Warburg walked to the window and peered into the room, obviously angry. Tense, and white to his lips, he said, "Hang one of the proprietors of East India Company from Blackfriars Bridge. Then Alex von Cleve and his Templar associates will know we are serious."

A titter petered out after Rothschild placed a postcard-sized image of an eight-pointed red cross on a white field in the center of the table.

Schiff, Europe's financial godfather, cringed. He existed with the blessing of this centuries-old order, the Templars—a military order of knights dedicated to guarding the roads to the Temple of Solomon. Schiff scanned the room and let his gaze settle on the fireplace.

"Our relationships must be absolute and secret. The Templars have never violated a trust. Our lives depend on a singular notion—we cannot allow our arrangements with them to become known. We have paid their required fees. Our funds have been spent. We have retained their order to retrieve Frederick's document.

"Let's hope this ordeal ends soon. Ruthlessly devout, the Templar will kill any man in this room who violates their trust. Including you, Lord Norman."

With a sigh, Rothschild said, "Enough of death. We must keep our focus on stopping Hitler. The companies associated with the circle of friends remain steadfast as Keppler predicted—I. G. Farben, Krupp, SKF, Siemens, Allianz, United Steel Works, the Conti Rubber Syndicate.

"The circle of friends has forty members. Eight are executives of I. G. Farben. Keppler and Farben Bilder organized this group. We must not harm these individuals. We are attempting to take over the seven industrial companies they represent."

Rothschild continued, "Max, when you, Mendelssohn, Wassermann, and Hitler signed the order reappointing Dr. Schacht to be president of the Reichsbank in January '33, did you have any idea he would create twelve billion marks' worth of armaments through this secondary currency, through these ME-FO bills, these short-term instruments?"

"How could we know?" Max Warburg exclaimed. "In '31, Creditanstalt, the largest bank in Austria, collapsed. Currency was withdrawn from German banks in Austria by the Reichbank, and by July of '31 those banks collapsed. By '33 we had to do something.

"With a single stroke, Schacht's four percent, ninety-day, ME-FO bill drew vast sums from the coffee cans of Europe. This secondary currency helped stem the tide of hyperinflation and helped put Germany to work. Unfortunately, the doctor made Hitler nearly invincible."

"We must not forget," Rothschild went on, "Dr. Schacht, and you, Lord Norman, are both members of the Bank of International Settlements. In fact, Lord Norman, you are the godfather of Schacht's grandchildren."

Max Warburg yelled across the room. "Dr. Schacht confiscated five million marks from the Allianz Insurance settlement for Kristallnacht. No Jew received a shekel from their claim."

Disgusted, Wiseman shouted. "The good doctor also tried to mortgage Jewish property last December to secure a $1.5 billion-dollar loan from Credit Suisse."

"Schacht is a clever Jew," Victor said. "Hitler fired him from the Reichsbank. Unfettered, Schacht convinced Credit Suisse to extend credit to Hitler as an economically sound decision for the Swiss economy. Now the doctor is looking for a new home. He knows Hitler intends to rid Europe of the Jew. His hands are not clean."

Victor paused, shook his head, and continued. "Our banking houses supporting our efforts have been brought online. J. H. Stein, Cologne; British South Africa, Johannesburg; JP Morgan, New York; Hong Kong-Shanghai, Hong Kong; Societe General de Belgique, Amsterdam; J. H. Schroder, London; and Hambros Bank, Berlin.

"The newspapers favorable to Himmler's ascendency are *Wolff/D.N.B.*, Berlin; *Reuters*, London; *Havas,* Paris; and the *New York Times.*"

Rothschild stopped pacing to gaze out the window. Better than anyone else he knew what lay before him. "Frederick's document in that wayward pouch is specific. It's all inclusive. The document is our death warrant—a Nazi warrant that will include the members of our families."

A consensus is not science, but a consensus of fear can become fact. At first Rothschild did not notice the silence. He remembered some talk the night before. Tense, he put in again.

"I'm guessing, but I think Ten Downing is being fed false intelligence by a divot within their ranks. A spy within MI6. Ten Downing is convinced their commando team is carrying sensitive documents detailing the Windsors' involvement in Asian markets.

"The Vatican is also frightened. They too believe their Asian dealings are outlined. Their fear is magnified now that communist guerrillas killed Tonkin's bishop."

John Schiff cleared his throat. His face was still. Sometimes his eyes smiled, rarely his lips.

"Alex von Cleve is the only link in the chain that would use subterfuge to leverage the Windsors and the Vatican. I'd wager that Templar lied about the contents of that pouch to solicit fees from the Vatican and England. I'd also wager that von Cleve is an outlier and that his Templar master does not know about his tangential contracts."

Rothschild gave a short nod. "That's a possibility. The Templar know the Catholic confessional is the most profound intelligence tool ever devised. Sub Rosa. From murder to deceit, any sordid detail is willingly given to a priest—to shame the devil. The Vatican made billions of pounds trading on these secrets over the centuries."

Schiff said, "If von Cleve is an outlier, if he has lied to his masters, they will kill him. But before they do, he will kill anyone to keep his secrets."

Throwing his hands open, Wiseman spoke. "As a group, we are responsible for this travesty. Mercenaries are killing England's special-service troops—for money. God help us. What have we done? For the first time in our lives we are threatened. Even Sun Life Assurance Company as compensation broker for these arbitrage specialists is mentioned in Frederick's document."

Standing by the open doorway, noting his own departure, Max Warburg exclaimed, "Steiner—Three Fingers to some—should have taken the document from the British team when he met that team in Haiphong."

"Wait a minute, Max," Schiff was sweating. "Who is Steiner?"

"He's one of the mercenaries killing British special-service troops. He's been in Lord Norman's employ for years at MI6."

Lord Norman drank his sherry and placed the empty glass on the table next to his chair. Isolated he shook his head. "Steiner operates under Mother's rose, Max, as do many nefarious characters. Almost all of those rankers are foreign born. How you came to know of Steiner, and of his involvement in pursuing these documents worries me."

Max Warburg pointed at Lord Norman. "Admiral Sinclair and I have been friends for years. Since moving my business operations to London, he has funneled intelligence to me daily. He knows I loathe Hitler."

Schiff asked Lord Norman, "Can your operative retrieve these documents without killing more special-service troops?"

Lord Norman waited for a long time in silence. "I fear it's a bit late for intervening tactics. Steiner's an intractable sort."

"Well Lord Norman, what do you propose?"

"To avoid getting our skirts fouled with blood, we need to retain a broker who is purchasing exports in the far east and has listed shipping assets. Rubber, exotic woods, raw silk. A contractor we can leverage."

Max Warburg held nothing back, sensing it was time to force Lord Norman out in the open. "It's the good Lord's skirt that drips with blood. Did you retain this Steiner to intercept our special-service troops, causing many to die?"

This question drew no reply.

"Men have died to save our ambitions, Lord Norman. You put Steiner and von Cleve in the same frame. You and you alone must stop their carnage. And by God, you, and people like you are also expendable. Who you hire to solve your problem is, indeed, your problem."

In spite of this, Lord Norman maintained a solemn dignity. For weeks he had pressured Gordon Dewar to withdraw von Cleve and all the other mercenaries searching for the classified documents. Unable to tighten the trace chains on Dewar, he wired Victor Rothschild.

Thankfully, Sir Nigel Stuart had ignored his entreaties.

* * *

London. The Athenaeum Court Hotel. 26 August 1939. 1730 Hours, GMT.

Physics was Johnny's hobby.

A second scotch, burly and red faced, drew him from safe harbor, as if the decision to order it caught the dispense waiter's eye. Look there, there among the cubes, tiny remnants of thought are dodging the light stems shooting from the inner ice. Scotch whiskey mixed evenly with Drambuie, too smooth for the novice, its golden threads eddy—the melting ice gives each thread motion and, therefore, energy.

The day was well-nigh gone.

Listening to the murmurs, those light huffs of laughter playing lyrical notes, Poston sat waiting for William Hockey in the Athenaeum Court Hotel's historic lounge, a male redoubt of fusty relics, and the trappings of battles lost. Nicely appointed, this lounge could disguise betrayal while serving the treasured whiskeys of the world.

Framed with massive stones, the room's expansive fireplace gave the nod to Britain's historic military campaigns. Valor's carved into dark, oak panels wrapped the lounge, drawing at a man's conscience—the room the radiance of England's past.

Russia will invade Poland—Germany first. The Bosche will pour into the low-countries—through the Ardennes and crush France using the tank maneuvers they have practiced in the Strasbourg Region of the Black Forest. Poston watched as Hockey checked his hat and overcoat with the valet, ordering his usual—a jar of brown ale. As Hockey approached, he saw something else, as well. Hockey's eyes were locked in ice.

To know men, Sir John had told him, was to know the outcome of every encounter. But with this Druid there was no surety.

William Hockey's hands, the knuckles of his hands, knurled and knotted, gave notice to young Poston; the man's strength should not be tested. He remembered the pain of the last handshake, and the red-flecked lines mapping the man's cheeks.

"I expect Dewar to arrive shortly," Poston said.

"He needs to enjoy his time. There's not much left."

"What have you discovered, Willie?"

"Give me a minute."

Quiet and reserved, his demeanor set with anticipation, Hockey sat to his beer. Finished, he put the empty glass aside and leaned into the arm of the overstuffed chair.

"Dewar's been on the move, smuggling opium," Hockey said.

After summing the particulars and presenting his findings concerning the death of Sir John Poston, Hockey ordered another jar of stout. "The duke of Hamilton, Rudolf Hess, and Gordon Dewar—these chaps have been smuggling ganja and opium into Europe through the ports of Bayonne and Marseille for five years, probably longer."

Noting a man over listening to his words, Hockey stood to the man's side, spoke briefly, and waited as the man and his guest left the lounge.

Once the air had cleared, Hockey opened the tobacco jar perched next to his chair and sat into a nod. "Drugs are a nasty business."

"The duke's a member of the Dungavel House in Scotland," Poston said.

"That he is." Hockey filled his pipe and set it on fire. "He's desperate for money."

"You should smoke a pipe, Johnny. This tobacco's the best in the world—close cut, dark, and moist. Your cigarettes are merely twigs." The pedestal ashtray perched between their chairs was of luxurious cut glass made brilliant by a polished-brass gooseneck lamp. Hockey turned off the lamp. "This room holds a deepening wealth. Rich greens and maroons, mahogany, and oak."

As though dismissing Poston's silence, waving his hand over Poston's drink, Hockey said, "Hess has Dewar tied to a lesser criminal syndicate. Street thugs. After Sir John framed the picture, Dewar had him killed to keep his shipping and warehouse assets in play."

After Hockey's intentions became clear, Johnny noted, "If the duke's not involved in the day-to-day operation, let's focus on Dewar."

"Fair enough. The duke's a pawn used for political leverage."

A red eight-pointed cross, tattooed on Hockey's forearm, was set at the hollow of his cuff, purposely visible for the wayward eye of a man at a nearby table, more a warning for the man yet to arrive—Gordon Dewar.

The sommelier handed Hockey a bottle of thirty-year-old Mortlach Whiskey for inspection. With a nod, Poston raised his glass for a top-up. The bottle was placed on the lamp table along with a wedge of Tornegus cheese and two glasses.

"Try the cheese, Johnny. The smell belies its sweet taste."

Poston turned aside to shade his expression. For years, elements of London's past, including William Hockey, had been trying to soil the lineage of Dungavel House in Scotland, recollecting scenes only now occurring. Hockey often cast this fine veil, a skein weaving the duke of Hamilton into the opium trade.

Poston poured Hockey a drink. "So, who killed my father?" With a shrug, he suggested, "A bit of backtracking led to MI6 and Dewar, I judge."

"Unlike Dewar, even Illiad had an occasional good day."

"Brain-skip is the muzzler's latest malady."

"There is a bit of fog remaining. We can assume the duke, Hess and Dewar are still active in the drug trade and we can proceed accordingly. Dewar uses MI6 as a foil, directing events and subordinates as though he's hemming Mother's linens—her knickers actually."

"Who killed my father?"

"I assume Dewar ordered the assassination."

"Who killed my father?"

"A man named Alfred Gosden."

Poston started to speak. The cast of Hockey's eyes bore him off.

"It's complicated, Johnny. Gosden abused Captain Hardin's mother years ago, in Tucking Mill, in Cornwall. To balance that ledger for Captain Hardin, I asked the admiral to assign Gosden to MI6. Right now, he's being posted to Cairo. Your brother can manage the rest."

"A military prison, I judge."

Noncommittal, Hockey set his glass aside. "Here's Dewar now." Hockey stood and braced his shirt cuffs higher, glancing at his tattoo. "Stand easy, Johnny. Let me rattle the wanker."

Gordon Dewar looked haggard. His trilby hat had lost its crease. His eyes had taken a back bench, dark voids in a maze of sun-burnt patches puzzled together by exposed veins. Breathing as if he had narrowly escaped the poor house, he stared at Hockey, recalling the misfortune.

His assailant must have seemed wider than he was tall.

Poston handed Dewar a drink, then went on to discuss William Hockey, who Dewar found just in front of him. "Gordon, this is William Hockey, a lifelong friend of the Poston family. Willie's the Tyler of the Masonic Lodge in Cardiff. He's come to London now to update me on family business."

"Mr. Hockey..." Extending his hand, Hockey turned into a shadow, leaving the firelight to accent half of his face. Dewar looked into the sand-gray hollow of Hockey's eye—the wet, sand-gray expanse. He winced as Hockey's grip ground his knuckles. Knowing Celts started the day at sunset, Dewar stiffened, staring at Hockey's tattoo.

For Poston a sense of knowing consumed the room.

Dewar picked up the bottle. "Mortlach Whiskey...judging from the many brands on by, this must be an occasion, Johnny."

Poston contained his humor with his glass. Dewar seemed unsettled, frightened by Hockey's presence as he took several sips of his drink.

Poston bumped Dewar's shoulder with his hand. "We need your help, Gordon. Your influence with Admiral Sinclair and MI6—matters relating to black-market dealings in Cairo relating to Operation Snow White."

"I've a rather crowded schedule these days, Johnny. This Snow-White business has been a mystery. I'd be happy to lend a call on your behalf."

"That's a trifle narrow," Hockey implied. "I've found being educated is rather like the ritual killing of one's mother and father."

Suddenly—for no apparent reason except that Dewar's voice had been dry, brittle and condescending—Poston wanted to pelt the bastard. "Do fat people like you, Gordon, find eating a serious endeavor?"

As though removing a shroud of sacking, Hockey stood abruptly and set his back to the fire, casting his image on Dewar. "A fugitive of sorts has landed a billet in MI6," he declared, extending his right hand, exposing the cross tattooed on his forearm.

With a shrug that brought him next to Dewar, he continued. "Sir John Poston was murdered by this fugitive. Alfred Gosden. Why he was involved, I have come to know."

With clinched fists Dewar leaned back in his chair and looked left, into the foyer of the lounge. "Are you certain this man's billeted with MI6?"

Hockey reacted violently to Dewar's comment. "I am. You signed his branch transfer and appointment card." A black dagger appeared in Hockey's hand—the hand that had held his glass. The glass sat on the table at Dewar's elbow.

Dewar hurriedly left his chair and stepped away from Hockey. Pointing at the dagger. "Damn, man. Put that away. Are you certain Gosden's the killer?"

As though believing his question had been answered, Hockey let several seconds pass. Levelling the dagger, cutting side up, he leaned toward Dewar. "I have his accomplice lashed with stopper knots, eeling in the fens near Kidwelly, waiting for his day." Hockey laid a photograph of Gosden, Dewar, and a third man standing in front of Potter's Bar in Lyon, France, on the table next to his glass, and rotated the photo so the other men could examine it.

"We're all waiting our end, Mr. Hockey." Dewar seemed to be evaluating. "Even worthy prossies are sharing woolen knickers these days."

"Your wait is nearly over." Angered by the irony of this bent, Hockey stepped away from Dewar. Toasting his glass, he leaned on the chimneypiece.

"Call me Willie, Gordon. I know this sounds a bit dull. As your enemy, I'm the closest thing to a friend you have."

Dewar sat down. "Gosden's a new hire," he said, swirling a finger in his drink. "He clerks for a man named Berryman. I don't know the third man in that photograph."

"A casual dalliance, I suppose. I am sympathetic to your delusions. Where's Gosden?" Hockey asked, holding his dagger into the firelight, and rolling it over in his right hand.

"He's been posted to Cairo—Berryman as well."

"Do you know why my father was killed, Gordon?" Johnny asked.

Suddenly suspicious, Dewar took his pipe from his jacket and slowly stuffed it with the dark tobacco. After lighting the pipe and several satisfying draws, he spoke through the haze. "Of course not, Johnny. On a dock, at night, in London? It's unclear."

Hockey's foot nudged Poston's as he picked up the photograph and sheathed the dagger. Pouring Dewar's drink on the fire, Hockey backhanded the smoke as it rose in front of the chimneypiece.

"Be well, my new friend. The men responsible for Sir John Poston's murder will be offered to their God in pieces."

Watching Hockey push his way into the cab with Dewar, Poston wondered if this was Dewar's last cab ride. Hockey's dagger had appeared by sleight-of-hand—ten inches long and reed thin.

Returning to the lounge Johnny sat by the fire. He was worried. Who is William Hockey?

He was a lifelong friend of my father's. But is he a family friend? Or is he a Mason dedicated to balancing Sir John's ledger? Is it probable that's what he does? With a raven's allure, he balances ledgers as a matter of course—for fellow Masons.

If Hockey has one of Sir John's killers hidden in the fens, he means to kill the man. I need to warn Lewis. If Hockey has made decisions about Alfred Gosden and Gordon Dewar, I'm certain he means to kill them as well.

* * *

Garmish, Germany. 26 August 1939. 0630 Hours, GMT + 1 Hour.

Morning had come with more snow. Samuel Eaton, vice president of J. P. Morgan banking house, sighed audibly, his sleepless night rushing into a grin as he pushed down on the rising stem of an old companion. Only the motion counted. With clipped spires of recognition, Petra's clinical image flashed, calculating and more aggressive than he remembered.

A church clock struck the half hour.

He rarely fantasized. It was wildly reckless, but her image had sparked his recall. He had never been with such a controlling, demanding woman. That she was a Nazi seemed to have piqued the opportunity and sent him wild. Immoralities aside, he was drawn to the woman.

Ice coated the rim of the windowpanes. Snow continued to gather in drifts, corrugating the enclosed courtyard. Gusts blew funnels of snow flurries around the remaining sedans. Lounging as though vigilance were presupposed, men in greatcoats blocked the exits.

I'm boxed in. If I live through this deal, I'll need to disappear.

Ashamed of his eagerness, Eaton could not discuss the arbitrage scheme with anyone. Its exponents and derivatives were well defined, centered in those stark pools of light just beyond the first betrayal. International financial transactions generally produced a sea of fragments, featuring an abstract urgency topped with a smile.

This deal was topped with an assurance of death.

He now realized the directors of J.P. Morgan had offered him as a straw man. Earn your fees, sucker, and if you live, we might consider your future. He wanted to tell the US State Department about the scheme, to mellow his sense of isolation. But who would they tell? Anyone with the information would become a threat.

Listening to the first imitations of the morning, the tattoo of carts running across the tiled, hallway floor announced breakfast—a tray of cheese and meats, hard-boiled eggs perched in flowered cups, fresh breads and rolls, butter, marmalade, coffee, juice, and milk.

Petra filled two small plates and poured coffees. After a brief silence, she nudged Eaton's plate. "You must eat, Mr. Eaton."

"I need more than food." Eaton looked at Petra for agreement and found a blush-colored stare. As they considered one another in silence, Sam chided himself, his infidelity. He had asked Angie, his secretary to spend the Christmas holidays with him in Hawaii. She had declined.

Petra stood and began dressing. She was well turned out. "I have the details for your contribution to the arbitrage plan and will give them to you in New York."

The woman's intention to travel to New York startled Eaton and loosened an urgent factoring of conflicting scenarios.

"You are not a brave man, Mr. Eaton. Perhaps I can help."

Eaton's brow arched, calibrating his confines, regretting his greed—more his lust for this dangerous woman. He found this road in high school. A road built by use—a road for fast cars and bundles of cash.

Understanding the events of the past twenty-four hours were no longer tangential fantasies, he whispered, "Honest answers. That's what I need." Eaton extended his legs to relieve an ache in his right knee. Speaking with a manufactured insistence, he asked, "The man controlling the meeting, who is he?"

Petra's expression grew cold. As though hardened by a pulsing surge, she exhaled. "He's Austrian, and he's dangerous. I don't know his name, and you don't need to know."

A fleet of Mercedes sedans formed a queue on the drive leading to the chateau, waiting to be directed into the courtyard. Staccato commands came from the guard post. Loading bankers separately in the seclusion of a stone archway, the soldier controlling departures allowed a barely perceptible nod to bring the next sedan forward.

Flurried snow whirled in clouds as a massive Grosser Mercedes cut through the fog. Eaton's memory was warping—objective experience giving way to fantasy. His thoughts were in knots.

Emerging obligations and conflicts of loyalty marched to a roulade of questions, blowing the bloom from Eaton's life.

And why did George Harrison, governor of the Federal Reserve Bank of New York, recommend J. P. Morgan Bank to the Austrian? Or was J.P. Morgan the root of this tree? Is Harrison involved in the arbitrage scheme?

With the federal funds rate in the United States being manipulated, this deal will either be a money pump, or a graveyard.

"Our flight's been delayed." Petra spoke with a seeming sense of purpose. "The early snows caught the whole of Europe gathering wool. We depart tomorrow at zero nine-thirty hours." The use of military time confirmed Petra Laube-Heintz as a soldier—a Nazi. Berlin Center trained.

"We have a suite at 148 Judengasse." She raised her chin with a hint of satisfaction.

"I need to cable New York." Eaton reached for his valise.

"That's been done. Your secretary at J.P. Morgan has your flight details. As does John Dulles at Kohn Loeb, and George Harrison at the Federal Reserve Bank of New York."

* * *

Burma. 27 August 1939. First Light. 0430 Hours, GMT + 6.5 Hours.

Dawn found angular shafts of light blending the shadows on the beach. Mellowed by a sea mist and a thin ground fog, palm fronds waved before a calming breeze. Standing inside the jungle's veil, Hardin waited for the village to come awake.

His survival depended on instinct and patience.

With the fens as a pillow and a thick Welsh coating, Hardin had spent the night in hiding—dreaming the tales of his father's childhood antics, amid images of a small Welsh village. A sliver of sunlight lanced his sleeping area, featuring a small bamboo viper.

Awake, he peered at an odd shape near the beach, the surf backlighting its unusual form. Expecting the jungle to collapse on his bamboo dingle, he stepped away from the tongue of the pale-brown snake.

Gravity set to the throbbing in his thigh. His fear should have such substance. The odd form near the beach became a bush in the dim light before dawn. The time had come for Hardin, code- sign Doc, to run for the rally with Uncle Dingo.

Grumpy's expression of relief as he died came to mind. The image cradled the dark voids that were Hardin's own. Linc Jensen had been a good mate. He deserved a better end.

As if ordained, the village was empty—no chickens, no pigs, and no people.

Tu appeared next to Hardin without making a sound, her eyes fostering grief, competing for space with her swollen cheeks and bruised brow. A machete hung at her back. A sock filled with rice hung across her chest. A leather water bag hung at her shoulder. And a chicken hung from a hemp rope belt.

"We leave today. My father wants to talk to you."

Accepting her charge, Hardin followed her north along the edge of the vegetation, skirting an isolated stretch of beach on the south end of the lagoon. Sweating with fever, he favored his leg to ease the pain. Tu climbed a hidden chimney of rock and slipped through a narrow crease.

Inching through the gap, Hardin found himself standing in the cave where the villagers kept their equipment. Dissected by crisp shafts of light, the interior lay in daylight, and the rock entrance casing shone a vibrant, emerald hue. Water flowed from a long crack in the rock ceiling. Fish netting covered a cache of ammunition and weapons near the back of the cave.

Where were these rat bags when Tu was being raped?

Kneeling by a clear pool, he splashed cold water on his face. His mouth tasted like rain-soaked leather. Pebbles at the bottom of the pool danced alive as shadow and light exchanged calls. He wiped the water from his face and drank his fill. Looking carefully around, he was puzzled by what he could see. He coughed to gain attention.

A woman rose from the fire, her dark face smeared with dirt.

Grudgingly, a man uncovered a pallet of equipment. Beyond the man a figure appeared, in the light for an instant and out of it into a side tunnel.

Hardin heard a mutter of voices. One was slightly louder. The old man—Tu's father.

Well, I'll be damned, Hardin thought. I'll bet these men ambushed the bandits down the beach. That's the gunfire I heard.

The old man must be leading a local guerrilla unit—supplied by the Americans by the look of these cases of grenades and this talk box. The men I spotted carrying carbines must be from another village. They're siding up to fight the Japs.

The odd-looking wireless was covered with matting stitched together with strips of bamboo. It sat apart from the other stores. The manufacturer's tinplate on the unit was stamped SCR-543. A skein of black wire encased the antenna and mingled with the smoke of a small fire and ran out through an air vent.

This is beautiful. Look at this equipment. This militia could stop a small band of pirates, Jap prickers, or the trailers chasing this bloody pouch.

Behind him Tu was busy sharpening her machete.

Hardin adjusted the frequency band and keyed the wireless handset. "Snow White, this is Grumpy. Come in, Princess." Hardin fumbled with the volume knob as a stark rush from the transceiver's speaker echoed in the cave. Desperate to talk with his extraction lead, he tried to whisper but his tongue was so thick he had to pause.

Hardin keyed the handset again and nearly screamed. "Snow White, Snow White, this is Grumpy over." Hardin spotted the silhouette of a man with his chin on his chest, sleeping on a chair in the black mouth of a side tunnel betrayed by a glint off his carbine.

After a moment of silence, Uncle hollered. "G'day, Grumpy. Good to hear you're about. The bottle's broken, over." The mission-code for Rangoon was bottle—the port of Rangoon was finished.

Hardin detected a questioning in Uncle's voice. The Aussie needs to know I'm wounded. Hardin keyed the transceiver. "Bounce your balls, Princess. The castle's damp, over." Damp—ops code for commando at half throttle.

"No worries. We're off to pester some curly dirt, Grumpy." Curly dirt—ops-code for Port Blair, on South Andaman Island. Pester—ops-code for stores and bunkering fuel.

"An apple-a-day, Princess. See you in Piccadilly." An apple—ops-code for seven miles.

"Mind the seeds, Grumpy." Seeds—ops-code for guerrillas.

Hardin dropped the handset on a bag of rice and searched the deeper confines of the cave. Near the fire Tu was talking to her father as he caressed her swollen cheek.

Tu pointed toward the cave entrance, handed Hardin a sock filled with rice and slipped out through the entry crease. Standing on the beach below the chimney of rock, a haggard grin was all he could muster. The young girl was going to lead him on a ball-jarring trek. Shouldering his kit with a series of shrugs and loading a round into the breach of his Hart MK1, he found her staring at the blue distance of the horizon.

The sun was straight up, bunching their shadows.

The deep ache in his thigh had thickened, sending jolting shocks into his ankle. The bottom of his foot was on fire. His right calf had swollen beyond the seams of his pant, forcing him to slit the pant leg and tie it closed.

Excess fluid in his lower leg was crippling his stride. Fever was fogging his vision. To make the rally and stay ahead of the hounds, he had to move faster. To survive, he had to accept Tu's directions and keep pace.

Amid the perpetual rustling of the palms, Tu stood silent, listening. Kneeling, she dug a handful of soil and cast it aside. The ground was moist and would hold Hardin's lopsided tracks for days. The game trails had become mere threads.

With every sense alert, Tu chose a trail that didn't exist. With quick short steps her sandals left no mark on the floor of the jungle—her stride subject to the gaps in the vegetation. In tune with the jungle, in sync with its mood, she kept scanning the treetops as though judging the movement of the leaves—the odd flutter.

She kept working south. Occasionally she stopped. Listening. Each time she changed direction—east. Always east before turning south again.

Assuming she understood the situation better than he did, Hardin forced his pace. Wincing as salt seeped into his wound, he pressed on. He fell and fell again in the next mile. As the day wore on, it took him longer to gain his feet.

*   *   *

Diamond Harbor, India. 26 August 1939. 1340 Hours, GMT + 5.5 Hours.

Men whispered. Von Cleve's hands were not tied, and he was not blindfolded. Exhausted, his face lacerated by diesel-soaked slivers of wharf decking. Squinting and yawning, he gently massaged the lacerations on his face, listening for a familiar voice. A man in the adjoining room spoke hurriedly, a hard, north-country German—precise and controlled.

An Italian spoke as if on stage. A Malaysian seemed to mock them both. The sequence repeated itself and telescoped into an ordered pattern. The German was in charge.

The Thule had ordered the death of the Warburg attorneys. Their assassins had also neutralized his bodyguards and shanghaied him. Why?

To date, his unearned mortality had been shaped by the protocols of a closed and secretive military order dating to the first Crusades. Scrupulous and reliable, the order had a complex network of operatives capable of protecting any client the world over—a military order of power, with wealth derived from being the first international bankers.

After torturing and killing Templars for heresy, the Vatican and the king of France had confiscated their property. To escape the purge, they loaded their ships with provisions and treasure, and more than fifteen thousand members of the order vanished into an underworld of chaos, finance, and retribution.

In the fourteenth century, in fewer than ninety days, the Templars fell off the earth, along with their vast fortunes. Even with communication systems tied to the average speed of a horse, the unwitting could not fathom a Templar cell's existence.

Avignon's pope confiscated the order's known liquid assets. The order's real-estate assets outside France and England were pledged by papal bull— to a more compliant military order, the Knights Hospitaler—the Knights of Malta, the Union Corse, the Assassini.

With their Templar masters charged with heresy, tortured, and executed in public squares throughout Europe, the remaining disciples went to ground—creating the most secretive banking operations in the world— Credit Suisse, Switzerland, and Enskilda Bank, Sweden.

The Templar had controlled the trade routes through the Alps, assuming a mantle of trust, meting transit tolls of indescribable sacrifice. Ruthless in their devotion, their guardianship of the way, these knights became the gatekeepers for non-travelers along these trade routes.

Now they were mentoring the world's notable merchant bankers. Cloaked in obscurity, their contracts contained a query: "What does your greed want for itself?"

Ion Crilley was a clandestine director of Credit Suisse. Fine-featured, with a strong face, his eyes burned hatred in their crystalline depths. A master assassin with decades of work along Africa's eastern rim, he was currently targeting non-travelers near the Bay of Bengal.

Crilley was Alex von Cleve's operational control, his master.

That von Cleve was careless enough to be wounded had forced Ion Crilley to reevaluate the South African's ability and his worth. His orders to von Cleve had been clear: "Deliver the pouch and its contents to a *dubok*—a dead-drop in Durban, South Africa."

Ignoring Crilley's directive, von Cleve's contracts with the Vatican, the Thule Society, and Compensation Brokers, Ltd. although mutually exclusive, were specific: eliminate the British SOE Team and deliver the pouch to Cairo—each contract specifying a different drop site.

As the door to the room swung silently to the wall, a model of the Thule—young, blue-eyed, and Indo-Aryan to his core—spoke, maintaining a refined, chiseled expression. "Well, von Cleve, a good many have died since you arrived in Diamond Harbor. Eleven at last count. Doing business with you is dangerous."

Von Cleve never responded to statements. For years he studied the precepts of the major religions of the world. The Thule was the Anti-Christ, replacing the cross with the swastika, reversed in its pattern to reflect the swirling rays of the sun as seen from the northern ice. The man confronting him was freshened by these swirling rays—a fresh plant, an apprentice.

"As you wish, von Cleve. You were the one ambushed. My superiors have directed me to treat your wounds. We have a meeting in the north to discuss our contract with you."

Von Cleve remained silent. He had to escape Diamond Harbor and regroup.

*   *   *

Lufthansa Flight 392. Enroute to Marseille. 26 August 1939. 1130 Hours, GMT + 1 Hour.

Reuters: August 26, 1939
Sir Carroll Starr's Death an Apparent Suicide
Sir Carroll Starr, deputy governor to the Court of Proprietors, East India Company, was found hanged this morning from Blackfriars Bridge. According to his wife, Sir Carroll's diary...

Petra read the bold headline from across the airplane's narrow center aisle. Few would find significance in the article. The second sentence caught her eye: According to his wife, Sir Carroll's diary was missing from their home. Scotland Yard is uncertain as to a connection with his death.

Petra thought of an operational reference and found Starr's execution in the arbitrage plan's briefing framework. His hanging was designed to create fear, confusion, and uncertainty within England's financial community. That he was executed sooner than scheduled meant the plan's sequence was accelerating.

Why wasn't I informed of the change? she wondered. If Eaton has no connection with Starr, someone he knows in New York will have.

"We have first-class tickets departing Marseille tomorrow morning—a flying boat, the Dixie Clipper. Pan American Airways Flight 193. We'll arrive at LaGuardia's marine terminal."

"What did the tickets cost?" Eaton asked.

"Six hundred and seventy-five dollars each—round trip. Stein Bank is your host." Weeks ago, over a late lunch, Harrison, head of the New York Fed, had informed Eaton that Stein Bank was Hitler's Endowment Bank. And Schroder Bank was being used to wash industrial levies for Hitler and other notable Nazis.

"I thought you worked for Schroder Bank." Eaton was enjoying the sparring.

"On occasion. Schroder Bank and Stein Bank have shared the accounts I am responsible for. Working accounts for routine expenses."

Eaton's chest tightened. Petra Laube-Heintz was obviously a well-groomed Nazi. He did not want to return to England or Europe. Why did she mention the round-trip ticket cost?

"When are you returning to Germany. Miss Heintz?"

"In good time."

*   *   *

London. Hansom Cab, Piccadilly Circus.
27 August 1939. 1840 Hours, GMT.

Put off by the traffic noise, Lewis Poston set his teeth. "I don't have the foggiest idea what cargoes our steamers are carrying, Johnny. My inquiries are being referred to a Benjamine Schaat, at 13 Rue du Four, Paris."

Squinting to filter a sharp cone of light, he held a small white card under the overhead lamp, so his brother could read it: Benjamine Schaat, 13 Rue du Four, Paris. Then he sighed from worry and relief and spoke his latest fear—the cold calculations of the moneyed.

"So far, this rather damp bastard has ignored me."

"13 Rue du Four is the Sorbonne—the University in Paris." Johnny had a habit of opening and closing his left hand when someone should agree with his conclusions. Waiting for Lewis to respond, he could have milked a stable of cows. Johnny continued. "That's why the address has been haunting—it's the Warburg Institute's former headquarters, an offshoot of a powerful merchant banking family. Some of them have relocated to London.

"If Poston and Sons' operations are profitable, our moss-grown wards will ensure their investors stand quiet."

Not for a moment did Lewis doubt his brother's logic. But why take him seriously? he thought, adjusting his frame, sitting sideways to better see his brother's expressions. Johnny, the theorist, had a habit of parsing words to fit probability outcomes he had already deduced. Lewis found the habit annoying.

"It's a demand note, Johnny. If the investors catch us with an empty pot, they can call the note and force us to sell off the assets."

Giving his brother's comment the customary waiting period required for facetious retorts, Johnny shot back, "Or they can ship a load of coal to Newcastle. Today the margins aren't high enough to sell the company at a profit and pay the note. They can make more money trading currencies."

"My research indicates these bankers have had more than a bit of good fortune." Lewis set the *London Business Journal* on the seat. The article concerning British Petroleum's problems in the Congo was not well documented.

"Merchant bankers and politicians—given the world's vibrational state, their lies are always partly true. Given enough time we will never find the strait of it."

Lewis smiled as the cab navigated London's streets with a rural ease, a darkened crucible indifferent to Gordon's Gin or any of the other doings beneath King Street. Johnny's comment went unchallenged as an elongated shadow leaped onto the wet cobble-stone pavement, raced from the curbside toward the cab, shortened into a blur, and vanished in an instant.

He did not want to spend another day in the filth of Cairo. But duty called. His schedule firm, he was booked on a flight to Alexandria in the morning for a meeting with the first governor of British East India Company. The subject: recommendations for the replacement of a deceased company ordinal, Sir Carroll Starr.

"Lewis, do we have a steamer in the Bay of Bengal, near Rangoon?"

"Why do you ask?"

"Just burrowing about. Silent clapping for now. Snow White has a steamer in the Bay of Bengal. Rangoon is logical given the rest of the puzzle—drugs, contraband, commandos."

Johnny rolled the window down and laid his hand out to catch the rain. Sandbags and barricades, sandbags and petrol pumps, ration cards and delivery licenses, blackout visors, blackout curtains, white footboards, and khaki-green paintwork—London, in turn, tense and expectant. Luxurious flats becoming a maze of East End squats.

"What kind of transceivers are on our steamers, Lewis?"

"First rate, I'm told. Capital technology. Hallicrafter HT-Series."

Johnny nodded and went on. "See if this bit of sauce gives it flavor, Lewis." Drying his hand with his handkerchief, looking quite smug, as though enamored of his insight, he exclaimed.

"Suppose I told you MI6 bought the note on Poston and Sons, Ltd. And the foggy squirrels are using our steamers as Q-boats. Decoys to smuggle drugs and the lot with Snow White as a cover."

Lewis sighed, and his mind's eye found the words *bloody daft*. "Well, you'll have to see about that, won't you? It's your scrubbing that will get us killed."

"Read the telegrams I've sent you, Lewis. I'm on the beam on this one. You'll see."

"Don't send me any more telegrams."

Neither man spoke until quiet had reached its limit. Then Johnny called to the driver, "Drop us at 6 Stanhope Gate, Park Lane, the Astor."

Gordon Dewar, subaltern to a dying admiral and MI6 D-Section chief for German Affairs, sat in the subscription room in a deep leather club chair as though a stuffy bag, grinding his mind with reams of data.

The last communication he received from Sir Carroll Starr lacked the usual clarity. The words were rambling and frantic. Dewar was certain the words were not meant for him. The meat of the message was intriguing: The Imperial Policy Group is fully funded. Inform Arthur Tester. Control is out of sorts.

Reading the message again, Dewar thought of his consorts at the Saint Ermins Hotel. He and Tester often shared their delights. Policy groups, institutes, endowment funds—these swells have all sorts of shills to hide behind, he mused.

Whiskey coated the rim of the heavy tumbler as he passed the glass through a billow of smoke, drew at its aroma, wishing he had liberated a bottle of Admiral Sinclair's twenty-year-old single malt. Some whiskey, that. The old boy is losing track of time and place.

Dewar had decided Sir Starr's death was not a suicide; it was a warning—a financial message from I.G. Farben's intelligence chief. Whether Starr's hanging was a directed execution or an extemporaneous expression, if Max Ilgner authored the target list, Dewar would top out for the same consideration. There was nowhere to run.

Smuggling drugs into southern France had been profitable and relatively safe before Max Ilgner and Rudolf Hess discovered the operation. Threatening to provide the details of Dewar's enterprise to the Corsican syndicate in Marseille, Hess demanded money—one thousand pounds per month.

Hess could sully the pope with his grin.

Knowing the Nazi had turned his own father over to the Gestapo for anti-Nazi sentiments, and the Nazis had sent Hess's father to a concentration camp, Dewar decided to suborn the zealot until he could arrange a hit.

Killing Hess would not be as easy as killing Sir John Poston—nor would it be as dangerous as kidnapping Hardin's wife. Witnesses aside, as ruthless as he was, Dewar could not harm a woman. She was being held in the house Dewar purchased from Alfred Gosden. If Hardin didn't make it home, his wife would be released. If he did, Dewar needed the leverage to get out of England.

Where he could go was complicated. The Corsicans controlled the elicit trades from Bombay to Marseille, including Tripoli and Algiers. The Nazis had infiltrated South America and many of the islands in the Caribbean. The world was shrinking.

Dewar's expression hardened in postponement when John Poston arrived, his brother at his heel. The Poston family represented everything he found inconvenient.

His jaw fixed with an ivory bite that would chap a weasel's ass, Lewis Poston toiled into a chair. "Gordon Dewar, how good of you to sponsor the Poston boys on such a miserable night. I do hope you don't mind if I join you for a drink, old chap."

Dewar twisted his mouth to demonstrate a thread of sacrifice and gestured to the nearest chair. "Not much leeway, Lewis. I'm sure we can sort your obligations."

"Well, fair enough. I see you've boiled your indignation into the usual bumf, Gordon. Always keen to sing *Tipperary* or some other dated ditty while you polish a bit of brass."

Casting a hand aside, Dewar spoke abruptly. "Have you rinsed out Grumpy's doings, Johnny—the SOE team survivor? Mother's spymaster, Blinker Hall, is on his heels. He insists the pouched documents are explosive, papers exposing Mother's financial doings from the Med to Asia. Blinker has a pair of letters he's on about—CS and ES. What do you make of those letters, Johnny?"

Johnny cast a cautious glance at Lewis. The spy master and Admiral Sinclair met for lunch routinely, and Johnny had been given the letter puzzle by the admiral days ago. "One set might be Credit Suisse—CS. The other set might be Enskilda Bank, Sweden—ES. Both banks have been corresponding with Hitler's lot at the Reichbank in Germany and in Argentina."

Dewar raised both palms to stop the disclosure, realizing the intelligence data being discussed was graded: *Most Immediate*. "Johnny. You just violated the Official Secrets Act."

"Bollocks. If you knew the answer, Gordon, why did you ask?"

Dewar spread into a cautious brace. Scratching at the chair's leather side with a plodding rhythm as though drumming the legions, he sipped his drink in short waves.

"Just backtracking information flow. And your access, Johnny." Looking at Lewis, he asked, "Are Poston steamers working the channel?"

"Trying on a new skirt, are you, Gordon?" Lewis asked, moving his pipe aside.

"Yes, we're in the channel," Johnny replied, interrupting. "Last quarter's report listed shipments from Hong Kong to Durban and Rotterdam." Johnny stopped talking when Lewis nudged his shin.

Dewar hesitated. "Should be easy to trace." Knowing neither brother was privy to the workings of the Ceylonese cartel controlling their father's business. Dewar had written the cartel's operational policy documents.

"How's British Petroleum these days, Lewis?"

"You do seem over weaned tonight, Gordon. As nosy as your boys at MI6 are, I'd be surprised if you didn't already have the answer. The admiral must have stacks of intel ledgers casting all the actors—oil, rubber, pot ash, pig iron, silk, diamonds, ganja, opium."

Dewar ignored the jab. "Just being polite, Lewis."

Known for his studied deference, Lewis set fire to his pipe and offered Dewar his tobacco. "Well, all right, Gordon. We're just pulling tits, really. The Japs will cut off Burma's crude and Java's crude. The Arabs are pressuring us to help expose Jewish terrorists in Gaza. European Jews are trying to escape the Nazis and settle near the Temple of Solomon. And British Petroleum's moving into the Congo. It's a busy time."

Johnny stood to catch the chief steward's eye and asked for a glass of water. "What are your friends at the Vatican planning, Gordon. Will they remain mute if Fritz invades Poland?"

"I'm sure Fritz and the pope are in concert. Time hardly exists for that grim theology, busy as they are, trying to reconcile their investments with their faith."

"Are the colonies running out of gold? India, South Africa?" Lewis asked.

Dewar finished his drink. "Speaking of gold. East India Charter paid a sizable commission for the elimination of our team that jumped into Tonkin."

"Unforgiving Catholics. Our team found the documents they want kept secret. Ten Downing wants the papers kept secret and the commandos don't know it." Johnny sat with his right hand extended as if coaxing an explanation.

Dewar accepted the gesture with a sarcastic grin. "Rome believes Team 7's carrying a diagram of the organizational structure for their East India smuggling apparatus extending from Hong Kong to Bombay. Enough detail to jeopardize centuries of preaching."

Johnny fixed Dewar with a knowing grin. "I wonder who fed the Vatican that load of horse shit." Johnny accepted his water from the sommelier with a nod. "Someone is pulling a long bow on this one. Did you carve yourself a bit of that pie, Gordon?"

Dewar lit his pipe and adjusted his chair. "After being ambushed, what's left of our special-ops team must be running. If this Grumpy is wounded and slogging through the jungle, he and his mates are in a tight spot—up against the next second."

"What's left! What's left! You poncey bastard!" Lewis reached across the table, snatched Dewar's necktie, and jerked him against the table, splashing Dewar's whiskey into his lap. "We're not playing skittles, jackass. Grumpy's a friend of mine. Bloody hell." He flipped Dewar's tie over his head, then threw Dewar into his chair.

Seething with rage, Dewar's plum-colored face was twisted as he wiped a palm across his eyes. After a period of silence, he cracked a facetious grin. Poston, the pompous shit, just told me he's been briefed on Snow White's details. That puts Johnny in the frame for willfully violating the official secrets act—for treason.

Dewar coughed through a hack. Lewis declared, "Your calculator seems to be shedding speed, you ponce. Say something perceptive so Johnny doesn't have to stop whatever he's doing and call a flap wagon."

"Very well—as it goes, SIS thinks the false trail concerning the Vatican was created to mask a spy doubling out of Whitehall." Dewar smugged his expression, savoring his guile.

As if assuming Dewar might turn more reasonable, Johnny sat into a brace and nudged his brother's foot. "Snow White's lads were browned off before they jumped into Tonkin—bowled out by the umpire, I'd say. You're the spy, Gordon. Why else would you bounce about such an obscure operation?"

Dewar stood and set his glass on the chimneypiece. "Fair enough, I suppose." Knocking his pipe on the hearth, he picked a pernicious grin as he packed it with fresh tobacco. "Try this shoe on, Lewis. Two British Petroleum representatives were shot in a go-down in Diamond Harbor yesterday—legals from BP's headquarters in Ankara, Turkey."

Surprised, Lewis asked, "Were you aware of this, Johnny?"

"No. And I don't believe it, either."

"Playing hopscotch on the duckboards, Gordon?" Lewis asked.

Dewar coined a knowing smile. "We have operatives combing the docks in Diamond Harbor, searching for a tall, white South African. We have limited information about the man. Our signal monitoring station at Lion Rock, on Ceylon, intercepted messages sent from Diamond Harbor that referenced a Portuguese steamer. These signals could have come from this man or his organization."

"Are the signals tied to Snow White?"

"Who would know?" Dewar's tongue ran the rim of his glass. He was satisfied his hate and anger hadn't gone anywhere after all.

"Here's a guess," Johnny put in. "The prime minister, Admiral Sinclair, and now you, Dewar—eyes only. Snow White's in chamber and hallway. It's your incessant fussing that's melted the wax."

"Nonsense, Johnny. My inquiries have been limited to the doings of SOE personnel. Nothing out of bounds, I assure you."

"Come now, Gordon. You've been preening with a fourth feather since you started tracking the Vatican in '36—since your liaisons at the Berlin Olympics. Since you and the duke of Hamilton danced off to play an odd game of sausage. I've been informed the French premier was a guest of yours."

As Dewar registered the duke's name, Lewis left the table to make a phone call.

Dewar waited as Lewis walked away, then said, "The duke's a rather dapper old sod." He tamped tobacco into his pipe. He and the duke had left Woolwich on the same day, with the same resentments.

With an instant of silence so intense, Johnny could hear his heartbeat, Johnny said, "Give this a rattle, Gordon. One of the deviants chasing Snow White—the Vatican, Whitehall, or Fritz—had our lads ambushed."

"We don't know, do we, Johnny?" Dewar scanned the room, pausing while Lewis sat. "MI6 would never bugger their own lads."

"Any member of Snow White's Team 7 that escapes Burma and finds his way to England will kill you, Gordon. If they don't, Hockey will."

Sitting down, a blackening seemed to grip Lewis as the geometry of his face grew more abrupt. His photographic memory liked to gallop through the years—the transactions, the names, dates, cargoes, go-downs, locations, his father's shipping files.

"My, my, my," Lewis whispered, turning from the table. "All of Poston and Sons' steamers are of Portuguese registry." That MI6 was tracking a Poston

& Sons' steamer didn't seem likely. "You're nose deep in this, aren't you, Gordon? All a-fuss as you troll for cover."

"One of your learned observations, I suppose," Dewar said.

Instantly, Lewis had a grip on Dewar's throat. "I've another observation. You and your friends are killing special-service troops." Pinning Dewar into his chair, Lewis twisted his tie. "If I find you've a hand in killing those lads, I'll blow your useless balls off."

"Someone's killing our lads, but it's not my doing." Dewar eased into a deep breath, tugging the tablecloth flat, still confident he could outmaneuver the Poston boys.

Johnny sat silently factoring data, staring at his brother.

Lewis braced his younger brother with a short huff and nudged him on the shoulder. "It's folderol, Johnny. Gordon wouldn't put a hoof wrong. He's too busy licking at stern duty. Padding his pay book and all that. Take me to the hotel. I'm scheduled on an early flight from Shoreham."

Again, Lewis pinned Dewar into his chair, hesitated, laughed, and threw his whiskey in Dewar's face. "Take good care, Gordon. You should keep a white feather in your lapel."

For Lewis, admitting his brother was right about Dewar required the second coming. But then, his brother was at bottom a statistical genius and an excellent judge of character. Too gentle for life outside of London, for the world away from England, Johnny was where he needed to be—at Admiral Sinclair's right hand.

*　　*　　*

New York. Pan American Marine Terminal, LaGuardia Airport. 28 August 1939. 1950 Hours, GMT – 5 Hours.

"Thanks for meeting me, Joey." Eaton smoothed his shirt at his waist, relieved his secretary hadn't come as well. "Joey, allow me to introduce Petra Laube-Heintz, a representative of Stein Bank in Germany. Miss Heintz, this is my friend, Joseph Telleli." She smiled and cocked her head, acknowledging the introduction.

Sam watched Joey shift his weight into a guarded stance as his eyes flashed a quick stabbing glance at the woman standing behind him. Joey's gaze seemed to pour cold fire as he scorched the woman's frame, etching his thoughts on a new canvas.

Joey kept glancing at her.

Sam and Joey had become friends during a fight over marbles in the second grade at the public school in Waterville Valley, Vermont. Parting ways after high school, Sam had slipped into the isolation of moneyed connections and greed. An obsessive-compulsive, sad at times, jealous at times, Joey had made the effort to stay in touch, to help his friend.

Eaton waited for a punch line as he tried to interpret the confusion in Joey's face. Joey's eyes kept straying to a set of pins that defied beauty—to the tall woman.

"What's the matter, Joey?"

An easy question, but Joey paused, then shot a backward glance at the woman and grabbed Sam's sleeve. "Sam, we have to talk. It's your secretary, Angela." Petra turned and walked toward a newsstand.

Joey pulled Sam to a window overlooking an empty departure bay and gestured with a reluctant sigh. "Stand still, Sam—please."

Sorting incomplete portraits of his dealings with Telleli, Eaton pushed him into a column. "What the hell is it?"

"Jesus—I don't know how else to tell you. Your secretary died yesterday, killed by a hit-and-run driver. It's damned strange. Cops think it might be murder."

The shock of silence caused Eaton to stroll along a series of windows. With shame knotting his throat, he extended a hand to the window frame, waiting for Joey's next comment. Joey had met Angela in Atlanta seventeen months before and, taken by her fancy, found her a teaching job in New York City.

Eaton screamed into the iron bridgework of the airport's ceiling, "Murder? What the hell are you talking about?" Searching the crowd for suspects, ignoring the stares, he pushed Joey away.

"In front of her apartment on Long Island. Yesterday."

Eaton's head shifted with an awkward shudder. Breathing more rapidly, his chest tightened as a weal of pain crested his forehead, leaving him dizzy. Sitting on a metal bench along the window fronting the departure bay, Eaton shook his head slowly.

Conflicted, the pace of his thoughts accelerated. He looked at Petra. She was talking to a stranger. He wanted to be rid of her—to amend his deceit.

"Who would murder a secretary?" Eaton's heart hung in his chest.

"I don't know. I'm sorry, Sam."

As Petra moved closer, Joey stepped aside. For an instant, he drew his eyes nearly closed as if questioning how this beautiful woman fit into Eaton's life. Eaton acknowledged Petra with a nod. Joey stepped to her side—strangers helping Samuel Eaton.

Eaton and Joey escorted Petra to her cab. "I'll see you at the office tomorrow." Eaton expected the German to help him organize the accounts necessary for the arbitrage scheme to function. He no longer cared whether Mr. George was right about the doings of his secretary.

"Good morning." Eaton smiled, admiring his new secretary. Their eyes met, and he was suddenly wary. What was it about the woman's beauty that bothered him?

"Good morning, Mister Eaton. I'm Dorothy Stuart. I've been transferred from the South American loan desk to fill in until you find a secretary."

"Dorothy Stuart. I'll try to remember."

"I'm constantly on the go, I'm afraid, wandering all over the shop. I'm scheduled to travel to England and Europe for meetings as the bank's emissary.

Dorothy stood five feet plus nine in her stockings, with a ripe-peach hue to her cheeks that set her auburn hair ablaze. She was a distraction, her smile a mingle of admiration and sensual familiarity. And she was gorgeous.

After reading her file, and several calls to the South American desk, Eaton knew Dorothy Stuart was well connected. And she was unattached and wealthy. Her work schedule was flexible, and she seemed to do as she pleased. Daily, excepting the weekend, from eleven in the morning until early afternoon, she ate a modest lunch near the ice rink in Rockefeller Center, and finished the *New York Times* crossword with a pen.

"A message for you, Mr. Eaton." Dorothy used her index finger to guide his attention to the telephone log, ruffling the page, permitting her expression to register Eaton's lack of response.

Joseph Telleli called...important...will call back.

"John Dulles is waiting for you in the lobby."

Eaton's thoughts bounded through a continuum of events, trying to construct a sequential testament for his secretary's life, parsing his reflections with the circumstance of her death.

Jousting with the nagging insinuations concerning the arbitrage plan, he tapped Dorothy's desk for luck. A stiffness rose in his chest as he eased away from the counter. The office lobby seemed to have a sinister cast. Holding the *New York Times*, John Dulles toasted with his coffee cup when Eaton lumbered stoop shouldered into the lobby area.

"I'm busy today, John. Can we meet tomorrow, say half past one?"

"Of course, Sam." Dulles grimaced. Having helped script the arbitrage plan, he had agreed to monitor Eaton's time, and document who he met with in New York.

Being a senior vice president at J. P. Morgan provided Samuel Eaton with amenities well beyond accountability. Any conceivable expenditure was presumed to be a function of image, assigned to an impressive address, and allocated to proportionate outcomes.

A meeting with John Dulles or his brother Allen could absorb several thousand dollars.

John Dulles had completed his studies at the George Washington University Law School well before Eaton had finished his studies at the London School of Economics. They had become acquainted through a series of loan transactions negotiated by Dulles for the Congo Syndicate with J. P. Morgan.

J. P. Morgan's intelligence arm had been tracking the Dulles brothers, their transactions, and their associates for years. Eaton knew that John and Allen Dulles had been negotiating with Adolf Hitler and the Reichbank on behalf of Kuhn Loeb Investment Bank since January 1933.

He therefore decided to keep the quiet-spoken brothers at arm's length, given their possible association with many of the companies involved in the arbitrage plan.

By extension assumed they had access to Nicholas, the Austrian responsible for orchestrating the plan. If correct, the Dulles brothers could well end Eaton's career and possibly, his life.

Dorothy's voice rang through the intercom.

"Mr. Eaton, Joseph Telleli is on the line."

"What is it, Joey?"

They talked for several minutes, primarily about the Yankees. As the phone fell silent, Joey addressed the purpose of his call. "I found eighty-one thousand dollars in cash in Angie's apartment—stuffed in a book satchel."

"How is that possible? She was a receptionist. She worried about making rent."

"Damned if I know. Where did it come from?"

"This can't be good. She never asked me for money. Even for groceries."

Eaton sat on the corner of his desk, took a pearl-handled switchblade from his coat pocket, and snapped it open. Admiring his letter opener, he asked, "Did her building super let you into her apartment?"

"I have a key."

Eaton exhaled to gain control. Seconds vaporized into a distillate, into a cluster of barbed granules—cold facts. Matching scenarios, his headache gained steam as he mentally paged through his secretary's finances.

"Are her parents wealthy?" Joey asked.

"I don't know. I don't think so."

"Well Sam, if it was murder, there had to be a reason." Joey coughed. "It happened while you were in Europe. Was your account compromised? Money missing?"

"Hang on, I'll run a quick check." Eaton put Telleli on hold and asked for his account balance. "You are right, Joey. The money was debited to my investment account."

"Do you think Angie could pull that off?"

"That seems unlikely." Eaton calculated the odds, his eye tracking the clock's second hand deciding the answer came with one sweep—or perhaps at twelve.

"Holy shit, Sam! The timing's too cute. Maybe the hit-and-run was a setup."

"For what? What are you talking about, Joey?" Jesus, what's going on? Eaton thought. Eighty-one large in cash—in a book satchel—with Steinbeck, I'll bet.

"You're a fool, Eaton. You and your big-money games. Listen. The men you're playing with like winning."

"We lost a friend, Joey. And we don't know why."

Dorothy's mood changed when Petra Laube-Heintz eased from the elevator, extended her hand, and announced that she was the representative from J. H. Stein Bank of Cologne, Germany, here for an appointment with Samuel Eaton.

The dossier compiled by MI6 on the woman for Admiral Sinclair was detailed—Petra Laube-Heintz was a well-educated financial warden of the Nazi state. She was shockingly beautiful. She managed Hitler's personal accounts. Her brothers had joined the SS.

Ushered into Eaton's office, Petra sat in the stenographer's chair at the side of his desk. Scanning the pictures behind his chair, she crossed her legs as if offended by what she discovered.

"Can I call you Sam?" she asked, mustering a cockish tone.

"I suspect you have a complete file on me." Eaton was not interested in small talk. Then he alerted. As he moved the water pitcher, he searched the photographs on the credenza behind his chair—no names.

"Have you forgotten our time in Garmish?"

"What companies are we funding?" he asked, changing the subject.

Petra hesitated, seemingly put off by the question. "We are dealing only with banking houses. The companies remain numbered accounts. The transfer margins and intervals for those companies will be sorted at Credit Suisse."

Eaton alerted to the change in Petra's demeanor. This arbitrage deal's starting to smell like a setup, he thought. Odds are the companies will not realize they're being primed for a raid.

"Why are six banks involved in the arbitrage instead of seven?"

"The specialist who collapsed during the meeting in Garmish died in his room. His bank had doubts and withdrew from the plan yesterday."

I wonder if the man was murdered. Poisoned?

"He might be the lucky one. Who's setting the spot price of gold?" Eaton wanted the projected gold-price fluctuations to hedge his own arbitrage plays against those the European bankers had scheduled.

"I don't know. The United States has fixed the price at $35.00 an ounce."

* * *

London. The Intelligence "Hole" beneath Whitehall. 28 August 1939. 0730 Hours, GMT.

Soaked, the rain had come in wedges, thick at the top. Deeds—leaseholds, copyholds, and charters—all had been flooded and jokingly assigned to the Royal Navy's Damage Control Department for shore drills.

For Johnny, a dry-land, warm-weather spook, the rivers had run bank-full for weeks.

London was girding for an invasion. The city's grimy cellars, with their low, windowless rooms, had been requisitioned by stern air raid precaution (ARP) wardens, each with a tuckbox for his gas mask strapped to his web belt, a tin hat to catch the first brick, and a handbell with a bright red handle to alert the weary.

A lamp's glint marked the chief warden's white helmet, and showed fitfully in his eyes, mingling with the fires of another rehearsal: air-raid sirens announced, and Londoners ran. The stranded ran into the muddy trenches dug in the park.

The admiralty received approval from the Cabinet to convert twenty-five merchantmen to armed merchant cruisers (A.M.C.'s) with eight 150mm guns, and two 76mm guns each. Twenty-three thousand reservists have been called up. All regular-service leaves have been cancelled. Night bombing raids will be coming. Poland will be for practice.

Before long, warders will be running London's streets.

Fostering a startled awareness, anxious they were, these valets for London's bowels, preying on strangers, baton in hand, herding stragglers down stone passageways, keeping them in the dark, hoping the poor souls would take root.

Even the babies had gas masks. Gas masks sprang from cardboard boxes, followed by a lout staggering, his mask in full flower as he hurled a stone at the window of the German embassy on Carlton House Terrace.

Sandbags lay in bundles strapped with twine. Some had removed their twine and thrown themselves about. Other bags had filled themselves. Some bags laid about, demanding to be stacked into a fashion—a crosshatch or perhaps a twill.

Gas masks and tin hats, what else could there be? Johnny wondered. All running-boards and bumpers must be painted white. Lamp posts and curbstones, as well. That's something else.

Fewer and fewer lights shone on the streets of London. In many neighborhoods, except for the trash fires, no light shone. Plaster saints, cast-iron and brass saints as well, seemed to fume and fret and posture in the dark, no longer revered for their memory, their spotlights dead—no longer needed for Mother to carry on. Field marshals and horses stood stock still, watching out for the children being shipped to the country's outlying farms.

As August 1939 was wearing out, a crush of probabilities, some 1,473,000 children, schoolteachers, and young mothers were sent packing.

Johnny began walking the streets at night, more to keep his sense of proportion than to lend a hand. He was becoming quite well versed in the art of filling sandbags. He did wonder where the children would be after the war ended. Would their parents be alive, or consumed in a rectory fire? Would their home be destroyed?

Standing in the entry of the dispensary, challenging Sinclair's chief surgeon to a duel if he didn't come clean, Johnny asked how long the admiral would live. "Sir Hugh will not last much longer. Clearly, not the war."

"Be specific, doctor—weeks, months, a year?"

"Three months, tops."

When the admiral entered Broadway's SIS briefing room the next day, Johnny noted an air of resigned inertia in Sinclair's stride. His boss was on short rations. Three months to live looked farfetched.

"Johnny, I thought I'd pop down. How are you, lad?" he asked, a sparkle in his eye like the memory of an old smile.

"I'm doing well, Admiral—mill walking mostly."

"Well good on you, Johnny." Sinclair got hold of a newspaper. He passed over the first page and began reading. Somberly at first, and then smiling, he scanned the next page. Dropping the paper, he said, "I miss my kinship with your father. He was a wonderful old git."

Johnny held nothing back, sensing it was crucial to give the admiral a full bottle, in detail. "William Hockey, a family friend, has sorted Sir John's death. He was murdered after discovering opium being smuggled into Europe using his company steamers."

Seconds swept the clock before the admiral acknowledged Johnny's comments.

"So...now we know." The cast to his eye lacked anticipation. Banging the dead ashes from his pipe, he gave Poston a warm nod. Wincing as if a stitch had bit his side, the admiral's expression bore the conflicting lines of pain and satisfaction.

Starting again, drawing a deep breath, he suffered a hacking cough. "Dreadful business, smuggling drugs." Sinclair had said it once before, and it reminded Johnny of his father.

"Raw silk will be expensive if it's available at all." Johnny lit a cigarette and waited for the admiral to sit down. He knew, in a general way, that his boss had handed the reins of Operation Snow White to the Poston brothers. "Sir, three men orchestrated my father's death. One is a vicar's son working for you, Admiral—Alfred Gosden."

Sinclair sat at the desk next to Poston's with a sigh. "I don't know him, I'm afraid." His expression hardened. "A vicar's son, you say."

"Sir, I've taken the liberty of having him posted to Cairo, to help with a special project he's uniquely qualified for. He'll be supervised by my brother, Lewis. Not openly, mind you."

Raising his head, the admiral agreed. "I see—straightaway then."

"He's already in Cairo." After a brief pause to confirm the admiral's inference and watch him light his pipe, Poston continued. "Gordon Dewar may have been involved in Sir John's demise, but just yet, we've failed to put him in the frame or determine his role."

"Dewar's a complicated man. He doesn't seem the kind geared for rough country. Have you found specifics that indicate he's working with the Bosche?"

"No. He has met with Hess in Malta, Marseille, and Lyon and with Max Ilgner, director of I. G. Farben, International's intelligence arm in Malta."

"Recently?"

"Dewar's been traveling to those cities on a routine schedule for three years—well before Operation Snow White kicked off."

"What do you make of it?"

"I believe Hess and Ilgner have compromised Dewar. I believe they have tied him to an opium smuggling operation and are demanding money and intelligence for their silence."

"And this Gosden works a back channel for Dewar."

"Yes."

*   *   *

Burma. 28 August 1939. 1320 Hours, GMT + 6.5 Hours.

South, they went, skirting the roadway to the east, resting at odd intervals.

Linc Jensen had died to save Hardin's life. Packing a deepening sense of obligation, Hardin was desperate to reach the Ross Island rally, and find his way to England. His dead mates had become part of his soul. Die if he must, he would honor their sacrifice.

He stumbled, staggering beneath the driving rain. His boot soles had separated, sucked apart by the dense clay. As he fell flat on his face, he lay still. When he did not try to get up, Tu's bamboo stave revived him. Taking an offered hand, he was able to stand.

As they pushed their way out of a patch of elephant grass, without a sound, they were surrounded. The character of the jungle holds true for these warriors, Hardin thought.

The strange men were a meld of vegetation, flowing into a definition, then vanishing, snapping into view as if thrown onto a canvas—stoic faces dusted to a pale gray. The canopy hung into a wall of vines and bamboo forming a continuous trellis.

Frightened, Tu stood into a flash of recognition. Fingers extended, she burst into a harried cadence of padded chatter, badgering a leaf pod with her left hand, gripping her machete with her right hand. Hardin counted nineteen men, all the picture of rigorous silence, all carrying American weapons and equipment.

Tu wiped her face with her left hand and set it at the front of her left shoulder. Cinching her fingers around the handle of the knife sheathed behind her neck, she seemed determined to die fighting.

With a series of tocsins, the men moved in unison, disarming Tu and Hardin, and forcing them onto their knees. Making a pretense of being agile, Hardin extended his right leg to ease the pain. A large white man slid into the circle and held a knife, cutting edge up, under Hardin's chin.

"What have we here?" he asked, examining Hardin's weapon.

So, I can quit, Hardin thought. Does my luck have a limit? Not much of a last hoorah. No final charge. No drum and fife.

Hardin had fallen without a shot being fired.

After a deep breath, he concentrated on the cadence of his pulse, on the throbbing of his leg wound, finally the rhythm of the raindrops falling on a large leaf. The roots near his boots had been freshly scarred. The tang of Linc Jensen's bowels hovered near his thoughts.

The intense heat under the canopy mixed with the cool soil to form a ground mist—steam.

"Let me see your face, cowboy." The words rang with a cornpone accent.

Hardin's mouth went dry. His chest ached, tossed by a surging heart rate and irregular jolts of adrenaline. Rotating around his stave to ease the pain in his thigh, he found the potato contours of a rural expression framing a pair of translucent, gray-blue eyes. Burnt with resolve, he waited. Motionless. Realizing one wrong move would get him killed.

Hardin gave the man his full attention, measuring the man's hawk-like eyes. Suspicious spasms stitched the man's angular jaw. Blond hair sat atop a weathered face, layered in patches as if shorn with a knife. The man's uniform had been stitched and stitched again, indicating a detail a reckless man would ignore.

Be careful, Grumpy, he thought. Aim off—lead the target—judge the wind.

A boot heel hit Hardin's chest, knocking him on his ass, splitting the tender hide on his wound. He squinted into the foliage. He could feel the warm blood. His throat welled with bile. A hand seized the front of his shirt, jerking his chest upright.

Instantly vulnerable, Hardin put pressure on his right leg to relieve the cramping, permitting a facetious curl to register his discomfort. The jungle-worn stranger twisted Hardin's right boot to read the identity disc woven into the laces.

"Grumpy. Is that your name, jackass?" The flat side of the knife's blade traced the length of Hardin's jaw, stopping at the point of his chin. Holding the blade under Hardin's left eye, tearing open a breast pocket on Hardin's shirt, the stranger caught the light-tan piece of cloth that fell out and read the message written in Burmese.

"Well, Grumpy, this rag claims you're the native's friend, and you want their help."

"That's a goolie-chit." Hardin braced, glistening with an even, dry indifference as the stranger started to speak.

"Well, my boy, elementary school must have been a real pisser for a boy called Grumpy."

His body wasted with fatigue and desperate for rest, Hardin wondered if he would live to greet the morning. Stalling for time, stalling, and watching, a heart-and-arrow tattoo on the stranger's arm caught his eye—an American army tattoo.

With time running down, Hardin took a chance. "Well GI, who are your goons?"

Stooping, the stranger retrieved his knife. "Goons! It's a damn good thing they don't know much English. These men are Kachins: native recon dicks drawn from the 3rd Battalion of the 20th Burma Rifles. Kachins are of the old thinkin'—morons like you are best shot and left to rot."

Hawking and clearing his throat, Hardin asked, "Why are you in Burma?"

"We're huntin' bandits—Jap prickers. Drifted south to see what the slimes were savagin'."

"American Ranger?" Hardin asked, pointing at the tattoo.

"Slim Pickens, long range recon, US Army, Provisional."

"British Air Service. One of John Dill's dodgy boys. And if you're Slim Pickens, I must be Andy Devine. Call me Jingles."

With a gathering deceleration, both men relaxed into a vagrant banter, weighing odd habits, their gestures muted by suspicious ciphers. Hardin's British axioms sparred with his New York instincts—on the verge, his speech hurried. The Kachins had all leveled their weapons on him. Tu set her right hand near the hilt of a knife she had strapped on her thigh. Wild-eyed, frightened, she seemed ready to explode. When he caught her eye, he shook his head once.

"Well, Jingles, you're about as Brit as I am." When the American's knife blade fell flat on Hardin's leg wound, his throat seized. Death had many faces. "It's sixes and sevens this go-round." The American dropped the goolie-chit in Hardin's lap and lit a cigarette. "Gin up some balls, New York, and do the blimey-dance again—without the horse shit."

"I worked on the docks in New York for a time."

Hardin searched Tu's sector of the jungle. Her eyes told the story. Swallowing to gain control, registering the knife's pressure, he started again. "I was the team leader of a long-range-penetration team. We were ambushed right after we crossed into Burma. We exchange identity discs as standard procedure. Grumpy's the only disc that made it out."

The American was sharply interested. "Who hit your team?"

"Cambodes, I think. Mercenaries. And a Dutchman, a solo tracker." Hardin turned and faced the American's challenge. Taking the small leather bag from his rucksack, he showed the American the contents. "Here's what's left of my mates. The bastards are counting thumbs."

"Are the slimes still doggin' your trail?"

"I don't know. Probably."

Watching the Kachins inventory his kit down to the sealed pouch, Hardin gestured to his right. "You can help us. I need to use your wireless to confirm an extraction."

With a slight nod, the American ranger handed Hardin a Webley, MK4 Floating Knife—special issue for American paratroopers and rangers. "It's an extra—it floats. Might come in handy on a water jump." True enough. Hardin might end up in the water.

The natives dressed Hardin's kit, uncovered their transceiver, and gave Tu her machete, her knife, and a chicken. Two men rigged a small canvas dodger over the wireless, and one man held the antenna upright. The rest of the natives formed a perimeter thirty meters from the transceiver.

"Grumpy here, Princess." Tu hung the chicken on her hemp belt. "Talk to me Princess, this is Grumpy, over."

With a protracted crackle, the rush of noise from the wireless shook at the hollow. "G'day, Grumpy. Good to hear your voice." Uncle's words came stitched with static. With the sound came the stark realization: he must convince Uncle Dingo he will make the rally.

"We're fingers out, Princess. The pie's in the oven." Code-extraction in five days.

"We're pulling tits-duty, Grumpy. No worries—add a bit of sweetener." Code-Uncle needs an extra day to make the rally.

"We have brown sugar, Princess." Code-Doc is wounded.

"No worries—good hunting, Grumpy." Hardin eyed Tu, then acknowledged the completion of the transmission with an assuring nod. He sat upright and struggled with his balance as he rose. "Thanks mate. Princess knows I'm upright."

"Cigarette?" The American peered through the squint of his right eye. Turning into Hardin's face, he waved a hand through the smoke near his face and offered Hardin the pack. "The jungle's gettin' kind 'a crowded. Malayan Chinese Communists have guerilla camps at most every turn. They aim to kill every Jap they run across."

"I don't want to bump into those boys."

Eager for a Lucky Strike, Hardin grabbed the smokes. Smiling, he admired the graphics--the green wrapper and gold bull's eye. He toasted the air with the pack and grinned to acknowledge the stranger's gift. With a gesture assigning the balance of the pack to Hardin's care, Slim Pickens extended a hand.

"Take this. It's penicillin. Should help heal that wound."

Hardin read the label on the packet: *Sodium Salt of Penicillin. Contains 5000 Florey Units. Keep Below 45*₀. "It's over a hundred degrees. Does this stuff work?"

"Can't hurt. Change direction now and then. Trackin' you is easier than followin' a chuck wagon." The ranger let smoke curl past his left eye and flipped the cigarette into the jungle.

The American ranger came clean finally, words Hardin needed to hear. "The monsoon's over. You need to be up and movin' before the trees have a shadow."

That made sense. Hardin memorized the stranger's face, the weathered grains that ran from his temples to the corners of his mouth. He released the man's grip. And then held up the MK4 floating knife with a nod.

"Thanks for the knife. I could use a couple battle dressings if you have any spares. After being bent for these many weeks, I need a favor. A call from you through your signal relay to report the body of a British soldier ten kilometers north of here. Describe the identity disc. No equipment or weapons."

The American turned to leave, then said, "Roger that. Here. We're do for a supply drop in two days." He handed Hardin three battle dressings. "Keep your head down. Lots of Jap prickers drug smugglers in this neck of the woods. You're breaking foliage with that leg of yours. Don't stop for over an hour. Stay off the coast road."

Rain swept into the upper reaches of the canopy. The mountain natives remained silent. With the snap of a finger they popped through the cracks in the foliage and vanished.

Almost at once there was a packet of quick shots. Moments later the American ranger appeared on the opposite side of the clock. "There's three less Cambodes. The Kachins are carvin' 'em up. Do you want their thumbs?"

Hardin shook his head. "Those bloody bastards came a long way."

"How 'bout their ears?"

"No. Be good if you and your Kachins backtrack our trail a few miles."

"Can do. Keep your head down, Grumpy."

After the ranger was gone, Tu appeared wary as she pulled Hardin in the opposite direction. She immediately picked up a bounding search-and-move stride using the stratagems known to natives of the jungle, threading aggressively into the maze, walking backward at odd intervals to check for trailers.

Occasionally she stopped and looked around as if to get her bearings.

After hours of being driven, Hardin was pleading for rest. With his hands he tried to explain he needed a slower pace. Finally, she stopped. Hardin dropped his blood-soaked pants and put a fresh battle dressing on his wound. Then injected himself with the penicillin.

This girl's going to kill me yet.

Tu eased their pace. By twilight they had traveled another three hundred meters and settled into a natural rock shelter near a small stream. Tu started a smokeless fire with bits of dry bamboo and set to preparing a meal of rice and chicken.

Hardin elevated his leg, removed the battle dressing, and squeezed the excess blood onto the ground. Tu took it to the creek, washed it, then gave it to Hardin to be used again.

Knowing that fear feeds on delay, Hardin dusted his wound with sulfa powder and left it exposed to the air while he ate.

Damn good luck that American crossed our trail. We might catch a break after he sends that false signal through channels.

*   *   *

Germany. Berchtesgaden, Bavaria. 28 August 1939. 1840 Hours, GMT + 1 Hour.

Albert Speer found Hitler's attraction to trifles annoying, a mixture of arrogant impulse provoked by long-winded calculation and episodic resentment.

Since joining the Nazi Party in 1931, he had become one of the Fuehrer's trusted confidants. Why he wasn't sure. His maximizing industrial production using slave labor seemed to actuate Hitler's demons. And yet his production successes left him at odds with many of the Nazi party's elite—Hess and Martin Borman in particular.

The map room was expansive and ornate. Larch logs filled the mammoth stone fireplace, warm and noisy. A 1939 *Michelin Guide for France* lay open on a cabinet near the window. The corporal's going to invade France using Michelin as a guide. The Nazi Blood Flag stood to the right of the chimneypiece.

Hours passed before Hitler entered the map room. Hitler walked to the fireplace and dropped an envelope into the fire. That done, he moved to the map table and set both hands on the table. Looking at a map of Poland, he spoke with a questioning tone. "The British are demanding Germany agree to an immediate settlement with Poland and form an alliance with Britain."

Hitler stood away from the map table and unfurled the folds in the flag.

To this point Speer's attempt to label Rudolph Hess as a spy had failed. A document had been left at his mail drop in Berlin connecting Hess to Victor Rothschild and England's MI5. After presenting Hitler with the missive, the Fuehrer glanced at the first page and then set the document in the fire as well.

Speer had lost the habit of listening or asking why. Carefully framing his response, he thrust a hand forward. "Production schedules can be maximized if enough Jews survive. Healthy Jews are more efficient."

"More efficient than what, Speer?"

Pleased with the provocation, Speer discreetly reached for his cognac. Suddenly cold, aware he, too, was expendable. Raising his cognac snifter, he said, "Unhealthy Jews, mein Fuehrer."

Hitler turned and walked to the map table. "In the final solution, Speer, Christianity will be trapped in a sea of Indo-Aryan ritual. The Jew will be deported. Germany's production schedules will not be subject to any religion."

Speer spoke cautiously, guiding his tone, aware he must conceal his disgust. Adolf Hitler wanted to wrap Europe in a cocoon—to wring the joy from Europe's flowers and nurture the spoils with social gradations of Aryan ritual tied to ancient celestial seasons.

"Accommodation with the Vatican will be essential to gain support of Catholics in Bavaria and Switzerland, running Credit Suisse, mein Fuehrer."

"Perhaps, Speer. Perhaps."

*   *   *

Diamond Harbor, India. 28 August 1939. 1200 Hours, GMT + 5.5 Hours.

Seven hours earlier morning had come to Diamond Harbor, India. The hammering rain that trailed the monsoon was now a colloidal mist, specked with bits of charcoal and dense enough to obscure the windscreen of the white Ford sedan.

The sedan had settled into its frame, metal on metal, the rutted roadbed assaulting the tires. Von Cleve's facial wounds barked with each jolt. The knots used to tie his hands told of a taut seaman. That his hands were tied in front of him told of inexperience.

The driver's a follower of the Thule, a disciple of Guido von List, a druidic cultist promoting Rossenkunde as fundamental to Aryan destiny. He's keeping notes for a debriefing.

For von Cleve, the driver was ripened fruit—an Indo-Aryan from Calcutta, complete with blond hair and eyes so strangely blue, they appeared to be antique.

Von Cleve admired the depth of the Thule and the rituals of the New German Order. But Guido von List had organized a secret cell, the New

Templar Order, in Prussia, challenging centuries of secrecy. The Nazi SS symbol, the doubling of an ancient Nordic rune, the Sig-rune, was designed by von List in 1933. Guido von List's "Seig" for "victory" became Hitler's variant.

Defying the edicts of Europe's Templar masters, von List convinced Hitler to build a system of "Order Castles," *Ordensbrugens*. Dedicated to a new Order of Teutonic Knights, the castles reversed Napoleon's edict of 1609, thus reestablishing a German military order of knighthood, and rewarding the more conspicuous affiliates of lesser military orders.

Guido died for his treachery. A Knight Templar killed him in 1919—Ion Crilley's father.

Von Cleve sat motionless, watching the driver's reactions, and timing his habits, waiting for that interlude when externals would fog the man's senses.

Logic brought patterns, sequences, and alternatives. He had to break contact with anyone outside the chase, to create space and gain time. Von Cleve focused on the driver, watching his movements, anticipating a pattern—a weakness. Whenever the traffic slowed to a crawl the man glanced at a newspaper lying on the front seat.

The sedan eased through traffic—a rolling coffin. The backseat grew smaller during a flurry of turns. Von Cleve measured the driver's neck.

Suddenly the driver yelled. A cow vaulted onto the bonnet, shattering the windscreen. The sedan swerved through a series of violent turns. While the driver was brushing bits of glass from his lap, Von Cleve laughed quietly and removed a cross hidden in the cuff of his pants. With a mounting rhythm, he rolled an eight-pointed cross over in his hand and began cutting the rope with its sharpened edge.

Von Cleve shook his thoughts free. He must focus to survive. He shifted his shoulders to square himself in his seat. The rope fell away from his wrists. Now he needed another cow.

The route from the docks of Diamond Harbor to Calcutta's international airport wound into the human sewer he expected. The sedan's brakes pulsed to a stop. Mired in a bovine sludge, busily engaged, the driver's eyes dropped to the newspaper.

Von Cleve kicked open the door, jumped into the crowd, grabbed a man hauling a two-wheeled cart and threw the man and the cart into the side of the sedan, trapping the driver inside. As the driver's pistol came level with the windowsill von Cleve threw a second man into the line of fire and dove crashing into the confusion of the market.

Pushing people out of his way, von Cleve ran through several stalls selling vegetables until he was out of the market. Free of the congestion he ran uphill, away from the traffic. After being ambushed for the first time in his life, he needed time to recuperate. He judged his worth as a primary target—millions of pounds. I've been worth more.

The Thule will keep trying to kill me. And, if the Vatican wants me dead, they will dispatch assassins from Malta.

Considering the ambush in the go-down and his capture, von Cleve decided the Thule must have discovered his competing commissions and therefore intended to kill him, intercept the message pouch, and use the documents to leverage the Vatican, Whitehall, or whoever thought they were exposed.

He had been careless, as had Leenstra, his cousin. Their targets, the commandos of SOE Team 7, were more professional than they had assumed. For anyone to escape ambush twice on such a well-known ratline was thought to be impossible—especially during the monsoon season. Yet that's exactly what happened.

More proficient and more ruthless than any other mercenaries he encountered in Southeast Asia; the Cambodians had failed. Brett Leenstra, a master assassin trained on Corsica from the age of nine, was butchered by the target in a counter ambush.

Informants operating along the Malayan coast had confirmed at least one commando had escaped the first ambush. If that's so, von Cleve thought, there's probably more commandos still alive, and those men will be difficult to find.

In a strange way, he was excited. As in the old days he was competing against good men.

Von Cleve kept heading toward the Hooghly River. Once he found the river, the Templar redoubt stood on the far shore about three kilometers to the east. He was risking his life. Crilley, his Templar master, might well have him executed.

Only those elevated beyond the purview of Masonic ritual had access to this sanctuary—direct descendants of Templar Knights driven into hiding in the fourteenth century, men for whom secrecy remained sacred.

Von Cleve was not one of these men.

Hours later he approached a man folding a net. "I will pay for transport across the river." Accepting a five-pound note, the fisherman pushed his skiff into the stream.

The temple overlooked all of Calcutta. The stone wall surrounding the property was a warning. To the masses, the stone wall isolated a family of wealth. To von Cleve, the wall formed the outer shell of a prison. His neatness lacking, he expected to be searched.

Von Cleve let the tension flow from his massive frame as he passed through the archway.

A heavy iron gate latched behind him. The sound announced Crilley's control. The Soldiers of the Passion of Christ would die for his safe passage if Crilley had ordered them to guard his life.

"*Caveo Dominus*, Alex," the old adversary said, extending a hand and inviting him into the chancel, then waving his arm in an arc as if noting the flowers. Palm trees grew there, and vines trailed from the garden trellis.

Von Cleve stood within a stone arch and searched the perimeter of the chancel. "Ion Crilley—it's been since Rota, in Spain. Rota's where you last tried to kill me."

"You killed nine of my men in that exchange."

"Yet known to all, I have always been an outlier. You tried to measure my worth with apprentice bowmen." A few yards in either direction and he would be exposed to every bowman in the priory. "Am I a welcome sight, or has my time expired?"

"Perhaps both are true—I have not decided." Crilley seemed to be evaluating the scars on von Cleve's face. "I have accurately predicted your outcomes for quite some time."

"A gift of sorts," von Cleve whispered.

Somewhat relaxed, they sat in the priory, whispering of times past, recounting clients, money and assassinations, the assignments they had worked together.

As though bringing himself to a decision, with his voice muted by cupped hands, Crilley said, "We lost track of you on the waterfront in Diamond Harbor."

"What happened?" von Cleve asked abruptly, pushing an insistent tone. Unable to resist, he screamed, "I lost seven men."

"They've been replaced?"

"Of course. Expendable Sepoys. You know who was responsible for the raid on my headquarters, don't you?"

Crilley's expression conveyed a wily shroud of distrust. He leveled his gaze on von Cleve's sutured face. "You caused the raid. You and your incessant demands."

"Ah. What are you looking for, Ion Crilley?"

"Alex, almost all men would be executed for what you have done. You have violated many of the precepts of the Strasbourg Constitution—principally those governing loyalty. You accepted multiple commissions for the same transaction. You must choose one and return the others. The temple will keep the pouch and its contents."

Von Cleve registered the challenge by stepping in front of Crilley. To be accused of violating the covenants of the Strasbourg Constitution, a founding Templar document, was to be accused of heresy. His chest heaved in quiet rage, his expression casting the illusion of impatient fatigue. *I must choose my words with care and be mindful of my adversary's archers.*

"We have had our difficult times, Ion. This is not one of them." Von Cleve stopped and searched the priory and the garden beyond. His cold, abrasive tone had caused Crilley's posture to stiffen.

"But even if you find my conduct treasonous, your hands are too slow." Then he laughed, gripping a dagger with an eight-inch blade in his right hand, cutting edge up. He plowed on. "The Templar have contracted with the Vatican for centuries—and the other principals for over a century. We satisfy the three contracts by securing the pouch. If we keep the pouch, our fiduciary will be complete, and our financial leverage will increase ten-fold."

Von Cleve cultivating a resonant mood brought calm to Crilley's face. After a group of men in brown robes streamed through an archway, Crilley's orders became clear. *Stand ready to execute von Cleve.* As the tension in the priory rose with uncertain life, the former allies drew pleasure in knowing Templar transactions were centripetal.

Von Cleve's commissions and the documents contained in the pouch would be kept by the Order and remain a secret—available for viewing upon request.

An arrow passed within a feather's brush of von Cleve's mouth and sank into the wooden spar near his right shoulder. defiantly resolute, setting his feet apart, von Cleve waited for the second arrow to find his chest. He could bury his knife in Crilley's chest and die taking the next step. Or he could sheath his knife.

Rolling the knife over in his hand, he said, "The Vatican, the Thule, and Compensation Brokers, Ltd., will pay an annual sum—a dear sum. The three clients will remain silent knowing the contents of the document will never surface in the public domain."

Crilley moved his heavy frame to the edge of the bench and slid an eight-inch dagger into his right hand. "You are a dangerous man, Alex." Appearing detached, Crilley seemed to be waiting. He was peering into the recess beyond a stone arch.

Crilley threw his dagger and buried the blade in the chest of a lead archer.

Von Cleve spotted the hooded figure as the man fell behind the arch and was immediately replaced by two archers. Crilley held a hand to his heart as if answering a signal.

Has a tocsin been sent? Will I walk out of here? von Cleve wondered.

"You judge me too slow. You might be right, Alex. Perhaps tomorrow we will find out." Crilley, as though promoting the glow of promises fulfilled, retrieved his dagger, and slid it into a leather sheath above his right ankle. Von Cleve now knew he was a target—but why?

"Lucien and Steiner have fallen to Romanism or some other unruly perversion," von Cleve insisted. With a long stride, he moved behind a statue, his pulse marking his facial wounds. An archer crossed the priory and dug his arrow from the spar. Three more archers joined him after he turned from the priory.

Acknowledging the relentless heat, von Cleve accepted a cup of water and described the waterfront ambush for Crilley. The facial characteristics and the clothing of the men firing from the doorways of the go-down in Diamond Harbor were unique.

"The assassins are members of the Thuggee Religious Society, a cult that ranges in the north of India, near the town of Jubbulpore. My grandfather killed many of these zealots in the Kaffir wars on Africa's Cape."

Crilley spoke softly. "We have the details of Lucien's separate contract. The documents in that pouch have the wealthy of Europe scurrying for cover. We have issued orders to Singapore's master to terminate Lucien. We know who else recruited him. England's MI6."

Von Cleve drank the cold water, letting his system settle with the relief he needed to foster. Thuggee loyalists operating near the Bay of Bengal would be the target of retribution for the Diamond Harbor ambush and kidnapping.

Crilley leaned on the well curb and splashed water on his face. He asked, "Alex, did the Vatican's Prefecture of Extraordinary Affairs actually send bankers to Diamond Harbor to challenge your abilities?"

With the force of twelve-pound cannon shot, Crilley's words slammed into the redoubts of logic. Does Crilley know the Warburg agents were traveling as Vatican bankers? Von Cleve considered the question with care. He's guessing.

"They were not bankers." Von Cleve garnished his tone with cynical amusement, his mouth set in vicious, calculating lines. "Bankers use cryptic sentences. They were solicitors. Typically fat, and their English had an unctuous ring to it."

Von Cleve drew his face into a studied resentment. Wary of Crilley's hands, those paws that could marshal a dagger weighted with rage, he knew Crilley could sink his dagger into a man's chest at distances reserved for strangers, where men stalked with ease.

Balancing alternatives, von Cleve extended cupped hands into the well, then washed his face with the cool water. Noting Crilley's location, he searched the darkened priory again.

Crilley's been ordered to kill me.

Stepping to the left, judging the archers' line-of-sight, von Cleve took another step putting the well and the stone bench between Crilley and himself. Two men in brown robes swept through a hallway not twenty meters to his left. Archers. With a concluding sigh, he offered, "My would-be assassins have common habits, and predictable methods. They are stupid."

Having called Crilley stupid, he waited. Crilley didn't respond. Von Cleve continued. "I can assign probabilities to Lucien's next three moves. And since each is mutually exclusive, I can adjust my countermeasures as he runs." An arrow nicked von Cleve's ear and shattered against the stone wall behind him.

Blood dripped onto von Cleve's shoulder.

Crilley walked around the well and stuck his index finger into von Cleve's chest and whispered. "Stupid as we might seem, Alex, we know where Lucien is and what he's planning."

With blood dripping from his earlobe, von Cleve stepped into Crilley's face and slid the blade of his knife under the cross that hung against Crilley's chest. "And so, Templar. By disposing of me, you can make somebody atone for these contracts and liquidate a Templar debt at the same time." When Crilley drew his eyes into slits, von Cleve nicked his ear with his knife.

"What's next, Templar?"

Crilley extended his hands to the side, away from his body, and stepped backward.

"If you're finished with these childish displays, Crilley, you can do something useful. I have already located Lucien and I will kill him. You, Crilley, can locate the pouch."

Crilley handed von Cleve a copy of *L'Osservatore Romano*, the Vatican newspaper, and pointed to the second column inside the front page. The brief article started with a few kind words of tribute for the men murdered in India, then issued a pledge of concern for India's unwashed and life's common victims.

Then, with religious flair, the piece mentioned financing the expansion of the convict settlement at Port Blair, on South Andaman Island, in the Bay of Bengal. The convict was von Cleve, and the settlement was the Vatican's agreement to pay von Cleve's additional fee.

"As you surmised, the men killed in your warehouse were posing as solicitors for British Petroleum," Crilley confessed with a grin. "You were the primary target."

"So, does this inquisition have an end, Crilley, other than my execution?"

Von Cleve suppressed a nasty grin and adjusted his belt—death had a design. Drawing the blade of his knife to Crilley's stomach, von Cleve grabbed Crilley's throat and whispered, "One more arrow, and we will both die today."

Nodding toward a corner of the priory as though anxious to end the encounter, Crilley said, "We have a man flying into Rangoon tonight with identity papers in your name. Lucien may have a team waiting for him. You're scheduled on Eurasia Flight 27, to Singapore, at zero five-hundred hours. That's if the monsoon continues to soften at a decent rate."

Releasing Crilley's throat, von Cleve thrust his index finger into the man's chest. "Lucien's mine to kill. I have use for him." Watching Crilley, he waited for those telltale spasms that always twitched near the Templar's mouth when the man was irrational.

"This is Robert McPhee, Rangoon's former harbormaster." Through a hesitant shuffle, Crilley presented a grainy picture. "He flew into Port Blair and met with a man we do not know."

As if alerted, Crilley arched his shoulders and scanned the priory. "So far the trapline from Tonkin to Alexandria has Lucien, MI6 and MI9, a harbormaster, Sir Nigel Stuart, a commando team, the SS Iron Knight, three interrelated financial contracts, and sensitive documents—mixed with competing interests."

Von Cleve sheathed his knife. "I know the sort of men Lucien hires. At least one man is dead—Leenstra, my cousin. The British agents hounding that tramp steamer work for England's MI9. The Cambodian mercenaries Lucien hired were careless."

"The documents in that pouch are explosive."

"For my clients, the contents of the pouch will be secured for all time."

*   *   *

Cairo, Egypt. Shepheard's Hotel. 28 August 1939. 0530 Hours, GMT + 2 Hours.

Lewis Poston picked up the newspaper. "*The Illustrated London News*: Britain's Territorial Army is "Called to Colors." Lewis loved the sublime, tasteful suspense.

"Mother's preparing for war I suppose. And, on a Saturday."

In the City of Gold—at Cleo's Club or Shepheard's, a man could buy prosperity, even with counterfeit currency. Opportunity, spiced with intrigue, brought dark skins and light skins to Cairo from the far reaches of the world.

Lascars and Copts, Indians and Persians, Englishmen and Germans—Cairo bristled with money and sudden passion. Much of it served with ice.

The heat came suddenly as it often does in Cairo, an airless heat replete with the stench of a thousand open sewers, jasmine flowers, spices, desert dust, and burning charcoal. The sun shone a striated gold across the horizon, its cast refracted off billions of ionized dust particles.

Standing in the shade and listening to the call to morning prayer, Lewis tucked the newspaper under his arm. He gauged the hand-cut stone curbing that framed the sidewalk in front of Shepheard's Hotel. Every bit the Englishman, his white silk shirt and linen trousers began their daily ritual of refracting the sun's rays.

The anxious whispers of a clatter of German nationals stopped when a corrugated door rolled nosily into the rafters of the two-story building across the street from the hotel.

Somewhat eager, Poston watched the chemist inventory his shop with a relieving sense of satisfaction. His smile welcomed Poston into Sinclair's English Pharmacy. Poston acknowledged his host and sidestepped between the narrow shelves, looking for a bromide, and enjoying the lively gossip of three young women.

He waited for the chemist to wrap the merchandise the women had purchased. After the women left, Lewis set his bromide on the counter.

"Will that be all, Mr. Poston?"

"Yes. Thank you, Sammy. What else are the ladies looking for?"

"Who would know? Those three could baffle the wise. Always perfume and powders... French letters." Accepting the evasiveness of the chemist's answer, Poston turned on his heel and strode into the street.

Sinclair's English Pharmacy sat in the middle of the block, nearly centered on the marbled facade of Cairo's Foreign Office. Shepheard's Hotel promoted its expansive courtyard as the headquarters for military officers, civilian contractors, Axis spies, and smugglers rummaging the Suez for a bit of gold.

Sinclair's, along with an Anglo-American Book Shop, an Indian jeweler, and an emerald dealer who claimed to be appointed by Queen Mary, framed and opposed the elegance of the terrace of Shepheard's main entrance, providing the sundries and the unmentionables an officer or a gentleman required.

Trying to relieve a pressured chest and a boiling stomach, Poston arched his back, wondering if French bromides had been formulated for industrial use.

His flight from Malta had encountered a storm over the Mediterranean that pitched a stewardess to the floor. Using the best of bedlam, winds attacked the planes fittings with double-jacks and pressure pockets dropped, then caught the plane and tossed it arse over tit.

Poston ambled gingerly, anticipating, waiting for the bromide to work its magic.

Wondering why the meeting with the first governor of British East India Company concerning Sir Carroll Starr's death had been postponed, Poston decided his briefing with a representative of the yet-to-be-announced Special Operations Executive promised to be boring.

As his system continued to percolate, he noticed a gentle movement in the taxicab parked across the cobbles of Shari Kamil, in front of Shepheard's. The black Ford glistened with its white fenders and foot boards. A white stripe ran across the doors below the windows, and a white *S* was centered on the passenger door.

For a fraction of time so brief it was not part of time at all, Poston was consumed, too sensually stupid for mere graphics. A beautiful woman sat in the back seat. Boyishly bright, he leaned to the fore, stepping a tiptoe forward. The woman's hand moved as silk on a soft breeze.

As new grass finds the dew, waving before a coloring sky, Poston found himself striding confidently toward the cab with his mouth locked in a grin. Reaching for the passenger door, his cheeks were on fire.

"May I be of assistance?"

Her lips glistened when she smiled—the crimson shore of an ivory sea. High heels firmly met by uneven cobbles, adjusted as she accepted Poston's hand. Appearing mature and assured, she leaned back, accenting a figure no man could imagine—the trace of her playful expression a true reflection of his own.

"An Englishmen?" Her words were thrown over her shoulder with a bit of fetch, as she read the hotel's elegant marquees. "Yes, perhaps you can." Enjoying her dash of sensual spice, Poston sailed dead downwind. The lady swept his frame like a jeweler, landing on his polished shoes.

"Splendid." Foolishly struck, he stared as she adjusted the strap of her handbag over her shoulder, augmenting the shape of her figure. Her nipples were erect, pushing against a cream-white silk blouse. He thought the thought before he focused on it, then he blushed.

"Allow me to introduce myself—Lewis Poston."

"It is a pleasure, Mr. Poston. I am Dorothy Stuart." With a slight nod the driver placed an overnight bag near her high heels and smiled as she counted the fare into his hand. Abruptly, as though offended, she locked her vapor-blue eyes on the cab driver and dismissed him without a word or a gratuity.

Lusting, saliva ebbing through high tide, Poston swallowed so he could speak. Fashioning a plan of canceling his scheduled appointments, he wondered if the lady had a cold streak. She was simply out of place, her damask complexion soft and aglow. When she set one foot away from the other, he marched to the top of her nylons.

Poston geared down to half-throttle.

Dorothy conjured a mysterious grin, ever ready to mock the priorities of the masculine world. Part of her charm undoubtedly lay in her attitude toward well-heeled men—the touch of a spoilt woman, well-schooled in music and the arts, and a smattering of manners.

Responding to a thumping cadence, Poston flew out of the broken clouds into a clear dawn, his morning parade stretching the linen, his satchel in league with the guard-chain on his watch. Perceptive as well as attractive, Dorothy Stuart smiled through a quiet sigh. As though measuring the affect she was having on this dapper sod, Dorothy adjusted her blouse.

"You're an American from New York City by the sound of it." Poston was pleased he hadn't stammered. "I'm sure you're exhausted, Miss Stuart. Are you booked here at Shepheard's?"

"Yes. I am is the complete answer. I've come to Cairo to secure my husband's footlocker, or what's left of it. He's been listed as missing in North Africa."

"The Western Area is truly unforgiving, I'm afraid."

"The Western Area. Is that what you call it?"

"That, or out in the blue."

Dorothy seemed amused by Poston's skylarking. "Sir Nigel's cable mentioned a storage depository in the basement of Shepheard's Hotel."

"Yes, of course. The hotel promotes registered bag storage." Poston counseled a grin, permitting his expression to muster delight; at the same time gesturing toward the marble entry of Shepheard's. "For the modest fee of four cents a month, the hotel will store a ditty-bag in its basement— payment due in advance of course."

As though accepting Poston's folly, she stepped through a sachet and found her knight staring at her. "Eighteen-twenty—one, eight, two, zero— that's the claim-tag number."

Poston blushed. "Forgive me. I have a bit of work on at the moment. May I buy you a drink or dinner later?" Caution leaped at him.

"Yes. I would enjoy some company. A less formal encounter. Leave word with the concierge prior to five o'clock."

The woman's well-traveled. But Sir Nigel has not been operating in North Africa for weeks. Is this woman his wife or an intelligence blind? —a honey trap?

"Splendid." Admiring the woman's figure, he managed a sheepish nod, hoping to coax her to share a bit of fortune. Speechless, primed for opportunity's knock, Poston synchronized his watch with the brass clock perched behind the concierge desk.

"No harm in giving fate a sporting try, I suppose," he whispered to himself. If she's an intel blind, I'll need to be careful. Find out who she works for.

As Dorothy approached the reservations desk, he cheered his prospects, searching the sun for highlights of the woman's fancy. Energized by a rush of small thoughts, he smiled. He needed a bath. The dry-polish he gave himself earlier, the smell of it, leant a rural delight to his masculine world.

Hailing his luck, he found himself wandering about an embroidered hem—that, and where the woman had found nylons. Wonderful as advertised, nylons were somewhat of a rumor—to be available as a lead-in to the '39 Christmas shopping season.

In the turn of her hand the woman had exuded a grace of proportion—nothing less than symmetry—a sensual equivalence.

With a devilish grin, he refocused his lens and turned to search the interior of the hotel, looking for Berryman, Mother's messenger, the hallway cyclist newly assigned to the Special Operations Executive, Force 133 Provisional, in Cairo.

Who could possibly feed Berryman's vanity?

The expansive terrace at Shepheard's Hotel had become the designated watering hole for Cairo, the Suez, and North Africa by summer 1939—a luxurious, Wednesday-market boardroom. Secrets were for sale—the cash price based on the degree of dishonesty the buyer expected.

Poston understood the knack of it; the sellers would give it a full chisel. This hotel, along with the Muhammad Ali Sport Club, and Cleo's Club, had become the world's commodity exchanges. Products from pot ash to troop strengths were sold in Shepheard's den of wicker, wrought iron, marble, and granite.

The edgings of urgency and deceit scrubbed each pledge. The well-dressed shook hands.

The floors, where exposed, gleamed. The polished, hand-cut stone sectioned into one-foot squares dashed in all directions. Ceiling fans swirled, and fresh air vents drew the smoke from hundreds of cigarettes, cigars, and pipes without the hint of a breeze. Tobacco jars sat erect, pungent with short-cut Syrian Latabra.

The reception area flowed onto an elegant terrace overlooking a tiled center court. Persian carpets lay among opposing stone columns and ran the length of the terrace. Ivory carvings of cats and serpents stood watch. The carpets softened the voices, and the music masked the words. In motion, as if black and white photos are clearer, servants and waiters moved through the room as confidential wards, without being seen and seemingly without hearing.

Poston stopped near a group of British officers and filled his pipe. After tamping the tobacco, a waiter offered him a light. Spotting an empty table on the far side of the terrace he requested a whiskey, and then worked his way through the crowd.

A dark walnut grand piano sat in the middle of the upper terrace, bobbing in a sea of small wooden tables and low-back wicker chairs—hundreds and hundreds of wicker chairs—some with rolled, hollow wicker arms, others with wooden arms wrapped in strands of wicker fastened by an ornate pattern of brass tacks.

These tables can assume any formation, he thought. Today they are arranged in dozens and dozens of private clusters—for islands of scoundrels to hatch their schemes of victory and gold—military scoundrels as well as civilian scoundrels.

British No. 61, buff khaki uniforms, many with short sleeves and short pants with long socks, others with blue or gold shoulder cords and no ties, a few with ties—uniforms flanked by civilian suits of one cut or another.

Guests of Shepheard's were attended by dark-skinned hotel staff in brilliant white robes, scarlet waist bands, and scarlet fez. The meals superb and the whiskey a delight—the game became quite civilized, expected really. With proper groveling and ample cash, private property was routinely deleted from the air-raid target list.

Poston selected a wicker and iron table set tight against a wrought-iron railing bordering the upper terrace overlooking the hotel's massive center court. The lower court boiled with activity.

The waiter stood erect, his stare placed afar, motionless as Poston settled into his chair. Remaining silent, the waiter handed him a whiskey and a note indicating Poston had twenty minutes to wait—to absorb Shepheard's contradictions.

"A glass of ice, if you would."

Delighted with the remnants of the woman's perfume, he set an ear to the din and adjusted his chair to monitor the courtyard below. Piano music filled the background with motionless delight, loud enough to interrupt the emphatic, its rhythm keeping pace with the hum of anticipation. Mixed with a chorus of waiters and attendants, the music masked those angered outbursts—those mingles of rage and contempt.

Shepheard's Hotel, a Swiss operated hostelry, advertised grand accommodations, sumptuous meals, French wines, and endless liaisons—an intelligence nightmare or dream, depending on a spy's point of view. Poston examined his valise. A Walther PPK, and an expendable Caseros silencer were strapped to the underside of the lid.

Waiting for Berryman, a man who couldn't hit the ground if he fell, prompted great boredom, and set Poston's disposition into bottom gear. Brushing his primary school intellect for the encounter, he saw Berryman and a man dressed as a linen draper stop to talk with an elegant, dark-skinned woman near the piano. She seemed anxious to escape.

Berryman dotted the air with a pencil and wrote an entry in a notebook.

The piano player started singing "As Time Goes By" just as Poston's glass of ice found the table followed by Berryman and a rather cumbersome chap, Berryman drawing a chair and extending a paw. The linen draper had a rather oblong body, a protruding chin, and eyes perched over high cheekbones. Berryman, on the other hand, had not matured. He remained a tiny, bespectacled man with tight lips, wire-rimmed glasses, and a pencil at the ready—never a pen.

Branded by Admiral Sinclair as a fatuous clot, Berryman's presence in Cairo loosened a flow of speculation.

"Sir Lewis Poston, allow me to introduce Alfred Gosden."

For Poston, Gosden's name rang with a sharp knell. Anger came easy to him. Suddenly on edge, Poston didn't shake their hands. Rage consumed him as he stepped away from the table.

Here's the bastard who killed my father. If my silencer was screwed on, I'd blow the blighter to buggery right where he stands.

For seconds, five at most, Poston remained motionless, aware of his abrupt, sinister change of mood. He walked to the piano without speaking—reckoning he asked the dark-skinned woman for a light. Arriving at the end of his calculations, he accepted the admiral's insistence he tolerate Berryman, returned to his chair, and with guile shook Gosden's hand.

"It's been years, Berryman."

"Yes. Time does run by." Berryman pointed, seemingly accepting Poston's challenge. "Gosden's our newest lad in Cairo. A minister's son. A cover for God's obligations, I suppose."

Purposely bored, Poston's disdain for Gosden creased his expression as he peered through the iron railing at the sea of diners seated in the lower courtyard. Here sat the bastard he planned to kill. Are there outliers? Who else is involved?

Berryman ordered a scotch with plain water. "As you may know, Lewis, we are in the throes of establishing Force 133 as part of a proposed Special

Operations Executive—all hush-hush. GHQ Middle East has yet to be informed of the proposal." He sat back, extending his fingers to conclude the introduction, admiring Poston's whiskey.

Moving his glass in circles, Poston said, "And the Security Intelligence Middle East unit, (SIME), a deception organization, will also be headquartered in Cairo, running a medley of controlled enemy agents."

"Yes. Sinclair gave me a brief on that security intel unit. SOE Force 133 will be cooperating with them in the eastern Med and the Suez primarily."

"There's more than a good bit of trading these days, Berryman," Poston said, fostering a pernicious grin. "There are pirates from around the world buying and selling—have a look." He swept an arm in an arc implicating the entire crowd.

"These golden entrails drift into nothing—agents, spies, franchises, syndicates, contracts. The admiral briefed me on Force 133."

"He did?" Berryman lowered his jaw and began cleaning his glasses with the tablecloth.

"I suppose you've also been informed the Royal Navy's Mediterranean Fleet Headquarters is moving from Alexandria to Malta this month."

With a nod, Poston agreed. "The move to Malta and keeping the Suez in Allied hands are the primary reasons for the creation of SOE Force 133 for the Med."

"Yes, of course." Berryman's breathing accelerated, as if he were anticipating. Whispering, he changed the subject. "What do you think caused Sir Starr's suicide?" Berryman glanced at the nearest cluster of men as he leaned into the table and adjusted his chair.

"That's the charm of it." Poston fell into whistling under his breath, admiring a tall, dark Sudanese woman—the tight shape of her carriage and the elegance of her stride.

"I'm not following." Berryman's words bit the air with a fading presence, as if his authority were set aside. "Can you be clearer?"

Annoyed, Poston's voice blundered in upon the twit. "Imperial snobbery makes its own leeway. Don't you agree, Berryman? You're one of Mother's lads."

"Starr didn't have the bounce for treachery. With his mindset moored at high tide, Mother used him to sort the incoming debris."

Gosden blurted, "Is that your view of the matter, Poston? Starr was a spy, so he tethered himself to Blackfriars Bridge?"

Poston peered at Gosden's oblong face. A gnawing told him he should take out his PPK, put the silencer on the weapon and shoot the bastard between the eyes.

"You're no bright spark, Gosden." Poston looked at the ceiling, trying to restrain his rage. "Sir Starr won the Military Cross on the Somme. You were bellowing for more tit while he carried his bat for England in the last lot."

Gosden grabbed the arm of a passing waiter nearly throwing the man into an adjoining table while demanding immediate service.

"Control yourself, damn you," Berryman hollered, standing to help the waiter.

Enjoying Gosden's reaction, Poston peered through the wrought-iron rail. "Starr did not hang himself. The good knight was murdered. Someone has sent up a balloon."

"The Household wants to know what the devil Starr's been at," Berryman said, dropping his spectacles on the table.

"What part of the Household?" Poston arched his brow to caution Berryman's query.

"I didn't find out, did I? MI5 probably."

Delighted with his agility, Poston's photographic memory found Gosden's name in his father's personal files correlated with the name Mary Hardin. The vicar's son, along with another thug, had abused Mary Hardin in Tucking Mill, Cornwall.

"You're a bit overdone, Berryman." Poston said. "Starr was tooling sleds for the Round Table—for Lord Montagu Norman at the Bank of England and Adrian Ailes—with Victor Rothschild at MI5 as his shield." Poston sat waiting for Berryman's register to ring, for that hesitant oscillation the slow witted require to focus.

Remounting his spectacles, Berryman said, "Do try to be clearer, Lewis."

"Very well, I can think of several reasons to kill Sir Starr: to pull in loose ends or to sever ties to a field operation that's gone off. The execution is a classic bit of deception."

"For the Round Table?"

"Or the Bank of England." Poston chimed, gesturing for a top-up. Leaning into the table he whispered, "Starr was brokering transactions with a chap named Walter Fletcher, a London rubber broker who has a network known as the China Syndicate."

"What sort of brokering?"

Berryman's either lying, or he's matured in the trade, Poston thought.

"Bartered transactions—rubber for diamonds, silk for pot ash, pig iron for oil, currency arbitrage, that sort of carry-on." Lewis's mood sharpened as Berryman sat closer, fishing with leaky charm.

"For the Round Table—for Lord Norman?"

"Try to keep up, will you, Berryman? It's all a circle. Taken left-wise or right-wise, one fact remains. The Household sanctioned the fox Starr was trapping."

"Ah, but we don't know that do we?" Gosden charged angrily, smashing his prosecutor's wig into center court. "Jesus. Who else is involved in these transactions? Poston and Sons, Ltd.?"

Judging the warning an insult, Poston nipped at his drink. Measuring the silence, he decided shooting Gosden would be a worthy christening for his PPK.

"No harm in your chasing God, I suppose, but we don't do Jesus here in Cairo." Poston held the edge of the table to check his anger. "You'll never find the center of that circle, Berryman. I'd give Starr's murder wide currency. Someone else will die in turn. Mother will see to it."

"Fair enough, I suppose," Berryman said.

Enjoying the joust, Poston bumped Berryman's arm. "Gosden here is your miserable skivvy. A disease meant for the poor. He's from Tucking Mill, in Cornwall." Then came a silence so intense, Poston paused to measure the sod's alarm.

Berryman sat cradling his drink near his chest.

Pointing with his thumb, Poston went on. "Stupid here's a fugitive. He did a runner from Tucking Mill to keep from being hanged. He and his mates abused a woman in the keg locker of Webb's Public House. I'm right about that, aren't I, Gosden?"

"Retribution was paid on the nail!" Gosden raised his chin, a stiffening set to his eyes.

"With a vicar as your shield, I'm sure it didn't cost you a penny."

Gosden leaned back, gave Berryman a moment to respond, and when his boss remained silent, took hold of his glass, and drank.

Donning a dry, facetious grin, Poston decided to sum up the rotten bastard. "That's a justified Christian for you, Berryman—a moral Goliath dragging God around like polished brass, coating his pride with Dettol disinfectant so he can bully-shag old women."

Berryman nearly fell as he came erect. "No need to pry the past, Lewis. That water's run by." As if annoyed by Stupid's posture, he moved the man's glass away from his own.

"I doubt Captain Hardin would agree," Poston continued. "He and a good many Masons have been forecasting your demise, Gosden."

"Who's Captain Hardin?" Berryman asked.

"He's a special-service commando. Stupid here bully shagged his mother."

Berryman moved his chair away from his aide. "I intend to find the individual who scrubbed your file, Gosden. Until I do, you'll be restricted to headquarters, and the essentials of boredom."

"Send him across the English Bridge into the western desert, into the Blue." Poston laughed. "Better yet, post him on the docks in Alexandria. They can hang him from the boom gate."

With a sagacious expression, Berryman said, "But as to Starr's death. We can start our inquiry here in Cairo by sorting through the sand Fletcher's been sifting."

"Fletcher's a minor rubber broker. An old saw. He isn't important."

Narrowing his eyes Poston leaned into the wicker arm rest on his left side. He started tapping his glass on the table near Gosden's hand. Come on you bastard, take a swing at me.

Waiting, fixing Gosden with an icy grin, he said, "If the circumference of a circle shrinks, velocities increase, and intensities magnify. And, if an ordinal of considerable power such as Sir Starr is hanged from Blackfriars Bridge, it's never by some forty-schilling freeholder."

Berryman seemed ready to run. "Old train smells can be burdensome. Don't you agree, Lewis? Tucking Mill... Blackfriars Bridge...?"

"Yes, old smells definitely carry a dim notion." Challenging Gosden's glare, Poston smiled a vicious smile and asked, "Who sent you to find the Grail this time, Berryman?"

"Dewar, I'm afraid." As if resigned, Berryman rubbed his face with both hands.

"It would be Dewar, wouldn't it? That voelkish bastard is deuced clever sending you off to hunt for the fox he's been grooming, slanging my family with a nimble toss." Poston took a quick look around the terrace and stood into a brace. "I've a rather crowded hour on. If you need help with crude-oil prices, that sort of carry-on, give me a ring. You have my number."

"Very well." Berryman started to usher Poston toward the lobby. Reaching for his glass, he swirled the drink as they walked, tossed it off, and set the glass on the piano. "Gosden's a bit of a prig, I'm afraid—over-weaned. Steeped in the English tradition of watching people work."

"High-school acne aside, Berryman—that bell's been rung. God made the twits first—for practice. If Mother needs to fill the frame, Stupid there will do. She won't bother to hang him."

With smoke billowing through his teeth Berryman asked, "Who killed Sir Starr?"

As Poston drew Berryman near the piano he whispered, "And you made wage in the Temple district of London—a Templar church at its center.

Blackfriars Bridge is the gateway to the Temple. To be hung from Blackfriars Bridge is a centuries-old warning—a Templar warning."

"Do they exist?"

"If you want to live to see London again, Berryman, you better strike your sails before you dip an oar in the Templar's Pond."

*　*　*

New York City. J. P. Morgan. 28 August 1939. 0730 Hours, GMT – 5 Hours.

Perfume's trace lingered in the confines of the velvet panels of the elevator. Or so it seemed. For Eaton the allure of Germany's banker lingered.

Eaton caught his weight, stumbling into the corner. The elevator jerked to a stop, responding to the hands of Mr. George Brown. Mr. George had been guiding the elevators at J. P. Morgan banking house longer than Eaton had been alive. A lean, tall, solid-oak black man with an infectious smile, George had a gracious manner and a greeting derived from his English heritage—his porter's charm provided a perfect cover for being a sports bookie.

Mr. George kept another book. A diary he could use to augment his wage. Neatly recorded, his extemporaneous notes of conversations were complete with temperament, dates, times, weather, and clothing descriptions.

"This is your stop, Mr. Eaton." George half closed his eyes as if trying to draw a comment from Eaton. "I'll miss seeing Angie. The lady was a lovely woman."

"Thanks, Alex. Angela was lovely."

Stepping onto the gray and white marble that framed the entry to his exclusive office suite, Eaton looked back toward the elevator. Suspicion mixed with grief. Something did not jive—facts or events or both.

"Am I being followed?" he whispered; unsure the words were his. Watching the elevator doors close, he began juggling the facts concerning the arbitrage scheme, facts containing snippets of familiarity, their sum giving way to a mosaic of greed.

"I must isolate financial anomalies, define the tolerance limits for each anomaly, and estimate the probability associated with likely outcomes," he whispered. "With any luck, I can leverage this Nazi arbitrage play."

The day before, Joseph Telleli, the passionate Italian, had confronted Eaton with his theatrics, plunging headlong into accusing Eaton of being sullied by greed. Joey seemed wired to an undercurrent of menace, chasing any person who might be responsible for Angela's death. To reconcile his friend's demands, Eaton had accepted Joey's willingness to attend his secretary's funeral in Georgia with a gesture of commendable regret. Only time would leaven his mood.

Anxious, he stepped onto the Persian weave, involuntarily sorting the patterns in the carpet. He stopped in front of the reception desk. Dorothy Stuart, his new secretary, had taken another holiday, leaving his office exposed.

"Forgive me. I've forgotten your name."

"That's all right, Mr. Eaton." The receptionist smiled and set his messages on the counter. When she started to speak, he held up his hand. Glancing at the phone logs, he did not move nor answer her. As the secretary started to speak again, he spoke proudly.

"It's Susan. Your name is Susan."

"Bravo, Mr. Eaton," she said, checking the air with her pencil. Distracted, he continued to cast about, reminding himself—confirming data and origins. Susan's simple delight ran counter to his suspicions.

"You have a busy morning. Mr. Telleli is waiting in your office. He is charming."

"I know, Susan. Joey's quite a charmer." Gripping the handle of his office door, he realized his mistake. "Susan, will you apologize to George for me? I called him Alex a moment ago."

Alex. Who in the hell is Alex? Without an answer, he found Joey looking through the wind-blown rain at the city below. Dressed in blue dungarees and a wool jacket with a fur collar, Joey took a deep breath as if cautioning his words.

"Is there an explanation for the beauty of that Kraut, Sam?"

"Probably not. She's affiliated with Stein Bank in Cologne, Germany, and has sizable accounts at J. P. Morgan to sort out."

As if dismissing Eaton's answer as a dodge, Joey set his thumbs into the waist band of his dungarees. "I converted the money I found in Angie's flat to silver and had it delivered to J. P. Morgan yesterday."

"I'll establish a transfer account for her parents as soon as the account is certified."

"Murder and cash, and you show up with a minxy dame who's the chancellor's daughter."

"Damn, Joey, stop insulting the woman. She's a banker's functionary. That's the extent of it. I need to ensure J. P. Morgan's business with Stein Bank is quickly sorted out."

Quiet once more, Joey slapped both hips and poured a glass of water.

"How did the funeral go? Did her family welcome you?" Eaton asked.

Joey grimaced as though allowing Eaton's comments to furrow into a natural revulsion. Grudgingly he shared the details of his visit to Georgia. "Angie's family was more than gracious. The simplicity of the funeral was refreshing. Angie had fifty-six cousins. Her mother asked me to say hello."

Eaton had not expected this response. Regret ready to the surface, he whispered through a crooked smile. "I'll bet Angela was her reason for living. She raised a beautiful child."

For Eaton, a brooding quiet consumed the office: the chair where Angela took notes.

Joey smirked. "Sam, I'm not buying your bullshit about that Kraut. Banker, my ass. I'll call you if I want to talk." Without shaking hands, he left the office.

Eaton wanted to scream—to tell his friend he didn't kill Joey's girl. Instead, he said, "Thanks a lot, Joey." More words came to his mind, but it was a time that left few memories.

He needed time to reflect—to think. After dismissing Joey's anger, he reread the latest cable from Credit Suisse outlining the currency transfers required for the day. With nineteen transactions, over five hundred million dollars were to be shuffled through J. P. Morgan. Five other players were in the game—four-point-nine billion dollars transferred in one trading day.

This plan is brilliant—free money for Europe's industrial giants, giants devoted to Germany's resurgence as a world power. A scheme executed when the Reichbank is washing confiscated gold, he thought.

"Excuse me, Mr. Eaton. Your nine o'clock appointment has arrived."

"It's eight-thirty."

"I'm aware of that, Mr. Eaton."

Without responding, he started scrutinizing the wire transfers. Lifting the crystal water pitcher perched on the cabinet behind his desk, he jiggled the glass to settle the ice. Not wanting to meet with Petra in his office, he stared at Susan.

"Mr. Eaton?"

"Send her in, Susan." He drank to relieve a bite in his throat.

Petra Laube-Heintz, born on September 4, 1914, near the Bavarian town of Bad Reichenhall, in the shelter of the Austrian Alps, grew up working in the fields near her father's home harvesting hay, sugar beets, potatoes, and such, tending the neighbor's cows and goats, and growing as a young girl should. She spent her free time hiking in the mountains, swimming in the cold Alpine lakes, and competing with her brothers over any money their village had to offer.

Sundays were spent tending the family gardens and pruning the trees and shrubs in the graveyard next to the church. Petra talked constantly as a child, to herself and to anyone who would listen. The priest found her company amusing and decided to teach Petra how to read and speak English. Insisting she keep her ability to speak English a secret, as he had himself. He introduced her to the northern and eastern dialects of German as well.

A wood carver, her father, Manfred, specialized in carving the religious figures associated with the Catholic Church and the farming life of Bavaria. When the demand for his carvings fell and the Catholics became less vocal, he accepted a commission to carve the architectural details designed for the Eagle's Nest, a project expected to last more than a year.

Hildegard, her mother, was much younger than Manfred. At six feet, her fifteen stones and her temperament were well suited for a butcher's assistant. Wary and afraid after three thousand laborers converged on Berchtesgaden to work on Hitler's mountain retreat, she cried when the New German Order consumed her sons.

In January 1937, with her brothers joining the Gestapo, and her father working on the Fuehrer's Bavarian retreat, Petra began training as an arbitrage specialist at J. H. Stein Bank in Cologne, Germany. Her fluency in English was essential.

More to the point, her beauty stupefied men.

After laboring on staff, a promotion found her managing the *S* account for Heinrich Himmler. Initially frightened by the exposure, she buried her fear in research. She was relieved to find there had been women making loans for centuries in Germany. Almost all were wives or widows of prominent Jewish bankers. And, as early as the fourteenth century, 50% of the loans in northern France were made by women. These facts buoyed her confidence.

Because her efficiency and cunning were natural, she was promoted to the international arbitrage desk, retaining control of Himmler's *S* account.

Her current assignment—suborn Samuel Eaton.

"Good morning, Mr. Eaton." Petra forced a soft Bavarian voice and glanced about the office with a contrived patience until Eaton's secretary cleared her vision and the door latched. Her black suit was tailored as if stitched to her frame.

Eaton's silence seemed to contain a message.

Judging the silence to be a constraint, Petra moved the chair to an area behind and off to the side of the desk, where she could gauge Eaton's gestures. "I trust the currency transfers were clear and in order." Crossing her legs into Eaton's view, she met his glance by adjusting her hem.

"Aversion and attraction are twins," she said.

"Yes, the plan's clear." Badgering the transfer documents into a stack, he said, "The volume has been increasing with one constant being an account at your bank. The other accounts have been gorging."

The office absorbed an inexplicable chill. Responding, she reset her legs, leaving them apart for a second, for that incomplete picture. Pretending to be embarrassed, she adjusted herself making way for Eaton's ungovernable surprise.

"Gold's at the apex, don't you agree, Mr. Eaton?"

"What's at the apex?" he inquired.

"Happiness." Petra projected a fabricated disdain.

Eaton's stare, penetrating and unnerving, seemed to cause discomfort. She rose and strolled to the bookcase, her body moving in synchrony, uprooting his intent with intimate vibrations, delicious morsels of enriched sexuality.

"More a vortex, I'm afraid." He concluded his comment by dropping the transfer documents on the floor beside his chair.

"A vortex creates velocities that allow you to stay on the rim."

"Who are you?" he asked.

"A banker, a farmer's daughter..."

He fell silent. A farmer's daughter, he mused. With a wry nod, he set his foot on the fund transfer documents. "An expensive pen and a plausible manner do not make one a banker."

"I'm learning how to be a banker. You'll have to settle for what you've been told." Her voice had changed patterns assuming the brusque formality of the North Country.

Petra started to speak, then tightened her lips as she walked to the door of the office and stood there, waiting. She knew all about Eaton... the man was ambitious and hungry for wealth. She opened the door to let herself out and recanted. "Can we meet for a cocktail this afternoon, Mr. Eaton?"

Deliberately playing with Susan's scheduling controls, she celebrated Eaton's discomfort.

*   *   *

New York City. The Cloud Room in the Chrysler Building. 28 August 1939. 1230 Hours, GMT – 5 Hours.

Max Ilgner, a hard bitten, dangerous man, was afloat in the protocols of a growing German trade. His biting sarcasm and durable memory worked in concert, and his mind operated with a ferret's intensity. Demanding loyalty, he insisted on the confirmation of the origin of intelligence data to minimize process variability.

The six arbitrage specialists involved in the planned takeover of the industrial companies represented by Keppler's circle of friends had lost their dearest loved one—on the same day. Eaton had lost Angie. And yet, three of the six specialists were life-long associates of Ilgner's.

Erratic and ruthless, he excelled at being Farben's chief spy. The Dulles brothers, the merchant bankers in New York and Europe, and the European crime syndicates trod with care when dealing with him.

At Ilgner's insistence, much of Germany's industrial base, including I. G. Farben, advocated for the ascendancy of Heinrich Himmler as the new German monarch.

In keeping with this undercurrent, and close hauled to the arbitrage scheme's objective of raiding companies to gain control of Germany's industrial giants, Ilgner had suggested I. G. Farben become one of the scheme's targets. Patience being a hallmark, he decided to wait until the bankers behind the scheme were overcommitted, and their money was irretrievable, before he exposed the Warburg-Rothschild consort to Hitler's henchmen.

In turn, with I. G. Farben insulated from the raid, if the stock price of SKF, International, fell, he would exercise Farben's option to purchase a controlling interest. Max Ilgner dreamed of running I. G. Farben, International, of being the genius to bring synthetic oil to the world market on a massive scale.

Last April he killed the man being groomed for that job. He slit his throat.

"Max!" Tapping the table, Allen Dulles drew Ilgner's attention from his menu. "The gold transfers from Austria, Czechoslovakia, and the Settlements Bank to the Reichsbank have stabilized the Reichsmark."

Ilgner thought the attorney looked worried. Listed as the attorney of record for SKF, International, a Swedish company funded by Enskilda Bank, with headquarters in Stockholm, SKF represented sixty percent of Allen Dulles's billing hours. And SKF, International, ranked as the Dulles brothers' most valued client.

With manufacturing plants in Sweden, Argentina, Germany, and the United States, Nazi Germany was SKF's best customer. Hugo von Rosen managed SKF's Philadelphia plant and sold ball bearings to the Nazis through a company in Argentina. Armies on the move throughout the world ran on SKF ball bearings, including America's army.

With Hugo von Rosen, a lifelong friend of the Dulles brothers, being Herman Goering's first cousin, von Rosen's affiliation with the Nazi Party was well-known.

Sensing a change of mood, Ilgner put in. "Is a problem developing, Allen?"

"Not with Farben or SKF Philadelphia. The gold transfers to the Reichbank are disturbing Asian markets. China's currency was based in silver. After they converted to 'legal note' issues backed by their national banks, it's anybody's guess what the Chinese yuan is worth."

"Farben will stay with US dollars. France will devalue their currency within the year. That will strengthen the Reichsmark considerably for a short period of time."

"What may I do for you, Max—tickets to the World's Fair perhaps?" Not waiting for a response, he declared, "They're featuring a smoking robot."

"I've no time for trivia, Allen. Farben, US, wants to sell thirteen million dollars of unsecured paper before the end of the year. We want you to arrange the sale of these debentures with Charles Mitchell, at National City Bank."

"Of course..." Dulles seemed cautious. "Word on the street is one-half of one percent of Farben's European wages have been impounded and placed on direct deposit in a locked account at the Reichsbank."

"The Fuehrer's prerogative." Ilgner waited until Dulles registered his agreement. "The Reichsbank also levied an impound on Krupp's wages. And the Reichsbank has set in motion a plan for workers throughout Germany to deposit a portion of their monthly paycheck to accumulate a down payment for a Volkswagen." Ilgner scoffed at the notion any worker would own a People's Car.

"Dr. Schacht continues to guarantee import markets."

"What did you expect?" Ilgner shook out his napkin. "Disposable income in Germany will be sparse for the next ten years." Alerted, Ilgner's head snapped to the left, his gaze centered on a tall woman near the restaurant's entrance.

"Do you know that woman, Max?" Dulles asked.

"Yes. She works for Kurt von Schroder at Stein Bank in Cologne." Ilgner bunched his napkin near his plate. "The industrial levies ordered by the Fuehrer are paid to an endowment account at Stein Bank, well insulated from the Reichsbank." Setting his spoon aside, Ilgner became silent. A cold, distant cast came to his eyes. His tone now cold, he routinely took the pulse of those he did not know. "Who's her escort?"

"Samuel Eaton, the senior vice president for international accounts at J. P. Morgan."

Dulles rose from his chair and extended his hand to a young man passing nearby. "James Warburg...Allen Dulles."

"Yes, of course, Mr. Dulles."

"James, I want you to meet, Max Ilgner, of I. G. Farben, International."

Shaking Ilgner's hand, Warburg's smile flushed in recognition. "My uncle Max is in Hamburg. Do you know him, Mr. Ilgner?"

"Max Warburg and I are lifelong friends. And before his death, your uncle Felix was helpful to me while acting as Germany's commercial attaché in Stockholm."

Raising a finger, Dulles said, "Young James just finished working as the director of budget in Washington, DC."

Ilgner nodded a storied understanding. "Your father helped write the Federal Reserve Act for the United States. Back then, he and I would meet for cognacs and prose on about women and controlling the currencies of the world."

A young woman eased her hand under Warburg's arm. Sheepishly he extended his hand to Dulles. "We have a short lunch break. It's good to see you again, Mr. Dulles. Give my regards to Uncle Max and Cousin Friederich, Mr. Ilgner."

Ilgner's attention was drawn to Petra Laube-Heintz. Suspecting her presence in the United States meant Stein Bank had decided to expand its investments, she might be playing with the arbitrage scheme's central purpose.

"There is a partially illuminated genius orchestrating the cost of US dollars in circulation," Ilgner declared. Donning a rueful expression, he fumed. "If it's not a Rothschild, it's a Warburg... or a Schiff... or a Wasserman... or a Speyer." Taking a drink of water, he laughed as Petra steered her escort to an isolated corner table.

"Well, Max." Dulles adjusted his napkin across his lap. "Standards help us measure who is ahead. Who will earn their brokerage fees?"

"Regrettably, the French have no money."

*   *   *

The Bay of Bengal. Port Blair, South Andaman Island. 30 August 1939. 1930 Hours, GMT + 5.5 Hours.

Gripping the steering wheel, Hawkes cleared a hole in the fog coating the windscreen. *If McPhee doesn't shut up, I'm driving back to Ritchie's.* Barely able to keep track of the roadway, listening to McPhee's bafflegab about his former maid, deciding he should shoot the Irish twat, he was simply too sober to think.

Robert 'Darkie' McPhee, with his disagreeable grin, was another sort, a footling, a bloody hard-knobbling perpetual expense.

Quitting drinking was easy for Jeffrey Hawkes; he had quit dozens of times since the Royal Air Force showed him the door. Giving it the best, his current consumption remained an excusable distraction.

That Chennault was considered the essence of military decorum annoyed Hawkes. That Chennault had requested a firing squad for him annoyed him as well. The request had the ordinary airmen whipped into a lather—pilot officers took note. His efforts frustrated, Chennault sent five military tribunals after the cashiered pilot, declaring charge upon charge.

Hounded by the adjutants of the RAF, whose wives had celebrated his lust, Hawkes dipped a wing and vanished into the cash economy of the British penal colony at Port Blair, on South Andaman Island.

Hawkes nipped at his pocket flask, a solid silver memento of his early days. He wore his RAF identity disc on a leather thong around his neck. The disc proved he was once a flying officer, for only the RAF had a Line six on their discs. The war correspondents, Warcos, he ran into were happy to spring for drinks and a decent meal. Better yet, the lumber brokers provided airplanes for him to fly.

The rear leaf springs of Hawkes's wagon waltzed with the front shock absorbers, leaving the undercarriage to settle and sway like unsupervised fat. The mud coating the headlamps left the roadway in a muted haze, in stark contrast to the golden hue of the dashboard lights. With the headlamps set on high beam, the motion of the wagon threw looping arcs of light across the mat of the jungle, each loop featuring an unexpected jar.

"We're close to airplanes," Hawkes said. "I can smell 'em."

Gaining form in the soup, Port Blair's airport perimeter security lighting cast a glow into a churning sky as the airport's control tower leapt from the fog, disappeared, emerging seconds later as a larger complex waiting to pounce.

Hawkes drove as if in a trance, assuming the messages he received were accurate. The owner of the Silver Bar on Rangoon's waterfront had verified McPhee's story.

Since then, he and McPhee had been coaching each other's greed. Agreeing to be temporary friends, they sobered into a silence. Hawkes's mind ran through cycles of plots and counterplots, winding up McPhee, and then scuppering the mick and dribbling off with the gold.

Hawkes ran his right hand across the top of the dashboard, adjusting the heater lever to low throttle. Patting the dash with affection, he paused. "I bought this beauty for a case of grog I pilfered from the docks. She was a mistreated contract carriage in this penal sewer. She liked to cough until I had her all kitted out and plugged in."

"She's a bit of a galloper, don't you think?" McPhee asked, adjusting his weight into a jarring roll. "I mean fair play. Fanny's arse is slapping her thighs. If I'm not giving her dashboard a go, I'm nose deep in her cushion."

"Rather like stumping up an old rhino, eh, Robby?"

"A rhino's a bit much these days, Hawker. Even standing on a box I'd get a snout full. A saucy bird would be a turn. A scubber would keep me out of the nick, she would."

"A man has to get his end away, Robby."

The vagrant chit-chat stopped when the landing lights bordering the runway ignited, pouring an obscene fire into the night, the lights refracting off a blanket of whirling, torn clouds, sending hundreds of grazing birds into a blinding scram.

Above the lights the sky went blank.

Eurasia Airline Charter Flight 833, suspended in a boiling flurry of clouds, dropped from the gloom onto the airstrip. Hidden from view, Hawkes and McPhee waited in a jungle recess near the reception hangar. Two shackled convicts and three young Asian women took the stairs from the plane and trooped across the tarmac, each in the hand of a member of the Sikh Militia who controlled the penal colony.

"A full house—three tarts and two rotters." Accepting a curious grin, Hawkes sparred with his reflections of the strangers he saw in Ritchie's Pub. "How were the sods who blew up your shop decked out, Robby?"

"They weren't wearing a chain, and half stepping." Shaking his head slowly, McPhee gave his balls a toss. "Those guarders are big, woolly bastards."

"Sikh Militia. Commanded by Mother's, First Northamptonshire Regiment." Hawkes turned his face into the shadow, suspecting a poster may have been circulated for his arrest. "Those convicts will be turned over to the police guard at Aberdeen Jetty."

"Mother's MI9 agents are a pair of derky slags. One's tall and the other's a bit stumpy."

Hawkes gave a collusive nod. "One is tall and trimmed up as a quick-set hedge. The other's short and a bit dumpy, gushing about like a glory-blown sod."

Picking at the hollows of Hawkes's face, McPhee lit a cigarette and nodded with satisfaction. "Hawkes, you god-bobbing bastard...Go on, give me the rest of it."

"Mother's hounds are in Port Blair, Robby—latched to a booth at Ritchie's."

"Sod on... Now...? Bloody hell..." McPhee started into the spill of a hangar light and stopped as a British officer approached the women. Squinting under a pair of red-orange eyebrows he added, "Those blighters dropped in on an unscheduled flight."

Hawkes took McPhee by the swivel and pulled him into the bushes to a vantage where they could monitor the runway and keep an eye on the station wagon.

McPhee straightened his shirt. "It's the odds I gave you, Hawker. I was knowing that Portuguese tramp is worth a quid or two."

"Shut up, Robby." Hawkes searched along the grass verge at the far side of the airstrip and found the airplane—the silhouette of a British Airway dual engine, twelve-passenger Wellington, with its window curtains fully drawn. The interior of the aircraft soaked in a filtered hue; the crew certain to be bored rigid. Hawkes had flown these assignments in Malaya.

The pilot and crew are probably still on board—on standby status.

Listening for an odd sound, Hawkes tamped a Dunhill against his thumbnail. Mindful of the Sikh Militia used as prison guards, he cupped the cigarette into his hand and lit it.

"Those rotters will be randy as ferrets by week's end." McPhee pointed with a bent thumb, implicating the prisoners as if remembering his time in the nick.

"We better clear off, Robby."

"That one bird's a saucy bit, Hawker. What say we give her a lift? Do a bit of cracking."

"We better shift ourselves, Robby." Hawkes pointed to the station wagon. McPhee failed to move. Hawkes spun him into the brush and nudged him forward. "Sikhs like their knives. Worse, I know who those brown birds will be working for. He doesn't like blokes from Dublin."

"A Londoner from Seven Dials is who I am."

"Skivvy-shit is what you are. Besides, all Micks are from Dublin."

The ride from the airstrip was filled with one wind-up after another—each tied to leveraging the ship's captain into a jam and capturing the gold after foxing the Household's ghillies with a limp leg and a twist. At bottom, challenging the Crown over an unknown cargo seventeen miles from the Cellular Jail Penal Colony at Port Blair left Hawkes thirsty, waiting to be salved.

Nearly a year ago Port Blair's head copper had escorted Hawkes through the Cellular Jail to show Hawkes his future, insisting the pilot fly an illicit cargo run each month to Colombo, Ceylon. The decision was an easy one—free whiskey or a jail cell.

The stone-and-brick circular stairway of the jail gave certain notice. At forty feet across and ninety feet high, it framed an arched stone portico into a world of pure hell. Seven stone wings radiated from a central tower, each wing designated for a level of punishment—a degree of torture and death. The windowless cells advertised as stone coffins.

The Indian Freedom Fighters resisting British rule found themselves shackled to a damp wall, in solitary confinement. Hawkes's freedom depended on his avoiding Chennault's friends.

Buffeted by onshore winds off the Andaman Sea, the station wagon sat near Harbor Ring Road at a vantage above and north of the quay designated to receive the Portuguese flag.

Knowing he was a terrible marksman, Hawkes found the grip of his Browning (HP), thirteen cartridge, 9mm, released the safety, and fingered the trigger carefully. The harbor and the quays were empty. The scene held a comic fascination.

Moonlight made clear the jungle bordering the roadway. The wind had lost its drag, and the tall grass lay still. A raw dampness tinged the air. The interior of the station wagon held memories for Hawkes—the deaf ear of a temporary mate and the savor of ingratitude.

He used this jungle vantage whenever a cargo bound for the illicit trades of Port Blair was ripe for picking. The wagon sat in a hollow of eight-foot foliage. The engine of the oxidized black hulk stirred with the hum of old fiddle music, skipping a beat at odd intervals, and coughing to add percussion. Hawkes would wait for the old girl to nearly clap out, then feather the throttle until she shuddered to a smooth purr.

Women, he thought. Some take forever.

Laughing at himself to ease the boredom, Hawkes let the Browning slide to the bottom of his coat pocket. Normally, he enjoyed sorting the intricacies of Port Blair's games. The downside of this game, this dicey-do of pestering the Crown, left him no safe harbor.

Would he side-up with Gum Tree 'Darkie' McPhec, or the ship's captain, or throw in with Mother's lads so he could become an RAF pilot again?

"Here we go, Robby." Hawkes pointed into the night at a black sedan approaching the far edge of the adjoining quay. "Mother's lads are in that sedan. Buggers have their headlamps off."

The outline of the car looked as though it had been cut from the haze encasing the bunkering dock, then perched upon a rack of petrol drums—its occupants more confidential than the glow of their cigarettes. Remembering with disgust the sacking he suffered at the hands of British snobbery, Hawkes continued to evaluate his decision.

"Do you be keeping a weapon, Hawker?" As if countering his mate's reluctance with a feverish insistence, 'Darkie' McPhee burst into good humor and shouted, "Something special, besides a bloody breechloader."

Unpredictable as he was, Hawkes snapped at McPhee. "A revolver... Why would any bloke give you a weapon?" Without pause, Hawkes grunted, then sighed in resignation and pushed the chrome button. The glove box door fell open, spilling a pool of yellow light into the front seat.

Keen with anticipation, he handed McPhee an old Webley-Fosbery, six-round cylinder, .45. "Short range only, Robby—six, Single Action Army ball cartridges—nothing beyond twenty meters. That beauty's a relic."

"I could hit those bastards at sixty meters with a hood clapped over my eyes." McPhee shook a cigarette loose, and shouted, "With my bloody cock on fire."

"And drive that front sight blade by the boards and into your bloody forehead."

Having decided the risk of McPhee being armed could be reconciled with a single shot, Hawkes slipped into the madness. "You're an amusing bugger. Dribbling with grog while Mother blows up your flat—your future really. And she's decided to stalk the balance of your miserable life. Leave out the bollocks, Robby."

"I haven't had my bollocks out."

For all his blimpish remarks, 'Darkie's a decent bloke.

For Hawkes the next hour brought a swelling sense of urgency. Knowing McPhee was felony prone, with no mind for a plan, he decided to ditch 'Darkie' if the British agents got too close. Unemployed for months now, his habits and his station wagon had become well-known for the oddments on South Andaman Island—too well-known. If Mother's lads tied the Ford to McPhee or the steamer, he would have to abandon the vehicle and leave South Andaman Island.

With Hawkes smoking Dunhills and McPhee smoking Players, each new fag met a consuming sigh and more questions. Why were Mother's lads laying siege to a tramp steamer? And where were the dock bulls, the lorries, and the dockers?

It's a setup. Hawkes decided. Mother plans to seize Captain Corcoran and his crew.

The Portuguese flag eased from the night, past Port Blair's deep-sea jetty, slid along the quay's fender piles, and threw her starboard lines over the bitts. Silent, as if unmanned, she came to a stop, leaving a ribbon of water between the quayside and her hull. The harbor was deserted.

"That's our steamer." McPhee rolled down his window.

"Robby, the agents have gone missing."

"It's a trap the bastards have, I'm certain."

Hawkes searched the folds and the shadows near the agent's sedan.

He had spent months nurturing an agreeable and harmonious relationship with Port Blair's chief magistrate, sharing the spoils of larceny. I'm making a good deal of money. If I offend the colonial pleasures of the Crown, I'll head the queue waiting for a vacancy in the Cellular Jail.

The clock on the dashboard shone bright; its luminescent dial sounded each strike as if the second hand was plodding in mud and driven by cast-iron gears. The clock's pale glow half-lit the faces of too much drink.

McPhee's breathing had accepted the clock's pace by the time the ship's crew flowed onto the apron. Corcoran came bounding down the apron, a seaman's skip, heading for the harbor strand, flipping his cigarette into the water at the last turn.

"That's the captain—the big man in the khaki shirt."

Watching the crew crowd onto the strand, Hawkes spotted the MI9 agents running toward the steamer with their weapons cradled at high port, their stride that of portly men.

"Latch on to your vitals, Robby. The war's on."

Hawkes depressed the clutch and slammed the transmission into bottom gear. With the synchrony only chaos could fashion, the wagon leaped careening onto Harbor Road, slid sideways through a turn, raced downhill, and slid to a stop at Corcoran's feet. McPhee threw open the rear door as the agents opened fire.

"Get in, Captain! It's a trap!"

Sitting on the sill of the passenger window, McPhee fired across the hood of the wagon. Corcoran dove headlong onto the backseat. The wagon lurched into the roadway. Hawkes swung the wheel and stomped on the gas pedal. The wagon accelerated up a long hill, racing into the night, into the moist, steaming, rural fragments that fashioned the penury of the Andaman Sea.

"Who are you convicts?" Corcoran screamed, leveling the barrel of his Webley Mark 4 at McPhee's head. As though sensing the circumstance, his throat tightened, and his mouth turned dry. Glancing at Hawkes, he released and reset the cylinder.

"Convicts, are we now?" McPhee hollered. "I thought it my duty to save you, Captain, after giving your tramp an early sailing from Rangoon."

"Yes, of course—Rangoon's harbormaster. Let's all have a piss." Corcoran's words settled into a barbed fence as he spun the cylinder on the Webley. The metallic notes brought silence. He placed the gun barrel at the nape of McPhee's neck.

"Is this one of your wind-ups, McPhee, or do we three make a full meal?"

Irritated, Hawkes had had his fill. "Kark it, Captain." Slowing the wagon, he turned into a secluded patch of jungle next to a bamboo hut. "Although McPhee's something of a dosey turd, he did send you on your way. And for his trouble, Mother followed him and set a trap for you here in Port Blair."

Turning into Corcoran's weapon, McPhee peered at the cylinder of the Webley MK4 and pushed the barrel aside. "You brought the buggers into Rangoon with you, Captain. A faulty door latch—that's what saved me. The bastards came one gust from killing me—blew my flat apart with explosives tied to the bloody door."

"Amitol—nasty work, that Amitol."

With its headlamps angled at high beam, the agent's sedan shot past the bamboo hut and dropped into the night.

Corcoran reset the muzzle of his Webley inside McPhee's left ear, watching Hawkes's hands. "And with proper squadron spirit, you lads came goolies to the wind, to rescue an old mate," he said, rolling his words with a facetious whine.

Hawkes scoffed and backed the wagon into the darkened roadway. Without delay he pulled on the headlamps as the old Ford gained speed heading back to the port. "Where to, Captain?"

"Back to my ship, or I shoot McPhee." Corcoran bloused McPhee's ear with the barrel. "Put your paws on the dashboard, Harbormaster."

McPhee extended his hands, and Hawkes started beating on the steering wheel. "Holy jumped-up shit. I don't give a toss. Shoot the derby bastard."

"Bloody hell, Hawkes, shut your fucking mouth."

Hawkes burst into a howl as the lights of the port came into view. "Here we go. I'm either driving to Ritchie's Pub to drink myself into a crawl or to your ship for a bit of gold and safe passage. Your go, Captain."

The station wagon roared onto the quay's front apron and slammed to a stop, with Hawkes staring down the barrel of Molly's Model 1897 shotgun. The large sailor placed the barrel of the shotgun under Hawkes's chin. One shot would take out Hawkes and McPhee.

For more than a while Molly had searched the buildings along Harbor Road. Spotting Uncle in the backseat, he grinned. "I got these fuckers, Captain."

"Give us a tic, Molly. Do we have enough fuel and water to reach China Bay?"

"Water yes. For fuel if we gain the offing. She'll need a good sea."

Corcoran poured three mugs of rum and settled into his chair in front of the steamer's radios. Evaluating the strangers, he slid the Webley into its holster under the radio mount. Mindful of his rendezvous south of Ross Island to extract Hardin and any remaining commandos from Team 7, keeping Mother's goons from forecasting the steamer's location was critical.

Operation Snow White had degenerated into sailing routes Mother found unlikely. All the while refueling and taking on stores without being sequestered.

Wounded, Hardin might be run to ground by the hounds. Hawkes and McPhee are wild cards—traipsing dribblers—either complications or temporary allies.

"Those could be Mother's lads," Corcoran said. "Or they could be Axis spies. Whoever they are, killing me seems to be part of their mission. I'll give you cash to waylay the sods. They should be in Singapore."

The three men sipped rum and laid a track for the move to Singapore. Convinced he might have to ditch Hawkes and McPhee somewhere along the ratline, Corcoran gave each man one hundred pounds, three hundred US dollars, and a promise of eight hundred pounds after they waylaid the agents.

Hawkes sat at the chart table placing the one-hundred-pound notes on Rangoon, Port Blair, and Singapore. Suspicious, he said, "Robby..." Hawkes motioned Corcoran to his weapon. "Robby, you're either toggled to Mother's boys, or you've stumbled onto matters of the Crown."

Huffing and snorting, pacing with the determination of a pig in heat, McPhee crushed his cigarette pack into a wad and threw it at Hawkes. "Now there's a cracking plot, eh, Hawker? You and the sailor here, a pair of nob-sharing wank-socks."

"What are you twatting on about, McPhee?"

"If it's gold, you don't lick it off the rocks."

Corcoran pushed his chair against the wall. "What jack is yours mick—amounts to whatever swag I give you."

"You bastards are clobbered—a pair of soppy twats." McPhee picked up his crumpled fags. "A drunk pilot and a swagman jacking as a boat driver—you lot are a pair of brown-tongue roaches. I know my onions. I was knowing when I clapped eyes on you, Captain, when gold's about you couldn't be trusted."

Hawkes fell over a stool when McPhee's weapon leveled itself on his chest. As McPhee reached for Hawkes's money, Corcoran brought the barrel of his revolver down on McPhee's wrist and kicked McPhee's feet out from under him, slamming the Irishman's head into the deck.

Hollering for Jesus and holding his wrist, McPhee's insolence ran to seed when Corcoran drove a boot into his kidney.

"Next time I'll blow your bag off."

"Did the agents show you their warrant cards, 'Darkie'?" Hawkes asked.

"'Darkie', again?" McPhee held his wrist as if it might fall apart. "Mother had Rangoon's chief magistrate guiding the bastards about. Is that enough brass to stand on? Bloody hell—sort it out. It wasn't a fucking I.D. parade."

"That's the extent of it, is it?" Hawkes asked, leading McPhee to think. "You were left to carry the can while the agents did a runner?"

"When they left my shop, one of the twats dropped a ten-bob postal order—with a street number written on the back: W.I. 13 Rue du Four, Paris."

Corcoran entered the address into the ship's log, unloaded McPhee's weapon, threw it to him, and keyed the ship's intercom. "Molly, can you join us? Bring Olive with you."

Hawkes started sorting his money. "Mind you, I don't care a damn about your blarney, 'Darkie'. Loaded or not, hide that revolver before Molly and Olive come calling."

Molly entered the chart room barrel first, ready for a punch-up, eyes wide and steady. Lately, the chief engineer met his day ready to offend anyone with a cock.

"The tall one is Hawkes. You met that twat lying on the deck, in Rangoon. McPhee was Rangoon's harbormaster. They're going to meet us down the line, Molly—after they deal with the bastards who tried to kill me tonight."

Sizing the man standing by the chart table, Molly chimed, "Weak stiffies if you want my view. In need of wire leads, they are."

"At half-ten show them off the quay."

"The ship's agent said there'll be a delay in taking on stores, Captain. The dockers voted for a work slowdown. They're on a reorg. At zero six the dockers are set to start hard-timing."

"We can't wait, Molly. Find out how much money the dockers want."

"Six hundred quid." Molly watched Corcoran unlock a cupboard under the radio mount and count out pounds' sterling. "The dockers said with no moon, it'll be dark enough to cut the painter at half-three, and drift before we run."

Molly took hold of McPhee's left arm above the elbow. McPhee stiffened. Trying to protect his wrist, Molly threw him into the passageway.

With Hawkes following at a fair distance, Molly directed the Irishman to an empty ward, nudging him with Olive's barrel.

"Go on…" McPhee pushed the shotgun's barrel aside.

"Don't tempt me, Paddy. Wait for a better time—after your balls have dropped."

"Grumpy, this is Princess, over."

Holding a mug of gunfire, strong tea laced with rum, Uncle was beyond going off. He had been transmitting on one primary frequency and a secondary frequency for the better part of the morning with not a hint of feedback. The transceiver's silence was aggravating. For Hardin to make the rally, he should be within earshot.

Grumpy—there's a good mate, an uncomplicated bloke.

The steamer was scheduled to refuel at 0030 hours and sail at 0430 hours. Ditching the harbor pilot, he threw lines at 0300 hours. With the outgoing tide, the steamer cleared the exit buoy and dropped over the horizon before first light. With the steamer's route listed as Singapore, Mother's lads would fly to the island ahead of the boats scheduled arrival.

Once the SS Iron Knight was overdue for its port call in Singapore, Lloyd's Shipping Index, headquartered at Speepen Place, Colchester, in the English county of Essex, would be informed. Lloyd's Shipping Intelligence Unit would consult their maritime casualty records to confirm there were no missing or sunk vessels in the Bay of Bengal.

That done, the Index would pass the matter over to the editorial desk of the List and inform British Royal Naval Intelligence. Coastal patrol flights throughout the Bay of Bengal would be activated as would Royal Navy coastal patrols sailing from Colombo, Ceylon.

Uncle had to pick up Hardin and run—west to Bombay, the Gate of Tears, and through the milky, stinking waters of the Red Sea to Suez, and then on to Alexandria.

Trapped on a steamer, how will Mother kill her prey? Sink the boat in open water in the Indian Ocean. The bastards will blame the loss of ship and crew on a U-boat. Uncle's musings led him to the bottom of the chart table for a cigar and another shot of rum.

"Once in the Indian Ocean we'll sail well south of the shipping lanes," he whispered.

With the wind three points to the port bow and the sea flat, Snow White's primary rally point west of the Malay Peninsula laid one finger south of Mergui's southern limits, the sighting taken from one mile west of the outer limits of the Mergui Archipelago. The rally point was near the southern end of Ross Island, a dangerous reach of water—a reef-strewn patch controlled for centuries by coastal pirates.

*　*　*

Burma. Mergui. 30 August 1939. 0610 Hours, GMT + 6.5 Hours.

Dawn found Hardin watching the gray of morning filter through the canopy. Tu had started a small fire with scraps of dry palm leaves. With the end of a pencil-size burning cane she gently seared the edges of Hardin's leg wound, then scrubbed the wound and seared the edges again. Lifting his shirt, she burned a leech from his back.

The penicillin the American ranger gave Hardin seemed to be helping. Unshaven, bleeding at every divot, his essentials were the only trophies the leeches hadn't cratered. Tu sprinkled his leg wound with sulfa powder, applied a fresh battle dressing, and tied it in place with strips of from his old blouse.

Using the cane to light a cigarette, he drew deep on the fag and burned the leeches off his lower legs. Forced to travel on dry ground, their route traced the coastal roadway between Tavoy and Mergui, crossing the bridge at Palauk at night to avoid detection.

Moving at night in the rain had been shear folly. His backtrail was littered with the hollows he formed falling into the foliage. Tu communicated with hand signals she had refined into a calculus, prompting Hardin to keep moving. Tu spoke in quick French, laughing whenever he stumbled, giving him a lift if he needed it.

It'll be tea and medals if I get through these next few hours.

Dawn brought ambient noises as foliage began to absorb the heat, followed by a stillness that was menacing. Sunlit streaks of sea-purples and pinks raced over the canopy out to the horizon, some adding reds to a slumbering sky, some echoing as a strobe.

Palmate leaves reached for the surf and ran from a wash of empty shells. The sea was empty, empty to the horizon. Beyond lay his next challenge.

The turbid waters of the inland waterway that ran north and south along Burma's western shore, churned in stark contrast to the clear, calm waters of the Mergui Archipelago. Monsoon rains had transformed the river deltas into a roiled stew, its upland sediment staining the sea.

Watching the sky, stopping near the mouth of a small stream twenty meters from the beach, Tu dropped her kit, pulled out a dry bird's nest and struck a match. Adding a small bundle of sticks, she set a cup of water in the flame. The smoke from the fire hung below the first layer of leaves before being dispersed by the dense vegetation.

A hours' rest was not enough.

Moving through the unbroken jungle, maintaining a brutal pace, Tu kept pushing. The noise of the rain had forced her into a pattern of running abeam at odd intervals, then folding back on their route-of-march to listen.

After the rain stopped, Tu lifted her chin as though setting an ear to a sound. Moving quickly, she signaled Hardin for silence. A trailer had found their tracks—one, no two. The jungle hung wet. In the hot, thick, clinging air, nothing moved.

Hardin pushed his stave into the mud and swung his weapon from his shoulder. Sector by sector he searched his flanks. The girl sank into a deep squat and fixed her gaze on Hardin. Her eyes flashed, but she was silent. He rubbed a knuckle in each eye to clear his vision, then held up his index finger, betting the tracker was operating alone.

Steiner, he thought.

A harsh flash came with the roar—a wall of rain swept in from the sea. Dark and light, the jungle absorbed the rain for a step and seemed to gain weight. Hardin dropped his stave and grabbed a limb on the nearest tree for balance.

Just as suddenly the downpour stopped.

Hardin wondered how the tracker would strike. Steiner's a Kraut—an arrogant ass. He'll never see the girl coming.

Her tactics were precise—classic bush-ranging moves. Providing the trailer with a silhouette, she flanked his movements using the wind-battered jungle as cover then appeared in silhouette on the opposite side of the clock. Repeating the move, as though lulling her prey with predictable moves, she became a familiar companion before she disappeared.

Curious, Steiner exposed himself. As she spoke, he turned his head. She bashed his face with a bamboo rod, crushing his nose.

Dropping his French Thompson into the mud, Steiner fell, screaming into cupped hands. Blood poured between his fingers. As the Kraut reached for his weapon, she slammed the end of the bamboo rod into his mouth. Steiner's teeth erupted into a jumble, highlighting a blossom of blood. His right cheekbone was crushed, leaving his eye to droop unsupported. His nose sat smashed, a glob of viscous sludge.

With a foot on Steiner's throat, she threw his Thompson into a bog. Sizing her prize, she toggled his hands across his back to the opposing ankle with three-foot, hemp lines. Inspecting her work, she jerked each line, tightening the knots. With a vicious yell, she rammed the butt of the cane into Steiner's kidney driving him to crawl.

Forcing him to stand, she tied a hemp lead around his neck and started east, away from the roadway. Running as if she wanted to gain distance from the ambush site.

Steiner fell. She struck his balls—over and over, crushing his right hand with the end of the bamboo rod.

Soaked and covered with a dark mud, Steiner had to skip his step to stay erect. The girl was on course for a fishing village situated seven miles north of Mergui—for food and shelter. "Fresh eggs and satay," Hardin whispered. "Lemongrass soaked in peanut oil and grilled in banana leaf; food, a dry hut and a transceiver, that's what I need."

Approaching a village this time of year is dangerous, he thought.

Tu continued to prod Steiner. Twice she slammed the butt of the bamboo rod into his kidney. Twice she unsheathed the machete and laid the blade on his face. Twice she stopped his step and whispered in French.

Minutes became hours. Sweat became grime. Leeches boiled from the mud.

The trek was a brutal mix of bogs and coastal vines. The sole on Hardin's right boot gave way to the suction of the mud. Stumbling from one handhold and searching for the next, he slumped to the ground at the base of a tree. Tu stopped for a smoke.

Tu tamped a light brown, long-cut tobacco into the ivory bowl. Speaking softly at first, her French broken in translation, she accused Steiner of hiring the Cambodes that raped her.

Hardin didn't care.

Tu beat the man as if to leaven the memory of her rape.

Steiner fell in stages, flailing, trying to ward the blows. Prodding him to crawl, she coaxed him onto the roadbed of the bridge at Kye, unsheathed her machete and struck her prey. Devoid of mercy, she severed the tendons above Steiner's heels sending him writhing—crawling into a rain-swollen ditch.

Jesus was the focus of his rage.

Fighting to muster a breath, he drew a branch under his chest to keep his face above the thick, leech-infested water. Fighting to draw air enough to scream, he begged Hardin for help, for the *Pervitin* tablets in his rucksack.

Pushing Hardin aside, Tu rolled Steiner onto his back. Her machete's blade sliced through the joint at the front and below Steiner's kneecaps. He faced a painful death. The mud that had quartered his boots now anchored his crawl.

Hardin pulled Steiner out of the water onto the road and set the Kraut's rucksack near his head, so he could eat his crystal meth tablets and his bag-rations if he got his hands untied.

"Who hired you to kill me, Steiner?"

After a slight shrug, the German mustered a sigh. "Somebody hired Lucien to intercept the pouch you're carrying." Steiner was gaining a withered yellow complexion. Losing blood had emaciated his face. "What's in the pouch? What am I dying for?"

"I don't know." Hardin opened Steiner's rucksack and took out the small blue-and-red tube of *Pervitin* tablets, unscrewed the lid, put a tablet in his enemy's mouth, and poured the remaining tablets on the ground near Steiner's face.

Steiner drew a deep breath and closed his eyes. "Lucien thinks you are a hard man."

"I felt empty after my team was ambushed. At times I still do."

"We are fools, *mein freund*—you and I." Steiner laid his head on the ground. "Tread carefully, Englishman. Lucien's friends infest the Devil's Neck with their cohorts." Steiner gave a short coughing hack. "They control the drug route across the Neck."

Lucien could not be far away. All of Mother's ratlines had choke points.

The Devil's Neck, the Kra Isthmus was a thirty-five-mile-wide finger where Burma turned into Thailand, a choke point south of Mergui.

Using hand gestures, Tu changed direction.

By afternoon Hardin was exhausted. Yet they made better progress now. Running out of time, he needed to find a boat, sail west around the north end of King's Island, and turn south to reach the rally point near the southern end of Ross Island.

Staying off Route 8, the main road, to avoid the patrols of Burma Frontier Force #2 stationed at Tavoy and Mergui, had been simple enough. The Gurkhas would find Steiner and attribute his death to bandits or Jap prickers.

After a day of ranging south and west, of catching and balancing his weight, the girl's relentless prodding brought Hardin's manhood and his wound to a boil. By keeping pace with this devil, even his sharp eye was closing.

Time, and again, her machete flashed, slicing the jungle vines. The sun broke late in the day, setting the thatch atop the village huts aglow, leaving the doorways dark hollows.

Bamboo huts and temporary frames for drying fish nets, sat in a clearing screened from the sea by staggered strips of foliage. Natives began approaching from the south. A small sailboat barely fit for salvage sat at anchor, its sails rolled to preserve the tatters. With her insistent chatter and three hundred French francs, she hired an old Burgi fisherman and his boat.

The heat of the jungle reached out across the water. Hardin welcomed the sudden feeling of space around him. The open water. Cooler air. The dark blotch was the jungle set against the cream-colored beach.

Fearing without knowing why, he opened and closed the breech of his weapon. Drifting in a tidal rip one-half mile from shore, he spotted a Malayan sailboat, a prahu coursing through the slackening tide. The old fisherman, became quiet, wiped his face, and struck the sail.

Hardin's thoughts returned suddenly to Steiner. Why did he warn me about Lucien? Odd when a man thinks of it. These pirates might work for Lucien.

Hardin checked the round chambered in his Hart MK1. As the prahu approached, the old seaman stiffened his back, and his attention fixed on the prahu's crew. Our fisherman recognizes these pirates, he thought. The bastards will try to kill me and rape Tu.

"Keep a sharp eye, my bloody arse," he whispered.

Weighing the risks, selecting the pirate he would shoot first, with nowhere to run, he boarded the prahu with the girl at his heel. Leveling his weapon to cover the foredeck, he waited as Tu stepped past the cabin door. With her rucksack against a bulkhead, she drew her machete and set the blade behind a wooden crate. Her lips moved as though she were counting. Four pirates manned the sloop. Hardin scanned the deck, locating his targets. A bolt-action carbine leaned against the bulkhead near the cabin door.

These wet-smuck bastards better have quick hands if they try to rape this jungle flower, Hardin mused. Losing their life to such a small child will be a surprise.

On edge, Hardin's eyes offered no clue. Instantly, the prahu's captain demanded money. Translating, Tu opened Hardin's kit, and, with a quick nod handed him one hundred US dollars.

Holding the money in his left hand, Hardin leveled his weapon on the captain's midsection and pointed at Tu. After Tu and the captain exchange heated words, a wireless was set on the deck near Hardin's feet.

The Model-200 transceiver was an antique. The light wind and the mackerel sea meant the monsoon had run its course, and wireless signals should sound clear. "Princess, Grumpy here." Hardin released the push-to-talk button. Instantly, Uncle's voice came crashing back.

"Been prancing about, have you, Grumpy?" The relief in Uncle's tone rang through.

"The apple's on the stem, Princess." Uncle needed to make the rally before twilight.

"The dough's sticky. A bit of a Welsh rabbit."

"Give my regards to Broadway, Princess." Hardin wanted to proceed through Port Blair, bypassing Singapore, avoiding a possible trap.

"It's the old maid, Grumpy. She's been having one of her dos." Two facts are emerging, Hardin thought. Lucien doesn't work for Mother, and Uncle is diverting to a secondary ratline.

Hardin didn't respond.

Uncle transmitted, "The tart favors her short-arm inspections. Mind your foreskin, cobber."

"Is the pie in the oven, Princess?"

"Pasty-pie, Grumpy—cook's choice."

Hardin shook at the words, sifting through this newfound urgency. The British government had Uncle on the run—but why?

"I mean fair play, Grumpy. The tabby's got hold of our front shirt and she's got a leg over. Turned into a bit of a slag, she has." Shaken, Hardin leaned on the deck rail sorting the warning shot Uncle had fired.

"The apple's well baked, Princess."

Hardin tossed the handset to the pirate coaxing Tu's attention and handed the money to the captain. Switching off the transceiver, he nodded and sat into the rhythmic clatter of the old steam engine. As he tracked the nearest man, the man standing near the carbines pulled a pistol from his belt and held it near his leg. Ignoring the man, Hardin decided the small pirate with his hand fingering the butt of his knife would trigger the attack.

As if aimless, Tu ambled into the confines of a rope storage area in the bow to a point where she could strike three of the four pirates. She perched her rump against the rail and peered at the man with the pistol.

Hardin used her ploy to move to the port rail and stopped where line-of-sight forced the pirate inside the wheelhouse to lean out of the door to locate him.

With a three-hour run on the slack tide and with softening winds, the prahu would make the rally minutes before twilight. The reefs and channels near the south end of Ross Island were not navigable at night. Any delay in the prahu's arrival at the rally point, or delay in the steamer's pickup, would force the prahu to anchor out, exposing the mission to Japanese coastal patrols.

Alerted by a smooth, barely detectable motion of Tu's hand, Hardin hacked a protracted cough. Tu cut the hemp anchor line ensuring the prahu would have to remain under power after they reached the rally. As he brushed the front sight of his weapon with his shirtsleeve, a clean-limbed pirate took stock of his kit, his eyes darting from side to side.

Hardin had to gain control of the prahu.

*   *   *

Cologne, Germany. Stein Bank. 1 September 1939. 0900 Hours, GMT + 1 Hour.

Petra's gait was hesitant as she set her teeth and entered the headquarters of Stein Bank, a chamber that was the essence of any number of German financial centers. Frightened by the ritualistic isolation, she found worry in the eyes of a clerk and the secretary, their hair trussed in a tight bun that left their ears swept rearward.

Joy to the world, Petra.

She had been detained upon entering the Frankfurt Bohnhoff, escorted to a first-class lit carriage aboard a train bound for Cologne, and searched from top to bottom. "*Fokus*," she whispered, measuring the silence between the harsh reports of Frankfurt's train station. And, as if she could make sense of her predicament, the only information she gleaned before being arrested —the name Nicholas.

So, what do they want?

Arriving in Cologne, more shocked than frightened, Petra nursed her last cigarette. With her arms cinched to her side, as Abwehr agents pushed her along the arrival platform, through the Bohnhoff's center court, and into a black Mercedes sedan. Taken directly to the Headquarters of Stein Bank in Cologne, her eyes scanned the building as she stepped onto the curb.

Her wardens were harsh, clinical Nazis, with eyes that looked to be glued in place. Catching a breath, her resolve dissipating, Petra absorbed what could logically be assumed—her eventual death in a woman's work camp.

Certainty came with accelerating events in the summer of 1939. Austria, Czechoslovakia, and Yugoslavia had battered their sovereignty for German favors and allegiance. And now in September, Germany was invading Poland. Germany was slaughtering civilians.

Desperate to relieve her fear, Petra drew a deep breath. All my movements and schedule of meetings over the past month are well documented—times, dates, and objectives. All my activities have been approved at the highest levels of the bank. She rehashed her activities, recounting appointments, and transactions. There were no requests for additional assets. And Stein Bank had not requested confirming data.

Who will be here besides von Schroeder?

Not caring to create suspicion with fear, Petra remained visibly unmoved. As she was roughly handled, pushed from escort to escort, her hard leather heels echoed on the granite floor. Her throat grew tight as she approached the massive wooden doors of the director's chamber of Stein Bank. Standing alone she found the isolation frightening. A chill came with the granite fronting the massive entry of Kurt Baron von Schroder's chambers.

"Miss Heintz," Hess began, his voice spiking her name, his tone projecting a seething free of misgivings, his large frame braced next to Petra. "Miss Laube-Heintz, you are sleeping with Samuel Eaton, JP Morgan's arbitrage specialist. Explain."

"Before you begin," von Schroder put in. He stepped around his desk with what appeared to be contrived caution. He stopped to tamp his pipe, making eye contact with the men in the room.

"You know Max Ilgner, I. G. Farben's intelligence director."

Eaton's correct, she thought. The arbitrage scheme flows into a vortex, then swirls down a rabbit hole dragging dolts like me with it. *Fokus* Petra.

As she took stock of their faces; she searched her mouth with her tongue. A foreboding came with the ritualistic carvings on the wooden doors, deep carvings charred in their recesses to flatten the sheen. Evoking a response, Petra's legs grew heavy.

My mouth is so dry.

Five men sat arrayed as a phalanx of established wealth—all except Hess who stood in front of von Schroder's desk clutching a stack of paper.

In the spill of her obvious fear, Hess became conciliatory, his brow arching over a half grin. "Please sit down, Miss Heintz."

Defiant, she remained standing, deciding to be aggressive. "Samuel Eaton's greedy and easily manipulated. Sex obscures any reservation he might assign to Stein Bank—he will support J. P. Morgan's participation in any transaction we suggest."

Setting his pipe aside, von Schroder asked, "Why did you travel to New York?"

"I received an invitation," she lied.

"From Samuel Eaton?"

"Yes. He's an energetic tool."

Suspecting von Schroder may not be privy to all the details of the arbitrage scheme, Petra had to choose her words. Her boss could disrupt the scheme with a trading policy directive and not know what he had done. In that regard he was more dangerous than any of the other men.

The room grew close fostering a daunting silence.

Ilgner began to guide the confrontation with a lighter tone, prompting with kind words—complimenting Petra. Ilgner seemed to be admiring her.

"Who killed Eaton's secretary?" Hess asked, his tone a quiet, contained anger, his face spiked with anticipation.

"I do not know." She went on staring at him, her eyes a blank slate.

Ilgner mused as he strolled along the windows overlooking the evening traffic on Wilhelm Strasse. "Gentlemen, Miss Heintz has met a rising star. Mr. Eaton can help us. He isn't Jewish and seems to have a tenacious longevity."

Pointing at von Schroder, he became enthusiastic. "Eaton's Catholic! Somewhat removed, I judge. That might help our negotiations with the Swiss."

Von Schroder set a file to the corner of his desk. The mood seemed to quicken. "Your liaison with Mr. Eaton was well timed, Miss Heintz. Your absence was not."

"I understand."

"We support your liaison. We can use Eaton to reach deeper into General Motors and the DuPonts." Von Schroder spoke with a boyish pride.

"A note..." Ilgner's tone was calculating. "Eaton has routine dealings with Allen Dulles and his brother John—valuable conduits for I. G. Farben." Putting on an overcoat, he continued. "Allen Dulles is connected to American intelligence interests in Bern, Switzerland—European financial and counterintelligence interests."

"You may leave, Miss Heintz."

I must worry about Hess. He is a brutally vicious, she thought. He would enjoy sending me to the woman's concentration camp in Saxony. But Ilgner's the man I fear most.

Petra had plunged into a pool of fashioned solutions, none derived from reasonable assumptions or facts. Cold, her legs as heavy as anvils, she looked without seeing. Sitting in a taxi speeding down Wilhelm Strasse, she lit a cigarette, relieved to be free of von Schroeder's chambers.

I need to find Eaton and warn him.

Why had traveling to New York created such a reaction? And was anyone else at Stein Bank involved in the arbitrage scheme? She had seen Max Ilgner once before and thought it was in New York—but where? She remembered. Ilgner was sitting with Allen Dulles in the Cloud Room at the Chrysler Building.

If Ilgner's the man who created this inquisition, he has a secondary plan brewing. The other men might be dangerous. Max Ilgner would have me shot.

*   *   *

London. The Berkeley Hotel. 1 September 1939.
1750 Hours, GMT.

On a sunny Friday. Headline: *The Illustrated London News,* Nazis Invade Poland.

An air-raid siren woke Poston—a siren announcing a new world war. As Nazi jackboots sounded in the distance, Section C of MI8 patrolled the airwaves, sorting long and frequent bursts of wireless activity.

Johnny had spent the night at Admiral Sinclair's home, sorting data and answering the admiral's questions. The day before, his flat in Pall Mall had been sacked—his papers burned, his suits cut to ribbons, and his whiskey stolen.

"I can replace the suits, Admiral. The whiskey's the real loss." Poston noted a weariness about Sinclair that had not been evident in weeks past.

"Do you take restricted papers from the office, Johnny?"

"No, sir. Sacking my flat is not an intel matter. I 've jabbed a nerve with my inquiries. Someone has sent me a warning."

"Our spy, perhaps?" Sinclair drew air through his teeth as he raised his brow.

"More than one, I would guess." Poston laughed to himself. Setting fire to the Balkan Sobranie tobacco he tamped into his pipe; he was almost too exhausted to smoke. "I've reserved a room at the Berkeley Hotel. They've put on twenty-four-hour security."

Sinclair pressed his hands on a desk and measured them as he spoke. "We are in for a nasty fight with the Germans. And more of that dreadful chicken pie.

"London has a curious resilience. One that thrives on chaos." The old sailor seemed to question his tone as he came erect. "Operation Pied Piper begins today. Evacuating the children will take five days, or more. Blackouts have begun. BBC television is shut down for the duration, and BBC Home Service radio starts broadcasting today.

"With the army mobilized, all men aged eighteen to forty-one will be drawing a full issue of new clothes, rifles, and kits."

"What's the status of Bletchy Park? Is your Code and Cypher School operational?"

"The first personnel arrived on 15 August. At their request, today all telephone services with countries abroad and ships at sea have been suspended."

Leaving the MI6 complex, Poston walked to his tailor on Seville Row. After a fitting, and a steam pressing for his wrinkled suit, he walked to the Berkeley Hotel. As a lark, Poston set the room charge to Dewar's social account.

The twit won't see the bill for at least a month.

Poston drew deep at the aroma of his coffee. Excited discussions, less private than before, have London's peerage in a frantic scramble. The streets are crammed with lorries and tray- trucks and more busses than yesterday. And troop trains are departing on the hour heading for staging areas near the Channel.

Bombers heading for France fill the sky.

Waiting for Dewar, he watched a man scurry across the road carrying a satchel that looked familiar. Dewar stepped out of a cab, took the satchel, and handed the man an envelope.

Did the old boy just pay for a delivery?

Drawing on his pipe Poston watched Dewar check his hat and satchel into the cloak room.

As if expecting an escort, Dewar surveyed the lounge. Always keen to be the judge, peerage was a constant barometer for him. Picking his way through the lounge, his gait and manner reminded Johnny of a poorly fed hound.

I'll bet this club chair fits the twit's arse perfectly, Poston thought.

Feigning respect, Johnny stood, hesitated, and extended his hand. "I took the liberty of setting the whiskey to your account, Gordon. With all the confusion, I hope you don't mind."

"I would insist. It's Friday, and it's my show." Dewar caught the sommelier's eye and ordered a whiskey and cheese. "The admiral informed me your flat was sacked yesterday."

"With all your informants, I'm surprised you had to wait for the information."

"Let's call a truce, Johnny. Anderson bomb shelters are springing up everywhere. Even the statues are looking for a lift. Now that the war's on, driving around Piccadilly at night will be riskier than driving in Warsaw."

"The Nazis won't stop with Poland," Poston proposed. "They'll pour into Holland and Belgium and come crashing through the Ardennes."

"I believe you are right. But only the Admiral is listening." Accepting his drink, Dewar seemed content. "We're in the fight now. The RAF is sending ten squadrons of Fairey Battle bombers and two squadrons of Hurricanes to France tomorrow."

"Just so—The Advance Air Striking Force. Admiral Sinclair informed me this morning."

Giving no sign of having heard, Dewar pressed his lips together, grabbed the tub of salt and set to his order of chips.

"You're off to Rome, I'm told," Poston said, pressing for intel.

"I'm surprised you've been informed. Sinclair, I suppose. It's Mother. She's rather inconvenient. She's having one of her dos."

"I'm told it's one of your dos."

"You've clocked onto it, have you?" Dewar fixed Poston with a cold-eyed stare as he smoothed the tablecloth. "Mark the difference for me, would you? In one go if you can."

"You've been putting about like a rutting boar—the duke of Hamilton, Tom Mosley, Dr. Tester. Have these expensive chaps met, or are they bonded in separate storage?"

"Liaisons are a ruthless business without a ray of hope. Linguistic elasticity, even with a familiar voice, will accentuate the machinations of Ten Downing Street," Dewar said.

"Does Mother know you're heading east?" Poston asked, drawing Dewar's attention to the fireplace with his left hand and stealing his cloakroom claim-chit with his right.

"Now I'm heading east." Dewar's expression drew to a blank as he smoothed the tablecloth again. As if casting for a response, he leveled his gaze. "By God, now there's a turn up." He began to muse softly. "You're the watercolor, Johnny. I'm the oil. I am quite incapable of lending my salt to the opposition."

"Always at a gallop—that's the spirit, Gordon, flying your mahogany Spitfire with a shout. The truth seems to lay behind the pictures you paint, don't you agree?"

Knowing Dewar was involved in Sir John's murder, Johnny had to bide his time. Admiral Sinclair wanted Dewar fed with false leads to compromise Rudolf Hess.

Dawning a facetious grin, Dewar whispered, "I'm rather bored. I will share a gram with you. Whitehall has assembled a list of pilgrims, and I've taken the liberty of lightly coloring your brother's name. I hope you don't mind." His voice had fallen into a rasp. He squinted, drawing at his whiskey, his jaw straining.

"You don't have the stuffing for this, Johnny. Once in the frame as a traitor, Lewis won't be able to defend himself against the allegations I'm preparing."

Poston stood abruptly and dumped his drink in Dewar's lap. When the old boy tried to stand, he threw a straight left into his jaw followed by a right cross splitting his ear. A single strand of blood ran down the side of Dewar's neck. He raised his hand and leaned into the chair.

"Stuffing is one thing the Postons do have, you frilly bastard. If you go after any of us, you'll find the rest will come running, along with our friends. Someday Hockey will be calling."

Storming out of the lounge, Poston presented the claim-chit and took the satchel. The satchel was filled with one-hundred-pound notes.

That old punter is running bags for Dewar's drug operation—in London.

Shortly after arriving in Alexandria, Lewis posted a letter that left Johnny fumbling with loose tiles. His visit to London had prompted concern.

Johnny,

I arrived in Alex without a smear and found the chancellor's bit, bestrode a ranker from the embassy guard, nose well down, her scratchers fully engaged, one yanking on his hair, the other cinched on his chat-bag—on the lounge in my office. Rather revving, as you might imagine.

That said, with the international financial houses and the madhouses of government creating new liaisons, our SOE Groups are forming up in order, countering Germany's expansion into the Mediterranean and Japan's expansion into Burma. The prime minister's not amused—all hush-hush, mind you.

You may remember Sir Nigel Stuart, an intel type from Singapore. He's been enlisted to head SOE Force 136 Group A, for Burma, headquartered in Calcutta. Group B's slated for Colombo, Malaya. He is a dangerous, complicated man.

Stuart speaks French and Mandarin fluently. His Africa desk is with HQ Signals Liaison Unit (SLU) 1, tucked in a closet of the St George's Hotel, in Algiers.

Stuart works MI6 operations in Algiers and Marseille, tracking the centuries-old slave trade: white women being abducted from Europe and other locals along the northern rim of the Med, are sold into Africa through the ports of Tripoli and Algiers.

You met Stuart at the Trocadero Restaurant in Shaftsbury. He's an understated, powerful sort with eyes that could cube good scotch. He informed me one of our steamers, the SS Iron Knight, is lying off the coast of Burma and is nose deep in Operation Snow White.

Be careful how you push about London, Johnny. Money is changing hands in the sewers of our fair city.

Additionally, Gordon Dewar may have ties to I. G. Farben, Germany...the Imperial Policy Group, London...and Rudolf Hess.

I've been quietly enlisted by the admiral to oversee Force 133 for the Med region from an obscure office in Alexandria. In my spare time, mind you—all hush-hush.

A chap named Berryman is trolling about Cairo. He believes he will be heading up Force 133. He has a subaltern you'll loath—Alfred Gosden—the man who killed our father. Be mindful of Dewar, Johnny.

Give Sis a hug and kiss for me. I'm sure Linc will be home soon.

Until I see you again, Lewis.

Alone in the taxi Johnny reread the postscript of his brother's letter.

PS: Our steamer, the SS Iron Knight, operating in the Bay of Bengal took on scrap iron in Port Kembla, New South Wales. Check Lloyd's Index. Find what you can.

*　　*　　*

Cairo, Egypt. Shepheard's Hotel. 1 September 1939. 1540 Hours, GMT + 2 Hours.

If not for the rhythm of the piano music, Dorothy Stuart's hips may have been tied to a softening Nile breeze. Poston marveled at the grace of the woman's stride, her spiked heels carrying a voluptuous figure as though the curves were made of silk. The refinements of the waiter and the beauty of the woman, together, in motion, left Lewis hidebound, standing in front of his chair, nearly speechless.

Poston searched Dorothy's figure, her legs, wondering where the run in her stocking had gone. "You are a beautiful woman."

"Well, thank you." Prompting the waiter as he pulled out her chair. "I'll have a bourbon with ice and a glass of water."

Accepting the waiter's courtesy, Dorothy set her purse on the floor, extending an open hand. "Please do sit down, Mr. Poston. You're smiling that smile again." When his smile grooved into merriment, she brightened.

"Any luck with your husband's kit?"

"It's bad news, I'm afraid." She lit a cigarette. "Perhaps he's picked it up. If so, he's in the fight. That, or he's gone off with one of these dark beauties who are on station."

Poston leaned into the table. "I've some local resources here in the Med region. Tomorrow I'll make some quiet inquiries. John Stuart, you say?"

"Nigel actually. John is less formal."

"Sir Nigel Stuart? I've met the chap. If my information is correct, I may know where he's lounging these days. Nowhere near Cairo, I'm afraid."

"Nobility requires no accounting. He fancies being a nimble sort."

Pursuing notions, Dorothy and Lewis talked of travel and family and war, snippets spiced with inferences designed to guide the blind. The evening meal and drinks were willing consorts—Poston interested in New York City and sex, and Dorothy interested in London and finding her husband.

Raising his heavy cut-glass tumbler, Poston proposed a toast. "Here's to you, Dorothy Stuart, and to a wonderful evening. You're a lovely woman."

"You're a rogue, Lewis Poston."

"I thought I was doing rather well. Can I get a message to Sir Nigel?"

"Tell the cad we spent the night wondering where he'd gone."

*   *   *

Eurasia Flight 93, Port Blair to Singapore—to the City of the Lion.

Eurasia Flight 93, from Port Blair to Singapore flew right into a monsoon squall. Bouncing about, Hawkes held sway as he read the lead story in *The Illustrated London News*, August 31. The article touted the bulwarks of Singapore's formidable redoubts. Situated on the empire's far-eastern flank, security experts agreed those who were able should leave England for the safety of the island retreat.

Bad advice, Hawkes mused as he pushed McPhee's snoring carcass away from his shoulder.

Hawkes assumed Mother's budget shortfalls left the ramparts of Singapore posted at low tide in her majesty's war room—too far from the fight in Europe and impregnable. And true to form, the backbenchers governing Singapore island grew more boastful by the day, flattered by Mother's defensible assurances.

Sodding twits, Hawkes thought. Comically insular is what these islanders are. He circled the article's last sentence—the declaration of the day concerning the Japanese army: The Malaysian problem will never reach Fortress Singapore.

The Japs are more than a Malaysian problem. Singapore Island, the Gibraltar of the East is isolated. The Japs are going to walk in from the north.

Hawkes found the article in the *Straits Produce* paper equally absurd. Featuring the largest dry dock in the world, with enough petrol storage to operate the British navy for nine months, the article declared the island impregnable.

Bollocks. The British navy isn't here.

Even my mates in the Republic of Singapore Flying Club are around the bend. The fools loaned the club's four Moth seaplanes and five Cutty Sark seaplanes to the Straits Settlement Volunteer Air Force for coastal-patrol flights.

Nine paper kites. They'll be shot to ribbons, and their reports will be ignored.

Dropping the papers, Hawkes found McPhee's gaping mouth on his shoulder again and a stream of saliva flowing down his sleeve.

"Is that absolutely necessary?" Hawkes shoved McPhee's drooling rag-box off his shoulder, wondering if Irish manners were ever properly governed. McPhee jerked awake, looking lost, his expression swept clean.

Annoyed, McPhee gave Hawkes the finger. "Leave it out, fly-boy."

"Try to keep a short lip, Robby!" Hawkes checked the area near his seat.

"Your gear's a bit tight, Hawker." McPhee stepped into the aisle.

Jousting with McPhee's penchant for suspicious inquiry, Hawkes sighed. He grimaced as he imagined what Paddy would declare as the purpose of their trip. He shook his head after McPhee started river dancing in the bathroom queue, desperate for his turn at the convenience-tube, crimping his cock at odd intervals, an Irishman giving his heritage proper acclaim.

"You should audition that dance at the Royal Albert Hall," Hawkes countered after McPhee returned to his seat. "With a clothespin and a ribbon on your cock."

"Bugger off. Having a piss on this plane is a fucking scrum."

"Here's a piece of piss for you, Robby. If RAF security personnel are checking the passports of arriving passengers, I'll get nicked, and you'll be having it."

"You'll not be needing money, Hawker," McPhee said, extending a fetching hand. "That way Chennault can't steal it."

With Chennault headquartered at the Tengah RAF base, Hawkes had to be careful. Chennault had issued a warrant for his arrest on charges of dereliction of duty and gross misconduct. Hawkes could move about the island if he didn't run into anyone he knew.

Eurasia Flight 93 began its descent with a lurch, banking east over the Singapore Strait. Hawkes had flown this route for years; he expected the turn. His stomach tightened when the aircraft swung west. Worried he had not responded to any of the queries concerning his RAF reserve-duty status, he was braced for a confrontation with airport security personnel.

Bucking unusual headwinds, the airplane pitched from side to side, fell and climbed, and barely found its course. As passengers fell about trying to gather their belongings, the airframe rocked, setting the landing gear with a jolt. The plane's Pratt & Whitney Hornet engines moaned, laboring at the slower speed.

The landing pattern extended well to the east of Singapore proper as the Junkers 52/3mce settled into its final approach running west over Changi and touching down with an unexpected jar. Then, as if free, Eurasia Flight 93 ran flat and smooth, taxiing to a stop in front of the terminal.

"Look there, Hawker." McPhee stumbled, pointing to the wall behind the customs desk. "There's an alert poster just there with your picture on it."

"Shut up, Robby. Give me your identity card and passport."

"Why?"

"When I hand him our identity cards and passports, step back where he can see you, cuss a bit of Irish and button your pants."

The customs clerk shuffled the identity cards, laughed at the dumb mick, and stamped both passports. The custom check lasted fewer than thirty seconds. They were British, and they were welcome.

*   *   *

Singapore. Paya Lebar Airport. Friday. 1 September 1939. 1310 Hours, GMT + 8 Hours.

"**D**amn Chennault and his bloody posters. Good thing Singapore is the world's waste-bin—a haven for thieves and itinerant sailors." Hawkes lit a cigarette.

"And drunk pilots," McPhee added, billowing cigarette smoke.

"Shut up, 'Darkie.'" So far Hawkes's luck was running true. Showing McPhee, the headline in *The Strait Times*, "Germany Invades Poland," he studied the wall map of the island. Locating the RAF Aerodromes at Tengah, Sembawang, Seletar, and Changi, on the map, Hawkes ran his finger along the east-west axis north of the city and located the civilian airport at Paya Lebar. There was more air traffic than he remembered.

"It's a bar those sods will rummage," McPhee said.

"They landed on one of the military bases."

Jeffery Hawkes was acquainted with RAF operations having landed his Hudson Bomber on all four fields. RAF Base Tengah had the tightest security of the lot.

Standing in front of the terminal at Paya Lebar Airport, he gave himself a lecture. Being shackled to McPhee, a man steeped in Rangoon's sewers, had become tiresome.

"Robby, look for the twin-engine Wellington. She's a tail dragger, the Wellington is."

"I checked the tarmac. Not a whisper."

"Odds are they're parked at Tengah—the RAF base in the Western Area. Let's find a cab."

"Flying Officer Hawkes. Is that you?" the cab driver cheered.

"It's Jamison—Flying Officer Jamison—at least for now Wesley. I'm on the dodge and you need to forget you saw me."

"I miss your father, Lord Jamison." The driver set his meter and put the cab in gear. "He was always quick with a hand up." The driver glanced in his rearview mirror and found a nod.

"I'm more forgetful these days flying officer. With the Straits dollar worth two shillings four pence sterling, a good bit would do me well."

Heading north on Bukit Timah Road, turning east onto Choa Chu Kang Road, Hawkes asked Wesley to stop the cab fifty meters east of the main gate of the Tengah Aerodrome. Army coppers walked their post near the guard shack. A British Bedford three-toner sat on the far side of the guard shack, filled with troops.

Hawkes spotted a Wellington unattended on the near verge of the vast dirt runway.

Sweating and in need of a drink, he climbed back into the cab. "Our lads will be wired to the Long Bar at Raffles by now, enjoying a Singapore Sling."

Hawkes and McPhee stood on the verge of Beach Road staring at Raffles Hotel. A colonial jewel, Raffles' white stone gleamed in the sun. Stunning, as if alive, the hotel was a three-story tribute to Colonel Stamford Raffles.

"Here's twenty quid for the lift, Wesley. If we need another cab, we'll ask for you."

"I'll give you my home number. Let me know as soon as."

Hawkes took the number, put a five-pound note on the front seat of the cab and shut the door. Turning toward the hotel he said, "Only top shelf here, Robby." He spoke with a welcoming gesture, inviting McPhee onto the granite walk leading to the luxurious entry.

Cocking his indifference, McPhee laughed. "I'll be craving a banger and a pint, Hawker."

Drawing the Irish twit to a halt, Hawkes warned. "You bloody lizard. Borrow a bit of brass and try not to pant in Irish."

"Full stretch, Hawker, it looks like silent clapping could do it here."

"It's the MI-niners we're looking for."

A dark cast edged the elegant stone trimming the hotel windows. Bright and deep, braced, and vigilant, the entrance stood ready for a royal occasion. Just inside an oak portico, doormen and their aides ushered guests along. Raffles boasted a sense of permanence, a sense of place.

"This was my father's favorite watering hole."

With the look of the Irish about him, McPhee seemed to gain a curious husky quality. With a ripple of laughter, he said, "Hawkes, you plummy twat. You're just a drunk pilot."

"I was a legacy in Singapore's social flimsies, awarded a membership at Singapore's finest gentlemen's club—the son of an English earl. After father secured my membership in the Tanglin Club, at 72 Emerald Road, I mocked the offering as an old boy's musty game."

"Your father was an earl, and you were too slobbered to harvest his life's work."

"Not only did my father own the Singapore Ice Works, but he was also a director in the Chartered Bank. Perhaps the biggest English bank around these waters." With a reflective nod, Hawkes continued. "My father rinsed me out after I embarrassed him. One of the Tanglin Club's, Chuckers-Out, a notable named P. D. 'Panjang' Lawson, a six-foot, seven-inch lad, chucked me out of the club one Saturday night. I was drunk then, and I'm still a drunk."

"I regret what I said to my father."

Resisting a yawn, Hawkes inventoried the faces in the lobby. He remembered his sobering words. "Well, Father, you, and your nobs have massed your money into grand stacks, broad baskets of insanity, really, and what have you found?"

"Comfort, I suppose."

"Now that you and your friends are nearly clapped out, you'll be judged soon enough— fibered bags of the Household's rubbish is my guess," Jeffery had replied. "Crushed velvet."

With that, his father bid his son calm seas, toured Tanglin Barracks to add nutmeg to fond memories, and departed for England.

Years gone by, Hawkes hated what he wanted to be—a whiskey-drinking, cashiered pilot. He often pictured himself in front of Raffles, parked in a Bentley, greeting a gorgeous woman as she stepped into the car. In his dream his father merrily shook his hand, gave him three hundred pounds, and bid him a fond evening.

Now, settling into the Long Bar, Hawkes noted the hum of a tight-lipped drone playing upon the air vents. Secrets filled with empty chatter drummed among the tables. He scanned the reaches of the lounge.

Serving their whiskeys, the barman rapped the bar, calling McPhee's knowledge box to order. "Mother's increased the income tax," he declared, "from five-sixths to seven-sixths on the pound. Paying for the war, I suppose."

"Paying for her ghillies cracking half-cocked 'round the world, she is," McPhee snorted.

Hawkes gave the Irishman a cautioning eye, waited as the Chinese barman registered McPhee's ignorance, then finished his drink in one toss.

"We're off, Robby."

Stopping before he entered the foyer, he spotted the British agents near the main entrance talking with a lieutenant he recognized from Singapore's Imperial Guard. Hawkes nudged McPhee back into the lounge.

"There's our lads, Robby."

"Who's the third bloke?"

"Alexander Barracks Imperial Guard. I wager the sods are alerting him to Corcoran and that steamer. I need a whiskey." Suddenly morose, Hawkes started shaking. His trembling was jousting with a cut-glass bowl filled with olives. He was sweating as if he had run for miles.

"Get hold of yourself, Hawker."

He gave McPhee a nod, tossed off his second drink, ate a handful of olives, and ordered a third drink. "I'll hang if Chennault gets hold of me."

"Hedge about, Hawker—making a meal of booze." Hawkes turned full circle and ordered another drink. McPhee waved the barman away. "Bloody hell, Hawkes. Having a skinful should give it some stuffing."

Gulping the whiskey and sniffing the empty glass, Hawkes gained his feet. "We need the lads' room number if we're going to kill the bastards."

"For God's sake, Hawkes. Sit your arse down. What are we going to kill them with?"

"I don't know. I've never killed anybody."

As a gold piece, worth twenty-schillings becomes a pretty penny, Hawkes and McPhee sat in the lounge staring into the foyer. Neither man moved for the next hour.

* * *

Calcutta to Singapore. Eurasia Flight 27. 1 September 1939. 0430 Hours, GMT + 5.5 Hours.

Friday's Eurasia Flight 27 departed the biscuits of Calcutta on schedule, bound for the caviar of Singapore. Von Cleve enjoyed the island city for its obvious class. Sitting in a jump-seat in the front row of the plane's passenger compartment, the seat with space for his legs, he read Crilley's instructions again—neutralize England's agents, operatives, and remaining members of its special-ops team. A picture of Corcoran and one of McPhee, both stamped *Neutralize*, came with Crilley's instructions.

Crilley enjoys (ed) these edicts, he thought.

The day before the tail of a monsoon had raced down the funnel of the Malacca Strait and battered Singapore's Changi Province with cyclone winds and torrential rains—a year's worth of rain in eighteen hours. From the airplane, von Cleve counted three bridges across the Changi River that had collapsed.

Travel on the island will require flexibility.

Von Cleve marked Crilley's intel reports confirming the MI9 agents' reservation at Raffles Hotel, and the Portuguese steamer, SS Iron Knight, sailing to Singapore. And dimly, in the back of his mind, something whispered, "Corcoran won't get trapped in Singapore." No matter where he's heading, any special-ops soldiers on board will need Royal Air Force assistance—a Wellington or some other long-range aircraft to get out of the Bay of Bengal.

A light rain greeted von Cleve as he stepped from the cab. Raffles Hotel was a redoubt he cherished for her many delights—a refuge he sought from time to time. And, Raffles came with Phillip, a concierge who was a fellow traveler.

The concierge claimed to be the man von Cleve grew up with—paid well. Both were true. Von Cleve placed a photograph of McPhee under the lip of the counter at the concierge station. With a shrug and a slight twist of his mouth, Phillip turned his head and lifted his chin, indicating the entrance to the Long Bar.

Von Cleve then described the British agents down to their unkempt shoes.

"For reasons unknown to me room 246 has been under seal for days." Phillip's voice drew the heavy dull tone of fear. He wrote the words "Alexander Barracks" on a pad and remained silent—the one-hundred-pound note was rare indeed.

Taking the stairs on the bound, von Cleve stopped on the landing to survey the foyer. After making eye contact with Phillip, he turned and looked down the corridor. An Imperial Guard sergeant was standing in the corridor, feet apart, with his back to the wall. Gathering his thoughts, he walked up to the soldier and asked for a light. When the guard relaxed, took a step away from the door to room 246, and reached for his matches, he slit his throat.

Von Cleve caught the man as he fell and pulled him away from the door.

Catching his breath, he picked the lock. With three quick steps he slipped into the room and viciously drove his knife into Pucker's body, cutting-edge up, lifting the blade through the man's heart and shoving the dead man across the room. Mutt burst from the bathroom wrapped in a towel. Von Cleve ripped his belly open, jumped to the side to avoid the mess, and drove the knife into the man's eye as he bent over to catch his cascading bowels.

Two men dead—sixteen seconds.

Excited, he wiped the knife on the bedsheet and stepped into the empty hall. He dragged the dead guard into the room and closed the door, leaving a trail of blood on the hall carpet. If Harbormaster McPhee came calling, he would land in the frame for murder. Death's circle always came with tangents.

As before, the killing was never enough.

Sauntering down the open stairway overlooking the foyer, von Cleve fastened the loop securing his knife in its sheath behind his neck. Blood stained the finger slots and the weathered swales of his right hand. Killing Lucien's shills had been exhilarating.

That the dead men claimed to be British agents means someone sponsored by, or within British intelligence hired the Frenchman. I assume the agents were sending Lucien situation reports, and any time lapse in these sit-reps will force Lucien to alter his next move.

Lucien will come to Singapore.

Acknowledging Phillip, von Cleve laughed as McPhee approached the concierge's desk. Pausing on the stair to light a cigarette, he watched McPhee scurry toward the Long Bar, stopping to glance across the foyer before entering. Moving to a vantage near the porter's station he saw McPhee standing nose to nose with the familiar face of Jeffery Hawkes.

What did Phillip tell the bastard?

While the pilot waved his hands as if choreographing a dog fight, McPhee jabbed the air with an index finger. He was barking at one of von Cleve's old files—Flying Officer Jeffrey Hawkes, a cashiered pilot. Last known location—Port Blair, on South Andaman Island.

Von Cleve put a bounce to his step as he left Raffles and headed for the harbor. Within thirty minutes he had the docking schedule for a steamer of Portuguese registry sailing from Port Blair. Rangoon's harbormaster, Flying Officer Hawkes, a Portuguese steamer, and two men running gates for Lucien—a puzzle with simple-minded pieces.

The steamer's docking schedule is a ruse.

McPhee was frightened as he spoke to Hawkes. "Some bloke asked the concierge for the agent's room number. Not ten minutes ago."

Hawkes held up his fifth scotch. "Describe him for me, Robby."

"A big man. Dutch—South African accent. The concierge said he had strange, deep, green-brown eyes and an uncomfortable smile."

"If the concierge remembers all that, he can describe you right down to the button trapping your stubby cock."

McPhee led the way up the stairs. When they reached the landing, Hawkes grabbed his arm. "There's blood on the handrail."

Standing near the door to room 246, McPhee pointed at the blood smeared in a downward arc on the wall. "You first, Hawkes."

Hawkes eased the barrel of his weapon against the door. Unlatched, it seemed to open itself. Dissecting the scene as it came into view, he ushered McPhee into the room.

"Holy Mother of God," McPhee whispered. "There's a Guard's sergeant in the corner with his throat slit." Fear pushed Darkie's face through a series of expressions.

Watching McPhee's mouth move, Hawkes couldn't hear the words

Blood stained the elegant furnishings—even the fabric landscape murals hanging on the walls. The taller agent's body lay in a sprawl, his body parts spread in a trail from the nightstand to the steam heat register mounted beneath a massive window. Blood ran in an arc across a richly embroidered silk curtain.

Hawkes stood near the window overlooking the courtyard, watching dozens and dozens of dinner guests enjoying a dance band and a sumptuous buffet. He decided the second agent had been flayed from the sitting area near the bed on into the bathroom and lay head down in the tub, his vitals piled on the floor.

"And I'll be for runnin'. Three dead." McPhee emitted a long sigh and tried to light a cigarette. The stench made him retch.

"These sods were baked-off by a pro," Hawkes whispered, avoiding the blood smeared on the interior of the door, ushering McPhee into the hallway. "This South African is sadistic. Nasty bastard prefers a knife."

With a calculating cast to his eye, Hawkes followed McPhee down the stairs. "We need to shift ourselves, Robby. I'm betting the concierge and the assassin are in this together."

Moving at a brisk pace along Beach Road, they needed to get off the island before the gates of Fortress Singapore closed. The flights scheduled from the civilian airport were limited, a 2330 hours' flight to Kuala Lumpur. Hawkes paid for the tickets and led McPhee from the terminal onto the tarmac.

"Your bag's a bit tight, Hawker."

"If the Guards shut down the island, I'll need more than booze."

Hawkes hands shook as he lit a smoke. Watching the airport security detail working the night shift, absorbing the silence, he listened for the guard-post phone. The flight would be canceled if Singapore's exits were put on alert.

"Have you seen Changi Prison, Robby?"

"Charming little flat, is it?"

Talking as he exhaled, Hawkes jokingly explained. "After the guards cane your Irish ass, you'll be singing the beauty of a good hanging. It's easy to come to Singapore, Robby. If we're fit in the frame for murder, we'll never dance again."

* * *

Rally Point, The Mergui Archipelago. 30 August 1939. 1440 Hours, GMT + 6.5 Hours.

Appearing weary and unconcerned, Tu widened her stance, her vicious smile telling Hardin she was ready to strike. Slipping the pirate's carbine over the side, she gripped her machete.

With the quiet of a viper, she warned Hardin with a nod—death ran but a fetch away. When the prahu's engine geared into low range, the bow dipped into the water, forcing a moment of balancing. Pirates stepped for a foothold and reached for a handle.

Hardin leveled his weapon on the cabin door.

The girl's machete sliced the throat of the pirate as he raised his pistol, penetrating to the base of his skull. She spun on her toe and slammed the blade into the spine of a second pirate as he reached for his carbine. His scream brought the captain into the doorway.

Hardin shot him with a short burst.

Trapped, the fourth pirate extended his hands, pleading through a smile. The swiftness of her attack left him without a weapon. He turned and threw himself over the side of the sloop. Tu sank the machete into his calf as his feet cleared the rail.

Hardin waited until the wounded pirate surfaced, then hollered obscenities while firing a nine-round burst from his Hart MK1, blowing apart the man's head. The pirate's body sank into a school of sharks, his blood erupting from the turbulence, then clouding the crystal-clear water.

With the last pirate lying on the deck moaning, writhing in pain, Hardin drove the butt of his weapon into the man's mouth. Grabbing the man's arm, he rolled him over the side. The slaughter reminded him of the kill zone of his team's ambush. All but the stench.

Pissed off, he rolled the last two bodies into the water. Grinning as if nothing had happened, Tu washed the blood from her machete and sheathed it at her back. Hardin slung the Hart MK1 over his shoulder and reached for the rail.

Watching the captain's body drift away, Tu stood to the rail with a vengeful shout. Churning the water, a swarm of sharks harried the remains.

She enjoys the killing, Hardin thought.

The girl worried him. Far too efficient to be a peasant, her skill rang of a trained assassin. Her movements too smooth and automatic—too well timed to be anomalies. An apprentice steeped in an ancient art—a wisp dispatched to ensure Hardin's escape from Burma.

Dispatched by whom?

Hardin shook his head and keyed the handset on the prahu's transceiver. "Princess, this is Grumpy, over." Static rushed into the wheelhouse.

"Grumpy, you dunny rat. Who's your mother, over?"

"High tea, Uncle. One cup this time."

"Are we ticklers or tarpots, Grumpy?"

"A bit of both, Uncle—no debris, over."

"No worries—we're chasing a new moon, Grumpy." Uncle would be at the rally point near Ross Island by twilight.

Relieved, Hardin set his weapon down and rubbed his face with both hands, then keyed the handset. "See you in Piccadilly, Uncle."

With the prahu's steam engine marking time with the current, Tu leaned against the rail, her yen welling to high tide, took out her ivory pipe, and tamped it full. She smoked only the highest grade of opium.

*   *   *

Cairo, Egypt. The Mena House Hotel. 1 September 1939. 2030 Hours, GMT + 2 Hours.

Primrose marigolds set the mother of pearl and the polished marble mosaics afire, flickering and posing as the candlelight winked and danced. The luxury of the Mena House Hotel was known the world over, famous for its mint tea. Like Raffles in Singapore, the Mena House was designed for, and catered to, the top shelf of society—the tall poppies.

A large brass ornamental scarab sat a perch near the reception counter, its head polished by years of those wishing for luck.

But time was a premium in September 1939, worth gold, and other ratable soils. Germany had invaded Poland, and Russia had mobilized her surprise. Dominion troops from Mother's colonies had been called to muster. Australians occupied the Mena House—a rowdy, outback band of brazen roustabouts.

The hallways were full of them—even the hotel linens were rumpled.

Lewis ordered the spaghetti with tomato sauce, a dish recommended by Admiral Sinclair and made famous by Bennini, the head chef. Bennini had created the dish for his favorite customer, Egypt's King Farouk. Spiced to perfection, the portions attracted the Australian officer corps and their sergeants.

Poston found the bag pipes a distraction as he hashed the method he could use for killing Gosden. The admiral discussed operational casualties with the prime minister last week—using percentages as though the war was a secondary issue. So, I guess if a tactical operation isn't in the queue, I'll shoot Gosden with my PPK. Berryman too, if he gets in the way.

To match ruckus with ruckus, the hostelry booked a dance band from The Black Watch, the elite Scottish regiment. The drums sounded at 2100 hours. Minutes brought the fifes and the incautious women.

For me, and these Aussies, tonight the world can go dance on a volcano—or go straight to hell. No woman's safe if she's with this crowd—not tonight.

Sudanese waiters swirled through the crowd balancing trays of drinks and sorted delights. Dressed in baggy pants, embroidered white linen shirts, cut away small black satin jackets, a scarlet sash and red fez, the waiters streamed from the kitchen and bar, a continuous offering of food and drink, their empty trays soon piled with dishes and assorted debris.

Laying a napkin over the spots where he had demonstrated the ability to scatter spaghetti-shot onto the linen tablecloth, the ginger hue of the palm fronds caught his eye. The palmate fronds hung still in the lifeless air.

Fed up with tracing the golden threads in his whiskey, Lewis drew Dorothy's alluring smile to mind, determined to find if the lady's marriage to Sir Nigel was a fantasy. When she first looked at him in front of Shepherd's Hotel, there had been something very cunning, very knowing in her grin, an unconscious awareness such women have, worldly, old as time.

Taking his drink to the courtyard, he sat at a table well away from the other guests. Shadows reached across the swimming bath and left the tops of the palm trees glowing in the sunset.

Grateful the sultry, coastal humidity had dissipated, Poston stood into the bath of a ceiling fan. A porter asked his name, nodded, and gave him a note from the head chef. Digging a chip of ice from his drink he read the note.

During World War I, an Austrian general was found running naked, chasing a young woman through the lobby of the Mena House Hotel. It seems he was forgiven by an Austrian Army Regulation:

"An officer may wear any costume appropriate to the sport he's engaged in."

Amused by the Austrian regulation, Poston tucked the note in his shirt pocket. His view of the desert was eerily peaceful, rose colored, and difficult to describe. A morning rain had washed away the pounce that draped its talcum shroud over Egypt's delta. Cairo's suffocating, dung-laden air had been pushed aside, to ebb offshore and return with the relentless heat of a new day, gathering the city's smells, lingering with the open sewers, the dead bodies, and the fetid trash—the manmade centerpiece of this Muslim metropolis.

He realized even when the day was still, the wind played in the desert. In the gathering of dusk, plumes of dust circled into the deep blue-purple sky. At this time of the day, Egypt's deceptively beautiful, he thought.

The Great Pyramid of Giza sat atop the palm trees, offering the heavens as if knowing Poston's worth—his thoughts—killing and sex. This country is complex—an outpost combining the strange life of the Nile delta and the nomadic life of the desert.

The Egypt he had imagined in his youth did not exist. The concept of *maleesh*, that outcomes can't be helped and do not matter, or that God's will ensures a more satisfying tomorrow, was pure horse shit.

Poston read his brother's cable again:

Lewis,

Willie Hockey found Sir John's end. It's been confirmed. Alfred Gosden stabbed our father. He's in Cairo fetching bread for Berryman.

Willie has the lot. "C" has been informed.

Johnny

So now that Johnny agrees, I wonder who Hockey will deal with next. Alfred Gosden will die praying for the devil, the most sinful vicar of all.

Poston fingered the trigger of his PPK. I can't just walk up and shoot Gosden. I'm too well known. I've been in this region too many years. I'll recruit a local and make it look like the Brotherhood did it—Sammy perhaps. Better yet. Hockey's a nomad. He can do it.

Put Hockey in charge of this borehole and the lot would be quick-marched into the sea.

Gazing at the heavens, wondering what he might find on top of the pyramid, he found himself watching a group of rankers from the Australian army cavort in the pool. Shaking his head, he whispered, "The Mena House is not the place for these dirt diggers."

Knowing William Hockey's loyalties—that he worshiped in the Temple church on Bodmin Moor, that he and Sir John were travelers and 33rd Degree Masons, and protecting each other's family was his oath — Poston drew his eyes to narrow slits. Planning the resolution of his father's murder would take a good deal of patience.

I wonder if Hockey knows why Dorothy Stuart's mucking about in Cairo.

The memory of Dorothy's nylon stockings, more the fabric buttons holding them in place, jolly-jumped through Poston's mind, banging on the instruments in the percussion section and setting steel to his humping tackle.

His glass empty, he toasted a lovely fantasy.

* * *

The Andaman Sea. Uncle's Steamer. 1 September 1939. 1420 Hours, GMT + 5.5 Hours.

Perceptive and fiercely determined, Captain Corcoran had an uneasy feeling about the crew and didn't have a handle on why. "Molly, come up to the port bow."

"One Hail Mary and a bit of the rest would do," Molly barked as if not wanting to be disturbed before breakfast—anytime, really. Molly handed his captain a cup of coffee, admiring the horizon. A trail of sparkling diamonds ran from the sun across the sea.

"We've a loose chipping on board, Molly."

"Sixteen men, that's the lot," Molly barked as if being blamed for the spy.

"Mother has a transceiver on board. One of the crew is working with the agents we beached—a signals expert. My guess he's older and has a technical specialty—explosives."

Running with the current, Uncle's estimates were made smaller by a flat sea. Scanning the northern horizon, he judged the need to dock in Port Blair for fuel, water, and stores before clearing on to Bombay.

Uncle knew, in the Andaman Sea, the tail of the monsoon drew typhoon winds through the Andaman Islands and the Mergui Archipelago, sending green water in ten-to twelve-foot walls crashing into any sod standing abaft of the hawse pipe.

It was sea boots and oilskins for ships caught in that upheaval. Heading hard to windward to ride these seas, Uncle had been agile enough to keep his flush-deck Portuguese tramp afloat.

Today's sea was calm.

The peach-orange distance of the sunrise lay on the water, black where the wind had gone. The sea stood aside—its current and storms saved for another day, a day when he held a mug of rum—eight points to starboard.

Molly took a small ledger from his shirt pocket and studied the crew list—misfits all. Each sailor had stumbled from one of the world's exits, each with a hitch. They had been flushed from prosperity into this bay or that. Ashamed as they would be, they were taut seaman. One old man had tarred pigtails and bled a Stockholm tar.

Rough men they were, yet almost all preferred to avoid fighting. Some preferred to read. Never worried unless the specter of being beached raised its head—merchant seamen recognized each other from Liverpool to Hong Kong, Rangoon to Suez, and Grant Road in Bombay to Malay Street in Singapore.

At the edge of a dream, each had won and lost. Without exception, each had been given a match to light his own fire, and each had been set adrift. Life's flotsam, they rode the tail of any monsoon. In common they worked for one man—Uncle Dingo. Loyalty came with the job.

"With this sea or in it," Molly whispered. Born under a gun, Molly was a Jack.

Molly inventoried the seamen working near the well-deck and checked the names of the crew on his ledger—his ragman's roll. He counted four tar-pots, seven taut hands, four lascars, and two ticklers. With a flick of his pencil here and a flick there, two sailors remained in the frame—the ticklers, the short-service seamen he shipped in Alexandria.

"It's one of the ticklers, Captain."

"When you lash the bastard, scrub his name from the crew listing, toss his kit in the sea, and burn his passport."

"Odds are he's a good swimmer."

"Olive Oil can help him along." Uncle started to light a cigarette, grimaced and threw the fag over the side. "I want his transceiver out of service, and the frequencies he's using."

Watching his crew lash the two ticklers with half-inch chain, Molly tested the shackles at their ankles and hands. Then he had them suspended over the side of the steamer, hanging at the end of a davit-hook.

With a hatchet-faced tickler swearing in German, and a rough looking tickler singing words in Welsh, Molly loaded Olive Oil, his Model 1897 trench shotgun, stroking her twenty-inch barrel and kissing her butt.

With hand signals Molly had one man, and then the other, lowered into the sea. Trolling, as he explained, for God's assassins. Delighted with this bit of sport, he uncoiled his black snake after the crane operators dropped the men on the deck.

"One of you lads is a taut hand. The other works a dosshouse for Mother— dipping his wick in the captain's business."

Asked to decide, the crew, each in his way, picked his man. With a thumb or a nod, wagers as well, fifteen men picked the lad from the fens as a loyal seaman—the Welshman, Grigor Madog. Topping out at five foot and seven, a stolid, heavy-featured man, Madog turned his massive chest, his scarred face marking each sailor, catching their eye. With a nod, as though welcoming their loyalty, Madog shook lose the stevedore lashings and let the ropes slipped through his fingers.

Seemingly amused by the swim, Madog bared his teeth, then raised his big, coarse hands, "If it's trouble you're about…" he turned on his left foot and threw his right fist into the mouth of the German still suspended from the davit hook. "I take trouble as it comes." Giving a nod to Molly, he waved a hand over the rail, then bunched his shoulders and hit the German tickler again, crushing his nose and pulping his lips.

With a hand to the crew, he smiled a reckless smile. "I've been wet me whole life. I won't forget your choice this day. I'll buy each man of you a jar in time."

Molly signaled the crane operator to hang the German over the bow, his tiny, inset eyes even with the railing. Smiling a smile he used when sorting out a pub, Molly leaned over the rail and bade the crane to swing the man closer. "Hill sixty in Flanders: the shell holes, the crump-holes, were full of mud and water—bodies and weapons. Hundreds of bodies. A bad show all 'round. Good men died in the mud southeast of Ypres on a bloody June day. Lads dying in a jumble—bawling the word *corpsman*—I was shot dragging my lieutenant from a crump-hole."

The German tickler spit at Molly.

Instantly Molly black-snaked the bastard's face, ripping flesh from his cheeks and splitting his left eye socket. As if satisfied, Molly set fire to a cigarette and signaled for the crane operator to bob his prey in the bow wash.

When the German threw his guts into the sea, Molly screamed, "That's a good lad." With his prey hanging near the railing, blood dripping from the man's left eye, Molly adjusted the sling on his trench gun. Placing the barrel next to the seaman's ear, he fired a load into the sea. Speaking while the bastard shouted his German shouts, Molly decided. "And for me there's the smell of a bleating Kraut such as you. Tell me, doxy, tell me where the transceiver is, and you'll live to see England. Or take your fancy for glycerin's twat and lick your way to hell."

Upside down, the man's eyes bulged beyond their reach. His hatred was measurable.

Molly rolled his shoulders and reset his feet. "This swim will be a bit of an up-scuttle. I'm going to jury-slice your wrist a bit so God's lads can smell your treachery." Unsheathing his knife, Molly caught the man as he swung near the rail and set the point of the blade on the mess that was the man's chin. "Hear me, you Kraut bastard. Hope is a slippery whore. Vaseline, she tells me there's no need for a coal trimmer such as you to touch bottom."

The doxy set his teeth and spewed words through the blood streaming from his face. "The wireless is in the aft lifeboat—port side."

"That's a lad."

"Mind the booby trap—bang-putty."

Enraged, Molly stabbed the traitor in the throat. With the man's blood flowing into the bow wash he sliced the hemp line tied to the man's ankle lashings and laughed as the Kraut splashed into the foam beneath the tramp's bow.

With Gregor Madog by his side, Molly brought Mother's wireless and a one-quarter-pound tube of Nobel's Explosive No.808 plastique to the wardroom. Uncle was eating a banger.

"Full rations for that Kraut. We'll give him a bit of quarter, Molly. No rum. Sir Nigel's lads can sort him at the turn."

Molly gave Uncle a slight nod but didn't respond. The bastard had spit at him.

"Bang-putty's rare in these parts, Captain. Priority issue. A jar of beer says that bastard worked for Sir Nigel."

Noting Molly's use of the past tense, Corcoran set his head on a cant. "You hang a good tale, Molly. Even if it's not true, the Kraut won't get shot running."

With an hour of daylight remaining, Tu had the prahu tacking to intercept the steamer outside a maze of coastal reefs. Scanning the steamer with a long glass, Hardin spotted Uncle standing near the bow looking back at him.

"Uncle Dingo knows what an extraction's about."

The instant Hardin mounted the davit-hook, the prahu cut its lateen sail and fell astern. He stood looking after the prahu, waiting for a signal. Tu appeared on the rear deck, held Steiner's French Thompson over her head, fired a burst into the air, and ducked into the cabin.

"Thanks for the help," he whispered.

Hardin slung his rucksack over his left shoulder and carried his weapon in his right hand. Not knowing who he could trust, he planned to stow the pouch, and what was left of his gear in a locker. If no locker was available, he would keep the pouch with him.

Reflecting on his mission, his dead mates—especially Linc Jensen, Hardin found Molly wiping the sea spray from his shotgun—from Olive's butt. Molly gave him a nod, cradled the shotgun over his forearm, and escorted Hardin to his bunk without saying a word.

Bubble dancing with his eyes nearly closed the long, hot shower left Hardin weak. Having existed on short rations and adrenaline for weeks, his muscle tissue from stem to stern was spent. Exhausted, he was grateful to be alive—too relieved to sleep. Wearing clean dungarees and a seaman's sweater Molly had taken from the ship-store's slop-chest, he washed his teeth with sips of rum as an Indian medic tended his leg wound with sulfa powder.

Grateful for the rum and the fresh battle dressing, Hardin shook the bottle of Atabrine the medic had given him, to measure its contents.

"Atta boys! I haven't had any malaria drugs for weeks."

"You've been fortunate. These jungles are brutal."

"Drinking rations of watered rum and citrus powder, and I still picked up yellow jack or malaria. Maybe both." Relaxed by the rum, he took his leave from the dispensary and rolled into his bunk.

Hardin came awake sitting into a crouch, clutching the pouch and his weapon. Lightheaded, sweating profusely, he set his feet on the deck. His leg wound ached as he limped along the passageway and into the tramp's saloon. Accepting a plate of eggs, beans, chips, and a baked tomato, along with a cup of fresh coffee, he laid the pouch and his weapon across his lap.

"I've been longing for a proper meal." Hardin sat to the table, dabbing blood from his lips.

"Slow down, cobber." Uncle lit a cigarette. "Too much food can be sick-making."

"I need a shave and a haircut."

"Bad luck cutting hair at sea. You'll have to wait on that until you're beached."

With his mug held high, Uncle had a warning. "Mother's got her hounds tracking this tramp steamer. We also have Jap prickers, German agents, and mercenaries. If they all have plastique explosive, we're not safe in any port."

"Plastique and French Thompsons. Three ambushes and seven dead commandos will never be enough. The Cambodians who ambushed my team cut off my mate's right thumbs. Their employer knew my team had eight commandos. When they only got seven thumbs, the Kraut and the Dutchman were their back-up. They were tracking us from the jump.

"That girl on the prahu killed them both."

After wiping blood off the side of his cup, adding five spoonfuls of sugar to his coffee, he opened on his beans, savaging his eggs with a heel of toast. Ravenous, he gasped for air for the food he ate.

Topping up his cup with rum, Uncle held his forearm flat and laughed as he exercised the hips of his tattooed lady. When Hardin calked his head and smiled, Uncle laughed. "I'll bet those pirates thought Sheila would do a runner. Swim for it."

"She's absolutely jungle. Too brutal for this squaddie. She ambushed the Dutchman just as he tried to lift my rucksack out of an ox cart. Split his head like a melon without so much as a scrap of fear. She left his body jumbled like a dog's breakfast."

Molly entered the saloon with an ear-battering bellow, lugging a plate of food enough for five. A sailor of the bulldog breed, he sat facing Hardin, enormous and ugly enough to scare a copper's horse.

"Hello, squaddie. You've lost weight. Is your humping tackle fit for work?"

"Ah, Molly. Your humor's a bit like mud."

"If you don't stop quick-stuffing your meat trap, I'll be lashing you to the aft rail with your arse rigged for volleying fire, and you wallowing about with the whaling hab-dabs."

Hardin set his fork down and shook Molly's hand. "How's Olive Oil?"

"Olive stands her post. The old sweat purrs at the touch of these palsied fingers." Continuing to eat, he pointed at Hardin. "You and your tuckerbag need another soaking. That pongo stink of yours will catch the odd eye." As though in warning, Molly drew an off eye to his captain.

"No rum ration, cockroach, and plum spiced rice balls and too much salt. I'll sweat it out in a few days. Besides, the jungle smell's better than that wet-coke engine room air you fancy."

"No worries." Uncle pointed with his mug. "You mentioned two ambushes."

"The Kraut tried his luck near the coast. That Burmese tart left him no hocks to stand on. Cut the tendons at his heels and the joint below his knees. She laughed when he tried to crawl. She kicked his head repeatedly, ending the slaughter by splashing mud in his face."

"Why is she helping you?" Uncle asked.

"I don't have the foggiest. But she knows how to kill—with a machete."

"Who hired her?"

"For a mate, Uncle, you ask a lot of questions." Rigid, his eyes alert to the changing mood, gripping the trigger on his weapon, Hardin turned to face both men.

Molly pushed away from the table into a brace. Uncle cautioned his engineer by tapping the table. Molly picked up his mug and set it aside, clearing the space between himself and Hardin.

Silence gripped the saloon. Hardin stared at Molly waiting for the big man to finish his move. Then he put in, "Whoever hired that wench hired a trained assassin."

"Give us our own, Molly." Corcoran waited while Molly left the saloon.

"Mother's field operatives want you dead. And the highborn want you in the frame." Uncle looked into the dim bulkhead light as if searching for some reason. "Whoever they are, they've been briefed on the details of this operation."

"Who do you work for, Uncle?"

"On paper it's Sir Nigel—I presume he's still with MI6. He claims to be rehearsing for a posting with the SOE group siding up in Ceylon." Molly stood and adjusted his waistband. A sheathed dagger was perched on his right hip.

"He's highborn," Hardin said. "He could have hired my Burmese escort, to pad a ledger—a gong for the aging—tales of helmet plumes, noble acts of valor in the Bay of Bengal."

Uncle and Hardin left the tramp's saloon when five sailors came to eat. Sitting in the chart room Uncle adjusted the volume on the transceiver and poured two mugs of rum. "Stuart's contracted with Lucien in the past. But the ambush that took out your team doesn't fit a Lucien-style operation—too many weapons. You thought they were Cambodian. Lucien wouldn't risk a foreign hire in Southeast Asia."

"If you know that much about Lucien, is he trying to kill me, or is he just chasing this bloody pouch?"

Uncle banged the char from his pipe and swept the ash onto the deck. "That pouch might contain the curly dirt he's after. My orders are clear—haul you to Ceylon—simple as that."

Uncle leaned into the passageway and spoke to a passing sailor. Standing near the radio mount, he scratched his cheek with the stem of his pipe. "Tell me, squaddie, if you and I work for this secret special-ops executive, who does Stuart work for?" Tossing the pipe onto the chart table, he lit a cigarette, and studied the fire on its end. "I'm guessing he's off the books—on Admiral Sinclair's quiet list—close hold."

"That idea would incite someone."

Molly entered the chart room, slammed his chair around and swung his leg over the saddle, eye-balling Hardin as if the squaddie had slandered his mother. Uncle handed him the rum bottle.

Hardin shrugged. "I'm sure this SOE bullshit is off the books. We were told it wouldn't be official for seven, eight months. And, if Winston has his way, SOE won't happen."

Staring at Molly, Hardin took hold of the rum bottle and filled his mug. "If my mission isn't sanctioned, only Sinclair, Dewar and Stuart know I'm here."

"Out of sanction, we're anybody's game," Uncle said.

"Of the three men, I trust Sinclair," Hardin said.

"Stuart can keep secrets—Dewar can't." Uncle took his Webley revolver from under the radio mount and opened the cylinder and checked the loads. With a satisfied grin, he said, "Molly, we need to find out if Stuart's working alone. If they're coordinating, I'm guessing Dewar's betraying Stuart and the admiral."

"Dewar's briefing for Snow White in Candle Creek was total shite."

"Recap your mission details for me," Uncle said, scratching both sides of his face. Uncle folded his arms across his chest. He hadn't touched his rum.

Hesitating, suspicious and not knowing why, Hardin decided to change the mission—to leave out the dead Catholic bishop to see whether Uncle would react—to decide whether his old friend had the mission's time sequences.

"We jumped into Tonkin at night with an equipment drop of weapons and ammunition for Ho Chi Minh and his Viet Minh guerrillas. The equipment drop was a ruse. Our primary objective was the rescue of a special-service sergeant being held in a prison compound near the Chinese border. Then we were to divert to Haiphong to rendezvous with one of Nigel Stuart's lads—all hush-hush."

"What special-service sergeant?"

Hardin straightened his leg to ease a cramp. Uncle seems surprised. Not mentioning the bishop was a good idea.

"We were a bit late. The commando we were sent to rescue was dead, flayed—head to toe—strapped to a bamboo bed in an abandoned hut. After we set fire to the hut, we found his kit nearby, stowed between layers of thatch on a nearby roof."

"Any personal items?"

"This pouch, that's the meat of it—no identity disc." To cover his lie, Hardin raised his mug. Wondering why Uncle queried the personal effects of a special-ops soldier, he asked, "Did you know the dead man?"

Turning away, Uncle nudged Molly. "Stow Hardin's kit—next to that wireless we found." When Uncle reached for the leather pouch, Hardin tucked it under his arm.

"Don't piss me off, Captain," Hardin said, grabbing the breach of his weapon.

Molly stepped to Uncle's side, with a knife in his right hand, cutting edge up.

Hardin set his weapon aside. "This pouch is mine to deal with. Leave it that way. You drive the boat, and I'll shoot the bastards trying to take the pouch."

"Toss the damn thing over the side."

"Nice try, Uncle. It's worth more than money to someone. As long as I have it, I can keep looking for the bastard who set up the ambush of Team 7. If we aren't on the same side, you can toss me over the side."

"Helping you keeps my crew in the frame."

"Your mission to extract Team 7 and transport the team to Ceylon hasn't changed. And it's nearly complete. Mother will ignore you if they think Linc Jensen got beached in Ceylon."

Hardin finished his rum and lit a cigarette. "I saved your sorry arse near Candle Creek.

It's your go, keeping me alive."

"Fair dinkum, cobber." Uncle stood to the chart table, then looked puzzled. "How are you going to dodge the Royal Navy and marines on station in Ceylon?"

"Molly's the butcher's dog. Either way the cat jumps, he can lie to 'em." Hardin stepped away from the radio mount and offered Molly the floor. "He's good at it."

"You're a jungle worn pain in my arse, squaddie." Molly closed the breach on his shotgun. "I'll tell Mother's lads a story and watch the bastards ponder the ball-weight of Olive's load."

After Molly left the chart room, Uncle described the events getting to the rally point: Rangoon, Harbormaster McPhee, Flying Officer Hawkes, Mother's MI9 agents, Port Blair, Sir Nigel, the second transceiver, Nobel's No.808 bang-putty, and paying to have the British agents neutralized in Singapore.

Beginning to understand Uncle's dilemma, Hardin asked, "The would-be MI9 agents tried to kill you? Is Stuart involved?"

"I don't know. The sods either work for Stuart, or they're for hire. I'm guessing they're all after that pouch. If Lucien sorted the puzzle when you met him in Haiphong, he decided to hunt you down, even if he had to chase you into Burma. And if those MI9 lads made a good guess, they've decided to chase you all the way home."

"They'll die trying."

"My guess is the bastards don't work for Molly's lieutenant." Shaking his head, Uncle chewed on his kola root, then offered an open palm. "Why would Stuart be involved in such doings?"

"For money!"

"You might be right, cobber. Snow White's off the net. Anything's possible when you're operating under Mother's skirt," Uncle answered.

"You and Molly knew about the pouch. My Burmese tart and her father knew. Linc Jensen knew. Everyone else is guessing. Let's claim I don't have a pouch, or anything more valuable than my rotting cock."

Uncle gave out a howler and started exercising the naked lady tattooed in a forest of curly hair. Flaunting her trotters to Hardin's laughter, Uncle joined in. "Eff-all, cobber. With or without a pouch, even my tattoo knows you don't have enough sense to get killed."

"It comes 'round to Lucien. If those agents are his doing, it's money they're chasing."

"Lucien and his whole ruddy crew were briefed on that pouch before you jumped into Tonkin. Lucien decided you found it when he rinsed you out in Haiphong."

Alert to the changing inflection in Uncle's tone, Hardin realized Uncle was the only man who had dealings with all the characters, including the MI9 agents.

"Do you know Lewis Poston or his brother, John? Sir John Poston, their father, sponsored me into the army. He was a friend of my family."

Uncle lit a cigarette. "Don't know those lads. But Poston and Sons, Ltd., is the registered owner of this steamer."

Hardin alerted. Swells like the Postons have durable memories and extremely long ties. Could the Poston brothers be Stuart's control?

"Lewis Poston works in Alexandria—fronting as a British Petroleum executive. Sir John told me Lewis worked outside of MI6. His brother John works in MI6, D Section, abreast of Dewar—quiet work, I'm told. John is London to a brick, so they say."

Uncle stubbed out his cigarette. A sailor set a pot of hot tea on the radio mount. After mixing rum with his tea, Uncle held up his mug of gunfire. "If this boat makes Egypt with its gear in one bag, will Poston sort the players?"

"I'm not sure." Hardin had noted uncertainty in Uncle's response, as if Lewis might know Uncle's file. "He's well connected and will know the color of each player."

"Not many mates around these days." Uncle picked up a fresh chew stick, frayed the end, gave his teeth a quick once over, and tucked it in the corner of his mouth.

Uncle banged his knuckles against the locker as if beating the measure of the tide while exercising the naked lady tattooed next to his watch.

"After I beach you in Ceylon, the bloke who could help you is a cashiered pilot. Flying Officer Jeffery Hawkes is one minty sod. I'm told he's a good pilot."

"Is this pilot hung on a wire somewhere?" Hardin asked.

"I paid Hawkes, and a paddy, to fly to Singapore and waylay the British agents who have been dogging this steamer. When Mother's sods tried to rack me off in Port Blair, Hawkes and McPhee dove right into the fight. Saved my life. If that pilot's alive, he's trying to get back to this boat and collect some money."

"Those agents aren't working for Mother," Hardin declared. "They may be on the old lady's pay book, but they're running out of bounds for some dodger familiar with the time-lapse details of this operation."

After a second splash from the rum bottle, Hardin said, "Tell me about this pilot."

"Hawkes is a right sort. A dodgy sod. Twice told, he was busted to pilot officer for mixing whiskey with fancy flying. With a winsome smile he waltzed on a bit of brass and was reinstated to flying officer status. When he destroyed a third airplane, Chennault decided to have him shot."

Hardin noted a faint bit of admiration in Uncle's description. "So, he can fly but he can't land. I could jump into Egypt, I suppose—last thing the wanks would expect." Belching, losing his vision, Hardin fell into a quick stride, grabbing the bulkhead abutting the chart table.

Dry heaves brought more dizziness and a sudden fever. Stomach acid mixed with rum erupted into his throat. Stumbling, reaching for the pouch he collapsed.

Malaria. The image of tortured bodies set itself in a bloodstained frame, raking him as though the serrated edge of a commando's knife. The air in the cabin smelled of a dank hollow. Shivering in the sweltering heat, he strained to fill his lungs with air. The blankets covering him reeked with heavy, jungle-smelling sweat.

After drinking his fill, Hardin ambled into the chart room, stepped to the chart table, and picked up the pouch. Surprised to find the seal unbroken, he dropped the pouch on the table. If Uncle Dingo works for Sir Nigel, why didn't he open the pouch? Mother's lads tried to kill him. And he made the rally to pick me up. Laying it out, he's decided to fly solo.

As Molly entered the chart room sliding Olive Oil from his shoulder, Hardin said, "The guts of this pouch must be barbed with bits of steel."

"Or wired with bang putty," Uncle replied.

His suspicions simmering, pausing for a moment, Hardin asked, "If Stuart knew the pouch existed, Admiral Sinclair and Dewar knew—all before Team 7 parachuted into Tonkin. And, if you knew, why did you ask me about a squaddie's personal effects?"

Hardin waited. Molly remained standing. The cabin grew smaller.

"Fair dinkum, cobber." With a slight nod, Uncle drew at his cigarette. "Lucien's a for-hire slag—a bloody mercenary. He and Steiner and that Dutchman, Leenstra, jumped into Tonkin a fortnight before you lads, escorting a shipment of American weapons and supplies for Ho Chi Minh. His second insertion this year."

"How do you know?" Hardin asked, trying to caution himself.

"Stuart's been running the equipment drops." Uncle's comment wasn't a question. It was a mistake. He just admitted he knew far more about the pouch than he had let on.

"So, Team 7 found the pouch, and Stuart hired Lucien to intercept it!" Hardin declared, casting a sounding line. "Lucien was looking for it after his equipment drop."

"Not likely."

"Why ever, not?"

"Stuart doesn't have any money." Uncle cleared off the ash at the end of the cigarette and stubbed it out. "Lucien demands money up front. He's Dewar's hire. Not Stuart's."

"You're starting to piss me off. Who do you report to, Uncle?"

"On paper, it's Sir Nigel."

"Don't give me a bunch of paper shit. Is the bastard a friend of yours?"

"He's too far up the flue for this sailor." Uncle took another bottle of rum from an overhead locker and mixed two mugs of gunfire. Handing one to

Hardin, he said, "After our first radio contact, when I realized you were done over, I decided to stop breaking shite and become a bit rum scuttled—to help you, Grumpy. We can't trust anyone, including Stuart."

Molly alerted to the comment and tossed off his gunfire.

Palms up, Hardin said, "Well, that puts paid to it, doesn't it?"

"For you, perhaps." Uncle laid his forearms on the chart table and started brushing his teeth with the kola root. "Stuart's been canny enough to keep us bobbing about. If I'm right, he thinks we're bound for Singapore."

Hardin laughed. "We're on a ten-knot flush-deck tramp. We won't be hard to find."

Pushing Uncle's forearms aside, Hardin located South Andaman Island and Port Blair on British Admiralty Chart 514 and with his finger traced the initial bearings for sailing to Bombay. Flying would be easier, he thought. I need a pilot, an airplane, and an airstrip—and fuel.

Drawing at the aroma of the rum-laced tea, Hardin decided to hang another baited line to test Uncle's loyalties. "Lucien's an agile sort. Pressing on, he'll do anything for money."

"No worries." Uncle poured rum into Molly's mug. "Lucien needs mobility. He has enemies in Hong Kong, Rangoon, Singapore, as well as Port Blair. And his picture's posted on the wanted ready board at the Cellular Jail in Port Blair."

Uncle took an intel flimsy from a slot in the radio mount. "Team 7 was airborne on their way to the drop zone when this information was transmitted. 'Protected documents have gone missing—last in the possession of a Catholic bishop in northern Tonkin.'"

"Who initiated that comic cut?"

"Don't know. The message was relayed by flight ops at RAF Station China Bay, Ceylon."

"So why did you ask about Team 7's mission?"

"Bad habit—asking cobbers like you for credentials. You're the last team to muster. One team went missing. I put the other teams through the same drill."

"Team 7 was the only SOE team dropped into northern Tonkin."

"Don't forget Lucien's lot."

With that reminder, Hardin finished his gunfire tea. "And with Lady Luck trooping her colors, Team 7 bumbled around, found the pouch, and the chase was on."

"I wager Lucien's lost a packet of money." Uncle set his mug on the radio mount, picked up a pencil and began tracing a route on chart 514 to South Andaman Island—Port Blair. "I'm surprised he didn't kill you in Haiphong."

"I didn't have my kit with me."

With Uncle's tramp steaming close to the wind, Hardin conceded that Uncle and his crew would remain in the target frame as long as anyone chasing the documents thought Linc Jensen was on board. *Once I jump ship in Ceylon, I'll have a bit of leeway. A few days. For insurance I could cache the pouch in Port Blair or leave it in one of Uncle's lifeboats.*

Still suspicious of Stuart's allegiance, and Uncle's loyalties, Hardin decided his best chance of reaching Alexandria was to hit the beach and hitch an airplane ride with the likes of Flying Officer Hawkes.

Wondering why Uncle mentioned the ready board at the Cellular Jail on Andaman Island, Hardin asked calmly, "Why Port Blair, Captain?"

"Fuel mainly. Water and stores. Port Blair because Stuart expects us to sail to Singapore. The Royal Navy's been sowing the Singapore Roads with sub-surface mines. It's a nasty bit of water. Thanks to those paint chippers it's a bloody obstacle. Port Blair first. Then Colombo, Ceylon, and with luck, Bombay, the Gate of Tears, and the rancid waters of the Red Sea."

"It won't take Stuart long to realize we're on a different route."

Uncle answered. "By that time, we'll have the fuel and stores we need to make the run to China Bay. Besides, Stuart will have his hounds waiting in Colombo."

*   *   *

Pall Mall, London. John Poston's Hotel Room.
2 September 1939. 1300 Hours, GMT.

John Poston had jammed the knuckles of his left hand when he hit Dewar. His right hand was in good shape. His left hand was purple from knuckles to his wrist. He dropped his theater tickets in a bin. Mother had closed the West End theatres in the Strand.

The world has gone mad. White bumpers, white curb stones, blackout curtains, and the paintings in the National Gallery have been moved to Wales. *And the dotards have issued an order to euthanize London's pets.*

He spent the morning drafting a situation summary for Operation Snow White. In short, German radio cross traffic in the Bay of Bengal continued to interfere with extractions, and operational control out of China Bay, Ceylon, had lost contact with Team 7 and its team leader, Captain Edward Hardin—Sir John's godson.

Snow White was in the soup and the admiral was not pleased. Poston's summary would not help Sinclair's disposition. Snow White began as a simple long-range-penetration mission to assist with an equipment drop for Viet Minh guerrillas. Once completed, Team 7 was to move overland gathering intelligence on Japanese activity along a prescribed route into Burma and Malaya, and rally with a tramp steamer for an extraction.

The bits about a Catholic bishop and protected papers had been added to the mission by Admiral Sinclair at the insistence of Victor Rothschild in MI5.

As events progressed, the operation became an escape and evasion nightmare with the remnants of Team 7 on the odds. Worried, Johnny did not know whom to trust. Somewhat isolated, he was left to discover facts known to Admiral Sinclair before Operation Snow White was active—well before Team 7 jumped into Tonkin.

For Poston, the admiral's secrecy meant the pouch and its contents were a priority for the royal household—for the Windsors. And a great deal of money was in play.

Money—it's always a game of money, Johnny thought. Rothschild in MI5. These immutable swells never use their own money.

A bad show really. War reparations aside, not one of Europe's banking houses wanted any member of Team 7 to tell his story.

Johnny read the intelligence decrypts again. The corners on the decrypts were curled and frayed. MI5's conclusions included a summary written by Rothschild concerning a meeting that took place at the House of Hesse.

*   *   *

Berlin, Germany. 2 September 1939. 0900 Hours, GMT + 1 Hour.

By summer 1939 European banking houses had become less visible. The reason, the increasing velocity of currency trading had produced profits far exceeding the estimates the Landgrave of the House of Hesse predicted.

Max Warburg and John Schiff were treated as mere financial functionaries after traveling to Berlin to pay respects to the Landgrave. This was a ritual, a routine, a quarterly visit for these bankers—social in more reasonable times.

Remembering the Landgrave's propensity for changing the terms of any agreement; Schiff became furious after being handed a sealed envelope and asked to leave. Visibly shaken, he and Warburg were miles away before Schiff opened the envelope and read the note.

"We've been put on notice," Schiff said. "One or more of our bankers has subverted our arbitrage activities."

"It's not one of our bankers. Read the note aloud," Warburg said.

> The House of Hesse is dedicated to the independence and prosperity of I. G. Farben, International. Any interference with our goal will meet with extreme measures and produce collateral chaos in financial markets.
>
> Credit Suisse and Enskilda Bank are twins. Born of riches accumulated in centuries past, their representatives are masters. They create social disturbances correlated with a desired schedule of financial anomalies.
>
> Choose your tangents wisely. X

Rothschild's intel decrypt had also been a warning for Schiff and Warburg.

> Our takeover plan has merging variables that could well be at odds. The Templar and their banking houses—Credit Suisse and Enskilda Bank, and now Farben's intelligence arm—Ilgner's NW 7. Centuries pass, Max—in secrecy.
>
> You should note, the Landgrave always signs his warnings with a hooked X—a symbol from centuries past.
>
> To insulate ourselves and isolate Ilgner, we must delete all mention of I. G. Farben from our takeover plans. Ilgner is dangerous, duplicitous.

*   *   *

John Poston's Apartment, Pall Mall, London.

Poston had found a copy of Rothschild's intel decrypt in the admiral's waste bin. The banker's warning was predictable. Merchant bankers were the first to seek shelter when money was swirling down the pan. He knew more than he wanted to know about John Schiff and the Warburgs.

Years before, Paul Warburg had published an article claiming to know the origin of the wealth at the bottom of Credit Suisse and Enskilda Bank. Finding a conspiracy in any disc of light, Paul had become an exciter of uncertainty, as though he were purposely creating suspicion.

He died of natural causes just months after publishing his findings.

Paul Warburg may have been right, Johnny thought. If so, challenging Max Ilgner or these banks will be problematic—an endeavor without a safe haven.

Tamping tobacco into his pipe, Johnny took a deep breath. He was scheduled to give a lecture at Cambridge in the afternoon on Chaos Theory.

Causing chaos and opportunity to collide to leverage the stocks of European industry was common during the First World War. Given that Germany cannot prosper without I. G. Farben, this new war will generate far more chaos and far more opportunity.

If one could mix Credit Suisse with Enskilda Bank and combine their assets with I. G. Farben's intelligence assets, one could easily generate the money and information needed to take over Europe's industrial base.

Is that what the documents in that pouch expose?

After writing the Federal Reserve Act for the United States, Paul Warburg, Sr., and the world's central bankers were confident almost all borrowers would struggle with the eighth wonder of the world—compound interest.

"More chaos—more opportunity," had been Warburg's creed—a creed with a footnote:

"Simple-interest contracts are boring. Any borrower can prosper."

John Schiff, Victor Rothschild, and Allen Dulles were scheduled to meet in nine days at 13 Rue du Four, Paris. The purpose of the meeting: to refine the sequence and timing of financial disturbances, thus maximizing the uncertainty in markets around the world.

Estimating a thirty-eight percent drop in stock prices across the board for the target companies, the conspirators, using currency arbitrage, would generate enough cash to buy controlling interest in the companies. Once in control, they planned to buy the balance of the outstanding shares over time, using the company's own money.

The opening salvo of the raid had a six-hour window.

Failure would cost tens of millions of pounds. If exposed, death would haunt the banking houses of Europe, and many prominent bankers would find their end on Blackfriars Bridge. They too had a master.

Johnny had aligned the details of a massive financial raid. A document search at Electra House the week before, had exposed an internal memo of MI6's. The Catholic bishop killed in Tonkin was scheduled to be escorted by an indigenous contact to the French embassy in Haiphong to board an American navy ship bound for Hawaii.

If the Vatican can sell the documents to the Americans, both the Vatican and the Americans know what the documents detail. Given that the Vatican has the best forgers in the world, if the documents are under seal, the seal could be a forgery. My guess is the pouch contains a sequence document for raiding the stocks of Germany's industrial giants—a sequence document that exposes individual conspirators and their affiliates.

So, what do I know? One or more special ops rankers escaped an ambush, their whereabouts unknown. A hard lot, if they get out of Burma, they'll be difficult to neutralize, and they will kill anyone to evade capture and reach Southampton.

With all of Mother's intelligence services and her military assets employed, the probability of capturing or killing these men is ninety-plus percent. Burma, Ceylon, India, the Indian Ocean, the Red Sea, Egypt, Malta, Gibraltar, on to England.

Linc Jensen and his mates don't have a prayer.

*   *   *

Marseille, France. Pan American Airways Marine Terminal. 2 September 1939. 1150 Hours, GMT + 1 Hour.

Pan American Airways, Dixie Clipper Service, Flight 173 had been held in a pattern of weighting and unweighting as headwinds and shear winds buffeted the aircraft and occasionally let the sky fall away. Expecting turbulence, Eaton's stomach had boiled into an antic mess, leaving his thoughts swimming in a slurry of annoyance.

His secretary's death had been classified a homicide by the Long Island Police and attributed to a rash of property crimes associated with the rising cost of illicit drugs.

A dull cadence had sounded her death.

Eaton's cousin Joseph Sheehan was a good Catholic boy running bags for King Joe Ryan, the head of the Longshoreman's Union on the New York docks. Sheehan was assigned as the head gunsel for King Joe's brother, Tough Tony Ryan, doing whatever Tough Tony had in mind.

A grifter at heart, Sheehan was plenty rugged.

Eaton had invited Sheehan for dinner after his secretary's death and asked him to keep his ears open for any information concerning the hit-and-run. Sheehan agreed.

Days later the cousins met for a highball.

"I went to Tough Tony's office for coffee as usual. And here sits the Mad Hatter, Albert Anastasia. So, the Hatter tells Tough Tony some Port Washington guy pays him twenty large to ice a black broad out on Long Island." Sheehan set fire to a cigarette.

"Thanks, Joseph. I owe you one."

"That you do, son."

As Sheehan left the bar, Eaton handed his beer to the bartender and ordered a double shot of bourbon. She was murdered when I was overseas. After I was mired in the arbitrage scheme.

The eighty-one large is a warning. Fostering a matrix of conflicting emotions, Eaton's greed lay in a tempting grass that was not grass at all, but a soggy, ruderal, undulating marsh.

Negotiating this boggish fantasy left him no ward of comfort. The arbitrage scheme had become a mosaic of performance standards, each assigned tolerance limits and graded on an incongruous scale, calculating probable outcomes.

Eaton could waltz these arbitrage margins in his sleep. So why kill the woman? Did she know something? Whatever the reason, Angela was dead.

Sitting in the Pan American Airways marine terminal in Marseille, Eaton began correlating names and facts. He started with the Bank of International Settlements.

Onerous reparations for World War I were levied on Germany and paid from J. H. Stein Bank in Cologne, Germany, to the Bank of International Settlements in Basel, Switzerland, for distribution to countries and companies holding outstanding debts.

The Settlements Bank had been established by treaty and organized by four men: Dr. Hjalmar Schacht, who became the president of the Reichbank in 1933; Joseph Rist, deputy governor of the Bank of France; Lord Montagu Norman, governor of the Bank of England; and George Harrison, governor of the Federal Reserve Bank of New York.

Today, Settlements Bank is washing money for the German State contrary to their charter.

Thinking about the bankers, Eaton found his way outside, whispering, "Dr. Schacht is definitely a Nazi. Rist is a close associate of Herman Goering's. Lord Norman's a close associate of Rudolf Hess and the godfather of Schacht's grandchildren. And George Harrison is a close associate of John and Allen Dulles."

I know Settlements Bank stopped distributing reparations in 1931 at Schacht's insistence, well before retiring debts. And now, instead of facilitating the payment of Germany's debt, the bank has become a shell, a conduit for laundering money.

The artificial exchange rate of the German Reich mark versus the French franc is being supported by international banking houses, including Settlements Bank, with help from Joseph Rist, Lord Norman, and George Harrison. My guess is Germany's engaged in the organized plunder of the French economy.

A pair of prominent New York bankers were protégés of Dr. Schacht's—Charles Mitchell at National City Bank, and Winthrop Aldrich at Chase Bank. "Both banks are active in the arbitrage market, including joint ventures with Enskilda Bank, the Bank of England, Credit Suisse, and Hong Kong-Shanghai Bank," he whispered.

Dorothy Stuart's research gave Eaton pause. She had penned her cautionary advice.

Petra Laube-Heintz provided lodging for you at a luxurious home located at 148 Judengasse, in Frankfurt—a home owned by the Rothschilds. Stein bank made the arrangements. The home is the birthplace of John Schiff, the head of the Kuhn-Loeb, Co., a Cincinnati-based investment firm.

John Schiff married one of the Loeb daughters.

The Dulles brothers are attorneys for the Kuhn-Loeb, Co., and Allen Dulles represents the Swedish company SKF, the largest ball-bearing manufacturer in the world, with plants in Philadelphia, Argentina, Stockholm, and Schweinfurt, Germany.

Sam be careful. The Dulles brothers are not what they appear to be. They are tied to Sweden's Enskilda Bank, in Stockholm. Enskilda Bank is a correspondent bank with Germany's Reichbank. Enskilda Bank is the primary lender for BOFORS, the German munitions and steel consortium with partners such as US Electrolux Corp, SKF, and International Telephone and Telegraph Corp.

There's a group of industrialists known in quiet quarters as "Keppler's circle of friends." They are ruthless and aggressive. Their Blood Religion is searching for breeding stock. Their Blood Flag, with its swastika, is their crucifix. They are certain Perceval found the Holy Grail. If you are German and you are not blond, you are in trouble.

The Dulles brothers represent many of the individuals heading up these companies. The brother's sphere of influence has rough edges. SKF Philadelphia is run by a relative of Herman Goering's. The head of SKF is a friend of Goering's. I.T.T. purchased a 10% share of the German aircraft company Focke-Wulf. The head of I.T.T. was a partner in Enskilda Bank and National City Bank, and the head of US Electrolux was a partner in an Argentine bank with Enskilda Bank as its principal correspondent.

The club is exclusive. In some respects, Max Ilgner is more powerful than Hitler. He is the intelligence chief for I. G. Farben, International. NW 7 is the company's intelligence arm. Max Ilgner speaks French and Dutch. He is dangerous.

As a Celtic knot seldom used will loop without end, opportunity mixed with chaos forces currencies to collide. Eaton's perspective of events was neither common nor realistic. Greed and deceit papered the walls of his mind. To speak aloud of the arbitrage scheme within earshot of any stranger courted death. Eaton set fire to Dorothy's memo.

Thoughts of New York were less frequent now. Whatever happened, Eaton was isolated.

Petra Laube-Heintz was separated from the din of Marseille's marine air terminal by her striking appearance. Dressed in a black suit with a velvet lapel, her beauty topped a pair of legs that made her nylons seem obsolete. She smiled a crafty smile. Her eyes amused by Eaton's anxiety. Having the answer already, she had scripted Eaton's next move.

"Hello, Mr. Eaton. Are you measuring curves or searching shadows?"

"One always leads to the other."

Easing a hand under his arm, she nudged his shoulder. Eaton stepped away. After reading Dorothy's message he no longer trusted the German banker. "Miss Heintz, do you know John Schiff, or the Dulles brothers?"

"I do know who those men are. I do know they either work with or represent almost all the monied players in Germany. I'm sure they do not know me."

"Money's racing these days—accelerating." Eaton drew at the fragrance of her hair. To harness an impulse, he checked his grin.

With an expression of solemn intensity, Petra wet her lips. "Stein Bank has deposited over three million in gold in your account at Credit Suisse. Each deposit date-stamped and recorded. By the end of next month deposits will exceed five million."

Frightened by the woman's declaration, that the deposits were well recorded, Eaton realized he was being framed as a Nazi collaborator.

*   *   *

Alexandria, Egypt. East Bay Dock-Basin. 2 September 1939. 0630 Hours, GMT + 2 Hours.

Dorothy Stuart had been awake for over an hour.

Utterly charming, Lewis Poston had been a gentleman, tempted yet reserved, courteous and unassuming. That was until he woke in a rush to find Dorothy, in one clandestine move, had locked hold of the bell end of his humping tackle, wrenched his pride, and led him on another romp through the escapades of sexual intrigue.

An elegant lady, she intended to hold serve—to be theatrically thrilled. To keep her hound at bay, she orchestrated a thoroughly delightful morning.

Agreeing to meet Lewis for breakfast, Dorothy hurriedly checked out of Shepheard's Hotel. She stopped near the curb and waited as the proprietor of Sinclair's English Pharmacy rolled the corrugated door of his shop into the ceiling and adjusted a handful of bottles displayed near the front counter. She saw the chemist check his watch as she entered the cab. The chemist exchanged tocsins with the driver.

The chemist knows who I am.

The cab driver's ruddy face, hooked nose, and bushy eyebrows looked familiar. Dorothy looked again. Something marked the man's brow—an unwarranted brooding, as if he were following instructions. Trapped in the sedan, her thoughts raced through the gathering mass of humanity as the cab approached the market. The Bedouins, the baggage-coolies, the porters, the slaves—all were born with four hands. As the cab cleared the confines of the market square, she caught the cab driver watching her.

Arriving at the Cecil Hotel she swung her shoulder bag to the ground. The bag jerked and skipped through space. Too tired to care, she paid the driver, withholding the gratuity. She looked up and down the road. An old twinge and a sense of unease crept into the day, as if someone were watching her. Relieved to be free of Shepheard's Hotel, she waited for the cab to turn the corner before she entered the hotel.

Cecil Hotel, the base for British intelligence operatives passing through the Med. The senior staffs of MI6 and MI-R maintained elaborate suites, complete with transceivers and weapons. Scout vehicles were on call.

Sir Nigel's locker was empty.

Several sealed envelopes were in her drop-box, along with a translated copy of the latest issue of *Akher Sa'a* magazine, the signal encryption service for the Muslim Brotherhood in Egypt.

The instructions from MI6 were unusual. They directed her to travel to Basel, Switzerland. Whitehall had arranged a meeting with the chief of counterespionage for the Abwehr to deliver a sealed envelope. Benti was an old friend Dorothy admired.

Reading the second note, with a sense of triumph she enjoyed teasing her right nipple. Sir Lewis Poston was proving to be rather inconvenient, annoying—an oil executive with a monstrous appetite for sex, and at least one other vice.

Dorothy Stuart,

To prosper in this region of the world one must keep their word.

I have an arrangement with every concierge in Cairo. I will do my best to keep my promise and locate Sir Nigel.

Until we meet again,

Lewis

The following morning a new British Morris Commercial PU 4x2 truck from Maspeth Barracks pulled to the curb in front of the Cecil Hotel, driven by a strapping young brown job. Admiring the sergeant and his clean truck, Dorothy tucked her tongue into her cheek, pointing at the Morris. "My goodness, I must be rather important."

"Only top-shelf, Mrs. Stuart. I am Sergeant Evans, Third Battalion, Coldstream Guards. We need to hurry if you're to catch the next flying boat to Marseille."

With the gear box lever near Dorothy's knee, she smiled as Sergeant Evans changed gears as often as possible.

She was flattered. The young soldier was dashing.

"Where are you dispatched from, Sergeant Evans?"

"From BTE. The headquarters for British troops in Egypt—the Semiramis Hotel. I've scored a victory of sorts. It's plush, and the dining hall serves good food."

"Better than the Western Desert. Can such a victory survive itself?"

"No, ma'am. I'm a squaddie. Sergeant Major detailed me to drive a canvas sided, AEC Matador, on supply runs to the front—that two-way rifle range. Daily runs."

Alexandria's East Bay was a rancid backwater, too shallow for shipping. Sheltered from extreme tides and high winds by a natural red-granite finger, the bay harbored hundreds of small boats and amphibians. With international demand for passage to and from Cairo and Alexandria increasing daily, businessmen and spies alike would pay any amount of money for a flying-boat reservation.

Carrying seventeen first-class passengers and a full load of mail, Imperial Airways Flying Boat *Caledonia* was a luxurious mode of travel. A round-trip from Southampton to Bombay fetched $825.00-US, with stops in Gibraltar or Marseille, Malta, Alexandria, and Aden.

With her ginger-blond hair clustering in waves, lightly caressing her shoulders, and her beauty jousting with a harness as though unsupervised, Dorothy hurried from the truck, passed a row of Bedford D39 tray trucks, and ran onto the quay where the *Caledonia* was moored.

Fretting, as if attracted to the man, Dorothy was sorting the ramifications of dodging Lewis Poston, deciding he might be her intel boss.

Seldom as content as she was now, a smile came to call. Lewis had been an energetic handful. Lewis was handsome in an honest way—with a trace of humor in his flat black eyes. Or was larceny his sense of purpose?

Searching for her passport, she discovered a small hole in her shoulder bag—a clean round bullet hole. Remembering the bag's antics in front of the Cecil Hotel, she quickly scanned the rooftops of the nearby go-downs for snipers and searched south along the quay. Fifty meters of open ground lay between her and the *Caledonia*.

A sniper tried to kill me.

Running onto the wooden gangway servicing Imperial Airways, she quickly inventoried the other flying boats anchored in the harbor—Rangoons, Singapore IIIs, Shorts, and an assortment of lesser French airframes. Shuttles from Marseille, she thought. Stepping into the plane she presented her ticket and her passport to the attendant.

Seated away from the doorway on the harbor side of the cabin, she pulled down the window shade. The bullet had grooved the top of her compact and lodged in her diary: a .303 caliber slug. An omen, she thought. I can use this spent round with the right adversary.

Fingering the hole in her shoulder bag, she decided Egypt was rife with contempt, layered with greed, and filled with terrorists sympathetic to Nazi Germany—the Muslim Brotherhood.

She had come to Cairo to meet with Sir Nigel and pick up a sealed pouch containing restricted documents. If the man isn't in Cairo, and Lewis Poston knows he isn't in the Mediterranean region, why did Admiral Sinclair send me to Cairo?

And, who wants me dead?

Her mission-orders from MI6 were specific. She had orders to secure the sealed pouch and eliminate anyone who interfered.

Looking out the window of the plane, the lush vegetation encasing the Nile trailed south to the horizon, a solid ribbon of lush, green vegetation. And yet, Egypt remained a dung-covered, cultural enigma.

Dorothy's eyes were heavy, sentinels for a body that needed sleep.

Chasing the sun west down the Mediterranean Sea, with no ball lightning or storm squalls to badger the plane, she drifted into a deep sleep. Jarred awake as the plane's pontoons nosed into the water, she grabbed her shoulder bag as it slipped off her lap.

Malta's Lower Fort Saint Elmo, a massive stone structure situated on the tip of the Sciberras Peninsula, controlling the entrance to Valetta's two inner harbors, had kept Malta's secrets for centuries. In the lee of Valetta's strand, the crew bade good day to passengers and offloaded the mail. Dorothy held her small pistol as she evaluated the new passengers—unarmed, well-fed businessmen. One man looked familiar. Was he following her?

Next stop: Marseille to catch a train to Basel, Switzerland.

The waning moon made the stars brighter and left the lights flickering along the harbor strand to split the darkness into squares. Scoundrels gathered in the smaller squares and spoke in hushed, angry voices in quick French.

The night chill gripping Marseille's harbor was foreboding. Being shot at was not a new experience for Dorothy. Being singled out by a sniper was a new experience. She rolled the slug over in her hand. A .303 caliber—fired from a nearby window or rooftop.

That was Cairo—the flea pit. This was southern France, the underbelly of the Corsican Syndicate. Even with limited knowledge of the actors in the Rhone River region of France, she knew the actors played many roles. Always a target, a woman of her beauty could lose her freedom in the alleyways near Marseille's harbor.

The demand for female slaves in Africa was raising.

White women abducted along the northern rim of the Mediterranean were sold into Africa through the ports of Algiers and Tripoli, and into deeper Africa through Khartoum.

Contraband brought a premium in Southern France in September 1939.

Jews and other émigrés escaping the Nazis filled the dismal byways of Marseille, exchanging names and achievements as if the past might one day meet tomorrow. A semaphore of winks and hand signs had emerged, its secrets becoming one of the cultural possessions of the Jews' underworld.

A codex of hard dread was gathering. Dorothy tried not to see the Jews. But they clustered as a sorrowful blot of white, without dimension.

The humble Jew, she thought. They suffer because life's burdens must be carried. They will bare cruelly the atrocities of this war.

Dorothy repressed a shudder. Drawing the shawl around her shoulders, she entered the Saint Charles Railway Station. Frantic with the noise of human clutter, travelers jammed the station's ticket queues.

Escorted by a young gendarme, Dorothy boarded a Gotthard Railway Line's twenty-passenger, first-class carriage, complete with a bathroom and a kitchen. The interior of the train to Basel was luxurious. The seat cushions are a rich, deep, rose-red velvet. How fitting, she thought—easier to clean off the blood. My sniper can join me at any of the seven stops between Marseille and Basel. Lyons, perhaps, or Lausanne, or Olten.

Standing in the dark, staring through the window, she found the night as the carriage rolled under the semaphore signal gantry. With the train gaining speed, she sat and leaned into the velvet cushion. The station lights rushed toward the rear of the train.

The glow of the city grew faint as she peered into the night, imagining an undulating landscape of hayfields and quaint farms. Switching on a small brass reading light, she sat whispering her greatest fear. In a few grim sentences, having avoided death, she knew she could not kill Lewis Poston.

A silver brocade carried the length of the headrest.

Facing the front of the train, she gripped the handle of her, six-shot, FN Baby Browning, .25 ACP, pistol. Setting the shoulder bag on her lap, she inventoried the detail of the compartment—the delicate bobbins, the elaborate fretwork, the brass luggage rails. With the coolness of old linen, she distilled the train's clatter to a single sound—the havoc of her heart.

If anyone had followed her, they would strike before the first stop at Valence.

When the conductor opened the door, she remained seated, handing him the ticket with her left hand, the Baby Browning aimed at his center-of-mass. He punched a hole in the ticket, holstered the punch, straddled the doorway, scanned the companionway, handed her an envelope, and closed the door.

> US Consulate, Marseille
> An émigré will accompany you on your next trip to New York.
> Hiram Bingham IV, US Vice Consul

Basel, Switzerland, was a refreshing, orderly expression of relief and calm. Although Dorothy slept soundly during the trip, dreaming as she often did, Cairo had come full circle. Dispatched to Cairo to liase with Sir Nigel

Stuart and pick up a protected document, she instead had her way with a British Petroleum executive who may have blossomed into a British spy.

A sniper had tried to kill her. Was the attempt connected to the Cecil Hotel, or was it a derivative of her tryst with Poston? Did Poston want her dead?

Her suite at the Castle Garden Hotel was luxurious, complete with a hot bath, a bowl of damsons, and a light Merlot wine. Shedding her clothes in full view of the garden, hanging the nylons to the drapery draws, she arched her back, gazing at the woman in the cheval glass, turning the full-length beveled mirror on its pivot.

Discerning, pinching her nipples to muster her lust, Dorothy admired what she saw. The charm of her compass lingered in the hue of the glass.

Lowering herself into the bath, she sighed and touched herself. With a splash of jasmine oil, she rhythmically massaged her thighs.

*   *   *

Singapore. Raffles Hotel. 2 September 1939. 1210 Hours, GMT + 8 Hours.

Posing as a free-lance journalist from Durban, South Africa, his oft used ruse when visiting Singapore, von Cleve had a stop to make before setting a course to Raffles Hotel—his *Illustrated London News* forged identity card in hand.

Presenting his credentials to the public information officer at Alexander Barracks, he set a picture on the officer's desk and asked, "Do you have information concerning this man? His name is Lucien. He operates throughout Southeast Asia—an abrasive rather dangerous man who is running truth's tightrope."

"He's a gotch-eyed bugger, that one. Strange deep-set nervous eyes. A sly bastard. We've an alert on. What's he done?"

"He scammed my paper out of fifty thousand pounds."

"Does he have a last name?"

"Not so far."

Deciding McPhee and Hawkes could be dealt with if they became a problem, von Cleve decided to focus on the French-American. If Lucien is in Singapore, he'll be waiting for that Portuguese steamer. With an alert on, he'll hide in a whorehouse or a remote bay.

Standing across from Collyer Quay, von Cleve watched a fellow traveler traipse toward him, oblivious to his near-run fate. Phillip, Raffles's evening concierge, a man of habit, hiked to work each night at 1920 hours, crossing the Singapore River on Collyer Quay and turning down Change Alley between the Singapore Rubber House and the Winchester House.

Over the years von Cleve had memorized Phillip's habits and schedules. He had searched the man's house and knew who the man's friends were. Von Cleve paid Phillip for information, girls, drugs, and other illicit sundries.

Today he intercepted Phillip near the general post office. Placing his knife atop the concierge's shoulder, von Cleve pulled him into the shrubbery next to the building.

Lapsing into the profane, von Cleve seized the man's throat. "Well, my friend, now we have icy waters. Rather sudden, I'd guess." The concierge avoided von Cleve's glare. "What have you told the harbor police and the Imperial Guards about the killings last night?"

Staring across Clifford Pier into a dust-blue twilight, his eyes filling with fear, the concierge drew air with a series of short breaths. With the knife at his neck drawing a drop of blood, Phillip took hold of the edge of his desk. "I described the Irishman who asked after the dead men, right down to his list-shod heels and the whiskey he prefers."

Releasing the concierge, von Cleve sheathed his knife and poked the concierge in the chest with his index finger. "Here's fifty pounds for your loyalty. If I find you've lied to me, I'll slit your throat." A month's wages could promote any story in 1939.

Obviously eager to be rid of his assailant, the concierge's expression fell into an expectant insistence. "If there's anything else, leave word for me at Raffles."

Poking the concierge in the chest again, von Cleve began churning words. "No messages, Phillip—ever. Here's a picture of the man who killed your guests. His name's Lucien. Call the guards at Alexander Barracks and modify your description."

Grateful for something of value, the concierge blurted, "That chap passed through Raffles this morning—before dawn."

"You're just on to work. How do you know this?" Von Cleve asked.

"I'm on a double shift. I saw him leave the hotel."

"Perfect. When exactly?"

"Between half four and five. He caught a cab."

"Inform Alexander Barracks. Show them this picture. Tell the duty officer that on the night of the murders, this man mounted the stairs and a few minutes later ran from the hotel."

When Phillip took a step backward, von Cleve drew his knife, refracting the sun's rays into the pallor of Phillip's face. "I'm going to escort you to the hotel, Phillip. I am concerned about your hospitality. You'll call Alexander Barracks, so the authorities can close the exits. You'll receive an investiture for your unblemished record—your dedication to stern duty. That...or I'll kill your family."

Von Cleve watched Phillip enter Raffles through the main entrance and walk through the foyer. Dabbing at the spot of blood on the side of his neck with a handkerchief, Phillip put on a splendid show, replacing the afternoon concierge with his usual enthusiasm.

As the man stood away from his desk, he handed Phillip a sealed envelope. "I'll have that envelope before I leave," von Cleve whispered.

Wrinkling his nose as he stood at the entrance to the Long Bar, offended by the flat smell of American tobacco, he scanned each face.

Watching Phillip place the receiver into its cradle, concluding his call to Alexander Barracks with a nod, von Cleve ordered a scotch with plain water and waited. Leaving his glass on an open table, he gave the waiter a signal to reserve the table, crossed the lobby, and mounted the stairs. Standing near the wrought-iron railing on the mezzanine he began categorizing faces. The habit had become tiresome—a loathsome iteration derived from years of counterespionage work.

An expensive-looking gentleman engulfed in luggage stood at the reception desk. Attempting to register, he was repeatedly interrupted by a woman many times his girth who needed a third leg to stand on.

Shouting, as if mounting a rampart, fostering the scram of chaos and intrigue, Alexander Barracks Imperial Guards burst through the entrance and consumed the lobby, corralling the guests and closing the exits. With guards surrounding the concierge's desk, the guards' sergeant forced Phillip into a brace.

The fat woman waddled backwards, catching her weight at odd intervals.

With an air of disgust Phillip danced a masterful dance, waving his arms, exclaiming this offense and that offense, finally presenting the photo he discovered behind the heat register in the room where the men were murdered. Yes, he was changing his description. "This is a picture of the man who ran from Raffles—from my hotel."

With redoubtable resolve, he stuck to his account, declaring the man was in Raffles early that morning and ran from the hotel. Military gibberish aside, yearning for a French leave, Phillip stepped away from his station and offered the guards' sergeant his phone. As the guards left the hotel, von Cleve walked to the concierge station.

Gnawing at the inside of his cheek, Phillip was short of breath. "Fortress Singapore is sealed." Fear flickered in his eyes, then went out.

Von Cleve whispered through the smoke of his cigarette, "Once that Frenchman realizes the airports are closed, he'll head for a remote harbor."

"Alexander Barracks must be a frightful place." Phillip set his pen aside.

Presenting the concierge with a one-hundred-pound note, von Cleve whispered, "You are still alive, Phillip. I'd be grateful for their service if I were you."

"This envelope just arrived." Waiting for his assailant to respond, Phillip ordered a bottle of wine from the Long Bar for the walk home.

Surprised, von Cleve studied the seal. Calcutta—a crown backed by crossed swords with an eight-pointed red cross—Crilley and his archers.

Alex,
     Lucien has interest in a sloop anchored in Chu Kang Bay, in the Western Area. The province is patrolled by the 22nd Australian Brigade, part of the South Australian Army.
     Ecce Dominus

How does Crilley know where Lucien keeps a coastal sloop?

"Where's Chu Kang Bay, Phillip?"

"It's a remote area." Phillip took a map from a shelf behind the concierge station and spread it out. "Here. North and west of Raffles Golf Course, west of the RAF base at Tengah. There's a live ordinance firing range north of the golf course. Unexploded ordinance. Stay on the road. No overland travel."

Von Cleve took the map. "I know we won't talk of these murders again, Phillip. If we do, I'll slit your vitals and pray while you bleed out."

Von Cleve found himself well along the waterway before he hailed a cab. In one fluid motion, he entered the backseat, closed the door, drove his knife into the driver's ear, exited the opposing door, hauled the driver's body from the cab, and dumped the body into the waterway near Collyer Quay.

Grateful for the suddenness of training, he wiped the cab driver's blood from his hand and drove the knife into the seat cushion to clean the blade. Pushing the seat back to extend his legs, von Cleve read the cab driver's license card. "Now I'm Wesley Hogan, a cabby who lives on Victoria Street."

Reciting poetry to lessen the tension, he motored north and west until he found Choa Chu Kang Road. He slowed the cab to a crawl, watching the guards at the main gate of the Tengah Aerodrome detain a civilian truck.

Motoring away from Tengah, too fast for the visibility, the road ended without warning. Bounding over ruts and clumps of vegetation. Believing being stupid curried favor, he jammed on the breaks, sending the cab careening sideways down a narrow cart path. When he pumped the breaks, the cab slid on the wet grass and came to a stop at the edge of a bluff that fell one hundred feet into Chu Kang Bay.

Black cutouts of trees framed the horizon, leaving hollows for the assassin to examine. The soft yellow lights of a dozen sloops dotted the bay.

Lucien can't escape in a small sloop. He'll just keep changing bays. Deciding to hide the cab, von Cleve stepped on the accelerator, crashing the cab backwards into a patch of elephant grass that consumed the vehicle within thirty meters. The stern light ignited on one of the sloops, and its searchlight panned the crest of the bluff.

"You woke the bastard up, VC."

The bay was the size of an exaggerated mill pond. From left to right, he examined each sloop. All but the one boat seemed buttoned up for the night. When its engine caught fire, its bow and stern lights grew brighter. A man stood to the for' deck and started hauling in the anchor. His voice was clear in the cold, crisp air. He was cussing in French.

Clouds gradually engulfed the moon. Restless yet engaged, using the vegetation as a backdrop to disguise his frame, von Cleve selected a route to reach the water's edge without covering open ground.

Dropping into a crouch he set an ear to the sound of a vehicle approaching from the direction of the Tengah Aerodrome. Retracing his steps, he ducked into the elephant grass just as the sloop's searchlight beam crossed his heels.

A white cab skidded to a stop near his feet. If not for needing the tall grass, he could have touched the car's boot. "Now who might this be?" von Cleve whispered.

Lucien bounded from the taxi, shouting obscenities. The cab driver demanded his fare and moved toward Lucien. The Frenchman's knife flashed in the searchlight's beam. The driver stumbled backward into a wedge of elephant grass.

"Ah, *mon ami*, let's not do this dance."

"My god, this is hilarious." Von Cleve shot Lucien in the knee, dropping him to the ground, then waved at the driver with the barrel of his weapon. "The Imperial Guards are looking for this man. His name is Lucien. He killed a cab driver. Call the guards from the gate at Tengah."

The cab sped off trailing a bloom of exhaust fumes. As the drone of the cab's engine grew faint, von Cleve shot Lucien in the other knee. The muzzle flash was brief.

Von Cleve drew the hammer on his weapon. "Ah, Frenchman. My cousin Leenstra is dead, and Crilley blames you for his misfortune. You've found bedrock, ill-stared if you like. You will have time to suffer in Changi Prison—Changi Gaol. You can learn to paint in penal servitude."

"I will find a way to send you a message," Lucien seethed.

"It's a contentious world. You can paint murals in Changi Gaol—tributes to the art of death and dying. Subjects you know well."

Propped on his elbows, Lucien tried to reply. He collapsed. Searching Lucien's coat, von Cleve found a long leather billfold tucked in the lining. Holding a bank note to the starlight, he whispered, "Pay to the Order of the Bearer Forty Thousand Pounds Sterling. Oversea-Chinese Banking Corporation." The three bank notes totaled 120 thousand pounds.

Bank drafts drawn on Oversea-Chinese Bank are favored by the Vatican for their dealings throughout Asia. The Vatican must have hired the Frenchman to intercept the documents.

Balancing his knife on his forefinger, von Cleve flipped it into the air and caught it with his left hand. The blade, perfectly balanced, had done its work well. The Whittingslowe Fighting Knife was a gift from his father, purchased in Australia for his eighteenth birthday.

Nudging Lucien's head, he whispered, "You bastard. You will live a life of misery in Changi prison, in the terror of solitude," his voice harsh with satisfaction. "You and the rats."

He set his knife on an open patch in the cart path a few meters from Lucien's body for the Imperial Guards to find. Then he picked up Lucien's Malay Creese.

The Malayan blade was perfectly balanced—a master's tool.

Suddenly alert, he set an ear to the drone of a vehicle approaching from the east. Stepping into the foliage at the verge of the cart path just as the Imperial Guards' truck arrived. He waited before easing between two trees. He found a game trail paralleling the roadway. Once around a clumped of bamboo, he stepped into the roadway and started running. He had to get to the civilian airport and purchase tickets to Port Blair, Colombo, Ceylon, and Bombay—the ports where the commandos might seek refuge.

With Lucien under arms, the remaining targets are few—the commandos and anyone giving them aid. First off, he needed a docking schedule for the commando's steamer. Fighting the northwest tidal flow in the Malacca Straits and the mines the Royal Navy had sown throughout Singapore Roads, a steamer sailing from the Andaman Islands would probably dock late the next afternoon.

Invigorated by his newly acquired wealth, von Cleve imagined the luxury of Raffles and those sexual pleasures he richly deserved.

* * *

Malta. The Old Drill Hall at Lower Fort Saint Elmo, 2 September 1939. 1030 Hours, GMT + 1 Hour.

Gordon Dewar's research had convinced him Malta was the best neutral ground for meeting any of the operatives MI6 dealt with in the Mediterranean region.

The redoubts of Malta had weathered the centuries as Christian ramparts. The Old Drill Hall in Lower Fort Saint Elmo echoed with a distant call to arms. From Corsairs to Royal Marines, the towns of Safi and Hal Far and Valetta were lost and liberated over and over.

In September 1939, England's finest fusiliers occupied the island of Malta—Mother's household janissary guarding a rock, the merchant shipping hub of the Mediterranean Sea.

Merchant seaman from Hong Kong to Halifax sang of Malta's delights—and of her prison. A strategic way station in the middle of the Med, Malta sat her perch. Mindful of her role, she serviced the allied vessels supplying the vitals of war.

What of the Knights of Malta—the Assassini? Dewar's intelligence decrypts indicated the descendants of this military order still operated from a remote mountain valley above the town of Safi. Over the years, Dewar had paid them in excess of a million pounds of Mother's money for their loyalty and information.

He knew the Nazis had paid them far more for intelligence on England's naval operations.

Dewar held his breath as the plane banked to approach the airstrip for landing. Too frightened to sleep, he spent the thirteen-hour flight resisting his chronic superstitions. He did not want to meet with, let alone talk to, Max Ilgner, or any of the operatives from I. G. Farben, International's intelligence arm, NW 7.

Judging the meeting to be a trap, searching the interior of the terminal's operations building, he missed the last step and fell onto the runway matting at RAF Base Hal Far.

Damn Lord Norman, he created this mess, Dewar thought. He and his favorite—Harrison, the governor of the Federal Reserve Bank of New York—raffish, greedy bankers.

Entering slowly through the stone arch that led to the Saint Gregory Bastion of the Old Drill Hall, Dewar came to a brace and scanned the interior, sector by sector. Three newly mounted quick-fire 6 pound-10cwt, 57mm guns looked over Valetta's Grand Harbor. A pallet of ammunition sat below each gun mount. A monk's table sat in the middle of the central staging area of the bastion. Richly stained and battered, the dark table was from another time, hand hewn and permanent, like the fort itself.

Battle standards hung as shutters arrayed in pairs.

The massive stone walls cast a muted haze, dark near the floor and rising thirty feet to a lattice of ancient oak rafters. A firing mezzanine extended the length of the interior of Saint Gregory Bastion, fed from each end by an elaborate, oak stair system.

The three-inch thick stair treads had been worn into foot-swales by eager defenders. Winches and pulleys strung with hemp ropes hung at the loading bays, ready to haul ammunition and provisions to the mezzanine.

The stone floor was swept clean as if polished by hand—worn smooth by the sandals and the boots of archers and riflemen, armorers and medics, runners, and slaves. Shafts of sunlight from a lattice of high and low firing ports lanced the hall, fondling a colloidal talc.

Viewed at the proper angle, worn paths were discernible leading to and from the lower firing ports, paths defined by a subtle river of tan. For centuries, soldiers mounted these ramparts, Christian ramparts. Where had their blood gone? And whose blood would come next? Dewar thought he knew. The upshot was not difficult to surmise.

A well-used ship's holystone sat on the floor near the lower firing ports. I could bleed out on this floor, and it would be clear the next day.

Max Ilgner and Rudolf Hess stood in a cubicle near the monk table, whispering. Irrational guardians of the secrets of Vril, stuttering old Norse eddas, Dewar mused. Merely contemptible if they weren't so dangerous.

Dewar walked the perimeter of the bastion clockwise through a series of light shafts, dragging a vortex of golden dust from the tips of his shoulders, swirling into opposing contrails to mark his passage. He winced as his leather heels rang crisp against the stone floor.

A dry knot stung his throat as he came to rest in front of the monk table. Ilgner possessed a grace. Hess, a ruthless man with a calculating aspect, well-honed in the art of servile flattery, was fated to the Nazi blood oath.

"Gordon Dewar, Mother's newly minted 'second' in England's Special Intelligence Service! We have been expecting a resolution to these wayward documents. Your ledger of incompetence led to the hanging of Sir Carroll. He was one notable. Who should be next?" Ilgner shrugged, gestured to a chair, and sat facing Dewar; his psychological reach that of a wind-blown, wide-spreading tree.

"I see your predicament, Max," Dewar agreed. "Special Counterintelligence Unit 104 will have the answer in due time. If you are in a hurry, hang anyone you like."

Hess lit a cigarette and pushed the box of Alpenrose matches toward Dewar.

"You're hired, Hess. MI6 needs a doxy little match girl."

"Enough!" Ilgner shouted. "Who should we hang next?"

Dewar frowned, disgusted with Hess and Farben's henchman. "Who indeed!" He chimed. Using a wooden match to light his cigarette, he looked at Ilgner patronizingly. A tongue of black stain ran the length of the monk table. Pitted and deeply scarred, the table held an eight-pointed cross inlay at each end of the stain.

To hell with these ghoulish bastards.

Laying the burning match on the nearest cross, Dewar let it smolder. "Farben and Krupp are integrals in the Nazi State. Join forces with me, Max, and hang a confidant of Hitler's. 'Fraulein' Hess here will volunteer." Watching Hess, Dewar flipped a lit matchstick across the table between the two men.

Watching Hess, his complimentary wave of death's Nazi ring, knowing Hess was too emotional to listen, Dewar shouted, "Check the Nazi's shoes, Max. Look for the rot that billows from his heels." Hess sat without expression, as if his subconscious had found his shoes. When Hess clenched his fists, Dewar held up an open palm. "With heathenry's preference for female cruelty, it's logical the bankers responsible for this hostile takeover of Europe's industry would offer a Sir Carroll, or even you, Max."

"Lord Norman is next on our list," Ilgner asserted, his voice swelling in volume.

"Well, of course," Dewar continued. "Lord Muck, the governor of the Bank of England—who indeed. And I assumed we gathered in the bowels of Malta to discuss the price of wheat middlings." He smiled, admiring the soldier painted on the Players cigarette box—the tall mustached, swarthy lad from the 5th (Cumberland) Battalion, the Border Regt. 1916.

"So, Max, you've identified your quarry. And yet Hess cultivates bad form with his astrologer. Hang Haushofer, after he tells us what's to become of Hess."

Irritably, Dewar stood, shoved his chair away from the table, and sat. That his ambition if realized would take him to a villa in Argentina, he preferred to remain in London. Never delusional, he knew he would be killed if he continued to deal with or provide intelligence information to these Nazis.

"Dewar, your world is colored by men like Hess. Hiding the horror of their soul behind a brooding veil and resolute hatred. Your Elysium is a composite of gentlemanly treasons."

More composed now, anger struck Dewar. "Swimming between wind and water, are we Max? You can ensure this hostile raid gets tangled in its own undoing simply by alerting the other companies. Then you can hang a confidant of Victor Rothschild's—a tempest-tost."

"Don't be stupid." Ilgner pinched his brow. "If the financial disturbance generates sufficient uncertainty, all parties will profit, and Germany's industrial base will be wrapped into a well-funded cartel."

"And so, Herr Dewar..." Hess, his voice strained, leaned forward and placed his palms on the table. "Stein Bank has established an account in your name, with records showing a history of deposits dating to January 1933. The Nazi Party has been rewarding you for your loyalty and steadfast support—your absolute obedience."

Dewar now understood the implied purpose of the meeting. He was frightened. Hess, the crafty Egyptian, had set a trap—a paper trail tying Dewar to the Nazi Party.

"Are you the messenger of some deity, Hess? No unholy ingredients. A Worthy sent to mediate between the sacred and the profane?"

Caution joined with a sharper focus as two soldiers entered the drill hall behind Hess and started talking with Ilgner as if welcoming a friend.

Ilgner shook hands with the officer and ushered him to the table. "Gordon Dewar, I want you to meet Dr. Bonello, the surgeon for the King's Own Malta Regiment stationed here at Fort Saint Elmo and a lifelong friend. Private Agius is his aide. The doctor knows you are a traitor to England and has agreed to castrate you should you fail to secure the documents.

"That done..." Ilgner accepted a cigarette from Hess and dismissed the surgeon. "That done, you can hang yourself."

Considering Ilgner's propensity for violence, Dewar offered an alternative. "You are often near something clever, Max. Why spend your capital on Hess and his hideous, gorse-bush brow? A dolt, who seeks an alliance with English notables to ensure a safe landing should this Rhineland illusion fail. Hess is Matilda, the hoarfrost of the Nazi Party."

Ilgner did not often smile. He made an unarticulated sound as he offered Hess the floor.

"And so, Herr Dewar, you continue to insult me. No matter the outcome, you will be on my list for retribution." Hess raised his chin as his eyes swept over the drill hall. "The Thule, the Vatican, and the Warburg Institute have paid vast sums of money for these documents. We have information MI6 paid money to the Templar for these documents. Is this true?"

Ignoring Hess, a tangible sureness mixed with a mounting sense of purpose set Dewar on edge. He chose a tone of cautious seething.

"There's a perfect fury to competition, don't you agree, Max? You've come to Malta all mist and darkness, threatening deathly recourse as though such folderol would produce these documents. I suggest you brand Hess for the weather he's causing. Nazi breeding stock requires a narrow forehead, long limbs, and blond hair. Hess has none of these, yet his family pedigree is traced to 1800, garnering him a greater Aryan Certificate—a greater Aryan with a bald spot bright enough for a landing light."

Nodding as though agreeing, Ilgner pressed on. "Is England's money involved?"

"Someone in the 'hole' below Whitehall invested British capital in this mess. Why, I do not know. I doubt they would deal with the Templar. MI6 and MI9 have information an American long-range penetration team found the remains of a British soldier in Malaya near the western shore, with the identity disc of a missing special-service brown job."

"Where are the documents?"

Dewar feigned a nervous comedy. "Indeed. Where's the Holy Grail? Why not ask Perceval, or the Fisher King?" Dewar struck another wooden match, held its flame to the center of the table, and flipped it into the air. "If I may, Max. Your fabled intelligence network will use the documents to leverage the conspirators and insulate Farben. So, you threaten me as though I were a fatling? Your threats mean nothing to me. If MI6 wins the race, I'll be thick boiled along with any English banker involved."

Weighing the wind-waves of Ilgner's mind, lacking due concern, Dewar spoke angrily. "Who, where! Who the hell cares? Time is meaningless. The documents either no longer exist, or a field-operative will offer them for a price."

"Many men go missing during conflicts such as these," Ilgner suggested.

"Do you think you're bulletproof, Max?"

"I want those documents."

"Max, since I will be one of the first to know when they surface, we must do this again."

Taking in the challenge, Hess shouted. "You won't be hard to find, Herr Dewar. Your consort, Lord Norman, should not have implicated my friends."

With simplistic zeal spiked with a caustic grin, Dewar declared, "You're flying blind, Hess. Your self-image is quite unreal. You don't have any friends."

*   *   *

The Andaman Sea. Uncle's Tramp Steamer.
2 September 1939. 1330 Hours, GMT + 5.5 Hours.

Guiding Lucy's hips with the tendons in his forearm, Uncle waited for Hardin to stop pacing. The commando's walking without a limp and gained too much speed for close quarters. The short-sheet—he's like an animal in its den. Captain Corcoran knew the squaddie needed to be free of the tramp steamer's confinement.

Uncle studied the well-worn chart. Worried about throwing lines in Port Blair right after the gun fight with the British agents, he decided: set a course during the day as if he intended to dock in Port Blair and change tack after dark, Mother's coastal patrol flights would not pick up the change until well after dawn, giving Hardin a window to evade capture.

Did the steamer have enough fuel to make China Bay? Maybe. If the weather held. Knowing green water crashed without warning from the north in the Andaman Sea, sailing this route was a gamble—one Uncle would take to beach Hardin and get his crew out of the target frame.

Uncle drew a track on Admiralty Chart 514 with his pencil, bypassing Port Blair by sailing through Ten Degree Channel south of Little Andaman Island, north of the Nicobar Islands.

Setting the compass rose to the chart, he estimated the line-of-bearing at 263 degrees for the first leg. With the wind variable from the northeast, Uncle had to gain the tide, and the tramp's bearing would require constant monitoring through the island chain.

Throwing his shoulders back, he slammed his mug on the chart table. "I don't give a toss what you want! Sit your arse down." Hardin sat opposite Uncle. "That's better. Listen, cobber. We've a decision to make. Mother's hounds will not expect this tramp to run off the chart, so we give them a dead bearing for Port Blair and sail for Ceylon instead. There's 273 Squadron at China Bay, right near the beach on the north side near the town of Trincomalee."

"Not quite Piccadilly," Hardin said. "Running for clear sky, if I keep heading west, eventually I'll reach Alexandria."

Uncle pushed up his shirtsleeves and set his outsized forearms on the chart table. "Mother may try to board us. If she does, Grigor Madog, our stout Welshman, volunteered to be Grumpy and surrender as the only survivor of your team."

"Grigor might be a good lad, but McPhee's my choice. Paddy owes the crown for blowing up his workshop." Mug in hand, Hardin searched the chart for China Bay. "For me, operation Snow White's come down to killing the bastard who directed the slaughter of my mates."

His expression swept clean; Uncle's eyes were measuring his mate. "It's a killing mood you're in, cobber. We're off to China Bay."

"Is 273 Squadron a seaplane outfit or land based?" Hardin asked.

"I drive steamers, cobber." Uncle poured Hardin a shot of rum and a larger shot for himself. When Hardin registered the difference, he gave Hardin the bottle. "Molly has 273 Squadron with Seal seaplanes and a half-dozen Vickers Vildebeest IV's. You could jump from those airframes."

"Any airplane will do, except those short-range kites. The Indian Ocean is a long stretch. Those crates will leave me swimming."

Savoring the warmth of the rum, Uncle continued. "That Vickers Vildebeest can carry extra fuel tanks with a total load of nine hundred pounds of fuel."

"How far?"

"You being down to a foreskin and shriveled balls, we could add eight hundred pounds of juice, a Mae West, a yellow doughnut, and take odds—see if you can stem the tides."

Molly showed his unshaven chops with his huge hands cradling three cups of coffee. Uncle added a splash of rum to each cup and offered Molly the bottle for a welcoming swig. Seemingly at one with a bit of rum, Molly eyed Hardin. "You're a worry, squaddie. This deck is jungle smelling, Captain. End to end. I say he sleeps on the boat deck 'til he simmers off."

Ignoring Molly's notion as he offered Hardin more rum, Uncle issued his orders. "We're running for the airstrip at China Bay, Molly. Give us full steam."

"I've been to China Bay, Captain. It's tricky sailing, that—by guess and by God, dancing around the rocky outcrops near the Foul Point lighthouse. That airstrip runs from the beach on Malay Cove, northwest to China Bay. It's but one-a-me above a good sea. May not be eight feet in elevation—a dirt strip, at last look."

The three men sat in silence, as if measuring the miles, judging their chances. Uncle knew almost all men feared Molly. But not Hardin. He was more alert to the big man's moods. Molly's face had been scarred so often, the conflicting lines of anger and joy fooled many an adversary. If the notions of rum came to call, these lines would jump into a dance announcing Molly's steam-driven rage.

Molly and Sir Nigel had been comrades. They must still be of one mind, Hardin thought. They fought together in Flanders Field. In a toss, will Molly side with his lieutenant and leave the crew floating light boned? Or will he side with Uncle?

Molly and Uncle started to speak, both men giving way to Hardin's open palm. "You'll need fuel from royal stocks by the time you reach China Bay. Mother expects to waylay this boat— makes no odds to that twat if it's in Singapore or China Bay."

Uncle set his massive forearms next to Hardin's mug and put a kola root in his mouth. "Mother's always looking for an echo with a light of hope in her eye. She'll nail your colors in the end." Uncle directed a small light onto the Nicobar Islands sector of the chart. With a finger, he traced the pencil-track he wanted to follow.

"Can we make China Bay, Molly?" Hardin asked.

"You'll be clown-white if we do," Molly blurted through a swig of rum. "Fuel for Royals only. That's what the lads at China Bay will say. A quid says we throw lines in Colombo."

"Can we make China Bay?" Uncle asked.

"A nasty run to Northeast Ceylon by the looks of it. A two-penny stamp says we make China Bay. A quid if we have a low and falling glass."

"Sir Nigel controls royal stores throughout Southeast Asia." Uncle hesitated, waiting for Molly to respond. "He might bugger our fuel to trap us." Uncle shrugged. "Poston and Sons contracts for fuel and stores in Colombo and Bombay. If Stuart interferes, we'll know soon enough, and Grigor will stand as Grumpy, and be hauled to England in chains."

"No worries. Grigor's Welsh. He was born to be a garbler." Molly collected the mugs. "Captain, you and Sir Nigel were weaned on different patches—sandstone and red brick. I respect you, but I fought beside my lieutenant." Topping off his mug with rum, he left the cabin.

Uncle shot a warning glance at Hardin.

As the sound of Molly's boots fell away, Hardin measured the miles to China Bay on the chart. "If Stuart discovers I'm aboard, you won't be able to buy fuel anywhere."

Tired of Hardin's whining, Uncle started brushing his teeth with the frayed kola root, spitting out a loose twig. "Sir Nigel's hounds will be in Singapore."

"Can we find Hawkes?"

"Don't count on Hawkes, cobber. The drunk could be in a chokey— in Singapore."

* * *

Singapore. Raffles Hotel. 2 September 1939.
2330 Hours, GMT + 8 Hours.

Irritated, von Cleve flashed an angry grin and lit a cigarette. Not listed on Singapore's docking schedule, the Portuguese steamer would need a port within a two-day run—Port Blair.

Insisting Phillip give him the key to room 346, he settled into the suite as if never having visited before. Relaxed for the first time in weeks, he enjoyed fondling the young Burmese girls who knocked on his door.

Undressing while the girls sat motionless on separate chairs, he laid the Malay Creese on the bed between them. With their fear exciting his urges, he flew into a rage.

With flight reservations confirmed on Eurasia Flight 87, scheduled to depart Paya Lebar Airport at 0500 hours, he would either send the whores on their way and wait for Phillip's wake-up call, or check out and leave their remains in the bath.

If the weather held, he would be in Port Blair on South Andaman Island nine hours ahead of his quarry. If his calculations were correct, the steamer would need fuel.

His next move: Bombay, on India's western flank.

* * *

Colombo, Ceylon. Tramp Steamer. 5 September 1939.
1710 Hours, GMT + 5.5 Hours.

Years ago, in the Silver Grill on Rangoon's waterfront, Captain Baxter Corcoran tried to beat Clive Mauldin to the floor for his arrogant bullshit. Unable to humble Molly, Uncle eventually realized underneath a dense spread of mischief that was Molly's mind, the big man's irreverence was spot on.

Sailing for China Bay around Foul Point had been too risky for Uncle's liking. Despite having a steady barometric glass, with a heavy sea running, the winds near the coast of Ceylon had been three points to starboard at twenty-three knots, causing the steamer to begin rolling her scuppers under and taking on water.

Throwing lines in Colombo, Uncle took stock of the British naval presence. Reading the harbor pilot's daily log, he noted the Southampton class cruisers, HMS *Manchester,* and HMS *Gloucester,* had returned from a nine-day patrol in the Bay of Bengal and were refueling, bound for Bombay on the late tide.

The harbor pilot had said the kipper kites overhead were spotting for local fishing vessels. As an aside, he added that Colombo's Coastal Liaison Command had twelve Seal seaplanes stationed at Royal Air Force/Fleet Air Arm Station, China Bay, and half of them were conducting coastal-patrol flights, day, and night, searching for Japanese submarines and surface ships.

After the harbor pilot went ashore, Uncle sipped his coffee and read an intel intercept with a sense of occasion. "Stay clear of Singapore. Damn I'm good at this shite."

A British India Steam Navigation Company steamer, the Sirdhana, ran into a mine in Singapore Roads and sank. Loss of twenty lives.

Standing at the port rail, mesmerized by the bustle on the quay—loading supplies, unloading garbage, and bunkering for another run, Uncle wondered about Hardin's physical condition. Not keen on having the commando stowed in steerage, he couldn't leave him adrift, either.

MI-R, Whitehall's guerrilla-warfare research group, had ordered Uncle and his steamer to remain within the bounds of the Bay of Bengal and the Andaman Sea to extract all of Operation Snow White's long-range teams.

With members of Team 7 reported to be on his steamer, Uncle knew if he scheduled a port call in Bombay, the steamer and its crew would become as expendable as Hardin. Mother's lads, whomever they were, would use the steamer as a target-of-opportunity.

That Hardin had a hitch in his stride was of no mind, just one of life's lumps—thick spittle. "The toe-rag's boots are tied," Uncle whispered. "The plain of it, he's loose change."

Uncle dropped his mug into the water. Snow White is finished, he thought, catching a glint off the mug as it disappeared. Waiting for Molly to return from shore leave, he reckoned the odds of Molly's drinking and whoring was as ever as a Sailors' Home needed repair.

The crisp bounce of Molly's conduct would thoroughly aggravate the local roustabouts.

Sunset shot through the clouds a bright orange and purple. Matching wits with these bursts of light caused Uncle to start talking to himself. "What am I doing running around this giant billabong, playing wank-sock for Sir Nigel or any of Mother's sods?"

Shaking a cigarette to his lips, he drew air through the flame, swallowing rum-saliva as a chaser. The parts of the sunset that weren't badgered by shingles of cloud had a look of vastness. Coning the ash on the end of the cigarette, squinting, he found Molly's hay-baling frame walking toward the gang packing Sir Nigel by the stacking swivel.

Stuart must have an airplane on hand. Only way he could catch up.

Molly slapped Sir Nigel in the head, cussed a friendly cuss, and shouted, "Keep your hoppers in gear, you gormless toe-rag. Under your bloody stride."

Breathing through a cautious sigh, as if the words were his own, Uncle returned to his cabin to receive the pair's harrowing story of conquest and treachery. With their bowels rumbling in tune, the pair guffawed and spat like crapulous louts. Molly and his lieutenant had set their mugs into the door frame as one, apologizing and gushing useless words.

Once inside the cabin, the confusion led to declaring they were bounced out by half of Colombo. With both men drunk, the after coating of Molly's shore pass became apparent, and Uncle could imagine their valor in detail. "Well, look what Snow White's done to you tottering dongers," he declared. Neither man responded nor changed expressions. But for Stuart's broken nose, the curiosity became annoying.

"What should I expect, Molly?"

Molly shook his head. His face resembled a bad knee.

Smiling as though he enjoyed his leave, Molly donned his story-time face. "We were cutting our sails when some highborn stoke hole tried to mince Sir Nigel's cobblers with a stool, and a pack of sailors jumped on my back. Until those bastards tipped in, we were for Meg or Peg or any whore at all—even Susan."

Appearing crippled by disorder, Stuart changed tack, came erect, cold, and sober, and far less benign. "Where's Grumpy, Baxter?" he asked.

Molly stared at his lieutenant.

"Baxter, is it, now?" Uncle asked. "Sniffing after the sergeant's shilling, are we?" Uncle moved his chair behind the chart table, keeping Stuart in view.

"I'd say if I was. Wouldn't I?" Stuart's voice ground with a righteous canter. The grip of a pistol under his jacket crept into view. "Where is he?"

Uncle ambled over to the radio mount. "After the storm blew itself out, we raised the house flag trying to find a signal. China Bay stopped transmitting." Keying the handset on the radio several times, Uncle let it fall. "We can't raise Lyon Rock or Singapore."

Molly's shoulders quivered as he came erect, pushing his back against the bulkhead. Uncle knew Molly had done his best to get Sir Nigel drunk.

"Let's not scrub 'round it, Captain. That commando's on board this packet, and I want a word with the squaddie."

Drawing a weapon from under the radio mount, Uncle leveled his Webley on Stuart's broken nose. "I apologize, Molly. I know your lieutenant comes from the earlies, but if Grumpy stands his post, your lieutenant means to kill the lad. Search him carefully, Molly. Lock him in an empty cupboard and bar the scuttle."

Molly didn't move. Stuart slammed an elbow into Molly's midsection and reached for the weapon tucked in his waistband. Instantly, in full cry, Molly spun on the balls of his feet, and drove a right hook into Sir Nigel's broken nose and caught him before he fell. Chin-strapping him against the wall with his forearm, Molly took the revolver from Stuart's waistband and threw it on the chart table.

"You disappoint me, Molly." Stuart gargled the words, his head pinned against the wall.

"Grumpy's a good lad." Molly grabbed Stuart's throat with his free hand. "He's born of the fens and the tin mines. I'll flush you through the scuppers before you lay a hand on the lad." Molly took hold of Stuart's belt and threw him against the radio mount.

Bleeding profusely, Stuart kept with his nasal drone. "You're off the rails, Captain—a spendable traitor is what you are. Regulation 18B—Mother will hang you for this."

"That's not likely." Standing, holding his weapon near his thigh, Uncle measured Molly's resolve. "Bloody Nigel. What a swishy name—Nigel. Many of the lads are dead, and you're sniffing their bones. You've graduated from tooling Mother's sleds to skewering good lads. One of the old bag's bog walkers. That's what you are."

"No promises, Captain!" Molly shouted. "With any luck the bastard will crawl back through his arsehole and break his fucking neck."

Uncle shook his head. Molly was a loyal seaman who on any other steamer would be tagged an old tar-pot. A man not to be trifled with, a sound-judging man, he could be slow thinking. For Molly, a sound thought had to soak for much of a day.

His brief tribute to Hardin's family origin—the fens and the tin mines—would answer Stuart's question about who was running the ratline from Burma. With this information, the home front minders could arrest Hardin's family.

Linc Jensen had never set foot in fens.

To keep Mother at bay for a few days Uncle set a course for Singapore. Once outside Colombo's channel buoys he intended to chart a course for Bombay.

* * *

Basel, Switzerland. Hotel Castle Garden.
5 September 1939. 2030 Hours, GMT + 1 Hour.

As an intelligence operative for the "Baker Street Boys" in London, the British Security Coordination Group in New York, and Roosevelt himself in Washington, Allen Dulles looked forward to the many unexpected intrigues. It was essential to keep one's personal plans a secret.

The volume of gold flowing into the Reichbank had brought him to the Settlements Bank in Basel, Switzerland. The volume had become alarming. Finished with his meal, he read the telegram again. Max Ilgner thanked him for his prompt work on I. G. Farben's debenture sale in the United States:

> I have been thoroughly briefed on the financial disturbance planned by a consortium of banks scheduled for the first week of October. Only the noteworthy are involved in the raid. Including your friend at J. P. Morgan, New York.
>
> I've known about this federal-funds rate disturbance for some time and am surprised you and your brother had no knowledge of the plan, given your dealings with many of the prominent merchant bankers involved.
>
> I expect to have a priority on your time. With no claims of a conflict of interest. Your law firm must be prepared to defend I. G. Farben across the board.
>
> Advise immediately,
> Max Ilgner

Scouring the intellectual depths of Max Ilgner, a man who regarded himself as ascendant, Dulles found a chorus of disturbed reflections. A second reading focused on the word *noteworthy*. Hoping the ever-dangerous Ilgner would not learn his complicity in the takeover plan, Dulles mused. "For God's sake, I helped draft the plan."

Agitated, he sat in silence. Victor Rothschild at MI5 and his brothers were part of the noteworthy, as were Schiff and Warburg. Any undoing of the plan's schedule would highlight Lord Norman's agreement with Dr. Schacht to transfer Czechoslovakia's gold from the Settlements Bank in Basel to the Reichbank.

If George Harrison, the governor of the Federal Reserve Bank of New York and a close friend of Lord Norman's, was on cue, he would raise the discount rate without warning, thus tightening the credits markets and restricting investment capital. What's more, the move would draw large quantities of gold from Europe to the United States, where the Federal Reserve Bank could leverage it, thus putting more pressure on the Reichbank.

More disturbing for the markets were the daily phone calls between Harrison and Roosevelt fixing the spot-price of gold. And what's become of Poland's seventy - five tons of gold?

Dulles had not slept well. The veiled threats in Ilgner's cable frightened him. Placing the cable in the ashtray and burning it, Dulles considered what the planned financial disturbance might yield. Companies and investors around the world would be scrambling to cover margin calls. Spreading the ashes of Ilgner's note, he decided to sell his current German holdings and purchase a short in Germany's largest companies, except I.G. Farben.

Stirring the ashes of the cable to further dissemble the words, Dulles stood into a good-natured recognition. Sporting a peevish grin, he waved to Dorothy, his psyche attracted to her unmarried status, and other less sinuating trifles of life.

Walking through the dining lounge Dorothy eased past the fireplace. Conversations drew to whispers. Her beautiful lines and bright, lilting style drew the attention of the men in the room, as if they were anticipating her seat selection. She spotted Dulles and knew she had to send him on his way before her liaison with the German agent.

Be patient, Dorothy. Let the gentleman speak first. He likes the sound of his voice. A master of words, his arrogance will not guard his lies.

Her primary advantage, she knew Allen Dulles was a spy. And, he had been submitting false billings to the Bank of International Settlements for years.

"Dorothy Stuart, what are you doing in Basel?" Dulles asked, offering her a chair.

"I'm meeting a Nazi spy."

"You could do that anywhere in Europe."

"How would you know, Allen?"

"Let's call a truce."

Reluctantly, Dorothy decided on the abridged version. "I've been to Cairo looking for my husband. Sir Nigel's last communiqué mentioned Shepheard's Hotel in Cairo, the Castel Garden Hotel here in Basel, and Potter's Bar in Lyon."

"Your husband? I assumed you were a single woman jousting with the world."

"Many men enjoy that view, the damsel in distress—paper-twits mostly. But you're right. I'm not married."

Put off his stride, Dulles offered a retort. "A gentleman wouldn't invite a lady to Potter's Bar." Unsure why, Dulles blushed as he hailed the waiter.

"You're right of course. But what makes you think I was invited?" She asked, presenting her cigarette for a light. Blowing smoke over her left shoulder, she continued. "I may be a widowed mistress, however. As usual, Sir Nigel's location is a mystery. I've had no luck here in Basel. My search in Cairo led to the Blue of North Africa and the jungles of Southeast Asia. Those remote regions of the world are dreadful."

"The Mediterranean basin is suffering an upheaval as well—from Gibraltar to the Adriatic," Dulles said. "I have refused to represent clients who require my travel to Africa."

"More interesting the rate at which the Polish navy is losing capital ships."

"Closer to home I suppose."

"Why are *you* in Basel, Allen? I thought the Settlements Bank gave all the gold it was hoarding to the Reichbank—to appease the Nazi state."

A deal of wall space was given over to the blank cast on Dulles's face. Why this intelligence operative, this high-powered attorney was familiar with Potter's Bar, a notable French resistance hub, was an issue for Dorothy to sort later. Her first thought was he may have ties to Harry Bingham, the US Deputy Consul in Marseille.

"Allen, it seems every Swiss national is training for war."

Dulles appeared hesitant, embarrassed.

"Seriously, Allen. Even the tractors are being armored."

"It's a dangerous time." Dulles smiled, then preened his lapels. "The Swiss are surrounded by countries who have negotiated sovereign barters with the Germans. Soon the whole world will be buying war bonds. Even Americans."

Accepting Dulles's comment as inert, Dorothy ignored his suggestive glance, his inspection of her assets. Deciding instead to rend the tissue of the dandy's day, to lay his work as a spy at London's most prominent post, E.C. 2, she decided to challenge the man's loyalties.

"Samuel Eaton indicated you have an office in Rockefeller Center—on the thirty-sixth floor, an adjunct of the proposed headquarters of British Security Co-ordination. Just down the hall in room 3603. And of course, the boys at BSC will supplement the doings at 64 Baker Street in London and, by extension, MI6, Section D, and the Baker Street Boys."

A Speed Graphic camera could not have recorded the flash of shock that half-crossed the attorney's face. Seemingly nerved, Dulles followed the revelation with a quizzical expression, his eyes projecting themselves into another time and place.

"Those arrangements are Sinclair's doing," he declared.

"You're the attorney who represents ball bearings, synthetic oil, synthetic rubber, and munitions—all materials essential for the German war machine. You're a director with the Bank of International Settlements. The bank that transferred Czechoslovakia's gold to the Reichbank. And you, Allen, are a spy privy to secrets the Nazis must uncover to win this war."

"And you're a secretary at J. P. Morgan."

She caught his sleeve as he stood up. "MI6 has a copy of your billing records, Allen—for the past six years." Dulles turned to examine his reflection in the window, so she continued. "Otherwise alert men seldom notice servants. The exceptions being bartenders and secretaries—servants rarely suspected of crimes."

Standing more erect as though a serious matter had become critical, Dulles excused himself. "I've a train to catch in an hour. Give my regards to Sir Nigel."

"Shall I make an appointment for you with Admiral Sinclair?"

"I'll pay my respects when I touch down in London."

As Dulles gathered his composure, Dorothy let him off the hook. "Sir Nigel will turn up. Like you, he's above himself at times. Unlike you, he prefers the ladies in Lyon and the wine at Potter's Bar."

Dorothy Stuart enjoyed her liaisons at the Castle Garden Hotel. She could relax, knowing the Swiss owners were paid well by MI6: forty thousand pounds per month, ensuring secrecy. Sitting near a tulip-wood window well, sipping a brandy, she was hunting for a spy.

Dusk had come early to Basel, yet the hotel was stubborn about turning on their terrace lights. Wearing a white silk blouse and linen skirt, with nylon stockings, Dorothy brushed a lock of hair away from her brow. She had sent Dulles packing with a veiled threat.

What to do now, she thought. Find Benti and leave Basel.

She sat at a small Victorian table between acorn-shaped, crystal candle lights. Set against the wall, near an ornate pair of cut-glass doors that opened onto the hotel's spacious gardens, her meeting with Eccard von Bentivegni, the chief of Section III of the German intelligence agency, the Abwehr, promised to go unnoticed. And yet, something was amiss.

The Abwehr's chief of counterespionage came starting out of the shadow and glided into it again, his expression reflecting the hours gone by. Benti was definitely Prussian, the concentrated essence of any number of scoundrels. Dorothy knew he could brook no rivals.

From his headquarters at 74-76 Tirpitz Ufer in Berlin, Benti, and Admiral Canaris had been conspiring Hitler's demise for so many years, a nave full of Christians could not have fashioned a crowning circumstance as illusive. Benti blamed Chamberlain's appeasement initiatives for delaying the removal of Adolf Hitler.

"Benti, how lovely to see you again."

With a lustful smile, he admired Dorothy's frame. "Dorothy, you look radiant. Nylons are an expensive rarity in Berlin."

Given the subdued chatter in the bar, she cautioned Benti to lower his voice. "The export of raw silk is controlled by the Japanese. Your newest ally."

"Germany will be embarrassed by that alliance. How's Sir Nigel?"

"He's gone missing in the Med. He'll turn up."

Benti looked around the bar and shook his head. "Why are we meeting?"

Dorothy handed Benti the sealed envelope she was ordered to deliver.

"Is this message sensitive?"

"It must be." Sensing movement on the terrace Dorothy leaned into the table and whispered. "Route Nationale twenty from Paris to Lyon has tens of thousands of refugees fleeing your guns. Worse, SS operatives in Bavaria are abducting young girls, raping them, and either killing them or selling them into slavery."

"This war is retched."

Samuel Eaton and Petra Laube-Heintz entered the lounge from the holograph fencing the garden terrace, passing within inches of Benti's chair. Dorothy lowered her chin and adjusted her shoulder, pretending to search her purse. "Benti, you must leave at once."

"What's happened?"

Absorbing a sudden wave of recklessness, she whispered, "The couple walking to the bar—the man is my assignment at J. P. Morgan bank. The woman is a German agent. A dedicated Nazi. She will recognize you immediately."

Eccard von Bentivegni stepped onto the terrace and disappeared.

Deciding her presence in Basel was personal; she ordered a sherry. After all, J. P. Morgan's arbitrage specialist had no legitimate reason to be in Basel.

With this chance encounter rousing in her a sensation of delight, Dorothy walked to the bar and put a hand on Eaton's shoulder. "Mister Eaton, how lovely to see you." Giving Petra a nod, Dorothy nearing laughed. "I see you've found an escort."

Momentarily balled up, Eaton stared at his secretary. Shaking his head and straightening his jacket, he found his voice. "Dorothy, why are you in Basel?"

"A lovely city for a getaway, don't you agree?"

"I do agree."

"Don't be alarmed, Mr. Eaton. The usual work awaits in New York; papers to be read and initialed, papers to be read and burned. I'm off to Southampton after a short stop. I've a morning train to Marseille to see a friend."

"Dorothy, you remember Miss Heintz from Stein Bank in Cologne."

In a damp beckoning way, Petra's muscular Nordic expression seemed to pack a slightly hostile, suspicious blend. With an air of nicely judged modesty, she slipped her hand under Eaton's arm.

Eaton turned away.

"Forgive me. I've been rude. I assumed she was your companion." Amused by Eaton's predicament, more the ice coating his honey trap, Dorothy pushed on. "I've never met, Miss Heintz, I'm afraid. When are you due in New York, Sam?"

"In a week or so."

"You'll excuse me. I'll let you get on. I'll keep the coffee hot." Dorothy left the lounge, checked out of the Castel Garden Hotel, and took a cab to the Euler Hotel, across the square from the train station. Her file on Petra Laube-Heintz had been an interesting read.

Fencing with educated men always had humorous components. Especially when they were driving without a license. Eaton's like a little boy. He's out of his league.

*   *   *

Kuala Lumpur, Malaya. 5 September 1939.
0330 Hours, GMT + 7 Hours.

The plane was a converted Vickers Wellington IC.

Pan American flight 237 bound for Bombay, had a short layover in Port Blair. Delayed by weather for what seemed an eternity, the flight crew boarded the aircraft. Hawkes sat trembling. Sweating, he had been nursing the near-empty flask for the best part of an hour. Dabbing the pocket-pistol on his tongue, he savored its last morsel of whiskey.

Anxious, Hawkes needed a refill.

The Wellington reminded him of any number of clumsy crates, a lumbering whale that couldn't out turn its tail. He shook his head after reading the news dispatch: "The German Luftwaffe shot down five Wellingtons from No.9 Squadron RAF over the Elbe estuary yesterday... 2 September: Passenger liner Athenia was sunk by a German submarine between Rockall and Tory Island."

If this is the true guts, Mother's in for a bashing.

McPhee slept as only the dumb can. Bunched in the scramble of his coat, he would smile at odd intervals after coddling his balls. Hawkes was enjoying McPhee's antics until a man he recognized boarded the plane—a South African with green-brown eyes, his former banker—the man who called in the note on the only house he ever owned.

Hawkes held a newspaper to hide his face, wondering if the South African remembered who he was. Von Cleve took a seat at the front of the airplane. Wearing a herringbone jacket, the banker fit the description of the man Raffles' concierge had described to McPhee.

Assuming McPhee would burst to life with the roar of the airplane's engines, Hawkes woke the Irishman, placing a finger to his lips. He grabbed McPhee's arm and pointed. McPhee turned white. Certain von Cleve would recognize them, Hawkes handed McPhee a section of the paper to hide behind.

"I wager he's the ripper who killed those Brits, and the Guards Sergeant," Hawkes said.

Awake with certain fear, McPhee had to relieve himself. If his cock weren't piss-tight when he approached the convenience tube at the front of the cabin, his sausage stopped functioning after von Cleve queued up several meters behind him. Begging his cock to get on with things, for mercy, and for less foreskin, McPhee took aim at the desert lily. Frantic, he spun around, fumbling with buttons, dribbling piss on the deck as he scrambled down the aisle.

"He's a nasty bastard, that one." McPhee twisted spastically.

"Shut up, Robby—dry your hands." Annoyed by McPhee's alarm, Hawkes whispered, "We'll stay on the plane until he gets off, and on the tarmac until he leaves."

"This bollocks has a bad cess to it."

The four-hour flight seemed endless, as if snails were dragging a striated slime line behind the wingtips. McPhee kept spying on von Cleve, standing, and sitting like basic squat-jump training, desperate to finish a piss.

As von Cleve left the airplane, McPhee let out a sigh. Quiet for a spell, Hawkes wanted to scream. "Bloody hell...With your charades, up down, up down, I thought we were done. He played at being a banker the last time we met."

"What's that—how long have you known the bastard?"

Monitoring the tarmac and the route to the terminal, Hawkes gave a slight nod. "He's a libertine. Morally unrestrained. I met him at the racetrack in Kuala Lumpur before the Royal Air Force gave me the door. His name is von Cleve. He's a Dutch South African—a financial fixture of sorts. Top shelf that one."

"He sorts people out with a knife."

"And I think he enjoys it."

*　　*　　*

Marseille, France. Tram Line 68. 8 September 1939. 1030 Hours, GMT + 1 Hour.

Dorothy cheered her good fortune as the man Admiral Sinclair called Harry stepped from a black sedan, license 3075-CAG, with Auto-Ecole painted in white letters on the driver's door. He stood on the platform, looking up and down the street, boarding the tram just as it departed from the stop at Saint Pierre Cemetery.

Hiram Bingham, IV, the newly assigned Deputy US Consul in Marseille, was alone. He's never without his bodyguard, she thought. The warning made her nervous. His suit coat is unbuttoned. Something is wrong. Restless and disturbed, she stood and gathered her skirt, pressing the palms of her hands to her hips. Harry is supposed to have an émigré in tow for me to escort through customs in Lisbon.

Harry cinched his hand through the leather ceiling strap, catching his balance as the tram negotiated a turn. A striking beauty, Harry was a master of Comstockery, boasting the sanity of the Tenth Worthy, a paragon of chivalry on par with Joshua and David. Harry's feathers were preened into a plume.

"Hello old Bean," Dorothy whispered.

Dorothy fancied his quirks as a lesser crime. She warned herself as she sat down.

Sexual liaisons are dangerous. Her body, however, followed the edicts of her desires.

An old woman and a shabbily dressed young man exchanged reactions— to Bingham. She had seen the old woman in the airport. The man had his hands concealed.

I'm being followed and at least one of them has a weapon.

Dorothy slid her right hand around the grip of her pistol and set her left foot. She raised her left arm as if to relieve a knot in her left shoulder, while scanning the passengers for a trailing eye. Clumsy, she had not spotted the tail or the rhythm of their movement—the sequence. The woman was neatly dressed and well-seasoned.

I'll shoot the man first.

Talking quietly as if he were selecting vegetables for a stew, Bingham played at stifling a yawn and took a seat near Dorothy. "Marc Chagall is the émigré you were to escort. He's a Jewish painter of some renown. From his conduct, I'd judge his work is abstract."

"Is your émigré learning to drive?"

"We're all learning something. The Auto-Ecole Company is a front. Chagall panicked, and we didn't have time to find him. We do have a replacement émigré for you. A mischling who had her German Blood Certificate confiscated by Berlin's Office of Racial Research. Muriel Gardiner is a psychiatrist. Her parents were arrested after falsifying their application for lesser Aryan Certificates—in Bamberg."

Opening her handbag, Dorothy screwed a silencer onto her Baby Browning.

"Your efforts have borne fruit, Harry. I'm being followed. Stay on the tram after I get off near the harbor. You know my schedule into Southampton. Have your liaison ensure the doctor gets on the plane and does not acknowledge me. What's she wearing?"

A mist filled the air as Dorothy left the tram and ran out of the station. The young man followed her to the harbor. Three blocks away from the harbor she ducked into an alleyway and waited. Within minutes the trailer appeared. Dorothy shot him in the forehead, took his wallet and passport, and calmly walked away.

Those trailers must have a target.

The wind was freshening when Dorothy presented her ticket.

With her head bent forward and her body drenched with sea spray, Dorothy ran across a jetty of pontoons and nearly jumped into the plane. With a grin of recognition, she handed her wet shawl to the steward, who hung it near a heater at the front bulkhead. Noticing her white dress, and the chill she was fending, the steward wrapped a blanket around her shoulders.

Dorothy watched Muriel Gardiner follow Bingham's instructions. After a debriefing in London with the Baker Street Boys, the émigré would be taken to America for a debriefing with Allen Dulles on the 36th floor of the Rockefeller Center.

Fog filled the English Channel and coated the Imperial Airways marine terminal at Southampton with a cold mist. England's dawn was wrapped in gray muslin, heavy and depressing, coating the horizon of the Isle of Wight. A line of landing marker buoys fought an insistent chop. Dozens of small boats filled the waters of Spithead, and lorries lined the roadstead off Gilkicker Point above the spit, to witness the marvel of transatlantic flight.

Seated in the last row of Imperial Airways Flying Boat *Cabot*, one of two S-23's flying the northern route to New York, Dorothy checked each passenger. The twelve were either young, over-educated girls, wealthy businessmen, or well-traveled women.

Mailbags filled the space behind her seat and the empty seats in front near the bulkhead. Her luggage was tucked under her seat.

Thirteen passengers, how unlucky, she thought. I'll have to ask the airlines for that black porcelain cat. Smiling, she recounted Sir Nigel's investiture. Thirteen members of MI6 had celebrated his knighthood with the usual fare at the Savoy in London, overlooking the Embankment. Kaspar, a black, three-foot porcelain cat, was seated as the fourteenth dinner guest—Sir Nigel's request—for luck.

Sir Nigel Stuart posing as her husband was an MI6 charade designed to give cover to her travels throughout the Mediterranean area of operation. Her immediate assignment: sort out George Harrison's role in the arbitrage scheme. To do that she had to copy Eaton's arbitrage files before she met with Harrison, the governor of the Federal Reserve Bank of New York.

Airborne, west of Foynes, Ireland, chasing daylight, Dorothy laid her pistol on her lap under a blanket, set her hand to the grip, and fell into a deep sleep.

*   *   *

Colombo, Ceylon. Tramp Steamer. 11 September 1939. 1050 Hours, GMT +5.5 Hours.

Charting a course to Singapore with Colombo's harbormaster, Uncle planned to clear the exit buoy on course and sail that bearing for an hour. Then he would set a line-of-bearing to the southern tip of India and a second bearing north to Bombay.

He was enjoying this game of catch. Normally, annoying the crown raised such a ruckus, the pure-blind deskbound twats in London would start buggering each other. Operation Snow White was extreme—a traitor was killing special-service troops.

Knowing being refueled and refit rarely brought calm seas, Uncle hesitated before he lit his cigarette. Bullshit aside, a trap was closing on his tramp steamer. Chuffed over the contents of that pouch, Mother will try to sink this tramp in open water somewhere between Bombay and Aden and leave my crew to reach for the bottom.

Incognito, driving a 7,745-ton, tramp steamer at ten knots, Uncle was a sterling catch—he asked no questions. So far, rescuing Hardin from Burma had been routine. Now he and his crew stood as Hardin's shield. Did they have a choice?

Hardin can light his own fire. Besides, Uncle thought, the man's more at home on a jungle trail than on this flush-deck steamer.

Uncle exercised Lucy's hips trying to pucker her pussy. Pleased with such sport, he scrubbed his whiskers. As the commando followed Molly into the cabin, Uncle detected an impatient posture. Molly had a mug in his hand looking for a ration of rum.

Hardin pushed Uncle's feet from the chair as he sat. "This tub's a trap—for all of us."

Uncle laced his hands behind his head. "No worries, cobber. We've a message, patched through China Bay last night. From the Yanks. Translated, it says a Yank recon unit found a body north of Mergui, Burma—bones and boots—a brown job by the look of what's left of the uniform. With a red and green composite identity disc stamped Grumpy."

"I have Grumpy's identity disc. A Yank ranger with dead looking eyes waylaid us for a look-see. He and some small brown men were trapping for Japs in southern Burma. They surrounded us before we knew they were there. I asked him to send that message through his wireless-relay network. He kept his promise."

"So now that you've carked it, what say we make you a sailor?"

"Sure. Why not? I can sandpaper the anchor. Then Molly can show me how a tar pot sorts out a dive—in Bombay."

Nodding, Molly filled his mug. "That's flat. Guzzling louts are like jumble sales, each has his price. Bit different in every port."

Coughing smoke, Uncle stood abruptly. With a cigarette on fire in each hand, he declared, "No worries. After London sorts that intel flimsy, if Dewar thinks the Americans have the pouch, the frilly ponce's arse will be tighter than a twisted lanyard."

"As old as he is, that's not possible." Hardin ran his fingers through his hair. "Dewar's been sorting cards from the start. Mind you, he only moves when the rain runs along the rooftops—he's more protected in a storm. If he believes the message, he'll embrace Snow White's demise."

Uncle dismissed the idea. "There's more to this bull shit." Uncle rubbed his eyes with a thumb and forefinger. "By now, Dewar might be out of the loop. How do we know he's after this pouch? Or even knows about it? The box he's in would make it impossible to hire foreign fighters without Admiral Sinclair's approval—and money."

With a sigh, Hardin made a decision. "If Sinclair knows about the pouch, Dewar and John Poston know as well. Only one of those men would kill special-service troops."

"Who hired the Cambodes?" Uncle asked.

"I don't give a toss who hired them. I'm going to sort out Dewar. And then any other bastard who ends up in the dock."

Not for lack of a response, Uncle changed the subject. "That Yank ranger you bumped into is lucky your tart didn't skewer his tackle."

"We were lucky. The Yank's team moved without making a sound. They could have punched our cards in seconds."

Hardin took another bottle of rum from the overhead locker and handed it to Molly. Watching him fill the mugs on the chart table, Hardin picked up the intel flimsy.

Uncle said, "I gave a copy of that message to the harbormaster in Colombo. The old duffer is sending it through channels up and down the line. He informed the air force this morning. They told him to bugger off—they were too busy to hunt for a down-market brown job, with Mother posting their best pilots to England and France.

"The Lysanders of 26 Squadron are on the way to France, and 230 Squadron made the water jump from Seletar, on Singapore Island, to China Bay. All available Spitfires are transferring to England before the end of October."

"Great. We can hide in the mess—be a load of scrap iron," Hardin said.

"Not likely, that." Molly held the rum bottle to the light. "More, a load of sour owl shit." Molly took his leave with the bottle.

"That Yank message will give us cover for a few days," Hardin said.

"That's a stretch, cobber," Uncle said. "You've become the Household's most immediate rubbish. Mother wants that pouch—she and her minders. You leave tonight and make your way to China Bay. Once we throw lines Mother will shift her skirts to Bombay. If she doesn't know you're gone, we can lead her on a chase. To stay alive, you need flexibility. Afoot you can modify your mode of travel."

"So, that's it. I'm to take my leave?"

"That's it—have a piss. We've turned the last leaf, you and me. We part ways here. Too many frightened clots think you're on this tub—too many wealthy clots. We sail for Bombay and on to Port Sudan, halfway up the west bank in the Red Sea. Stuart will be off the net until we weigh anchor in Alexandria—longer if Molly keeps sorting him out."

"I'll look for you in Piccadilly, Captain."

For an unholy break, the two men peered at each other, their friendship keen. With a nut jostle and a swig of rum, Uncle summed the day by crushing both fags and rummaging in a bushel of charts. "If Piccadilly's still providing horizontal entertainment for sailors, look for Molly. He has a bit of luck left in his tucker bag."

"You have that feeling, do you, Uncle?"

"One of us is going to die. That's the duck's guts, cobber."

Uncle held a decrypt of a day-old transmission, then handed it to Hardin. "Odds are Mother's twat's so tight a jack couldn't drive a spike home. Her Chain Home Radar failed, and Spitfires started shooting at Hurricanes, and the Hurricanes took a piss and answered back. One plane and one fighter pilot were lost. Most planes were not even hit."

"She's jacked because they can't shoot."

Uncle lit a cigarette. "Happened on six September—four days ago. The Warco's are bleating on about it—cartoons. The whole duffel. Ed Morrow called it, 'The Battle of Barking Creek.'"

"Barking mad is what it is." Hardin shook Uncle's hand. "There will be more broken biscuits before this bullshit's over."

"The British Navy broke some yesterday. The British submarine HMS Triton, torpedoed the British submarine HMS Okley, with the loss of fifty-one sailors."

"The lads are dribbling to give Fritz a good rattle. A gong for killing the first Kraut."

"The Admiralty is scuttling cargo ships in Sherry Sound, Scapa Flow, as blocking ships to restrict entrance to that harbor."

Uncle lifted a weapon from behind his chart barrel and handed Hardin an M1928A1 Thompson—along with a spare, thirty-round magazine box. The Yank's newest infantry weapon was fully automatic and designed for issue to paratroopers. The American Thompson had a rigid form and a heavy, dark wooden stock.

"That beauty's well-tended—Stuart's doing. He doesn't need it. You need cover. Mother's weans are searching for a Brit."

"Are you certain Stuart's after the pouch?"

"Molly is. Leave your Mark MK1 on the boat."

"That puts Dewar in the frame along with Lucien for ambushing my team. No matter the Household; it's Dewar's nuts I mean to stake—Dewar and his tuneful choir."

"Lucien may have hired the Cambodes. But I doubt it. That kind of money came from on-high. Bankers. Or MI6."

"I don't care. Dewar lied when he briefed Team 7 at Candle Creek in New South Wales."

"No worries." Uncle poured them shots of rum. Lighting a cigarette, he shook his head.

"Don't get too many ruffles in your shirt, fair knight. We're the lads from the fens and the outback. We're the ones for Traitor's Gate and the Tower of London."

"Alexandria's a turn and a dance from China Bay—a long way if I don't find a pilot."

"There's a panic to lost hope, cobber." Uncle handed Hardin an envelope containing one hundred thirty pounds and three hundred American dollars. "Stuart doesn't need the money. Be careful where you spend it."

Uncle stepped to the cabin door when a scuffle erupted in the passageway.

Molly presented Stuart's swollen face in the doorway for inspection, with an introduction. "Sir Nigel Stuart, this is my mate, Captain Edward Hardin." Stuart remained silent. "It's a fine soup, apologizing for this nobleman. He's unemployed these days— first on sickbay's Binnacle List—can't find his salt or his school tie."

"Sir Stuart..." Hardin finished his rum and offered the mug for another shot. "For my mates, it's been a bloody sweat, crawling through the slops of Burma. Hereditary officers like you shout their passing, and we squaddies double-out and quiver. Mother has run seven good men to ground. For that I'll feed bits of you to the eels. The fens are beautiful in the spring. Your relatives will be proud to know you've snowdrops for a pillow."

Sporting a broken nose spread from pupil to pupil, cheeks rumpled with welts, and an expression akin to symmetric confusion, Stuart remained silent.

Poking Stuart in the chest, Hardin asked, "Who hired Lucien?"

"Lucien's doing more to stop the Japs than you special-service squaddies ever could. He's made five equipment drops into northern Tonkin. I've known him for years."

"You willing to die for that Frenchman?"

"When Lucien finds out I'm out of the game, he'll double his efforts to kill you."

"Better ten of you should fall than a single commando," Hardin shouted.

"Another time, Molly..." Uncle waved a hand toward the door. Stuart had something else to say, but Molly had shoved off, dragging his prize by the nape of his neck.

Pinching his eyes as he changed focus, smoothing out a chart, Uncle drew a finger across the Indian Ocean and landed in the Red Sea. "Molly insists we gare-up in the Red Sea until we have confirmation you've made Alexandria. If you need safe haven, we'll be at anchor on the western side, sixty to eighty miles north of Port Sudan."

Doubt seemed to prompt the fragments of a hostile mood. Rumbling and vibrating, announcing Hardin's departure, engine notes from deep within the steamer beat the rhythm of the end of his stay. Opportunity was the driving consideration.

"I'm tired of looking at you," Uncle said, pinching and spreading the legs of his favorite tattoo. "Tired of listening to those lousy Japs broadcasting dance music from Radio Jakarta in the Dutch Indies, and those Vichy Frogs broadcasting from Saigon." Exercising the tendons in his forearm, shaking Lucy's assets, Uncle went on. "No worries. The Free French broadcasts from Brazzaville in North Africa come through when the wind is true."

Who is Uncle's control now that Stuart's off the net? Hardin wondered. Stuart comes from on-high. He has money enough. Blank pay-books. I'll bet he knows who hired the Cambodes.

Uncle finished his rum in one toss and poured himself another. "Stay clear of Palestine, cobber. Two British divisions are headquartered there— the 7th and the 8th, plus a go-down full of loose chippings: The Royal Dragoons, the Royal Scots Grays, Palestine Signals, 54 Field Company, and 2 Wireless Company." Uncle handed the troop list to Hardin.

"With Stuart off the net, how long will Mother let you bob about?" Hardin asked.

"I won't stand in the dock for what I'm doing. I'll be shot.

"As long as she's a plate short of a meal, she'll keep sorting the slag heaps around the Bay of Bengal. Once I turn west, she'll know I've abandoned the operation. And if she thinks there's a commando on board, she'll sink this tub and watch us swim. It's the independent chaps who worry me. They deal in opium mostly."

"What independents?" Hardin asked, concentrating on the immediate.

With the wind freshening outside, Uncle donned a cotton flying helmet to measure its fit. His expression set to a quizzical look. "Dewar's a barker—a quailer. He has the courage of a cockroach—a Bombay runner. Lucien's too extreme for the twat. Sort it out, cobber. The trackers your Burmese tart butchered were independents, worked outside British Intelligence."

"Taking Mother's money!"

With an expression akin to turning over a last leaf, Uncle set to his cigarette and blew the smoke down the front of his shirt, coaxing smoke from his right sleeve. Pointing with his chew stick, he said, "Could be it's the old slag. I'm not convinced. Full on though—I'm guessing Lucien has three or more employers."

Given this sea of fragments, conjecture aside, Hardin tried to dismiss Uncle's claim.

"I'm running from a pack of hounds. The closer I get to Alexandria, and England, the more grazing fire there will be."

Acting as if he were distracted, tapping his fingers to the rhythm of the engine notes, brushing his teeth with the kola root, Uncle set his massive forearms on the chart table. "Grab hold of your piss tube, cobber, and be on your way."

With suspicion welling, still measuring the destination, Hardin said, "The air base at Ratmalana has long-range aircraft. China Bay can barely handle a Vildebeest or any of those cloth covered kipper kites."

"After you reach China Bay you can lay up—be on holiday—mud, fire ants, bird spiders, beetles, snakes, fuck-you lizards. All the usual delicacies. Air operations are primitive, casual. They're using elephants to haul their kites around the airstrip." Uncle stood, arched his bask, and redressed his humping tackle.

"One thing is certain. You need more than this ten-knot steamer."

Sweeping the air above the chart table with his hand, Uncle set a finger on the south end of the island of Ceylon. "Molly's hired a coastal-sailor to haul you around the south end of the island. Up to three days depending on the weather. You'll pay when you land."

"Why China Bay?"

"You're out-of-bounds, jackass. Stay out—rack off. I've been sailing around that island since this mission started. Ceylon's a bloody outpost. Make your way to Trincomalee—to China Bay. It's a backwater compared to the naval activity at Colombo. And Colombo's air base at Ratmalana is crawling with nib-sniffing royals." Uncle handed Hardin a pint bottle of rum. "To keep you warm."

"Here's to a good bit of luck."

"No worries. The intercept station at Lion Rock sent this intel flimsy last night. The engineers laid Marsden matting on the airstrip at China Bay. Might be long enough to take tricycles and tail draggers—Wellingtons." Uncle blew smoke down his shirt again, shrugged, standing more erect as the smoke filtered through the buttonholes.

"There won't be a brown bird waiting for you, and there won't be any lamps. And, with elephants shitting on the airstrip day and night, there's bound to be a good bit of chaos."

"Just canned rations—bully beef and dung beetles."

"No cobber. It's bully beef and ten sweets. It'll be like eating vanilla custard in a latrine."

Long after Hardin had gone, Uncle had Stuart on the foredeck tied spread legged, with his arms tied to the top of the canvas dodger covering a lifeboat. With Molly watching, he ruthlessly black-snaked the man. Having taken a cup too much, it was ten lashes, then twenty, each go followed by a testament to the courage of the commandos Uncle had known.

Long ago he measured Hardin's depth—long ago after the commando saved his life in the stormy waters near Refuse Bay, in New South Wales. Hardin was a miner and a longshoreman—a docker, a wharfie. The cobber is worth a packet of any number of royals.

Now, as never before, Uncle was willing to reciprocate, to lose his life to save his mate's. This time, for the first time, he would step forward.

"You've had your innings, Nigel. You should have kept your oar in your own boat." Snapping the cat near Stuart's head, Uncle spit over the rail. "If killing you keeps that commando alive, you'll die where you stand." Blood stained the rags of the royal's shirt.

Choking out his words, Sir Nigel Stuart said, "There are too many of us, Captain."

*   *   *

New York. The Cloud Room in the Chrysler Building. 11 September 1939. 1240 Hours, GMT – 5 Hours.

George Harrison, the arty, sagacious twit elected governor of the Federal Reserve Bank of New York, operated in a cocoon of silk and lace and a continual state of doubt and confusion—a front he cultivated. Liking the uncertainty of the illusion, he pestered the minutia of his trade, insulated from the hardship raising discount rates would cause.

For this dingy-faced man with gray, receding hair and a singularly bulbous nose, facilitating the raid on Germany's industrial giants was at first a lark. Victor Rothschild and Max Warburg had formulated the sequencing and had Allen Dulles encourage Harrison participate by opening and closing the discount window at the Federal Reserve on cue to stimulate the flow of gold.

The telegram from Dulles had few words: Dorothy Stuart is an MI6 operative.

"Damn this pen." He hurriedly scribbled in the notebook he kept in the breast pocket of his suit: (1) Massive amounts of gold flowing across the Atlantic. Not difficult to suggest the cause. The Bank of England and the British Gold Exchange are washing gold for the Nazi State—for the Reichbank. (2) British gold exports for 1939 have increased five hundred percent over 1938 levels. Ontario's monthly gold production is at a record high. England may ship her liquid assets to Canada for safekeeping. Find out where!

Dorothy appeared as he finished writing. "There's a piece of gold for you, Georgie," he whispered to himself, holding his napkin over his mouth. "If she were my secretary the funds rate would go up daily—twice on a good day. Early afternoon at a minimum."

Dorothy had stopped at the reception desk and was using the phone, looking at her watch, slowly shaking her head.

Harrison's jealousy of Eaton and men like him had driven Harrison into the clutch of the business editor of the New York Times. He wasn't being paid enough for manipulating the federal funds rate, so he was negotiating an advance on a story he could tell—about well-known bankers, about notables being hanged.

His book of slights listed Samuel Eaton's particulars, including estimates of Eaton's undeclared fees and false expense reports. Harrison kept Eaton's information in an envelope marked for mailing to the Internal Revenue Service on April 16, 1940.

Dorothy hated the fat blowhard. Knowing Harrison's capacity for betrayal increased daily, MI6 had given her intel briefings concerning the auditors of his life, the merchant bankers he so envied, detailing his promised golden parachute and million-dollar soft landing if he were to be terminated.

With such greed mounted on the hob, warmed for the taking, she also knew Eaton continued to amass a personal fortune—in gold held outside the United States—leverage that left Eaton subject to arrest and prosecution for violating President Roosevelt's Executive Order 6102, should he smuggle the gold into the United States.

As Dorothy eased her way through the Cloud Room, Harrison sipped his brandy. "She doesn't look like a spy." Standing and offering her a chair, his thoughts of discount rates had vanished. "You're a ravishing beauty."

"Thank you, George."

"Has Samuel Eaton found his stride with these arbitrage opportunities?"

"Yes. He also found a Bosche temptress ensconced in Stein Bank, in Cologne—a cold, dangerous woman. MI6, Section D believes a British national working for Kurt von Schroder, the director of Stein Bank, is directing her activities."

"I've been informed you work in British intelligence. How long have you been working for the Brits, Dorothy?"

"Does it matter?"

"No, perhaps not." Assuming Eaton would pay dearly for his gold, Harrison mixed his satisfaction with a questioning frown. "Samuel Eaton hasn't been at his desk for some time. I've received several queries from our German and English friends."

"Give him room. He'll turn up."

"He may be out of time."

"Are you tightening the credit markets on cue?"

"Yes—twenty-five hundred basis points. The market expects a modest move in the opposite direction, an easing of credit. Shock waves will result."

"Be careful how you present your motives. Documents prepared by Frederick Warburg detailing the hostile takeover have gone missing. I've been assured your role is detailed in these documents."

Harrison put down his drink. His complexion blushed livid, as ruddy as a winter berry. Water glass in hand he walked to the window. Gasping, he drank the water and steadied himself.

Returning to the table, mumbling to himself as if fending the ungovernable, he seemed to be drawing a curtain. "If the raid and subsequent takeover of the industrial firms supporting Hitler are successful, the documents will become a badge of honor."

With a sly grin Dorothy raised her brow. "Honor and shame are twins, George. Each has its reward. If the raid fails, the Nazis will send agents to deal with all of you."

"Does MI6 know who killed Sir Carroll Starr?" he asked.

"A reprisal, I'm told. Sir Starr threatened to disclose sensitive matters concerning the owners of Enskilda Bank and their connection with the demise of the Inter-Allied Control Commission."

"My god. I have knowledge of those sensitive matters."

"Drink your brandy, George. You may be next."

* * *

Ceylon. Sailing North to RAF Base, China Bay.
13 September 1939.

Armed with his trench gun, Molly hailed a cab and escorted Hardin to a small boat landing twelve miles south and east of the Colombo, Ceylon harbor. Molly spoke to a fisherman in low tones. Hardin could not hear. The captain of the coastal-sailor was a stocky, sloe-eyed, confident bugger. His clothes were stained and torn, his face weather beaten, and his eyes were always moving. Leaning his head to the side, he looked at Molly with a conjuring eye, then ignored Hardin's hand as if he had been lied to.

"Keep Olive filled with good oil," Hardin said, giving Molly a nod.

With a dry chuckle, Molly said, "Olive holds her prime, squaddie."

Hardin stepped aboard the coastal-sailor and stowed his kit, including Stuart's Thompson, in the wheelhouse. The chill felt good. The fisherman threw lines and took hold of the wheel.

"We're late for the tide, Yank. The wind's up. Find something to hold on to."

"I'm not a bloody Yank."

Hours later, with the tide on the flow, six-foot seas running from a nor'easter crashed against the coastal-sailor, tossing the craft from crest to hollow. Heading hard to windward, the more water that washed the deck, the more antics Molly's fisherman displayed.

The jackass is unstrung. He's hit every bloody wave.

The man's face was striped with cracks and gray with age. As the thirty-four-foot coastal-sailor ran in and out of small coves, he would shout at the wind screen and dance with his balance, jumping in the air to keep from being tossed aside.

That he's Molly's friend should have been my first clue. With this jackass scoffing with the surge of this tub's engine, I'll die trying to muster my bag.

Hardin burrowed closer to the bulkhead, waiting for his arsehole to erupt. His balls ached. His eyes were filling with pain. Well beyond upright, he was heaving his fearful guts out. Blobs and bits of salt beef clung to his beard, his sleeve, and were cascading onto his boots. In blissful unison with the sea, Hardin tried to keep from spewing again.

"Salt beef. The lads call it 'Old Horse'—horse shit is what it is."

By nightfall of the second day he could barely sit, let alone stand. His beard was encrusted with stomach rumblings and the scruff under his nose was caked with hard and soft globs of bush oysters. Naked, on his knees, he held his pants in the bow wake, trying to wash the shit away.

The morning of the third day the sky cleared. Still naked, his uniform completely covered with squeam, Hardin had no illusions. Survival would only come with a good bit of luck.

The fisherman's eyes offered no mercy.

"We'll lay off the coast a mile outside the lighthouse at Foul Point and wait for nightfall. It'll give you time to scrub the cabin and wash your scurvy arse."

"Do you keep a ship's log?"

"You daft git. Not with Molly involved."

Sailing past the Sacred Hill of the Three Temples near Trincomalee, the captain rammed the boat's prow into the sand in a quiet cove near the south end of the runway at RAF Base China Bay. A herd of elephants was crossing the runway heading away from the beach.

His uniform cold and wet, Hardin paid the captain and stepped into the surf.

In reverse, the boat plowed its way to deeper water, wheeled in a tight arc, and set into the current. When he could no longer see the fisherman, Hardin dashed across a mat of dry seaweed and slid through a cluster of palm trees. The boat turned its side to the beach and the captain began sweeping the beach and the airstrip with a searchlight—back and forth.

"What's he bloody fucking doing?" Hardin whispered. "Is he signaling my arrival?"

Against the backdrop of vines Hardin knew he was invisible if he remained still. When the boat disappeared around the point heading south, he held the breech of the Thompson into the moon's glow and checked the load. Then he removed the cartridge box, checked the following spring, and reset the box.

Not a star showed to relieve the blackness of the sea.

Tucked in a dense copse, he cleared a sleeping area. An intermittent onshore breeze billowed the leaves. Fireflies filled the palm fronds set against the night sky. A fine ground-mist swept ashore, lending a thickening cast to the night, making the stillness seem empty.

As was his day these days, Hardin found pleasure in cultivating hate. As a way of thinking matters through, he would kick-start his rage by recalling Dewar's mission-briefing at Candle Creek—the incessant grind of his voice— the way the quill-driver's tone would change pitch before accelerating. Whenever Dewar tried to avoid eye contact, a criminal weakness linked into his glance—his words timed as if he were counting breaths.

Dewar's body language never seemed to match his voice. Packing a vexed look, he seemed to forget himself between questions. The moron had lied. Locating the team's drop zone in northern Tonkin, he used an old French map, slapping the damn thing with a wooden pointer.

"You there. Listen up. Winds are variable. We expect you to land here. Eight kilometers southeast of your objective. The rice paddies will be dry."

The details of the operational briefing were bunk—the paddies were flooded, and the drop zone was a grass-covered stretch of dry ground less than a kilometer from the target.

And so, again, the ambush came calling. The memory, the brutal carnage, the image, the screams of dying men. Hardin dozed for minutes, jousting with the roar of small arms fire.

Hardin took stock of China Bay's airstrip. The matting glistened with moisture, refracting the light from the watchtower and the pilot's dispersal hut. Tiny darts of light, variegated in color, shot from the yellow ground markers at the far edge of the airstrip, ran a course across the matting, pointing at Hardin as though announcing his presence.

A fifth dart was interrupted by a mound of elephant dung.

Easing through a patch of wet grass, the route to the pilot's dispersal hut became an endless weave as the grass gave way to islands of large tree roots and dense undergrowth. The ground was a lattice of vines and decayed leaf bogs.

Expecting the surface bunch grass to be solid footing, he slipped off a buttress root and sank to his crotch. Cussing his stupidity, he crawled onto the buttress root and searched for a path to hard ground.

Shivering and covered with mud, he crouched where he could monitor the comings and goings of flight operations. Hardin laughed at the doings of this remote outpost. 273 Squadron's flight operation's shack was a public house, filled with beer and song. With no time for war, last week's urgency had fallen to raucous hallooning.

"They're a carefree lot."

Crawling to within ten meters of the pilots' dispersal shack, Hardin could read every word. According to the ready board, the lack of enemy activity had taken the squadron from coastal patrol duties to anti-aircraft cooperation flights. Listening to the chatter, Hardin surmised that boredom had led to the mock dogfights the pilots were on about—aerial arm wags dedicated to the brown birds on the game.

From the chatter, the pilots and their crews had been queuing up for mock dogfights in the Vickers Vildebeest IV's. At eighty-two knots the agile biplane rolled and dived with ease. Squadron Leader Burgess had put an end to the antics, sacking eight pilots and posting them to the Air Striking Force in France.

After numbing days of this and that, Hardin had all the useless intelligence he could stand. 273 Squadron, a reconnaissance unit at RAF Station China Bay, was indeed a flying circus. An assignment with few worries and fewer realities.

"No gongs for these lads—no fat black type above the fold in the Saturday paper."

Fire ants had invaded his sleeping dingle. He lit a match to determine the ants' route of march as he carried his kit through a maze of lanais to the base of another rosewood tree. Sagging against the tree, he removed the skin-dressings covering his forearms. Asleep, dreaming about Katherine and the bakery in Ashchurch, suddenly, and without a sound, Hardin sat erect with his Thompson ready to fire.

With a shrieking, booming crescendo, the night crashed into a frantic recital featuring the chaotic screams of dueling packs of rhesus monkeys, their gamboling encounters badgering thousands of fireflies, sending the nocturnal beetles into a rolling bloom of tiny lights.

He set his weapon across his legs and scrubbed his face with both hands. Tracking a wave of belly-lights through figure eights, Hardin decided he would have a better chance of escaping if he went to town and found Uncle's friend.

With the jungle canopy bending toward the sun, dawn sparked a light-gray shot with orange. Riffs in the cove's tidal current cast the sunlight from eddy to eddy. The creamy-white sand beach with its purple hollows and gold stripes seemed to regret being discovered.

Soaking wet, shaking, his throat was raw to the swallow. With hunger gnawing at his ribs, he decided he would even enjoy a ration of salt beef.

His vantage was secure. Piles and piles of elephant dung were strung across the airstrip and clustered at the front of the pilot's dispersal hut. As though sucked into a vacuum, the jungle near the airfield's chance-light went quiet, leaving a hollow knell filled with an ambient chorus.

Listening, peering into a black curtain, a rushing sound slipped through the grass, a rhythm too even to be a man. Hardin's skin began to crawl. His fever spiked. Malaria's death-cycle bit him, its charm a two-edged blade.

Will I ever get out of Burma? Hardin tried to find Linc Jensen's face, but the other faces kept coming, their smoldering eyes, their bush hats, and their devotion. Linc was there, somewhere.

Tu, his Burmese escort was a short, bronze girl. She was dark, cunning, and she was lovely, yet he had difficulty remembering just what she looked like. He told himself he was around the bend, but the fact remained, his recollection of her was no longer distinct. Had he really had sex with her? Or was that an illusion.

Accepting the due he deserved, a chill shook his chest. Fighting for air he leaned against the tree and extended the telescope. One eye watching, he steadied the look-stick to read the signs bordering the operations terminal entrance—RAF Coastal Command, and Ceylon Naval Volunteer Force (CNVF).

A Ceylon for Tea sign advertised the primary mission of RAF Base China Bay. Scanning the pathway leading to the terminal with his look-stick, Hardin spotted the fisherman who brought him to China Bay ambling toward the watchtower, chatting up what looked to be an officer—the wing commander. Cussing his luck, he focused on the fisherman.

The fisherman has my bush hat bunched in his fist. There's no quality to that toe-rag.

The stillness filling the morning shattered when hundreds of birds took flight—from the airstrip, from the trees, from the sea. Pilots were running from the control tower and dispersal hut. Monkeys sat frozen for a moment, then screaming, ran inland for forty meters.

Hardin fell against a palm tree as the ground rolled and shook. *Earthquake!* Windows in the flight operations building, the watchtower, and the pilots' dispersal hut exploded and crashed from their frames. Hardin checked his watch—0901 hours. The date, 13 September 1939. The tremor shook China Bay, giving the lighthouse at Foul Point a full measure.

For seconds, or many minutes, the matting on the airstrip galloped in place, rolling end to end, flipping elephant dung into the air, and rolling again. Sago palm trees arched, then swayed and shook their locks. Clumps of bamboo shoots banged their hollow drums.

Thousands of the monkeys of Ceylon screamed their shouts as each, and the rest of the animals turned again to stare out to sea. They turned to run, but as one they stopped and sat slack-jawed, pointing out to sea—Leacock's horsemen were cresting the horizon.

With almost all the runway matting displaced, and ground crews racing about, Hardin laughed at the confusion and changed location, moving inland.

Waiting for the aftershock he realized all was deathly still. When the sea raced away from the shore, he silently screamed, "Holy shit!"

Grabbing his weapon and his rucksack, he started to run inland. Holding to a course near the airstrip, he ran west toward higher ground.

Still climbing, he watched the sea crash into the jungle along the shore, snapping the palm trees near the chance-light.

Surge-waves pounded the airstrip for nearly an hour forcing a mountain of airstrip matting against the side of the pilot's dispersal hut and the operations building.

"I'll never get out of this dump."

*   *   *

Paris. 13 Rue du Four, Paris.
Universite Paris I Pantheon – Sorbonne.
13 September 1939. 2120 Hours, GMT + 1 Hour.

Still fearful, Petra stopped crying. She read Kurt Baron von Schroder's urgent communique again, this time parsing the words. The last words seemed empathetic. She had not been trained to be sure of things. The farm girl had native intelligence, but she couldn't judge, though she knew, the level of hell she had entered.

If Rudolf Hess is willing to order a woman's execution, I may be next.

Suborning men like Eaton for merchant-bankers will end my life one day. Being summoned by the financial wizards of the Nazi State means something is amiss with the arbitrage scheme.

Sam must be in trouble.

Instinctively honest, Eaton had become remote—angry. Their liaisons had grown more reckless, more sexual, his body a mix of strength and rage—his passion mellowed by bouts of loyal fondness, as if Petra were his mate.

Accepting memory's glow, a feverish tenseness drained like liquid from her limbs. This was her first journey to Paris and her first journey by train at night. The train was a *rapide.* An immaculately dressed porter escorted her to a first-class sleeping car with end entrances and vestibule, and a cabinet de toilette—a blue light shown above the compartment door in the corridor. The porter lowered a bed from the wall and fluffed the three pillows, offering Petra his hospitality on call.

Too tired to carry her fear, Petra peered into the night. Faint outlines of the French countryside shone as gray lines on a blackboard—a barn and a grain bin, and a farmhouse with a pale-gray plume of chimney smoke. These rural images brought Petra to her home in the Alps, in Bavaria.

The railway station lights had vanished as if switched off. Surely a farm would have a light for her to enjoy. In the black of this night, she admired her reflection in the window of the railway carriage: tall, with a slender waist; long, black, radiant hair; large, full curves; and the quiet eyes of a spider—*die Spinne*.

Brooding. Petra did not want to be a Nazi or be fond of Samuel Eaton. Or did she? Several times Petra stood near the window and looked into the night. Did she fear JP Morgan's banker? How could she?

Eaton had taken her beauty as if it might run off, celebrating her first steps from the hot bath, then lifting her against the wall, using gravity to help him plumb the depth of her carriage. And again, during breakfast, stumbling onto the balcony—suspended over the balcony rail, in view of a sidewalk cafe, her racking gasps keeping alternate time with Eaton's thrusts.

How easy it is to make a lover, she thought. Do I need this man, his glances of recognition, the irony of his words, his quiet contempt, the secret amusement in his eyes?

Expecting a thoroughly bad night, Petra fell asleep watching the dawn gain the rooftops, farm after farm, listening to the rack-rail wheels—their rhythmic, abiding charm.

Eager to be moving on, she came awake with a start. Uncomfortable, she rose and scanned the compartment. A door down the corridor slammed open. A woman began shouting her denials in German. That the woman was beyond reason was obvious. Petra tucked the Lugar into the waistband of her skirt and drew the curtain covering her compartment door aside. Watching the woman being escorted from the carriage, she thought she might be next.

For several hours, she imagined her fate. The constant clack of the wheels set a drumming cadence as she marched to the firing squad wall. The noise and confusion in the station masked the sound of the shots and she died in a cleaning closet. A bunch of Rhine Monkeys shot her and tossed her in a river.

Yet she arrived unmolested and alone at 13 Rue de Four.

Petra knew the Warburg Institute had relocated to London in 1933 followed by Max and Felix Warburg and most of their assets. Without warning, Dr. Schacht, the head of the Reichbank, had summarily closed Max Warburg's banking business in Germany.

The Institute's Centre d'Etudes de Politicque Etrangere, at 13 Rue du Four, Paris, was a shell, a convenience for the Warburgs, the Rothschilds, and the von Schroders and their related financial dealings.

Braced for an iteration of her summons to von Schroder's headquarters in Cologne, Petra rang the bell. The butler was a fit young man. The entrance was elegant, the door a plank of darkened oak, brass bound with large, flora carvings.

The carpet was an awkward mix of muted colors from dark primrose blue to dark greens and black browns. By contrast, Hess was a brilliant mix of unbridled neurosis, standing with his hand on the latch of what must have been for him celestial gates, his pernicious nature being that of Saint Peter's at the founding.

The carpet even makes Hess seem pleasant. Then she wondered, why is he at this meeting?

The carpet left Petra's stride unannounced. The quiet seemed to gain weight. She drew a deep breath to bridle her fear. Her legs were numb. As if for auction, expecting to be directed to death's queue, she stood erect in the center of the room. Max Ilgner, Kurt Baron von Schroder, Rudolf Hess, and Victor Rothschild all sat in the library, enjoying a sherry.

Why is Rothschild here? Is MI5's money involved?

Von Schroder set his left hand to his lapel and arched his brow. "Miss Heintz, urgent complications are developing with the hostile-takeover plan for controlling the industrial giants represented by Keppler's circle of friends. Documents have gone missing."

Is Keppler a British agent?

Ilgner set his sherry on an arm rest. "You will be prepared to neutralize Samuel Eaton. We will not tolerate loose ends. Do you understand?"

"Yes." For Petra, the shock was difficult to take in. A log fell in the fireplace, and she stiffened. The pewter clock on the chimneypiece chimed half-one, striking a pang in her chest.

Ilgner has me marked for execution. Agents of Ilgner's NW 7 will have me followed to find Eaton. Surely von Schroder and Rothschild are not part of this.

Victor Rothschild approached the window overlooking Rue du Four. He seemed cautious and out of place. With a conciliatory tone, he glanced at Ilgner and said, "Miss Heintz, you are not in danger." Standing next to Ilgner's chair, he continued. "So far this is a story of hyphenated idiocy whose making has consumed much virtue."

Rothschild returned to his chair. His smile was utterly charming. "We need your continued help with our arbitrage investment strategies. Assist Samuel Eaton in converting his gold deposits at Credit Suisse into US dollars and transfer the funds out of Europe—to Enskilda Bank, perhaps."

"Will Credit Suisse convert gold for a US citizen?"

"Yes, that bank will welcome the opportunity. Since the collapse of the Gold Bloc in '36, gold transfers to the United States have increased dramatically. Remember the US Reserve Act fixed the price of gold at $35.00. For now, it's legal for a US citizen to own gold held outside the United States."

When will that window close?

Too late, the right thing to ask, Petra did not ask aloud. Paris is occupied, she thought, with Jews, thieves, and dead lovers. Musing at the glow of an elegant light shade, a tiny black dot lingered near its edge. The dot darted to the rim of the shade and a spider sat next to Rudolf Hess, peering, waiting for a vibration.

These Nazis and Jews cannot hear much reality.

*   *   *

Geneva, Switzerland. 14 September 1939. 0740 Hours, GMT + 1 Hour.

A light fog whispered as the sun's glow crested the mountains east of the railway station. The mist clinging to the station began to die away. By the time Eaton finished his cigarette, travelers expecting a train had swirled into queues.

The Swiss were bracing for war, young and old. The French were fighting with each other. Republican Spaniards were looking for a home and another fight. Soldiers of stripes and plain were running toward the field, not evil or wishing to be, more just willing to celebrate evil's day, with little sense of collective identity.

Rich, eight million dollars so, Eaton found himself running as well. Touted as an intellectual who instantly knew the margin of a deal to the one-sixty-fourth, Eaton was touted as a financial spark. His letter of resignation from J. P. Morgan had surprised the old minion, Mr. George, and Joseph Telleli as well.

Without a breeze, he wired his resignation to New York. The scheme's money-transfer requests accumulating on his desk would remain unanswered. J. P. Morgan would find another such cog—more in league with the kikes who fashioned the arbitrage scheme.

Did the rags of his greed need mending? After abandoning his post as an arbitrage facilitator, Eaton was on the Austrian's disposal list. He knew too much. Nazi goons would scour the continent, the world, to eliminate him. His death was only a matter of time. Weeks.

He had thought of hiding in North Africa. In Casablanca. But the Vichy French were essentially Nazis, and yesterday French navy vessels exploded in Casablanca harbor while off-loading mines. Three auxiliary mine sweepers. Three trawlers, and a minelayer cruiser.

Rain fell in waves through brickets of fog as the passenger queue braced for the next arrival—the morning train from Paris. The chill felt good. Eaton waited for an ex-patriot. Petra Laube-Heintz had become a refugee.

Moral ambiguity aside, Eaton knew his time in Europe was limited. This would be his final trip to Geneva. Sorting the risks of the arbitrage scheme and the untaxed fees he had garnered; his next move could prove fatal. Accepting the risks with a false bravado, he blinked when Petra popped from a crowd of ragged immigrants.

Briefly in relief he held up his hand.

Never quite free of his desire, he found the hollow at the front of Petra's skirt and traced its image with a grin. Early as it was, he imagined a tryst—in the railway carriage. Selecting from the few things he thought to say, Eaton spoke an edited version of his thoughts.

After Petra set her bag down, he said, "You have beauty enough for two."

Understanding his grin, muted by a cupped hand she spoke with a lightened tone, "There's a certain relief to being exhausted. Don't you agree, Sam?"

In the tautness of excitement, his impulse was to disagree. Hopeful, he latched on to a crisp stride. "Of course—we can eat breakfast before we rinse out my Credit Suisse account."

Petra made no answer. Did he startle her? Had he interrupted her thoughts? Were her hands tied more tightly than his? Eaton secured her bag and followed her through the station entrance and hailed a cab. She seemed remote, detached, and more cordial than familiar.

As though isolated from the gathering roar of Geneva's war-weary morning, Eaton and his escort ate omelets and jam in a small restaurant. Her brooding held his attention; her mood that had been assuredly complete was far less alive. She seemed to be watching him with a hint of intrigue, as if waiting for an expectant flaw.

"What the matter, Petra?"

"Nothing!" Hesitant, as though not caring to create undue urgency, she urged, "We must convert your gold holdings to US dollars."

Concentrating on the immediate, permitting an expression of concern, he creased his expression into a morning smile, swallowing as he did so. "I've resigned from J. P. Morgan. I'm scared. I'm running, and don't know where to go. I thought the remote forests around Geneva might be considered unlikely. I could become a stranger."

"Europe is filled with strangers."

Petra covered her mouth, glanced to the left and to the right. Offering a slight shrug as if to allow herself a stage, softly gesturing with her palms, she whispered, "Sam, the arbitrage plan has been compromised. Copies of the plan's financial circuit diagrams are missing. If these copies fall into the wrong hands, you and the other traders will be assassinated. You must leave Europe at once."

With an odd set to his eye, an odd sense of recognition, Eaton realized Petra Laube-Heintz had been the implement used to facilitate his participation in the arbitrage plan. She had been selected to suborn a man prone to infidelity. Angry for being such a schmuck, his dream of financial freedom was just so—a dream gathering near the edge of a fog-coated London street, perhaps Bishopsgate or Old Jewry.

Codes, ciphers, Nazis, Jews, assassins, drug dealers, secrets… those thoughts lingered with him and came to visit this day. Eaton dismissed his fear. "There's a bank in Windward Islands. I could wire the funds to Martinique."

"You're new to this world, Sam."

Without responding further, Petra's concentration seemed absolute. Eaton watched as she excused herself and maneuvered the waiter to a darkened corner. As the waiter's focus followed her lead, she laughed and beckoned Eaton to follow.

Eaton stepped to Petra's side.

"I have fifty US dollars for you if you escort my friend out the back of the restaurant and on to the main office of Credit Suisse," Petra whispered.

For Eaton, in September 1939, gold was survival's currency. For the waiter, US dollars were gold. She tucked the escort-fee in Eaton's jacket pocket.

With a flash of mischief, she kissed Eaton as if saying good-bye, mixing her words with a tear. "I'll wait in the restaurant for another coffee and take a taxi to Credit Suisse."

Petra followed Eaton to the back door of the restaurant, then returned to the table. Warming her hands on the side of the coffee cup, she scanned the sidewalks. She was being followed.

Is Eaton marked for elimination?

Petra emerged from the elevator at Credit Suisse as Eaton entered the front door. "Sam, the principal bank in Martinique is a correspondent with the Reichbank. Baron von Schroder may own it."

Eaton remained silent. As they strolled across the lobby, he grew more confidential. "The world's getting smaller." He wasn't sure the words were his.

"Put the money in Asia—the Oversea-Chinese Bank." Petra was nudging his shoulder as if they had finally met, chattering like a tourist. "That bank does not correspond with the Reichbank and is cautious with their dealings in New York."

The gold conversion took over an hour.

"Petra, you must come to New York—escape Europe and the war."

Born of a rural nature, Petra's patient smile was an instant adhesive. As though a child trying to cobble pieces of two puzzles together, her expression pleaded for understanding.

"Sam, you cannot go to New York. The arbitrage plan has principals in New York."

Convex, concave, convex, concave, the temperance of rage suddenly mixed with too much loud pedal, its synthesis among the most exquisite of the creations of mankind. Eaton's face creased as his eyes narrowed, his hands clearing the air with swift motions.

"How long have you known?" His voice was cold and contained a threat.

She took a series of long breaths before saying, "I was informed after I returned from New York. I'm frightened—for you and for me. I've asked for a taxi."

First searching for a word of revenge, its residue, feeling ashamed of his strident tone, Eaton shook his head. Hearing the exhaustion in her voice, he tracked Petra's gaze into the terminal. A tear perched on her cheek and ran slowly to the corner of her mouth. She was crying—softly.

"The northern flying route to the United States from Southampton via Foynes, Ireland, and on to New York is scheduled to close in eighteen days—on October third. Nazi agents have moved into Ireland and will be watching anyone trying to get to your country."

At that moment, in an approval of sufficiency, Eaton allowed her his confidence. With this new sense of certainty came recognition. Petra had been a Nazi. But she was no longer a threat.

Out of earshot, with ideas racing, he decided to address a more immediate problem—how to hide in plain sight. "So, I'm afloat in Europe's sewer. Hiding from German agents."

Before he finished speaking, she shifted her frame, sidestepping his holdall. A brief, trembling smile flickered on her face as if she were grateful for Eaton's forgiveness.

Speaking through her tears, she set her hand to his elbow. "Sam, you need a Swiss passport and a new identity. Once in hand, travel east from Lisbon. Take the train to Lyon and go to Potter's Bar on Rue Saint Catherine, Number 12. Rue Saint Catherine is short and wide in front of the bar, running east and west in the La Croix-Rousse Quarter."

"Potter's Bar?"

"Yes—a forger frequents Potter's...specializes in identity papers and passports. He drinks expensive Macallan Sherry Oak quarter whiskey. His eyes are shocking; a white-blue-gray. He plays the harmonica. Eight hundred US dollars is the current price for a Swiss passport."

Although Petra's fear was less apparent, Eaton set his arms to a fold. "Is this forger known to the Nazis?"

"The Abwehr call him Cager. The man's brilliant." Gathering herself with a deep breath, Petra lifted her chin. As if looking for a safe haven, she said, "He's an Argentine—a master, Adolphe Kaminski. Don't mention my name."

Surprised by Petra's frailty, Eaton chided his cruelty. Her tears welled up again. When he closed the gap between them, she invited herself into his arms and kissed him on the cheek. She cupped his cheeks and kissed him as if saying good-bye.

"Whatever you decide, don't go to New York, or the US."

"Will you come with me?" he asked genially.

Appearing conflicted, frightened, she stepped away and searched the bank's lobby. "I'm being followed, Sam—by the Gestapo. There's but one end."

With his thoughts inextricably tied to the geometry of her stride, Eaton flashed a quizzical smile, and Petra Laube-Heintz walked out of his life.

*   *   *

Port Blair, South Andaman Island. Ritchie's Public House. 14 September 1939. 0850 Hours. GMT + 5.5 Hours.

Having arrived on the shuttle from Kuala Lumpur, Hawkes engaged McPhee in a quiet discussion, tucked into the darkest corner of Ritchie's Public House. With his flask filled to its limit and his breakfast eaten, Hawkes scrubbed at the whiskers on his jaw. "You need to shift yourself, Robby."

"Not now, Hawker. I'm tracking a rare beauty at the moment."

"Before you inaugurate another tale, if our South African stops for a crumb, you can join him and say hello."

"Just so..." McPhee changed seats and pulled down the brim of his hat.

As if on cue, von Cleve barged into Ritchie's Public House, secured a cup of coffee, tramped directly to the table behind McPhee, and sat in a chair facing the door. Without hesitation, von Cleve asked over his shoulder, "What do you know about flights to Bombay?"

Hawkes, with his newspaper on high, started burbling covering fire, adjusting the paper and his voice. "A flight-schedule is posted near the door you just passed through. There's a mail flight on Thursdays at half-twelve."

"Thank you."

Without so much as a tart's kiss, von Cleve made tracks for the door. After examining the flight schedule, he left Ritchie's Public House, leaving his cold, calculating, ability to kill without remorse sitting next to McPhee.

With a rush of curious humor Hawkes asked, "So, Robby, if I may ask, is that shit I smell?"

"Leave it out, Hawker," McPhee shouted as his chair flew sideways. He flew into the isle smashing his face into a dish cart.

Spilling a bucket full of dirty dishes, a waitress screamed, "Earthquake!"

The guts of Ritchie's Public House burst violently into a scram—glasses, mugs, plates, and bowls; pots, pans, garbage bins and waitresses. Shouts scudded from wall to wall as panic and chaos took hold.

Snaring his coffee cup as it vaulted off the table, Hawkes stumbled from his chair and slammed into the wall. The windows shattered, exploding from their frames.

Dodging the flying glass, McPhee leaped over a chair, followed by the plate containing his breakfast. Cussing, he tried to stand. His foot met a bucket of dirty dishes careening across the floor. With damnation's sulfur stinging his nostrils, he crashed backwards into a platoon of frantic chairs. Bruised and hollering, he scurried under a table.

"Now that the floor's down to a quiver, I need another drink," Hawkes declared. "One minute of bedlam, and Ritchie's is a ruin. The epicenter must be nearby."

Looking like he just crawled through the path of a cyclone, McPhee became a never-failing braggart and declared, "This is bloody bullshit. Two bob says Rangoon's chief magistrate is too clapped out to sound a tidal alert. With any luck, the bastard's too drunk to get to top ground."

With a clipped British accent, Hawkes mimicked a flight controller, "Coastal Command China Bay, hear this, scramble your Vildebeest IV's, and order those bumbling jacks from the Singapore Flying Club to scramble their kipper-kites, over."

Sporting an indefinably foolish expression, his coat stained with breakfast delights—canteen medals, McPhee opened a pay-book filled with indignation. "That South African. First, he says thank you, then he gins up an earthquake to announce his leavings. I'll wager the bastard's breath would curl the bark off a gum log."

"So, Robby, is that shit I smell?"

"A fucking frenzy, that we know." McPhee lit a cigarette and picked his way to the entrance of the pub. With customers searching for belongings, and the bits and pieces of Ritchie's shattered and strewn, McPhee drew a long drag on his fag. Through a mouthful of smoke, he asked, "Where's the Ripper?"

"Just there at the curb. Odds are he killed the local director of the Hong Kong and Shanghai Bank, eight months back, and hung him in the Singapore Ice Works." Hawkes stepped away from the window when von Cleve turn around.

"I do remember one gram, Robby. The blighter has a cross tattooed on his arm—a cross from the Temple District of London."

"One of God's gallopers, is he?"

Von Cleve's cab drove off.

Hawkes took a nip of his flask. "He's a butcher, that one."

"So now that the Ripper's off to Bombay, we can close our pay-books."

With a one-corner smirk Hawkes shook his head. "I've never met a bog-trotter who didn't gain weight. Think Robby—Rangoon's out, Singapore's out, my Ford's been tagged, and they've a prison here that's worse than Changi. This isn't a game. We can't get out. We're in the soup to the end."

Hawkes ran his finger down the flight schedule posted next to the door and held it on a flight to China Bay—1740 hours, a Lysander from 26 Squadron RAF.

"We'll stand by for that Lizzy. I probably know the pilot." Hawkes was beginning to shake. He desperately needed a bottle. "If that Lizzy's full, we'll catch the train, the Singapore-Kuala Lumpur Express."

*   *   *

Ceylon. RAF Base China Bay. 16 September 1939. 1400 Hours, GMT + 5.5 Hours.

Elevation 5 Ft.—so read the forty-foot sign painted in sixteen-inch high white letters across the front of the fight operations building at RAF Base China Bay. The windows on the building were gone, and a dark line near the roof's eves marked the height of the tidal surge caused by the 6.0 earthquake centered near South Andaman Island.

At least half of the airstrip matting was uprooted. Elephants in harness were dragging huge, squared logs across the airstrip where the matting was still flat to clear the mud and debris.

I've been adrift for forty-nine days, Hardin thought. And my new laager is under water, one meter of mud, and bloody elephant shit.

Captain Edward Hardin's uniform was striated with red and brown mud, sand and seaweed, and assorted bits of jungle debris. Warmed by the sun, laying on a dry pile of thatch, free of marauders, Hardin dozed when he wasn't laughing at two pilot-officers blagging away the day shoveling debris from the pathway leading to what Hardin assumed was more confusion—flight operations for 230 Squadron RAF.

Eventually the sunset compassed the horizon with trims of turquoise, salmon pink, and crimson—universal signals for ending the day's work.

As if satisfied with their repairs, the pilots assumed an idler's slouch, smiling as they opened a beer. Toasting the idea of flying off to war with a torrent of garlic gratitude, each in turn came to attention, assumed a ceremonial expression of disordered intensity, and in tuneful unison started singing:

> *'I don't want the sergeant's shilling,*
> *I don't want to be shot down;*
> *I'm really much more willing,*
> *To make myself a killing,*
> *Living off the pickings of the ladies in the town;*
> *Don't want a bullet up my bumhole...'*

Suddenly, as only the brass can, Wing Commander Crow appeared. As the silence grew mischievous, one pilot and then the other, considering each other, handed the Old Man a beer and stood-to again.

Toasting a beer with each hand, the Old Man sang on:

> *'Don't want my cobblers minced with ball,*
> *And let it be to Susan,*
> *If we're going to lose 'em,*
> *Or Meg or Peg or any whore at all.'*

Then, with a beer to each pilot, he toasted, "And here's a toast to Her Majesty's Submarine *Odin*, for sinking a Japanese patrol boat in the Straits." Tipping his tile with the edge of a beer can, the wing commander turned on a heel and entered the flight operations building.

An odd one, that officer, Hardin thought. His arms don't swing when he walks. Must be the beer he's harboring. Uncle's right. Security at China Bay is a circus.

Growing restless, Hardin stood up. His leg ached as never before. His frantic effort to gain altitude and avoid the tidal surge had taken its toll. Trincomalee's isolated nobs of higher ground were covered with red-brick bungalows, laced with palmyra and coconut-leaf fencing and spiced with temperamental canines.

Hardin spent two nights fighting the maze. Covered with mud, huddled on top of a rickety goat pen the first night, and perched in a tree the second night. The airtight cylinders in his kit had kept his matches, cigarettes, and heat tablets dry. A third cylinder was filled with rum.

Encrusted in a mold of dry mud and goat shit, he shed weight between steps, leaving a trail of red-brown flakes near his boot prints. At the edge of a pool of clear, cold water, he knelt and filled his canteen. Moving around the pool, he found a small stream flowing toward the airstrip. Grateful for the fresh water, he stripped, washed his uniform, and took a bath.

Passing the last hut on his way to the beach, he stumbled into a carpet of tiny flying beetles. Fighting the hum of thousands of wings, he ran through a stand of palm trees and stopped to brush himself off. The ground he crossed was pocked with crushed beetles where his boots had hit the ground, and their guts packed the odor of sweet dung.

This was another kind of weariness. Tired of fighting a dull fatigue, peering ahead he saw a coastal-sailor anchored in Malay Cove. Molly's fisherman was in China Bay.

A warning beat at his mind.

Skirting the runway matting, sprinting in short spurts, threading his way through the vines and grass, mud, and debris, he brushed off the remaining beetles and crawled into a hollow. Somehow the ground shone an oily brown, as if it were polished. Searching the clearing for wires and booby traps, he leaned against a rosewood tree. The ants were gone.

The tidal surge had left a beaverlike berm of logs and mud on the beach side of the hollow and washed the hollow bare, leaving the ground laced with exposed finger roots.

The thought of another night in the jungle made the pilots' dispersal hut more tempting. Drawing his fingers through a pile of soggy leaves, through a crevasse near the base of the tree, he found his bush hat. That damned fisherman, he thought. Why's he tracking me? There's a metal container of some sort in the hat—a booby trap.

Twice he started to unfurl the hat, only to stop and check for wires. Satisfied, he gently shook out the bush hat. A flask partly wrapped in wrinkled paper fell between his knees. Waiting for the explosion, picturing his balls being blasted right past his ass, Hardin wanted to scream.

The handwriting on the paper was Uncle Dingo's. Now Corcoran's sending me bedtime stories. Fighting the oncoming shades of night, Hardin held the message into the glow of the operation terminal's security lights.

Drop your cock, Cobber

Airstrip construction China Bay was completed 5 September. First landings were 13 September. Flight operations are chaotic. Primary school at best. If you get in a jam, make your way to the Welcombe Hotel in Trincomalee and ask for my friend Paddy O'Shaughnessy. He's so disagreeable, nothing's right with him. He's a good lad.

Here's a bit of whiskey to take the chill off. If Hawkes shows his face, he's a right proper drunk. Loves the wobbles more than pussy.

Urgent scuttlebutt. The Chinese have female battalions. Let's side-up, cobber. We'd have bags of tall tales and anxious women. Stern duty and all that.

Have a piss, Uncle Dingo

"Bags of tall tales and anxious women," Hardin whispered. "Have a piss." *Tall tales* being their authentication code to certify the message's origin. Flight operations at China Bay did have the makings of a game of skittles, boasting brown parcels toggled to any pilot who jumped the odd queue— routine missions fashioned into a blistering scram.

Hiding near the flight line, listening to conversations, Hardin learned that a squadron of Bristol Blenheim MK1's flew into China Bay from Seletar, on Singapore Island, on their way to London. Mother needed the airplanes— more so the pilots. Additionally, 26 Squadron was moving its Lysanders to France to join the Advanced Air Striking Force in support of the British Expeditionary Force.

If I can stow away, a Blenheim or a Lysander would do the trick, Hardin thought. Those crates have enough range to tackle the Indian Ocean.

The taste of the rain not yet fallen, mixed with the smells that were a matter of habit, brought an unnerving calm. Hardin sensed he was being watched. He slipped out of the hollow down to the beach and searched west past the end of the runway. The beach was deserted. So was the verge along the runway.

The stench of uprooted and rotting vegetation thickened the cool night air.

Listening to the wind barge through the foliage bordering the beach, Hardin counseled his spirits. He waited a minute, then another. He expected a sound. As if canceling all furloughs, a China Bay pilot hollered as he toasted his beer, announcing the first casualty listing of the war was expected on 19 September and would be posted in the pilots' dispersal hut.

Who will be the last man on the final list? After unscrewing the lid on the tube containing his dry matches, he cupped his hands and lit a cigarette. Drawing on his smoke his chest shuddered through a quieting. I need to see that list. See if my mates were found. See if they were worth their salt. See if I made the list.

Hardin pulled his bush hat closer to his eyes.

Setting an ear to the drone of an inbound aircraft, he eased through a patch of tall grass to the end of the runway near the base of the chance-light. A Liberator VI loomed into view in the north. As if a black cutout, the night wore the airframe to a shadow, only to have the airframe tear a hole in the curtain. Reacting to this monster, loons and gulls burst into the air, wheeling as one, filling the landing lights with hundreds of wings.

The haunting screech of a loon echoed in the night—forlorn and melancholy.

The ground crew set chocks to the wheels of the Liberator with a good deal of fanfare and gave the aircraft commander a thumbs-up. The ground crew steadied the hatch to welcome two passengers and the five-man flight crew to China Bay. The flight crew stood in a tight circle lighting cigarettes one after another. A mail bag was thrown from the aircraft.

With miracles and wisdom splashing about, both air crews moved off, declaring the Liberator, the Queenie II, was too long for the length of the matting, and except for the engine rattle, the whole affair was damned good flying.

There's a pair of cogs in civvies, Hardin thought. They might be Hawkes and McPhee.

"Damn, that was a rough landing," one said, coaching the other man away from the plane and around the plane's right wheel.

Out of necessity, keeping a low profile, Hardin frog-marched across the matting and crouched behind the chance-light. With his line of sight cleared, he tracked the flight crew as they approached the watchtower. The civilians ambled away from the aircraft and burrowed closer into cover near the base of the chance-light, five meters from Hardin.

"Mother's in trouble, Hawker," McPhee whispered. "If those low watts are pilots, she's in for bashing."

"She's been buggered for centuries." Taking a step forward, Hawkes cocked his head, extending his hand as though noting the chance-light.

Hawker must be Flying Officer Jeffery Hawkes, Hardin thought. And that sawn-off rat bag must be Uncle's harbormaster. I should be so lucky.

The way an animal skirts a fence, Hardin worked along the verge of the matting. Waiting until the last airman entered the flight operations building, he retraced the move, stepped onto the matting, and sank into a deep squat.

To relieve the pain in his thigh, he lowered his right knee to the ground and leveled the Thompson on McPhee's center of mass. In a triumph of instinct, he snapped the selector switch on the weapon to automatic fire.

The metallic tattoo rang cold, changing the tenor of the night.

Mindful of the crewman still on the plane, Hardin whispered, "Flying Officer Hawkes and Harbormaster McPhee, do stand still." The silence came with a question. "If you move, you won't take a second step." McPhee turned into the voice.

Tapping the airstrip's deck with the butt of his Thompson, Hardin said, "That's when almost all men die, Harbormaster—between steps."

With the wind freshening, Hawkes searched the periphery of the airstrip, seemingly fostering a knacker's sense of recognition. "Steady on, Robby. With the heft of that weapon, I'd wager the damn thing aims itself."

Hardin remained in a deep squat, hidden by the base of the chance-light. "Captain Corcoran believes you're in Singapore, Hawkes. Conducting a bit of business, he's paid you for—pounds sterling and dollars, I'm told."

Hardin waited as the remaining airman climbed out of the hatch and stopped in the spill of the plane's shadow to bum a light from McPhee. He saw Hawkes stiffen as McPhee's face caught the tail of his eye. Quick to form a trio, Hawkes pushed McPhee aside and offered the airman a light.

"Thanks for the lift, mate," Hawkes declared.

"No worries, mate. We're hoofed off to France—the lot of us—Advanced Air Striking Force needs a hand. Colombo first."

"Bash on, no matter," Hawkes yelled as the airman jogged away.

As with all thoughts unspoken, for the better part of seconds, Hawkes stared at McPhee's face. Shaking his head, he dropped his cigarette and crushed it with his boot. Watching Hawkes draw near McPhee, Hardin heard him say, "You stupid wank—you bloody, stupid blighter. I've a gram for you, Robby. The lad squatting near the cheeks of your brain, is Grumpy. He's put 'paid' to a good many accounts since he dropped off. He's packing a weapon with an automatic switch. If you run, Paddy, you'll be buried in a mound of elephant shit."

Ambient sounds increased in volume as the runway lights chased each other. The chance-light turned black, leaving the watchtower and the dispersal hut aglow. Within seconds, gulls and loons filled the air, landing on the airstrip's grass verge, the grass heavy with dew.

"I mean fair play, Hawker. The sodding bastard isn't worth the candle."

"Apologize, jackass—before I rip your bag off," Hawkes said, spitting the words.

McPhee's breathing became erratic.

Suddenly, deliberately, Hardin took a stride and slammed the butt of his Thompson into McPhee's balls. The harbormaster crumpled into a heap groaning and gasping for air, sprawled on the matting. Hawkes dropped into a squat and pulled McPhee's head and chest off the ground.

Alert, Hardin scrubbed his face. I might have to shoot the Paddy. Focusing on the watchtower, listening to a far-off sound—a lanyard's warning, a high-tone metallic twang, dinging the flagpole with a short and insistent meter. For Hardin, the rhythmic knell brought the dead—a call to muster for his mates.

Hawkes helped McPhee to his feet. "It's difficult to judge the recoil of some weapons, Robby—least said, soonest mended and all that. Speech mechanics might help your blunt mind." Hawkes's words came with a hesitant abrasive voice. "With your bag in sensitive health, throbbing with great thumps, I suggest you give silence a go."

Hawkes stepped aside with a nod and ushered Hardin to the fore.

Hardin handed McPhee a pack of cigarettes and Hawkes the pint of rum. "If you're looking for sympathy, McPhee, it's in the dictionary between shit and syphilis. Next time I'll shoot you." He grinned a guarded grin and moved a few feet away.

With a consoling gesture, Hawkes offered McPhee a slug of rum. "You see, Robby, your dribbling just got your tackle confused."

With McPhee coddling his equipment, and Hawkes coning the ash on his cigarette, Hardin decided to polish their piggish wits and help the immigrants focus. "This game has many facets, McPhee. Allowing you to be a shit bag isn't one of them."

Measuring the pilot's slack posture, Hardin continued. "I've been running Mother's ratline in Southeast Asia and the Bay of Bengal for nine weeks. My team's been butchered—three ambushes and a rucksack full of treachery."

Sensing hostility in McPhee's silence, Hardin pushed the Thompson's barrel against his midsection. Allowing the moment to be suspended, Hardin raised the barrel to McPhee's throat. "I'm done negotiating with rubbish like you. Molly's waiting for you, McPhee—in Colombo.

If you don't show for stand-to, you'll be dead within a week—or now, jackass, if it's a treat you're needing."

"Molly's a good mate," McPhee declared, his face twisted in disgust.

His face purpling with rum, Hawkes asked, "Well, Grumpy. May I call you Grumpy?" The pilot seemed to have lost his thought. "Ah, yes. You'll find the Irish are popular with themselves. You'll find with McPhee here; Irish lore is rich with residual fantasy—a perverted science if you like. Don't you agree, Robby?"

"Bugger off, arsehole."

As they had exploded into the night, the runway lights went out. McPhee turned with a lurch. Hawkes grabbed his shoulder. "Stay easy, Robby."

"Are there rations on that Lysander, Hawkes?" Hardin asked.

"Yes—the crate has quite a load, I'd say."

"Fill this parachute bag with as many rations as you can carry."

Drawing Hawkes and McPhee into the tall grass at the verge of the matting, Hardin dropped to one knee. "That Liberator's on its way to the RAF Base at Ratmalana, near Colombo. Get on it, McPhee. From the air base, make your way to Corcoran's steamer."

When McPhee didn't move, Hardin nudged him with his weapon. "Get on it and stay there."

"Shoot me, squaddie, and the whole base will know what you're on about."

"If I shoot you, I'll have to shoot Hawkes."

Hawkes took hold of McPhee's neck and threw him toward the aircraft. "On you go, Darkie. Get rusted to it." Turning toward Hardin, he said, "I'll get as many rations as I can carry."

After Hawkes was back on the ground, McPhee stuck his head out of the hatch. "It's good luck you'll be needing Hawker."

"Bang on, Darkie."

"Hawkes, you're coming with me to do a bit of flying—as a pilot." Not caring whether McPhee had the sand to stay in the chase, Hardin followed Hawkes into the jungle near the chance-light, the Thompson's barrel resting on his shoulder.

* * *

Colombo, Ceylon. Uncle's Steamer. 16 September 1939. 2010 Hours, GMT + 5.5 Hours.

With the tide ebbing at the bottom and the moon just past full, the harbor at Colombo, Ceylon, held starlight, the rancid smell of bilge and the insatiable revulsion of low careers. As India's night outruns her dawn, as merchants find their wares, sailors wake up in every livery and crack, stumbling from this door and that, measuring their step—downhill toward the harbor.

McPhee found the Portuguese steamer refueling and taking on stores. With his usual nonchalance, he mounted the gang, and the lights went out. Molly's fist landed on the side of his jaw the way a double jack strikes home.

Stabbing the collar of McPhee's coat with a docker's hook, Molly handed the hook to the nearest sailor. "Drag that Irish shit to the captain."

And drag they did—three sailors taking turns on the hook, allowing McPhee's feet to kick about. They left him on the saloon floor and drank gunfire—hot tea mixed with rum. An hour later, full of rum, they escorted one-each Irish shit to their captain.

Cleaning his weapon, Uncle tried to keep from laughing. "Good to see you're upright, harbormaster. I see a jack did a bit of backhauling on your jaw. Molly has some experimental loads for Olive Oil he wants to show you. You remember Olive—Molly's shotgun?"

Remaining silent, McPhee's knees collapsed as he sat—his face still and ridged. His lower jaw no longer favored his nose, and his teeth no longer meshed. This was Harbormaster McPhee's final hand, and he was a lousy gambler.

"Now then, harbormaster, there's the matter of the intel blokes Mother has sniffing after Snow White. The cane toads you were paid to neutralize. Scuttlebutt has them flying into China Bay last night on a hop from Port Blair. You owe me money, harbormaster—Molly, actually."

With a tone packed with studied insolence, McPhee barked, "Me and Hawkes were the blokes on that crate. Those blighty boys you fancy were done over. Skewered by a for-hire slag big enough to fill this room—a South African, says Hawkes. The ruthless bastard carved the agents open and spread their guts across a fancy suite, from the steam heater to the tub—in Raffles Hotel, no less."

"Where's Hawkes?"

"The South African killed an Imperial Guards Sergeant as well."

"Where's Hawkes?"

"You'll be knowing some bloke dropped a sight on us. Called himself, Grumpy. Ordered me onto a Lysander for this rendezvous, this jaw-jacking. He took Hawkes with him."

"What was this bloke wearing?"

As if caution had joined with laughter, McPhee hollered. "He's a jungle-slag. A bloody squaddie. In the dark he looked like a nig-nog." McPhee then described Hardin's weapon. "I'll be meeting the lad again."

Uncle snorted. "Grumpy's a changeling. A nasty sort—he'll kill you next time."

Molly entered the cabin carrying cups of coffee, measuring the cant to McPhee's bite.

Handing Uncle a coffee, he uprooted McPhee and set him on a locker next to the radio mount. "Your mug was begging a jacking, Paddy. Now that you're a rare card, the slappers will be strutting their twats."

Uncle huffed. "McPhee here needs mending, Molly. He needs to pass for Hardin. Clothes, hair—whatever needs adjusting."

"Half-a-meter first off—plus balls and a cock."

"Be helpful, Molly."

Uncle Dingo drew a light rag through the rear sight of his Webley MK4 revolver and blew lint from the cylinder. Dropping a round into place, he held the mauve cartridge-issue box and read the label. "'Twelve cartridges; revolver, .380 inch, 24 June 1939, M.Q.' —looks like the right ammunition."

Easing himself to a safe distance from Molly, McPhee asked, "And who would Hardin be?"

Uncle set his revolver on the radio mount. "Captain Edward Hardin. He comes from the fens of Wales and the tin mines of Cornwall—from the 1st Duke of Cornwall's Light Infantry and the commercial docks of New York City. He's the lad you met on the airstrip in China Bay.

"Captain Hardin is Grumpy—Operation Snow White's surviving bush-ranger. He's the lad your South African and Mother's weans mean to kill. We're going to help him get to England."

"Snow White's having an operation, is she?"

McPhee's notions seemed to be hanging at full length. Molly gave him a quick feint to the jaw, causing the Irishman to fall into the chart table. Grunting, giving his courting tackle a vigorous boost, Molly said, "Grumpy's bigger than your runty half-jar, Paddy—hands as big as butcher blocks."

*　*　*

China Bay, Ceylon. 26 Squadron RAF.
17 September 1939. 0200 Hours, GMT + 5.5 Hours.

Hardin needed dry clothes—and a gallon of tar-pot coffee. "Damn this yellow jack." He set his hand against the tree trunk and tried to stand. Halfway up, he fell backwards.

The day before, he searched the clearings and the jungle to the east and west along the beach. With no outposts or roving sentries, and no evidence that RAF China Bay was worried about a Japanese invasion, he knew his presence in China Bay was secure.

"Come on, Doc, get off the ground," he said to himself.

"You've got malaria, cobber," Hawkes chimed. "A chilling fever comes with Burma's dragon, any time of day. I'll escort you to water as soon as I can see the ground."

Dangerously dehydrated, Hardin had to reach the pool even if he had to crawl across the open runway. If he burnt dry, his sweat controls would shut down, and he would die within spitting distance of a British aerodrome, fresh out of spit.

Thankfully the air was wet—it was always wet.

Smelling the air, a sweet drift of rain swept in from the bay. A squall played along the beach. Hardin set his cup at the outfall of a large leaf to gather water. He held another leaf to his mouth. Within minutes, fifteen minutes, sweat began to bead on his forehead.

Bathing in a putrid sweat, his temperature steady, he peered through the vines.

Captain Hardin had been over the mountains and through the jungles of the whole of Southeast Asia and more than once had been on both ends of automatic-weapons fire. Rugged and tall, with a face the cut of chattered boot leather, he sat demolishing a can of bully beef and washing it down with rainwater. Seven thousand miles from England, toggled to a cashiered pilot, a stranger he must count on.

The mist enveloping the landing strip undulated like a delicate scarf; a fine, light yellow mist set aglow by the lights of the watchtower. A fog rose from the runway matting, creating a layer of cloud twenty meters high.

The sky was a mix of dark grays atop a black void that was the jungle canopy.

Finished eating, he took stock of Hawkes's worth. Comfortable, the pilot seemed to favor an unworried grin. As if relaxed, Hawkes described the murder scene in Raffles Hotel, emphasizing the ruthless nature of the killer.

"Von Cleve's the man's name—a South African with a pair of strange eyes. I'll not forget those eyes. I met him in Kuala Lumpur, where he played at being a banker. He's a banker of sorts—a for-hire sod with his Templar cross."

"I've seen that cross on some high-born—in England. Does he know where you are?" Hardin asked. "Or if you're flying again?"

"He might. I don't know." Hawkes stepped into the light of the watchtower. "He's a clever one, that one. If he's chasing you, he'll catch you."

Cupping his hands to hide the glow of his cigarette, Hardin took a long drag. Soaking wet, shivering, he lost his balance. Suddenly shaking, chills ran over the whole of his frame. He reached for the pouch, missed it, and fell through a tangle of vines.

The Atta-Boys he took to fight malaria had come too late.

Dreaming, his mental frame-shop held a snap of the instant Tu's machete entered the Dutchman's skull. The assassin's left hand held the front grip of his French Thompson, swinging the weapon to fire. His right forearm was exposed. Captured for all time, in still frame, shone the symbol of a justified Christian—an eight-pointed cross tattooed in red.

The sequence did not stop. For hours, the Dutchman kept dying, again and again. The man had eyes like a cannon's bore—crosshairs centered in the backlight of long black tubes.

With a flash of light Hardin saw himself hiding in a clump of bamboo. The Java boys were still raping Tu. Her father was screaming, yet his mouth was closed.

Weak and exhausted, Hardin's vision gradually cleared. The air was heavy with heat. Covered in mud, he waited. For what, he did not know. Behind him, in a tunnel of grief, the confusion of the ambush played on.

Tu's jungle came alive, the sounds of the monsoon and the echoes—the ambient echoes.

Finally awake, free of his recall, Hardin shook at the chill in his chest. At first, he did not know where he was. He was near a small harbor. Near an airstrip. A golden mist was drifting through the palm fronds overhead.

Hardin's face was streaked with mud. Flying Officer Hawkes grinned. Sitting up, Hardin searched the jungle near the chance-light.

"You're a hard case, Grumpy."

"Well flyboy, you didn't run. Are you in for the haul?"

Handing the weapon to Hardin stock first, Hawkes put in. "Watching you is amusing.

For me it was you and your brace of shakes, or China Bay's stockade."

"These dribblers are too bloody fancy to have a stockade."

Hawkes sighed and stood. "Well squaddie, you've acquired a special kind of luster, mixing malaria with yellow jack fever. I want to bask in the glow."

"You find that entertaining, do you?"

"A challenge is what it is. The Royal Navy Medical Service has a hospital in Trincomalee."

"A stockade of sorts."

Scanning the airstrip, Hardin marveled at the glow above the mist in the east. The beauty of the jungle at dawn was unmatched—a time when the morning mist eddies from the trees and the air begins to vibrate with the heat—a time when the ambient noise of the vegetation warns of the jungle's mood. A hundred yards beyond the freshwater pool, a sloping hill showed blacker in the gray of dawn.

"Before McPhee and I left Singapore, the Alexander Barrack Guards arrested some bloke for the killings at Raffles. He'd been shot in both knees."

"What's the bloke's name?" Hardin took a deep breath, welcoming a shaft of cool air.

"Sounded French."

"Changi Prison has a hospital of sorts—Roberts Hospital." Hardin was relieved. He found Lucien's fate ironic. The consummate soldier, the Frenchman always played his hand with abandon. With this turn he would die a stranger. "Lucien's a Yank. He's one of the jack-wagons trying to kill me."

"Lucien sounds right." Hawkes pulled Hardin to his feet. "Thanks to this jaunt of yours, and Corcoran's rusty steamer, Singapore and the Andaman Islands are off limits for me. To get out of the Bay of Bengal region, I've got to steal an airplane. To do that, we need to drink with the lads flying the Vickers."

"You're out of whiskey, and I'm out of water," Hardin said, bending to pick up the pouch. His left kidney ached and seemed heavy.

With a glance to check for the dung-removal crew, he stepped onto the western edge of the airstrip, using the foliage to hide his frame. Instantly the hair on his neck bristled. Hardin's fisherman was standing near the flight operations shack scanning the area near the chance-light with binoculars.

"What does that bastard want?" Ducking into the jungle, Hardin started busting brush. The four-hundred-meter trek to the freshwater pool seemed a mile.

Stirring the pool to hide his face, drinking a few swallows, he sat onto his left haunch. Kneeling near a cluster of large, fresh cat tracks, he snapped the selector switch on his weapon to automatic fire, and waited, signaling Hawkes to be still.

The tiger hung in the air as if on strings, ten meters from Hawkes.

The roar of the Thompson consumed the space beneath the canopy, each round exploding as if shot from a piston-driven plunger, each round pounding the tiger's side as it fell away from Hawkes's body.

Visibly shaken, Hawkes walked around the cat's body. "Bloody hell. I didn't hear a sound. Look at the size of that monster." Examining the cat's front paw, he ran his thumb and forefinger along a claw. "Five hundred pounds. Six if he chewed off my tackle."

"Your tackle weigh that much?"

"Ask any Abigail."

With his eyes scramble sharp, Hardin stroked the smooth stock of his weapon—the sudden Thompson. He found himself between laughter and tears.

"The cat likes whiskey-soaked pilots." Hardin sank into a squat.

Hawkes was shaking and sweating. "I'd have a piss if I could find my balls."

"That cat owned this pool." Hardin hurriedly picked up the empty shell casings. "Muster your bag, pilot. We've got to get to town."

It took sixteen hours to trek around the airbase and reach the town of Trincomalee.

With pilots and missions changing daily, flight-operations China Bay greeted each new flyer as a fresh experience. Hawkes introduced Hardin as a returning ranker from Z-Special Force, and himself as himself. After excusing Hardin's torn and scarred uniform, he choreographed his antics while interrupting the football match on the pitch in Kuala Lumpur as a legend twice told.

Swelling in the wretched heat, his tale of derring-do focused on his slightly tight flying skills, and on Chennault's attempts to have him shot.

Providing a back-slapping reception at the lesser venues in China Bay, Hawkes found his mark sitting at the bar in the Welcombe Hotel, in Trincomalee—another pilot officer who worshiped his drink, a vainglorious, credulous apprentice.

Too drunk to stand, with his cock tin hatted, the apprentice pilot snorted his delight while his whistle bait joyously jumped to conclusions, hollering with glee, enjoining the moon. Hawkes and Hardin eased into the pilot's bungalow with the girl watching them, hollering, and slapping her prize, then closing his cheeks with both hands and twisting his head into a pillow.

The tart commissioned to play with the pilot was monkey-wrenching the blue job's balls when Hawkes took the pilot's identity disc and uniform.

*   *   *

Bombay, India. Templar Compound. 17 September 1939. High-Noon, GMT + 5.5 Hours.

Amused by the world's growing shaft-alley system of barter, von Cleve believed any agreement between a scoundrel and a gentleman favored the scoundrel. And so, the Nazis set the Junkers of Prussia and the Jews of Europe on the southbound roads to hell.

Shocked and humiliated, these pilgrims expect the tracks of common decency to be cleared. With their chests branded and their property and gold confiscated, they'll scurry from hovel to hovel, disheartened successively.

Marseille was a city littered with worn-out shoes.

Von Cleve worked the world over as it stumbled from one sovereign declaration to the next, pausing every few months to gain perspective. His team in Yugoslavia had been executed, for what he did not know. His team in Poland had gone underground and fled to Sweden. His political contacts throughout Europe were stretched and some were evaporating. Many, no most were wealthy Jews.

His French team had joined a Resistance cell headquartered in Casablanca.

Dr. Schacht, Hitler's banker since 1933, had proposed a sequence of sovereign-barters that proved he was a devious scoundrel. Von Cleve had laughed when country after country, in a fit of relief, announced the remedy they preferred, ceding their sovereignty.

"These countries are stupidly welcoming the Nazis." Von Cleve talked to himself to create a sanctuary for reflections. "Poland and the low countries will be mere impediments. The Germans will eventually control the Baltic, the North Sea, the English Channel, and the Suez. Raw-product shipping lanes."

Austria bartered her gold and her exports to the Nazis for sovereignty. Romania bartered her oil and her exports to the Nazis for sovereignty. And Yugoslavia bartered her copper and her exports to the Nazis for airplanes— one hundred airplanes. All in good faith, gentlemen signed agreements with the world's leading drug addict.

Von Cleve thought of himself as a gentleman's contractor, a man sworn to honor his commitments. He had promised three powerful organizations, Compensation Brokers Ltd., the Vatican, and the Thule—merchant bankers, the church, and the occult—he would retrieve sensitive documents lost in Southeast Asia.

He had taken their money—their gold.

Having failed to intercept the documents in Burma, and losing his trackers in the process, he cut his ties to Lucien. He crippled the Frenchman and set him in the frame for killing the British operatives in Singapore.

I don't know if the men I killed worked for England, he thought. If they did, England's MI6 has blood and money involved in retrieving those documents.

The entrance to the Templar compound in Bombay was hidden from the roadway. The stonework, the finest to be found in western India, marked an edifice of flowers and light, the home of wealthy merchants. Breathing deeply to ease the tension, as if the harsh reality of this sanctuary might blossom, von Cleve pushed a worn entry stone into a canted recess. The muffled rush of water falling into a cistern played its music. The weight transfer drew a stone door aside exposing a chiseled, rose-colored, granite, cross-shaped slab.

His way wrapped in a shivering coziness, and a cascade of bougainvillea mixed with lavender, enjoying the scent, he meandered along a tunneled pathway between a pair of winding mosaic walls, admiring the arbor's structure and its brindled stone. Anticipation rode his shoulders as he prepared to defend his fate.

Crilley's questioning in Calcutta had been a dangerous game. At this juncture, von Cleve had a clear idea of life's sums. As he had eliminated Lucien from the game, Crilley seemed ready to eliminate von Cleve.

Stopping, he listened to stone grinding on stone. The entry reset itself with the doom of a heavy soul. Drums sounded from opposite reaches of the cloister. The pathway's mossy verge was springy, and root veined beneath his feet.

A stone-encased ambulatory extended to the right and to the left, each arched hollow featuring the outline of a dark-brown robe. Confined, von Cleve traversed a series of small, cross-shaped slabs leading to the center of the cloister. He stopped and waited for his eyes to sort the gloom inside. If Crilley meant to kill him, the attack would be immediate.

Von Cleve stepped from the arbor. The sky broke open—the color of lemons. Climbing a short flight of steps, he noted Crilley's inability to adjust his conclusions. In a silent, studied motion von Cleve remained cautious—he had to appear comfortable while keeping track of the man's hands.

Crilley stood erect, as if a statue—five meters away.

Judging the mood of this dispassionate assassin, given Crilley's cold, placid, lifeless face, von Cleve knew no man's eyes gave off light—Crilley's were no exception.

Crilley shifted his head back. His expression belied a hint of isolation, his ire. His eyes remained centered on his visitor. "Welcome to Bom Bhaia, Alex."

With equal ceremony, searching at his back, von Cleve set his hand to his dagger. "Lucien's been dealt with. Unfortunately, he had arranged to sell the documents to the drug cartel he works with in the Neck of southern Burma. He'll die beyond notice, I expect—Changi Prison, perhaps."

"Changi's been confirmed. His knees are in pieces. He cannot stand." Crilley gestured to a stone bench and sat down. "Your tactical loose ends are few."

"Perhaps..." Von Cleve searched the cloister's garden. The sun's rays broke in linear patterns through the expansive trellis. "Exchanging gifts with that steamer does not interest me."

"It should. Sir Nigel Stuart's gone missing." A harsh note crept into Crilley's voice. "We believe he's on that boat."

In a calm, acidic voice, von Cleve gathered Crilley's ignorance. "The Brits will continue to hunt for the lone survivor of their special-operations team—not to secure his safe passage, but for the documents in the pouch he's carrying. If Stuart gets in their way, they'll kill him too."

"As danger grows, the British become less nervous; when it's imminent, they are fierce; when it's mortal, they are fearless."

Crilley's right hand dropped to his right ankle. Reacting, von Cleve landed several meters from the bench. From nowhere, the Malay Creese appeared in his right hand, held low with the cutting edge up. Warily, he started forward. Crilley extended his hands away from his body and placed them, palm down on his knees, his manner unaffected by von Cleve's move.

Robed men, the mullions of Crilley's frame, ran toward Crilley from separate directions. "Stand fast," Crilley ordered. With the wave of his hand the monks disappeared. A stirring followed their footsteps. A large monk remained.

As if rising from the ground, the monks reappeared arrayed as one. The large monk stood in front of them wearing a white tropical habit. He was holding a sandalwood box.

Stepping forward, acknowledging von Cleve's keepers, Crilley whispered, "That steamer's the only target we have not rinsed out. The documents are on that steamer if they exist at all."

Raising a pant leg, Crilley unsheathed a knife and threw it. The knife turned twice, missing von Cleve's head by the width of the blade. With the dull pitch of a hammer driving a wooded peg, the knife found the sandalwood box—the knife's blade vibrating as though a tuning fork. White and brown clad monks stood still as if nothing had happened.

With a voice that seemed confined, Crilley spoke, stirring the water in an oval pond, drawing a wave to the edge as if his mind had found itself.

"That British special-operations team is of no import to our fiduciary." Crilley handed von Cleve a folder. "Our intelligence operative in Cairo identified one of the men. That's a picture of a commando—Captain Edward Hardin. He was the team leader for England's Operation Snow White. His operational code sign is Doc. Our intel group think he escaped Burma with the documents you are chasing."

"Am I the only man here chasing these documents? If they exist, how do we know Doc has the documents? Or that he's alive?"

"Before Lucien went to Singapore, he interrogated a fisherman who hired his boat to the commando near Mergui, Burma. The fisherman took a soldier and a young native girl to meet a small coastal pirate vessel. Ross Island was mentioned as their destination. The soldier fit Captain Hardin's description. And he was carrying a sealed leather pouch."

"Lying. That's Lucien's specialty!" Von Cleve became strident. "If that commando had a pouch, it would have been hidden inside his rucksack."

A white clad monk placed the sandalwood box at Crilley's side and walked away.

"We tracked the steamer to Colombo, Ceylon."

Watching Crilley draw his knife and push the sandalwood box away from his hip, von Cleve braced in place. "Lucien solicited a third-party contract for retrieving the documents—with a drug cartel. If that squaddie got out of Burma, he was on that steamer. By now he must be on foot and that sailor's using his steamer as a blind."

"That could be the reason the steamer diverted to Ceylon." Crilley laid his knife on his right thigh. "The ship's captain doesn't trust his minders. Our intelligence network monitored wireless intercepts out of Malta confirming MI6 as the money source—over a million pounds."

"A rogue agent in MI6?" Von Cleve's caution had joined with an idea. "A spy?" He decided to earnestly agree with Crilley's conclusions. To buy time.

Understanding Crilley's inflexible nature, von Cleve's comments and answers had been measured. Weary from his travels, his expression creased through a quiet sigh. "Ion, that soldier's a hard man. Wounded, he's run for weeks through a monsoon-laden jungle and killed two world-class trackers."

Scanning the perimeter of the cloister, he continued. "The witless in England who are responsible for this soldier's travails should pray he never learns their names. Your spy's a bit of fluff compared with this man. If he unties the operational knot, he will kill anyone in the frame."

For a long chilling moment Crilley kept his eyes on the sandalwood box. "I have counseled Compensation Brokers, Ltd., to remain calm, to no avail. I told them we located the documents."

Noting a slight hesitation in Crilley's voice, von Cleve raised a finger. "Lies and logic aside, these bankers are a waning moon—the sons of rich cowards. Heighten a banker's fear, and he becomes more pliable. If not Lord Norman, hang his consort, Gordon Dewar. Or better, hang a midlevel banker—a Speyer or a von Schroder."

Drawing his eyes into narrow slits, knowing such hangings had been scheduled, Crilley offered von Cleve a veiled ultimatum. "The Thule and the Warburg Institute were informed yesterday that we have located the soldier who has the documents and will complete the contract in the next few days. The Vatican no longer seem worried by these documents."

"I don't know if I'm worried or not. But a week's not possible." When von Cleve reached for the sandalwood box an arrow stuck in the post where his head had been. "Jesus, Crilley. You Bodmin bitch. You haven't even located the soldier. And if you do, you won't tell me. You are setting me up. Putting a target on my back. Why else would you look up my clients?"

"And thereby hangs the tale. Your exposure is of your own doing. Time wears on."

"Does the Thule have resources in Bombay?"

"Of course," Crilley declared. "After we eliminated Thule operatives in Diamond Harbor, the order paid us a fee in excess of our demand, and their suspicions that we are dealing with other parties' lost urgency."

"They killed a monk—a man of God."

"Yes! Now, as cold as charity, they want my help, and you dead."

Von Cleve snatched Crilley's knife from his thigh and offered it to him, blade first. "One of your archers will have to do your work." When Crilley didn't reach for the knife, von Cleve threw it in the pond. "The Thule will have sailors in need of work. Lascars from the Indian Merchant Navy would be best. Have an oiler and a coal trimmer queue up for that steamer when she docks in Bombay. The Indian Ocean can be rough this time of year."

*   *   *

China Bay, Ceylon. 26 Squadron RAF.
18 September 1939. 0230 Hours, GMT + 5.5 Hours.

Standing on the tarmac, identifying the three Vickers Vildebeest IV's on ten-minute standby, fueled and loaded with bullets, Hawkes's mission was down to finding enough booze to smooth his kinks and muster his senses.

At 0230 hours, Hawkes and Hardin were wheels up on a routine coastal-patrol mission.

Heading for the RAF Aerodrome on Worli Island, in southern Bombay, Hawkes nipped at his flask, convinced the sauce made him a better pilot. He hated India—that patch of hell where filth and slavery met in a disused church.

Worli Base, the home of 24 Squadron RAF, remained the Royal Navy's worst posting—a sodding scab located on Worli, one of the seven islands reclaimed to form Bombay City.

"Worli's famous for a pair of odds," Hawkes proclaimed. "The first is the Tower of Silence, where the local Parsi take their dead to be eaten by vultures. The second, the island has the only racetrack in the world where the horses run clockwise."

"Is Worli Base near the vulture's pantry?"

"No! Other side of the island. It's an RAF transit camp. If we're lucky we can just become another temporary hire. There's bound to be lots of comings and goings."

"Why are you helping me, Hawkes?"

"I'm not. You're just a Welsh squaddie who needs a lift." Nipping his flask, Hawkes set the stopper. "I'm taking you to England because I'm on my way to join Mother's Air Striking Force. In France if she'll have me. If she's a tart, I'll be in prison—compliments of MI5 at Wormwood Scrubs."

"With your eyes swimming in booze, this operation might not end well."

Admiring his flask, Hawkes smiled. "Stealing Mother's airplanes is a game she'll hang me for. Time will tell, old boy. If you keep my flask full, I'll be able to drive."

After five hours of flying, running on fumes while carving holes in the night sky above Worli Base, Hawkes followed a Lysander into its short-final approach to the airstrip. Avoiding the runway lights, he set the Vickers on the verge in a patch of tall grass and cut to an apron along the side of a darkened hangar.

He thumped the fuel gauge with a stubby finger. The needle didn't move. Parked well down the flights from the watchtower, near an isolated maintenance bay, the Vickers needed petrol.

"I can speak an airframe fitter's language." Larceny in full swing. Hawkes laughed. "Give me some of Corcoran's money. I'll find us some juice."

"Get some food."

Fifty minutes later, his grin marked with simple delight, Hawkes arrived at the maintenance bay riding the fender of a 1938 Bedford Bowser brimming with 100-octane gasoline—gravy for the Vickers. Haggling for an age, with Hawkes trying to outfox a fair-haired chief airframe fitter, the mechanic settled for a spiff of fifty pounds to top off the biplane.

"Your nameplate says you're Longley." Hardin tapped the fitter's chest.

"Cullen Longley if you need the whole of it."

Hardin studied the watchtower for several seconds before his gaze returned to the fitter as if deciding what Longley intended. Does the fitter want to roll Hawkes over to his section chief? Or does he want the money?

Hardin didn't trust the man. We will see if Longley needs the adventure.

Sheltered by the weight of fifty pounds, the fitter pulled a bundle from the cab of the Bowser and presented Hawkes with two Irvin jackets lined with fleece, the RAF Eagle, the Shitehawk, on the shoulder badges, the breastplates adorned with a small pin—a caterpillar.

Longley gave his nose a twist, stuck his finger through a blue ring of cigarette smoke, swirling the last ring into a spiral. "The pilots those Irvin jacket's belonged to were members of the exclusive Caterpillar Club—prop-jockeys who bailed out. The caterpillar and silk being the link."

Their faculties minced with larceny, an airframe fitter, a pilot, and Mother's latest complaint jabbered like jay birds.

"Are these jackets bad luck?" Hawkes asked, admiring the caterpillar pins as he measured the fitter's grin. "I mean fair play, are these lads still flying?"

Adorning his expression with great innocence and a cheek-filled show of nonchalance, Longley cleared his throat. "Those bus drivers were pictured in the RAF's, *Tee EM* magazine last month—in the 'Lessons Learned' section. They were placed in jankers for pilfering the Squadron Commander's victuals, being clobbered on the Old Man's wine, and practicing landings on the Old Man's tart in the Old Man's quarters. They were shipped out the next day.

"They're in France dodging those flaming onions the Kaiser uses to paint the sky."

"And I got the door for a lousy cart-up landing that rattled a football match." Hawkes's tone offered as much disgust as the whiskey allowed. "Or did I hit civvy street because I'm a guzzling lout, farting the periods as I speak?"

Hardin could only grin. "You do drink a lot of booze, fly boy."

"Nobody checks this end of the flights." Longley went on, scanning the airfield. "Roll your kite into the brush and put that camouflage net over her. You're down the flights to the end. The chance-light's just there."

"Hawkes let's leave this shit hole. Let's take off before it gets dark."

"There's a flap on just now," Longley chimed. "Flying Officer Hawkes's mug is plastered on 26 Squadron's ready board. I believe the orders are clear, shoot on sight. The short of it—China Bay has a Vickers searching for your bird. Colombo has a Spitfire from Special Survey Flight—Number 2 Camouflage Unit—searching. And Heston Flight has a Beech searching."

The mere prospect of flying without a proper ration of whiskey left Hawkes juddering.

"I'm done over, cobber. Even with a scam, let's give this tin basher his due—tiggerty-boo." Wagging a finger, he pillowed his head in the fleece of his new jacket.

Comfortable, he declared the obvious. "First off, I need sleep."

"Where to in this paper kite?" Longley asked. "Must be a short hop—north or east."

"West," Hardin blurted, instantly stupid.

"You'll be in the drink." Longley offered Hawkes another cigarette.

Mistrust set its cap in Hawkes's eye. Kensitas Cigarettes were rare indeed. The chief fitter's a drummer. He's a scrounger. Hawkes was excited.

A half hour passed with jabs of small talk before Hawkes could muster a thought. "Here's a rattle." Handing Longley, a twenty-pound note, his expression reflecting an ample amount of larceny, he asked, "Can a wrench like you procure good food and decent whiskey?"

"I can. Stay out of sight. This maintenance bay's storing a Wellington on the signed-off charge inside. I don't know why the RAF has that kite red lined. The crate's in good shape. It's equipped with an overload tank."

Still measuring the fitter's sail, Hawkes pointed at the Wellington. "Does she fly?"

"Wimpey suffers from the riddles of technology, I'm afraid. She's an agile sprite. The bird has her gremlins. She has her sense of occasion—goes unserviceable without a hint—all three lights go red. I gave her a formal forty-hour inspection. Pitch controls, magnetos, petrol cocks, flaps, compass, gyros…there's not a rivet out of place—nothing I could find."

Hawkes threw his head back with a laugh. "I knew a woman like that once."

"Was it Abby's pitch controls or her petrol cocks?" Hardin had to ask.

"T'was the flaps on her magneto."

Yep. She's the bird I wanted to marry. She had a bit of a shudder as I recall."

"Good you're an agile lad. She'd have worn you to a whisper."

With a quick nudge of his balls, Longley searched across the airfield at a blinking light, and frowned as if unsure of its meaning. Pausing before he started toward the Bowser, he raised idea's hand, and turned into a grin. "The lights on that kite were in the green when she flew in. Juice will cost you lads another three hundred quid."

"Let's make it three hundred quid for the crate, two large Sidcot flying suits, two parachutes, and four bottles of the Old Man's whiskey," Hawkes emphasized his request with his hands.

Looking across the airfield, humor pounced on Longley, and he began to dance. "Flying Officer Hawkes, you are a blistering sot."

Singing a furtive limerick, "The long, the short, and the tall," while filling the Wellington's tanks in the dark, left Longley with a mischievous grin. "The old Bowser's damned near empty," he declared, holstering the nozzle.

"Will the engines on this lovely turn over?" Hawkes asked.

"The trolley's accumulator will flash up the old bird."

"Whiskey first."

*   *   *

Germany. Bad Reichenhall, Bavaria.
18 September 1939. 1850 Hours, GMT + 1 Hour.

Petra tried to match her father's stride. The stride she remembered. The long loping steps she remembered—her chest out, her head held high. Her attempt didn't last. She was too cold. Her memories of summer, the ring of an empty pail, the lowing of the cows, these were gone now. Her wool shawl was soaked and pulled her frame to a forward lean.

For weeks, she had thought of old fences, yesterday's winds, the fields, the flowers, the cows. Ever homesick, her eyes sought distant pools.

Storms came to the Alps from north and south. Granite spires clashed throwing bolts of lightning through clouds so black, the light shown in striated shades of gray, tinted with angry clusters of dense, frozen water. Once a placid mountain valley with cows and children adorning the fields, cropping grass, and bunching edelweiss, her home was an enclave, girding for the ravages of the Nazi storm.

This storm was more violent than any Petra remembered.

An old tree fell without a fuss.

In the heart of the valley, where tors faced off and relieved their harshness of size by sheltering the farms with their shoulders of granite. Here Petra had rested; her childhood had drowsed. Torrid sheets of water now burst from the rocks that defined her youth.

Petra wanted to visit her father's grave without her brother knowing she was in the valley. Walking at first, a squall nearly knocked her off the path. The church was a kilometer from the train station, up a small hill.

A lightning bolt flashed above the spire exposing the jagged arc of the horizon. For an instant, the tors stood aloof, unmolested. Then, the lightning climbed the granite faces: splintering clouds along the way. The wind stirred and grew stronger and struck across the field.

Petra stumbled on the verge of the roadway and fell into a tangle of gooseberry bushes. She shook her head and screamed. Her spontaneous anger was followed by a rush of boisterous chatter. She was covered with mud, and her Shetland sweater was filled with bits of bramble.

Thunder touched one rock face, cracked against the next, barging down the valley, playing arduous music. Dark and even darker greens defined the valley—trees and grass and leaves gripped the valley floor. The river was cresting.

Drenched with layers of sleet, Petra turned from the roadway and ran through a field. And then there was the wind—withering trees as fence rails quivered. Water flew from the tree limbs.

The stone, arched, lych-gate at the entrance to the churchyard measured three meters at its crown and two for its waist. The gray-flecked granite was green and brown with moss. Bracken lined the base of the wall; burdock choked the flagged granite entry slabs. Dead leaves clung to a wrought-iron cross.

The priory notice board was blank.

Looking for her father's tombstone, the graveyard of the old church seemed alive with mischief, as though one memory and another had decided to trade—a footman for a railway man, a rapist for a thief. Flashes of lightning highlighted one gravestone after another.

There was a new head stone near the south wall.

Light and dark storm clouds seemed to join near the church—death's after-mark, tawny and encrusted with purposeful streaks. In the corner a tinker was trading with a tailor.

And yes, there was the new grave, a man beaten of his dream. Her father. A ceremonial expression of sadness and relief consumed Petra. Her father had been ill for years. It had started with pain in his joints. With his feet swelling, eventually he could not walk.

The priest waved to her from the church, beckoning her to come in.

Mud found Petra's boots, and water soaked their seams—the mud of a fresh grave—the best of muds. Surely God was aware of the mud. Comforting, the bright granite headstone, free of lichen and mold, shone a bright spark in the rear rank of Christendom.

Sobbing, Petra touched the top of the stone. An emotional sureness set her heart to full cycle. The stone held numbers and her father's name—her woodcarver's name; the words crisp and clear, the letters and numbers splashing with rain.

No more was needed. The engravings illumined the past with tender sentiment.

My dear father must be wet and cold. I can't believe he's not thinking anymore, weighing his oilskin tobacco pouch, stoking his charred briar pipe, scratching his cheek with its stem, testing a knife's edge, a figure in his eye.

A warning light hung in the recess of Petra's grief as she entered the church. The priest wrapped a blanket around her shoulders and told her the story.

A week had passed since Manfred Laube-Heintz quit his job carving the intricate Bavarian scenes, the cultural details for Hitler's Eagles Nest. Nearly finished with his contract, three small woodcarvings of farm scenes remained, a confrontation with the foreman over his workmanship and pay, followed by a confrontation with his SS supervisor over his conduct, left Manfred no leeway. He assembled his tools in a leather holdall and returned to his farm.

Manfred Laube-Heintz was hanged in his barn by the Gestapo, by his eldest son, Karl.

The priest whispered to Petra. "Karl raped a twelve-year-old girl in Bad Reichenhall. Some say as many as four. His SS uniform gives him illusions. He shouts and dances widdershins around the church." The sharpness of his words was an index of his quest for retribution.

"I was twelve when he tried for me."

"The girls have vanished. I believe they were sold."

Holding her mother, Petra was shaken. She was afraid of her brother. Drying her clothes near the fire, drawing at the scent of paraffin, wet fir boughs, and fresh pitch, a shiver climbed from her thighs through her frame.

Sensing her mother's fear, she picked up a Nazi uniform jacket with a darning needle stuck in its shoulder, and asked, "Does Karl come here?"

"Karl goes where he wants these days."

The wind continued to howl, and thunder echoed down the valley. Something slammed against the window shutter. Petra dropped the blanket and set the iron bar across the door. Cold air pushed through the cracks on the sides of the window.

Each time Petra looked at her mother, she found worry in her eye. It had rarely been so. She drew her mother near the fire.

Remembering fragments of her youth, one memory was clear. When her father caught Karl tearing off her clothes in the barn, he beat Karl with an oiled leather harness strap—the same harness strap Karl knotted and hung his father with—in the barn.

A trembling hand cradled Petra's cheek, and a cracked, wrinkled thumb wiped at her tears. Against the low light, she tried to weigh her mother's grief. Her mother appeared frail.

With her hair cast against the fire's medley, her mother made a heavy swallowing sound, and said, "Karl has a driver now, Petra. He rides in a black sedan giving orders and demanding attention. Some men are evil, Petra. The Fuehrer is evil. Karl isn't altogether bad."

"The priest knows young girls from the valley have vanished?"

"Ja! You must leave. Karl's heart is spoilt. Sometimes he eats breakfast here. If I know what I feel, he's not finished with you Petra."

*　*　*

Bombay Harbor, India. Uncle's Tramp Steamer.
19 September 1939. 1830 Hours, GMT + 5.5 Hours.

Lashed to the cast-iron mooring bollard on the front apron of Victoria Dock, north of Carnac Basin in Bombay harbor, the tramp steamer sat facing south—motionless in the pale-brown water of a flat bay. The harbor, normally laden this time of year with debris distilled from inland carnage, had been rinsed by an irregular surge of clear upland flow.

The essence of the harbor remained one of weary making. Chit-coolies ran from quay to quay waving messages, dingoes dressed in rags.

Uncle was hyper-alert. The air didn't feel right, the day a bit pear-shaped.

Squinting into the sun, focusing on the horizon beyond the city, he found solace—setting nature's cap to the bustling traffic of the waterfront. The serenity of the far-off scape ran counter to the wet harvest that defined Bombay's docks. Infested with rushing gharries and frantic street coolies vibrating with the unrest reminiscent of an ant heap, the docks were pure bedlam.

For a half hour plus twenty, the dock bulls, garbage passers, and lesser wharfies scurried like raft spiders along the front apron, bolting from hither to yon in a human leach pool.

An outcast in the thinning crowd near Victoria Dock, Molly strode all aback with certain delight, back-hauling two bodies. Temporary seamen, lascars, Uncle thought; ticklers.

Tracking a small raft of garbage as it found a path between the steamer and the quayside, Uncle stepped to his left and slipped on an oily rag, barely catching his fall. A fire bit his forearm as he fell over a stanchion, praising his sudden fright with a bit of mild god-bobbing.

Suddenly, with startling clarity, the snapping sound of a bullet burning the edge of his ear caused Uncle to twist away. A second bullet ricocheted off the rail where his hands had been and rammed into the bulkhead above his head, followed by the report of a second rifle shot.

Scrambling across the boat deck, he dove behind a canvas dodger. The sniper had fired from a rooftop in Black Town, west of the harbor strand. Twice Uncle started to rise. Twice he counseled himself for patience. Sheltered by hatch covers and a steam-pipe housing, he ducked into a companionway.

With bunkering under way, he sat in the chart room drinking rum. Stiff and sore, Uncle dabbed at the bullet crease across his forearm. With vengeance suspended above the ghetto of Black Town, he considered trying to find the shooter but gave up.

Nigel's dotards just tried to kill me.

First obscure and now elusive, for Uncle the shooter was no longer a ghost—no longer an abstraction—and his mission should have been obvious. Kill the ship's captain and the vessel would remain in Bombay Harbor until a new man signed on. Meanwhile, Sir Nigel would be rescued and launch an investigation, claiming Uncle had gone off the rails, was harboring a fugitive and was guilty of treason.

Unsure of the depth of the treason, Sir Nigel will demand the Traitor's Gate for all my crew, and, if alive, I will be put in chains in a Royal Navy stockade, in India, and left to rot.

Molly will steal into the sewers of Falkland Road—into the Pill-House District with its wooden cages and prostitutes, its drugs and filth.

At midday Molly awoke from a haze. He had slept badly, rolling around with a near-empty bottle of rum clutched to his middle.

Splashing water from a brass-bound wooden bucket, he turned the mirror away from the sun, deciding the damn thing made his face look like a well-worn relief map. As was his habit after a whoring drunk, he held court near the aft rail, looking into a pale, cornflower-blue sky. After seeing to the weather, he drank the last of his rum, and read Uncle's message. "Molly, a bloody sniper took two shots at me this morning."

The ticklers he signed on at the Sailor's Home on Thana Street to sail the leg to Jeddah were taut hands, seasoned with an animal vitality and in proper fighting trim. He had hesitated to accept their papers after he heard them speak German. But this was 1939, and their physical traits were of work and the fear of being beached.

For a sailor, being beached brought a special loneliness.

Molly, who preferred sailing the seas alone, had stood his post in the spring of 1915, and for years in Flanders Field—a Foot from 1ˢᵗ Battalion of the Royal West Kent. His salt unfettered; England was his home. Yet through the ensuing years, Mother had hardly been his friend. And even these fibers were being driven by the musty odor of lost time.

Now I'm going to kill Sir Nigel as if he were a stranger. A useless water clerk. I'm a squaddie of sorts, and in my own way, I'm poison. Rumsquaddled, I've no reason for the choice. I'll splice the main brace, and then I'll kill him just the same.

"A sailor must remember, it's one hand for yourself and one hand for the ship."

Clouds hung in the gaps of Molly's mind. Fear for his captain had settled along the seams of his face—weathered seams laced with the grime of being betrayed by his former lieutenant. Sporting the splendor of boiling rage, he set his eye to the rear sight of his Pattern 1914, MK4 Lee Enfield Rifle, and scanned the maze of dockside streets and the strand along the waterfront.

If I locate the sniper, I'll drive a solid through his chat bags.

With the Enfield's battle sight set at 300 meters, he could adjust her aperture rear sight to 1,600 meters. Molly and his P14 had fired many a round in Flanders Field. Modified for the .303 cartridge, his lady had a five-round integral magazine and the accuracy of a carpenter's plumb. Scarred by rocks and quartered by mud, she had barked on cue in June of 1917.

Ginger whiskers grated on the worn grain of the carbine's stock as Molly examined the man he found in the carbine's sight—the vagaries of his dress the confirmation of his origin. Life being one of enduring, Molly excused the man. Wishing a cool breeze, he wiped the sweat from his cheek.

Twilight brought an iridescent hue and a welcome breeze. The distant clouds were encased with an orange-purple crust. Gaslights, where they fluttered, defined Bombay harbor. Late as it was, the harbor strand was ablaze with commotion. Sailors and dockers, whiskied into boiling fits, were fighting over well-fledged young birds.

For Molly there was a quality to being alone—the calmness of not caring.

The stench grew heavier in the cooling air. The ashes of the past, the human salvage featuring the roil of British imperial snobbery, brought a smolder to Molly's eye—a steady hate. Yet his eyes never seemed to lose their gleam.

Incensed by Stuart's attempts to kill Hardin, the red carpet of poppies in Flanders Field came to Molly's mind—April 1915, again on Hill sixty in June 1917—the dashed Huns, the mud, the rain, the graves with those makeshift tree-branch crosses—rows and rows of flimsy crosses.

A muddy rest camp—a stiff's paddock.

His chaplain, "Tubby" Clayton, singing, raising his mug of muck, cheering on the lads at the Everyman's Club at Talbot House, in Poperinge.

And then, with loud, piercing, rhythmic cries he dragged his platoon leader from the fight. His hands swollen into ham hocks, he struggled with the small tin box—Hypodermic Syringe Field Kit, the Morphine Flask, morphin sulfate, $1/8^{th}$ grain. And then loaded his mate into a shell-torn wagon of the Friends` Ambulance Unit.

My God, what have they done with the stretcher bearers? And where has the doctor gone, Major John D. McCrea? There's Bonneau, his dog.

"In Flanders Field the poppies blow, among the crosses, row on row."

Today Molly had lost more than he had gained on that day in June 1917—surviving the carnage the field marshals called the Battle of Messines.

With Sir Nigel's betrayal, Molly lost the value of his recall of that one vivid, motionless scene.

Embracing morphine's echoes, Molly hated thinking. He calmly traced the frame of a wog, drawing the rifle's sight across the man's chest. Deciding he should relax and toss darts instead; he leaned the weapon against the rail and lit a cigarette. Again, in Poperinge, Belgium. The brothels Molly knew well—Fancies, the Poplar Tree, Pug Street.

As light and shadow chased each other, a chop ran along the surface of the bay. Tucked in a tarp without his rum ration, fishing for a shot at a wog, Molly tired of the charade and dashed down a companionway into a passage heading for the tramp's saloon. Following the insistence of his captain's voice, he ducked into Uncle's chart room.

With the wound in his forearm seared and beginning to pulse, Uncle shouted, "That bloody fucker." The sniper's bullet notched a furrow across the tattoo of his favorite tart. Lucy, his Mayfair Mama, no longer had tits. He laughed through the cigarette smoke as her hips sprang to life, accentuating the lust her captain admired.

"Damn good thing I've a locker full of rum," Uncle said.

With a plodding gait, Molly strode to the chart table, his expression sporting the remnants of Vaseline, a memorable tart. "The derby bastard's more than a fair shot." Molly turned Uncle's forearm, so he could better examine the damage to his captain's tattoo more closely. "Took her bouncers right off, he did."

"The sniper's second solid clipped my ear as I fell. Means the shooter knows his target. Good oil, that. It ties the bastard to Stuart—MI6 or MI-R."

"Bloody shot was a near-facer, titts and all." Molly was grinning through a swig of rum.

*   *   *

London. Blackfriars Bridge. 19 September 1939. 0330 Hours, Greenwich Mean Time.

A vast, heavy veil of fog had been gathering for days, a fog clinging to the stench of the last neap tide. The River Thames ran bank-full, forced to the well-curbs by rain-sodden winds pushing the North Sea racing through the English Channel. Bottled by high winds, the sour-brown stench of the river wafted, offending the usual drab following.

William Hockey, the Poston family's principal janissary, leaned into the wind and the rain. Standing in a familiar alcove on Blackfriars Bridge he waited for two Stumpie barges filled with garbage to clear his vision. With the help of two devotees, and two shots of morphine, it took well over an hour to suspend the Duke of Hamilton over the iron and stone railing.

Tired and wet, Hockey watched a cargo boat push against the tide, biting the wind, its green and red navigation lights barely visible. A blast from its horn was answered by a shrill, piping whistle. Riding the tide, a Watson motor lifeboat towing a bumboat appeared for seconds only to vanish as it cut under the bridge.

The three men lowered the Duke of Hamilton kicking and screaming over a small ledge into the turbulence of the boat's wake.

Filled to its lip, the river danced with a chop, first dragging, and then throwing the condemned man's feet into the air, drawing and jerking his fat body at rope's end—the frantic motion firing globs from his exhaust. As if celebrating some long-ago victory, the Duke of Hamilton tossed his arms about, the rope wrenching his neck.

Throwing his head banging onto his left shoulder, his tongue lapped hungrily at his lapel. The man's wreck of a face grew heavy and wretched— without a suitable reply.

For Hockey, the Duke of Hamilton's death throes were in good voice. He deserved to die a drug smuggler's death. Hanging this banker will cause a bit of chaos, Hockey thought. The traitor tried to wake the echoes with his roaring.

Blackfriars and Templars were up and fed. Even the Jews were relieved. A despicable man hung from Blackfriars Bridge. The execution order had come from Pretoria, South Africa, through the Contraband Control Base at Haifa.

William Hockey strolled through Hyde Park as if the rain had stopped—a stroll made straight while measuring the worth of the duke's life and the life of Gordon Dewar. The Lady's Mile has not been used today, he noted.

The trees drooped and seemed to soften their shape.

Hockey showered in the transient billet made available for veterans at the Red Cross Headquarters on Seymour Street, a half block north of the park. Dressed for church, he put his wet clothes, including his shoes and worsted trousers, in a donations bin and set his tie to the center. He was meeting young John Poston in the canteen on the ground floor.

The canteen's serving line was crowded. Johnny seemed preoccupied.

With a plate of beans, sausage, eggs, baked tomato, and chips, Hockey ate in silence. Hamilton's agony had been complete. Knowing the fat man was too weak to climb a rope, Hockey had left his hands free to worship a glimmer of hope. Gargled English had been mixed with gusts of wind and the surging rain.

"John Poston, will Mother ever have an investiture to dub you a Knight of the Realm?"

"Don't be daft. With Mother's shifting feuds, we'll have to wait."

With a tired and unpuzzled smile, Hockey said, "Captain Hardin's wife is alive. Katherine's being held against her will in a churchyard house in Tucking Mill, in Cornwall. The lodge has determined two men are minding her needs. She appears to be in good health. We have determined her guards are MI6 harriers and working for Dewar."

"Katherine's alive. Does Hardin know?"

"We've sent word to Lewis. I don't know if he's found the captain, or if the captain's alive."

"Dewar better find a hole—somewhere in the smithereens."

"We've also confirmed Dewar had your father killed to gain control of your father's shipping assets. Probably to expand his opium-smuggling operation in southern France. Now he's trying to isolate you, and anyone who might search for answers."

Johnny quartered his baked tomato and poked the air with his fork. "Are you sure about Dewar? I wonder how he proposed to gain control of our shipping assets."

"Indirectly. He purchased the note on your father's shipping business to gain control of the profits. That failed. Now, for Dewar, anyone who looks into your father's death is a liability." Hockey finished his meal. "By now, you are as well, Johnny."

"Probably. Dewar didn't purchase the note. A German banker named Schiff bought it."

Accustomed to the symptoms of faithful espionage, Hockey took note. "That's a worry. Schiff has financial ties throughout the world. He's Austrian."

"He could be Austrian. But really who cares. Time will make Dewar more reckless. These international bankers won't tolerate his polycentric approach to life."

Nodding agreement, Hockey said, "We believe Dewar hired Gosden at MI6 to control Gosden's location. He gated you in MI6 Section D for the same reason. Then he kidnapped Hardin's wife, faked her death, calculating your father would have Hardin posted abroad."

"And you, Willie?"

"Yes, I've considered that. The Duke of Hamilton hung himself from Blackfriars Bridge last night—too stormy for my taste."

"The duke was a consort of Dewar's." Poston calked his head. "Does the admiral know?

"I assume he's been informed."

"Can you help Hardin's wife?"

"By now Admiral Sinclair's lads have arrived at Gosden's old home in Tucking Mill with a restless thump of hooves. Katherine's kidnapping will shift to the Ashchurch area and be kept under seal." As if sensing Poston's concern, he added, "The admiral and I are lifelong friends, Johnny—from our lodge in Cardiff."

"If that beautiful woman is harmed, I'll kill Dewar," Poston said.

"What's Dewar up to?" Hockey asked.

"He's assigned to Sinclair in Broadway, a complex of cubicles beneath Whitehall," Poston said, pushing beans onto a heel of toast. "On call around the clock, his travel banned."

"That won't work."

Hockey sat admiring an elderly woman approaching the adjoining table. Her face was a fold of time, tethers of laughter and chains of vivid tragedy. Fending for herself, she wore a coat of woolen tatters pulling at her frame, yet her eyes danced on crow's feet.

Hockey rose and stood next to her and laid an open palm and pulled out her chair. Alert, and obviously surprised, she gave a slight nod. From edge to edge, her tray brimmed with food. An orderly laid a plate next to her tray that held a mound of custard for afters.

"If she goes 'round for backups, we'll escort her home," Hockey insisted with a grin.

Smiling as though admiring the woman's determination, Hockey sat and leaned toward Poston. "Dewar's working a back channel for the royals, Johnny. Rudolf Hess is involved. As are Victor Rothschild and a good deal of money—German industrial money."

"Willie, how do you know this?"

"The lodge owns Saint Ermins Hotel. Members of the lodge have been spying on Dewar for nineteen months. He plays fancy at Saint Ermins— twice a week."

"Ring me when Katherine's safe."

* * *

Bombay, India. Worli Base, 24 Squadron RAF.
20 September 1939. 0530 Hours, GMT + 5.5 Hours.

Sleeping inside the Wellington Mark 1, having his eyes wired to a thoroughly bad night, Hardin came awake to the persistent rattle of the maintenance-bay door. The chief fitter looked inside while talking with an officer standing on the apron in front of the door, giving his pilots time to hide. Hawkes and Hardin gathered their kits and crawled to the tail section of the cargo bay—trapped inside the Wellington.

"We need to flash up these engines, Lieutenant," Longley said, handing the officer a clipboard with a form to sign. "This crate's scheduled to fly to France tomorrow, this week at the latest. Wimpey's on the signed-off charge here about, but the boys in France aren't so picky."

"Where did she come from?" The officer moved a signal pad and slipped into the cockpit.

"She's one of the birds the New Zealand Air Force refused to keep, six all told."

Longley hooked the accumulator to the engine leads and gave the officer a thumbs-up. The engines juddered, coughing as if unemployed convalescents. Fifteen minutes of run time left the engines in fine tune. The officer signed the form Longley presented and left the hangar.

Hardin peered out the airplane's hatch to find Longley setting a tool bin for breakfast in the corner of the maintenance bay—white tablecloth, cloth napkins, silverware, salt and pepper shakers, eggs, bangers, potatoes, and coffee.

"Bit of a slap-up for you scoundrels." Longley handed Hawkes a fork. Again, there was something in his eyes. As though he was at grips with a foe.

"Artificial elegance, I'd say." Hawkes flicked a nervous glance and cheered a scrap as he touched his bottles of embalming fluid.

Longley shook his ruddy chops. His mockery sharpened. "Business before pleasure, gentlemen. Flying Officer Hawkes needs to have a swig of whiskey, then initial Form 78—an Aircraft Movement Card. After a second belt, he must sign Form 700 taking responsibility for this beauty from the ground crew."

"Well, tin basher, is your name on those forms?" Hardin asked.

"You're a sharp lad. Do you need a cipher clerk?"

Stifling a response, Hawkes followed the fitter's instructions, slurring his initials and signature. The three men sat to their meal. Hawkes raised his coffee cup. "To the men who keep the aircraft flying, no matter the weather or the cost."

"There's no cost to me." A maverick in Longley's eye led to an expression of poker-backed reverence as he lifted his cup, exclaiming, "That missing Vickers you flew in on might be a fading beauty, but the betting pool's in full bloom. The squadron exec is holding one hundred and thirty quid for the man who finds her. As soon as you lads are wheels up, I'll discover your foul treachery. A mate of mine gets twenty pounds. He has the watchtower from ten-hundred hours until dusk."

"You're a grifter." Hardin nudged Longley's shoulder. The fitter reminded him of the union steward who fronted as his best mate in New York. His steward always had a con going.

"And you blighters are on the dodge."

"Not actually. I'm a flying officer on my way to the Air Striking Force in France. And this brown job is a special service lad back from Burma."

"England just lost the aircraft carrier Courageous. The crew tried to swim for it. Lost 518 sailors southwest of Ireland."

"Bloody cold water." Hawkes stood and walked a few steps.

His breakfast finished; Longley sprang to his feet. "There are parachutes and five days' worth of provisions on board. With Wimpey's gremlins on the loose, I'd keep those parachutes at the ready. After a bit of dead reckoning, odds are you'll both be touching silk."

"I can't swim," Hawkes said, nipping at the bottle.

"I'll leave the flash-up trolley. Use the accumulator if the engines get stale. We have never met. I don't want to find a trace of your leavings in my maintenance bay tomorrow."

Forewarned, assuming Longley was a harmonium in need of padded hammers, Hardin began wrenching about, jabbing his parachute, and kicking his prospects, forcing Hawkes to drink. A Druid appeared, perched, and laughed—Longley's a tinker who will bleed us, and roll us over before nightfall.

Caution joined the ache in the middle of Hardin's forehead and raced into its natural warren. As his stomach turned over, he put his fork down. The sausages were the first he had eaten in fifty-five days. He savored the potatoes, and the coffee was hot.

A nagging hand remained outstretched—Longley's hand. His eyes were never still. Hardin detected anxiety in the fitter's delivery, as though the man's voice had run sharp—accelerating with anticipation, as if a vascular dam had given way, his stammered words issued while gazing into the sky.

Training his look-stick on the flight operations terminal, Hardin found the fitter in full animation, refueling the Bowser with an orchestra of mates 150 meters away. After a series of swift hand motions, Longley pointed at the maintenance bay, checked his watch, and pointed at the watchtower.

"We're leaving now," Hardin declared.

"We're due off at twelve-hundred hours," Hawkes countered.

"We're already late leaving. Get in and start driving."

The engines of the Wellington fired to life at first spark. Hawkes, the picture of relaxed intrigue, had the stick in one hand and a bottle nudging his essentials.

"Hawkes, there's a man on a headphone at the top rail of the watchtower."

"He's alerting the ground wallahs. He's got a hand on the Aldis Lamp to give us the green if we pass muster. Get that Thompson ready."

Rolling down the runway to find its end, the headphones barked requesting aircraft status and mission status. Reaching the end of the tarmac, Hawkes ignored the requests from the tower and turned into the wind.

"Step on the gas, Hawkes." Hardin's pulse was revving faster than the plane's engines.

As a ground crew armed with short magazine Lee Enfield rifles sprinted toward a Bedford three-toner, a yellow, 1938 Commer tray truck careened off a stanchion, lost control, and ran into the side of the Bedford. Longley stumbled from the Commer waving his arms.

"All in good time, cobber."

Hawkes screamed, "Tally Ho," gave her the boost, and pushed the Wimpey to full throttle, charging through the heat waves, heading for the chance-light.

"Worli tower, this is Wellington 667. We are outbound on the signed-off charge, bound for Frog Land. Bit of a water jump. Wish us luck, Worli, over."

"Roger, Wellington 667. Identify yourself, over."

"McPhee's the name. I'm transit on your listing. Disc number 173. As of yesterday, over."

"Roger, Wellington 667. Good luck."

"There's your parachute, Hardin. I don't know who packed it. There are initials on the rigger's card. It's just me, your lonely bus driver, and good whiskey keeping you from harm—needle, ball, and air speed pressing on no matter—chasing the sunset."

As the mountains fell away, the river delta widened, the vegetation thinned, and the coastline rose to greet them. Hawkes had to drink. He was driving his bus over open water.

A single-stacked coaster was running north near the shore.

The Indian Ocean ran before him; an endless sweep of glass pitted with wind chips. A British Shoreham Class sloop scored the sea, heading west a few miles from Bombay harbor. With his look-stick Hardin read the sloop's name: HMS *Fowey*. Except for roaming flocks of loons and flurries of gulls, the balance of the sea ran untouched to the horizon.

Using the plane's intercom Hardin asked, "How did you get tied to McPhee?"

"Gum Tree 'Darkie' McPhee's a right sort—worked the angles at Trinity House to become Rangoon's harbormaster. He had a colonial-style flat and a live-in comfort girl." Hawkes didn't seem to welcome Hardin's questions as he drank a gulp. "Darkie's kept his baggage trim."

"When did you meet?"

"Ten, twelve years ago, in Port Blair. On his way to a pub, he sold me a Halfpenny Rose Red stamp in mint condition for ten pounds. I sold the stamp for one hundred and forty pounds the next day. McPhee also introduced me to a clatter of lumber brokers—for a ten-pound fee, mind you. McPhee gambles. That's his grind. Always needs money. He was convinced Corcoran had gold on that steamer."

"What happened in Singapore?"

"Mother's agents were flayed and spread over a luxury flat in Raffles Hotel. The assassin damn near bottled us in Port Blair. The son-of-a-bitch sat right behind McPhee in Ritchie's Pub, asking about flights to Bombay."

"Do you know this SOB?"

"Von Cleve is South African. Well healed. A banker. A vicious one. Big, well dressed, black hair, greenish eyes. Carries a knife."

"A banker who carries a knife. How old?"

"Don't know. Has a cross tattooed near his right wrist."

"Corcoran has a tattoo."

"This tattoo's the symbol of an old military order. Our banker's a traveler. That swell Corcoran has chained below deck has the same tattoo."

"Sir Nigel Stuart."

* * *

Cairo, Egypt. Shepheard's Hotel. 20 September 1939. 0900 Hours, GMT + 2 Hours.

The escape-and-evasion ratline extending from Hong Kong to Alexandria, its weaves more complex than a Cornish fulling mill, led ghillies and stalkers to the Red Sea and on to the Mediterranean—rats, snakes, and whores of odd sorts mostly. A tramp steamer owned by Poston and Sons, Ltd., was running this ratline.

Manned by long-dentured tarpots immune to Mother's favor, the steamer ran at ten knots. With lamps burning and no reason to be, seamen one and then another drew his longbow in defense of simplicity. They'd be better off on a road mending gang.

Operation Snow White seemed simple enough. "And where is my nephew? Where is Linc Jensen?" Poston whispered, lighting a cigarette.

Dressing his tender cock and his balls to the right, he sat in the wicker chair and signaled the waiter. Shepheard's Hotel served an elegant meal in the morning. Needing a soothing lotion, Poston whispered, "More to the matter at hand, who the hell *is* Dorothy?"

Adding brandy to his coffee, he leaned back, drew at the aroma of her stationery, set an ear to the din, and read the three-day old cable again.

> Lewis,
> Please forgive me. I was recalled to New York. I had a lovely evening. Here's to those times.
> Dorothy

Exhausted, his equipment was volunteering for duty—on its own—without regard.

A voracious lover, a woman prone to protracted shudders, Dorothy was too intelligent to be a corporate secretary. Coaxing him with sensual gestures, too agile for his imagination, he feared she was a spy. Not an Axis spy. Her inquiries focused on money, on British Petroleum's currency arbitrage strategies, all the while demanding more rhythm from the percussion section of his lower back.

That she worked at J. P. Morgan in New York, a bank aggressively courting German industrial companies, was critical when factoring Stuart's ties to MI6 and MI-R—and perhaps Gordon Dewar. She lied. She was not married. Admiral Sinclair confirmed Stuart a bachelor. Yet she declared Cairo a stop to find her husband's kit.

So, who was this lady using Shepheard's Hotel as a dead drop?

Returning to his flat, Lewis found his clothes strewn across the bed. Intruders had ransacked his flat and dumped the contents of his holdall on the kitchen floor. What were the bastards looking for? After gathering his clothes and repacking his holdall, he examined the folder containing his proposed British Petroleum contract with the Protectorate of Aden. Nothing.

A page from his scheduling notebook had been torn out—the page detailing his first encounters with Dorothy Stuart.

Taking a last scan around the hotel room, he began dissecting his encounter with the lady. Stepping to the curb, he waved to the chemist across the street and hailed a cab. He was bound for Alexandria's east bay.

Not wanting Corcoran's steamer to reach Alexandria before the details of Operation Snow White were rinsed out, he requested a twelve-man reconnaissance team be dispatched to Sharmel Sheik at the southern end of the Suez Canal, for a look-see. Trusting few, Sergeant Dirk Jensen's selection as the recon team leader was tailor-made for the operation. Dirk was Poston's youngest nephew, Linc Jensen's younger brother.

A safe bet. He'll scour the Red Sea to find his kin.

Standing on the natural red granite finger that protected the east bay of Alexandria's harbor, Poston braced as three soldiers walked toward him. Jensen was a step ahead of his mates. He was a large man with square shoulders and a cumbersome stride—a familiar stride.

Poston extended his hand to Jensen's sleeve. "Dirk, a good many vultures are trying to kill your brother. Each a fading memory. MI6 contractors as well as foreign operatives have had a go at Linc. He needs help. He probably doesn't know he's carrying sensitive documents that have the royals and many of the world's bankers spending great sums of gold and hard currency to find him—to intercept those documents."

"What's my brother's status?" Jensen flipped his cigarette into the bay and took a step closer to Poston. "Is my brother dead or alive?"

"We believe he's on a tramp steamer entering the southern end of the Red."

"The northern run through the Suez takes eleven to twelve hours. There are delays. The currents are still running south, north of Great Bitter Lake."

"The tramp has not joined the queue to transit the canal."

"You don't know if he's alive—do you?" Jensen walked to the edge of the apron and looked into the setting sun. "Your worthless intel twats will get us all killed." Lighting another cigarette, he turned. "Let's start over. What if this tramp isn't in the Red?"

"Proceed to Aden. That tramp needs fuel. Poston and Sons, Ltd, maintains a contract for fuel and stores in Aden—none in Port Sudan. The Sudanese are servicing German cargo vessels."

"If Linc's on board, we'll find him. If he's not on board, I'm going to let the air out of any bastard in my way."

"Before you strike the flag, Linc, there's a wrinkle to be ironed." Poston shook the young man's hand. "A bit of a windflaw if you like."

"What the hell's a windflaw? Is there a separate target?"

"Just so." Poston lit a cigarette. "Monkey bread, really. A liaison snout. One of Snow White's traitors will be going with you. A D-Measure priority—straight from Broadway."

"Do we know this shit bag?"

"He gets up in regular style, but he's not part of the crew. He's tied to the bastards who bowled out Team 7 and left Linc to do for himself."

"If you've identified the bastards who killed my brother's mates, are any of them still alive?

"Almost all of them." Poston hesitated, wanting to tell Jensen the rest of the facts.

"I'll shoot the fucker. It's what I'm about."

"Just the one casualty. In the confusion if you can."

"And the weather?" Jensen asked, casting about as though Poston had sounded an alarm.

"We've a brief respite between monsoons. If rain comes, it will be from the northwest. The met mechanics are predicting clear skies for a fortnight. Captain Corcoran's a cautious sort, likes to anchor well away from other ships with a long swing circle."

"What's the windflaw's name?"

"Gosden. He's a Methodist minister's son."

"Spaniel-eyed I suppose. All's well then. Gosden's just waiting for God."

"Right you are."

*　　*　　*

The Indian Ocean. Uncle's Tramp Steamer, 21 September 1939. 1650 Hours, GMT + 4 Hours.

After throwing lines in Bombay, the depth sounder watched the seabed fall into the deep ocean. With her empty ballast tanks acting as buoyancy tanks, the steamer made good time. Her quadruple-expansion engine had maintained a ten-knot pace. But the longer Corcoran sailed in open water, the more worried he became. Coursing atop a flat sea, unmolested between wind and water, the wireless traffic had been brisk.

Dispatch: 14 September, Kriesmarine Type IXA submarine U-39, depth charged and sunk off Rockall, Inverness-shire: 17 September: HMS Courageous-class aircraft carrier torpedoed and sunk southwest of Ireland: 20 September, Kriesmarine Type VII submarine U-27, depth charged and sunk west of Lewis, Scotland.

HMS Sloop *Fowey*, L15, manned by the Portsmouth Port Division, passed in the night on the tramp's starboard without announcing her presence or sounding a horn.

While looking aft, a destroyer's horn called once, and Uncle acknowledged her intent to pass with one blast. Flag-waggers aboard three Royal Navy destroyers signaled to pass the steamer on her starboard. At twenty-six knots, HMS Destroyers *Daring, Duncan, and Dainty* made short work of flanking the tramp on their way to the Med.

With each naval vessel to pass, he expected to be boarded. By now *Lloyd's Shipping Intelligence Unit,* and Lloyd's editorial staff, along with Mother's navy had recorded the steamer's coordinates, line of bearing, and where it was heading.

The Royal Navy Red Sea Force will board us in Aden harbor.

Admiring the speed of the destroyers, he spotted the convoy he expected—Convoy Red-1. Bearing down on the steamer from the west, passing three points on her port bow, passenger liners *Bristol Britannia*—the "Whispering Giant"—and *Duchess of Bedford* were bound for Bombay, escorted by Royal Navy Aircraft Carrier *Eagle* and Light Cruiser *Liverpool*.

Molly walked from the forward well-deck with a steaming mug of coffee. Under his arm was his latest reading material from the colonies, a dog-eared Batman comic.

"That balls-to-four watch has your headlamps at half-mast, Captain."

"Busy night. Set the dead lights to all portholes, Molly." Grigor Madog ran off to close off the portholes, starboard and port.

"We've two days to the Gate of Tears, three days to where we gare-up north of Port Sudan. That port's crawling with Nazis." Uncle lit a cigarette and took a long drink of coffee. "George Washington's coffee. Bloody colonials even abuse their own."

"Only the finest stores for our by-dollar liner," Molly chimed. "That Silex brews a stiff cup." Molly set his forearms on the rail. "McPhee gets off after we gare-up in the Red Sea." Molly peered over the rim of his mug, watching the temporary seamen scurry across the deck like Bombay runners, then dodge into a companionway.

"Taut sailors, are they?" Uncle asked, gritting his teeth.

"Franciscans, by the cut of 'em—a pair of burnt bearings. They get off in the Red."

"Give their bags a toss, Molly." Uncle dropped his mug into the sea to emphasize his order, set the old brass look-stick to his eye to scan the horizon.

Molly shook his head. "That mug was a gift from my mum." He spit, pointing at a wrinkle in the bow wash where he last saw his mug.

With a grimace, Uncle shrugged. "There's a boarding inspection brewing."

Backtracking toward Bombay, HMS Sloop *Fowey* appeared on the horizon, four points to starboard. The sloop would pass the steamer within the hour on her starboard.

Mother's sloop has orders to keep track of this tramp, Uncle thought.

Hours later, savoring a hot cup of gunfire inside the wheelhouse, Uncle heard the crew hollering. He walked to the foredeck and found the crew leaning over the rail, taking bets in several languages.

Stuart's feet were tied to the base of a davit hook with his hands tied to the starboard rail.

Molly had beat the temporary seamen until they were weak and barely mobile. Lashed in chain, the ticklers were hanging upside down from separate davit hooks over the rail. The crew had gathered for a seaman's trial. Molly was the sitting judge.

The ticklers were shouting their innocence in German, all the while pointing at Stuart.

"What have we here, Molly?" Uncle asked.

"There's never enough room to swing a cat, Captain. These slags were hatch-combing. The toffs tried to give Sir Nigel this toy gun." Molly threw the Baby Browning into the sea. "A jar says they're after Hardin's pouch." Molly held the loops of his cat to the fore, slapping the side of Stuart's face, driving his head into the rail.

With his lips pulped and bleeding, Stuart hollered. "I was given a D-Measure order relating to Hardin—execute immediately."

Deciding to teach the spy a lesson, Uncle drove his right fist into Stuart's midsection. Drumming his words, Uncle ordered, "Lash this cock to a hook and hang him in the sea. Drag him until he tosses his future."

"You can't wash Mother's laundry without undressing the bitch," Molly chimed. "You can live to see Dover, Nigel, or you can have a swim through the steamer's props."

Screaming as he went under water, time and again, the royal began begging for his life. Gagging and vomiting sea water, Stuart was dropped on the deck. Pushing vomit away from his face, he muttered, "All right. That's enough. MI5 and MI6—take your pick. The D-Measure order came straight out of the Hole below Whitehall, I'm told." Stuart set his forehead on the deck. His lips were white with pulp.

"Is there a cast to this bullshit we might know?" Uncle asked.

"Oh, there's a Rothschild in MI5, and a Warburg. Their money has brought more—Lord Norman and his minions—and Dewar at MI6. It's a list of men anyone could assemble."

"Prattle on, fair knight. You're pathetic, Nigel." Uncle picked Stuart up and held him against the rail. "Untie this worthless cock, Molly, and drag him to the chart room.

"And you, Sir Nigel?" Uncle pushed the muzzle of his Webley pistol into Stuart's chest and backed him onto a locker in the corner of the chart room. "You've a cross tattooed on your forearm. What should I make of it?"

"I'm a follower of the Lady of Wisdom."

"Wisdom, is it? You're a bloody nutter, that's what you are. A clever liar."

"By now I'm out of sanction. You're helping Hardin, and Mother probably thinks I am as well. Puts me in the frame with you and your crew—operational liabilities."

Uncle cocked the hammer on his Webley and put his finger to the trigger. "I don't believe you. Not anymore. You betrayed a friend. The loyal sergeant who saved your arse near that poppy field." Uncle fired the Webley into his laundry bag, inches from Stuart's hip. Molly grabbed Stuart, forcing him to stumble toward the door.

"Show Sir Wisdom the half-door, Molly. A sound lashing with stopper knots for now, both hands. Have a piss, Molly."

Molly moved like a bear stalking its prey, his shoulders firm as if loaded with pig iron, feet spread as though walking the "tarry plank" in a twelve-foot sea. Stuart had warped farther out of the straight than he imagined.

With the German ticklers screaming their wrath, lashed in chain, and hanging from davit hooks, Uncle's eye traced the bow wash, lingering on a paddock of foam. Searching down a tunnel, more a cone-shaped clearing in his mind, alone on the empty deck Molly would swing his cat and kill these temporary sailors as he had the Huns—Sir Nigel's Huns.

*　　*　　*

Airborne in a Vickers-Wellington, Heading for the Red Sea. 21 September 1939. 0130 Hours, GMT + 4 Hours.

Phosphorous, blinking bits of splashing life, jumped, and skipped across the surface of the sea. By the time the Wellington escaped Bombay's edgings of hell, the sun had raced away, spreading an unbroken pall over the Indian Ocean. Night by night the moon had given more of its light, waiting behind a shroud to expose itself again.

Hawkes edged the Wellington north-northwest. It's good to be flying again.

Hunting for the wind, he tacked back and forth across his bearing. If the airplane went into the red, he did not want to fight a stiff headwind. With a wink and a nod, Longley had been jokingly serious when he warned of the airplane's gremlins. Longley and Hawkes were drummers. Bidding up information to gain leverage on any straight answer was an essential part of their charm.

The squadron commander's whiskey was a common mark. Betting pools and honey traps, being a master drummer, Hawkes would do anything to cock the brass—steal a Vickers Vildebeest IV, steal a Vickers-Wellington I… steal anything, really.

Vague lies offered in an honest tone were Hawkes's specialty. Vague lies were as common as comfort girls in September 1939.

"Stop prancing about, Hardin."

"Piss off, Hawkes. I'm not leaving this bird until I'm over Egypt."

"If we make Egypt."

Hawkes cherished the freedom of being alone. Drinking whiskey, perched in the plane's conservatory, watching the Wellington's lights blinking red at odd intervals, he decided the only way to ensure Hardin survived was to have the squaddie jump from the aircraft.

Hawkes began shouting. "I gave you the station-to-station flight data. You jump into the desert along the coastal plain north of Jeddah, between the Red Sea and the Al-Sarawat Mountains, north of Obhur Creek."

"What, and then swim across the Red Sea?"

"If this bird's still stumping in the green on the approach to Jedda, we'll make a run for Egypt." Hardin would jump into the desert twenty miles south of the pyramids, expecting to meet Hawks at Shepheard's Hotel in Cairo, in ten to twelve days.

Both parachute-drop scenarios had Hawkes ditching the Wellington in the desert south of Cairo as near the pyramids as fuel would allow. Worried about the gremlins racing about the airframe, he stopped breathing when all three warning lights begin to blink red at odd intervals.

"We've got red lights." Hawkes had a death grip on the bottle next to his nuts.

Hawkes knew he needed booze—a need wedged like a clot of rice-hulls in his throat. He had plenty of whiskey. And a bottle reserved for the overland trek to Cairo. For days, and weeks now, he drank more and more, recounting the abrupt dislocations in his life. Now he was drinking to hide from those blinking red lights.

Determined to keep the Wellington in the air, he rapidly tapped the face of the fuel gauge.

The fuel consumption chart's "Howgozit Curve" confirmed he would be flying on fumes after he crossed the Red Sea. Drinking in swigs, the glow he needed to ignore his fear was taking hold. Those Bristol Pegasus engines are too heavy to allow this crate to glide. I need more power to keep the nose up.

"How goes it?" Hardin asked, checking the fuel gauge.

"I'm driving a bloody lead turd." Sitting on the port side of the pilot's station, Hawkes pointed at the flashing red lights. "We'll make the Aden drop zone. After that, this tart will be calling the ball."

"What Aden drop zone?"

"It's new." Hawkes tapped the fuel gauge. "On 11 September, ten days ago, a monsoon dumped three years' rain on Jeddah before midday. I'll wager that drop zone's under water."

Hawkes stuffed the empty bottle into a map holder and picked up his sterling flask to admire the engraving. "We've no choice. These red lights say you jump into Yemen."

Cruising at angels-ten the interior of the airplane was covered with frost. An isolated cloud crowded the moon. Suspended between a black sea and a star-filled sky, Hawkes counted the ships. There're three westbound destroyers heading for the Mediterranean. And Convoy Red-1 is heading for Bombay—an aircraft carrier, a destroyer, and two passenger liners.

Over the years, Hawkes had accepted an odd sense of recognition, a reckoning of his need for a reckless form of personal freedom—the lights of a passenger-liner's lounge, the music, the women… the good cheer.

Being three parts tight, Hawkes fell in with the image of romance, of the wealthy women who would be sailing the seas to Bombay—their winsome smiles coaxing his humor. With one bottle tucked in his kit, he set the bottle intended for celebrating Hardin's parachute jump on the metal grate next to his seat—a nip or two away.

The airplane lurched, coughed, shook, and started to fall. He yanked on the controls. The bottle next to his seat did a pirouette, slammed into the radio mount, rebounded, and tumbled down a ladder through a series of near breakouts, and shivered on the bomb-aimer's window in the nose of the aircraft, splashing whiskey into a puddle.

Hawkes sobered instantly, cussing his loss. He could smell smoke. One of the plane's green lights blinked red, then held red.

The starboard engine ran in splendid trim. The port engine continued to cough—each cough spewing flames through the flame-dampener, the "Christmas Tree" mounted below the cowling. Balls of sparks burst from the dampener, fractured into showers, and bounced along the airframe, spewing into the swirls generated by the contrail at the aircraft's tail.

"You fat tub o'shit." Hawkes screamed at the airplane. Trying to light a cigarette, the match broke and fell from his hand.

He shouted his best, frantically milking the left engine's feathering knob. As the port engine coughed to the rhythm of his feathering routine, the engine's propeller began wind- milling at twelve hundred rpm's, threatening to become uncontrollable and spin off into the fuselage—or space.

"Check the skin," he shouted. "I think we're on fire."

"We are." Hardin pointed at the bomb-aimer's window. The broken match had set Hawkes's whiskey afire on the bomb aimer's window.

Hardin turned and started climbing the icy incline through the passenger bay toward the plane's tail section.

The skin on the port side of the Wellington near the tail was also on fire, opening a hole, exposing the geodesic grid that formed the frame of the aircraft. Climbing uphill past the navigator's station and on through the dwindling arch of the upper passenger bay, dragging a wool blanket, he spotted the fire.

An ever-expanding hole near the cramped tail section was ablaze at its edges. Lying on his side, reaching through the duralumin bracing of the grid work, he smothered the flames.

With resin burns on his hands, he clamored downhill toward the cockpit across a sheet of frost coating the deck of the upper passenger bay. Hardin's feet shot out from under him, and his head crashed into the decking.

Recovering, he glanced out the Perspex windows over the left wing. The wing tip was spilling a contrail of condensed air mixed with sparks.

The propeller turned slowly and stopped. Seconds passed before the engine took hold, blowing stuttering plumes of sparks. The sudden power surge caught the airplane at angels two.

Climbing to nine thousand feet, Hawkes's hands shook. Sweating profusely, his prospects bleak, he thought, no matter the mission, Mother will castrate me for commandeering this gremlin-infested tricycle rejected by the Kiwis.

"Mother's mahogany shit-heels are going to grind me to a pea," he whispered. "The bastards have my file. They know I can't swim."

Finding the wind moderate from the southwest, he turned northwest, searching for the land-water contrast of the coast of Oman. Five minutes over land, he turned southwest, keeping the coastline of Oman and Yemen on his left flank.

He opened the bomb-bay doors to test the drag.

"Get a move on, Hardin. We're eight minutes out."

Hawkes picked up the blanket Hardin used to put out the fire in the tail section and dropped it onto the fire below his feet.

Good whiskey deserves a better end.

Keeping the white seam of the coastline at a constant elevation, three inches up on the port-side windscreen, hunting the wind, he checked the radio compass needle. Rotating the loop antenna atop the aircraft linked to the aircraft's degree indicator, he was searching for the homing beacon from RAF Base Khromaksar in Aden. He needed to be one-degree south of the signal on his final approach to the drop zone.

"This is going to be tight, cobber. If you jump too soon, you'll end up in a crater. If you jumped too late, you'll end up in the water."

Standing behind Hawkes, suddenly alert, as if a round had snap-passed his head, Hardin rubbed his face. Hoarfrost glistened on the radio mount.

Blinking to gain a clear focus, Hawkes knew he was in trouble. A shimmering sheen of high-quality malt lay near the edge of the bomb-aimer's window.

"The old rhino's stumping in the green, cobber. As heavy as those engines are if this bird dies, she'll drop like soggy knickers."

Hardin started rocking back and forth to warm his feet. "Open the bomb bay so I can check the lower weapons bay—the airspace between the bomb bay and the bomb beam. That overload fuel tank could be a problem."

"It's open. The lights of Aden will show on our right." Hawkes slapped his hand on his thigh to force blood to his fingertips. "I don't trust this bird."

"Fair enough—where's the drop zone?"

"At twelve hundred feet, you jump onto the boot at the southeast end of an isthmus—between Aden Harbor and the Gulf of Aden. You'll land east of Steamer Point. The terrain's beastly rugged. You'll have twenty seconds of drift if you get a full chute.

"If you land in that crater, you'll break your bloody neck. If you drift too far, you'll either land on the Elephant's Back, a volcanic outcrop in the Gulf of Aden, or you'll land in the gulf. Either way, you'll get the rough end."

Hardin climbed onto the platform in the nose of the aircraft and started clapping his hands and closing and opening his fists.

"I'm leaving an Enfield Mark 3 for you, Hawkes. And three, ten-round magazines. Depending on where you ditch, you may be in for a fight."

"That's a proper gong, cobber."

"It's a good weapon."

Checking the fuel gauge, Hawkes said, "When I give you the go, don't hesitate. The winds are moderate from the southwest. Even a mild breeze will drag that heavy chute like a dry leaf."

Hawkes pushed the stick forward. "We've the Gate of Tears to the west, and the Red Sea. At twenty-five count after you jump, I'm turning north and west. Don't bugger this up."

Hawkes extended his arm to mark his words and toasted the air with his thumb. "Good luck mate. I'll look for you in Cairo."

"Look for me in Piccadilly."

The lad's nuts. I fear we will not see his like again.

At home jostling the stick, Hawkes yearned for a drink. His face cast a rheumy expression. His breathing picked in four-four time, at odds with a pulse that was off the chart. Experiencing relief, he would deliver on a promise he made to himself—he would help this lad on his way.

For the first time in years, he was doing something positive—no money, no shady deals, no lumber brokers, no whores—keeping a promise to another man. More important, keeping a promise to himself.

"Pay attention, Hawker," he whispered to himself. "The approach to this drop zone has got to be spot on."

A long, black gap, a slit-trench lay between the side of the over-load fuel tank and the edge of the bomb-bay door. Freezing, Hardin leaned his shoulder against the bomb beam and clapped his hands. With the plane descending into warmer air, he took off his gloves.

Deciding to secure his drop bag around his waist under the thick webbing of his parachute harness, he rechecked the folds in his drop line to ensure the coils would play out. He was jumping a heavy US Army, T-4 parachute. Adding a drop bag left him with no ability to guide his descent.

After wrapping the Thompson in a blanket, he put a sock over the barrel and tied it to his left leg, stock down. The magazine boxes went in the map pockets of his pant legs. He divided his rations and medical supplies between the drop bag and his map pockets. He taped his canteen to the barrel of the Thompson.

With a deep breath, he shrugged into his parachute harness.

Standing on the upper rim of the bomb bay door, his static line hooked to a cable, his left hand held the drop bag line. His right hand on the bomb beam, he whispered, "If Katherine's in heaven, she would be in the way here."

I should be jumping into France.

"Go, cobber," Hawkes screamed.

At the sound of Hawkes's voice, Hardin kicked the drop bag loose and stepped into the night. The prop wash grabbed his feet and laid him on his back. The belly of the Wellington swept passed his face. The rivets near the rear wheel housing looked loose.

*　*　*

Lyon, France. Potter's Bar. 21 September 1939. 1430 Hours, GMT + 1 Hour.

Construction as sturdy as a ship's casement, the sally port of Potter's Bar was a patchwork of well-worn tarry planks fashioned into a shield that could out-latch unwanted intrusions—Vichy police.

"So, this is Potter's Bar." Whispering to himself Eaton could barely hear the words. He muscled the door open. Standing inside and to the left of the door to allow his eyes to adjust to the dark interior, he thought, *their faces look to be soaked in brine.* Petra had supplied him with intel related to Potter's Bar, along with recent news clippings.

I could use Petra's company about now.

Inside, in the stutter of a cultivated confusion, Petra's intel listed a secret passage existed near the keg locker that led to Traboule 30. With cat-faced cobbles, the archway was used by Resistance fighters and criminals to escape the Bosche and the police.

After an abortive raid on Potter's bar a policeman was missing. He was last seen in the bar using his nightstick on a man near the keg locker. The raid seemed to set the stage. The next night the police headquarters was bombed, and parts of the missing policeman were found in the debris. On the second night, the police chief's home was bombed.

That was in June 1939.

Peaceful now, the square in front of Potter's Bar was more round than square. As purged as the square was, a brisk, cool breeze picked at this cultural redoubt—a borough comfortably lined with honey locust trees, atlas cedars, and small shops, trinkets, and foodstuffs mostly. Cat-shaped headstones paved the square.

Tables sat in clusters along the sidewalks wherever a meter could be found. Kindred men filled with yesterday's reasons, wiled away the day and the night. Lyonnais silk workers (canuts), their hands knurled, were long past their Jacquard looms. Their talk was of war, and of losing Japan's supply of raw silk—and young girls.

Par amnesia was in vogue in Potter's Bar.

Out of place, a merchant among thieves, Eaton's attempt at casual wear framed him as a banker or a manufacturer. He drew deep on his cigarette to ease his nerves. Once seated across from the bar, he kept his eyes moving, careful not to stare at any stranger as he typecast the man's face.

Petra's forger plays a mournful harmonica and sits alone.

The bartender was a big, well-set-up man with a hawk-like face. A white scar ran the length of his right forearm. Eaton knew one wrong move and he would not leave Lyon alive.

Putting down his glass, he considered the situation. The rum was of good quality. Absorbing without ciphering French, and bits of German and Spanish, he fell in with the rhythm of the bar. Secrets, with their interludes, seemed to be well supplied.

Groups of men ate as one.

A chessboard clacked, drawing the eye of a master in waiting posted a nod away, near the dusty window on the street.

An awning of smoke lay amid the oak rafters, its tail, drawn through a lattice of old muskets, moved loosely past the keg locker, parsed by the horns of a large stag, and on to an arched doorway. I'll bet the smoke leads to Traboule 30.

Too quick to remember, Eaton found a man sitting at his table holding a shot glass, a harmonica showing at the breast pocket of his shirt, something rolled up in his hand. Guile marked the man's expression. Hard living marked his eyes—eyes that lay as flat as holy stones.

"I'm due for a quarter shot." As the man raised his empty glass to the bartender, Eaton noted the conviction in his tone. *This must be Cager.*

The stranger set a caustic grin, his lips parting over stained teeth. A hard, cynical light came into his eyes. He was a stout, leather-skinned man, wide across his cheekbones.

Three men drew chairs and sat behind Eaton. Another man laid the blade of a dagger on Eaton's right shoulder. Cager's eyes clung to Eaton, riveted there as though deciding the stranger's nationality. There was an animal keenness to the man's bearing. Built like an old spike keg, Petra's forger was a survivor.

"I'm Samuel Eaton."

Cager smoked quietly for a few minutes. "I don't care who you are. If you're stupid enough to use your name, why did you come to Lyon?"

Without reacting, Eaton hesitated, waiting for another weapon to appear. Keen to be on his way, he slid four hundred US dollars across the table. Cager counted the money. With a nod the dagger on Eaton's shoulder was sheathed and the men behind him returned to their tables.

"A friend suggested Potter's Bar. I have an urgent need to be Swiss."

"You're Swiss by half. If you have the rest, come with me."

"What should I call you?"

"Nothing."

Tossing off his drink, Cager led Eaton past the keg locker, through an arched doorway, into a small, enclosed plaza, through the stone arch of Traboule 30, along a series of stairs and hidden pathways, across a matting of old straw, and into a cave, a dugout—a hillside cellar of sorts, tucked behind a tangle of shrubs.

Eaton was breathing heavily when the light came on. Only then did he see that Cager had a Mauser tucked behind his waistband.

"Many call me Cager. If you mention our liaison to anyone, we will find you and kill you."

The air was moist with the smell of damp soil and fresh straw. The dugout seemed to welcome the hue of the green glass lampshade. With a welcoming gesture the forger sat to a padded stool and a worn trestle table.

Zeiss field glasses filled an ivory case perched near a bottle of Macallan Sherry Oak whiskey. A Walther PPK lay in a pile of pencils within reach.

The hours hung in silence with Cager wearing a jeweler's eye. Covering his work from the cavalcade of dust tied to a lorry rumbling overhead, he seemed to admire the opportunity. Presenting his art with a nod, his eyes gleamed like a cat's in firelight.

The passport was perfect. Samuel Eaton was Frederick Borruck, a Swiss national.

"You must stay here until morning," Kaminski said. "I'll be at Potter's."

Offering Eaton his hovel, its coffee, whiskey, and soiled bunk, Cager donned a fisherman's cap and left with a nod and a firm fist. For Eaton, one large whiskey was all.

No longer asleep, his whiskers bristling with a thick residue, his jacket smelling of the smoke in Potter's Bar, Eaton sprang to. The shadow-reach of Petra's form riled his senses—not to mention his tackle. Reflex brought him upright, confused, and somewhat worried—wondering why she had come to Lyon.

A tremor passed through his frame. Ideas chased across his face. Cager had escorted Petra to the hovel and was busy setting to his workbench. A siren wailed on the street above the dugout. Men were shouting in the distance. Waiting for nothing, Eaton knit his brow.

With a silence building between them, Petra's voice quivered. "Are you going to line up in a circle, Sam? Or straighten yourself and say hello?"

Eaton had ideas about that, but he kept still, thinking it out. His mind was a raucous place by his own account. He glanced at Cager, he looked at her, a little confused. "Why are you here?"

Talking in clipped syllables she recounted her visit to see her mother. Gradually she finished her story. "I don't know if I'm worried for my mother." She held a small wooden figure of a farmer holding a scythe. "This carving was my father's gift to my mother and me. For refusing to finish his work at the Eagle's Nest, Papa was executed by the SS—by my brother, Karl."

Then, in the dim light, tears ran over her cheeks. "It seems even farmers are being executed," Eaton said, holding the wooden figure under Kaminski's work light.

"Cager knows I work for mad men. Von Schroder and the other bankers are no different than my brother. They are hideous chameleons—Jews are eating their own. They want to kill you and me now that we've become a threat."

Resignation came with a series of deep breaths, as if she had given up and did not care what happened next. Why did she turn to me? Is she out of sorts or are we playing chess?

Petra no longer seemed the cold, clinical Nazi.

Now in the dim light, color flew high in Petra's cheeks. Here for the first time, Eaton held the arm of a frightened farm girl. As her shoulders shook, she searched in fear and the suspicions blurring his thoughts began to drain away. And so, he thought. She's running from her life's work—from the Nazi state—from a cartel of Nazi bankers. And you know all this by looking at her face, guessing what wasn't said, so you can inaugurate another tale.

He drew Petra to him, and his face stretched into an expression of calm. Forget she's a woman and listen to her voice, the inflection, and the words. She's a refugee—as if another Jew. Put a red *J* on her passport and dress her in a torn woolen coat if it makes it easier.

"I'm growing nameless, Petra. You should, too."

Petra didn't respond. She couldn't keep a smile in place and wept softly. Red rings corralled her eyes as she lowered her head. Eaton reached for her shoulder as she leaned into his side. A truck on the street above geared down and rumbled the ground sheltering the dugout, shaking the hooded light, and dusting Cager's work.

The train ride from Lyon could not have been more confused. Partisans uprooted from civility by the porter's new uniform all looked to be hiding from a past that kept appearing.

Lisbon was over 1,300 kilometers from Lyon—a sixteen-hour journey, first on the 60cm gauge, Corsican Network's sugar-beet line, switching at the border to the larger, more conventional gauge of Spain's National Railway. Unwrinkled Nazi flags, the guidons of the future, checked passports and punched tickets, each keeper offering a word of caution.

"I need a cigarette." Petra held out a pleading hand, her expression harried. "I was stopped by the Gestapo as I was walking outside of Bad Reichenhall. When they demanded my identity papers, I shot them and ran down a muddy farm lane to the edge of the village, walked to the other side of the village and back to the train as if I was coming from the opposite direction. I think the monsters wanted to rape me."

"If the Gestapo connects you to the shooting, they'll kill your mother."

Agreeing, she said, "Anyone I know will be questioned."

*   *   *

Protectorate of Aden. Airborne, South of Aden Harbor. 21 September 1939. 2350 Hours, GMT + 3 Hours.

An instant too quick, an incomplete instant, the rear wheel of the Wellington flashed, lightly kissing Hardin's face.

Falling, lying on his back, the drop bag's line tugged at his waist, and his feet arced toward the earth.

The prop blast ripped the risers from the backpack, followed by the heavy T-4 parachute. With a snap and a pop, the canopy filled with air. The chute's harness tightened, seizing the tendons cratering his crotch, and with malice, the saddle and the harness strapping ruthlessly pinned his testicles to his ass.

Frantically adjusting his essentials, he cussed a stream of expletives, scolding the parachute and Mother England.

Unlike the night jump into the cloud cover over Tonkin, this jump was favored by the glow from Aden, a three-quarter moon, and unfettered starlight. Warm winds made a whispering sound in the suspension lines. Hardin had no time to think.

The drop zone was a maze of rock outcrops and long-fingered shadows. And he was falling too fast for a mountain-side landing. With onshore winds slowing his drift toward open ground, he knew he was in for a wigging.

With just seconds of drift left, he climbed his left-front shroud lines. Standing on the riser he jumped up and down trying to dump air from the canopy and increase his westerly drift.

The ground was a black nothing crashing toward his boots.

Here we go. Feet together, knees bent.

He was drifting southwest between volcanic ridges. Any change in wind direction and he would slam into the side of a volcanic up-thrust.

Once on the ground he had to keep the parachute from dragging him to his death. Gripping the suspension lines, dangling by his left arm, he unfastened the snap hooks and pushed the crotch straps of the parachute harness back between his legs.

Desperate, he scanned the horizon. His canopy slid below the jagged crest of the crater, and the wind vanished. His canopy was oscillating. His drift accelerated.

Could he do a standing landing on the rugged slope?

The glare of the landing lights of RAF Base Khromaksar dropped behind Mount Shamson's silhouette. Frantic, the change hampered his search. His night vision was sixty percent. At first it could have been a star, but as he drew nearer it became a small fire near the shoreline.

A fire—huddled figures—goat herders.

The animals might alert when I hit the ground. The men staring into the fire will have limited night vision.

Hardin had to avoid the locals. In this region of the world, where dozens of small tribes ranged through the mountains north of Aden, tribesmen would welcome a stranger into their village, serve him tea, and then kill him as if he were a goat.

I'll need a place to hide.

Standing on his riser, the canopy picked up a cross-shore wind and shot away from the goat herders, heading west and a bit north. Straddling the drop line, checking the campfire, dozens of goats were grazing along the beach.

"Bloody hell!" He could not see the ground.

In front of him lay Steamer Point. An isthmus housing the Royal Marines, the British Army, and the RAF. He had to avoid detection and find a boat.

Hardin lifted his chin. The instant his drop bag slammed into a boulder, he released the drop line, jumped from the riser, cinched his elbows to his side, fell to a momentary stop, and crashed into the ground.

The Thompson rang against a rock.

Landing on the crater's flank, his ribs cracked by the canteen's spout, his Thompson swung passed his face into a tangle of suspension lines, volcanic shards puncturing his hide.

Rolling and sliding, his head smashed into a shard. He kept sliding, falling. With a grinding cinch, his canopy wedged between rocks, and he shot out the bottom of his harness and slammed into a boulder with the Thompson jammed into his face.

Shocked and disoriented, he tried to breathe. Several of his ribs were cracked or broken. Unfastening the snap hook of the harness, he pushed his reserve chute off his face.

Cocking his head, he searched the area around the campfire. The goats had not been alerted. The goat herders huddled near the fire have no night vision.

They must be deaf.

The Wellington coughed in the distance. Rolling into a low crouch, Hardin faced the campfire. It's at least eight hundred meters away. Hauling himself up the side of the boulder, crouching, he began whispering his mind—all this for Grumpy's bloody pouch. If I chuck the damn thing, I'll never find the bastards who killed my mates. Fair play, they'll hunt me down and kill me anyway. What's in the pouch? Under seal?

Pouch or no pouch, Hardin was mired in the misery of Yemen.

"Where's my knife?" He was surprised by the resignation in his voice. On his hands and knees, he methodically searched the ground he was dragged across. He couldn't clear his throat without wanting to lie down.

Backtracking the skid marks, there was no sign of the MK4 floating knife. Cussing to himself, he spread dust over the skid marks to cover his trail. Opening his kit, he took out a roll of gauze. Holding one end in his teeth, he wrapped it around his chest and tied the ends.

He bundled the parachute, stuffed it into the drop bag, took the towels off the Thompson, wrapped a towel around his neck, and started ranging west toward Steamer Point. Walking in spurts, with three kilometers to cover to reach the harbor, he needed a place to hide before the gray of dawn.

The volcanic headland loomed black against the glow from the RAF Base runway lights.

The bare rock on the crater's flank was flecked with patches of polished lava. There was no cover on the crater, and he knew his back trail would be easy to follow.

I should have stayed on that Wellington.

Sitting under the awning of a large rock, Hardin gingerly massaged his rib cage. "Well, jackass. You cracked your ribs and squashed your chat bag."

Luckily, he cleared the RAF Communications Center and the No 222 Signals Squadron complex before the sky turned gray. The next group of buildings housed the Regional Headquarters of the British Provost and Security Services.

He waited for the sentries to change direction then moved quietly around the buildings, angling down the side of a swale into a dark hollow. Thirty meters past a motor pool, in the lea of a knoll, he stumbled into the apron fencing for the RAF Hospital.

The complex covered a good deal of ground. The interior hall lights in the one-hundred-year-old stone lookout came on as one, followed by the lights in the wards, announcing the start of morning rounds.

Skirting the fencing, Hardin stumbled and landed on his hands and knees. The ground was chalked with porous cinder like fragments of dark lava and rock. Arid and bare, with virtually no vegetation, even the night air held its dust.

Why did I leave the jungle—there's not a root alive in this soil?

If I check myself into that hospital, the orderlies will demand my serial number, seize my weapon, and kit, and turn me over to Mother's weans.

Cinching his hand around the straps of his rucksack he lumbered on.

Pick up your feet, Doc.

Playing tag with the faint starlight, he turned north and east, skirting the lower slope of the crater, heading for the Al Ma'ala District of Aden and the harbor. Rooftops grew into the horizon, their outlines black against the low dawn light and the far-off landing lights of the RAF Aerodrome.

Hardin moved quickly. The air was filling with burning sand. The rag he tied over his nose and mouth was damp and caked with a pale dust. Empty huts and animal pens forced him onto a hard-beaten path. A wall of rock forced him toward the beach.

The sun was gaining form.

Tired though he was, he had to keep moving. Shoving the drop bag into a hole formed by a mound of volcanic slabs, he cast sand over it, and brushed out the boot prints he could see. With the horizon showing a bit of gray, he needed to layup and find a boat.

Listening for an odd sound, he searched his back trail along the hard-beaten ground. Although a British Protectorate, a British officer taken in the remote areas of Aden would either have his throat slit or be sold as a trophy.

The terrain was devoid of life. The trees must be starving for water. Ranging downhill for hours, steeply at first, the descent had leveled off.

Anger came easily now, yet rarely interfered with his judgment. Images of his dead mates brought dreams of ritual killings. For Linc Jensen he would torture Dewar or any individual he found in betrayal's frame.

A breeze off the harbor, a river of air funneled by the rock wall, carried the stench of

Al Ma'ala around the crescent-shaped escarpment and out to the luxuries of Steamer Point.

Muffling a coughing jag with his hands, he reeled at the pain in his chest.

Bending his leg against the knot of his wound, he cussed the weight of the Thompson. The trail dipped into a ravine and then crested a low rise. Quiet except for the occasional rattle of small stones, he moved at a steady pace. Within minutes he found himself on the outskirts of the town of Al Ma'ala—a putrid squalor of goat shit and human debris.

One- and two-story buildings filled the land above the crescent-shaped beach, a hodge-podge situated along a straight stretch of road. The sidewalks, where they existed, were curbed with granite. Laneways, eight feet wide, and thirty feet long, opened onto intersections with multiple exits—each boasting a bubbling froth of beggars and deceit—each vowing to protect him not from death, but from misery.

Arched doorways were but black holes in the gray before dawn, governed by fragile brows. Empty wooden crates were stacked or strewn as though their worth were notional.

Candles glowed and then went out. Dogs barked. They seemed notional in their greetings, welcoming a stranger to the Arab street. An old man needed a crutch in the changing shades of dawn. Hardin watched him as his knobby hands shook, and his arms trembled when he tried to steady himself against a stack of salt bags.

A survivor, his life as futile as a rope of sand.

Horse drawn landaus began rolling toward the waterfront. The lights of an overloaded merchant ship beckoned shuttle craft to the ship's side, its Plimsoll-line well below the sea. Dhows framed the harbor's chores.

Wallahs began stirring in the streets, the well-dressed carrying clean shoes for sahib. Beggars, broken to the wheel, stung any passersby, old ones, young ones, some learning to walk. Those not begging were barely awake—drinking coffee and carrying trays of shoelaces or fly swatters, offering their sisters as a bonus—the stain of myrrh. But even the poorest beggar will, after a time, find the solace of a doorway.

Is it possible to live honorably in this place? Hardin wondered.

Beesti wallahs dumped buckets of shit into the harbor. The bare arse of a fisherman sat perched over the side of a dhow, shitting into the harbor—the sunrise no match for the stains.

Hardin turned north down a laneway. At first deserted, the narrow street erupted with life. He sought out the recess of a doorway and waited, as a camel laden with a bundle of tree limbs, drew a water cart past his boots.

Where the hell are the trees?

Broken crates cluttered the street. Old barrels—most empty, and bicycles with no means to cycle; these were the sentinels of Al Ma'ala. Worn canvas awnings covered the doorways.

Goats roamed the streets using earthenware pots as roundabouts, acting like pavement artists, scripting their canter as if mimes, stopping to raise their heads and stare—as if they knew how confused the humans were.

Darting across the road, Hardin skip-stepped through a loading bay into a stone warehouse perched on a hummock near the shore. Rats scurried as he burst into the go-down and eased himself into a corral of salvage and bags of salt.

His breath came in shallow gasps.

Preparing to move, he checked his equipment—Thompson, magazine boxes, medicine, food, water. I'm going to need another knife.

Covering his dingle with a canvas tarpaulin, he lay down. The smell was jute, or was it cinnamon? The minutes that followed never came quite clear. Dreaming, the face of a toothless street Arab, the old man, crept into his view.

Hardin came awake with his eyelids encrusted with salt. Drained of precious fluids, listening to the grate of his swollen tongue, how long could he hide? Drinking slowly, he held the water in his mouth, pushing it through his teeth, letting his tongue and the tissue inside his mouth absorbed the tepid liquid.

Peering through a space between the tarp and the top of piled salt bags, Hardin began to memorize his surroundings. Deck timbers creaked, and the loose timbers rattled as a dock-bull charged into the go-down in search of a bale of jute. A second dock-bull lifted a pallet of salt.

Dock carts and low bogeys wove along the apron outside the loading bay, dodging the laborers. Aden's harbor was a hive of foul smells and insistent chatter. Across a stone roadway a British army lorry was parked in front of an adjoining go-down's loading bay. The lorry sparkled in the sun, a mark on the filth of Aden.

Five, six voices. Laughing. Boots scraped the go-down's deck.

"There you are," a man shouted archly, his brogue that of a Brighton. Instantly sailors of all stripes were exchanging hands and lies—brags and stories of whores and drink—the brown birds of the east and their singing houses.

Hardin stopped breathing as he scanned their faces. Deliberate in his effort at self-control, he set the Thompson at the ready, and peered through a gap in the canvas. Nine, no, ten flyswatters had gathered in the go-down not twenty feet from his boots.

Merchant seamen by their looks. Roughshod, bulldogs, ruthless and malicious, but not stupid, they shuffled for a time, and separated into familiar clusters. Gathered for a smoke, they all had knives. One man carried a bolt-action carbine. One had an all-purpose awl; another fondled a leather sap looped at his wrist.

Why are these sailors in this particular go-down?

The chatter in the go-down rose before it suddenly stopped. The seamen stood and sheathed their weapons. Four men had entered the go-down wearing expensive sandals, linen pants, and short-sleeve silk shirts. The first man carried a riding quirt.

"My name's Alex von Cleve. It's my money you are wanting to earn. If you betray me, or lie to me, I will have you slaughtered and fed to the fish."

The shock left Hardin as he traced the man's face. Is this Hawkes's banker? The vulture hounding the ratline—Von Cleve? My God, the bastard's a monster. He's six feet plus a jar. The South African appeared to be a deliberate, vicious man—the sort with a quick-changing face, where thinking was never a visible process.

The Malay Creese tucked behind his belt made him seem even larger than his massive frame. Using the quirt, he panned the seamen. Then gave them a cloth packet.

"The picture I gave you is of the man I'm looking for. His name is Captain Edward Hardin. He's a British officer, part of England's special-service troops. I believe he's in Aden. When you find him, bring him to this go-down, and keep him out of sight until I arrive.

"I've given every man fifty pounds. I will pay an additional three hundred pounds for this officer. He has a leather pouch that belongs to me. I will pay eight hundred pounds for the pouch if it's under seal." Von Cleve tucked the riding quirt under his arm.

"You've had fair warning."

In the fading light von Cleve eyed the interior of the go-down, quarter by quarter. His measured smile, the sudden pause, the squint followed by a summing breath—he was peering at the ten sailors.

Why this go-down? An eight-pointed cross was branded on the fore-arm of one of the four, other silk-clad men. Sir Nigel's military order had foreign roots.

The four men separated themselves from the sailors, talking in Dutch. Casually, three of the men spread out, bracketing the exits. The implication was clear. Any sailor who tried to leave would be dealt with.

A sailor turned to leave, stopped, and turned toward the others. A Dutch sentry shot the sailor in the head with a silenced pistol. The shock registered immediately. Nine sailors stood frozen in place—indelibly branded, each with a proven strategy for locating scoundrels hiding in the Protectorate of Aden.

"Captain Hardin is hiding from the British military. He will either trek overland or head for the waterfront to find a boat. He's heading for Alexandria."

"He will not escape Aden," a Turk shouted. "We have many informants."

"Perhaps you do have friends." Von Cleve lit a cigar and peered at the tarp covering Hardin. "As you have witnessed, I am not one of them." Glisters danced in the big man's eyes—eyes harder than jacketed cartridges.

"Turk. Do not rush to your death. This man is dangerous." Von Cleve's escorts were in constant motion, tracing an arc between exits.

Hardin lay motionless. Acrid blooms of jute dust thickened the air underneath the tarp. He covered his mouth with his neck rag, taking slow, shallow breaths. He needed water.

Sweating, he wedged his empty canteen under a sack of rice.

The men left the go-down. As his team filtered out of different loading bays, von Cleve bellowed, "Captain Hardin's days are numbered."

Hardin raised the canvas at its edge focused on the doorway von Cleve had not used as an exit. If he spotted me, he'll use a different route to reenter the go-down.

Waiting for several minutes, Hardin grew faint. He was sweating profusely. Embracing malaria's charm, he passed out.

Hardin came awake with a start to find a rat half the size of his Thompson sniffing his boot. A quick jerk of his foot brought a rush of rats scurrying through the go-down, swirling blooms of dust with their tails. It must have rained, he thought. The loading bay's damp.

A deep, searing pain beat within his thigh. The gauze that bound his ribs had slipped to his waist. Slowly he drew the canvas off a jute bale. Standing with his weapon at high port, he swept the go-down from end to end.

Satisfied he was alone, he hobbled to the loading bay facing the harbor. A pale-tan dusting of jute coated his skin. Twilight was beginning its magic—a new night. The brief storm and the wet, west wind would bring an early dusk, reducing visibility. Hardin found a water catchment at the corner of the go-down. Skimming the dust from the surface of the water he submerged the canteen and drank his fill. Then he refilled the canteen.

I need to get out of this uniform.

As silence creeps, Hardin laughed. His humors in solitude included having sex with Lady Luck. She had raised her skirt and trooped her colors. To his regret, the sweets of her luxury had become a necessity. Hardin had seen his enemy.

Relieved Stuart had not hired the mercenaries; Lady Luck had shown him the face of his enemy. "They're a bunch of brutal bastards. That's certain." Lost were his primary avenues of escape: fishing boats, dhows, pirates, and steamers—Aden's harbor was off limits.

If Uncle doesn't throw lines in Aden, I'm in deep shit. A trek overland through the mountains to the Red would take weeks. Plus, where do I find a guide with a horse to pack enough food and water. A guide that wouldn't make me tea and then slit my throat. Or sell me to one of the tribes that would have a feast and then slit my throat.

*   *   *

New York. Pan American Airways Marine Terminal. Port Washington, Manhasset Isle, 21 September 1939. 0430 Hours, GMT – 5 Hours.

"Why are the virtuous so greedy?" Hockey asked.

Dorothy Stuart sipped her brandy. And then, hesitating, she looked at him, and flushed. "Who knows? I've copied Eaton's arbitrage files. He has made a good deal of money."

Accepting the files, William Hockey set his drink on the table and narrowed his eyes. "Samuel Eaton has become a problem—your problem. Kaminski has informed me Eaton purchased a Swiss passport and is going to ground. He's running. Last seen in Lyon boarding a train for Spain, I assume he's heading for the seaplane terminal in Lisbon to board a flight to Bermuda. He's traveling with the German woman who works for Baron Kurt von Schroder."

"Her name is Petra Laube-Heintz."

"Yes, I know. If you leave tomorrow, you might intercept them at Lisbon's train station or the seaplane terminal." Pouring Dorothy another brandy, Hockey was off to bed.

The seaplane base at Sands Point, near Port Washington, on Manhasset Isle was a short drive from William Hockey's estate. Flight check-in was in a new metal-framed hangar. The departure gate was connected to the aircraft by a long ramp and a floating dock.

As was her custom when flying east, she purchased the two seats isolated in the rear of the aircraft, in the first-class passenger compartment of the Boeing flying boat. Her seats were situated up a series of platforms, in the tail of the aircraft, adjacent to a luxurious lady's powder room. The accommodations suited her security requirements.

The twenty-six-hour flight went unnoticed.

The B-314, Dixie Clipper, was landing at Horta, on the Isle of Faial, in the Azores, when Dorothy came awake. Waiting on the dock, along with a businessman bound for Lisbon, a courier handed Dorothy a sealed cable from the British Radio Security Service, MI8—the envelope stamped priority, the cable stamped #54 Broadway.

My goodness. A missive from Mother's Special Intelligence Service.

Signed by the head of station at the British Passport Control Office in Lisbon, the order was specific: rendezvous with an émigré in Marseille and facilitate his passage to Lisbon for connections to New York. The date, time of day, tram line, and code name of the émigré were buried in a personal note from Hiram Bingham, US Vice Consul in Marseille.

Chaos is mounting in Europe, she thought, frantic émigrés, whores, and a double agent code-name Eggs—the world is a scramble. But Willie is still reasonable in light of this madness. Making sense because he's coldly predictable.

Emphatic, in a calculating way, Hockey had explained the specifics as he understood them, of the contracts targeting Operation Snow White. "Without a satisfactory conclusion to these contracts, the pursuit of those financial documents will continue. Sir Nigel understands this, as do I. The Templar have turbulent roots, loyal roots—a psychosis of sorts. They will keep their word. They will kill anyone, including the six arbitrage bankers or you to keep their secrets."

"Do you want me to warn Eaton?"

"He's yours to run." Hockey sipped his sherry. You had his secretary killed to gain access to the man. Warn him if you must."

"Good night, Willie."

Is Hockey Eaton's executioner? Or is his message meant for me?

A stylish, marauding crust formed in the west with the sun running from the night, its mellow distance aglow, and its charm gliding toward the rooftops along Lisbon's waterfront. Lisbon's marine terminal was new, enriched to its eves by expensive chaps smoking expensive cigars, guiding a lissome escort. For the flying boats, increasing demand had ticket prices on the rise. Padded chatter set its hum as Dorothy secured her bag.

A fog drift was forming on the harbor.

Confident without knowing why, she searched the interior of the terminal. She found Petra standing near the main entrance. Arranging a verdict, Dorothy walked around a column and found Eaton next to the German. His hair unruly, he looked a mess, scared as well.

Eaton saw her immediately.

"Samuel Eaton. Does J.P. Morgan have an office in Lisbon?"

"Why are you following me?"

Dorothy hesitated, considering Petra's timid demeanor. Guessing Eaton had reached out to the German for support, she became less strident. "To help. You can't go to the United States. New York is off limits. You're on a list for assassination. By I. G. Farben International's NW 7 intelligence group. Miss Heintz is on a collateral list posted by Baron Kurt von Schroder."

"How do you know this?"

"Ah. Mister Eaton. Do I dare trust you, Sam?"

"Get away from me!" Eaton exploded, furious. "Who the hell are you?"

"I work for England's Secret Intelligence Service, MI6. I have for years. J. P. Morgan is my current assignment. J. P. Morgan and Allen Dulles."

"My God." Eaton picked up his bag and threw it down.

"You need to run. The men behind the killing don't care about the money; they're worried about what you know. They have purchased municipal protections throughout the globe. Their lackeys will be stalking the flying routes to the United States, and the raw-product shipping lanes from the Panama Canal to the Red Sea."

"I've purchased tickets to New York using forged passports," Eaton said. As though searching Petra's expression for signs of support, he continued. "I've a place to hide. A small chalet in the mountain village of Zell am Zee, Austria, near the German border."

"Might work." Examining the passports, Dorothy handed Petra her spare wedding band. "Start acting like you're married and stop rubbing each other's ass. Are those your bags?"

"Yes—three bags, that's all." Petra stepped away from Eaton.

"Are there any identity papers or personal items in the bags?"

"My Lugar and ammunition." Eaton shook his head and looked perplexed as if evaluating the ramifications of Petra's declaration.

Dorothy confronted Eaton. "After you check your bags on to New York, give me the airline tickets. I can sell them in Marseille." Watching Petra kneel next to her bag to secure her weapon and ammunition, she continued. "Catch the first train leaving Lisbon heading east or south. Lisbon is crawling with Gestapo and many of the locals work for them."

*   *   *

Protectorate of Aden. 22 September 1939. 1110 Hours, GMT + 3 Hours.

Landing at RAF Base Khromaksar, courtesy of 8 Squadron RAF shuttling Bristol Blenheim MKI's from Alexandria to Bombay, Lewis Poston, the oil executive examined the details of a proposed contract between British Petroleum and the Protectorate of Aden.

Pushing a tuneless whistle through his teeth, he put the contract in his satchel and, dripping with sweat, entered the flight-operations shack. "My God, it must be a hundred and twenty degrees." Acknowledging the wireless operator's unit badge, a fistful of sparks, he waited in the queue to send his message.

Eager to be of service, more to be rid of a civilian twit, the wireless operator transmitted Poston's dispatch down-station for relay to London.

> Johnny,
> Sir Nigel Stuart. Find out what he's about. Having a go at Linc and his mates are my guess. A woman claiming to be his wife is swimming in the Med.
> A banker looking for her husband's kit. Nothing of the sort is the short stack.
> Lewis

Walking along Steamer Point, the crescent, passed the Indian-owned steamship coaling station, and east along the waterfront was a ritual Poston found fascinating—the confusion of men in tatty, faded gowns, disabled beggars, and the black-robed lepers shaking their handbells to warn the fit.

Heat waves waved.

A cool wind breathed in rushes between the buildings trailing a humid stream. Poston had accepted the company of two local Arab dragomen recommended by the Marina Hotel's concierge—a page and a chamberlain. In sorrowful contrast, one had a hungry eye, and the other had a nervous craw. The tall man was lean and unkempt. The other wildly untidy and twenty years the elder. Dressed in the rags of their work, they left a trail—a sweet, ebbing, foul smell.

Sorting their confiding gestures and toothless tirades, do what Poston might, the stroll was rife with incapable urgencies. Dodging sand-laced coins of spittle, Poston grimaced as he glanced at the harbor for relief. Why do these dolts have new sandals?

Poston admired the blues and browns of the harbor. If not for the flat blue sky, the light tan dust, an occasional patch of flowers and cannas, and the spindly pale green palmates, Aden would be devoid of color. Aden could boast of a single tree, but the British cut it down so the stunted palms would no longer be stunted.

For centuries Aden, known as the dull-gray eye of Yemen, had been the gateway to Mecca and its surrounds. Before the advent of the airplane, Muslim pilgrims bound for the hajj, from Arabia, the Persian Gulf, India, the subcontinent, or Indonesia, traveled via Aden and Jeddah. Throughout, even the dhimmi merchants of Aden made vast sums. Indian officials managed the Protectorate of Aden for the Colonial Office in London. Indian merchants and investors had constructed hotels and other luxuries, making Steamer Point, Aden's commercial hub.

Poston drew at the air. Was that nutmeg he smelled? Dodging a carriage hack and a band of urchins chasing a tourist, he waved when the last urchin called to him, "Sorry, *sahib*." In their wake, all went quiet.

A leper's handbell rang its lifeless song. A soot-grimed woman screamed.

A flicker of movement drew Poston's eye. The glint of a knife blade flashed in a shaft of light. Poston cautiously entered the go-down. A British soldier was cornered in a cupboard of jute bales. Shouting a vile Portuguese and Turk, three oil-stained sailors stabbed in turn at their quarry, as if by some protocol.

It was possible, Poston decided, to stir the shit in this cesspool and see who complained about the disturbance—might create dissension or a diversion. The remedy suggested itself when Poston handed his jacket to his escorts and started to engage the nearest sailor.

Just as he moved, he stopped. With each thrust of a knife, a fist half the size of a jute bale found a protruding jaw as a maul finds a spike. The three sailors were quick enough, but not so quick as the squaddie. In minutes the three sailors lay on the deck of the go-down, their knives tossed behind a stack of salt bags.

"If they're not dead, they definitely look the part," Poston declared.

As the squaddie leaned against the massive post, it was obvious the man needed help. His uniform was stained and torn, his face was weather beaten, and his eyes never stopped moving. He stepped with a minor limp and kept his free hand pressed against his rib cage. Kneeling, he rifled the pockets of his unconscious assailants.

The bastards looked dead, sure enough.

Stuffing money and passports into a map pocket, the soldier's cracked lips creased into a crepe-paper grin. As his lips split and bled, he likened a rural tune. Blood spotted the dust-laden scruff around his mouth. He sighed as if to lessen the tension and bellowed as he leveled his glare on the stranger.

"Thanks for the help, mate." The soldier leveled his weapon on Poston's chest.

"Perhaps I can be of help now."

"Not much linen where I'm about, jackass." Poston stood erect as the soldier secured his kit. "You're a pastel-colored jack-wagon with indoor skin and fancy sandals." As the soldier came closer, Poston braced himself. "Well Abigail, are those fuckers your doing?"

"Fair point, I suppose. My name's Lewis Poston. I'm with British Petroleum hereabout. I just popped down from Alexandria." The soldier acknowledged the name with a vinegar smile.

"'Just popped down'—what the hell is that about? BP's been oiling the queen's hinges for so long, second-table blokes like me will never know she's coming." Brushing at his disheveled uniform, the soldier set his right hand to the trigger housing of his weapon and opened his left hand in a gesture of truce—or was he demanding attention?

"Your English is good, Poston. Does it match your passport?"

Unmoved by the soldier's deprecating comments, Poston produced his passport for inspection. "Yes…May I buy you a pint?" he asked, gesturing as though the squaddie was the kind of man he hoped to find—that England needed.

"Here. Put on my jacket."

Seemingly wasted by weariness and in need of shelter, the soldier accepted his meal with mock respect. Commercial sorts in Aden's corner of the world rarely offered a favor to a filthy, unshaven, British brown job.

After eating his fill, and a large jar of Stella beer, the soldier lit a cigarette. Placing the edge of a vulcanized fiber red and green identity disc on the table, he snapped it flat and set a finger to its edge—*Grumpy* was inscribed on the disc.

Something about Poston had marked him in Hardin's mind, jarring him to question his instinct about the man. Something disturbed him. He paused, then said, "Sir John Poston was a man of means—a godfather to some."

"That gambit is rather singular," Poston nearly shouted as he eased away from Hardin. "Sir John was my father. Be careful how you use his name."

Hardin offered no reply.

Reading the disc, Poston traced the imprint. He hesitated and cocked his head, deciding the faint, red-brown stain was not blood. The stamped recess of the identity disc cradling the "rum" of Linc Jensen's code sign was filled to its limit, no longer liquid, lying as a dull crimson, scuffed, and muted by its journey. Is Linc dead? No, there's a picture of the lad here in my jacket. If this is Grumpy, where is my nephew?

Poston shook his head in denial. Drawing his glass through the pool of water at its base he rose to retrieve his hat, rolling it through his fingers, measuring its worth. Seated, he finished his pint in one go. There is no reason to judge this squaddie.

"I am Captain Edward Hardin—Sir John Poston was my godfather."

"Good God, the whole world is looking for you. Or someone like you."

"Grumpy died in Burma."

Poston glared at Hardin. "I'm damn sorry to hear that."

And so, this—this—is the legendary commando. The special service chap the world's trying to kill. I'll bet he doesn't know why.

The day turned hot, and then hotter. Brooms and dustbins met the morning. The granite walks blistered the slow foot. Dust whorls trailed in pairs behind Poston's sandals, leaving a trace on the walk.

Goats governed the laneways and the doorways. Better fed, they would shit again.

If not for the British army ambulance, nothing else would look dirty. Parked across the road from the entrance to the Marina Hotel, lepers formed a queue at the vehicle's side door, ringing a bell and waiting for sahib's medicine—chaulmoogra oil.

Bypassing the hotel's entrance, Poston ushered the commando into the Star Pharmacy to a chorus of pleasantries.

"A bromide, Surtag, for my friend," Poston chimed. "A razor and soap as well." He found Hardin studying the currency exchange. "In the Aden Protectorate the currency currently in use is the British Indian rupee. About thirteen plus rupees per pound sterling."

"Mother's bankers have their hands in everyone's pocket."

The hotel's stairwell was dark and smelled of heat.

The two-story building was stone from its foundation to its rafters—granite from a local quarry. An eight-foot veranda ran the width of Poston's room and was protected by a stone half-wall, topped with a rough-hewn rail and a three-arch wooden lattice.

The fly wire covering the windows was coated with a fine, light tan dust.

From the veranda, the view of Aden Harbor went from the open water of Front Bay on the left, to the Aliyah Cholera Quarantine Station, to Slave Island and Dhow Harbor on the right, and north on to the Salt Works with its hundreds of mounds of salt.

"There are three thousand six hundred and eighty-six acres of shallow salt pans in the Salt Works—Aden's primary export. Pump in seawater, let it dry, bag it, and sell it."

"Poston, I'm not interested in salt or this borehole." Shedding his shirt one sleeve at a time, wincing, Hardin searched the room. The left side of his chest was turning green and purple from the bruising where his canteen had been driven against his rib cage. "There's a four-man team in Aden led by a South African. He's hired nine sailors. You met three of them this morning. The bastards mean to kill me and take this pouch."

"Despicable..." After a brief silence, Poston took a photograph of Linc Jensen from his pocket. The lad stood erect in his Wolverhampton football togs, smiling, toasting a glass of ale in front of The Blistering Sod Publik House. It was the same picture of Linc Jensen on Gold Flake cigarette cards.

Hardin acknowledged the photo. "We were ambushed in Burma by mercenaries. Linc was the last to die." His thoughts went to Jensen's final sigh. "I've a small bag with what's left of my mates." Hardin dumped the severed thumbs on a small table. "Their cocks were fed to the rats."

"Are these trophies?"

"Are you as stupid as you seem? They're proof-of-kills. Bounties. One is Linc's."

"I see. You lost some good mates."

"Linc Jensen, Robin Wingrove... and the others."

"At least..." Poston set his jaw and turned away. "I have been looking for my nephew, for Linc." Hardin laid a towel over the thumbs. "I'll settle this with Stuart. I'm convinced he's nose deep in Snow White.."

"I know he is."

Hardin drew air through his clenched teeth. "Stuart's nose deep and dogging me. A South African is chasing this pouch as well. At times, they seem to be in league." He emptied his rucksack and spread his gear across the bed, separating the Thompson, its extra magazines, and the pouch. Suddenly his recall flashed, crushing the *L* pill against Grumpy's molars.

Holding up a magazine, he depressed the magazine's following spring, pushing, and releasing the spring to test its resilience.

Satisfied, he tossed the magazine on the bed. "Stuart didn't hire the Cambodes who ambushed my team, nor the two trackers. All were hired by the South African."

"Really? On paper Stuart works for MI9. He's been under cover, working North Africa's slave trade. Why would he risk exposing his identity?"

"Why indeed? Mother's after the pouch and I stumbled into Stuart's bailiwick."

A knock and the rattle of pans brought a dhobi wallah into the room just as Hardin covered his gear with the bedsheet. The young boy set a basin of hot water and towels in a green cubicle that passed for the bath, took a tray of iced tea to the veranda, and fled, leaving an innocent smile to hide whatever intelligence he had gleaned.

"Mother does have her days." Hardin sampled the tea. "If nothing has happened to Uncle Dingo, Stuart's lashed to a bulkhead, enjoying the luxuries of second-class steerage on that tramp steamer—your steamer, Poston." Watching Poston's eyes for a white-feathered spark, Hardin wiped off the stock of the Thompson, set a round in the bolt housing, and slammed the bolt closed.

"Uncle Dingo is Captain Corcoran, I presume."

"Right you are. Lord of a manor, are you—a tall poppy? A month of K-rations and bully beef will cure your highborn ways—your social constipation. That tramp steamer you own needs a scrubbing—and paint."

"I've never seen that ship."

"If Mother doesn't sink her, the scow will be in Aden by tomorrow."

With a suggestion Hardin could bathe and relax, Poston said, "There are a good many mahogany-desk jockeys looking for that pouch: bankers, priests, industrialists, back-benchers, royals. Bankers, mostly—Dewar at Section D, MI6; the silk crowd fancies the Metropole Hotel."

"And you, Sir Poston? Are you one of the hounds?" Hardin's vision was blurring.

"Not intentionally, I assure you."

Scenes of the team's ambush merged with the attempted rescue of the bishop in Tonkin. Hardin was flying toward the rear-wheel housing of the Wellington as he fell arse over tit from the plane. Pressing a thumb and forefinger to his eyes, he tried to relieve a sudden ache. Dizzy, he drew a long breath. He needed a cigarette.

"Do you have a weapon, Poston?"

Opening his valise, Poston stepped away to allow Hardin to inspect the contents. "A small caliber Walther PPK with an expendable silencer."

Hardin held up the weapon. "Hitler carries one of these."

"Yes, I know. Many operatives in MI5 do as well."

"Not much of a weapon." Hardin emptied the chamber and took the magazine from the weapon's butt. Nodding, he handed the weapon to Poston. "The last man carrying that pouch lost his head. A Catholic bishop." He closed Poston's valise and threw it on the bed. "He didn't carry a weapon."

"Lost his head?" Poston asked. "I wondered why the Vatican was in Snow White's knickers from the jump. Priests and private operatives alike contracted through the Vatican's Prefecture for Extraordinary Affairs—through an East India company. Seventeenth-century trade routes still provide cover for Vatican ratlines that honeycomb Asia."

"Who are you, Poston? You and your silk shirts and linen pants."

"As a British Petroleum oil executive, I've been imbedded with MI6 for a good many years. Secretly posted as the head of a provisional spy group—Special Operations Executive's Group 133 working the Mediterranean region."

"Were you briefed on operation Snow White from the jump?"

"Admiral Sinclair briefed me. Our Inter-Services Liaison Department has been flooding the intel relays with partially true data. Chicken feed mostly. My brother works for Sinclair."

"Silk and talcum playing baccarat, and the squaddie draws a five," Hardin said.

Ignoring Hardin's insult, Poston continued. "Intermediaries representing the Vatican, traveling as bankers, were killed in Diamond Harbor, India. They were meeting with a South African. Admiral Sinclair and others at MI6 believe the South African is a Vatican hire."

"Makes no odds to me. That libertine defies God and kills anyone he's of a mind to. He sent trackers to kill me in Burma and again in Malaya—took out all my team before that. Uncle said he butchered two of Mother's twats in Singapore. And shot at Uncle in Bombay harbor."

"Who put Stuart in chains?" Poston stood into the wash of the ceiling fan and unbuttoned his sweat- stained silk shirt.

"Captain Baxter Corcoran. The wild man we call Uncle. He's driving the tramp steamer you own." Hardin scratched both sides of his beard. "He has Stuart lashed to a bulkhead in second-class steerage." Hardin took off the chest wrap exposing his bruised ribs. "The tosser's damn lucky to be alive. If Uncle's chief mate had his way, Sir Nig-Nog would have gone for a swim."

Nodding, Poston poured an iced tea, stepped into an archway at the veranda's rail. "Stuart has a tattoo on his forearm—a small red cross. William Hockey, a lifelong friend of my father's, has that same tattoo, as did my father."

"You best tread lightly, Poston—on quiet feet—toe then heel." Hardin examined the Rengas sap scars on his forearms. One was still a bit pulpy. "Hockey's a hard sort. Cut from rough stone. I met him when I was nine years old. He has the gift. That half smile he favors is fair warning."

Nodding as if deciding, Poston went on. "Hockey's an incomplete portrait. I know he's dangerous, a 'People of the Book.' His ilk will kill anyone to keep a secret."

"'One of God's ruddy little games'—your father's words," Hardin said. "The South African and his associates wear the same shield. God's bankers. Knights of old and all that curly dirt." He picked up the Thompson and inserted a magazine box.

"Are you a killing man, Poston?"

"Not so far."

Reflective, as if ancient tocsins had forced a coded urgency, Poston fell silent. The special-service troops he dispatched had landed in the desert near the south end of the "Ditch," expecting to board the steamer anchored in the queue waiting to transit the Suez Canal—expecting to find Linc Jensen and Sir Nigel.

With a quizzical expression, Poston thought he heard footsteps in the corridor. Waiting, he whispered. "I believe the South African has decided Team 7's remaining commandos and the pouch are in Aden. I've yet to determine why Stuart is tracking Snow White."

Poston walked into the empty hall and returned to the suite.

Twice he started to reach for the pouch. Twice he hesitated, drawing caution from a nearly indiscernible hand gesture of Hardin's—a slight cock to his right thumb.

One disconcerting move and Hardin would kill him. The soldier was a throwback, a timepiece from a Welsh tragedy, with hands outsized for his six feet and some. Hands that looked as though soaked in walnut oil. The man had been primed by weeks of counter ambush evasion, and he was dangerous.

My father loved this squaddie. Does it matter that he's now a different man? Hardin has made courage from the slaughter of his mates.

As though cards shot from a child's hand, he rummaged through the days of his past. Briefing notes, cropped with sparks, shot from his father's files.

Dewar was connected to Poston and Sons Ltd.'s misfortune.

Johnny's details do find an end, Lewis thought. I considered Dewar to be a displaced twat who cultivated irrational dislikes. But Johnny's right. Dewar's a traitor.

Poston finished his iced tea and said, "I need to send a dispatch to Alexandria." After covering Hardin's gear with a blanket, he issued a warning. "Don't leave the room."

If I can find Stuart before Hardin does, I might be able to end this chase. And find out why Team 7 was run to ground. The signal he would send to Dirk Jensen would be mainly true:

> The steamer will be in Aden tomorrow. Sir Nigel is detained below deck.
> Grumpy is on board. Secure both men and their kits.

Stepping into the street, Poston found his escorts waiting to lead the way to the Postal Exchange. He decided to get Hardin to the British air base and a plane ride out of Yemen.

*   *   *

Protectorate of Aden. Go-down on Aden's Waterfront. 22 September 1939. 1930 Hours, GMT + 3 Hours.

The Nazi signals-listening post in Cairo intercepted SOE Group 133's transmission to an operative in Aden who alerted von Cleve that his target was still on a steamer in Aden Harbor. Amused, von Cleve checked the box magazine for his Browning (HP) for loads and whispered to himself, "How do the British brand stupidity with such a cold iron?"

Hoping the signals transmission from Southeast Asia, sent through American radio-relays describing the remains of a British soldier was a ruse, he calculated the odds, betting the remaining commando was on the steamer. But if the message was true, the Americans might have the pouch.

Captain Hardin's in Aden. After nearly killing three hatchet-faced sailors with his bare hands, he took their weapons, passports, and money.

No longer wounded, the Welshman will be a dangerous kill.

Von Cleve enjoyed watching the eyes of a man about to die. The soul would perch itself outside the mind girding for a disturbance—like the patterned maze produced when light beams collide—no longer a rainbow, more the bars of a codex.

"Killing that commando will be a bright spark." His voice trailed off, as if remembering. "With any target there's an easy way in."

For sport, he decided to wait for the three sailors to come awake before he shot them.

Closing his hand to relieve a kink in a tendon, he shuttled the pistol from hand to hand. The handgrip on the silenced, Ceska, CZ vz. 36, 6.35mm, double-action pistol was made for a woman. Bored with the stench inside the go-down, he shot each sailor in the head.

Standing in the recess of a loading bay, he measured the worth of their excuse—the persons in the town. For von Cleve, the natives were an ensemble of useless tools—untethered goats and goat shit prompting their way. Urchins and beggars vied for intersections, be they for streets or laneways.

Their critics, the lepers, scuttled about or sheltered in unused doorways. Hand bells chimed and the fit changed their ways—a pivot drew a bare foot from sandal to hot stone—a lifting, subconscious quickening.

A handbill nailed to the go-down's wall announced the movie *You Can't Take It with You,* was playing at the Regal Cinema, starring Lionel Barrymore and James Stewart. Remembering the Al-casino & Steakhouse served an excellent fare, he set a course for Steamer Point.

Settled into the comfort of the restaurant, von Cleve savored the coffee, adding honey.

The commando's in Aden. British intelligence believes he's on that steamer. I'll trap the steamer to ensure the target does not re-board after the British team withdraws.

$*$　　$*$　　$*$

Protectorate of Aden. Uncle's Tramp Steamer at Anchor in Aden Harbor. 23 September 1939. 2030 Hours. GMT + 3 Hours.

Molly cocked his head, sucking air through his teeth. "Something's amiss, Captain. Not since Flanders have I posted Mother's casualty listing next to my bunk." He set an ear to the port and cocked his head. The current washed the bow with a rush and a rhythmic slap. After a swig of rum, he said, "Hardin's mates missed the list."

Uncle drew deep on his cigarette. "That soldier's home at Steamer Point will have a full jar to measure soon enough. It's the Church of England's Institute for the simple, that's what it is—for crafty old sweats who fancy their tarts." He set his mug on the rail.

Half-past twilight.

The harbor looked a right mess, as Aden's harbor generally did. Dhows and lighters, small boats and sewage coursed through the tide. A tidal rip meandered from the small harbor inside Slave Island, around the island, and turned north along the isthmus to the Salt Works. The rip was chocked to its limit with debris, offering bits of garbage to any wisp of wind.

Anchoring out as was his custom, Uncle judged the depth at mean-lower-low water at eleven fathoms and set the anchor chain at five times the depth. Anchor chain raced from the hawse to the starboard, accelerated, and crashed to a stop. Links paused at the hawse hole and chinked their way into the harbor. Preferring a large swing circle, he expected the stern to drift toward the inner harbor with the incoming tide.

Watching Molly set the Jacob's ladder on the leeward side of the boat deck, Uncle realized HMS Sloop *Fowey* had followed him into the harbor and tied up at the royals' bunkering dock, its crew scurrying ashore, free to muck about the town.

Their off to the Union Club—the only club in Aden that allows women.

Leaving the chains and ropes to lie about, Molly switched off the masthead light—the sidelights, bow and stern lights went as one. Not as one, the insects stopped their wing beat, silent at first, replaced by brief spurts of confusion. Dead lights covered the portholes.

Brief periods of unrelieved darkness interrupted Uncle's vision. Pinwheels fell to the intermittent intrusion of the lighthouse at Balfe Point. Shot with a brilliant strobe at seventeen-second intervals, he retreated from the rail into the shadow of a lifeboat.

Aden must have snipers. The moon's out.

Barely glowing lights along the shore lay as shafts on the water, aimed at the center of his chest. Wherries, small lighters, and dozens of small shuttlecrafts sat idle, some with lights, the rest just black hulks. Dead calm, not a hint of breeze, a fish slapped the water.

Muzzle down as though judging the night, Molly handed his captain a mug of rum and leaned on the rail. He laid the barrel of his Model 1897 tart on the rail, settled his chest into the rail, and adjusted the shotgun's leather sling.

"If I have another go at Sir Nigel, he'll be simple enough." Molly turned his head, listening as if he heard an odd sound. "His teeth are so loose; they're dodging his bite. His laughing gear has a bend to it, and I've watered his rum." Molly used Uncle's fag to light his own.

"I've a proud hatred for that royal, Captain."

"Patriotic hatreds are best, Molly—Mother's choice." Tired, Uncle set his back to the ship's rail.

"Stand easy." He whispered his warning as he laid a firm hand on the barrel of Molly's shotgun. "We've visitors—marines by their looks. They're armed with those nasty MK1 Bren light machine guns."

Silence held sway. Measuring the threat, Uncle waited.

Dark figures crouched in various firing positions across the for'e deck and the hawse, their weapons keen for any movement in their sector of the deck. A man with an oblong torso stood erect as if he were not on the guest list. Although armed with a Bren, his manner was undisciplined. The other men were royal marines.

"If you would do me the honor to be surprised, Captain Corcoran."

"Of course, I'll pipe you on board—and who would you be?"

"Lieutenant Dirk Jensen. The lads are special-service troops. We've come to take Grumpy and Sir Nigel Stuart."

The oblong man jumped to Jensen's side and shouted, "Fetch the bastards, or I'll open up your virtue with this Bren gun."

The stock of Jensen's weapon landed on the point of the man's lower jaw as he opened his mouth for a second salvo. He collapsed. "My apologies, Captain Corcoran. There's always one new lad, I'm afraid. Gosden's a desk transfer—a chuffer if you like."

Molly shoved Uncle's hand from the shotgun's barrel, whispering, "I'll give the special fucker a transfer. A packet of lead balls to gargle."

Uncle whispered, "Have a piss, Molly." He knew if he didn't defuse the situation, Molly would open the dance with Jensen and the chuffer—one barrel each. Whispering again, he said, "Molly, you and Madog fetch McPhee and Stuart."

"We have our orders, Captain," Jensen said.

Uncle lit another cigarette and shuttled it across his mouth once, and back again. Then he took a long drag and blew smoke to his side. Watching the oblong man gain his feet and pick up his weapon, he waited for the next move.

"Mother's been trying to kill Grumpy. Are those your orders, lieutenant?"

"Pick up and escort—that's the order."

McPhee and Madog appeared on the far side of the raiding party with their weapons at the ready. The barrel of Molly's shotgun appeared from behind the port-side davit crane, centered on Gosden's chest.

"Stand easy, lads," Jensen said.

"Grumpy will go with you if he's allowed to keep his weapon," Molly declared.

Instantly, Gosden spun into a crouch, leveling his weapon on McPhee, screaming, and firing as he turned. Firing too quickly, the initial rounds tore chunks out of the wood decking to the right of McPhee's feet.

Madog shoved McPhee away and lunged in the opposite direction, falling as he tried to bring his weapon to bear. In the same instant Molly squeezed Olive's trigger, held the trigger in place and pumped a second load into the chuffer's chest.

Gosden's body flew sideways as his Bren gun ripped jagged holes in the wooden deck and blasted troughs out of the rail, the shot pattern trailing McPhee's body by hairs, one-in-four tracers arcing into the air.

Molly had been up to the wire so many times, with his weapon held at high port, he fumbled with the new loads. Listening as Molly racked a load into Olive Oil's breach, eerily silent men watched as the Balfe Point lighthouse pictured the scene every seventeen seconds.

The special-service troops, all in a crouch, focused on their sectors of the clock.

"Stand easy, lads. You may keep your weapon, Grumpy." Jensen set his weapon at high port; his face hidden in his silhouette. "We're away, lads. The dead man first."

Lieutenant Jensen stood into the face of the man called Grumpy—McPhee's face. Peering through five cycles of the Bathe Point lighthouse, Grumpy was too small to be his brother, Linc.

"Who are you?"

"I'm the bloke who's been looking right and rowing left. One of Mother's tarts—I'm Snow White's orphan, the brown bull of Cooley."

Jensen walked across the deck and bummed a cigarette from Corcoran, and asked, "I have orders concerning Sir Nigel Stuart. Is he available for transport?"

"Our liege fancies his morphine. Molly gave him the mate's rate on two hits. Your royal's there on the deck. He turned turtle, so we lashed him in a hammock. He's so knackered he doesn't know Christmas from Bourke Street. You and the lads will be drinking gunfire in Alex before he knows what you're on about—Molly's choice."

After Stuart was lowered away, Jensen climbed over the rail and mounted the Jacob's ladder. With his arms resting on the top rail, lighting another cigarette he peered at Corcoran.

"We won't meet again, Captain. If we do, you'll need more than a trench gun."

* * *

Lisbon, Portugal. Rossio Railway Station.
22 September 1939. 1550 Hours, GMT.

Acting as a party of three, a wheel within a wheel, two women enjoying the prospects of being with a wealthy banker; Dorothy, Petra, and Eaton took a cab to Lisbon's Rossio Railway Station. With three first-class tickets to Lyon, Dorothy had ensured the booking clerk would remember her purchase, more the loose buttons on her blouse.

With sensual gestures wrapped in scraps of ease, Dorothy exposed the top of her carriage, so the on-board porter would remember. Her lips made humor with her eyes as she seized the sense of occasion, gave the young attendant a peck on the cheek and a five-pound note.

"Watch my bag, would you? We're going to eat dinner." The porter hesitated through an amiable smile as if an oversight were disguised with flattery. Dorothy caressed his cheek with a light touch and asked, "Does the restaurant in the station have grand sangrias?"

Retrieving her bag an hour later, Dorothy asked the attendant to escort the trio to their assigned compartment. Before he could respond she gave him a kiss on the cheek and another five-pounder. As planned, Petra asked the porter to show her to the dining car. Dorothy gave Eaton a peck on the cheek, said goodbye and rushed out of the rear exit of the carriage, strolled from the railway station, and caught a cab to the British Passport Office.

MI6 and Admiral Sinclair's Double-X Committee had set up shop using Lisbon's passport office as a drop for their operatives. Dorothy was escorted into an office where she picked up a ticket for the China Clipper bound for Marseille.

Spain's war was not long over, and the service on the National Railway had yet to recover. In their private, first-class compartment, Petra did a strip tease, bathing in the basin with playful interludes. Eaton cheered. Eaton kept pace, discarding his clothes with flair, his humping tackle swelling on cue.

Petra switched off the lights and drew the window shade closed.

In and out of her main line, Eaton's tongue turned the windmill, teasing her shudders again and again. Petra was flush—her legs weak, and she was tender and dry. "It has an odd taste, that tool of yours," she said, smoothing cream on her face. Eaton fastened her nylons to her garter, setting the wire clasp over each fabric button as if scoring a goal, gently nudging her lips with his hand, admiring her scabbard, caressing her inner thigh.

Who could care of Spain or of Spanish Republicans when this woman was in flower?

Slowing steadily during the climb over the Col-des-Balistras Pass, the train seemed to coast as it approached the border with France and the small town of Cerbiére. As the train eased over the crest of the pass, it gained speed. The grasslands of Spain had given way to mountains and the promise of farmlands and the Mediterranean Sea.

"One war's ending, and another's beginning," Eaton said. "The bankers must be pleased."

"We change trains in Cerbiére," Petra said. "The Gestapo and their agents will be checking papers—detail by detail."

Estimating the danger, Eaton said, "The train to Lyon leaves in thirty-one minutes from Platform One. There can't be many eastbound platforms to choose from."

"If we are eager to be on our way, our papers in hand, the long coats will be less suspicious." Petra held her passport into the light and studied her new name. If she was thoroughly searched, if they found her Lugar, she and Eaton would be detained.

"Tie your hair back and muss it a bit," Eaton said, straightening the lapels of his overcoat. "You need to look crueler, Petra. Less attractive."

Raising her dress, she set the holster to her thigh. "Give me your handkerchief before you strap my pistol in its harness?"

Squatting on his haunches, Eaton drew the harness straps to their limit, and gently kissed her thigh, drawing at the aroma. Petra wiped her lipstick onto his handkerchief, rolled it and tied back her hair, mussing her hair over her forehead.

"Are you frightened, Sam?"

"You look a fright. But the Gestapo scare me more."

"These days they're looking for anyone to arrest. Republican Spaniards are being shot. Sympathizers are thrown in prison."

Eaton searched the station as their train slowed to a crawl. With vicious malice a policeman grabbed a woman as she stepped from the train on the adjoining platform, pushed her against a telephone box, and tore off her coat. As she begged, a man in civilian clothes nodded and began questioning the woman. Suddenly he shouted and threw her handbag onto the platform, spilling the contents onto the track.

When she fell to her knees and began picking up her money, he shot her in the back of the head. The gendarme jumped back and unslung his weapon from his shoulder. His uniform, but stitches from the last war, matched his helpless gestures as he laid his weapon on the ground.

Only the train and the German in civilian clothes were well defined.

As if treason were implicit in his expression, Eaton practiced his silent words. Without any apparent interest, and no way of approaching the situation with care, Petra elbowed him to be still and pulled him near a group of huddled figures.

"Act as if it doesn't matter," Petra whispered.

Making an effort at self-control, his thoughts quickened. "Those ruthless bastards." There was fear in his voice.

The railway station at Cerbiére was crowded. Dozens of French policemen armed with the PM Erma Mle-1935 submachine guns stood in pairs at the exits, searching faces with an air of arrogant certainty. The PM Erma's vertical wooden foregrip and perforated barrel shroud were menacing signatures, marks for the exigencies of wartime travel.

"We're next. I can feel it." So, now what, Eaton.

"Be quiet, Sam"

French railway officials and their German aides checked papers as if learning a new trade. Eaton gasped a silent gasp when security personnel escorted Petra to a separate queue, acting as though Petra was who they expected. When Petra began arguing in strident German, a French policeman flicked the air with an indifferent pen. Her bag was closed, and Mr. and Mrs. Frederick Borruck were directed onto Platform One.

Breathing a sigh of relief, Petra led Eaton out of the restricted area. "They are looking for a British woman—Dorothy perhaps." Checking the schedule board, she traced her finger over the route map. "We'll leave the train at this small village. Five kilometers this side of Lyon. We can make our way to Geneva through the countryside. We'll trek around Lyon and look for a farmer heading home from market."

*   *   *

Protectorate of Aden. Basse Café, Steamer Point, Aden. 23 September 1939. 0840 Hours, GMT + 3 Hours.

After the more than thirty minor Arab tribes who controlled the regions north and west of Aden proper had reached an accommodation with the British, Lewis Poston was able to negotiate several contracts for British Petroleum with the Protectorate of Aden. During his tenure, there had been no long-term certainty and fewer quiet days.

Twilight seemed to usher in the gunfire the Arab street used to celebrate its arguments.

Small-arms fire in the Gulf of Aden or anywhere in the Middle East could announce a celebration, a fishing feud, a pirate assault—any number of events. The percussion and rhythm of each chorus were so common, the incidents were often ignored. The pattern of small-arms fire Poston heard the night before was odd—the short burst of an automatic weapon and the answering roar of a shotgun—a three-second exchange—too short and too sudden.

I hope Grumpy's stand-in is safe, Poston thought. A crust of light, a rising mix of yellow and maroon, pushed the horizon to respond.

The dock basin lay quiet, confined, as it were, by colonial chaff. Tidewaiters manned the docks, their custom forms marked for arrivals. Three lighters approached the beach, with a beach-bound wallah shouting his hand.

I should have a response from Dirk Jensen by now.

Tourists and locals used the Eastern Telegraph Company's signals station at Steamer Point as their touchstone, not knowing the station was a British special-operations advanced signals center. Tourists, mostly—the locals were not going anywhere.

The heat was stifling—forty-three degrees Celsius and ninety-eight percent humidity—before breakfast could be mustered, let alone served. Hack carriages and gharries ran about, delivering the essentials for Aden to thrash its way into morning roll call. The layout of the streets and buildings of Aden had fallen prey to the intricacies of improvised plumbing—a seventh-century replica of confusion.

Exhausted by the continual drum of beggars and urchins, the badgers and cheap jacks, Poston had taken the usual abuse—so had his watch.

A thin mantle of dust greeted Poston as he sat at his favorite table near one of the harborside windows at the Basse Café. He read Sergeant Jensen's signal again, this time with a sense of relief— "A jolly good show. Remains not viewable." Brief and to the point. Gosden was a mess. Sir Nigel was under arms and Grumpy's stand-in was safe.

In turn, Poston relayed a short, false, encrypted signal down-station to the British Passport Control Office in Cairo: Grumpy's secure.

His declaration was accurate enough. Jensen's sloop, HMS *Grimsby*, made the Red Sea and would enter the ninety-mile-long Suez Canal within twenty hours. That McPhee was not Hardin would not be discovered by Mother's snouts for weeks now that Gosden was dead.

That McPhee was not his brother, must have set Dirk on edge.

The next morning, reading Cairo's reply, Poston marveled at the speed of gossip and the investiture announced in the morning bulletin from the RAF signals station. Gosden, the barmy wank, wasn't worth the candle.

Tribal Guards and five members of India's 2ⁿᵈ Battalion, 5ᵗʰ Mahratta Light Infantry, patrolling in the Western Aden Protectorate last night, found a body of a British officer washed up on the beach. The body of Lieutenant Alfred Gosden, a special-service officer, was transported to Saint Mary's Garrison Church, in Crater for burial. An honor guard from the 20ᵗʰ Fortress Company, along with Red Sea Force Commander, Acting Captain P. I. Gun, will attend the ceremony. Full honors will be observed with an investiture for Lieutenant Gosden as an Officer of the Most Excellent Order of the British Empire.

Finishing his meal, he examined Hardin's new passport. Lieutenant Colonel Sir Bernard Rawdon Reilly, the governor and commander-in-chief of the Colony and Protectorate of Aden, was a lifelong friend of Poston's. He suggested a colonial passport for Hardin would be less suspect and less restrictive for travel in the region. Passport 609 was set in a well-worn red passport jacket. Hardin had become Joseph Hitchcock from Liverpool.

I'll bet the man has a hitch in his cock by now, verging on those vinegar strokes. In good spirits, considering an appreciative smile, Poston decided his dealings with the commando, were lighted, here and there by a touch of irony.

Returning to the Marina Hotel, Poston hollered his arrival and opened the door. Hardin was lounging in a hot bath, smoking a cigar, with a bottle of rum stationed on a chair ready at hand. The Thompson was propped on a second chair, aimed at Poston's nuts.

Poston dropped Hardin's passport next to the rum bottle. "We're off to RAF Base Khromaksar later in the day. I'm in a scout car with a small detachment of lads from the 2ⁿᵈ of the 5ᵗʰ Mahratta Light Infantry. The teams looking for you will expect you to try to find a plane ride out of Aden. That's why you're on foot. Scout cars going anywhere in this region at night might get ambushed."

"The lord gets quarter-inch steel, and I get the door."

"Right. I negotiate contracts. Paper contracts for British Petroleum. You're a special-service squaddie and I'm helping you get home. If you want to be a primary target, ride in the scout car. I'll catch a cab."

"How far's this trek?"

"Precisely eight kilometers—tonight with a guide. Number 8 Squadron's headquartered at Khromaksar. If we don't meet up, ask for Squadron Leader Phillips. He's been briefed that you're working for me."

Poston walked onto the veranda and hollered over his shoulder. "Run the eight kilometers if you like. Your guide's a jolly sort."

"A royal marine?"

"They're a rough lot, as marines generally are."

As the main gate at RAF Base Khromaksar came into view Poston celebrated. "Looks like the locals took the night off," Poston yelled.

As the scout car approached the gate house, automatic-weapons fire lanced the night from three locations, killing the squad leader. As the dead man slumped out the door, Poston caught hold of his harness webbing and hauled his body into the center of the front seat. A sting bit Poston's bicep as he grabbed the dead man's carbine to return fire.

Poston dropped the weapon into the foot-well and tore off his jacket to stop the bleeding.

The squaddies in the rear of the scout car returned fire. The driver slammed the gear lever into bottom gear and stomped on the gas pedal. Sentries from the 2nd of the 5th Mahratta Light Infantry along the perimeter of the base responded with suppression fires, pouring tracers into a funnel at one location in the black desert. The scout car crashed through the gate with all its tires blown to pieces.

Nine hours later, Hardin strolled into the base dispensary and shook Poston's hand. "So now you qualify as a foot wobbler, or a jolly—your choice." He could barely distinguish the difference in the white of the gauze and the color of Poston's skin.

"Foot wobbler is my guess—the marines wouldn't have me." Poston held his linen jacket briefly to his face to stifle a cough before offering Hardin a chair. "A good lad died today. The contents of that pouch can't be worth the price."

As Poston's gaze hardened, he asked, "If that South African knows you're not afloat, he might have ties to the Nazi listening stations in the region." Poston slid off the examination table.

"If he is, he'll be waiting for me in Cairo," Hardin said.

"According to the Commander of British Forces Aden, Air Vice Marshal Reid, there's a German advanced signal center in Khartoum. The Krauts have been monitoring cross talk."

"Well, von Cleve's just one man."

Nodding, Poston put on the remnants of his soiled jacket. A corpsman had cut off the right sleeve, leaving the shoulder padding ragged and torn. "You jump into the desert tonight, Hardin. You're in the rear seat of a Vickers Vildebeest IV—a biplane from coastal patrol."

"Soiled. Sleeve missing. A bit rumpled. You've a linen jacket for any occasion, eh, Poston?"

*   *   *

Protectorate of Aden. Down the Flights at RAF Base Khromaksar, Aden. 24 September 1939. 0320 Hours, GMT + 3 Hours.

Hardin shouldered his rucksack, picked up his weapon and walked out of the dispensary headed for the airstrip. With Poston hard at heal, he stopped on the verge near the flight operations center. "Were you ordered to assist me?"

"Yes. Admiral Sinclair. I've also been ordered to secure the pouch and your rucksack."

That Sinclair wanted Hardin to give Lewis Poston the pouch containing the sealed documents, and the rucksack he jumped into Tonkin with made some sense. From the jump, Poston's arguments had been rife with such desk-bound logic.

But Linc Jensen told him to give the pouch to his uncle, Lewis Poston and no one else.

After swinging his rucksack to the ground, he opened the breach of his Thompson and checked the load. Suspicious, Hardin said, "If that's not in writing I won't give you a damn thing." With irritation on the rise, he moved away from Poston. "The pouch is the admirals to do with. But why does he want my rucksack? It's nearly done over." The question was well chewed but drew no reply. "Tell me who you are, Poston."

Silence.

"You're more than an oil merchant."

Doubt mixed with anger. Hardin turned on Poston with his finger on the Thompson's trigger guard. Over the weeks Hardin's face had taken on the patina of weathered rosewood. His eyes narrowed as if sorting an eminent threat—wild things held true.

"Reality has a certain beauty, Poston."

Their eyes met. Poston stepped away holding a Walther PPK aimed at Hardin's midsection. "You don't need to know who I am, Hardin." The folds of tangible respect played across Poston's face. "The field operatives chasing that pouch think the documents you're packing are in your rucksack. Now give it to me."

Opening the rucksack Hardin took out a water-stained picture of Katherine. Dropping the ruck at Poston's feet, he tucked the pouch under his left arm. "You're a stupid diddler, Poston. One shot from that pistol and I'd have cut you in half with this Thompson."

"I know. The Walther's not loaded. Here's a small torch and a medical kit."

"Not loaded. Fate or folly. Are you as stupid as you seem?" Hardin put the torch and medical kit in a small canvas sack with the rest of his personal gear and drew the draw string tight. With the Thompson slung over his right shoulder, barrel down, he threw the pouch to Poston.

"It's your turn. Under seal, that bloody pouch is as useless as a cock flavored lollipop." Hardin reached in his rucksack and removed the leather bag containing his mate's thumbs.

"I'll be keeping these to bolster my defense at my court-marshal. After I blow McPhee's brains apart."

"Don't get too many notions, Hardin. If Team 7 hadn't found that pouch, no one would believe it. The bankers, the royals, the priests, they're obsessed with fear. The ambushes, the relentless pursuit, the killings. The bastards will keep paying for the killing."

Poston put the pouch in Hardin's jungle-worn rucksack. "The lobby goblins are going to kill you anyway. You're contagious."

Hardin looked away, considered grabbing his rucksack. "They should be worried. The ropey turds I find are going to die."

"Save that bollocks for Admiral Sinclair. To Mother's intel, your mates are yesterday's wind, bleeding beneath your regrets."

"Just so, that. I'll dump those thumbs on the admiral's desk."

"Sinclair's dying of cancer. You'll be lucky to speak to him again."

Lewis Poston and Captain Hardin walked along the perimeter roadway of the airstrip at RAF Base Khromaksar. The clear sky and light ground winds, together with an ample moon, meant his third night jump would be easier the jump into Aden, and dryer than jump into Tonkin.

"Who's the pilot?" Hardin asked.

"Willie Hockey's grandson, Peter."

"It's a crowded dance, this boogie of ours." Hardin walked away from Poston, stopped, and turned around. Opening the breech and checking the round in the Thompson's chamber, he said, "I've half-a-mind to burn you down, Poston. You silk-covered twats piss me off. If I find you had no orders from the admiral concerning this pouch, we'll talk again."

"Shopping for another regret, I suppose."

Hardin poked Poston in the chest with his index finger and stood into a brace. "Listen, you've been given fair warning."

"I've some intel you may want." Poston offered Hardin a cigarette and lit both. "Fresh water's scarce in the desert north of Port Sudan. Bandits control the wells."

"I hope I land closer to Cairo than Port Sudan."

"This *djellabah* is the local dress. Wear it over your uniform during the day." Hardin tucked the shift into his sack.

"Anything else?"

"Yes. A support team's in place at the Mena House Hotel. It's a rambling complex facing the pyramids. If there's a disconnect after you get there, put on the civilian clothes hanging in the closet of the room we reserved, and proceed to the bar on the roof of the Metropolitan Hotel."

"What name's on the room?"

"Joseph Hitchcock. Cost: fourteen pounds per night. Includes meals as well as attendees."

"Any more cross talk?"

"Beware of well-to-do locals. They're tied to the Muslim Brotherhood and the Nazis."

"Jump with me. Hold my hand"

"Next time."

"Poston. Don't let me find you on the other side of this operation."

Compared with the Vickers Wellington, the Vildebeest III was a string kite. Light and mobile, the biplane was an all-metal, fabric-covered airframe, with single-bay unstaggered wings. Hardin took hold of the nearest strut and climbed onto the left wing.

The kipper kite's pilot, Peter Hockey, was a nineteen-year-old, boasting balls of brass. With a smirk that set authority aside, his air force uniform looked as if it had been issued from the secondhand bin—a cloth flying helmet with one ear flap, flying goggles with a crack in the left lens, a flying suit with no name tag or unit insignia, and an oilskin patch on one knee.

His firm handshake took Hardin by surprise.

With one hand on his essentials, the young jockey rang a peal, laughing as Hardin fumbled with his parachute trying to wedge himself in the navigator's seat of the Vildebeest.

The copilots for these kites must run chest high, Hardin thought.

"We're across the Red, then north. The drop zone's in the desert, flat ground some miles south of the pyramids. Winds are light and variable, fifteen knots from the northeast."

Hardin shrugged and held up a thumb. "Tally ho," he whispered. The end of the monsoon's striated shades had left the night sky an open window. Hardin looked forward to the warmth of flying at lower altitudes. Stepping off the wing would be easier than dodging the overload tank in the Wellington's bomb bay.

"A Wellington did some excavation two nights ago, a few miles south of the drop zone. The lads in flight operations have intel that the crate's frame is still burning."

Hardin nodded, deciding to change the drop zone and search for his favorite pilot. If Hawkes is alive, this will be like looking for flea specs in a pile of pepper. He sighed. His mother liked to say that whenever she lost her sewing needle.

The biplane bounced and fluttered north along the west coast of the Red Sea, flying at three thousand feet. A headwind set the Vildebeest at a slight starboard cant the pilot seemed to enjoy. At angels three, the heat rising from the desert floor was intense.

Thermals will slow my descent and extend my drift. If winds are gusting, I'm screwed.

Hardin searched the surface below the airframe. Except for the isolated cluster of masthead lights on eight ships, and the patchwork glow of Port Sudan, the Red Sea ran dark and gloomy, a black tendril twining khaki-tan deserts—the heat from these endless expanses of sand lifting gray, dust-filled funnels hundreds of feet into the air.

Those dust funnels could be a problem.

The desert sand was refracting the light of the three-quarter moon, glowing near the Red Sea, and fading to black in the distant west and east.

If my drop zone's far enough from the Red Sea, it should be dark.

Wedged in the back seat like a dry sardine, Hardin set his canvas bag against the narrow windscreen in front of him and crawled out of the hole. Sitting on the edge of the cockpit, he took hold of the vertical strut next to the fuselage and paused to set his bearings. Drawing a deep breath his cracked ribs barked. Ensuring the O-ring on his T-4 parachute was accessible, he climbed onto the lower left wing and arranged his weapon and gear.

Even a stand-up landing's going to be wobbly.

Spotting remnants of Hawkes's airplane, its outline a series of brief flares, Hardin stepped off the wing into the night. Air rushed past his face as he rolled a shoulder to relocate the burning hulk of the Wellington. The T-4 caught air. The jar sent a weal of pain through his chest.

"Damn these bloody chutes."

The Vildebeest circled above him, dipped a wing into the moon, and turned north.

Dumping air to land downwind from the Wellington, Hardin searched the dunes for signs of movement. Using the fire as a reference for the horizon, he landed on a hard patch of sand. Bouncing on his cracked ribs, not once but twice, he spit expletives as rapidly as he could muster the words.

With sympathy done over, he bunched his parachute—hand over hand.

Holding his weapon at high port, he approached the glow of the burning aircraft. If Hawkes is alive, he didn't drop any crumbs. The geodesic grid held the aircraft's ghostly shape. What remained of the aircraft's linen skin burned in small patches near the sand. A long trench had been plowed into the desert where the Wellington's belly staggered in, sliding until the props caught the ground and jerked the nose of the aircraft deep into the sand.

Hawkes's isn't in the aircraft. Shining the torch into the remnants of the cockpit Hardin spotted a broken bottle, but no blood. Tire tracks of one vehicle and a confusion of boot prints indicated Hawkes was picked up. Placing his parachute next to a small fire, Hardin donned the striped cotton shift and started walking.

After seventeen hours, with the toe of his right boot coming apart, his right thigh aching, his canteen empty, and his chest begging him for a rest, the sand was still firm, hot, and endless. Nearing the last pyramid Hardin broke into a chuckle.

Exhausted, he set the stock of the Thompson on the sand and knelt on his left knee. "That glow must be from my hotel," he whispered. "Must be three miles yet."

The Thompson was difficult to conceal under the cotton shift when Mr. Joseph Hitchcock checked into the Mena House Hotel. His room charge had been paid in full.

The concierge flashed his disapproval of the condition of his new guest, but Hardin pretended not to notice. Within seconds the hotel manager was beside Hardin inspecting his passport. After a brief glance at Hardin's face and the battle dressing on his arm, the manager asked him to wait, and led the concierge into an office.

The concierge returned with a small medical kit and a room key. Weapon in hand, Hardin followed a porter through the hotel lobby and into a wide hallway.

The hostelry was a raucous assemblage, a crimp of confusion. Incised emblems of competing patriots lined the walls. This destination for the wealthy had fallen to Australian army troops, British officers, and the hulks of sailors run aground.

My concierge is out of sorts.

His room faced the pyramids, isolated on the outboard side near the gardens and the pool. A rank of palm trees cast slender bars across the surface of the pool. Blue pointed lotus and white round lotus sat in an artificial garden pool amidst a paddock of yellow chrysanthemums, pale purple hibiscus, cornflowers, jasmine, and red poppies.

Noting the fragrance of the garden and the woman in the pool, Hardin switched off the room lights, opened the double door, and eased onto the patio. A disturbance drew at the air—eddies in his mind. Something wasn't right. Someone was watching, waiting. Quickly, quietly stowing his gear in a recess of papyrus near the patio, he slipped through the dark room and tucked the Thompson under a towel by the side of the tub.

Naked, he slid into the hot bath armed with a bar of floating soap. Shaving in the bath without a mirror had been a bad idea. Months of pursuit through Burma's jungle and beyond had left his face corrugated with insect bites and lesions. Standing in a tentative way, watching the Australians near the pool, he dabbed his face with boric acid ointment.

The medicine seized each divot as though boiling worms.

In the moon's spill he examined his reflection in the window—tall, bruised, muscular in a lean sort of way, and as freshly groomed as a jungle-worn soldier could be. Focused again, threw the cotton shift in a bin, washed his uniform in the bath, rinsed it in the sink, and hung it in the bushes near his kit.

Posing as a civilian, he put on the clothes he found in the wardrobe. Selecting a red poppy for his lapel, he smiled. The Lotus were beginning to close.

After a dinner of lamb and sweet rice, more relaxed than he had been in months, he retired to the lounge to sip snifters of brandy and listen to a reasonably good piano.

Laying his head on his forearms he fell asleep in minutes.

A jolt of fever brought the image of Linc Jensen to bear, rotting in the undergrowth of a raucous jungle. Linc Jensen's pennon stands just there, stiff against the wind. With his bowel cleaved, spewing its bile, Linc offered a final tear. As then...his team leader was prepared to run, yet his boots left a printed trace—Jensen's boots as well.

The unpastured, waving tufts of jungle grass had grown to match their bush hats, marking their way and how tall they had become. Linc had warned him as only a young man could: "If you fancy tomorrow, don't let Mother know where we are."

Jarred awake, staring at a face working its delight, Hardin tried to gain ground on what looked to be a foreign news agent, then laughed through an apology, accepting an envelope from the night porter.

Mr. Joseph Hitchcock,

24 September, the Japs bombed Haiphong today. Destroyed four hundred and twenty (420) barrels of Frenchy's corn syrup, one hundred and forty-three (143) cases of Canada Dry and blew off the masts of the French cargo ship Porthos.

Your appointment with Mr. Wimpey has been reset for Kasr-el-Nil Barracks, opposite the British Paymaster's Office... Date undecided.

A car will stand by at 0700, the next two mornings.

The Vickers Wellington's called a Wimpey. If Mr. Wimpey is Flying Officer Hawkes, the pilot ditched another airplane.

*   *   *

Paris. 13 Rue du Four. 24 September 1939. 1300 Hours, GMT + 1 Hour.

George Harrison was not well. Afraid to fly, he suffered nearly thirty hours on a flying boat from New York to Ireland. Then a train to Dover, a ferryboat to Calais, and a train to Paris.

Max Ilgner and Kurt von Schroder were the first to arrive at 13 Rue du Four, the Sorbonne, the Warburg Institute's former Paris headquarters. As Victor Rothschild and Max Warburg approached the complex on foot, George Harrison, the governor of the Federal Reserve Bank of New York, stumbled from a taxi.

Adjusting his coat, Harrison looked up to find them staring at him.

Tripping at the curb, catching his fall with his valise, appearing confused and out of sorts, he fumbled with the taxi fare, spilling dollar bills and coins on the cobble walk and into the gutter. Walter Schellenberg and Rudolf Hess arrived in a second taxi as Harrison chided his driver in French, demanding the driver remain at the curb, on call.

The institute's library offered a leather-bound greeting, books bathed in a subdued light, gathering the smokes of pipes and cigars alike, blending the aroma for the typically rich. Its hearth was encased in granite, its massive oak chimneypiece adorned with rich, ivory carvings.

A rick of wood sat pale brown to the lamplight, a mellow gold near the fire. A pitch pocket flared, announcing Harrison's arrival. Flush and glistening with sweat, his face was a mural of despondent grays.

Laying siege to a cigarette, Harrison found the remaining overstuffed chair ungracious, as though propped in a star chamber or in the center of Temple Church.

Sensing the banker were frightened, Rothschild placed a hand to Harrison's shoulder. As he leveled the light shade he said, "Our arbitrage transactions have been aggressive and well timed, generating one point six billion pounds—sufficient capital to purchase control of the select companies—excepting I. G. Farben, International, as we agreed."

Rothschild approached the side of Harrison's chair and gave him a cigar. "In six days, the United States Federal Reserve Bank will announce a federal funds rate increase. The increase is not expected and will be of such a magnitude, markets around the world will panic. Stock values will fall. We will make money on the way down, and if prices fall far enough, we will raid the companies."

Using a poker to liven the fire, Warburg asked, "George, what rate increase is necessary for this scenario, and is that the rate you intend to announce?"

Flush to the point of sweating, Harrison grimaced as he set the unlit cigar aside. Rates and margins were Warburg's domain. With the room as warm as his garden shed in high summer, Harrison rang for the sommelier and requested a glass of water. With a proper mixture of dignity and hauteur, morning coat and striped pants, the sommelier left the room.

Harrison picked up the unlit cigar, turning it in his hands. Why did I leave New York? This meeting's a trap. He accepted the glass of water, welcoming the interruption. "A fifteen-hundred basis-point increase will ignite the market," he said. "Many are betting on war-material contracts and the like. The chaos you expect may take more than one rate hike."

"Rubbish, George," Warburg laughed. "Talent doing what it can, I suppose you brought your wife to Paris."

Max Ilgner looked around the room. "Harrison is frightened and may betray us. I have words of caution for you George. Pass them along to your chairman. I. G. Farben, International, and the banking houses represented in this room will be risking enormous sums of capital shorting the stocks of the selected companies."

Again, Rothschild stepped to Harrison's side. "All in this room know we have but one opportunity to get this right—in one rate hike. Do you agree, George?"

"Yes, of course."

"Here's a token of my regard George. A pine-tree shilling from the colonies. I know you don't have one in your collection."

"The institute's kitchen has prepared a meal for you gentlemen," the sommelier announced.

Harrison stood to gain courage. Examining the rare coin. Inured to his fears, he placed the coin in his breast pocket and declared, "Who hanged the governor of the Bank of England from Blackfriars Bridge—Lord Norman? Who sanctioned such a thing? The scoundrels may as well have hanged Fenian again—Stoneway Prison, Blackfriars Bridge. We're jousting with ghosts."

Ilgner seemed to find the outburst amusing—rich men playing dangerous games. From the beginning of the arbitrage plan, he considered Harrison the weak component and decided to gradually withdraw I. G. Farben from the game.

Rothschild guided Harrison to the fireplace and waited as the others entered the dining room. "George, if you would. Call this number in London, Temple Bar 4343. Ask for Willie. He's an associate of mine. He'll answer your questions about Lord Norman."

*   *   *

London. The Intelligence "Hole" beneath Whitehall. 24 September 1939. 1410 Hours, GMT.

September 1939 was a month of uncertainty. Petrol rationing had begun.

The British Expeditionary Force in France needed men and equipment. The Air Striking Force in France and England needed planes and pilots.

Auxiliary Ambulance Stations were up and operational, manned by groups of Indian women. The Trent Park Hotel was requisitioned to house high ranking German prisoners. Every room was a "Mike Room," bugged to listen to captured senior officers.

British inmates with less than one year remaining on their sentence were released to make room for a possible flood of German prisoners of war. And because of projected food and medical supply shortages, over four hundred thousand pets in greater London were being euthanized.

Londoners huddled near their radios in the morning, listening until late, lying awake in the dark. Troop trains packed with joyous Brown-jobs rattled on—heading east. Bombers flew in all possible directions. Troop transport planes crossed the Channel in a continuous stream. And the children stood in queues—wide-eyed, with labels pinned to their coats, their worn, cloth knapsacks containing a fresh change of underclothes and a sandwich or two, heading west.

A tray truck carrying sandbags overturned, forcing John Poston's cab onto the sidewalk. He spent the morning helping the laborers load the sandbags into a nearby lorry. Tailored in Savile Row, his impeccable morning appearance had given way, and he was scheduled throughout the day.

Rumpled and soiled, he took the stairs down to the Hole two at a time and stopped in front of the security checkpoint.

"Are you John Poston?" the guard asked.

"Yes." Poston presented his identity card.

"I've a message for you, sir."

Poston read the message on the way to his desk. He may have found the answer to Dewar's cash. Not since scoring a double-first in the classics and math at Oxford had he found such a rush of emotion. Old answers had blossomed into "Why didn't I think of that?" and, "of course!" Amused to find Dewar fidgeting with a stack of intel decrypts, Poston wrote another false decrypt to further disorient the twit.

After waiting five hours for his meeting called by Admiral Sinclair, Dewar signed for Poston's false decrypt. Authenticated with Sinclair's stamp, directed to Dewar's attention, the decrypt detailed the findings of an investigation concerning a drug-smuggling operation in southern France.

As though winded, Dewar stood, sat, stood, and walked about, announcing he was going to the loo. Returning he began again, standing and sitting, each rendition featuring a fresh cigarette. Routinely obsessed with Sinclair's tardiness, Dewar launched into a tired carp.

"This memo's about drugs, Johnny. Now the admiral has time to mess about in slothful sloughs. There's a war on. I've a landlord's bill to pay, and Sinclair, the sick bugger, is off on a jag. He's quite incapable of intrigue." Obviously on the raw, Dewar paled and sat.

"Is it that you find power an ugly tool, Gordon?" Poston asked.

"This is the second time in a week Sinclair has rearranged my schedule." Dewar lit a cigarette and reached for the phone. He had a second cigarette burning in the ashtray.

Footsteps echoed from the hallway leading to the office. Dewar hung up the phone.

Sinclair was dressed in an exquisite leather shooting jacket and corduroy trousers. Pauper-thin, his complexion flaccid, he had been morose and angry for some time. Without greeting his wards, he let drive with a declaration.

"Dewar, you've been restricted to this complex—this office, actually." Dewar crossed his legs. He scanned the length of the ceiling. Sinclair's words seemed to storm along the crest of his imagination and crash into his need for mobility.

"I'm not well, Dewar. Cancer, the doctors claim. I require your assistance to be on call as it were—day and night."

Seeming to suppress an impulse, Dewar looked into the papers he was shuffling. "I've rather active files, Admiral. Planks to put in place for operations. Lyon to Cairo."

Sinclair started walking around the room, the way he often did, organizing the personal things on each desk. He seemed to enjoy looking at the pictures and then setting them in a different spot on a desk. Arriving where he had started, he said, "Bromidic might describe the logic you exude, Dewar. Either you're not listening or you're thick. Let me be clearer. I want to be able to talk with you, to see your face, on any tick of the clock.

"Poston will take over your field operations. You will ensure he's thoroughly briefed."

Dewar started into a nodding routine—seconds and a minute of nodding before he spoke. "Very well, sir." He continued his nodding with an expression that told of confusion and revenge, stacking papers as if he were oiling the hinges on his own casket.

Poston laughed to himself.

"Poston…" Wincing, Sinclair grabbed his side and began massaging his left flank. He continued. "I've been advised by Berryman, in Cairo, that we lost an officer. An Alfred Gosden was killed by hostile fire in Aden. He's to be buried at Saint Mary's Garrison Church, in Crater. Look after the details, would you?"

"Of course. A church parade and he lands in a distant rest camp." After waiting for Dewar to respond, Lewis continued. "I've credible intel indicating Lieutenant Gosden was part of a cabal smuggling opium into France. Account records mostly. And, that he had help from inside MI6."

Dewar stood stiffly. "Bollocks. Gosden's a new lad."

Sinclair stared at Poston and then Dewar. "The graveyards will be filled with new lads after this lot—old lads as well." Sinclair strained to stand erect and drew air into his lungs. "We'll all have the same gongs in the end." Fatigue took hold as he walked toward the door. "Guy's Hospital in London's sector ten is stuffed to its sheets."

Sinclair knocked the door with his knuckles. The instant he looked at Dewar his expression turned to anger. "You will be on-call or be sacked."

Waiting for the admiral to clear the area, Poston spoke in a whisper. "Gordon, this new man's death cleans your closet a bit." Poston set a file folder in front of Dewar. "You'll agree after you read those intel summaries. Comic cuts, mostly."

Dewar, a man with few illusions, glanced at the summaries, and set them aside. "Is your prose meant for editing, Johnny?"

When Dewar put on his jacket and dropped the summaries in a bin, Poston held up a hand and said, "Does the admiral know you're a spy?"

"Don't be absurd."

"Hockey has determined your frequent trips to Bayonne and Malta involve opium. And it's the reason you killed my father."

"Killed your father. Now there's a turn up. And who might Hockey be?"

"William Hockey's a traveler, as was my father. He's partial to my family. Hockey had questions for the Duke of Hamilton and Gosden. I suggested he meet with you."

Through clinched teeth Dewar whispered, "Well young man, the wonder behind your words is difficult to find." Nodding as if settling his thoughts, the larceny of his rage held sway, as his gaze hardened. Inspecting the end of his cigarette he looked at Poston. "Gosden was a friend of mine. A young lad with more than enough to learn."

"Are you smuggling drugs, Gordon?"

*   *   *

Protectorate of Aden. Uncle's Tramp Steamer, Aden Harbor. 24 September 1939. 0930 Hours, GMT + 3 Hours.

Brown, and sun-browned, the ship's chandler inventoried the stores as the davit-crane lowered the last cargo net onto the ship's deck. His hard jaw and careful, covetous eyes were at odds with a rolling gait that seemed to suit his build. His shore clothes smelled of myrrh as they had for years. Ending his count, Mohamed Hack lubricated his mustache with his tongue and wiped the mossy log on his sleeve.

A round shouldered man with old hard eyes, he had an irritable disposition.

Now relaxed, he started as though stung. A shadow had passed over his shoes, yet he was alone. Or was he? With cunning sitting atop a mountain of greed, Mohamed Eharral Hack was a shrewd negotiator. The ship's chandler for seventy percent of the commercial vessels passing through the Port of Aden, he was fluent in five languages.

As such, he knew Lewis Poston well—as well as he knew the Harbor Police Authority. Awash in money, he trusted no one—especially with the sale of ship's stores.

British intelligence listed Mohamed Hack as a leading East African businessman working out of Khartoum, in the Sudan. A Catholic, he was suspected of being the head of a cartel specializing in high-priced female slaves and was known to be the principal owner of a German cargo ship operating in the Mediterranean, the MS *Rothenstein*.

He courted contractors and British dignitaries with lavish parties, a diplomat's trousseau of seductive women, and a subversive docket of smuggling.

Soon after being awarded the British Empire Medal in 1937 for his business success in Aden and Port Sudan, Hack constructed a complex on Steamer Point featuring the Regal Cinema and the Al-casino & Steakhouse a hub for gambling and other pecker-fretted vices.

With a tribal intelligence network that was complete in every particular, he also specialized in the sale of sensitive information. The wireless transmission from Haifa instructed him to delay servicing the Portuguese steamer until von Cleve made contact.

Von Cleve. I should never have provided whores for that Turk.

Discovering a telltale pattern of notches torn from the ship's weather deck and the leeward rail, he set the ship-stores listing on a hatch cover. The three-foot stain on the wooden deck was blood. A holystone lay next to the companionway.

"The shots fired last night killed somebody."

Whispering, Hack's voice lost itself in the noise of the surf. He froze into a brace when he found a sailor watching him—a short, powerfully set-up man, with dust-rimmed, yellow eyes that blazed back with hate. Eyes that rarely looked into themselves. A sailor who would blacksnake Hack for a quid.

Is this last night's shooter?

Whispering again, Hack grabbed the ship-stores listing and scurried to the Jacob's ladder. Frightened, he missed a handhold and nearly fell, wrenching his shoulder as he caught the next rung. Looking at the masthead, he wondered, if he should have the harbor police inventory the ship's cargo?

Hack's office at the casino was a well-guarded den smelling of myrrh, aloes, and cassia—two shakes and a pile of goat merde from the rancid stench of Al Ma'ala. The complex had the attention of every intelligence service operating in the Middle East.

Secreted into the complex through a secluded parking plaza, Poston, Uncle, and Molly sat down to a sumptuous meal. Drinking Cork Distiller's Paddy Irish Whiskey and smoking Cuban cigars, the three men relaxed, their mission half forgotten.

"Mohamed Hack," Poston said, standing to introduce his associates. "This is Captain Corcoran and his chief engineer, Clive Mauldin. We did not expect such gracious hospitality."

Hack reluctantly accepted the gesture, then crooked a knuckle and stroked his mustache. "Yes, of course. I see you've been wounded, Mr. Poston. I hope your stay in Aden did not include such a difficulty." Hack looked at his watch anxiously, turning its face inside his wrist. Molly squared his shoulders.

Poston waved his hand as if the wound was minor. "Pirates, I'm afraid. Nothing for a ship's chandler to worry about."

Hack's lips separated exposing clenched teeth. "There's been some landward mischief these past days. I have a flying boat chartered to take you to Alexandria this afternoon at thirteen-forty hours. The pilot's expecting two passengers, but he has room for five with the limited cargo and mail he is carrying."

"You moved up our schedule," Poston said. Molly opened the breach of his trench gun.

Exposing the weapon behind his belt, Hack looked at each man. "It's not as though your garments were altered, Mr. Poston. The sunlight's the same. It's the dictates of the clock that complicates, don't you agree?"

"Why did you change our schedule?"

Obviously irritated, Hack began shouting. "Three sailors and a ragged beggar afflicted with hashish were shot dead in a go-down in the Al Ma'ala district. British army personnel were ambushed near RAF Base Khromaksar, leaving one merchant-sailor and a British soldier dead, and two British soldiers wounded. A British officer was killed on your steamer last night and his body dumped into the harbor. All crimes and bodies a mystery, mind you. And you ask me why I moved up your leaving?"

"Fair enough, I suppose," Poston said, handing Hack a customs clearance form.

"Your vessel is partially loaded. Did you intend to take on salt?"

"No. Shipping pig iron on flush-deck steamers is tricky enough." Poston set his right hand over the barrel of Molly's trench gun as the old chief swung it onto the table.

Hack reached for his weapon and nearly fell. Corcoran kicked the pistol from the bastard's hand, then took Hack by the throat and slammed him against the wall. "We just met and you're wanting to shoot us." Corcoran picked up Hack's pistol and emptied the solids on the floor.

Watching Molly as Poston removed his hand from the trench gun, Hack seemed ready to run. Through bared teeth Corcoran said, "That steamer of mine will lay up and remain at anchor until a new captain arrives. In the meantime, the crew is well armed and must be maintained."

"Yes, of course. My water clerk will service your vessel every morning."

"No one else. Only your water clerk will board the steamer."

"As you say." Corcoran pushed Hack toward Molly.

Poston asked, "You mentioned a British officer...?"

"Aden's information officer, Captain Stewart Perowne, informed me the British officer killed last night will be buried today in the British garrison cemetery in Crater—a captain. His body washed up on the beach near the salt bins—a shotgun blast to the chest."

"Did you shoot him, Hack?"

Hack pointed at Molly's trench gun and stormed from the room.

With his world growing more unstable, Molly scoffed a derisive huff, closed Olive Oil's breach, and stroked the wooden butt of his metallic tart. For the old soldier, the whole sea lay in his hand, a hollow memory. Sir Nigel, the man he rescued from the shell craters of Flanders Field, had betrayed him. And Poston was playing piss with a nig-nog, a despicable East-African.

I should shoot the dervish bastard.

For Molly, the sun cast gold jewels. In this close-huddled room, limp air filled the corners with a special hue—the color of betrayal. For Molly, Sir Nigel's roots had infected those corners, and the good Lord had become something less than a pennyweight. Yet he weighed more than this faded-brown East-African.

Poston won't care if I shoot that African bastard. But Uncle Dingo might.

Uncle set an off eye to Molly and gave him an agreeable nod. Sorting hundreds of men over the years, he found two to be true—Molly and Hardin. Not trusting Poston was a matter of lineage. For Uncle, as the day distilled the sunlight and the night-birds gathered, a ship's bell still rang over the cliffs at Camp Z, in New South Wales, the twilight blessed with bits of Darwin's rain near Candle Creek.

Molly is a taut hand, and Hardin is Welsh to his core.

For Uncle, the mention of MI6, that Hack was their whore, meant Hack was expendable. Rolling the Webley over in his hand, he admired his forearm, playing his fingers, remembering how Lucy's tits liked to wiggle. The wound the sniper carved through her virtue had healed to a purple welt.

I should shoot Hack. Why worry about that black bastard?

Uncle looked at his watch and scrubbed his chin. "These wicks of time burn on, Poston. Transporting Team 7 was my charge. Turning circles in the

Bay of Bengal, we ferried Hardin to Ceylon, and ferried McPhee to Aden. My mission is now a ruse. Mother dares us with her game of beat-the-clock. Our honor is clean, Molly's and mine."

Poston seemed pleased with Corcoran's declaration. "Yes. You have rescued a special-service soldier, a pilot who drinks too much, an Irish harbormaster, and your crew. Not to mention the documents the whole world's chasing."

Uncle rolled his pistol over in his hand. He wanted to pull the trigger. "You forgot Sir Nigel. We didn't throw him over the side." Uncle opened the pistol and checked the loads.

As for the weather, for Aden and the Red Sea, this was the turning of the year—the respite between monsoons would bring a surge in commerce for British Petroleum and East African nig-nogs like Hack. The war would bring intrigue for Poston and MI6.

*   *   *

The Mena House Hotel, Cairo, Egypt.

Landing in Alexandria's east bay, the French flying boat cut to a remote beach on the lee side of the breakwater. Poston, Uncle, and Molly stepped ashore. The twenty-nine bullet holes in the tail section of the aircraft ran in a tight line beginning inches behind the rear window—the result of the packet of small-arms fire the aircraft absorbed climbing out of Aden harbor.

"Those sodding wogs." Molly laughed as he lost count of the bullet holes. With one exception, numbers were a problem for Molly. He always knew how many rounds were left in Olive Oil's tubular magazine.

"The pilot told me the shear winds were bad getting out of Aden," Poston said.

"I met a whore who could fart shear winds," Molly declared. He joked with himself, knowing he needed to visit the brothels in El Birkeh, to see his old friend, Lady Fitz.

Sorting Molly's humor, Poston hailed a cab. "I've arranged a bit of luxury for you two at the Mena House Hotel. Telephone number 159. Top shelf this go 'round. You've earned a bit. Meals and hot showers. SIS is paying the tab. Fourteen pounds per night." Noting that Corcoran and Molly seemed unimpressed, he put in, "Keep your hands off the maids, Molly."

Molly smiled. "Ah, my lord. A proper porter will know a tart or two."

The khaki-colored streets of Cairo were filled with dust and rampaging youth. From the gates in front of the Gezira Sporting Club, to Abdin Square, to the El Azhar Mosque, to the British Ministry of Interior, young Egyptians were rioting, waving their useless employment cards, demanding the British leave Egypt. Mounted Egyptian policemen dispersed one crowd only to confront another.

The bloody wogs are expecting the Germans to win, Uncle thought.

Free of the city, the black Ford taxi eased along, following a Royal Army Service Corps convoy hauling ammunition and supplies to the troops stationed in the Western Desert. Trapped, Uncle Dingo was anxious to throw lines. Molly was asleep.

Turning south the taxi slowed to a crawl as it reached the elegant white wall that bordered one side of the road leading to the front of the Mena House Hotel, well south of Cairo. Stepping onto the red tile entry, Molly turned and searched the terrain from left to right, memorizing the vegetation, evaluating threats.

Uncle and Molly followed a porter through a foyer crowded with Australian officers, some with their ladies dressed for supper. At odds with their surroundings, filthy and packing weapons and field gear, they were hurried down an expansive corridor. Their room was at the end of the south wing.

Toe then heel, Molly used his soft feet, worried his bulk might damage the luxurious carpet. Finding no hammocks hooked to the walls of his room, he opened the double door to a patio and the gardens surrounding a pool. He alerted at the smell of curry wafting from the pool deck.

"Turn off the lights, Captain. We've dominion squaddies nearby."

Uncle picked up his weapon, checked the breech, switched off the lights, and stepped into the bathroom to have a piss.

Quietly setting his gear down, Molly scanned the vegetation beyond the pool deck, wetting his lips. As he scratched his grizzled chin, the wind grew cooler and howled a low howl. Molly stiffened and set his stance into a brace with his trench gun at the ready. His face was suddenly a blunt-jawed, leather-tough combination of strength and seasoned hatred atop a bull neck that consumed his powerful shoulders.

"Where are the lads, Molly?"

Recognizing Hardin's voice coming from the bushes near the patio, Molly remained still, evaluating an Indian soldier near the pool. The man was armed with a German machine pistol.

"Poston's in Alexandria seeing to Sir Nigel. We're to meet him in the morning. The captain's in the loo pestering his gear."

Setting an ear to the desert, Molly whispered, "Put out that cigar, cobber."

Hardin caught the patter of swift feet and the rush of dark shapes across the pool deck. Uncle stepped out onto the patio buttoning his fly.

The light globe over the patio was brief in its living, shattering the night with exploding glass as automatic weapons fire lanced the night, each round a tracer wired to Uncle's chest. Instantly, Molly was running. Hotel guests scrambled into their rooms and crowded deeper into the hallways. The garden and the pool deck were deserted.

At the crack of the first round, Molly had run forward as he had in Flanders Field, stuffing lead into the face of three men as they tried to reload their MP38 machine pistols. So, sure of their target, they had fired as one and had died as a torch carried march-order into hell. Maimed as men could be, the Indian soldiers had no face to express surprise.

At the crack of the first round, Hardin ran through the arbor and into the desert, his Thompson firing at retreating black shadows. He immediately returned to the arbor to retrieve his gear and reload his weapon.

Insane, cussing an incoherent, grunting rage, Molly threw the three bodies into a marble statue at the pool's edge and viciously kicked the bodies into the water. The pool's marble deck was awash in blood, an expanding stain, a swirling henna tattoo of rust-red brown.

Uncle Dingo was down, crumpled against a patio wall packing an indulgent grin. With his captain sprawled in agony, Molly threw the tables and chairs aside, lifted his captain, and laid him on his bed.

With blood gurgling from his mouth Uncle gasped, his eyes open, registering his final understanding. Cinched with pain he mustered a breath and said, "Have a piss, Molly."

Whispering as if a prayer might come out, Molly removed his captain's identity disc and pillowed his head. A respite for his friend, Molly lifted his captain's forearm and pushed the tattoo's hips around—the old rhino still didn't have any tits.

Hardin stood next to his friend and squeezed Uncle's hand. "You had that feeling, Uncle. You knew one of us was going to pack it in."

Wired with rage, Molly pushed Hardin away from the bed.

"You're home from the sea, Captain," Molly whispered. "May the angels of mercy have some left for you." Uncle Dingo died whispering a soldier's song he and Hardin had sung while drinking Darwin stubbies in the officer's club at Candle Creek.

Molly grabbed his gear and stuffed extra shotgun loads into his shirt pockets.

Molly found strangers in his way until his face showed reckless, blessing Olive Oil with new life. An Australian officer tried to impede his progress with a raised forearm. Molly imprinted the man's sternum with a perfect tattoo—a circle the diameter of Olive's bore.

Ranting the sounds of a mongrel dog, Molly reloaded Olive Oil in seconds and rapidly shot into each body floating in the pool, to watch the bastards bob.

Hardin ducked into the foliage near the arbor to retrieve his gear. Molly whispered, "There's more of the bastards on station, squaddie."

"I know. You and I are into the desert—fifty meters."

Lying in the grass under a patch of holm oak and palm trees, Molly organized his gear. "Give me Uncle's Enfield," Hardin said. "I'm going to circle the hotel and watch the front. If we get separated, tell Poston I've gone to Ashchurch."

"Does it matter who I shoot, Captain?"

"Not anymore." Hardin ran into the pathless desert and disappeared.

Molly counted the minutes, laying his front site on anyone he found worthy.

The door to Uncle's hotel room burst open, spilling light through the arbor. Molly eased his finger off the trigger guard and took up the trigger's slack, hoping one of the wogs would touch Uncle's body. A large white man stepped into the room and began directing the Indian soldiers as they searched.

Molly set his sight on the wog searching Uncle's body. The target was Olive's choice. Molly blew the nearest wog's body from his feet, his arse landing across Uncle's chest. The second wog's head punched a hole in the interior wall when he flew away from the trench gun's load.

If that's the South African, he just killed Uncle Dingo. Knowing Hardin needed help, Molly ran into the desert toward the front of the hotel.

*   *   *

Egypt's Delta. Fayid Barrack's Stockade, 25 September 1939. 0630 Hours, GMT + 2 Hours.

Sweating wasn't the half of it—a shaking frenzy wasn't, either. The shivering palpitations and the convulsions, they were more than half—they were the Blue Johnnies. As naked as a short-haired dog's balls, his uniform in tatters on the deck, Flying Officer Jeffrey Hawkes's skin was oiled to a grimy sheen—a pumpkin-colored grimy sheen.

Pore fungus held the day.

No longer a crapulent fool, days of jousting with delirium tremens, of shitting his uniform to its seams, had left him running from one pink spider and hollering at another, hoping, and praying a snake of decent size would lend a hand and eat the rats.

In the spirit of fair play, Hawkes had been given the smallest cell in the stockade so the guards could lay odds on the blighter ever catching up with himself. His Form 252, much more than a disciplinary charge, Hawkes was on an extreme fizzer, a routine sure to bounce his balls.

Fayid Barracks, derisively called the Glasshouse in Egypt's Delta, was the headquarters of the 4th Indian Infantry Division, 11th Indian Infantry Brigade. First Company of the 6th Rajputana Rifles stood guard mount for a stockade known as the 'Jollop' on the Nile. Not one Indian soldier cared about Hawkes or that he was puking and shitting his life into the trough of an open sewer.

Slavery and shit were integral oils of life's canvas.

Severely toweled up, sore to the touch, his knackers were all a-cock. As though wasted on curry, his arse was afire, blazed by a series of high-test ring-burners.

Charged with stealing a Vickers Wellington, an aircraft needed in France, of being too drunk to drive, and with destroying Mother's property, Hawkes had earned short rations, no toilet, and no shower, but enough water to lubricate the squalid corners of his cell. Three times a day the guards had taken to cold-pigging Hawkes—throwing a bucket of ice water on him, hoping he would dance into the jim-jams, become absolutely jungle, aim his cock through a series of quick squirts, and then shit himself again.

That stopped working, so the guards put No. 9 pills in his water. The laxative was an elephant rouser. An industrial grade torment, and quite reliable.

Captain John Lindsay and Corporal James Walker, both outback Aussies, like to bitch about being detailed to Fayid Barrack's Stockade as wardens—brass-hats. Set apart from their task, sobering Hawkes for a tribunal was the sort of filth they drove on about. Assuming Hawkes had manners stuffed somewhere in his tremulous chamber, that the pilot was somewhat more than a bucket of fog, the warders inspected Sir Lewis Poston's credentials, and the orders directing the immediate release of Flying Officer Hawkes.

Having processed a number of crying women, the warders laughed as Hawkes clanged out of his cell, engaging obstacles one and two, laden with the slime of something come out from hiding. Resisting the temptation to help the squalid sod, they gave Poston the Enfield Mark 3 Hawkes had been packing, the spare magazines, and a shackle key.

"You may have to loan him some air," Corporal Walker said. "For three days, he's been up to putty, trying to flog a dead horse."

These days without booze left Hawkes's legs shaking without word. Too early in the morning, emaciated and staggering, the stench of his crotch had curled the tongue of his boots—the brass eyelets had turned to tin. Thick-lidded eyes topped with dusty-black brows and cornered by scruff-covered sunken cheeks; Hawkes could have doubled for the most talked about scoundrel in Egypt—because he was.

Tucking the newspaper under his arm, Poston counseled his judgment. The flying officer he vouched was canted and bent, a stinking hairlegger, a walking piss tank, with breath lumped into gasps, his face suffused a frightful panic, and the scruff under his nose was clogged with hard and soft bush oysters.

Considering Hawkes with distaste, Poston decided he had sponsored a man destined to be a vicar's sexton. At bottom a realist, he said, "After you've cleaned yourself, and you're dressed, Flying Officer, we'll have a whiskey."

Soundlessly the tenacity slid from Hawkes's face, smoothing his brow, sparking a glister in his eye, and prompting a frightful grin. Hair had grown on his teeth.

"I've a bottle of Glen Grant Twelve waiting for us."

Poston was writing a letter to his brother when Hawkes climbed clean limbed from the prison innards, his jowls dismantled, gray, and battered. Whiskey brought Hawkes to the stake, his mouth reasonably shaped, as if an ice cube defined his future, and lent distinction to his haggard looks. Tapping his glass for a top-off, his thirst that of a camel, Hawkes's bribable nature ran abeam.

"Where's Captain Hardin these days?" Hawkes asked.

"For changelings like yourself, Flying Officer, he's hidden behind another whiskey."

"You should be good to beggars like me, my lord." Hawkes's third shot did not touch the tabletop. "Any beggar, really. Even stoked with larceny, your fate rests with sods like me."

"Right you are, I'm afraid. Your mate jumped into the desert using the Wellington you scratched as a reference. Looking for you, I presume. He jumped from a Vickers Vildebeest III, driven by a nineteen-year-old lad—nowhere near the designated drop zone."

"All three lights on that blooming crate went red," Hawkes declared. "The damn thing caught fire and went down faster than Peg's knickers." Seeming to measure Poston's reaction, Hawkes held his empty glass to the light. A suspicious curl set itself in his eyes, as Poston handed him a pack of fags.

"You set a trap for the lad, didn't you, Poston? You silk-covered cocks would shag any sheep in the paddock. That's what you swells are on about. You want that pouch before the lad gives it to somebody who can soil Mother's linen."

"There's a mole in MI6—an active spy spending millions of pounds to keep Hardin from reaching England." Poston's voice had taken on a quiet ease.

"I've a turn up for you, Poston. Hardin will kill anyone in his way. I don't think he cares who it is." Hawkes opened the cigarettes and set one to his lips. "Neither do I, actually. You, my lord, are just a polished, fancy wonk who gets sods like me killed."

Hawkes poured a fourth whiskey. "There's an assassin looking for that pouch, a South African—Singapore, Little Andaman Island, China Bay, Bombay, Aden, Cairo. He's well hated that's certain. McPhee, Hardin, and yours truly know what the Dutchman's knife looks like, and we're of one mind. What we understand about the man, what Hardin understands, you, MI6, and the king have never seen."

"I'm getting closer, Flying Officer. He wounded me in a skirmish in Aden and killed Captain Corcoran here in Cairo—just last night."

"Now that's a damned shame." Hawkes could not stop nipping at his drink. "He was Captain Corcoran to you blighters. He was Uncle Dingo to Molly and Hardin and the commandos in Team 7. Uncle was a salty horse—a green-water sailor—a Jack who was proud of finishing Scarborough Primary."

As though looking at life from a jail cell, Hawkes raised his chin. "Cut Hardin's tether and let him run. He's from the fens. Fix him a dinner of Welsh rabbit, and that Taffy will finish the job, and only the proper scoundrels will fall to his gun."

Poston presented Hawkes with a brass gorget plate designating Hawkes as a Flying Officer in the Royal Air Force. "Listen, Flying Officer. You can be reinstated to flying status with full grade and back pay. Or I can leave you with those British coppers in Bab-El-Hadid Barracks."

With eyes regarding something beyond their focus, the air one of futility, Hawkes accepted Poston's offer. "If you betray that squaddie, I'll kill you."

*   *   *

Cairo. The Mena House Hotel, 26 September 1939. 0130 Hours, GMT + 2 Hours.

After soaking his thoughts, Hardin was convinced the South African was being fed information by a spy in MI6. It can't be otherwise, he thought. There are too many players chasing that pouch.

With Uncle dead, my mission isn't about a sealed pouch.

For my mates, Linc Jensen, Dudley Sutton, Nathan Everett, Rory Campbell, Harlin Rogers, Emrick Blaney, Robin Wingrove, and now Uncle, I'll give the traitor his due—well-placed solids to shatter his bones. I'll leave him no pins to stand on. Like Steiner, he'll die pondering God's partisans.

"We've got to shift ourselves, Molly," Hardin said, bolting off the ground.

Running on heavy feet, Hardin and Molly scurried into a patch of brush sixty meters from the front entrance of the hotel.

Molly wiped sand from the Olive's housing and kissed her butt. "Indian troops are working with the South African. The three floating in the pool were Indian squaddies."

So, the South African killed Uncle. And Indian soldiers searched Uncle's body and his hotel room. Looking for what? If the man's powerful enough to purchase troops from the Indian army in Egypt, he can purchase anyone.

"I shot the first wog that touched Captain Corcoran's body."

"Good measure, that." Hardin settled his chest into the sand and took a deep breath. "I've a hatred worth bottling."

Hardin adjusted the sight on the Enfield as von Cleve and three Indians soldiers got into a British military sedan—Von Cleve ended up in the backseat, on the right side. Hardin lay in the sand nine feet above the roadway. Shivering, he set his cheek to the Enfield's stock. A stiff, cool northeast wind forced Hardin to close his left eye. Sand scratching across the surface of the roadway swirled into tiny, inverted cones.

Sighting the Enfield, he flinched when the driver switched on the headlamps. Resting his cheek against the wooden stock, Hardin drew the slack from the trigger. The rifle leaped. The solid hit von Cleve in the forearm. The second solid took out the front seat passenger.

Indian troops stationed near the hotel entrance began returning fire.

As Hardin ran into the desert, he turned to find Molly behind him. The echo of the Enfield's roar had lanced his youth. He just killed an innocent man—a brown, spare man.

With adrenaline packing a high-count, he found himself near the pool deck, near the arbor. The three bodies floating in the pool had joined hands near a surface scupper. Watching Indian soldiers pick up Uncle's body and carry him into the hallway, Hardin set his jaw.

"Find a vehicle, Molly. I'll be on the roadway fifty meters north, near the right verge. Caution lights only."

"Poston should be here by now, Captain."

"I know, Molly. We've got to tread lightly. Killing Uncle might be Poston's doing."

Running again, Hardin had run across the night, his memory stained with ritual death. He must kill one more man—Von Cleve—for Uncle and Mother England.

Muttering in the turbulence of grief, listening to himself, to his petty excuses—Hardin realized he was Molly's new captain, and wondered if he could keep the old tarpot from dying.

* * *

Cairo. Shepheard's Hotel. 26 September 1939. 1920 Hours, GMT + 2 Hours.

"Shepheard's Hotel!" Painfully sober, Hawkes stepped from the taxi in front of the hotel trying to match its opulence with the filth and the stench of his Indian jail cell. His crotch burned as if he was sweating pure curry. A pair of British military policemen stood some twenty meters off to the left of the entry, braced as if ready to react, their red-top hats, white Blancoed webbing, and shiny pistol holster at their hip.

Talking to himself Hawkes said, "Red Caps—Joeys! Me being able to see must be Poston's doing. The swell wants to be my wing weenie. I don't trust him. The man's not a British Petroleum exec. He's a bloody spy—a linen draper."

Hawkes paused before crossing the street to Sinclair's English Pharmacy. The MP's crossed the street in step. A lotion for my bung hole. A tranquilizer for the coppers.

Returning to the hotel entrance Hawkes noticed the sky turning dark in the east.

Worried about Poston's motives, Hawkes motioned to Shepheard's doorman and asked him for a light. The cigar he held up was so dry the damn thing went up in flame, igniting like a fuse.

Why did Poston have me reinstated as a flying officer—with back pay? Why would he help a man whose work's constantly done over by what I can't remember, a man who steals airplanes?

Any favor Poston offers me will be tied with long, costly twine.

Welcoming the shadows that consumed the city, Hawkes crushed the dry cigar. A poet at heart, he wanted to stop drinking, but the flask his father gave him was his friend. "I wonder if Mother knows she's purchased a cashiered pilot?" Hawkes enjoyed his play on words.

"She must be in a serious jam."

Watching Poston alert the coppers before paying for his taxi, Hawkes realized the royal was carrying Hardin's rucksack. Immediately suspicious, he mounted the curbstone in front of the hotel. The pot-bellied heat of the city street had converted his sandals into a drinking-man's trivets. Even the day's moon was parched.

"Why am I being quartered here and not on one of the aerodromes?" Hawkes asked.

"It's only for tonight." Poston handed Hawkes a room key. "To see Hardin on his way, we'll need you with a stick in your hand."

"On his way to where? That's the question. Did Hardin give you his rucksack?"

"Admiral Sinclair's orders." Poston showed Hawkes the dispatch. "You and Hardin are scheduled to fly out of Alexandria's east bay tomorrow."

"We'll fly out if you're not lying." Hawkes lit a cigarette. "If you are lying, graves registration will be digging a hole tomorrow afternoon." Hawkes stopped as he mounted the first step, turned, and said, "How would you like to be buried in this sewer?"

"You're a flying officer, Hawkes. Well worth a night at Shepheard's. Start acting the part and order us a cocktail. I'll join you in a few minutes."

Click beetles, grain weevils, locust, and dung beetles shouted and clicked their mating sounds. Hawkes wanted out of Africa and the Mediterranean. Watching Poston walk into the sea of chairs near a grand piano, Hawkes gulped his whiskey. For some reason, drink helped him start a cycle of better approximations, knowing he was more rational when he was half tight.

At the bar, Hawkes had his flask topped off. Then he found a table overlooking the center courtyard. Admiring the brown beauties, he ordered a scotch with plain water.

One more cycle and he would don his copper-toed boots. Issuing futile boasts about his lineage, he would gather his sleeves in ruffles about his shoulders. A worthy knight, his sword in hand, he would mount the bird and fly through hell. And if the bird was Meg or Peg, he would flail about, determined to get all tropical, and raise her glories to grand heights.

Poston scanned the sea of wicker chairs. Remembering Dorothy's nylon stockings, more the fabric buttons that held them in place, he found

Hawkes in the glow of a sheltering lamppost near the wrought-iron railing overlooking the central courtyard.

As he started forward a stranger with a bandaged forearm drew back a chair and sat at Hawkes's table—the South African. Warily, Poston stopped near an empty table, in the spill of the grand piano, to listen to their conversation.

"Why do I know your face?" von Cleve demanded. The big man leaned into the table, took Hawkes's glass, and tossed off the whiskey.

"You're a banker," Hawkes replied, his eyes bulging as if he wanted to piss himself. "From Kuala Lumpur. You're supposed to be good with faces."

"The racetrack. You're the chap who interrupts football matches. What are you doing in Cairo? Let me suggest you've been in the company of Harbormaster McPhee."

Sweating, Hawkes spoke when von Cleve's hand dropped below the edge of the table. "I lost track of that Irish twit in China Bay." Hawkes moved his hands off the table to keep them out of reach. "Since China Bay I've prospered—reinstated in the Royal Air Force with my captain's rank intact, with full pay and compensation."

"Not many men lie to me, Pilot Officer Hawkes."

"Well, two things are true, khaki's a lovely color, and somebody shot you." Hawkes pointed at the dressing on von Cleve's forearm. "With any luck, the shooter hit that cross plastered on your woggish arm."

"I'm going to kill you for that, Pilot Officer."

"Here? In front of all these people? There's a rather long queue for that, I'm afraid." Poised to lunge out of his chair, Hawkes set his right foot into an open aisle. To keep his fear in check, he declared. "I'm a Flying Officer, actually—on my way to France to support the British Expeditionary Force. The odds are not good for lads like me, flying Lockheed Hudson bombers— so lying to a bastard like you comes easy for me."

"I'm going to gut you like a goat."

As von Cleve tucked the Creese under his forearm, Hawkes rose and moved his chair several feet across the stone floor. When he spotted Poston, he smiled a taunt, and said, "Well, alright Dutchman. On you go."

With voices mingling in counterpoint, swelling in volume, Poston approached a table near the piano hosting five Royal Marines. "I need your help, lads. We've a pilot going down for six. I'll stand those willing to a night at Big Henty's Snooker Hall."

The marines stood-to at Hawkes's table, drawing posts to the flanks and to the rear of the large, green-eyed stranger.

Poston motioned for Hawkes to leave and ordered drinks for the five Jolly's. "We'll have a large beer and a large whiskey for each of these lads. Put the charge on that gentleman's tab." Poston waited for von Cleve to respond.

Then he pointed at the big man. In a voice quietly strained he said, "I see you've been shot. Last night, I presume."

Von Cleve's sudden move was not well timed. A marine's fist, half the size of von Cleve's head, crushed his right ear, lacerating the outer edge. A second fist broke his jaw. The Malay Creese slid across the granite floor.

Von Cleve, backed against the iron railing, lunged at the nearest marine, and threw him into the adjoining tables. As he raised his head to take on the next man, two marines grabbed him and pinned his arms behind him, and three marines beat him senseless.

Enjoying the carnage, Poston picked up the Malay Creese. Shepheard's concierge handed Poston an envelope as he was leaving the hotel. Hawkes was waiting at the curb.

Lewis read the message with a bit of caution.

Sir Lewis Poston,
    I'm due in Cairo shortly. The ribbons in my scotch seem to tie the ice with gold. There's an afterglow we should gather.
    D. Stuart

Does she know I have the pouch?

Exasperated by the woman's mobility. Certain she was a spy. Lewis decided to move Hawkes out of the city to a more secure location. "Flag down a taxi, Hawkes."

"What happened to my night of luxury?" Expecting a nebulous answer, he went on. "Mark Twain was right. Shepheard's is the second worst hotel in the world."

"Flag down a taxi."

"I'm in recovery. A bit of flattered blarney would do me. Better, let's see how you well-dressed nobs flag down rides."

"Hawkes, we're on our way to 250 Wing RAF at Ismailia, northeast near the Suez Canal. 55 Squadron has a Bristol Blenheim Mark I, for you to drive—Malta, Gibraltar, and Southampton."

"Where's Hardin?"

"He's waiting at the airfield."

"What's he waiting for? There are pilots in that outfit who can drive him home."

"Hardin wants you on the stick."

"He doesn't trust you, Poston. Or your spotted dick. And, neither do I."

With a nod, Poston handed Hawkes von Cleve's Malay Creese. "The marines were still beating your banker when I last looked."

*   *   *

London. Red Cross Headquarters on Seymore Street. 26 September 1939. 1700 Hours, GMT.

John Poston enjoyed measuring the Londoners he encountered at the Red Cross headquarters on Seymour Street. The canteen's serving line was full, moving a half-step at a time. Coffee and tea urns percolated all hours of the day at this hostel, one-half block north of Hyde Park.

Parsnips, onions, and baked tomatoes were aligned with bangers and chips, a right-by-square English offering for the lads standing a post—standard fare for London in September 1939. Victory Gardens blustered at those too lazy to lend a hand. The lads in Belgium, England's Expeditionary Force, needed the rations.

John Poston followed Gordon Dewar in the serving line, quietly amused, watching the dandy wince, as if evaluating his need to eat any of the offerings. His expense account knackered one day last week, Dewar was reduced in grade by half, his pay book subject to daily accounting.

Johnny sat facing the entry to the canteen and waited. Dewar took his seat. "William Hockey wants a word with you, Gordon—in person, tonight."

Without taking a bite, Dewar pushed his tray aside and lit a cigarette. He threw his charge a quick glance—a man sizing an adversary. Seemingly reticent, he said, "The old trees in Hyde Park bring an uncommon peace, a recumbent welcoming, more gracious than most." Coffee in hand he toasted the crowded canteen, passing his cup through an arc. "These old walls echo, I'm sure—charging the guns of time—musket balls and helmet plumes."

"Hockey expects a call at noon today."

"Johnny, when you're on a road with no end, is the clock always just at noon."

"Today it is. Hockey's at Temple Bar 4343."

"The Savoy. Of course."

Using his Aunt Margret's phone, Dewar dialed the Savoy and asked for William Hockey. The hotel's operator acknowledged his request with a seeming urgency. Dewar's astonishment turned to trepidation. Who the hell is William Hockey?

"This is Hockey." Gershwin's *Rhapsody in Blue* was playing in the background.

"Gordon Dewar, here."

"I'll be at Temple Church. I've arranged a private service for you at twenty-hundred hours. I expect to see you." The phone rang off.

Dewar shied at the words. He needed a new sounding line. The menacing tone of Hockey's voice added depth to his fear. Whatever Dewar might do, death's picture was becoming clearer. Run! To escape he had to hide in plain sight—fade to the middle distance of a common scene. Any common scene would do. Kenya or Argentina.

Dewar had money laid by—over a million pounds on deposit at Credit Suisse in Basel, Switzerland—the profit from his opium dealings. To survive he needed to cut ties with Rudolph Hess, Max Ilgner, and Victor Rothschild.

Aunt Margret will help. She always has.

Returning to his flat at half eleven, Dewar phoned MI6 to let his secretary know he would be in in the morning. Seconds after the first ring a clicking sound delayed the second ring. Dewar hung up. They've tapped my phone.

Drinking brandy, the noon hour went without a word. Packing a holdall with garments evaluated for their durability, Dewar took stock of his situation. John Poston had destroyed his life. I should kill that swell before I run—in the admiral's office.

His eyes narrowed as he neared Margret's flat. The woman waiting for a bus was too well dressed for the neighborhood. He crossed the street. Two workmen lounged on the steps of Margret's apartment house, both studying him with interest. He moved his holdall to his left hand. Their tin hats pegged them as block wardens.

Dewar's gaze held steady as he mounted the porch.

Passport in hand, he sat at the kitchen table for a cup of sweetened tea with the one woman he understood—his mother's sister. Almost all what Aunt Margret knew was darkness, for herself she could light another lantern—a wise woman and her crystals. Steeped in the occult, Margret was a knowing woman.

A slight, rather tall woman, with eyes that seemed dreamy, moved with a ghostly flow as she secured her cigars and a box of matches and sat at the table.

"I'm up against the bollards that frame Ten Downing, Margret. A John Poston or one of Admiral Sinclair's staff will be asking after me. I'm in need of shelter, a name, and a job.

Away from London, I'm afraid. It's Africa, or South America. South America seems reliable—Argentina, Brazil."

Irascible and ruthless, in a relaxed moment, with a severe look and a watchful grin, she drew on her cigar and asked, "How will you get on, dear boy?"

The wistful thrum in her voice alerted Dewar—as if she had known. Of course, she knew. She had the gift. And, she had been a bookkeeper in Warsaw for thirty years, keeping track of accounts for the scoundrels who owned the old Le Royal Meridien Bristol Hotel. There was no easy place in this woman's heart.

"I have money enough."

"There's never enough." She nipped at her gin, crushing her cigar in a wooden bowl. "Who else knows you have money? Each has a plan for your money, Gordon. Wealthy homosexuals are an unforgiving lot. They take infantile delight from deceiving anyone."

Aunt Margret lit a long, thin cigar. Her gaze seemed to harden and then fade to some illusory distance. "You have much to learn, Gordon. You won't find the world you once traveled. You must leave tracks as if you were confident and stand as nearby as your money allows. With luck, Mother's agents will decide you have left a false trail and turn their attention to more likely locales. The less you move, the more difficult it will be for MI6 to find you."

Aunt Margret attacked her cigar, drawing short leads until the damn thing glowed.

"Mother's lads are persistent, Gordon. Untethered, they are ruthless—under the rose. They will measure what I say and know it cannot be. I will mention Europe and let them decide. The unspoken better sways the future, Gordon." She spoke vaguely enough to warn Dewar off.

As the evening wore on, Margret's habits of hospitality converged to a cold center.

"Were you followed here, Gordon?" Silence drew Aunt Margret to her feet. There was a pistol in her hand. "Do you have a description of the men looking for you?" She pointed the pistol at Dewar's face. "You don't have any idea, do you, Gordon?"

Aside from the obvious, that MI6 would try to arrest him, Ilgner or Hess would order his execution. He took a soft leather sheath from his holdall. Extending the sheath across the table, he said, "That's the ten thousand pounds I borrowed from you eleven years ago, Margret."

"Muster your courage, Gordon. It's a decision."

With her pistol laying on the table still pointing at Dewar, she counted the money, whispering the numbers. "Where's the interest? You owe me three thousand pounds." With a sneer, she set the cigar to her tobacco-stained teeth, brushed her hair back, set her right hand to the pistol grip, and cocked her head. "Give me the money you owe me, you queer bastard."

Dewar fumbled with more bills.

"Not many ports have two seas, Gordon." Aunt Margaret set her cigar aside as she stacked the money. "You must have multiple escape routes."

"There are Nazis looking for me as well—ruthless, powerful men."

"God might care."

Margret escorted Dewar onto her back stoop. When he turned, she poked him in the chest with her index finger. "The Spanish burn their mattresses, Gordon—to keep the dead from returning home to sleep. Don't come here again. Be reluctant to give up the future, dear boy. Choose your friends wisely."

With his midgut tied in knots, Dewar needed sexual relief—a boy to fancy—Alistair. Increasingly anxious, ebbing of hope, he coaxed the taxi through its paces, smiling as it stopped in front of the Saint Ermins Hotel in Caxton Street, between the House of Lords and the Victoria Railway Station. Boys on the game knew their sums.

The boys at Saint Ermins were well tended.

Relieved, enjoying a quiet sherry, Dewar took off his bright red scarf and gently wrapped it around the lad's neck, rubbing his hand. He had been meeting Alastair Bagley for years, preferring the excitement of their near-public liaisons in Saint Ermins' cloakroom.

"Alastair, I have purchased a holiday for us in Basel, Switzerland—for queen and country." Bagley's joy was too vibrant to be concealed.

Dewar paused looking across the lounge. He was taking a chance involving this novice.

How much of a chance would depend on how quickly Dewar could wrap up loose ends in England and select a place to hide.

"You'll do this for me, Alastair." Dewar handed Bagley a well-worn British passport. "I prepared that passport some months ago, anticipating we might get away on holiday."

Alastair nodded, waiting. His face tightened, but he forced a smile.

"I've never been across the channel."

Dewar reached into an inside pocket and gave Bagley a train ticket to Southampton, a round-trip ticket to Lisbon, and five hundred pounds. "I used a recent photograph of you. It's on page three of the passport. It's not regulation, but I do have connections." Bagley thumbed through the passport's pages, smiling as he read the visa stamps—Algeria, Egypt, Switzerland.

Dewar shrugged, disturbed despite himself. His signature was perched below the picture of Bagley, and he knew the boy was too soft for anything but puffery.

"You'll be traveling as me, Gordon Dewar. You'll be living in Basel. The address of our holiday flat is in the folder with your plane ticket. You must keep a low profile. You're a decoy. You must be careful not to make friends."

For several minutes, neither spoke.

Opening and closing the passport, Bagley seemed to turn the idea over in his mind, and asked, "Where will you be, Gordon?"

"In France. I am siding up with the French Resistance for a counterintelligence operation. We're going to flush out a female spy who I've identified. I'll travel to Basel as soon as I can—a month at most."

Dewar coaxed his charge into the cloakroom.

"This is exciting," Alastair said. "Thank you for the red scarf."

Of course, Dewar thought. I'm setting the lad up as a decoy. Signing his death warrant. There will be other boys. In Argentina.

*　*　*

London. 26 September 1939. 1140 Hours, GMT.

Traveling from France, George Harrison landed at London's Heathrow airport and was detained on the tarmac by two of Mother's most distinguished coppers. "Mister Harrison, I'm Sir Vernon Kell, head of MI5, and this is my associate, Albert Corming, head of Metropolitan Police Special Branch. We want to speak to you. It won't take much time."

Punched with fear, Harrison nearly sang the words. "I've a flight in an hour."

"We took the liberty of rescheduling your connections to New York."

Whisked away in a black Bentley, Harrison was shivering with fright. Suddenly flush, his face felt florid.

If they're willing to hang a governor of the Bank of England, these men will hang anybody.

"Where are you taking me?"

"There's generally a beginning and an end to the encounters of life, Mr. Harrison," Kell said. "Victor Rothschild, an employee of mine at MI5, asked you to telephone William Hockey at the Savoy when you met with Victor and others in Paris."

"I intended to call him from Heathrow." Sweating, Harrison loosened his tie.

With a hint of humor, the coppers turned and spoke in subdued tones.

Kell lit his pipe. "You seem to have a rather routine mind, Mr. Harrison. Perhaps the River Thames will help you focus." The Bentley turned onto Blackfriars Bridge. "London is a city that has crushed more bankers than the rest of the cities in the world combined.

"I'll put you in the picture, Harrison. There's no longer any need for you to call Hockey, or anyone else for that matter." Kell handed Harrison a heavy manila envelope. "Hockey's instructions are clear and concise. You will follow those instructions without fail."

The Bentley stopped in the middle of the bridge and Kell opened Harrison's door and pulled him onto the sidewalk. As the Bentley sped away, special branch detectives confronted the banker and turned him toward the Temple district.

* * *

Cairo. Sinclair's English Pharmacy. 26 September 1939. 1400 Hours, GMT + 2 Hours.

Lewis Poston's white silk shirt was moist with sweat as he stood under a ceiling fan in Sinclair's English Pharmacy waiting to purchase a bromide.

Listening to the pharmacist barter with an Englishwoman near the front of the shop, he smiled and thought, Sammy has his ladies and his potions, and I have a pilot who drinks too much, an Irish sergeant who fancies his privates, a tarpot toggled to a shotgun he calls Olive Oil, and the three have a hatred for all things royal.

Looking across the street, charting the powdery dust swirling from a passing taxi, Poston spotted a group of Shepheard's porters, men drawn from Nubian and Sudanese warrior stock,
escorting inebriated English officers toward a military police van.

I wonder how Molly's getting on.

Even though well-seasoned, after Corcoran was killed Molly had become edgy, and more dangerous. A square-built man, he carried his day with a practiced gait, as if he weighed a ton, Olive Oil his one constant.

Darkie McPhee had become Molly's subordinate by a sleight of hand, after he was drunk. Flashed during his passage through the Suez Canal, he was enlisted into Her Majesty's Royal Army as a sergeant, detailed to Special-Service Troop, to the Special Operations Executive—a phantom assignment.

Molly was McPhee's section leader—a newly minted top sergeant.

Hearing of the death of Captain Corcoran, Admiral Sinclair, although dying himself, reactivated Molly with full rank and benefits. That only his next liberty separated Molly's future from his past gave the admiral no pause.

Clive Mauldin had been a loyal soldier.

Enjoying a smoke, Poston left the hotel and crossed the street where he sat in a storage room in the back of Sammy's pharmacy to read the admiral's orders—*Most Immediate: Eyes Only*. He used the storeroom routinely, paying Sammy a modest stipend.

His office echoed with the thump of the paddles of a ceiling fan. Poston found the rhythmic noise soothing. Iced tea in hand he read the orders again. The directions were detailed to the fork and on to a familiar road for the men still active in Operation Snow White.

There would be no variance from these directives.

Sir Lewis Poston is directed to secure the documents that are under seal in Egypt and deliver same to England upon request. Poston is directed to proceed to Marseille with a decoy pouch and aid the movement of individuals running Mother's ratline.

Sir Nigel Stuart is directed to assume command of SOE Force 136 Provisional, for Burma, and is to proceed to Signal Station—Trincomalee, China Bay. From that locale, he is directed to find and terminate enemy operatives peculiar to Operation Snow White. Stuart is to roll up the Burma section of the ratline.

Top Sergeant Clive Mauldin will escort Sergeant Robert McPhee to Southampton aboard HMS Sloop *Grimsby* via Malta and Gibraltar. McPhee will continue as Grumpy carrying a decoy pouch.

Captain Edward Hardin and Flying Officer Jeffrey Hawkes will fly via Marseille and proceed directly to Southampton.

Setting fire to the admiral's directive, Poston said, "Sammy, I'll be back shortly."

With Hardin's rucksack in hand, Poston entered Shepheard's Hotel and paid the desk clerk forty-eight cents to store the rucksack, in their basement for one year. The number on the claim-tag was 1730, a proper hour for a vintage scotch.

After tying the tag to the ruck, he opened it to ensure the sealed pouch was inside, and as a diversion, he gave the concierge the decoy pouch to store in the hotel's vault. Allowing a porter to lead the way, Poston followed the man down a concrete stairwell.

The basement was heavy with the stench of fetid heat. Even the dust refused to swirl as Poston's sandals struck each step. No longer white, the storage room was an open bay filled with mounds of duffel bags and assorted luggage. The porter unlocked the wrought-iron gate and set the ruck against the far wall.

Paying the porter twenty pounds Poston stepped into the storeroom and buried the ruck under a mound of duffel bags. Taking hold of a dusty rucksack, one with a claim-tag number of 217, he shouldered one strap, and with a bit of fanfare both he and the porter walked past the reception desk.

Waving at Sammy to ensure the chemist saw him with a rucksack, Poston took a cab to the Turf Club, on the top of the Metropolitan Hotel, and checked the decoy rucksack into monthly storage.

The lady won't know about the rucksack in Shepheard's basement, but she will be told about the one at the Metropolitan. Poston was having fun.

Dorothy used the Metropolitan as her operational headquarters. He knew she worked for British intelligence but had been unable to sort out her specific operational status.

*   *   *

Alexandria, Egypt. East Bay Dock Basin, 26 September 1939, 0530 Hours, GMT + 2 Hours.

Clumps of palm fronds quivered and rustled in the breeze as McPhee boarded HMS Sloop *Grimsby* with Molly, acting as McPhee's orderly, carrying McPhee's kit as well as his own. Making hay, posing as Captain Hardin, McPhee ordered Molly to stow his gear.

Furious over being drafted into the British army, as if a gust had blown his red hair into a fire, an angry idea came to McPhee's mind.

He wanted to take his complaint to the sloop's senior officer. Yet he could not. The crew, including Lieutenant Jensen, thought he was Grumpy, and the crew would not be debriefed until the sloop reached England.

And then there was Molly. Fuming as if about to burst, Molly hollered, "If you order me about like a coolie, you Irish shit, I'll take out your gobs one ivory at a time." Throwing their rucksacks onto the sloop's deck, Molly took Olive Oil from his shoulder and opened her breech.

McPhee stepped away quickly, knowing Molly wanted to lay Olive's butt on the side of his jaw. "If it's Mother with Hardin's ruck, why are we still trolling?"

"We're curly dirt, Paddy. Decoys for a bale of papers. And the admiral wants us to pack up the skivvies who've been killing special-service lads."

"The admiral, that's the man who drafted me into your royal-arse army."

*   *   *

Nile Delta, Upper Egypt. 250 Wing RAF Base Ismailia. 26 September 1939. 1300 Hours, GMT + 2 Hours.

Lewis Poston drove the jeep under the wing of the Wellington and unloaded an open five-gallon can filled with iced tea. Showing Hardin the offering, he said, "It's not fermented, but it's cold." Back in the jeep, he said, "I'll round up Hawkes and you'll be off."

"The ice has sand in it," Hardin declared.

"Look around. You're in the bloody desert."

"How about a cup?"

"Use your hand."

RAF Base Ismailia may as well have been posted in the seventh century. The tents had to be watered to keep from igniting, thus qualifying as the only possible spontaneous event ever imagined in this region of the world—God's will and the rest.

Slow the day if you will. What else can I do? The natives seem happy to be here, Hawkes thought. But then, what else would they be?

Too hot to take a deep breath, lizards lined the shade of the flagpole.

Hawkes dozed in a canvas chair; his head cradled in the shade. Broiling in the sun, his empty flask caught the wind, fell off a petrol barrel, and landed squarely in his lap. Finding the seam between his bare legs, the flask singed its image on both sides of the cavern.

His bulwarks breached; Hawkes let out a holler. Asleep when the flask hit his legs, he cinched his thighs to protect his nuts, thus seizing the glowing ember, thereby ensuring the burns matched the flask's full trace.

With a rectangle of boric-acid salve coating opposing burns, filling with wind-blown sand, he hobbled on bowed legs to the canvas water bag and soaked his bandana.

Ice would not arrive for hours if at all.

A sign next to the stand-alone tent read: *SDG*. Hawkes opened his umbrella, picked up a bandy-legged stride, and hobbled over to read the second line. Southern Desert Group. "These lads like it here," Hawkes whispered. "Damn it's hot. Chickens must be laying hardboiled eggs."

With his face contorted and his deck on a slew, Hawkes waited for the dust to settle before he made his way to the watch terminal for 250 Wing RAF. Drinking water like a battery mule, sucking on the spigot of the canvas bag, he wished for earlier times, in Singapore, drinking at his father's Tanglin Club, flying short hops for the brass.

Hawkes shook himself, and his face relaxed. Celebrating the cool water, he looked about. Discovering Poston mounting the stairs, he called out, "Where's our Welshman?"

"Just there—on that Wellington. You get to ride the leg to Malta. Then it's a flying boat to Marseille with you at the stick." Giving Hawkes a canvas holdall, Poston shook his hand. "Give Hardin this signal."

"My flask's empty."

"There's food and drink in that bag. And a medical kit. A Class-B uniform and a decoy pouch as well."

Poston continued up the stairs of the control tower and turned before he opened the door.

"You're on your way, Hawkes. This isn't cricket, but it's necessary. If you survive this go-round, you'll be posted to the Air Striking Force, flying cover for our expeditionary force in France and Holland. Good luck."

"I'll look for you in Piccadilly." Poston didn't hear him or wave good-bye.

Approaching the Wellington, Hawkes's eyes glistened with appreciation. "While the weather lasts." Lumbering from side to side, he stopped behind the wing and stood in the prop wash to cool off before entering the aircraft.

With Hawkes packing an Enfield, Hardin sharpened his grin. Accepting the holdall, Hardin warned, "We can expect trouble at every turn—in Malta and Marseille. And, in England."

After a brief pause, Hawkes read the inscription on his flask. With a nod and a smile to size up the situation, Hawkes mused, "We won't be safe until the grass stops growing."

He submerged his flask in the iced tea and drank. Then he filled the flask with whiskey. With his system mellowing, he said, "Poston gave me this envelope." He handed Hardin a small, dun-colored envelope stamped: *Most Immediate*, and turned to cleaning the burns on his inner thighs.

Hardin held the flimsy into the light near a tiny Cellon window under the wing. He scowled grimly and hunched his big shoulders, sensing the forces in play. Reading, he stood up and spoke softly to himself. "The royals tried to deprive me of my Katherine."

Captain Hardin,

Katherine's alive. She's in my care. She knows you're upright and trying to get back to England.

Dewar's in the frame for staging her death, her kidnapping and killing her driver. It's complicated.

Celts begin each day at sunset.

Hockey

The message brought him up short.

Permitting a silent scream to echo down the day, Hardin checked the moisture in his eyes, rising with the knot in his throat. Consumed with conflicting emotions, he read Hockey's message a second and third time—the crux now a stained adhesive. Controlling his joy and his rage, questions flowed from a surging lust for retribution—what of the closed casket?

Operation Snow White had boiled to a rancid char. Thankful for his survival, for Linc Jensen shoving him out of the line of fire in the ambush kill zone, Hardin battled a swooping hatred.

Tempered by the harsh ways of the jungle, strong in its sense of justice, ruthless in its demand for retribution, relentless in its pursuit, Hardin broke into a flashing sweat.

For minutes now, he thought of killing Dewar. Finding Hawkes with gauze plastered to his inner thighs, gargling, he laughed at his chances of reaching England in one piece.

"Hawkes. Does whiskey sharpen your flying skills?"

"Deadens the vocal cords so I can scream the lyrical version of 'bloody hell' when the dash lights on this crate start blinking red."

Until the grass stops growing, Hardin mused. Hawkes is a sage. Chennault wanted to shoot the bloke but had to settle for cashing him out of the Royal Air Force. Admiral Sinclair reinstated him. When the chat back came to why, Sinclair declared, "Simple. He's a good pilot."

The troop bay of the Wellington was packed to the ceiling with personal duffels, and down-station mail and sundries for Malta, Gibraltar, and Southampton. Hardin and Hawkes shared the troop bay with five air-crew members. Each man seemed lost in the drone of the engines.

Passed from hand to hand, the Thompson was inspected, unloaded, and loaded, and the magazine hefted for its measure. All in all, the heavy wooden stock rated the nods. Hawkes seemed eager to praise the weapon... and Hardin, for that matter.

That was until the commando passed his flask, and the damn thing went dry after one round.

*　　*　　*

RAF Base Hal Far, Malta.

The Hal Far airfield on Malta was covered with carrier-borne airframes—all the Fairey Swordfish—a cloth kipper kite affectionately known as the "Stringbag" by its crews. The planes were assigned to the carrier HMS *Illustrious*, anchored outside the harbor of Valetta.

The officers' bar at RAF Base Hal Far, was a hangar for sprogs—newborn pilots, their antics punctuated with derring-do, nut jostles, and the hand gestures of those maneuvers new crate drivers could recount with tangible humor.

Pilots can't talk without using their hands, Hardin observed.

Portraits of the Old Lags, time-expired men, lined the wall facing the bar. These men who had flown into yesterday's sun stood stock still, obscured by the misgivings and the mockery of what was to come.

With a sudden feeling of space around him, Hawkes said, "Hardin old boy. This whiskey and my flying is the most lasting relationship I've ever had."

"Shut up, Hawkes. We're due out from the Imperial Airways marine terminal."

Hardin surveyed the scars on his hands, then shook his head a bit. "What Poston didn't tell you is we queue up in three hours with the passengers for the flight to Alex. Then slip into the water and swim to the plane. You're driving a Stranraer Flying Boat."

"Just like that." Hawkes seemed shocked. "Did you ever think of that?"

"What?"

"How things cross your mind."

"Some things are so dim they must be holy."

"I can't fucking swim!"

Waiting to order a drink, Hawkes found a framed photograph hanging near the bar that reminded him of the silk crowd at the Tanglin Club in Singapore. The picture showed the winners of the Royal Malta Golf Club Spring Challenge Cup; Majors Hamilton and Tabuteau, Colonel McCombe, and Lieutenant Colonel Linton—all rigid in an unexpected way.

At least they're holding a beer.

The bar sat in an elongated archway, ranged from end to end with whiskey bottles. Centered in a wall of vertically laminated logs, each log was lacquered to a high shine. A *Shove ha'penny* board sat idle against the wall, its slate top lubricated with a fine dusting of French chalk.

Hawkes carefully evaluated a group of engaging young women. Sorting complexities, he decided the grog seller was a buxom lass with a winsome smile. The knots forming the lace atop her tit-carriage ran wing to wing—Double Carrick bends.

Three whiskeys and I could untie those knots. Two might do it.

Round tables allowed periods of confused dreaming, new pilots yearning for stern duty, all pledging to take on the Italians and the Germans. Each in turn choreographing a harrowing dogfight, in and out of the clouds, the sun— damn the sun, machine guns bursting with flaming onions, tracer rounds arcing under their belly, the holes in their airframe too quick to count, each hole a near facer nicking the navigator's pencil or the bomb aimer's shoe— routine-missions' stories—no flap-wagon casualties.

Sprogs all, still polishing their buttons, these lads declared in turn no man among them would play pussy and hide in the clouds.

Hawkes found his derring-do. Three Red Crossers, three sisters from Princess Mary's Royal Air Force Nursing Service, and two members of the Women's Auxiliary Army Corps, joined as one, rejoicing at Hawkes's sense of equivalence. Pilot officers all, Abigail's one through eight had latched on to Jeffrey Hawkes's larcenous smile, merrily recounting a rogue or two, laughing, one nurse, and then another estimating the measure of Hawkes's equipment.

With two whiskeys down and a third touching glass, Hawkes had a Red Crosser's tit in one hand while his other hand searched the confines of an auxiliary's skirt. Watching a nursing service dame drink his whiskey, his tackle skipped a gear and the Red Crosser slapped him.

Hawkes grabbed his empty glass, slammed it on the table, and shouted, "You daft cow. You bloody snotter."

"Grab hold of your mud hook, Blue Job, and get stuffed." When the Red Crosser screamed, eight dames took flight as widgeons do, and settled into a nearby pond, mingling with a raft of young lads from the Royal Irish Fusiliers.

As if reaching for a sober thought, Hawkes jokingly took a drink of water. "That flying boat's named after Mother's chat-bags—'the whistling shithouse.' The loo opens right into the air. When you lift the lid the blooming thing whistles."

"All's well then. You'll be right at home. Poston found you in an Indian Army shithouse, with you whistling from both ends." Hawkes accepted the flask Hardin offered and toasted the air, augmenting his grin by waving his tongue across his upper lip.

"From both ends at the same time, mind you. Poston claimed if I didn't accept his terms, I'd be locked in that Indian borehole until Chennault's pet goat shit a whistle. Damn shame Poston gave away all that lovely scotch."

* * *

Railway, Cairo to Alexandria. 26 September 1939. 1230 Hours, GMT + 2 Hours.

The square and gardens in front of the Midan al Mahatta, Cairo's railway station, was alive with natives. Thieves, pickpockets, boys selling beads and flyswatters, brothers selling their sisters, jugglers, whores, and porters. Mounted Egyptian police pushed crowds here and there. British military police with their red caps gathered in rings providing an oasis for any traveler.

Given their tenacious longevity nomads have no timely needs, von Cleve thought.

Assisted by the concierge of Shepheard's Hotel, the chemist from Sinclair's English Pharmacy, and the hotel's clothier and page boy, Alex von Cleve caught a cab to Cairo's main train station. Unable to move without his cracked ribs finding humor in any form of haste, he stood in the queue to purchase his ticket to Alexandria.

Faced with riding the Delta Light Railway from Cairo to Alexandria, in Upper Egypt, a distance of two hundred and nine kilometers, he purchased three first-class tickets for his oversized frame—the carriage seats barely fifty centimeters wide.

The first-class carriage on the light-rail system was a cosmetic version of a livestock lorry mounted on springs too far removed from its wheelbase. Any change of track, switch, stop and start, or short-radius turn set the carriage through an oscillation followed by a dampening rock.

Incensed, dodging a rusty tubular armrest, von Cleve caught his weight as the carriage kick-swayed and then crashed into the adjoining carriages, then lurched, swayed, and settled onto its haunches—an empty threat and something of a joke.

"These railcars aren't fit for camels."

For five hours, he fought the train's suspension—galloping on independent leaf springs too short for the carriage frame, settling through a protracted shudder, accented by sudden jerks to re-center the carriage's weight, and reset the wheels.

With the train paralleling the Nile near Benta, a raft of snowy egrets took wing and flew over the English Bridge. The bridge was open, allowing dozens of dhows, bluff-nosed feluccas, and motor barges to pass. Remembering all road-bound traffic from the Western Desert had to cross the bridge to travel to Cairo, von Cleve decided to hire an assassin to watch for his Englander, his commando.

The wound on his arm held its charm. The round had entered through the crux of the eight-pointed cross—perfectly centered.

Ion Crilley's communique was abrupt. Annoying. Sir Lewis Poston was not to be touched. "No, Ion. I will touch Poston or anyone to secure the pouch. It's the only permanent trace of my strategy," von Cleve whispered.

Not knowing whether the pouch was airborne or afloat, he decided the Welshman still had control of it. If the Welshman were afloat, he would be aboard the Sloop *Grimsby* and sail for Malta. If he were airborne, he could be anywhere. Von Cleve's contracts with the Corsicans allowed for such contingencies. One team would hit the *Grimsby* in the harbor at Malta. A second team would cover the arrivals in Marseille.

Knowing that a blind in British intelligence was also trying to eliminate Snow White's special-operations team, von Cleve decided to kill any British agent who took a hand in the game. Even an intel blind.

For now, I can ignore my contracts with the Thule, the Vatican, and Compensation Brokers, Ltd. What can they do? I have their money.

For the Welshman to reach England he needs a long-range aircraft.

At Dumyat, the end of the line for the Delta Light Railway in Upper Egypt, he hired a taxi to Alexandria. Arriving at the marine terminal, ticket in hand, he decided to eat before catching the flying boat to Malta.

*   *   *

Marseille, France. 26 September 1939.
1030 Hours, GMT + 1 Hour.

Dorothy found Marseille in a state of chaos.

Hats—straw boaters banded white—were giving way to winter's garb. Working hats, some for fishing, would have to endure the cold. Summer aprons and summer cherries had given way to falling clouds, as had dancing in the street.

Joy had given way to fears of war.

The queue outside the US Consulate had been growing for weeks, wider than the sidewalk, blocking access to neighboring businesses for hundreds of meters. Horse drawn carts sat idle, without horses. Young boys at hire and the sons of émigrés stood idle, ready to help pull a cart along—crates echoing with lost grandeur. Time attached a mystique to the lost—a life, a piano. Surely a grand piano. The story would be grand when the Jew reached Jerusalem.

Men waited, at times in a driving rain—jovial and angry, anxious to a fault, with coats short and long, some of the finest wool—not many.

Worn to a fray, some with unstitched hems, heavy coats pulled at hungry frames who had lost their resolve.

For Dorothy, Hiram Bingham was a friend. Harry was the Deputy US Consul, in Marseille. He wanted to sleep with Dorothy and never passed an opportunity to boast about his abilities.

Where are the women on the game? Dorothy wondered. Surely, they can't be far—tucked in a lockup along tramline C—nowhere near the docks.

Riding in a Wolseley provided by Bingham, Dorothy relaxed. She was keen to register the changing mood of this city the world called The Capital of the French Underground—the tall chimneys, the factory smoke, the maze of railway switchyards, the harbor's contraband.

After decades of disagreements, Corsican syndicates and labor unions had formed an alliance and refined the heroin trade, expanding their drug dealings into Southeast Asia. A British spy had been trading with them for years—five British intel operatives stood in the frame.

These same Corsicans controlled the prostitution trade in Cairo and Alexandria—Aden as well. The *un vrai* monsieurs de Marseille governed their syndicates as a community. Corsican footmen supervised street corners.

The Corsican Network of 60cm gauge trains, the sugar-beet line, dominated the Rhone-Alpes Region of France and the Rhone River Valley from Marseille to Lyon, serving as the primary distribution link for smuggling heroin throughout Europe.

For money, these syndicates would turn anyone over.

Is a refugee also an émigré? Dorothy wondered. Are they of equal status? If so, they require forgeries of equal quality, these Jews and Republican Spaniards. For money, the world will shun both with equal zeal.

As though defining Marseille's old port, the garbage and the filth, the rue la Carrabiere, the seediest street in all of France, was jammed with small carts. Wicker side baskets and dust-covered donkeys ran at odds, damming the rest, circling, and stopping, turning, and stopping, delighted to be starting and stopping.

Bars and brothels, grocers and brothels, trinkets and brothels, sidewalk stalls and watchers, the Corsicans controlled the facets of trade on rue la Carrabiere. If the watchers found a man with money, he was better off spending it than losing his life trying to keep it.

Standing on the upper-bastion of Fort Saint Nicholas, Dorothy whirled with the celebration—the confusion of launching the new bright-red fireboat built for the city's first Marine Fire Battalion. The sound of bells and horns filled the harbor as the fireboat's pumps shot arcs of saltwater to port and starboard.

"Dorothy, you are lovely." Bingham gleamed, giving her figure a complete appraisal.

"You're a cad, Harry." Yes, you are, she thought—your full cheeks, wire-rim glasses, and pug, self-assured smile. "Are you without an escort?"

"I'm never at a loss, Dorothy."

"I've come across a pair of Pan American tickets to New York from Lisbon."

"Always a help, dear girl..." He accepted Eaton's tickets. "Jews and Republicans are pouring into the city. And they don't get along."

"Let's not run off with the idea that they should. The Republicans will join the Resistance. The Jews will want transport. Are there enough ships? Or countries for them to go to?"

"Not anymore. The Resistance wants these Jews out of northern France, so they can fight the Nazis without having non-combatants clogging the villages and highways. These refugees are drifting like cattle—by the thousands."

"Well, Harry, facts are facts. They eat too much food, and they can't go north."

"Since Radio Normandie started broadcasting last June, private stations have joined the fray using the transmitter in Allours, France. Velvet voices are suggesting Marseille as a destination for temporary employment."

Dorothy shrugged contemptuously. "There's obviously no work in Marseille."

"The Resistance controls the transmitters, and they want the Jews and the other civilians out of the way."

"As long as the Resistance is ridding Europe of Jews, the Nazis will let them keep broadcasting. If you stay within your means, Harry, as close to US law as you're able, you will never handle the horde."

"That's true. In a few days, the Austrian 'Freiheitssender' starts broadcasting for Radio International and for Radio Normandie. One station is in Marseille, another in Lyon."

"How may I help, Harry?"

"I've been approached by a Varian Fry. He's with a group forming in the states calling itself the Emergency Rescue Committee, ERC."

"Outside US law, I presume."

"I assume so."

"That's good, Harry. I can work with him directly, and you can help without being flogged. You have lots of children of your own, Harry. Are these Jews yours as well?"

"Of course! Hitler fills the bucket with shemozzle and dumps it on the world."

"Enough of these Jews. I'm looking for an American ambulance driver. A Virginia Hall. She has a wooden leg."

"She's not in Marseille. Perhaps in Lyon."

With a sensual gaze, Dorothy stood more erect. "I'm staying at the Mascotte Vieaux Port Hotel. Will you join me for a drink?" At first Bingham, did not seem to have heard her question—then he nodded.

I'll ask him later, she thought.

With twilight shading the harbor sky to gray blue, Dorothy found the boats at anchor sat fixed in a black, glass mirror. She scanned the storefronts for reflections, sensing a foreboding, yet thinking about sex—about sleeping with Hiram Bingham.

His wife must be on holiday.

"Stop the car, Harry."

"Is there a problem?"

"Pull into the curb. I'll just be a minute."

The door closed after she entered the Pharmacie de L'Arriver and side-stepped behind a display. Behind the counter two salesclerks were arguing about money. Lewis Poston, ever the gentleman, was trying to purchase a bromide.

"Lewis Poston." Dorothy trifled a laugh. Apparently, her surprise had his tackle spinning in opposing circles, and banging against his thigh. "Did I upset your day, Lewis? It seems your stomach needs mending again."

"I seem to find you whenever I need mending."

"Let's have a drink in the bar next door."

Unlike English gentry, Dorothy knew Poston preferred female company. Smiling, he sipped whiskey as if summing her beauty. Dorothy admired the lust she found in his eye—the fantasy of an evening of play—of sailing his French coaster into Dorothy's estuary.

Dorothy met his grin by adjusting her straps and boosting her assets.

"Sir Nigel—has he surfaced?" she asked.

"Yes. He's in top shape—on his way to the Bay of Bengal—to Ceylon. We met in Alexandria and again in Cairo." Drawing on his cigarette, Poston creased his eyes with humor and snapped his lighter closed. "But I suspect you know that and a good bit more."

"Is it a cat you're looking for, Lewis—or what the cat might find?"

Torn between impulses, he said, "I am an inquiring sort."

"I'll just be a minute, Lewis. Order me a whiskey with ice."

* * *

Malta. Imperial Airways Marine Terminal.
27 September 1939. 1320 Hours, GMT + 1 Hour.

"Why are we taking a bus?" Hawkes sang the words. His balls still ached from his bout with the Blue Johnnies.

"The cab drivers on Malta work for the local syndicate." Hardin vaulted up the steps into the bus and took a seat behind the driver. After Hawkes was seated, Hardin said, "That Red Crosser was a horse-faced barker. Fully braced when she slapped your tools into a jangle."

"True enough, that. Even so, she did have crisp bouncers—nylons as well."

Malta's route-bus, the REO Speedwagon, was hardly that. The multi-colored beauty was so new the driver had rarely set a foot to the gas pedal. As the bus lumbered from the RAF Base at Hal far heading for the harbor, Hawkes listened as the driver whispered. "My beauty has a bright white top, dark-orange stripes along her hips, and light orange body. What a lovely girl."

Smiling and humming, the driver set his eyes in the shade of the green sun visor perched across the front of the bus like an eyebrow above the windscreen. Barely registering his passengers, he stopped the bus at each designated stop, opened the door, and waited for a few seconds before he drove off. Seventeen stops and no new passengers.

Hardin grabbed the driver's shoulder and pointed to the curb.

"We walk from here."

The buff-colored canvas holdall was frayed at its skids, but that wasn't Hawkes's problem. His flask was empty. Out of habit he kept hefting the flask, sniffing the lid.

Hardin stopped in the shade of a palm tree near a massive stone wall overlooking the Imperial Airways marine terminal and the harbor. "We're early. If anyone's looking for us, they'll have locals prowling the docks."

Drawing Hawkes into a recess in the wall, Hardin said, "Keep watch on the seaplane dock." As he opened the holdall, searching at his back as he uncovered the pieces of the Thompson, he raised the stock, hesitated, looked up and down the street and covered it again. Then came a feeling, a premonition of being watched.

"Hawkes, what's inscribed on that flask you keep sniffing?"

"The inscription is personal—my father's last words." Hawkes seemed nervous. With a distant stare, he hardened his jaw and wrung his hands. "I hope I end up close to home. If I ditch in the Irish Sea, I hope the Lifeboat Institute has a station nearby, at Foynes."

"Focus Hawkes. I'm going to shoot your banker if he's on that plane coming in from Alex."

"Should I start running?" Hawkes asked.

"I don't care."

Hardin wiped sweat from his neck and drew saliva over the salt tablet in his mouth. "Look at this Malta one-pound note. The note's dated thirteen days ago. 13 September."

"I don't care. Without whiskey, my life's a scrum."

Hardin dropped his face into the hollow of his shoulders as an AEC Matador, filled with British troops, with RAF Base Luga insignia, rumbled by.

"I wonder if those squaddies have any scotch," Hawkes whispered. Watching for the Sloop Grimsby he realized a muted, blue-purple hue of mounting intensity lay on the sea in the east. Flickering glisters caught his eye. And yet the water in Valetta's harbor was a dull blue-black.

The ships he spotted were a variation of the same dull color.

Expecting trouble after HMS Sloop *Grimsby* entered the port, Hardin assembled the Thompson and held the stock to his cheek. Leaning the weapon against the wall near his leg, he scanned the horizon, judging the range to the mouth of the harbor.

Convoys, escorted by the Royal Navy, loomed into view as black silhouettes, then merged with the horizon and disappeared. Sounding their passage, Hardin knew their crews would be suggesting a layover was in order—so they could don their shore-clothes.

Fond of Malta's delights, Hardin thought of Uncle, the stories and the smokes and the laughter they had shared. Uncle's chart room, with its radios and dim lights, rang with Molly's well-told exploits. By any estimate, Molly met every whore on the Asian rim.

Molly had frayed, oft-used shore clothes.

A flying boat dipped through Hardin's line of sight and drew his eye into the harbor that defined Valetta. Phosphorescent sparks of water flew from the plane's pontoons. Three flying boats rocked in the arrival queue for Imperial Airways. Passengers bound for the hotels streamed from the dock.

Hours passed while dockhands sorted and piled mailbags. Crates of foodstuffs and sundries found the top of the gangway where lorries picked up their deliveries.

Taking a rag from the holdall, Hardin wiped the sea salt from his forehead and adjusted the weapon's sight. Drawing a deep breath, he set his cheek to the stock. His beard reeked of stale sweat, burly enough to fill the divots left by the leeches and the ticks of Burma.

Hardin's rugged appearance fostered a weathered, storied expression of fatigue. With a coppery cast—his face no longer seemed an oddment of scars. He did not know how long he waited. Like his mission, like the jungle, time had become part of a boggish reality.

Anxious, he drew a bead with the front sight of the Thompson on a passenger to check the sun's glare. "Count the passengers, Hawkes. Something doesn't feel right."

"Did you kill the man who was watching us?"

"What the bloody hell are you talking about?" Hardin pointed down into the harbor. "The second plane in the queue came in from the east. Your banker might be on it."

"There was a man in the alleyway, just there. With a double-barreled shot gun."

"There's two alleyways."

"He's gone now."

"You're nuts, Hawkes. Suck on that empty flask and shut up."

A flight from Marseille carrying eleven women and three well-dressed men had docked. Merchants, Hardin thought. The plane from Alexandria brought women and children and one man, and he was shoving his way down the gang.

"That's him—the South African!" Hawkes nearly screamed.

Determined, accepting his charge, this ultimate summons, time passed as it had never done before for Hardin. Organizing the holdall so he could hide the weapon, he checked the chambered round and set the sight on von Cleve's chest. *Ninety meters.*

"Stand still you bastard."

Letting out his breath, he took up the slack from the trigger as he tracked the target. The Thompson leaped. The round took von Cleve's valise as he placed it on the boot of a taxi. The taxi lurched forward. A second round shattered the cab's rear window. The roar of the Thompson reverberated in and out of the narrow streets near the harbor.

"Damn that lucky fucker!" Hardin broke down the weapon, shoving the parts into the holdall. He and Hawkes ducked into a stairway, ran up an alleyway, scrambled uphill for several blocks, and caught a Speedwagon headed for the harbor.

"That bloody gun's a bit cross-eyed," Hawkes said, hefting the empty flask. "The documents in that pouch aren't shit to me. They're not worth dying for."

"I'll kill that bastard even if it means dying with him."

Von Cleve examined the .45 caliber round lodged in his Old Testament. He knew at first glance the round was fired from an Argentine Ballester-Molina or a M1928A1 Thompson with a noncorrosive primer. Both weapons were US Army priority issue.

No sniper would use such a clumsy weapon. I know its Crilley. He's tired of my being. Pushing air through his teeth, then drawing air until his ribs ached, he arched his back.

Before dawn, he would know if the Welshman or the pouch were in Malta.

Nearly an hour passed before von Cleve found the location the sniper had used. Standing behind the massive stone wall, he lit a cigarette. Scuffing the side of his shoe along the base of the wall a shell casing spun into the air.

Examining the brass casing, his expression creased into a grin. A Thompson, he thought. This must be my Welshman or one of his mates. From the corner of his eye, he saw a sloop entering the harbor. A commercial motor launch was approaching the sloop.

As the Sloop *Grimsby* dropped anchor in Valetta's outer harbor, the cabin door opened, and an interior light set the frame of a large man. If that's my wayward Welshman, I have a competitor on Malta, von Cleve thought. It's Crilley or MI6.

I'll have the Corsicans hit the sloop tonight.

Sitting in the captain's chair on the sloop, McPhee had had his say. Then he drew the short straw. Hornier than a pack of dogs, and now pissed, he wanted this shore time to join in the alcoholic heaving that would surely be Molly's treat.

Lieutenant Dirk Jensen and five men, together with all but one of the sloop's crew, boarded the ship-chandler's launch for a sailor's liberty on the town. Malta was well suited to servicing the Royal Navy—any navy.

The last to leave, Molly turned and kicked McPhee's boot.

"Irishman, can you swim?" Molly handed Olive Oil to the only Paddy he seemed to know. "Olive gets hot and tropical when she's loaded to her guards."

As ever he must, McPhee checked the loads in the trench gun.

Molly handed McPhee extra shells. "Two loads for ballast. Turn off the bow and stern lights and lay out near the bow, opposite the ladder."

"Piece a piss, Tar Pot."

Molly threw the decoy pouch into the pilot house. "If trouble comes you won't have much time. Use Olive as you can, then into the water. You're in for a cold night, Paddy. Me and the lads are off to find a liquor port."

"Take the last lad with you, Molly. So, I don't root him in the confusion."

After he turned off the sloop's lights, McPhee stood on the deck, watching the chandler's launch glide ashore. Laying out near the bow, he laid his head on a canvas fender. A steady breeze kept the ensign near the stern bouncing.

The harbor was a mat of dim, bobbing lights. Masthead lights swayed as a child's kite. Cock boats with sailors, whores, and contraband negotiated the harbor's imaginary roundabouts. Each image incomplete, a chorus of oarlocks sounded in tune— brass on wood and wood on leather— the oar's blades splashed rhythmic at times.

Wanting a smoke but not the attention, McPhee drank instead. He knew Molly for what he was, a hardened mate. But Molly was unpredictable since Uncle's death. Molly angered more quickly, waving Olive Oil around like a swagger stick.

With an eye on the head of the ladder, McPhee sipped his rum. Tired of the evasion game, if not for Molly he would ditch the sloop and swim for shore.

The South African would come—not in person, and not tonight. Running his hand over the trigger guard onto Olive's stock, as Molly would, he kissed his fingers and rubbed her butt—for luck. Setting his finger into the trigger housing, he laid the weapon across his lap. Enjoying a last bit of rum, he eased the bottle into the harbor.

Tired, he rolled his shoulders to lessen the tension in his neck.

Alone at last, drink taken, he dozed off. Catching the shotgun as it slipped through his fingers, McPhee set an ear to a wooden shout. An oarlock chunked brass on wood, leather on wood—a gun barrel. The knock of wood rattled among the hulls in the harbor.

McPhee thought he heard his empty bottle sing out—*chink*.

Shore lights mounted on the stone wall along the strand shone suddenly bright. Mounted at regular intervals, one light guttered with the wind, its image pulsing across the water. The sloop's gentle rocking motion was soothing. Another of the shore lights drifted off, leaving a channel of black tied to the sloop's stern, centered on the ladder. A third light dropped away.

The splash of a short chop announced the oncoming wash of a wooden bow. McPhee closed Olive's breach and braced himself. The first man seemed to vault over the rail. The second man's head vanished in the rush of lead balls as his beret cleared the rail. Keeping the trigger depressed, the shotgun fired automatically when McPhee closed the breach. The blast took the first man's chest in stride.

More men appeared at the rail simultaneously.

Dropping the shotgun, rolling into the water, McPhee plunged hand-over-hand down the anchor chain, released his grip, swam to his breath's end, and gently broke the surface. Taking a quick breath, he pulled himself underwater, swimming as he counted to thirty. Surfacing, breathing deeply, his strength waning, he turned to locate the sloop. A cock boat cut away from the stern of the sloop and headed for shore.

"Bloody fuck, that was close." McPhee could see the lights along the harbor strand. He yearned for the dodge of the nearest bar. He was cold and wet and determined to find Molly.

*   *   *

London. The Savoy, 27 September 1939. 1330 Hours, Greenwich Mean Time.

William Hockey sat to a jar of stout, waiting for Victor Rothschild and young Frederick Warburg. Dressed in corduroy pants and a tweed hacking jacket, his gray eyes lay flat in the seam of a tiring day. Knowing Rothschild started his afternoons with the drink, he took the liberty of having a bottle of the finest sherry sent to his table,

Young Warburg walked into the smoking room ahead of Rothschild. He looked to be expecting the worst. After they settled, Hockey wasted no time.

"Ilgner pulled all of I. G. Farben's money out of the arbitrage plan and put almost all of those funds in gold held at Credit Suisse," Hockey said.

"I expected such a move," Rothschild said.

"For your safety, Frederick, you will fly to the United States through Lisbon and Bermuda. Allen Dulles, a friend of Victor's, will meet you. Here's his phone number in New York."

"Does Uncle Max know?" Warburg asked.

"He suggested the trip. Your document's the problem. It's your mess to resolve."

Rothschild leaned toward young Warburg and spoke in a whisper. "You have an important role to play for this arbitrage to work. You will visit George Harrison, the head of the Federal Reserve Bank of New York, and insist he lower the discount rate dramatically on cue."

Hockey finished his stout and asked for another. "Your life depends on Harrison's performance. There's much at stake."

"What if that document falls into the wrong hands?" Warburg asked.

"Victor can explain it to you."

*   *   *

Cornwall, England. Tucking Mill. 27 September 1939. 0230 Hours, Greenwich Mean Time.

Gordon Dewar was adrift. His aunt Margret, a Celt, had the gift. Her warning chilled him to his core. After sending Alistair across the channel, he decided to hide nearby, in the least likely place any of his growing list of enemies would suspect. Hockey, the admiral, the Poston's, or any of their minions. In Alfred Gosden's cottage in Tucking Mill, his associates were looking after Hardin's wife.

Coursing down Tucking Mill's coal canal, keeping the shore reeds brushing the right side of the skiff, he guided the bow into a gravel raceway between two fingers of moldering stonework that reached into the canal's flow. The skiff's keel grated on the gravel and fell silent in the grass. Dewar pulled the skiff up the raceway.

The churchyard lay atop a terraced landscape dotted with miner's shacks and cottages—an uphill jaunt through the village of Tucking Mill. Wet and cold, Dewar checked his watch. It was nearly midnight when he crested the hill near the church.

Built as part of the stone wall defining the grounds of All Saints Parish Church, the thatch-roof cottage sat on a hill overlooking the town square and the River Connor.

A drizzling rain continued to fall. The church belfry was clearly outlined black against the night sky. Fighting a chilling breeze, Dewar found the well-head in front of the cottage gate. Flanked by maple trees in the center of an expansive cobbled square.

The cottage was a squat, one-story tribute to masons long past. Beautifully crafted, the stones were black this night, gray near the chimney top. A fire burning near its ember cast a faceted glow from a leaded glass window, each facet adorned with a partial rainbow.

"The fire must be in the study," he whispered. "I wonder if Gosden's dog's awake."

A low stone wall joined the lane and wrapped the churchyard. Maple and beech leaves had made an art of dying. Rain fell on them with a soft patter.

As wet as he was, Dewar's mouth was dry, and his tongue felt like a large stick. There was no movement in the cottage. The glow of a fire was barely showing.

"Something's amiss."

A misting fog ran in patches through the trees, one patch ran down the lane, running from a breeze harboring the remnants of yet another day. The moon peered once to cast shadows and brand the puddles.

Shivering, Dewar stood in the bushes across the lane from the cottage. The lanc was wide and flat where it split around the maple trees. The well stand was centered between the trees, its hand pump and spigot glistening in the hue of a miner's headlamp. Water ran in gradual surges into a small stone cistern.

The cadence to the miner's step was in sync with the rhythm of the falling water, the sound guiding his way. It was a miner's tune, his tired hulk accepting a quiet pace. Slightly tarnished, he was reaching for a warm room.

The shacks and cottages took notice with one candle to spare. In this muted glow the last colliers trudged. Tucking Mill would expire as it had for a century, one candle at a time.

The colliers of South Crofty, the black-tin and wolfram miners, each suffering in his own person, walked and then grew whole as he welcomed his wife and accepted the comforts of a warm fire and hot water for his bone-weary feet. An old miner, with gumboots for feet and black-out curtains for eyes, stopped to drink from the well-stand and moved on.

Gosden said he always left a key wedged under the letter box.

Expecting the pub to announce last call, waiting for one more song, Dewar decided to join the homeward bound. Stepping into the lane, he strolled with his head down. Pausing at the well- stand, he waited for a nearby door to close. Tracking along the wall bordering the cottage, his ear keen, he eased the wooden gate open.

Night sounds mingled, an assortment of shuddery. The cottage was quiet—too quiet.

Shading the window with his hand against the intermittent glow of the moon, he peered through the leaded glass. The room was semi dark. Sorting the ambient noises near the river, Dewar flattened himself against the wall.

The bell pull was dislodged from its mounting. He turned the key, eased into the front hallway, and snapped on a torch. Hockey! That ruthless bastard.

A man lay sprawled head down on the stairway. Blood coated the five lower steps and stained the hallway wall with short and long pomegranate-colored fingers. A second man sat at the kitchen table admiring his meal, his death too sudden to mask the wit in his eye.

Dewar stepped around the dead man on the stairs and searched the bedrooms upstairs.

Hardin's wife was gone. Worse, the man lying face down on the stairs had lived long enough to bleed out—long enough to tell a dying story.

Dewar's thoughts came in fragments—sanctuary, revenge, retribution. He would have the Poston brothers killed. And hire Hardin's execution as well. Then run. Not on a usual route, but one that would come with each day. First, a place to hide.

There are no rooms for let in all of England.

The children shuttled from London to the villages and farms had filled the beds between Cornwall and Edinburgh. Land wardens and draft wardens were scouring the countryside for odd caravans, out-of-date license plates, and draft dodgers. More daunting, the mothers of England were pitching in, watching for Nazi spies.

Dewar hesitated. The thrum in his ear stopped as he shut the door. There were no sounds except for the purl of the stream. Manchester, he thought. I'll go to the city. A cab to Camborne and a train to Manchester. Threading his way through a stand of spindly trees along the stream, Dewar pushed the skiff into the flow and sat to the oars.

*   *   *

Marseille. Rue la Carrabiere. 27 September 1939. 0750 Hours, GMT + 1 Hour.

The Mascotte Vieaux Port Hotel in Marseille ran a course between provincial and Old World. This unique edifice to a once-elegant merchant trade cast its façade over the spoils of temporary friends. Filled to its beam, the hotel's forty-five rooms were pledged in advanced—at times for hours, mostly for weeks and beyond.

A lonesome jewel perched across rue la Carrabiere from the old port of Marseille, the hostelry retained its elegance by ensuring the Corsican syndicate governing the waterfront was compensated. Paying its share of the security deposit, MI6 maintained a suite on the top floor overlooking the port.

As the desert-gray of dawn gained the sky in the east, Lewis Poston counted dozens of skiffs and chandlers' boats carrying ship stores or ferrying seamen. Morning had come with a thin layer of fog and only a hint of red in the sky.

The color of the water in the harbor ran from a deep blue brown to pockets of light blue and blue green, the shades mixing along a rip that drew itself out to sea. An Imperial Airways flying boat cut through the quiet and set to the harbor.

Naked, musing over his coffee, biting at its bitter taste, Poston inspected his tackle, laughing at his cock's misshaped attitude. The damned thing had a kink in it.

Dorothy danced from the hot bath abeam with color in her cheeks and wrapped her essentials in a white towel, leaving the folds to tease

Poston's fancy. Handing her a cup of coffee, Poston's desires began to dance. Chiding himself, he wanted to unveil his wounded tools and set his coffee aside.

And so, he did.

Following his lead, Dorothy cinched down on his linkage to iron out the kink and made a meal of the tender sod. Allowing such favor required a meal of its own, so Poston twiddled her dee. Dorothy's knees were wobbling when she stepped into a second hot bath.

"Why are you in Marseille, Lewis?" she asked, inviting him to join her.

"It's part of the territory I manage for British Petroleum." He smiled as he slipped into the bath, trying to keep his cigar dry.

"Really, Lewis—and Operation Snow White's an oil-exploration venture run along a ratline from Burma to Marseille." Purring softly, she ran her hand across his forearm.

Adjusting his weight, suppressing a shout, with a slight nod, he looked at Dorothy to gauge the depth of his folly. He had soused his tool in a honey-trap of the finest quality. "Why are you in Marseille?" he asked, leaning twice laid into her smile.

"I liked the fresh mussels."

Offering a mischievous grin, he said, "What do you know of Snow White?"

"So far she's an enigma."

With a confidant grin Dorothy stepped from the bath. "I work for MI6 out of New York. We're opening an office on the thirty-sixth floor of Rockefeller Center. My focus started with J. P. Morgan and spilled into your field of play."

Curious and more than perturbed, Poston asked, "And Marseille?"

"I am aware of the financial documents under Snow White's skirt." She lit a cigarette. "Hess and his spy in MI6 are trying to secure these documents, as are prominent German industrialists and bankers."

"Then you know Admiral Sinclair and my brother, Johnny," he said, drying his back.

"I know both men. The admiral's my godfather." With her bath towel on the floor, she sat on the bed and suggested Poston should join her. When he hesitated, she stacked three pillows, laid back and smiled.

"We can talk about our families when we meet again, Lewis."

After being barely able to muster his pride, Poston massaged his equipment, and put on his clothes. "Did you follow me to Marseille?"

"You're not that special Lewis. The admiral believes the traitor in MI6 is in league with Rudolf Hess and IG Farben International. I think the spy is doubling for the Windsors—for Mother. The governor of the Federal Reserve Bank of New York has been implicated as well."

"I take it Sir Nigel's part of your doing."

"Yes. I hope to see him again." Pouring herself a refill, she drew coffee through a sip and continued. "How special-service troops became expendable; I do not know. I suspect our traitor is one of many funding the chase."

Abruptly, he asked, "And Marseille?"

"The spy went to ground. We think he's here or in Lyon."

"Who is this spy?"

Donning a reflective expression, Dorothy pulled a crooked smile. The change in this man's expression is revealing, she thought. He may know who the traitor is. Dorothy looked around. Reluctantly, she put in, "You stay clear of Snow White. I have orders to neutralize him."

Leaving Dorothy to finish her breakfast, Poston hurried across rue la Carrabiere, heading for the Imperial Airways marine terminal. *Neutralize, terminate*—words and orders for the elite of MI6—words rarely shared. She had played her role with precision, her light, vapor-blue eyes now haunting wells of sensual deception, the taste of her sex too sweet. Drawing the smell of her from a cupped hand, Poston could think of nothing else but Dorothy's sexuality.

That the lady knew Hardin would run through Marseille, a decision made yesterday because there were no flights to Gibraltar, meant her intelligence network included locals, wireless radio operators, and couriers on station throughout the Mediterranean basin.

Stopping to watch a wagon load of wooden barrels go by, Poston went rigid when a hand seized his forearm, and then released its grip. "Stand away from me, Poston," Hardin said. "Do you twilight lads always smell like yesterday's pussy?"

Poston pulled away. "Why are you walking about?"

Showing no sign of having heard, Hardin assumed the slouch of a sullen rascal. "You bloody wanker. You're being followed by a pair of trailers. You're new to this game of chase, Poston."

"Where's Hawkes?"

"Why do you need to know?"

"I don't."

"You linen dandies are all alike. I gave you the pouch. Now go chew on the admiral's tackle and leave me alone."

"Is Hawkes alive?"

"The drunk's at the marine terminal, wedged in a queue—posing as a father of four." Hardin violently muscled Poston into a small cafe and ordered coffee. "Make a fuss of giving me some money—twenty pounds. I'm going out the back. You stay here and finish your coffee. Then go to your hotel."

"Your enemy knows you're in Marseille."

"Thanks to you." Hardin held out his hand for the money. "Half of France is in Marseille.

I don't trust you, and you're in this borehole."

Hardin stepped near the doorway and scanned the street. One operational aspect seemed certain: Poston's loyalties remained with MI6. "They're following you—the seaman in front of the butcher shop and the lass pushing a handcart."

As though waiting for Poston to measure the situation, he bummed the pack of cigarettes, made a show of threatening a cheapjack, and put the pack in his coat pocket. He pointed toward the restaurant's rear exit and shoved Poston into a chair.

"You're naive, oil man. If you return to Alexandria, you better start packing a weapon."

Poston had missed the tails—the merchant seaman window shopping and the woman pushing a handcart—neither and both were out of place. The seaman's face showed signs of recognition.

"Well-heeled men are trying to keep you from reaching England," Poston said.

"You're well heeled, Poston. And, you have a natural flair for being stupid." As if searching the dandy's face, Hardin's eyes creased to narrow slits. "The Sloop *Grimsby* was hit last night." He slid his hand into the holdall and set his finger to the trigger housing of the Thompson. "McPhee was the only man on board."

Watching the street, Poston said, "Yes, I know. Corsicans. Hired by our South African. McPhee killed two before he escaped. Corsicans—they took a decoy pouch." Nudging Hardin's holdall with his foot, he continued. "Give me your decoy. No need to confuse the bastards."

Free of the decoy, Hardin found a reminiscent smile. "Your nephew Linc Jensen was a good mate—a man to stand beside." He handed Poston Grumpy's stained identity disc.

Poston caught his breath and cleared his throat. "McPhee's proving to be the same sort. Irish, Paddy's piss tight over being drafted into the British army. Claims he's owed the Queen's shilling from each of us."

Poston held the identity disc off-angle to the light. Dried blood filled the stamped letters—nearly the same color as the disc itself. Pledging support, he flashed an understanding grin, appreciating the commando's gesture.

"McPhee's too smart to be gulled. The sloop's crew waited until all was blue before they ran a mick on him—got him so drunk he was washing words.

When his slur was down to dits and dahs, the sloop's captain enlisted him in the infantry."

"McPhee's not a man to quail or lose heart. He won't forget."

"He's Molly's to march." Poston knew McPhee would not give in willingly. "I've chambered a round for Dewar." Poston drew a Walther PPK from inside his jacket. "And another round for Snow White's banker—the bastard paying Dewar's bills. Two graves. It's personal."

"For a dandy like you, Poston, it's always personal." Hardin rubbed the linen sleeve of Poston's jacket. "What aircraft am I jumping?"

Poston tucked the decoy pouch under his arm inside his jacket. "I chartered the boat you flew in on—Hawkes is driving. Parachutes are stowed, rations as well. Good luck."

"Hawkes fancies that flying boat. Whiskey-waltzing a 'whistling shithouse' is a fitting way for a rogue to return to England." Hardin pointed at the merchant seaman near the entrance of the restaurant. When the sailor joined a party of new arrivals, Hardin ducked out the back door.

As the taxi turned into the curb in front of the coffee shop, Poston opened the front door and a merchant seaman shoved him into the taxi and Dorothy's waiting arms. Did she know he was given a pouch? Escorted into the restaurant in the Mascotte Vieaux Port Hotel, he realized he had been duped—by Dorothy or Hardin or both.

Dorothy pulled her chair around to Poston's side of the table and sat so he had to turn to look at her. With a flick of her hand, the waiter withdrew. Inclined to misjudge the woman's clandestine ability, he dawned an adjustable smile.

She cast an eye across the street—stiff necked and straight backed, with coffee served. "Who was the man you gave money to in the restaurant?" As if to emphasize her words, she lit a cigarette, exhaled, and uncrossed her legs.

Appearing not to notice, Poston chose a bit of flattery. "No one you should know. Then again, perhaps he works for you—Basil Davidson—MI6 D section."

She waited, her expression fanciful, then thoughtful and then hard as steel. "Basil is a much smaller man, I'm afraid." With a chiding gesture, she pointed the butt of her cigarette at Poston.

"The man in the restaurant gave you a pouch. Who is he?"

"I told you who he is." The cast of Snow White's bloodstained actors flashed through Poston's mind—Stuart, Gosden, Dewar, Lucien—and Dorothy. Are they in league? —he wondered. One or all of them are killing special service troops, trading lives for bits of paper. "The man's identity is not important. It seems delivering this pouch was his tribute to the men who died running through Burma's outback."

"One of the commandos, I suppose." She hardened her jaw, as if dismissing Poston's tripe.

"Perhaps he's been reading your bio—fighting for Mother in a miserable way." Taking the pouch from inside his jacket, Poston wrapped the strap around his left wrist. "Should you be challenged for your failures my lady, remember, nobility ranks above courage."

She leaned forward, her auburn hair hanging close to her face. "We believe there are protected documents in that pouch." Her tone set the stage for a confrontation. "Documents we must keep under the rose." Dorothy held a Browning in her right hand, extending her left hand. "Give me the pouch."

"What's your hurry?" Knowing Hardin had to clear Marseille's harbor, Poston wanted to delay the obvious. "On present showing, you're dual nature has you fondling the crown's nickers." Stalling for time, minutes even, Poston set the pouch on the floor.

With an expression of amused contempt, her grin seemed to last a long time. And then her eyes laced with ice. "Lewis, give me the pouch. There's nothing else for you to do."

"Who decided to take out Snow White's commandos?"

"Gordon Dewar's not without his talents, criminal and non-criminal. Mostly criminal. Admiral Sinclair ordered him to ground in the Hole below Whitehall—on a clockwise leash. So, the twat did a runner. He's compromised. A spy—he'll keep running."

Surprised by the lady's language, Poston handed Dorothy the cable he received from his brother. "He's running."

Lewis,
Dewar escaped England. Lisbon and Southern France are suggested.
   Johnny

Smiling as she might, Dorothy's expression seemed to cascade through an upheaval, and land in the quiet of a library, in the soft hue of a green lamp shade. As though reluctant, she stepped away from Poston and dropped into a chair across from him. She laid the barrel of her silenced FN Baby Browning on the edge of the table, coaxing him to respond.

"Drama has taken the fore, I see," Poston said. "Now you won't get blood on your blouse."

With an expression of weariness, she said, "I regret pointing this pistol at you. One last time. Give me the pouch." There was a deliberate space between her words. "I gave the Corsicans a dozen photographs of Gordon Dewar with instructions to shoot on sight."

A lean, hungry-looking man came to a stop behind her. The man's weapon disappeared, then was there again held loosely in his right hand.

Setting the pouch on the table, Poston stared into the muzzle of the pistol. "If it's not Dewar, it's your husband, Sir Nigel. Or..." Poston started to add Dorothy to the list, but other words followed in his mind. "I don't care. Jesus. A good many lads died transporting those documents."

"There will be more gloomy days for these commandos, Lewis."

There was something in her still, lovely face, that told Poston he was skating on thin ice. "Do you conflate mission outcomes?" he asked. "Should we meet again, I'll be carrying this PPK." When Poston set his weapon on the table, the Corsican lifted his weapon, drew back the hammer, and pointed it at the back of Poston's head.

For what seemed many moments he thought, wondering his words. "Do you put your hand to the killing, Dorothy? I mean fair play. Commandos. Spies. Who would care the difference?"

"Again, you're dressed in tired linen, Lewis, squawking through your clacker. Think. Dewar's mine to kill. His passport was spotted in Lisbon. Heading for Lyon—probably on the way to Switzerland. I have orders to terminate him—I'll tap his eye."

Shocked, with a suspended reaction, he then asked, "The passport's a forgery?"

"The admiral considered that possibility. My orders include impostors."

Surprised, his aim blurred, Poston found himself staring at a stranger. Amends aside, he said, "I'll look for a woman I once admired—at Shepheard's— near the grand piano."

"Not to push the bounds of propriety, Lewis, after Operation Snow White is rolled up, I insist you meet me in twenty-four land for a game of touch-me-not."

"'Twenty-four land' is code for Portugal. Why would I go there?"

"So, we can gamble at the Polocio and escape to Bermuda."

"It's time for a nightcap and you and your thug are pointing guns at me. That's no way to keep me on the boil." Poston took his PPK off the table and handed Dorothy the pouch.

For several minutes, Dorothy did not speak. Tapping the table with an unlit cigarette she scanned the restaurant, quarter by quarter. Securing the pouch, she placed it on her lap along with her Browning.

Alerting to the sound of gunfire in the harbor, she turned her head. "My associate standing behind you is on loan from the Corsican syndicate—here to help you on your way. Trust his judgment and do what he says. He's with me because he was paid by a South African to kill you and your pilot."

Poston didn't respond. No matter how he sorted the players, getting Hardin out of Marseille was imperative. Deciding how to work free of his predicament, he considered her warning. If what Dorothy said was true, the woman he had been shagging was running an intelligence network throughout the Mediterranean basin, including contracting criminals.

She casually introduced the Corsican, as if they were just enjoying a day's work.

"I am surprised the admiral would sanction that," Poston said.

"Don't be. He gave the syndicate a bag of gold."

Poston rose to leave, pointed at Dorothy's lap. "Good riddance."

She held up her hand and spoke to the Corsican in French. With a nod the Corsican seized Poston's arm and escorted him out of the restaurant.

If the syndicate hasn't been paid, Poston thought as he stood on the sidewalk, then I'm being set up—to lead the Corsican to Hardin. After searching the faces of the men at the curb, Poston started across the street. The hungry-looking Corsican had gained an assistant.

The gunfire in the harbor bore the heavy pulse of a .45 caliber weapon— Hardin's Thompson. I hope Hawkes is airborne before she opens that pouch.

Poston was pushed into a corner booth in the hotel bar. Minutes later, speaking in French, the nearest Corsican slammed the barrel of his weapon against Poston's head.

*   *   *

Malta. The Harbor Strand. 27 September 1939. 1150 Hours, GMT + 1 Hour.

Malta was going to bed when the sun rose.

Sergeant Robby McPhee looked a mess and walked a mess, his crotch lined with a crust of salt. With bleak, bloodshot eyes and a weather-burned face, he had swum the length of the Grand Harbor at Valetta against the outgoing tide. Exhausted, he sat in the entry of a trinket shop along the strand, looking for a live wire to hit up for a cup of coffee.

Entering the other-ranks club, as though flushed from a scupper, his boots sloshed with a sponging sound, the left boot louder than the right.

His bright red hair, bunched and afoul, left the peals of his brow jutting ahead of his vision, accenting an expression of wishful lunacy. His wind-burned face looked ready to burst with its swollen smile and week-old stubble. As he spotted Molly, the discovery seemed to blast his buttons. He became brazen, shouting vowels and hyphens of confused vengeance.

McPhee picked his way around the outer edge of the tables throwing his words. "Molly, you dag-sucking bastard. I've been hiding all night—doggo. I was in the harbor, and you did nothing but drink and whore your cogs off."

"Darkey McPhee. It's the bloody blue-light clinic for a blighter like you. Look at your sorry arse. I'll bet your short arm's buggered." Molly waited for the laughter in the bar to subside, finished his rum, and raised his voice, "I'm putting your pot on. Putting you up on a 252-charge. Your conduct and appearance are against 'good order and military discipline.'"

"Fair go, bum-brusher. At least my lips aren't shaped like Mother's twat. Or have you been brown-tonguing one of the lads here?"

Molly set his jar of stout on the bar, pushed a sailor away who was crowding his right shoulder, and punched McPhee full square, jarring his tats loose. The Irishman collapsed. Even Paddy's clothes collapsed, hiding what some thought was the whore's back-up.

The sailors in the pub nodded in unison—as if half fearing an encore.

Drinking rum with his feet cushioned on McPhee's arse, Molly bought drams for the lot with McPhee's money. When the Irishman started to muster, Molly threw a jar of beer on his head. "Where's Olive? My Model 1897 and me are of Flanders and Cairo's outback."

"A vintage year, 1897," McPhee hollered, trying to keep his voice even. He rubbed his neck and jacked his jaw back and forth. After tapping his teeth together, he said, "I dropped that oily tart on the sloop's deck and swam for it."

"If Olive's all at sea, Paddy—she's a prize for some wank." After ordering McPhee, a rum, Molly started humming the tune he like to think by. "Was Olive a taut hand, Robby?"

"None crueler—head and chest—dead certain."

"Olive's yours to find Paddy—before we wake."

Ranging past the taverns frequented by merchant seamen, McPhee did not expect to find Molly's shotgun, or Molly for that matter. As the hours fell away, McPhee stopped for a beer and a basket of chips. In the corner of the pub five sailors quickly gathered near a well-dressed man who gave each sailor money—counting as he placed the notes on the table.

After the man left the pub the five sailors walked to the bar and ordered beer. McPhee sat dumbfounded. A well set-up sailor in a heavy sweater had Olive Oil slung across his back. Nearly jumping from his chair, spilling his beer, McPhee ran from the pub.

For Molly, it's a tart for me to ask. One whore's laughter led to another whore's story. For a water-soaked fiver, the tabbies he asked had a grand idea where a dumb mick should look. Swishing their wares, they all claimed to love the old shaggledick.

Chatting up a tart in front of Hope Tavern, for a quid, a second tart hauled McPhee a half block where Molly had his courting tackle wired to a saucy young trollop in the alley behind the chief magistrate's office. Listening to their old slithery, her touch-hole sloshing and her exhaust firing shots, McPhee laughed a high *B*-flat, wishing the gas barrage would ignite and twist Molly's balls into a knot.

Recruiting his humor, he hollered, "Molly! It's cupid's itch and cockles for you this day." With no reply, McPhee put in, "Olive's walk-about up the road. Whoring with some beer-scoffing lascar—a bilge bailer by the look of him."

Molly shuffled from the alleyway securing his equipment, appearing at half-mast. With a thumb for his whistle-bait, Molly shook his head into a sobering grin. "A bit more choke and that lassie would have caught fire." Molly buttoned his pants as he spoke. "Show me, Paddy. Keep a weapon handy. I'm game for a tart up."

And there she was—Olive Oil—starkers, flashing her well-rubbed butt. Barrel down, she was consorting with a hatchet-faced sailor with shifty eyes, spewing a Sicilian form of hog fuel.

With music blaring and streams of beer flowing, Molly rushed straight at the man with Olive slung across his back, and threw a fist into the man's kidney, driving his weight to its limit.

Screaming, the man slammed into the bar and arched backward. Molly drove a left hook into the side of his head as he fell, keelhauled.

With a Webley-Fosbery, McPhee pointed at the sailors on Molly's right side who took a step forward. "Stand easy, lads, or I'll root ya. There'll be no more dick-waving."

Grabbing a handful of hair and holding the man's head off the floor, Molly jerked the trench gun's sling over the sailor's head, shortened the sling to its home, checked the loads, and leveled the shotgun on a sailor standing next to the bar on his left. Handing Olive to McPhee, Molly braced into an invitation. "Would you be wanting a go at this old tar pot?"

"You're an old jack who likes surprises." Drawing a pistol from his back, the young sailor and his Guernsey sweater fell where he stood. Quick-eyed or rum-eyed, the pub went quiet. Molly's gutting-knife had found a home, its hilt burbling blood.

Another man stopped his stride when McPhee drew his eye.

Molly leveled the trench gun on the man and grinned. "No worries—you won't need to pray. If hell's where you're rellies live, half-jack, I'll help you find `em." Molly eyed the rest of the men in the pub, measuring threats. Holding the trench gun over the bar, he shouted, "This is Olive Oil. Her name's etched on the trigger guard. Bar Keep, stop bobbing about in that back eddy, and read the scribe for these lads."

Molly grabbed the barkeep's hair and held the shotgun near his face. "'Olive Oil.' The name's scratched on the trigger guard, like he said."

"Shift yourself, Paddy," Molly said, pulling McPhee toward the pub's main entrance as he backed out of the door. Once in the street they ducked down an alleyway that led to the harbor.

HMS Sloop *Grimsby* sailed from Malta at 0400 hours bound for Gibraltar and her home port of Portsmouth. Top Sergeant Clive Mauldin and Sergeant Robert McPhee were in transit as well. Traveling on orders as Captain Edward Hardin and his aide, bound for the Chatham Dockyard in England assigned to the British Expeditionary Force in Belgium, they sailed on board HMS *Aphis*, a small, river gunboat returning from the South China Sea with three sister gunboats.

*   *   *

Lyon, France. Le Gare les Brotteaux Railway Station, 28 September 1939. 1430 Hours, GMT + 1 Hour.

For a railway station, the building was an architectural jewel. The Gare les Brotteaux sat in the 6th Arrondisement of Lyon, out of scale for its neighbors, yet made no difference to the hordes of refugees clogging the railways of France.

Keen eyed, Dorothy whispered. "Jews. Wool overcoats and the same hats." Standing near the station's main entrance, her eyes flickered over the interior of the station—hundreds of faces.

"If Dewar's smart, he'll become a Jew," she whispered to herself.

Poston's pouch was filled with useless news. Under the barrel of her silenced Browning, he gave her *The London Daily Mail's* sporting news. Fostering a contemptuous grin, she did enjoy their game of tidies and what-nots. There are more pouches.

After leaving the restaurant in Marseille, she had received two cables from MI6, Lisbon, stamped Passport Control. One stating that Lewis Poston worked for MI6, for her boss—Admiral Sinclair. The other stating that a young man carrying a British passport, traveling as Gordon Dewar, had boarded a train in Lisbon bound for Lyon.

Knowing Lisbon passengers bound for Lyon had to change trains at the French border, she waited. Her hunch about Geneva had been correct. But where was her spy?

In Lyon, Dorothy purchased a first-class ticket from Lyon to Geneva. She didn't intend to use it. John Poston's telegram to his brother suggested Dewar was in southern France. The intel decrypt confirmed Dewar was running.

Eager to be moving on, she entered the station and stood near the departure board. Noting a murmur of subdued talk, Dorothy stood for a moment looking up and down the reception plaza. Her briefing papers prepared by MI6 cited Lyon as the central hub for transit to Marseille or Geneva. That no one on the run could hide in Lyon. The Corsicans would pick them up and wring them out. Dewar's boy must be ticketed through to Geneva.

The rail system in the Rhone River valley was part of the sugar-beet line—owned and operated by the Corsican syndicate. They monitored the trains leaving Lisbon and Marseille, following any passenger buying tickets to Lyon.

The decrypt stated Dewar has a boy in London he fancies. Alistair, she remembered. He'll be anxious, nervous.

Sorting the passengers as they stepped from the train, she did not see any man likely to be a syndicate watcher. Spotting a likely young man stepping from the train, she unbuttoned the top button of her silk blouse and fell in behind him. The chill felt good.

This must be Alistair, Dewar's favorite. He stopped in the center of the station and was reading the arrival and departure board. He smiled as he looked about. He seemed frightened.

"I'm scheduled for Geneva. Do you see it on the board?" Dorothy asked, adjusting her shoulder bag, exposing her fortune.

"Yes, it's just there. Platform one, in forty minutes." As he talked, Alistair was watching the policemen near the station's main entrance.

"The train's in," she asked, centering the strap of her shoulder bag, extending her hand and leaning forward. "My name's Sister Lia."

With a look of shock, the young man accepted her hand. "Sister—I'm Alistair Bagley."

"I've a first-class compartment. If you're going east, you can join me. It's a short ride."

"Thank you, Sister."

Sister Lia closed the door to the compartment, drew the door's window curtain, and adjusted her blouse exposing her ample curves. Distracted, Bagley's eyes widened with the shadows of panic as he backed up. The Baby Browning coughed twice. Bagley collapsed with a look of soft horror. Dorothy took his British passport, Swiss passport, and his money.

"Now where is, Dewar?"

Stepping from the train she sauntered from the Gare les Brotteaux and hailed a taxi. Arriving at Lyon's passport control office, she gave the driver a five-pound note, and spoke in French. "You dropped me at a hotel, yes?" The driver gave her a quick nod.

If Dewar went to Lisbon, he's either heading for Bermuda or changing trains at the French border and is on his way to Marseille. Simply keeping one's promise is success of a kind.

Frustrated, Dorothy listened to her Corsican counterpart—Dewar was not on a train to Marseille. The cable she sent to her MI6 contact in Lisbon was succinct:

The punter's not in France.

*   *   *

Marseille Harbor. 28 September 1939. 1900 Hours, GMT + 1 Hour.

Standing at the top of the gangway leading to the flying boat dock, Hardin nudged Hawkes's shoulder. "We'll separate, create a diversion, then slip into the water, and swim to that Stranraer."

"I can't swim," Hawkes said, chafing his hands together.

"Christ in gaiters. I thought you were bloody joking," Hardin laughed, handing Hawkes the holdall. "Take one of the skiffs down the landing. No one will notice."

As if hypnotized, Hawkes looked toward the harbor. "We're not that bloody lucky."

The Stranraer flying boat Poston had purchased sat at anchor in the harbor, facing the wind, forty meters off the Imperial Airways dock. Listed as inoperable to blunt the inquiries of more insistent passengers, the plane was topped off with fuel, five days' rations and two parachutes.

They separated at the bottom of the gangway. With the Thompson wrapped in a blanket, Hardin mingled with a cluster of well-dressed men waiting to board Imperial Airways Flight 173 to Alexandria. With infinite care, watching the attendant hand-loading luggage and mail sacks, he ambled from the crowd and lowered himself into a maze of pallets and petrol drums.

Valetta had become a hungry town.

Hawkes wandered down the landing and stopped near a cluster of skiffs. When he couldn't see Hardin, he set the holdall in the prow of the nearest skiff, shoved off, and started rowing toward the Stranraer. A man standing on the strand overlooking the landing yelled and started running toward the gangway, firing a pistol at Hawkes.

The passengers on the landing panicked. Pushing and hollering, eleven sets of feet tried to mount the gangway as one. Hardin cleared cover immediately, cast off the bow and stern lines of the seaplane, and shoved it into the harbor. Glancing from the shore to the seaplane and on to the gangway, he spotted men with pistols pushing passengers aside.

Two men burst from a crevasse near the top of the gang and bounded down the ramp. Starting with the man in the rear, Hardin shot each man center of mass. A third man stood frozen at the top of the gang, staring.

Extending the sling on the Thompson, Hardin drew it over his head and slipped into the water. Using the drifting seaplane as cover, he swam to the Stranraer.

"Get in, Hawkes. I'll unhook the buoy."

With a pierhead jump Hawkes landed on his stomach on the left pontoon, as the play of several searchlights illuminated the Stranraer's cockpit.

Burbling bile, shaking, and sweating at the throttle, Hawkes started screaming at the three harbor police boats racing toward his new home. Tucking his flask next to his balls, he jammed the stick to full power, aiming the seaplane at the nearest police boat.

I'll be killed for a bloody Straits dollar by a bunch of two-by-twice scenery bums.

With searchlights bathing the cockpit and muzzle flashes announcing the arrival of hot lead, Hawkes pulled back on the stick. She took to the air, clearing the masthead light on the wheelhouse of the police boat by inches, small-arms fire shot through the cockpit, one round splitting the front edge of his seat, centered between his legs.

Hawkes grabbed the flask and drank until. Gasping for air, he couldn't leave the whiskey alone. After estimating the distance from the split in the seat cushion to his cobblers, he finished the whiskey in one go.

The shithouse whistling an incomplete chord brought a vague sadness that was almost a happiness. We're all misfits, more or less. The sum of our leavings.

"The French are menacing bastards," Hawkes screamed. "There must be a clot in MI6 working with von Cleve, besides our spy."

"You're spot on about MI6," Hardin said. "Try this for size. The admiral ordered us to land in Southampton with a decoy pouch. Must be a trap. I'm jumping into England near the Ashchurch Army Center. I know those fields."

"Hold on, Cobber," Hawkes said. "The desk-jobs would guess that sort of move. So far, they've killed Corcoran and damn near killed McPhee and Poston."

"What's on your mind besides booze, Hawkes?"

"Do you know how to pack a parachute, cobber?" Hawkes asked, something new in his still, cold face. "It's their last chance to kill you. An accident would absolve the whole of Mother's crowd—equipment failure."

"Poston secured the chutes."

Unsnapping the parachute packing flaps, Hardin screamed a string of expletives. His static line was cut free. Hawkes's chute was cut as well.

"You were right, Hawker. The static lines weren't hooked to the drag chutes."

"Fix my chute before you leave."

"I already did."

Hardin took a deep breath, trying to temper his rage. Amongst the thousands of flimsies and decrypts the MI6 had to sort each day, a spy had managed to rig his death. Jumping at three hundred and fifty feet, he would have augured-in, died in a rush in Katherine's backyard.

*   *   *

Bombay, India. 28 September 1939. 1530 Hours, GMT + 5.5 Hours.

The massive stone door ground open, stone on stone. An expanding shaft of light warmed the bougainvillea's luxurious drapery. The winding mosaic path drew von Cleve into Crilley's nave, the expansive arbor a wondrous confusion of shapes and colors.

Alone, von Cleve set the pouch taken from the Sloop *Grimsby* on a marble flower stand and filled a glass with water. The autumn sun, its reds and golds, pierced the foliage atop the arbor tying the stones in the floor with ribbons of fluttering lumens.

That Crilley appeared without making a sound, too pale to be alive, projected an evil unbalanced by good. Disturbed by a nerving pulse that set the bougainvillea's bracts to dancing, waving their flowers without weeping, von Cleve set his back to a large column.

"So, you have kept your promise. The pouch and its secrets rest with the Templar." Crilley took the pouch and examined its battered seal. Caution joined with a vacant stare as he cut the seal and offered the pouch to von Cleve.

With a voice quietly strained, Crilley's offering fostered a premonition. "Alex, you have earned the privilege of exposing these documents."

Trapped, a linkboy without a torch, von Cleve scanned the priory and peered into the reaches of the arbor. Dozens of silent men stared, their brown robes drawn with a bright yellow sash, their sandals unscarred, their feet washed.

Von Cleve lifted the leather flap. Hesitant, his eyes dilating, he stared into the hollow at the edge of a newspaper. Where are the protected documents? Briefly he thought of William Hockey's father, the man who had proctored his lessons eighteen years ago. Holding the paper into the sun, he showed it to Crilley.

"*The London Daily Mail*—what's next?" von Cleve asked.

"You're a dead man—that's what's next."

He searched the folds of the paper for a clue—a date, a headline. Nothing. Handing the pouch to Crilley, he found the man's eyes vibrating in death's dance. Stepping away from Crilley's reach, the priory, and its devoted wards seemed to fill with a silent scream, instantly drawn as Crilley spoke through a nod.

"You have less than a week, Alex. Nigel Stuart's in Port Blair on South Andaman Island. Lewis Poston just left Marseille. The location of the special-service soldier has not been confirmed. One of these men has the documents you agreed to retrieve."

"I'll start in Port Blair. If Stuart doesn't have them, he'll know who does. If the soldier has the documents Hockey will let us know. Poston's too exposed to be trusted with anything."

*   *   *

Ritchie's Public House, Port Blair, South Andaman Island.

Chuffed over being posted to the fringe of the Realm, to a down-market wallow in the Bay of Bengal, Sir Nigel Stuart handed his supper meal a splendid licking, flushing grand gobs of sausage with throat-knotting gulps of beer.

Ritchie's Public House served the best fare in Port Blair. For Stuart, dining at Ritchie's was akin to a horse enjoying a rick of second-cut hay. That he had forsaken an oath and had taken up Hardin's defense might one day bring a reckoning.

Today he yearned to join the British Expeditionary Force, to be again in Belgium—in Flanders Field with Molly. He could smell the fodder, the mud— the shell-crater's gravel clung to his back, his body bruised and battered as his top sergeant dragged him through the carnage. A shattered femur glistened white above ragged bits of flesh—showily vulgar. The hinges needed oil that day—no gate swung free.

The generals died in bed—their bowel well-tended, their feet washed to a creamy pink.

With three jars down and the last jar running from a short whiskey, he paid for his scavenging and stepped into the night. Waiting for a taxi, he was scheduled to fly to Malaya in the morning to oversee the delivery of a shipment of rifles. He was more interested in trolling the harbor for a bonnie lass than scrubbing the skid marks from Snow White's knickers.

Obscured by the glare of the lamp's light, a man was approaching Ritchie's—a large man. Instantly alert, Stuart drew into a deep shadow as von Cleve passed by.

This is not by chance. The man's come to kill somebody.

Stuart checked the loads in his Enfield No. 2 MK1 pistol and screwed the silencer into place. Admiral Sinclair's orders were clear—eliminate the principals complicit in Snow White. Killing von Cleve, a fellow traveler, would bring a reckoning, somewhere down the line.

Ornamental-iron trellises framed the roofed walkway leading to the main entrance to Ritchie's Public House. Supported by a rank of iron arches extending from the taxi stand at the curb to the oak entry, the walkway was encased in bougainvillea.

Tables and chairs sat in groups across the terrace sporting a variety of shrubs and plants. Stuart drew shrubs together framing the entry to the terrace, and sat in a chair twenty feet away, peering between the shrubs.

Relaxed by the drink, he sat bathing in a light mist with his Enfield lying on his lap.

Alert and not alert, he kept nodding off as he waited for von Cleve to come out of the pub. Four jars of beer and a whiskey were more than his limit.

As a startled animal reacts, he sprang away from his chair, stumbling, baring his teeth he screamed as he brought the Enfield into line. Von Cleve's stiletto arced past his throat as he fired the first of six solids into the monster's chest.

Kicking his chair backwards, the stiletto's blade flashed passed his face. As if hitching a ride, the blade seemed to change direction as each round found its mark.

Flailing and screaming, trying to dodge the flashing blade, Stuart fired his Enfield snub nose until it rang empty.

Teetering and convulsing, von Cleve slumped upright to his knees, slouched into a shrub, his arms extended to opposite sides of a three-foot pot, his head buried in the shrub's branches. He hollered, gasping for air. Blood pooled at his knees.

"Shut up, you bastard." Stuart kicked von Cleve in the side of the chest, and the monster fell free of his prop, his head parked in a pool of blood.

Fighting to steady his heart rate, Stuart drew rapid, gasping breaths, brushing debris from his clothes. He was soaking wet, shivering, and floating in adrenaline. Running from the terrace, away from Ritchie's, the Cellular Jail was on his mind.

After what seemed a mile, he stopped and hailed a cab for the airport. The next flight to Colombo, Ceylon, was scheduled to depart in five hours.

Six solids at point-blank range—he was certain von Cleve would die.

*   *   *

Airborne. Drop Zone: Ashchurch Royal Army Ordinance Center. 29 September 1939. 0020 Hours, GMT.

Presenting Hawkes with his parachute, Hardin said, "I tied off the static lines. Jumping at three hundred and fifty feet without a chute, we would barely be screaming when we augured in—a piece of meat and a jumble of sharp bones."

"If you got it wrong, I'll never know." Hawkes shook Hardin's frosty hand and gave him a nod. "I can't swim, remember?" Hawkes set his parachute in the copilot's seat. "Get the life raft ready for me to grab."

"Where are we?"

"We're grazing the stars on a westerly vector to clear Lands' End, nearly over Saint Mary's Isle, in the Scilly Isles Archipelago." Flying Officer Hawkes had radioed an IFF—Identification Friendly, followed by a distress signal to Southampton, purposely failing to identify himself. He then announced the aircraft was returning to Horta, in the Azores.

Southwest of England's southern extreme, using the lights of Star Castle on Garrison Hill, on Saint Mary's Isle as a landmark, he turned northwest topping the flashing beacon of Bishop Rock Lighthouse, and turned north toward Ireland. After a twenty-minute run, he set a course for Wales and on to Ashchurch, England.

Lifting out of the harbor at Marseille, the "whistling shithouse" had flown through a barrage of small-arms fire. The cover on the loo had taken a bag full of hits, producing a fluted, mournful tone. The holes in the lid whistled as one, the chord fluctuating between a seventh and the three flats of a diminished ninth, approximating an E-flat.

Years ago, Jeffrey Hawkes had been an accomplished pianist—his ear was keen. Laughing now, he tried to hum the notes. He enjoyed the irony. One of the holes in the toilet seat rang on a cant. Its voice was various and filled with an odd lilt.

Holding the "captains and coxswains' logbook for Royal Air Force marine craft," Hardin read the entry Hawkes had fashioned—who can be serious when Mother's about?

With the aircraft crabbing along at three hundred feet to avoid detection, Hawkes hoped the antiaircraft boys in Wales were drinking through the haze of a quiet night, singing rhymes to bolster the lads—patriotic songs of earlier times—the Somme and Gallipoli. He hoped the drone of a single airplane no longer brought farmers and shopkeepers from their sleep.

Coastal-patrol flights had become a constant reminder.

Reading the "Howgozit Curve," Hawkes calculated the distance—with light to moderate headwinds there was barely enough petrol to make the marine terminal at Foynes, on the River Shannon. Hardin started turning tight circles as a cat might when caged. His antics brought Hawkes to a blistering boil.

"Sit down, jackass. And stop reading the bloody gauges," Hawkes yelled. "Have a piss."

Hardin picked up his T-4 parachute and sat down. A traitor in Mother's crowd had sabotaged the chute of the last man standing. Poston had supplied the T-4's. That meant Poston was either a cunning operative or a useful dolt.

Whom should Hardin kill first? Wound tight—too tight, he kept lifting the Thompson and checking its breach. He wanted to talk with Willie Hockey. Then he would kill Dewar and anyone else involved in killing his mates.

With a one-corner grin, Hawkes toasted the air with his empty flask. "This bus driver's off to Foynes, on the River Shannon, for fancy Irish whiskey and a green-eyed lassie."

"Hawkes, you'll soon be in France."

"You won't be far behind me, cobber."

"I'm done being a brown job."

"Here's the latest from the colonies," Hawkes declared, as if to say goodbye. "Joe Lewis won the heavyweight title in eleven rounds. And the New York Yankees are beating the Cincinnati Reds in the World Series, two games to none."

"I'll look for you in Piccadilly, Hawkes."

"I'll be there."

Perched on the left wing, fighting the prop wash, Hardin waited for a thumbs-up from the best flying officer he knew. With a thumbs-up from Hawkes, he pushed himself into space, falling free of the wing, watching the aircraft's tail assembly flash by. Jumping at combat altitude, he was sorting the parachute's risers when he slammed to his knees, careened sideways and was dragged by the wind through a raceway of cows.

The grass was cased in crystals.

Mustered and smelling of the farm, measuring the rooftops as the gray before dawn lightened the roadway, he ran into a hollow. Grouse or golden plovers flushed from a tangle of briars. Dropping to the ground, his ribs rang with pain. The one star he could find seemed to accentuate the darkness.

By the time he reached Tirle Brook near the Ashchurch town square, blackbirds were massing in the treetops, and the mist that covered the brook at dawn was drifting away.

After the longest day ever, tired and wet, he stood in an alcove meant for trespassers near the front gate of the Ashchurch Royal Army Ordinance Center, staring at a sentry's Bren gun.

"Who are you?"

"Captain Edward Hardin. I'm a special-service officer just returned from Burma." Hardin's uniform was stained and torn, his face was weather beaten, and his eyes kept moving—checking his perimeter.

"Your identity papers are outdated, you have no identity disc, and you're carrying an American weapon, a Thompson submachinegun."

"Papers and identities are mission sensitive and the weapon's a special-service issue."

"That, or you're a bloody Kraut."

After being ordered around for the next thirty minutes as though he were a German spy, Hardin snapped, cold decking the two guards. Securing their weapons, he phoned the duty officer in charge of the guard mount.

He tried to phone Hockey, but the operator at the ordinance center's switch refused to place the call. Hardin didn't know the authentication code for calling off base.

He placed his kit and the Thompson on the pavement in front of the guard shack. Then he took the guard's weapons and set them on the pavement next to his kit. It didn't make any difference who the duty officer was. He would not kill Hardin unless he had orders to do so or became frightened.

Hardin turned on the floodlights, opened the door, and stood near the open gate with his hands raised to ensure the guards would realize he was not armed.

An olive drab Morris saloon car with military police stenciled on the door eased to a stop twenty meters from the guard shack, its lights on high beam. Now, as the guards separated, he recognized the man who stayed with the car.

Hardin raised his hands farther and stood at a brace, the silence broken by the approaching sentries loading their weapons. They wore gaiters and web belts and were carrying Webley .38 revolvers with wooden grips. Without a word, they searched him and took him into custody.

After being escorted to the center's headquarters, his left hand cuffed to an iron stanchion, he lit a cigarette, closed his eyes, and set his head against the wall. He thought of Hawkes and their sabotaged parachutes, wondering if his favorite pilot had reached Ireland.

The back door burst opened.

Two men in camouflage uniforms firing Bren guns instantly killed three of the four British soldiers. Uncuffing Hardin, they dragged him outside. The fourth guard crawled to the back door and saw the prisoner thrown into a lorry.

Sergeant Akens ran into the building with his weapon at high port followed by another guard. Calling the front gate, he warned, "We've Germans on the base. At least two men dressed in British uniforms are driving a lorry. Shoot on sight."

Calling the base commander, he said, "Sir, this is Sergeant Akens. Base security has been breached. Two Germans killed three squaddies and wounded a fourth man here at headquarters. They are driving a lorry and must be trying to get off base."

"Take a prisoner if you can."

"Sir they kidnapped Major Edward Hardin, a special-service commando."

At the front gate, three Bren guns opened fire at the oncoming lorry shattering the windscreen and the heads of the two men in the front seat. Hardin, laying as flat as the handcuffs would allow, crashed into the headboard when the vehicle plowed into a tree.

"Captain Hardin! You're awake."

"Well, damn if you're not Sergeant Akens. You've gained a rank. Congratulations are in order. Are you still a signals sergeant? Can I still call you Sparky?"

"I am. And yes, you can. You've been unconscious for almost a week."

"What the hell happened?"

"We don't know. Two British civilians dressed in regulation camouflage uniforms tried to highjack you and get you off the base."

"Are you sure they were civilians. British citizens."

"Yes. The intel boys confirmed both counts. They came from Manchester." With his mind trying to locate a reason for Hardin's equipment, Akens said, "I'm the sergeant-in-charge of the guard mount tonight." Akens stepped into the next room and sent the gate guards on their way. Returning with coffee he offered Hardin a biscuit and a chocolate bar.

"The base commander wants to know where you've been posted?" Akens asked.

"I've been deployed overseas for months. In Burma. I just parachuted into England. My papers are out of date and I've an American weapon. So here we are."

"Damn shame about your wife, Captain. Delivering that message was the hardest thing I've ever done. None of the officers wanted the duty."

"Paper officers never bleed much." Hardin rubbed his wrists, picked up his cup and sipped the hot coffee. "That message wasn't true. Katherine's safe."

For Akens, caution had joined with relief, and then with anger. "That's well over the score. Who are the derby bastards?"

"My friends in England have been sorting the cards."

With a nod, Akens said, "I'll stand easy."

"Sparky, I tried to use the phone earlier, but I needed the challenge and password." Akens wrote two words on a piece of paper. After Hardin read the words and gave him a nod, Akens set fire to the paper and set it in an ashtray.

"I don't want you to hear this, Akens." After a series of directory inquiries, Hardin was patched through the center's switchboard, and the phone rang clear.

"Hockey."

"Willie, this is Edward."

"Ah, and so it's Katherine's Welshman. Your mother claims you're fair-haired. I've seen no evidence of that these past months."

"How is Katherine?"

"Katherine's in fine fettle. Lovely as ever. Worried sick, as is your mother."

"Where is she?"

"Katherine's five months and so—stiff and sore and scared—in full foal, thanks to you. She wonders where you've been."

"Is she safe?"

"Yes. She's with your mother. I have men watching them—day and night."

"Where are they?"

"Not now, Edward. Not over the land line."

"All right. I'm at the Ashchurch Ordinance Center. I've been gated under arms."

"Be careful! Don't let them take you anywhere."

Sensing alarm in Hockey's tone, Hardin asked, "What's going on?"

"Port security killed a man and arrested three others inside the wall at the Chatham dockyard. The attackers opened fire on two squaddies as they came down the gang from a small river gunboat. The dead man had a picture of your team in his shirt pocket."

Deciding the targets were Molly and McPhee, Hardin said, "Those squaddies helped me escape Burma."

"They're in decent trim. 'Darkie', your Irishman, has a bullet burn on his neck. Bit of a scratch. And the big man coldcocked a guard."

"'Darkie' is Robert McPhee. The big man is Molly. Clive Mauldin. He's just been promoted to sergeant major. How did the Krauts get inside the wall?"

"They worked there."

"Sod-all. MI6 has spies, and Bosche sympathizers have infiltrated the ports—airfields as well, I suppose. Our expeditionary force is in for a drubbing."

"Do you have a weapon?"

"Yes. An American Thompson."

"Be careful who you talk to. I'll arrive before nightfall."

* * *

Lyon, France. Le Gare les Brotteaux Railway Station. 29 September 1939. 1850 Hours, GMT + 1 Hour.

Gare les Brotteaux railway station was groomed with the reverence of a Catholic mass. Atheists and Jews were converting to Hitler's blood religion as if Abraham had appeared on the Reichsmark. Civilization's boundaries had been redrawn. Orderly, obedient conduct defined the loyalty the Nazis required. With German agents loosely toggled to each French gendarme, another would bloom from hiding, pen in hand, and free of rust.

Petra had warned Eaton—Gestapo were scouring southern France looking for her. The grainy photograph they had was a picture of Dorothy—a side view. MI6, along with Hiram Bingham, had flooded the transportation routes out of Marseille with the photo at Dorothy's insistence, knowing if detained, her papers stated that she was a British member of the International Red Cross.

Eaton and Petra fell into silence as they waited on Platform one near a second-class carriage. Voices were approaching from every direction. Anxious to board the train to Geneva, Petra nudged Eaton's rib and whispered, "Keep a smile in your eyes, Sam. If fear rides your shoulders the Gestapo will notice."

Eaton gripped his holdall and looked at his shoes for an instant. Then his gut turned over and his fear returned. "These Nazis believe whatever they invent." He stood for a moment, watching the sun creep through the overhead trellis and pool on the platform.

"The Germans are everywhere."

French gendarmes roamed the platform, questioning arriving and departing passengers. They casually searched Eaton's holdall. Petra's bag was searched twice, pocketing her nylons.

Eaton rubbed his jaw. "What's going on?"

Petra caught something of his fear, and whispered, "Smile and give me a kiss on the cheek. Then pick up my bag and be attentive."

Anxious, they waited as the body of a young man was placed on a stretcher. Petra edged past Eaton, using the distraction to walk down the platform, and kept moving until she was near the carriage stamped on their tickets.

Eaton whispered, "Do you think Dorothy came through Lyon on her way to Marseille?"

There was no reply.

When Eaton caught her arm, Petra turned and slapped him. "Your secretary is a cunning, dangerous woman, with the power to hate more than most Nazis. I think she killed that man they are carrying out." As though emphasizing her point, her eyes chilled. "Did you tell her where we were heading? The country, the village?"

"Nothing. She'll figure it out—Switzerland or Austria."

"I prefer Austria."

"Good. We're heading for the village of Zell am See, in Austria, a few kilometers south through the Stein Pass from Bad Reichenhall. I purchased a chalet overlooking the lake, and a small flat in the center of the village."

"So, we tempt our enemy and hide in his courtyard." Petra's voice was brittle.

"It might be too close to your mother."

"And, if your secretary doesn't kill us, you can kill my brother."

It was almost dark when Eaton locked the front door to the chalet overlooking Zell am See. Satisfied he had done a proper job of finding shelter from the mad moneymen of Europe, he sat enjoying a coffee and the lake's beauty.

Ruthless bankers or Nazis, a distinction without a difference, he thought.

Fresh from her bath, devilish eagerness sprang into Petra's face as she slipped into a robe, spread her hair across her shoulders, kissed Eaton affectionately, and poured herself a coffee.

With a peevish grin she walked with a certain mirth toward Eaton. "Sam, I'm going to visit my mother. If she's having trouble with my brother, I'll bring her here. Do you mind?"

"You must be careful! I don't want any exposure. If you can bring her here without disclosing our relationship, you could live in town, and visit as often as you like."

Suffering something of a romantic failing, Petra's hands were lying on the table, quiet as stones. "My mother must grow old the way a river grows old. Gently."

Bad Reichenhall's old church was mottled with shades of brown lichen and gray and green moss. The worn swale at the entry to the nave ran the length of the granite step, saddled in the middle by centuries of reluctant feet.

Hans Marsh was Bad Reichenhall's vicar. At six foot plus five inches, he had only to smile to put parishioners off their game. Every day he drove his tray truck to the village so he could have lunch. On his way home he would stop at a nearby farm and cut wood. His wages consisted of enough firewood to keep his cottage warm until the next afternoon.

Raised in a rough way, at thirty-eight years old, the vicar was best left with a smile.

"You should not have come, Petra," the priest whispered, his voice carefully empty. "As is a custom, Karl has taken over your father's farm. Sadly, your mother is a servant in her own home. Karl continues his evil. Since his return, a girl from the village has vanished."

Pinching her features, Petra asked, "If your truck's in running order, Father, will you take us over Stein Pass? I've a place where mother can live in Austria."

"Of course, I'm due in the village for supplies. When it's safe, after the SS soldiers gather for beer, I'll pick up your mother, and we'll come for you."

Showing the priest her forged passport, she began to tell her story. "I'm Mrs. Borruck now, Father. I'm not married. Wealthy Nazis want to kill me. I know too much."

As if frightened by the familiar sound of a German staff car, his face rigid in its concern, the priest took Petra's passport and waved her toward the back of the graveyard. When she started to leave, he said, "Go into the meadow and hide. These Nazis intend to search the church."

Tucking Petra's passport into a pocket under his sash, the priest ran into the church through the chancel and down the cellar steps. Exposed for fifty meters in the garden lane, he pushed the small truck onto the roadway, and engaged the clutch to quietly coast down to the village.

Gathering near the wellhead near the front of the church, five SS soldiers hollered for the priest's wine. Karl, without a coat or shirt, lifted his hat and centered it firmly on his brow and raised his chin as if expecting applause. Suddenly enraged, he ordered his underlings to sack the church cupboards, locks and all.

Her brother stood erect with his hands clasped behind his back, surveying the graveyard.

If I shoot one of them, it must be Karl.

Petra unsnapped the band holding the Lugar in its holster and held the pistol near her side hidden in the folds of her skirt. She had qualified expert on the pistol range—shooting at paper silhouettes. Her brother would shoot back. She took a hesitant breath, trying to remember how many rounds were in the Lugar's magazine. There were four soldiers, each carrying a Lugar.

After shattering glass and splintering wood, the soldiers who sacked the church burst from the nave into the sunlight and presented their finds, their cheers swelling in volume. Nine bottles of wine sat atop nine prominent headstones in the graveyard. The dusty bottles glowed, absorbing the sunlight.

A young soldier marched straight at Petra.

Unbuttoned, he found her shoe with a full stream. A reflex she would carry for life, Petra moved her foot. The soldier jumped, seizing her wrist and jerking her into view. Petra swung the Lugar up to fire. He wrenched it from her hand and slapped her with an open hand knocking her to the ground. She rolled away from his boot as he kicked at her face.

"I've found a nymph," he hollered, grabbing her hair and jerking her to her feet.

Karl's stare seemed to grow to joyful disbelief. The sister he had been denied stood helpless before him—for the taking. With the graveyard sealed, he unbuttoned his pants and peed on their father's headstone, moving his cock around soaking the letters and numbers.

Seething with lust, he stripped off his clothes and threw them on the ground.

Karl snorted his contempt as he seized the lapels of Petra's jacket and blouse and ripped the fronts off, causing her to stumble and fall at his feet. When she tried to cover herself, he kicked her in the stomach. Then just as abruptly, he grabbed her Lugar from the young soldier and fired three rounds into the earth near Petra's face.

The earth erupted in front of her eyes as the rounds split the sod. Her head seemed to bounce with the impact. Or was it a mental recoil? If she begged for mercy, she would be giving her brother more pleasure.

After holding her Lugar for the soldiers to see, he tossed it to the nearest man. Then he ripped her skirt into strips and tossed the rags into the air. Exposed, Petra found herself suspended between two soldiers. Five heathens cheered when Karl seized her tits and forced her against their father's headstone.

She stood in nothing but a bit of her blouse and the sweat of his grip.

Karl grabbed her breasts, viciously squeezing them. He slapped her face. Hollering, he kept repeating the routine. Seemingly tired of that, he spun her around and leaned into her.

Sobbing, her tears met a chorus of shouts. Suddenly manic, Karl forced Petra's belly against the headstone, pushed her chest over its granite top, and raped her violently, alternating ports.

I'm screaming, and his friends are cheering.

Petra was thrown to the ground when he finished. Two soldiers picked her up and held her belly-down over the headstone. Her legs were covered with blood. Saliva flowed from her mouth. Numb, she no longer cried, she no longer screamed.

One after another, the SS soldiers worshiped the afternoon—sunshine, wine, and Karl's sister for dessert. Held over the headstone, the raping of Petra Laube-Heintz went on for hours. As if lusting for butchery, Karl celebrated his rage, throwing his sister to the ground and kicking her in the stomach.

Aiming her Luger at her head, Karl raised a palm. Naked and covered with sweat, he shrugged as if asking his men to join in the killing.

The youngest soldier yelled, "Not here, Karl. Not in the churchyard."

*   *   *

Southampton Marine Terminal, England.
29 September 1939. 1830 Hours, GMT.

John Poston checked and rechecked the signal logs at Southampton's marine terminal, fearing the flying boat carrying, his cousin, Linc Jensen had gone down in the Channel. The last wireless signal from Flight 173 was logged as the aircraft flew over the coast of Portugal—SOE code; 24 Land.

"Have you any more information from Horta, in the Azores, or Lisbon—mechanical difficulties, that sort of message?" Poston asked.

The signals corporal shrugged. "Two hours ago, we listened to an IFF transmission from an unknown aircraft diverting to Horta. The airstrip at Horta hasn't landed any diversion flights."

"No May-Day's or location status Tally-Ho's?"

"Nothing. In an emergency a flying boat could ditch anywhere."

"Their wireless must be tits."

Johnny sorted the chaos—a constant habit. Knowing something of his nephew's past, that his emotions never touched his reason, the young man could be lying on the beach in Lisbon. But the escape scenario Poston preferred—the flying boat was still bound for England but not to Southampton or Portsmouth. That meant Linc Jensen suspected a trap and was improvising.

Talking to a windowpane, Poston decided. "If the commando lands with the aircraft, the airstrip will be a farm field in Wales or in Cornwall on England's south coast. If he jumps into England, the drop zone will be the familiar fields near Ashchurch."

Checking the departure log for the continent, Lisbon in particular, Johnny confirmed Gordon Dewar's name. He had missed him by thirty-one hours.

"Admiral Sinclair, please, John Poston, calling." He wanted to alert *C* he had confirmation that Dewar had done a runner.

"Sinclair."

"Admiral, this is John Poston. Gordon Dewar's listed as a passenger on an Imperial Airways flight to Lisbon thirty-plus hours ago. No confirming data."

"That's been sorted," Sinclair said. "Yesterday a young man doubling as Dewar was shot dead in a railway carriage in a Lyon railway station—shot by one of our rovers."

Poston half-closed his eyes and went on. "Second issue, Admiral—there's no sign of our commando, code-sign Grumpy on the flying boat out of Marseille."

"The flying boat's on the River Shannon near Foynes, Ireland. Captain Edward Hardin parachuted into England. The captain's the only man who survived from SOE Team seven. He's code-sign Grumpy. He's gated at base operations, on the Ashchurch Ordinance Center."

John Poston's throat was full, his focus seemed to pinwheel, sparring with a confusion of vague shapes. Hot tears came to his eyes as he realized Linc Jensen was dead. Pestering the lord, he thought, perhaps Linc's merely gone. He was iron-shod. Serviceable, with a torrent of pluck, but never still, he stalked at a footballer's pace.

For half a moment John Poston could not find a grain of air. Stifling his rage, through clinched teeth he said, "Code-sign Grumpy was my nephew, Admiral. Sergeant Linc Jensen."

At first there was no reply. Then with a curious ceremonial expression of solemn intensity, Sinclair said, "Well…many of our days will fade into night, Poston. Most of our lads will die beyond explanation, or with an unnoticed passing."

Accepting the turn, John Poston needed to move on. "What's next, Admiral?"

"Let's not go on about it, Poston. Find Dewar."

*　　*　　*

London. The Savoy. 29 September 1939.
1300 Hours, GMT.

As one tangent might elude another, William Hockey found true north more suitable. He liked to run straight at a problem and let the impulsive make their mistakes. He deduced that the document pouch was in Cairo, and that Lewis Poston knew its location. He wanted his document discussions with Victor Rothschild and Max Warburg to be brief and cordial.

The fog that had settled on the streets of London had thinned and left the city cloaked in a soaking mist. Larch logs burned in the fireplace at the Savoy, casting a yellow hue throughout the lounge. Placing his right hand on the chimneypiece as the bankers walked into the room, he looked at Rothschild with genuine respect. For some time now, Hockey had cataloged Rothschild's duplicitous dealings with Berlin and London.

Knowing Rothschild preferred sherry in the afternoon, and not wanting the meeting to drag on, he presented the bankers a snifter of brandy as they sat down.

"I do apologize. Damp wood doesn't give off much heat."

Assuring his guests their secrets were safe, he suggested the hostile takeover scheme had been folly from the outset, declaring, "That others will learn of your involvement, they will be difficult to manage for a time. I suspect in the years to come we will find humor in all this."

"It's just business," Warburg declared.

Drumming his fingers on the arm of his chair, Hockey put in, "Many have died for your business." Hockey's response was intentionally abrupt. He admired Rothschild. He despised Warburg. And again, he knew why. As he stepped toward Warburg, he added, "One would need to be sufficiently demented to fashion such folly." Hockey removed his jacket, sat facing the bankers, and laid a piece of paper and a pen on the table between them.

When Warburg leaned away from the table, Hockey reached for the pen, ensuring the red cross tattooed below his shirt cuff was easy for the banker to see. Warburg's face carried a disgusted look as he waved the paper to Rothschild and set his brandy aside.

Hockey leaned into the table; coaxing Rothschild closer. "Benjamine Schaat gave me the original note drawn on the Bank of England for eight hundred thousand pounds, signed by Sir John Poston on behalf of Poston and Sons, Limited. Schaat is, and has been, my intermediary in this matter."

Pausing to sip his brandy, Hockey raised his glass. "Schaat represents the owner of the note, the Landgrave of the House of Hesse."

In a huff, Warburg asked, "What *is* Poston and Sons, Limited?"

"A small shipping firm headquartered in London, owned by the sons of a deceased friend. The landgrave wants you both to cosign the note as guarantors and pay the obligation with no recourse against the sons or the company."

When Max Warburg pushed the note aside, Hockey represented it for signature, choosing a tone of kindly condescension mixed with icy contempt. "Sir Carroll Starr and Lord Montagu Norman have fallen at the foot of your perverse ambitions. Their suicides were not expected.

I don't blame you for the weakness of these men. But I strongly suggest you follow the instructions the landgrave set forth."

Victor Rothschild signed the note and set the pen on the table in front of Warburg. As if perturbed by the tenor of the meeting, Rothschild had not touched his brandy.

For minutes, no one spoke. Hockey stared at Rothschild, discerning the man's expression as it gradually creased into a satisfied calm. The man has class, Hockey thought. Raising his brandy, he found Rothschild raising his and together they toasted the air. Turning in unison to look at Warburg, Rothschild seemed to grimace when Hockey lurched from his chair.

Savoring the revenge, Hockey nudged the paper. "Now, Warburg, you alone will pay this obligation without a hint of recourse."

"Why would I do that?"

"Because the landgrave knew you alone would object." Curling a grin to the right, Hockey drew air noisily through his brandy. "By now you should realize, Max, in the landgrave's world, you are no more important than Lord Norman or any other financial shutter."

"I'll sign it tomorrow."

"Are there no recitals you merchant-bankers understand? Warburg, I know your religion prompts delusive beliefs. So…here's a morsel for your piggish greed. I have the wayward documents you fear. If you sign now, you will have three days to pay off the Poston note.

If you do not sign, the landgrave intends to publish the documents."

Hockey tossed off the rest of his brandy. "We have put in place the mechanisms required to confiscate all of your assets in England if you refuse to cooperate."

John Poston was smiling when he arrived at the Red Cross headquarters canteen on Seymore Street. He was haggard, and his suit was a right mess. Continuing the rush of the day, he selected eggs and toast, and joined Hockey with a nod.

"Dewar's afoot, Willie," Poston said.

"We've located him. After he thought for a few moments, one of Dewar's fancy boys at Saint Ermins Hotel, gave him up. Dewar's hiding in Manchester. Instead of running, he made the mistake of looking for Captain Hardin's wife. Members of the lodge spotted him at the train station in Camborne and followed him to Manchester."

Poston scanned the serving line. "That doesn't make sense. He has plenty of money. He must think he can buy his way out of this mess."

"Money won't help," Hockey said. "He's swimming in an airless box."

"The admiral gave me orders to find him."

Hockey handed Johnny a Ceska pistol wrapped in newspaper. "There's no safety lever on that weapon. It's a small caliber. Short range—make sure he's dead."

Reluctantly accepting the weapon, Poston fought to show an undertone of fear. This was his first inkling of Hockey's expectations. "I'm to find him, Willie. To locate him."

Twice Hockey circled the room. Poston shifted uncomfortably in his chair. As if wishing the young man luck, Hockey put a hand on his shoulder and said, "Grow old, Johnny. Those four men standing near the door are all armed.

"Those lodge members will escort you to Manchester. Remember, Johnny, Dewar's the man who ordered your father's execution."

William Hockey had given the lodge members their orders—protect John Poston at all costs. The lodge members whispered during the trip to Manchester. Laughing at times, they seemed to have a natural appetite for the killing.

Intelligent, polished, a young man of great promise, Poston rolled the Ceska pistol over in his hands. He did want to avenge his father's death but didn't want to shoot Dewar. He had known the man for over a decade. How do you shoot someone you know?

"We're in Manchester, lad," one of the escorts said.

Well, that, was that.

Manchester was a city of dismal grays, choking on its prized possessions, its industrial byproducts—smog, stagnant air, and bushels of money. A dreary dust coated the streets with a layer of slick waste. Tire marks streaked the cobblestones.

He searched for escape routes as the sedan pulled into an alcove some eighty meters from a brick cottage. *So, this is it.* Smoke was curling from the chimney. A small warehouse was attached to the house. Its door was open.

The pistol was heavy. He was frightened.

"That's the house, lad," the driver said. "Don't mess about. Don't let him start talking—no time to think." Welding sparks flew in the warehouse, illuminating the dark space at odd intervals. "We'll handle the warehouse, lad. You look to the house. He probably has a weapon. Wait for us to enter the warehouse before you make a move."

Crossing the street, Poston tried to temper his heartrate. As the driver approached the warehouse Poston lit a cigarette. After a series of short breaths, he ground out the cigarette. Opening the front door, he eased down a dark hall, and tiptoed into the study. Dewar sat in a chair facing the fireplace, his head half-shadowed by the flames. He was wearing whipcord breeches and a wind cheater. He looks to be asleep, Poston thought.

The man had not moved.

Poston leveled his pistol on the man's head.

A whiskey bottle and empty glass sat on a small table to his left and a holdall sat on the floor near his feet. The man came bolt erect. Still facing the fireplace, he spoke in German, the words clipped, brutal. The stranger jumped to the front of the fireplace, weapon in hand, turning as he landed, firing as he screamed, "Ah, Johnny Poston, one of Mother's watercolors..."

Johnny felt the tug of the round on his left arm as he jumped to his right, flinching and pulling the trigger of the Ceska. The weapon recoiled and nearly hit him in the face. At three yards, he shot the man through his mouth, blowing his brains and patches of his skull onto the chimney and into the fire. Frantic, Johnny stuffed the Ceska in his coat pocket, and picked up the empty shell casing. The man's front teeth were splintered, and his skull was half empty.

Gagging through a frenzy, Johnny drew the Ceska and shot the stranger again. "You bloody bastard." Swelling in volume, he screamed, "Who the bloody hell are you?"

Awaking to his surroundings, stepping away from the body, he picked up the holdall and paused. The man's left hand bubbled in the embered crevasse of two logs. Dragging the man's hand from the fire, he whispered, "What have I done?"

As John Poston ran from the brick cottage, picking at the strings of time, his face carried a disgusted look. There was a ragged hole in his coat between his chest and his left arm. The bullet had burned the inside of his arm.

The sedan was running with a back door open when Poston reached it. Throwing the holdall onto the seat he jumped in. "I shot some stranger who tried to kill me." Poston closed his eyes and rubbed them with his thumb and forefinger. Hockey had managed the day with frightening simplicity and efficiency. But who was the target?

"Is the target dead?"

Gripping the Ceska pistol, he slid his finger onto the trigger. "I don't know. The man in that cottage is dead."

When Poston closed his eyes the dead man's face glared at him—his broken teeth—his body sprawled on the floor. Livid, his voice quietly strained, he put in, "Hockey should have known Dewar wasn't in Manchester. You blokes should have known."

"Ah, just so, that. Did you pick up your shell casings?"

* * *

Singapore. Raffles Hotel. 30 September 1939. 1530 Hours, GMT + 8 Hours.

Silent, as if lost, Phillip, the evening concierge, stood in the lobby of Raffles Hotel, staring at a picture of Alex von Cleve, afraid to breathe. A guard-sergeant from Alexander Barracks held the picture and continued to badger Phillip with questions. The man in the frame had killed a taxi driver and dumped the body in the harbor near Collyer Quay.

With a nervous scrap of laughter Phillip pointed to the picture. "Yes, this man stayed at Raffles on the night you mentioned... No, nothing unusual. He was in a hurry when he left."

Ion Crilley and Nigel Stuart sat in the Long Bar at Raffles in full view of the lobby, recounting the events of Operation Snow White, the variables of Team 7's mission, and cursing across the havoc of war their masters had created... the unrealized parts.

Always keen to astonish, his voice thick with folly, Crilley put in, "Just so, I suppose. There's little enough I know about wounds. Our von Cleve is alive. He's being patched up in Port Blair, on South Andaman Island."

Trying to stifle a yawn, Stuart waited. Then said, "That monster was full of himself when I shot him." Living another day, he clattered on. "His being alive is a load of damp tailings. I mean fair play; I shot that bastard six times with an Enfield snub nose."

Speaking through a grin, then scanning the lobby, Crilley shrugged. "He didn't notice—one round hit his chest, one in each shoulder, one in each arm, and a creased rib." Setting the drink aside, Crilley excused himself. "I'll be right back."

Walking into the lobby he looked carefully around before approaching the guard-sergeant. Looking at the picture in Phillip's hand, he said, "I know that man. What's he done?"

"He killed a taxi driver not far from here—drove a knife through his brain."

"Alex von Cleve is his name. He's hospitalized in Port Blair—gunshot wounds. He's a banker from Kuala Lumpur."

"How do you know all this?"

"He was my banker. I needed quinine. I was at the dispensary in Port Blair when the corpsmen brought him in. The man was in rough shape."

Crilley found Stuart ordering another round of drinks and holding a supper menu. "Nigel, what will we do about this leather pouch?"

"I think I know who has it. After I secure the contents, we'll meet in Pretoria."

"Are we done killing people?"

*   *   *

Ashchurch Ordinance Center, England. 30 September 1939. 0650 Hours, GMT.

A morning mist came with the clouds that filled the trees and farms. The airfield at the ordinance center was shrouded and pocked with great clumps of dark and light-gray cotton clouds, badgered, and bunched by winds just husky enough to lift the curtain, whorl it, and then lower it on cue.

Hardin's fag was out before it landed in the slit trench.

The squaddies I see are in for a bashing. These lads should meet Tu. That girl could train them to kill their enemy without looking back. But they won't have time. They seem so naïve. Many will die before they realize how sudden the killing can be.

Eleven weeks of bush ranging had turned Hardin from song and cheer to killing anyone he found in his gun sight. I've run from Tonkin to Marseille and that wasn't enough. And they took one last try—sabotaging my parachute just as I reached for home.

Linc Jensen died as a pawn, for nothing—for the king's nethers—opium, Corsicans, assassins, mercenaries, bankers, and lords.

Molly and McPhee have more honor than the Windsors—Flying Officer Hawkes as well.

And what of those men dedicated to the Lady of Wisdom—the Templar: Sir John Poston and William Hockey—the South African and Sir Nigel Stuart? Two are trying to kill me, one is trying to keep me alive.

Sensations came to Hardin, one at a time. The gripping tension that had governed his body seemed to right itself. "Is it just a game of money?" he whispered.

"Are you with me, sir?"

With his memories fading Captain Edward Hardin gave Sergeant Akens a quizzical grin, moved his pint of beer from between them, and looked into the young man's eyes. "Yes, I'm with you now. It's been a long grind."

"You're a bit barked up—nicks and divots and such," Akens said, handing Hardin his kit and Thompson.

"Just for show, Sparky."

Hardin was asleep in the transient billet when Hockey reached the base commander's office. A guard kicked his boot and he rose slowly.

"Your transport's here, Captain."

Lost for a moment, Hardin scanned the billet, then rubbed his eyes to clear his vision. Relieved he was nearly home; he mustered his kit. Before he followed the guard, he paused to glance around the room, then picked up his weapon.

His thoughts returned suddenly to Katherine as he found the old traveler enjoying a cup of coffee, being tended by Sergeant Akens as if he were royalty.

"Give us a minute, Sparky."

Waiting for Akens to clear the room, he said, "Good to see you, Willie."

"As ever could be, Edward."

Looking for an answer to Hockey's sigh, Hardin gripped his shoulder. "Pull up a sandbag, Willie. Is Katherine nearby? Is she well?"

"Not far. And yes. I have five men lodging in the town, working independently. They're experienced trackers. We're still doing a bit of blind flying on this one. Not sure the threats have been fully neutralized."

"Trackers? Can't the secret squirrels in MI6 give us a hand?"

"Relax Captain, we're not wasting rations."

Something was burning with Hardin, not killing's tight rope, but a caution born of experience. "Fair play, Willie. But I've been hounded for weeks and months." Handing the Thompson to Hockey for inspection, offering a spare magazine box as well, Hardin said, "That weapon's a short-range brawler. I'll let Dewar measure the bore before I shoot him."

"Just so, that...John Poston shot a man he thought was Dewar in Manchester last night. He used a caliber much smaller than yours at short range and blew the man's brains onto the fry of a well-banked fire."

With a message buried into his grin, Hardin took back his weapon and shook his head. "If that's John Poston Jr. you're talking about, I must have met someone else."

"Johnny's grown into the war." Donning a nicely judged Christian expression as if to temper moods, Hockey went on. "Dewar arranged the killing of Sir John Poston."

"Where is the skivvy?"

"We have him located in a warehouse he uses for smuggling drugs near Manchester."

"Drugs! He smuggles drugs. Is he alone?"

Hockey asked an orderly for more coffee and set his jacket aside. "No, he has a security team with him—at least a pair."

"Is Dewar as high as Snow White goes?"

"Dewar's as far as *you* go, Edward."

"You know too well Dewar isn't the last leaf."

"There's a calm to changing seasons. A silent knell works best. You can curry your ire and keep a distant log on any man you might suspect. Or relax and find a hobby to consume your after years. If you live with Katherine, she will insist you enjoy her company."

Hardin accepted Hockey's comment as he pointed at the tattoo on the man's forearm. Hockey gave a slight nod and handed him a new identity card and a passport—Captain Edward Hardin, complete with a clean-shaven dated picture.

Hockey put sugar in his coffee and stirred slowly. He seemed to be gauging Hardin's notions. "Your mother's staying with Katherine in your flat on the square in Ashchurch—Mary Bishop—a precaution for now."

"What on earth for?"

With a slight nod, he said, "We've found all the decoy pouches. The pouch with the documents is still afloat."

"No, it's not. I gave it to Lewis Poston. With any luck, he'll sell it for millions of pounds."

Hockey excused himself. A light step and a wink joined a smile when he returned. "A visit to Manchester will take a day or two. Dewar's yours to sort out."

Hardin's chest tightened as members of his team appeared in outline, as if coursing the crest of a ridge. As they vanished, he said, "It won't take long."

"Have you looked in a mirror? You're a bloody mess."

Farther away, the jungle canopy was as if a great spread of silk, billowing gently, a mosaic of greens caressing the horizon. Twilight had set in. Hardin looked at Hockey deliberately, his eyes vibrating as he said, "I don't trust many people, Willie."

With an aura of understanding, Willie handed Hardin a tattered piece of cloth. "It's your mother's. Mary popped that shake-rag to get your father out of Webb's Public House and home for his dinner."

"Our home was three terrace steps above the pub, but I remember the sound—an echo from the wind. Curlee Jones, our father's shift mate, always walked with him. He's dead now, too."

Hockey stood to adjust his trousers. He paused. The lore-keeper knew the dead had measured steps. With a shock of clarity, he seemed to realize Captain Edward Hardin was still in Southeast Asia. After he lit a cigarette, Hockey didn't mince words. "Captain, you need to decide where your home is—here with Katherine or in Burma with your dead mates."

Bitterly, Hardin turned away and picked up his weapon. After fronting Hockey, he held the Thompson by the barrel across his left shoulder. "Well sage, you're so damn wise. Put this on parade. What makes you think a mud-eater like me has a choice?

*　*　*

Shepheard's Hotel, Cairo. 01 October 1939. 1720 Hours, GMT + 2 Hours.

Hours and days of unrelenting heat left Cairo's olio of breathable air with a taste akin to charcoaled dung. Lewis Poston had not expected to see Dorothy Stuart but was delighted by the prospect. I have my faults. Indecision isn't one of them.

Tucked in a cul-de-sac formed by small tables and islands of wicker-wrapped chairs, British officers and their Indian counterparts, soldiers, airmen and sailors, rug merchants from across the globe, and Axis spies all bartered their wares.

The odds and sods of the Australian Imperial Force had arrived as well.

Lewis Poston set to a whiskey, annoyed by a Burmese officer who was scolding a waiter, standing, and then sitting, insisting the waiter treat him as a member of the Solar Race of Kings—a Red Peacock from Rangoon.

Harbormaster McPhee would have a comment about the man's lineage, I'm sure.

Sitting next to the balcony railing overlooking the lower courtyard of Shepheard's, he laughed quietly. This table had sheltered the battered hulk of the South African after the Royal Marines had stomped his carcass into a pile of loose chippings.

Sorting his memories, far behind Dorothy Stuart, Hardin held center stage. As he was told, Linc Jensen died in the Welshman's arms, willing his team leader a memory; an identity disc—inscribed with a code-sign, Grumpy. Holding the disc into the lamplight, tears welled in his eyes. The young man's blood held serve, filling the *rum* of the stamped code sign to its limit.

Sipping whiskey, keen to a sense of trouble, a disturbance rekindled a flow of adrenaline. Allowing the ice to settle, he found Dorothy gliding past the grand piano, a porter in tow, a gratuity in hand. After a brief exchange with the piano player and matching nods, the piano's actuating hammers softened their tone: *I'll Be Seeing You.*

"I have been seeing you, Lewis. I'm relieved you're in splendid trim."

"Here in Shepheard's, I suppose."

"A familiar place." Dorothy accepted a drink from the waiter.

Sharing a toast with a lady he admired, Poston set his drink down. "You pointed a gun at me in Marseille. Rather indelicate, I'd say."

"A bit of borrowed brass." Dorothy tossed off her drink. "Was it handbags-at-dawn when you shot at me in Cairo." Dorothy dropped her diary upon the table and stuck her left index finger into the bullet hole and pushed the diary across the table.

Hefting her shoulder bag, smiling a winsome smile, she tipped her head to the side as if waiting for Poston's retort. With a mischievous grin, she said, "A lady must defend her yield, Lewis. Besides, that bee of yours will never quit the clover." With her empty glass, she proposed a toast. "May Snow White rest in peace."

"This wasn't my doing." Poston held up the diary. "What pages have our liaisons, or did you avoid such folly?"

As if dodging galloping dominoes, Dorothy stifled a yawn. "Hardly a whisper dear boy."

"Ah, yes. Stain our dalliance with tinctures out of the East. Be aloof. Windy, utterly detached. Let's hedge about rather than confound the confusion."

"My God. You've been smitten." Dorothy's eyes burst aflame with laughter.

Embarrassed, Lewis began his challenge. "In full cry my lady, that church is under repair."

Seemingly amused, cocking a lustful grin, Dorothy set her handbag on the table. "Shingles of sand or lollies, Lewis, you can't lie for toffee."

"Even so, I am quite busy. But I do have a series of parallel high oblique aerial photographs for you to take to Mother. Each pair of photos was taken at the same time from a Lockheed 12A, commercial airplane, by our own operatives. Taken with F-24 cameras and a Leica, they show the layout of Axis airfields in the Vichy French controlled, Mandate of Lebanon, and on the Isle of Rhodes."

"Any German camouflage tricks—grass areas painted to look like runways?"

"A possibility. Examined together through a stereoscope, the photos third-dimensional quality will show any painted objects that lack depth."

"These should be helpful. But that's not why I'm here, and you know it."

Aroused by prospects of a lovely evening, yet leery, Poston lit a cigarette. "As one-pound sterling equals but four US dollars, you, and Snow White have no such constraint. Vigorous at the turn, you sport a weapon, and many attractive assets. I can guess why you're here."

"Fair enough." Her mood communicating itself, marauding, tossing morsels of sensual prate, Dorothy seemed to relax. "Willie tells me you have the document pouch, Lewis."

"Hockey mind you, must know that MI6 has the pouch."

"Shall we celebrate our liaison and break the seal?"

As if her fraid-hole was moistening, when Lewis returned from Shepheard's cellar, Dorothy's eyes seemed to ripple with applause. After he presented an old rucksack featuring claim-tag 1730, offering the pouch with a sigh of resignation, Dorothy rose and gave him a vigorous kiss.

Reluctant to end the moment, kissing Dorothy again, suggesting a remedy, he offered, "There's a man whispering in a wheat field. Do you know him, my lady?"

"You're a cad, Lewis."

He tried not to smile, but the General was marshalling his troops.

Wrapped in the business section of *The London Daily Mail*, a safe-deposit key slipped from the folds. While Poston examined the unmarked key, Dorothy casually put the newspaper back into the pouch, and the pouch back into the rucksack. The lead story above-the-fold of the newspaper concerned the ball-bearing company, SKF International, and Enskilda Bank, in Stockholm.

Slipping the security-box key into her shoulder bag, Dorothy toasted the air out over the balcony rail, and rubbed Poston's hand. "Do you need another bromide, Lewis, or are you hunting mice?"

Admiring this lovely woman, Lewis could but admit his needs. "Mice, I guess." Seeing Dorothy with the pouch, he mused. "You're a downy bird my lady." Her reply a quiet smile, he went on, "That pouch has been through a roaring. It's a mess. Admiral Sinclair can sort out why so many good men, so many good squaddies, have died."

Dorothy put a hand on the grand piano and smiled. "Let's meet at eight for dinner."

*   *   *

Manchester, England. 02 October 1939. 0300 Hours, GMT.

Cloudy skies and gales badgered the Bentley throughout the drive from Ashchurch to Manchester. Hardin slept during the trip. Parked at the Manchester airport, more to protect Hockey's Bentley than to protect the occupants, Hardin's escorts met a small, dark man inside the terminal.

"Is our friend in the nest?" Hockey asked.

"Yes, with one man."

"This is Captain Edward Hardin. Dewar is his to sort. Take your cab to the warehouse, neutralize the guards, and secure the area. The captain will handle Dewar."

"Do we meet at the same public house?"

"Yes, near the airport in an hour. To be safe, don't speak to anyone or use a phone box."

"Understood."

Armed with a silenced Ceska pistol, the driver picked the lock and ushered Hardin and a second shooter into the warehouse. A dim light shone above the door of a glass-encased office up a flight of open metal stairs. Hardin knelt near a wall on the main floor, listening for any movement nearby.

Hockey's associates split up, searching the main floor, quarter by quarter. A pistol coughed once in the right-front quarter, followed by silence. A rush of footsteps, followed by three silent shots, brought down a man at the bottom of the metal stairway.

Nervous, Hardin's thigh wound sang with the beat of his heart.

Time had fallen on its uppers when Hockey's associates met at the base of the stairway and signaled the all-clear. Setting the selector switch on the Thompson on semiautomatic fire, Hardin took to the stairs, careful to mount each step before proceeding.

Dewar slept with his head behind a pillow. A machine pistol lay near his right hand. Easing the weapon off the bed, out of Dewar's reach, Hardin stood for several seconds, then slammed the butt of the Thompson into Dewar's midsection.

Screaming, Dewar rolled onto the floor and came up firing a second machine pistol grazing Hardin's cheek and splitting his right ear.

Hardin went absolutely jungle as he dove to his left, firing as he fell. His first shot went through the bones connecting Dewar's right shoulder, sending him careening into a desk. Another round blew bone splinters from Dewar's left shoulder against the wall.

"Stand up, you greasy bitch."

Dewar lay helpless. Blood was flowing from both shoulders. He tried to put the barrel of his weapon in his mouth, but he couldn't hold it upright.

"Stay down, Dewar. Save your wet-work for the devil—the seventh level of hell's your next stop." Sporting a vicious grin, remembering Tu's vengeance, Hardin shot Dewar in both knees.

Dewar's scream arced through the warehouse as Hardin put a boot on his chest, pinned him against a bedpost, and set the barrel of his Thompson on the side of his lower jaw near his front teeth. Splattering teeth and bits of Dewar's lower jaw across the floor, Hardin wiped blood from his boot. Kicking a piece of Dewar's chin against the wall, he uttered a heathen laugh and screamed, "That's for Grumpy."

Turning to take a Frenchman's leave, he picked up Dewar's holdall. "Damn, I nearly forgot." He turned and fired one round into Dewar's crotch. "Take the night to die, you frilly fuck. Have-a-Piss—courtesy of Uncle Dingo."

With his tongue hanging free, Dewar seemed to be praying.

*   *   *

Ashchurch, England. 03 October 1939. 0530 Hours, GMT.

"Empathy's a heavy ax to grind, Captain." William Hockey's words rang clear.

Hardin stood-to an hour before dawn. For months now, fending betrayal had been the singular purpose of his life. Fresh from a killing, a torment gripped the morning. A subliminal glimpse of Katherine's beauty sparred with Hardin's finely tuned, reactions.

Katherine was so alluring—more than beautiful. A primary school teacher and, the loveliest woman a brown job squaddie could hope to know.

A hot shower—when will the British Army conquer that problem? Hardin washed his hair twice—it didn't seem clean. Can I ever relax. Be the man I used to be?

His hands were badly scarred, as was the index finger of his right hand. His right cheek had a fresh burn, and his right ear was sporting a notch. Both his little fingers were jammed, their knuckles swollen and discolored. Residual bits of thorn barbs had laid waste to his left palm, leaving calcium lumps at the base of each finger. The poisonous sap of the Rengas tree had cratered his forearms with divots the size of a bull's eye.

The horizontal bullet scar across the front of his thigh had cured to a tricolored laboratory exhibit—a twist of dough, baked twice for good measure, then used for a season as a grip-sock on a cricket bat.

Handsome, his face above his beard had weathered to a ruddy brown that escaped the balance of his body—except for the odd white where his mouth held sway. The ticks and mosquitoes had gone their way—not willingly. Leech welts on his back, chest, and legs held their posts as purple knots on a white field.

Hardin was a man to run the jungle with. Surely the admiral would have an investiture for surviving—for keeping his word. Or had the admiral tried to kill him?

No, the doors were mostly open. The Ashchurch town square was the same, yet it seemed smaller. The cobbles were swept, but now they were uneven. This was market day—Wednesday.

A general air of fatigue lined the faces of the farmers. Was it his imagination or was there a poor turn of sale? As though partners in harness, shoppers bantered.

The town clock struck high twelve, and no one paused.

The faces, vendors and shoppers somehow turned into Hardin's fond memory.

Hesitating, as if contrary to orders, even with his new battle-dress blouse, Hardin had nothing to commend his appearance. Stopping behind a well stand to dress his uniform, he practiced his greeting. He wanted to be normal, as the shoppers entering the bakery. They were lolling on about their day, not on guard.

Reaching for a memory of his mates, men who had lived savagely, who had endured so much, and whose hope was so small, he found their echoes and their shadowed smiles.

He had not expected their echoes. Banging from ear to ear.

As if without stamens, he wrestled with these knurled roots of time, with heart strings yearning for yesterday's wind. His wounds, old and new, bled beneath ambitious regrets.

Captain Edward Hardin was the essence of any number of men—possessing the character and demeanor expected of a serving soldier—a squaddie with a memory as a frayed, torn carpet. Looking at his hands, stopping in the entrance alcove of the bakery, he adjusted his sleeves and pressed the front of his blouse flat with his palms.

Tears at the ready, anticipation had his heart racing—more apprehensive than excited, he drew at the aroma of fresh bread. It was noisy in the bakery—a joyous noisy. Customers wishing to be first stood and sat. The tables were full of shoppers with bakery faces. The air was alive with cinnamon and hot sugar and fresh dough.

Hardin looked past the counter into the kitchen. The hair on his hands prickled. Willie's wrong. Killing is a place. It's not here in Ashchurch—not here in the bakery.

The roar of the monsoon, the thresh of the sea rain, the prop wash under the Wellington's belly, and so many dead mates—how would he keep these from staining his Katherine? Had he forgotten how to be proud?

I'll start in Ashchurch and remember this way again.

Mary wore a woolen dress and a bright woolen scarf. She raised her brow when she saw Edward and the wrinkles at her smile sprang with joy. Announcing her secret with her raised chin, she and Katherine sat at the table closest to the window. Mary busily began rationing a loaf of bread, adding butter and jam.

Mary smiled without warning. She seemed ready to sound her shake-rag as he stood to the back of Katherine's chair. Jumping and hugging, a cameo in the small bakery, Katherine gave out a joyful holler, started sobbing, threw her arms around Hardin's neck, and then, still sobbing, sprang backward to show her soldier their baby-in-waiting.

Katherine couldn't stop crying as she nestled her face into Hardin's chest. Let me look at her now. She'll never be quite this way again.

Pestering the lord, hollering through her tears, she took hold of Mary's hand. "Oh, what have they done with you, Eddie? Look at my Welshman, Mary. Where have you been? You must tell me the details—the cities and the countries—all your adventures."

Awkwardly hugging his pregnant wife, and kissing her for seconds and more, he gently convinced her to sit. Drawing a chair next to Katherine, he reached for his mother's hand, squeezing it as he leaned forward to kiss her cheek.

"You'll need a father's grace, you will," Mary said, running a hand through his hair. A single tear of relief seemed to carry her joy as she bunched her shawl in her lap.

Catching his breath, Hardin's words came with tears. "You're lovely, Katherine. So wonderfully lovely." He caressed her hair with a battered hand and pushed his face into it—to smell the smell he longed for in Burma, had dreamed about.

"Aren't I though?" Katherine exclaimed. "You wait until I get you home." She blushed a rose-colored blush, waving a smile for the bakery faithful, she had a job for her squaddie. "I hope you have a get-around left for me."

Five men swept the walks of the Ashchurch town square, their brooms a concert of changing moods, each brushstroke lifting an eye to gauge a shadow, their dustbins empty.

*   *   *

Postscript:

Tucking Mill, near Camborne in Cornwall, lost her first young soldier. John Chegwidden, a commando of 1 Special Service Brigade, Edward Hardin's only childhood mate, was shot by a sniper near Sword Beach on D-Day + 2 while securing the arrival of Field Marshal Montgomery's 21ˢᵗ Army Tactical Headquarters element.

Major Edward Hardin had landed on Juno Beach on D-Day in the second wave, along with three others of Monty's Tactical Liaison Officers, and had helped set up Monty's first Tac Headquarters in a nearby chateau.

South Andaman Island's chief magistrate arrested Alex von Cleve while the South African lay in the dispensary recuperating from his wounds and transferred him to the dispensary in the Cellular Jail, in Port Blair. Von Cleve stood in the frame, accused of murdering a taxi driver near Raffles Hotel, on Singapore Island.

The Crown's Court in Singapore heard the oral arguments. In tones more grave than necessary, Ion Crilley gave testimony as the prosecution's primary witness. Raffles's evening concierge, also a prosecution witness, was found floating in Singapore Harbor near Collyer Quay the day before the trial.

A jury found von Cleve guilty after an hour of testimony and twenty minutes of deliberation. Sentenced to life in prison, he decided to memorize the Bible.

The puce-colored Cellular Jail, constructed with the deep, gray-purple brick of Burma, contained 649, eight-by-fifteen-foot cells arranged in seven, two-story spokes emanating from a central guard tower, one prisoner per cell—solitary confinement.

Chained to a concrete bed mount for twenty hours each day, his massive frame withering, von Cleve's pacing ritual soon took on the peculiar, stunted amble of a human mole.

Alex von Cleve met his end in an instant—bayonetted in his cell in 1942 after the Japanese Army invaded the Andaman Islands.

Sir Nigel Stuart arranged Lucien's release from Changi Prison on Singapore Island days before Christmas 1939. Assigned to the Special

Operations Executive, Force 136 Provisional at China Bay, Ceylon, Stuart informed the Baker Street Boys in London that Lucien was too well-known in Southeast Asia to be effective.

Wheelchair bound, Lucien was transferred to SOE Force 133 Provisional in Cairo and worked for Sir Lewis Poston for the duration of World War II.

The Muslim Brotherhood executed Lucien in front of the Mena House Hotel, in the shadow of the pyramids in 1946, after he publicly denounced the Koran—a fairy tale.

Flying Officer Jeffrey Hawkes, never worse for drink, flying in support of the British Expeditionary Force, went missing when his Lockheed Hudson MKI Bomber, flying top cover for Operation Dynamo and the evacuation of Dunkirk, was jumped by a raft of German ME-109, Messerschmitts.

Shot full of holes, his copilot dead, his crew bailing out, Hawkes was losing blood. His bomber, trailing a sky full of smoke, resisted his grip as he turned out to sea over the North Atlantic. His final wireless transmission, a farewell to Mother England, was dedicated to Top Sergeant Clive Mauldin — "Scapa Flow, tell Molly I'll be drinking the Old Man's whiskey when we meet again."

The drink gradually died out of him.

A sterling-silver flask bearing Hawkes's name engraved on its side washed ashore years later on the north side of Stronsay Isle in the Orkney Islands, near Scapa Flow.

A bloodstained note found inside the flask read: "Here's to good whiskey. And if it's Top Sergeant Clive 'Molly' Mauldin, or Sergeant Robert 'Darkie' McPhee, or Captain Edward Hardin, tell them I'll be flying a vintage crate somewhere in Piccadilly."

A brass, eight-sided identity disc held its form, affixed to a brass lanyard, set to the flask as a waist and shoulder harness. Perfectly shaped, the disc was etched with a touching farewell: "To my son, Flying Officer Jeffrey Hawkes— God speed you on your way, dear boy."

Top Sergeant Clive 'Molly' Mauldin, along with "Olive Oil", his Model 1897 Trench Gun, were extracted from the beach at Dunkirk in a small fishing boat. Assigned to the Long-Range Desert Group, in Egypt, he was blown out of a scout car near Benghazi and evacuated to Malta, and then on to England. Molly returned to North Africa after four months and was wounded during a raid on a German petrol storage depot near Tripoli.

Molly's tramp steamer, the SS Iron Knight, a bulk carrier built for Australian Broken Hill, Ltd. to carry iron ore, was sunk off the coast of New South Wales, eleven miles off Montague Island, at 0230AM on 8 February 1943, by a Japanese submarine She sank bow first in less than two minutes with the loss of thirty-six of her crew. The fourteen survivors, afloat for five hours, were picked up by the Free French destroyer Le Triumphant and transported to Port Kembla.

Molly finished his career as Top Sergeant of the 21st Army Group's Tactical Headquarters defense troop—Phantom (GHQ Liaison Regiment), joining Major Edward Hardin and Field Marshal Montgomery's seven other tactical liaison officers for the invasion of Normandy and the European Campaign, landing on Sword Beach in the second wave on 6 June, 1944.

Top Sergeant Clive Mauldin discovered his end—at 0500 hours, 11 April 1945. Along with men of 2 SAS, he would become one of the first British soldiers to encounter the horrors of the Bergen-Belsen Concentration Camp—deloused—crumbed up.

Pass 173

The Bearer ___Top Sergeant Clive Mauldin___

 Is authorized to enter No. 1 Concentration Camp, Belsen, after dusting, on duty.

Signature of Holder   Comd

___Molly___   10 Grn

         Certificate of Dusting

This is to certify that ___Top Sergeant Clive Mauldin___ has been dusted.

 12 April 45   **Maj.**   OC 30 Fd Hyg Sec.

In May 1947, at the Royal Small Arms Factory (RSAF) at Enfield Lock, on the Lea River northeast of London, with Field Marshal Montgomery looking on, Top Sergeant Clive "Molly" Mauldin donated his scarred Pattern 1914, MK 4, Lee Enfield Rifle.

Thought to be the only Enfield in working order to survive Flanders Field, North Africa, El Alamein, Sword Beach, Caen, the Falaise Gap, Arnhem, crossing the Rhine River with Churchill, and the liberation of No. 1 Concentration Camp, at Bergen-Belsen. Molly's picture and the rifle are on display.

The picture has its irony. Molly is holding "Olive Oil" at port arms.

"I'll keep our brass rag handy, Robby. We'll meet again." Slinging Olive Oil across his back, Molly dragged his friend from the sea. Lifting McPhee into his arms, Molly swept the sea grass from his mate's face.

"You've played the bloody devil, Robby."

Molly cried a testimonial as he carried his mate across Sword Beach to the Casualty Clearing Station. Amidst the stench and the carnage, Molly straightened his mate's limbs, and fastened the buttons of Robby's battle jerkin. Molly filled out a VIP—casualty tag: KIA, Sergeant Robert 'Darkie' McPhee, personal enlisted aide to Field Marshal Montgomery.

"May God have a bit of mercy for you, Robby."

Sir Nigel Stuart continued to work for MI6 first in Ceylon and in Egypt, with the Special Operations Executive, Force 133 for the duration of the war. Working in concert with the Long-Range Desert Group, a special-operations detachment of the British army who became known as "The Desert Rats," Sir Nigel and the LRDG rescued nineteen young European women from Tripoli's slave market during the North African campaign.

John Poston left MI6 after Admiral Hugh Sinclair's death and assumed control of Poston and Sons, Ltd. The eight-hundred-thousand-pound note stamped paid-in-full was framed and hung in his office. The company's steamers and warehouse assets were levied by Mother to support supply and transport requirements in the Mediterranean Theater of Operations for the duration of the war.

The holdall he found when he shot the wrong man in Tucking Mill, had contained three hundred thousand pounds in cash and four bank notes drawn on "The Chinese Oversea Bank: Pay to the Bearer," amounting to two million pounds. Johnny traveled to New York City along the southern route and secreted the bank notes into a safety deposit box at J. P. Morgan Bank.

The cash was held in the London offices of Poston and Sons, Lt. for Major Edward Hardin, his wife, Katherine, and their young son Linc—to be drawn upon request.

Lewis Poston, reading the contract British Petroleum had negotiated with the protectorate of Aden for BP's refinery operation in Little Aden, found the words meaningless. Aden and Steamer Point would forever be tied to Lewis Poston's favorite Welshman and his antics.

Cairo, in turn, would be tied to the ambush that killed Uncle Dingo; Egypt's Delta to the sobering of Flying Officer Hawkes; Malta to the raid on the Sloop *Grimsby*, and Robby McPhee.

Marseille held the beauty of Dorothy's voluptuous assets and her Baby Browning.

Lewis continued his career with British Petroleum, working with MI6 and courting Dorothy Stuart. Sensing a change in the Middle East, that England's role would diminish, Poston requested a transfer to Bermuda.

Dorothy transferred to New York City, where she worked for British Security Coordination, BSC, in room 3603, on the 36th floor of Rockefeller Center, the unofficial headquarters for British Intelligence throughout the war. Allen Dulles continued his intelligence work throughout the war in room 3606, a skip down the hall.

Lewis and Dorothy married in 1946 and moved to the Poston estate near Port Washington, New York.

"Men have superior judgment, don't you agree, Dorothy?"

"Yes, you married me."

Samuel Eaton purchased a farm to raise sugar beets near Zell am See, Austria. He and Petra Laube-Heintz maintained their identity as Mr. and Mrs. Frederick Borruck, fearing the youthful Nazi werewolf teams operating throughout Europe and former SS thugs who had settled in Bavaria.

Once a year after the war, in September, Petra took the train to Bad Reichenhall. With flowers and money in hand, she paid her respects to the priest who had helped her escape. Insisting she be careful, the priest refused to let Petra board the train in Bad Reichenhall for her trip to Austria. He drove her as before, three stops down the line.

Her brother, Karl, had returned to the church the day after raping Petra—to visit the coliseum of his conquest. Raging, he pissed on his father's memory. When he seized the priest's arm, the priest's stiletto pierced his heart.

Buried next to his father, the headstone is blank.

George Harrison, governor of the Federal Reserve Bank of New York, betrayed the European bankers and lowered the discount rate by 250 basis points. Warned by Max Ilgner days in advance, none of the players in the arbitrage scheme held a short position in the stocks of the six target companies.

As World War II progressed, an operative with information gleaned from intelligence sources within the OSS, disclosed the timing of key allied invasions to Kurt von Schroder of Stein Bank.

Through currency arbitrage, von Schroder and his associates made 530 million pounds overnight knowing when and where the invasion of Algeria would occur.

William Hockey and Ion Crilley, lifelong travelers, devoted followers of the Lady of Wisdom, met at the Savoy each year on the winter solstice to drink a whiskey and recount the folly of Operation Snow White—from Singapore to China Bay, from Bombay to Aden, from Alexandria to Malta, and on to Marseille. As luck often flourishes within the chaos of war, the Templar made tens of millions of pounds chasing a document that was locked in a safe deposit box at Enskilda Bank in Stockholm, Sweden.

The financial circuit diagram remains there today.

Loyalty and secrecy—as directed, Hockey and Crilley continued to use the derivatives of the arbitrage scheme throughout the war, garnering three million pounds by leveraging critical intelligence data given to them by Allen Dulles at OSS, and Victor Rothschild at MI5—data specific to the tactical plans of the Supreme Headquarters Allied Expeditionary Force (SHAEF).

Knowing the exact timing and tactical makeup for the invasions of Algeria and Sicily, Hockey and Crilley generated profits for the merchant-bankers involved in the original arbitrage scheme in excess of one billion pounds.

William Hockey continued as the Tyler of the Masonic Lodge in Cardiff, Wales. Sponsored by the Landgrave of the House of Hesse, he became the head of intelligence for Credit Suisse.

Ion Crilley, sponsored by Frederick Warburg, moved to Sweden, and became the head of intelligence for Enskilda Bank.

Two neutral sovereigns—two Templar banks—a wheel within a wheel.

Godspeed.

Glossary: *"Dyin's Easy"*

British Slang, Circa 1939.

Snap	Picture
Kit	A soldier's equipment
Bags/Goolies	Balls
Humping tackle	Cock and balls
Manky	Rotten
Mother	The Queen
Browned off	Killed
Welsh fiddle	The itch
Abigail's	Women
Bouncers	A woman's breasts
Cloth-headed	Hungover
The Beano	Comic strip
Welsh rabbit	Bread and cheese
Doss house	Whore house
Barney	Fight
Have a piss	Goodbye/Piss-off
Sod on/off	Carry on/Get lost
Give us a tic	Give us a second
Jollop	Sticky situation
Cat-Lick	Catholic
Staff weens	Desk sods
Mahogany Spitfires	Staff desks
Yen	Craving
Fizzer	Disciplinary charge
Gormless	Worthless/Stupid
Nickers	Woman's underwear
Bumf/Bollocks	Bull shit
Flap wagon	Ambulance
Cobber	Mate
Under the Rose	Operating in secret

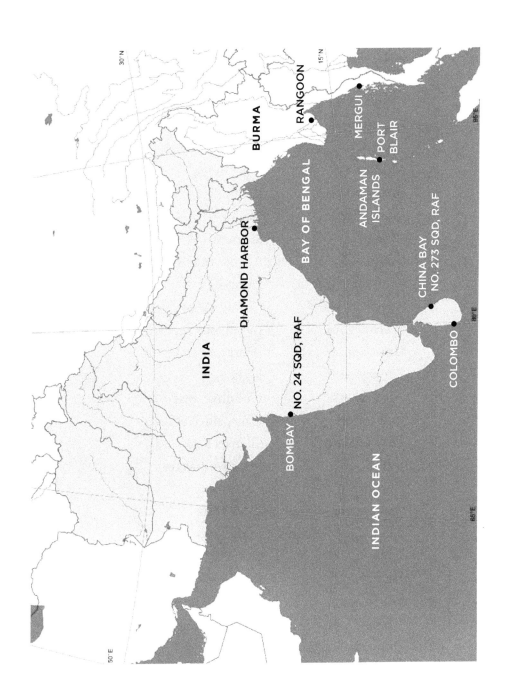

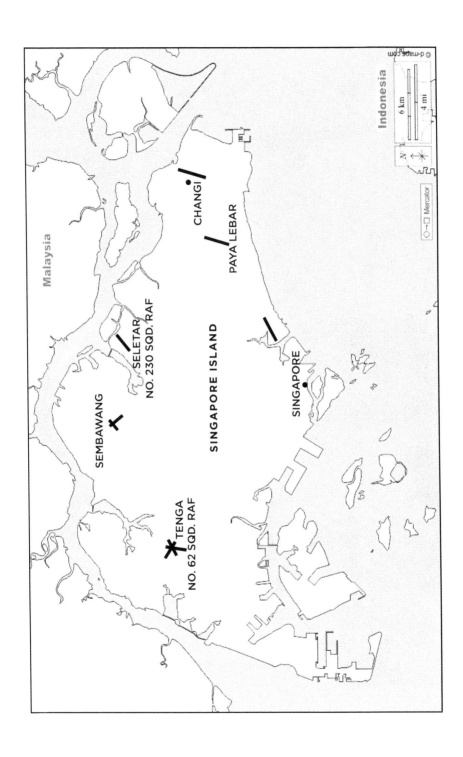

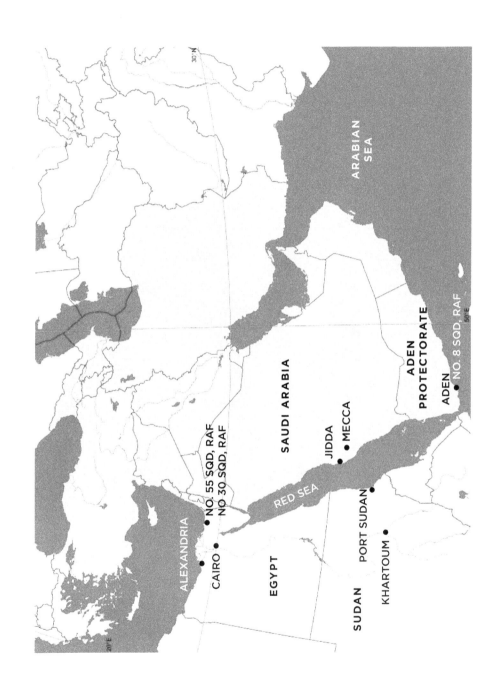

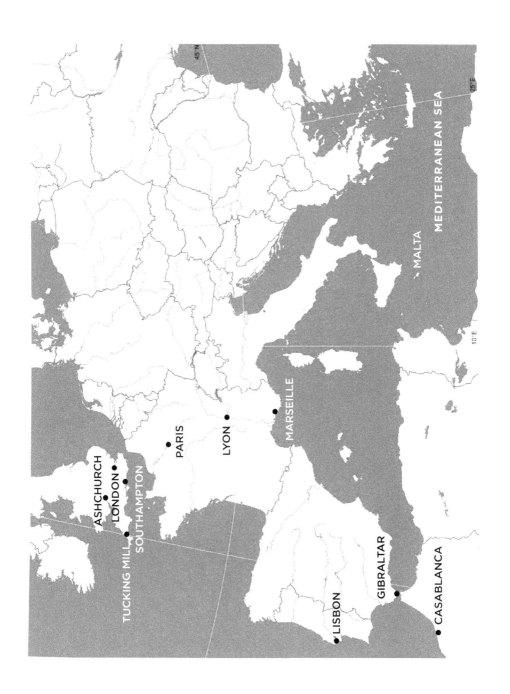

CPSIA information can be obtained
at www.ICGtesting.com
Printed in the USA
BVHW052157250123
657190BV00021B/318